For Jean, Anthony, Mary, Joan and Arthur with respect

Sarah Harrison achieved international success and acclaim
with her first novel, THE FLOWERS OF THE FIELD,
first published in 1980. She lives with her husband and
three children in Hertfordshire

Also by Sarah Harrison

THE FLOWERS OF THE FIELD
HOT BREATH

SARAH HARRISON

A FLOWER THAT'S FREE

Futura

A Futura Book

ISBN 0 7088 2527 3

Typeset, printed and bound in Great Britain by
Hazell Watson & Viney Limited,
Member of the BPCC Group,
Aylesbury, Bucks

Futura Publications
A Division of
Macdonald & Co (Publishers) Ltd
Greater London House
Hampstead Road
London NW1 7QX
A BPCC plc Company

PART ONE
1936

CHAPTER ONE

'Here and there, everywhere,
Scenes that we once knew,
And they all just recall
Memories of you'

'Memories of You'
Andy Razaf and Eubie Blake, 1930

AT one minute to six on the morning of 14 June, 1936, the black chicken on Kate Kingsley's alarm clock nodded up and down, in time with the ticking of the second hand, as it had done for the past fifteen years with only brief intervals for running repairs. The hour hand had already settled on the six, the minute hand was in the centre of the twelve.

The clock had a face painted like a chubby, smiling sun, with broad, wedge-shaped rays fanning out against a blue sky dotted with clouds like white cottage loaves. At the bottom of the clock face, above and on either side of the six, were the black chicken, forever pecking at an invisible grain of corn, and a haughty red and green cockerel with one foot imperiously raised.

The minute hand reached the middle of the twelve and the clock emitted a brief, tinny squawk before Kate's hand came down on top of it, sentencing it to another twenty-four hours of beaming, pecking silence. This is my last ordinary day here, thought Kate. Tomorrow, everything else begins. She wanted to go, but she didn't want to leave, and she was quite capable of accommodating these two apparently conflicting impulses. She knew very well that once she was on her way, the second would fade and the first predominate: Kate Kingsley, at twenty, was a very positive young woman.

Now she hitched herself up in bed and stretched her arms above her head. The brilliant East African sun was already sending long, inquisitive darts of golden light round the edges of the curtain on the verandah door. Kate linked her fingers behind her head and looked at her room, her things, beginning the conscious process of separation which would be complete this time tomorrow. There was her gramophone, and all her records piled on the table beside it, along with the box of needles; her bookcase, reflecting her taste from Kate Greenaway to Huxley; her cabinet of horses, beginning with the patchwork pony with purple wool mane and ending with the prancing glass stallion; her chest of drawers and wardrobe, containing the few bits and pieces in which she felt truly at home, and a vast quantity of clothes that she actively disliked; her desk, and the chair with the removable seat and the bedside table which her brother Joe had made in carpentry class – it needed a wad of paper under one leg – with the clock sitting on top of it. The clock, of course, she would take with her.

With detachment, she considered her room and the arrangement of it childish. It hadn't changed much in all the years it had been hers. She looked forward to a new room in a new place, in which to express the person she now was, with no purple-maned ponies and nursery-rhyme books.

Decisively, Kate pushed back the sheet and swung her feet out of bed on to the rush-matted floor. From the verandah she could hear the rhythmic swish of the houseboy sweeping. Somewhere in the not-so-distant bush a bird whose name she still did not know gave his sad, repetitive *oo-oo-oo*, with a dying fall.

She pulled her nightgown – a cut-down striped shirt of her father's – over her head, and walked naked to the chest of drawers. Her straight, thin white figure and fuzz of amber hair were caught briefly in the long mirror on the wardrobe door. Without deliberation, she selected a pair of faded cotton drill trousers and a white blouse from which she had long since removed the Peter Pan collar. To these she added: a striped elastic belt with a metal snake-clasp, a necklace of small coloured wooden beads, and a red and white bandanna which she folded lengthways and tied round her forehead and hair. Finally, she put on a pair of tennis shoes and, without glancing in the mirror, opened the door and stepped out on to the verandah.

Meru was at the far end, just completing the sweeping. He nodded and grinned gappily, his discoloured teeth jutting randomly and at odd angles from his pink gums like rocks in some ancient stone circle.

'*Jambo*, Miss Kate.'

'*Jambo*, Meru.'

He disappeared round the corner of the house, his once-white Chilprufe singlet flapping. Kate walked along the verandah in the opposite direction. The early morning air smelt of dryness, dust and tinder-brittle grass and foliage, everything scorched but for the moment still cool after the night. Flowering shrubs and herbaceous borders edged the expanse of desiccated yellow lawn. On the far side stood Joe's cricket stumps, a little drunkenly, since the holes had been re-used too often and were now over-large.

Kate thought she would go and see the puppies, the bastard offspring born to Thea's cross-bred bitch Dora just four days ago. Jack had made mother and pups an enclosed run under the verandah on the sheltered west side of the house. There were five dogs altogether on the Kingsley farm. In the pen near the driveway gate lived the guard dogs, two Rhodesian ridgebacks and an alsatian. Allowed in the house (on sufferance only, by Jack) were Thea's two dogs — her Staffordshire bull terrier, Cornet, and Dora, a more recent acquisition. Dora was a yellow and white labrador-spaniel cross, with a melting expression and an uncontrollable sex drive.

The puppies were quiet this morning as Kate jumped down the two wooden steps on to the grass. She saw the first little body lying in the sunshine about a foot from the chain-link wire that Jack had nailed up. She thought at first the puppy was asleep, but then she saw that the wire had been ripped back from its nail at one corner, revealing a dark, gaping hole. The puppies' silence was suddenly sinister. She bent over the puppy on the grass. It was dead, its tiny, blunt head almost severed from its body. It was so small and lifeless it looked like a little beanbag that someone had thrown down.

Kate pulled back the remaining wire. The massacre was total. The killer had been not just thorough, but frenzied. The bodies of Dora and her remaining three pups lay scattered about in the gloom. The hard-packed earth was sticky with blood. Dora herself lay on her back, nearest the wire. Her murderer must have called some hours ago, for she was stiff, her legs jutting from her body, flies humming round her open mouth. Down the length of her white stomach was a rent from which her guts spilled in a gleaming, serpentine pile. She looked as if she had been thrown forcibly backwards before the *coup de grâce* had been administered, and Kate silently saluted her for the brave fight she had undoubtedly put up. Kate did not cry: she had seen worse things, but rarely one which made her so angry. There was simply nothing left of all the life and warmth that had been there the day before.

She ducked her head back out, picked up the flaccid little corpse and placed it with the others, and hooked back the chain-link wire. She sat there on her heels for a second, the early morning sun beating with gathering strength on her back.

It was then that she had the powerful sensation of being watched. Along with the sun there was another beam being directed at her, as unmistakable as a tap on the shoulder. Without rising, she glanced behind her. There was no one there, but she caught a movement, no more than a ripple, amongst the shrubs behind the cricket stumps.

She rose, smoothly: nothing too sudden, not too much curiosity or bravado, wait and see. She concentrated on that little patch of green, fifty yards away from where, she had no doubt, another pair of eyes was fixed on her with equal intensity.

She did not have to wait long. Halfway along the flowerbed, where the shrubs gave way to Thea's lovingly tended delphiniums and michaelmas daisies, the visitor appeared. He emerged from amongst the flowers like a dictator from a group of sycophants, his front feet planted knuckles-down on the dried-out grass.

He was a huge, old, ugly baboon, standing over three feet at the shoulder. His wedge-shaped face with its broad, creased snout, and fierce little eyes set piercingly close together, wore an expression of disdainful hostility. A thick mane of grizzled hair hung almost to the ground from his powerful shoulders. As Kate watched, he stretched his neck and drew back his lips over yellow teeth in a silent laugh.

Kate's brain raced. Baboons were social animals, usually moving in large, structured groups with carefully observed hierarchies. But this one was on his own. So he was a rogue and an outcast, probably a former group leader nearing the end of his life. She had no doubt he was the killer.

He sat back on his haunches and picked at some parasite among the paler hair on his chest, studying it and then transferring it to his mouth with one surprisingly delicate front paw. Then he turned and began to slow-march away from Kate, tail aloft, the single beady eye of his narrow arse staring back at her.

'Murderer!' Kate's scream cut a slash through the sunny silence. 'Damn cowardly murderer!'

The baboon half-turned with a coughing sound, showing his yellow teeth again, afraid but fierce. Kate was halfway across the grass. She knew what to do, they'd had trouble with baboons stealing things from camp on safari. They didn't like noise, or direct attack. She pulled up one of the cricket stumps as she ran and hurled it at him like a javelin. It glanced off his back and he sprang into the air, landing straight-legged. He looked terrifying at close quarters, but Kate thought of his yellow teeth tearing the puppies, and his skinny paws clutching Dora by the throat, and ripping open her stomach.

'Bloody murderer!' Kate had not been reared in an environment where delicacy of speech counted for much.

She pulled up another stump, and then the third, scoring a direct hit with each one. He began to back off, chattering, his eyes cold and angry. Behind Kate others appeared, alerted by the noise, but she paid them no attention. She picked up a stone from the edge of the flowerbed and threw it at the retreating animal with the whippy wrist action that had caused many a run-out. It caught the baboon on the back of the head and he yelped and began to canter away. She pelted stones after him in a vengeful ecstasy.

'Bastard! Bastard, ugly brute!'

Grinning and breathless, she turned to see the rest of the

family dotted about like participants in a game of grandmother's footsteps. Immediately behind her was her twelve-year-old brother, Joe, looking at her with amused astonishment. Advancing behind him was Jack Kingsley, brisk and inquisitorial. On the verandah stood Thea, in a towelling robe and fluffy slippers. At the corner of the house, peering round anxiously, were Meru and the Kikuyu cook Jela, with a couple of goggle-eyed *totos*.

'What in heaven's name was all that about?' asked Jack. He was dressed and freshly shaved, and had probably been having breakfast.

'It was a great big nasty baboon,' said Kate. 'Didn't you see?'

'No, I didn't. Where did he go?'

'There,' she pointed. 'I hit him with a stone.'

'Good girl. What, enough to hurt him?'

'Absolutely.'

'He'll be back.' Jack looked at his foster-daughter up and down with dour admiration. 'Is it all right with you if I finish my breakfast?'

'Of course.'

'Thank you.' He began to walk back towards the house.

Joe came up to Kate. 'Kate Kingsley, white hunter,' he murmured, then rode the push she gave him and added: 'I say, where are my stumps?'

'Oh, sorry, I chucked them at the baboon. They're somewhere over there.'

'Decent of you to tell me . . .' Joe waded in among the delphiniums to retrieve the stumps. The servants drifted back to work, the drama over. Thea was in the middle of the lawn now, idly pulling at some spindly weed at her feet. The bull-terrier Cornet had waddled after her and was standing bandy-legged at her side, his tongue lolling from his mouth, his eyes slits in his smooth bullet-head. Suddenly he began to sniff, and then to make his way over to the run beneath the verandah.

'Cornet!' Kate called him, but he was inflexible. Idly, Thea began to follow him. Kate ran over to her. 'Thea, don't.'

'Hallo, darling. Heavens, what a start to the day.'

'Don't go over there for a minute.'

'But I want to see the puppies.' Ahead of them, Cornet whined and scratched at the earth beneath the wire.

'That baboon got Dora and the puppies.' Circumlocution was not one of Kate's faults. Thea whitened.

'What?'

'I found them about half an hour ago. He must have done it during the night. That's why I made such a din when I saw him.'

'Oh my God.' Thea began to hurry towards the run. Kate caught her sleeve.

'I wouldn't, honestly.'

'Nonsense, they'll attract flies,' said Thea, pulling away, but Kate could guess at the tears in her eyes.

She let go and went to sit on the steps. It was hot now. Two tiny brilliant firefinches were dust-bathing not three yards away. Kate watched the bright glitter of their wings and listened to the rustling and scraping of Thea seeing for herself.

Cornet came back first and settled down with a little groan at Kate's feet, his head on his paws. Then Thea sat down on the step by Kate. She smelt of talcum powder, but there was a bloodstain on the blue, fluffy edge of her slipper. Kate didn't look at her, but put out a hand and squeezed her knee.

Thea covered the hand briefly with her own. 'Poor, poor Dora,' she said. And then: 'I must go and get one of the *totos* to dispose of all that mess.'

'I'll do it,' said Kate, 'you're not dressed.'

'I know, it's disgraceful isn't it, and I've been awake for ages, too.' She ran her hands backwards through her tangle of black hair. Eighteen years' hard labour in East Africa had altered, but not extinguished, Thea Kingsley's beauty. The tanned skin of her arms, and of her ankles beneath the dressing-gown, was patterned with small scars from bites and scratches and everyday accidents, and a web of little lines had appeared round her eyes. But at forty-four her hair was still gypsy-black, her tall figure straight and slim, her manner one of unforced gaiety and optimism. Though she seldom wore make-up, and her clothes were mostly old and unfashionable, she would have drawn admiring glances in any smart European city. And her trump card was that she couldn't have cared less. Kate was suddenly, piercingly aware of how much she would miss her, and it made her brusque.

'Who shall I tell to do the clearing up?' Kate stood up briskly.

Thea shielded her eyes with one hand. 'Oh Lor', I don't know . . . what on earth's Joe doing in my flowers? Joe!'

'Fetching his cricket stumps. Who?'

'Um . . .' Thea re-addressed herself to the problem. 'Not Meru, he's terribly squeamish. Ask Jim, why don't you?' Jim was the gardener. 'Get him to bury them somewhere out of the way where this one won't dig them up.'

'Rightie-o.'

Thea smiled up at her foster-daughter. Against the sun, Kate's shock of hair sprang out from her bandanna like some wild, glowing halo, though she made an eccentric angel. 'Bless you, Kate,' said Thea. 'What am I going to do without you?'

'Plenty, I expect. Go and get dressed, I'll see to it.'

Kate went round the corner of the house to the kitchen door. Meru and Jela were standing there, gossiping. 'Where's Jim?' asked Kate. 'Meru, go and get on, please.'

'Watering,' volunteered Jela. The mouthwatering aroma of frying bacon wafted from the kitchen behind him. Jela was a first-class exponent of every classic English dish from bacon and egg to summer pudding, though he himself lived exclusively on maize *posho*.

'*Asante*.' Kate sought out Jim, by means of following the hosepipe attached to the kitchen tap. Thea had constantly told Jim that waterering plants in the morning was a waste of time since all the moisture was sucked up by the sun in a matter of minutes. But it was an operation which held a magical fascination for Jim. The turning on of the tap, the invisible flow of the water along the pipe, the sense of power to be enjoyed by placing one's finger over the mouth of the pipe so that the water jetted wherever you wanted it — all these were an endless source of pleasure to him.

Now his tall, stork-like figure was to be seen in the vegetable patch, directing the arc of water from the hose on to a row of already saturated lettuces. Apart from the watering, it was Jim's special talent to care for the garden while never actually being seen to do so. Kate's enduring picture of him was that of a lanky black statue standing motionless and laconic in his horticultural setting, usually accompanied by one or more of his insignia of office — spade, rake, edging shears — but rarely using any of them. He was a Masai, with that tribe's characteristic up-tilted profile, and an expression of unassailable hauteur which was probably, in Kate's view, just sloth and indifference. He had originally attached himself to the household by simply maintaining a presence until work was found for him to do, but why he had done so remained a mystery. For one thing, the Masai were not traditionally cultivators of the land, but shepherds, and nomadic. Secondly, it was considered sufficient for a young man, a *moran*, to bask in his maleness while others worked. A side-effect of this cult of the male was that Jim, when he had first arrived, had been all-too-visibly masculine, with parts that swung like an elephant's trunk and could be clearly seen from behind as he walked. In the interests of visitors whose sensibilities might be more refined than the Kingsleys', the problem of Jim's 'wedding tackle', as Jack called it, had to be faced. Thea had at last persuaded him to go at least partially clad, and now he wore his usual daytime uniform of a pair of cast-off khaki shorts of Jack's. They sat precariously on Jim's narrow hips, the wide legs flapping round his knees.

Now Kate unleashed a brisk volley of kitchen Swahili in his direction, killing several birds with one stone, chastising him for the indiscriminate watering, telling him to turn off the tap and not simply leave the hose trickling on the ground, and issuing orders concerning the dead dogs. He listened with an expression of ineffable disdain, but Kate wasn't fooled. She knew that Jim was almost pathologically idle, and only the sharpest and most direct approach would spur him to action. 'Yes?' she concluded, making a hurry-up motion with her hand. 'Get on with it.'

She literally stood over him as he strolled, with a studiedly *degagé* air, back to the kitchen door, and stood two feet from the tap telling the hard-pressed Jela, who was cutting bread at the table, to do it for him. A heated exchange began, which Kate cut short.

'Jim! The tap — off! Get on with the job now.' It was never clear how much English Jim understood, but he responded to her tone of voice. Sulkily, he twisted the tap, smarting under Jela's delighted, face-splitting grin. He then came to stand before Kate, like an attenuated ebony marionette, his long hands and arms dangling at his sides. His hooded eyes gave nothing away.

'Come with me.' She led him round to the other side of the house and showed him the run, the broken wire, and the corpses of the dogs, which were now beginning to smell strong.

'Aaaah . . .' Suddenly animated he crouched down, nodding and peering at the horrible mess. He didn't like dogs, so he was probably delighted, reflected Kate.

'You'll need a sack — wheelbarrow —' she made a putting-in gesture. 'All right?'

He rose and ambled off. Now his interest was engaged, she knew he would get on with it.

Joe had been driving his stumps into the rock-hard ground in a new place. He ran towards Kate, bringing his arms over in a fast bowling action as he did so.

'Bringing the *watu* to heel, are we?'

'Shut up.'

'This place will fall apart when you've gone.'

'What nonsense.'

'Honestly. You're so much more effective than Mum, they do things for you.'

'She's too nice, that's all.'

But Kate flashed him her quick, devilish grin. It pleased her to be thought of as effective, even a little fearsome. In sharp contrast to her foster-mother, whose main object was to establish good relations with her staff, Kate wished only to establish the kind of relations that got things done.

Jim ambled by, carrying a sack and a spade.

Brother and sister looked at each other and giggled.

'The phantom reaper himself,' said Joe. 'Poor Dora.'

Kate went back into the house and into the dining-room. Bacon and eggs were on the side, over a night-light. As she helped herself, Jela appeared softly and removed the empty toast-rack. While she ate he returned with fresh toast, and a pot of coffee which he placed on a coaster on the table, having first filled her cup. He hovered, shifting restlessly from one long, purplish foot to the other.

'*Musuri* Jela.'

He left the room, closing the door quietly behind him. Kate ate hungrily. She saw Thea pass the window, dressed now, and arm in arm with Joe, and then heard her voice in the kitchen, lilting and conversational, and Jela's chattering reply.

She finished breakfast and went along to her room to change and complete her packing. Meru was in the drawing-room, polishing the top of the piano, and wiping over the glass on the front of the family photographs which stood there. The first duty he performed with a duster, the second with the hem of his singlet, both with extreme thoroughness. The room was sunny, shiny with polish, bright and leafy with roses. In the grey stone fireplace stood a hand-painted china jug full of tall grasses, flanked by a copper scuttle and irons, and a huge African log basket. Cornet lay in the doorway.

Now Meru saw Kate watching him and made a face at Cornet, shaking his head. '*Kali.*'

Cornet rumbled menacingly.

'Be quiet.' Kate gave the dog a nudge with the toe of her tennis shoe. Meru applied the singlet to a miniature of Thea's mother, still muttering mutinously.

Kate went into her room. She poured some water from the pitcher into the flowery bowl, peeled off her shirt and washed. Then she put on underclothes and clean trousers and shirt, dropping the dirty ones by the door. Finally she removed the bandanna and looked at herself in the mirror for the first time that day as she brushed her hair.

'Carrots' Kingsley they'd called her at the boarding school in Nairobi, and Kate had no pretensions to beauty. On the other hand she paid only scant attention to her appearance and when she did she was quite satisfied with it. She was tall and slender (thin was the word she herself would have used); her hair, in her view, justified her nickname, though an impartial observer would have called it red and would have given its fiery brightness a second glance in any crowd; she had been spared the redhead's typical sandy lashes and her eyes were vivid and compelling in her pale face — narrow, upward-slanting hazel eyes. When she looked at herself in the mirror she met a stare that was watchful, alert and appraising. Hers was not a soothing or a restful presence, nor did she intend it to be. The impression she conveyed was one of intense and challenging self-knowledge, defying anyone to catch her out in vanity, complacency or self-delusion.

Kate's upbringing had been solitary by design as much as by circumstance. In spite of Thea's repeated invitations she had not brought school friends home in the holidays, preferring to walk and ride and drive out with Jack in the truck than be obliged to engage in more girlish pursuits with any of her contemporaries. At school she was industrious in class, excellent at games, and wholly self-possessed. She had not shown the least interest in running with the herd. In her early teens, when most of her peers played tennis for its social advantages, she did so to win. While they strove to be in fashion she remained resolutely outside it and apparently impervious to its allure: she dressed for comfort and to suit herself and the result was often strikingly idiosyncratic, so that girls who had lavished care and cash on their appearance suffered the uncomfortable sensation of having been effortlessly (and, even more galling, unintentionally) upstaged.

Luckily for her, Kate was sufficiently formidable to be neither ostracized nor derided for her individuality, but admired for it. She made no close friends because she didn't seem to need any, but she was popular in her way, and respected for her unshowy ability to stick up for herself and for others.

As regards the opposite sex, Kate was that perverse creature, a woman not endowed with conventional beauty, but who nonetheless held strong views on men. Thea, anxious for her foster-daughter's popularity, could at times have wished her less critical and aloof, especially since it took a brave young man to breach the wall of chilling indifference she had set around herself. Suitors of sufficient temerity were scarce enough, yet Kate had not the least intention of feigning interest in the eager, bumptious youths who occasionally put themselves forward, and they in their turn were soon discomforted by this acerbic girl with her sharp eyes and funny clothes.

Yet Thea knew Kate was far from cold. Apart from the naturally practical attitude to matters biological common to children raised in the country, there was in the young Kate an awareness of the physical and its power, an assertive sexuality of which only Thea knew the mainspring. Every so often that quality would burst through like a hardy, exotically flowering weed forcing its way between the stems of more genteel plants, thrusting itself towards the light, demanding attention: and Thea feared it.

One image in particular haunted her, a picture of Kate at sixteen after they had brought her back from a disastrous dance at a neighbour's. The girl in the back of the truck had been sulky, gawky, rebellious, awkward in her taffeta dress and court shoes. When they had got back to the farm Kate had simply jumped out, discarding the hated shoes and nylon stockings, and run off towards the paddock, a rustling, shimmering green wraith in the night. Thea had made to follow her, but Jack had put his hand on her arm.

'Don't. Leave her to it. She's only gone to visit Sailor.'

Thea demurred. 'She's in her best dress.'

'She loathes it. Give up the unequal struggle.'

'It's pitch dark—'

'That worries you, not her.' He put his arm round Thea and kissed her warmly, turning her face to his and kissing her again on the mouth. 'Stay here with me, Mrs Kingsley, I'll go after her in a little while.'

In a little while he did, while Thea sat anxiously on the verandah with Cornet. She did not bother to light the lamp. Joe was away at school. Only a faint light from the passage beyond the drawing-room crept across the verandah and spilled wanly on the grey, night-time grass.

She wished that she could, as Jack recommended, give up the unequal struggle. She wished she had not made Kate attend the dreaded dance or that, having done so, she had not made her wear the taffeta dress. Of course you couldn't force Kate to do anything. Thea had won what now seemed a Pyrrhic victory by gentle persuasion and a direct appeal to Kate's better nature. 'Do it for me,' she'd said, and much good it had done her. She could not understand herself. She knew Kate better than anyone, perhaps loved her better too, and understood her, and yet perversely sought to change her. Perhaps it was that exotic, voracious flower she sought to eradicate, that ineluctible growth which could only be Dulcie's.

Immersed in these gloomy reflections Thea sat in the near-dark, waiting, staring, not really seeing. So that when her husband and daughter did reappear they had, for her, an almost hallucinatory quality.

Kate was riding the pony, bareback. The green taffeta dress that suited her so ill now gave her the look of a female centaur, cast in bronze. Her pale, pointed face framed by wild red hair was impassive, almost haughty, though her eyes, as she drew closer, Thea could see, were fiercely bright. On either side of the pony's barrel-hard flanks the girl's long, white, tapering bare legs hung loose, but commanding. And beside the pony's head, one hand on its mane, walked Jack, slow and erect, courtier-like.

For that moment, as they advanced silently across the grass to bid her good-night, Thea saw them not as father and daughter, but for what they were — man and woman, not linked by blood or kinship but part of a primitive, atavistic pattern. She could change nothing. She was powerless. Like the *belle dame sans merci* and her helpless, ensnared knight these two whom Thea loved so much moved towards her. And when they stopped in front of the verandah they were silent for a moment, each thinking the other would speak first. Thea raised her eyes from her daughter's languidly drooping feet and looked into her face, and there it was, that challenge — unintended, she knew, but there nonetheless — that she remembered so well and which invaded her dreams and made her sleep restless.

'Here she is,' said Jack, 'I brought her to you.'

'Yes,' replied Thea. 'Good-night, my darling.'

If Kate replied she did not hear her. The girl turned the pony's head and rode him away into the dark in the direction of the paddock, leaving the two of them on the verandah. Her departure seemed to trail a wake of foreboding, so that Thea shivered, and went indoors.

For Kate the distant past was a blur. Of the first five years of her life, in Paris, certain images remained, though most had been wiped out by the memory's selective process. She recalled the small flat where she had been brought up by a woman she knew as Tanty — a corruption of the French *tante* though somehow Kate had always known she was no relation. Tanty had been strict, and conscientious. She had looked after Kate without evincing the least interest or affection for her as an individual. Kate could still feel the smarting strokes of the stiff hairbrush on her cringing scalp; the shiny, glacial cleanliness of the undersheet as she slipped into bed after one of Tanty's enthusiastic baths; the brisk rattle of the curtain rings when she came to say goodnight, her purposeful, rustling tread as she walked about the room, leaving the imprint of her assertive, tidy nature over Kate's childish disorganization.

As a child Kate had been much alone but not, as she recalled, lonely. She had never had other children to play with, there had only ever been Tanty and her with their quiet, clean, ordered, enclosed life. Kate had not known delight or excitement, but neither had she known misery or fear. This in spite of the fact that her earliest impressions were of a noisy time, when people spoke of there being a war on. They did so with horror and dismay as though war involved terrible things, but if terrible things there were, the young Kate did not experience them. All she knew of war was soldiers in the streets, boarded up shops and Tanty's frequent complaints that she could not get this or that.

Tanty was French, but she had worked for an English family in Wimbledon before the war and spoke English with an accent of tortuous suburban gentility. In Wimbledon – she pronounced it Weem-burl-den – she told Kate that she had been regarded as one of the family, and that Madame had wept when she, Tanty, had left. This was an anecdote which was told often, probably as a reminder of palmier days, but which never failed to baffle Kate. She simply could not imagine any adult weeping, let alone because of having to part with Tanty. But she would listen attentively, and Tanty was usually in a good mood after reminiscing on her past popularity and would give her charge's cheeks a tweak with cold, dry fingers.

By the age of four Kate was an astute little girl. She knew Tanty felt hard done by looking after her. Though they were comfortable in their little flat, safe now that the war was over, and they wanted for nothing, something was missing as far as Tanty was concerned. Kate realized this but was not old enough to see that that something was status. Since there was no one here of a superior nature to value her or compliment her on her work, Tanty operated in a vacuum. From time to time she would tell Kate, as though reciting something she'd learned by rote, that she was a war orphan, but that a 'kind lady' wished to see her looked after and had employed Tanty to that end. Kate knew her benefactress called from time to time, but she'd only caught sight of her on one occasion and that, she suspected, by accident.

She and Tanty had been for one of their little afternoon walks, and when they got back to the house there was a large car parked outside, with two people in the front seats, a man and a woman. As they went up the steps to the front door, Kate heard a woman's voice call 'Mademoiselle Paul!' – Tanty's proper name – and Tanty had turned sharply. Her grasp on Kate's hand had tightened, and her whole arm had gone very rigid, to prevent Kate turning round too. Kate had stood to attention in that vice-like grip while Tanty fumbled for her key, opened the door and then gave her a little push.

'Run along up and I'll be with you in a moment. *Dépêches-toi!*'

The use of French was a sure sign Tanty was rattled, she reserved it for occasions of the utmost urgency and importance. Inside the hall, Kate couldn't resist a peep through the chink in the door, and saw Tanty standing by the passenger window of the car, which had been wound down. The occupant was leaning out, and Kate saw her quickly-moving red lips, and her pale face, mysterious behind a wine-coloured veil. The lady's escort had got out and was leaning against the bonnet of the car with his ankles crossed, smoking. He was wearing an army uniform. It was only a short exchange, and when Tanty turned to trot briskly up the steps Kate had had to race up the stairs to the first-floor landing so as not to be caught in the act of spying.

A few months later, just after her fifth birthday, Kate was told that she would be going to Kenya. There she would have a proper home, *une vraie famille*, how fortunate she was! A friend would come and collect her and accompany her on the long journey, so there was much to do.

Kate was thunderstruck. The mere word 'Africa' was enough to terrify her. In vain did Tanty read from informative books and consult atlases. Africa already existed in Kate's mind. It was a landscape huge, tangled and hostile, populated by bloodthirsty hottentots and gigantic slavering beasts. She pictured herself living in a conical hut with no creature comforts, while dusky foster-parents with bones through their noses crouched on the mud floor, grunting to one another and stirring a noxious porridge with sticks. To no avail she voiced her fears to Tanty, who simply laughed at her foolishness and explained that Kate's new family were English, friends of the kind lady, and would be absolutely civilized.

At any rate, a great deal of sorting out and sprucing up now began, both of Kate and her possessions. This dreadful note of preparation brought home to Kate with fearful force the fact that Tanty would not be coming. Suddenly, at this late stage, she conceived, or at least fabricated, a real affection for her austere guardian. She followed her about, clung, literally, to her apron strings, begged her not to abandon her. But Tanty's line was always the same. She was so lucky that these kind people in Africa wanted to be her mother and father, she shouldn't be crying. But Kate was no fool to be so easily duped. She knew with the very marrow of her bones that the roles of mother and father, though she had no experience of either, could not simply be assumed by total strangers in a heathen land thousands of miles away, and that she could not be expected to love these strangers to order.

The 'friend' (of her new family, not Kate's) who was to accompany her turned out to be a Mrs Avery. She was quite the smartest person Kate had ever seen, though far from the prettiest, and it was obvious from the first that Tanty considered her a paragon. Kate disliked her cordially from the moment Mrs Avery asked how she was looking forward to the trip and then failed to listen to the answer. That is, she listened to the first few words with the brightest and most rapt of smiles, and then turned abruptly to Tanty who was hovering near and asked: 'Does she have any better shoes?' leaving Kate feeling stupid, with her remark stillborn.

That was the evening before they left. Mrs Avery spent the night in Paris — not with them, she had booked a room in a hotel — and the next morning she called early for Kate in a cab which was to take them to the station for the long journey south to Marseilles and embarkation for Kenya. That night

Kate cried bitter tears of fear and frustration, but in the morning, for the hated Mrs Avery, she had on the face of tight-lipped and implacable sullenness which she was not to set aside for some months. Dry-eyed, she kissed the belatedly remorseful Tanty, climbed into the taxi and sat looking out of the window as the two women said good-bye on the pavement. Her hands, in neat little grey gloves, were locked together, her teeth gritted, her brow beetling.

The journey took nearly four weeks. On board the liner for Mombasa Mrs Avery gave the impression of having lived there all her life, making friends with dazzling speed and behaving in a manner which was both energetic and amusing. In the morning she deposited Kate in the ship's nursery while she strolled on deck and refreshed herself in the first-class saloon. Then Kate had children's lunch and was packed off to the stateroom for a rest while Mrs Avery ate at greater leisure with her widening circle of acquaintances. In the afternoon she would either relax on the first-class sun deck, or take to the games deck for deck tennis or quoits, dressed in dazzling white with a silk scarf round her head, while Kate looked on. Then there was children's supper, an unappetizing affair with the nannies of the rich in attendance, after which Kate would once again be banished to read until bedtime. This regime did not actually bother Kate and she also absolutely refused to display any interest or curiosity about where they were going.

One evening Mrs Avery attempted to enlighten her willy-nilly. Kate had had her supper of fishcakes and carrots at six, Mrs Avery was off to dine at the captain's table and was obviously in excellent spirits. She came and sat on the edge of Kate's bunk, fiddling with the rings on her long, pale, bony hands. She smelt fragrant and was wearing a sparkly golden brown dress that went with her crinkly, sandy hair. Kate lay there rigidly, the sheet taut beneath her chin, wishing she'd go away so she could think her own thoughts in peace.

'Do you know, Kate,' said Mrs Avery, shaking her forearm to admire the jangle of bracelets on her thin, freckled wrist. 'Do you know, I used to go to school with Mrs Kingsley. Think, all those years ago! Well, perhaps not so very many –' she laughed gaily – 'so I know her terribly well. And you're *so* lucky she's adopting you.'

Kate was baffled. The word 'adopt' was the problem. To Kate, adopting was something you did with a 'tone'. And the adopting of a tone, as referred to by Tanty in accents of the utmost severity, was reprehensible. So the use of the word in connection with Mrs Kingsley and herself did nothing to allay Kate's fears. But Mrs Avery was chattering on.

'Of course it's a few years since I've seen Thea, so this is rather a special trip for me, too. Off to the dark continent without my husband, I don't know . . .' She shook her head and laughed again, it seemed she was talking to herself more than to Kate. 'But what fun it all is, don't you think? Or maybe you don't.' She suddenly turned quite a searching look upon her charge, so that Kate was obliged to give a taut little smile. She didn't want to cross swords with Mrs Avery or she'd stay even longer.

'Yes, it is,' she muttered, through teeth that, these days, always seemed to be clenched.

But Mrs Avery went on searching her face as if she hadn't heard her answer. 'What an odd little body you are,' she said.

Even the patronizing choice of words could not hide the fact that this was the first real interest she'd shown in Kate, and the first wholly sincere remark she'd addressed to her. The little grey dot that Kate had become glowed red for a moment, and was capable of further kindling had Mrs Avery only realized it. But she didn't.

'Anyway!' she cried, rising and smoothing her already smooth dress. 'Thea is absolutely one of the nicest people I know, and you and she are going to get on famously . . .' She caught sight of herself in the mirror and her attention was snatched away as she twiddled the little corkscrew curls on her forehead.

'Go to sleep soon. Night-night.' She switched off the light and went out of the door, closing it with a soft click, already glancing up and down the corridor for any of her numerous friends. The tap of her high heels died away and Kate, left alone in the dark with the strong, insistent thrum of the ship's engine, determined then and there to be so horrible to Mrs Kingsley that she would send her back to France on the first boat.

But unfortunately, when they finally disembarked in Mombasa in heat such as Kate had never dreamed possible, there, waiting for them was not Mrs, but *Mr* Kingsley, a character in the drama for whom she was totally unprepared.

To aggravate matters, he was clearly a person whose deep reserve actually matched Kate's own. As he greeted them, Kate felt that he watched from behind his face, using the niceties and formalities to conceal what he really thought both of Mrs Avery — whom he knew, a little — and herself. He was of medium height, but looked taller because he was very lean, and had reddish brown hair and a narrow moustache which emphasized the rather severe set of his features. So far from being black, or even dark brown, from living in such a hell's kitchen of a climate, he was pale, and dressed in a smart light suit and fedora. The plain fact was that all the strange sights and sounds of the weeks on board ship — the gully-gully men of Port Said, the baking sands stretching away on either side of the canal, breathtaking sunsets over the wild, rocky coast of Somalia — none of these had in the least prepared Kate for her meeting with this one taciturn Englishman. Her plans for loathly behaviour were thrown quite out of kilter.

Also, she was completely overwhelmed by the strangeness of her surroundings now that they were on *terra firma* and not gazing at it over a ship's rail. The rugged Moorish buildings of Mombasa shimmered in an incredible sticky heat, and the tall, scarred walls of Fort Jesus presided over the teeming harbour like a fierce old general. Around them on the dock swirled a babel of loud outlandish voices: they were buffeted by black and brown bodies and assailed by a smell the like of which Kate had never experienced: spices and strange foods, sweat, dung, dried fish, weird foreign plants and oils. In Tanty's view a nice fresh-airy nothingness had been the only suitable atmosphere for young girls to inhale, so here Kate felt guilty even breathing. Mombasa was still an Arab town, and the harbour was crammed with delicate wooden dhows, whose captains looked exotic and piratical in bright turbans, like something from 'Arabian Nights'. Amongst all this Mr Kingsley had taken Kate's hand in his, with a light, firm grip and said 'Pleased to meet you' with the utmost urbanity. Mrs Avery's exuberance was undiminished, she prattled on and gazed about her in excitement. But Kate felt crushed.

Later on, in bed in her room at the Metropole, she lay stiff with apprehension. As she stared at the ceiling, a huge lizard darted across it, paused for a second, throat palpitating, splay-toed feet clinging improbably to the plaster, before darting off to God knew what hideyhole, perhaps Kate's pillow. She would have swallowed her pride and gone to Mrs Avery in the adjoining room, but they had been allocated an African servant, tall and cold eyed in a white *kanzu*, and she imagined that he might be standing in the shadows somewhere with a dagger in the folds of his robe . . . So, with a moan of fear and misery, she went right down under the clothes and stayed there, sweltering, until she fell asleep.

The next stage of their journey was the train ride from Mombasa to Nairobi, due to start in the middle of the afternoon. That morning it transpired there had been some kind of mix-up about their trunks which Mr Kingsley went down to the harbour once more to sort out. Mrs Avery was keen to go with him, but he told her quite bluntly there was nothing she could do. Kate could tell she was mortified. She was a woman who prided herself on her competence, and here she was being treated like a useless ninny, and in front of a child, too. They sat in the unglamorous lobby of the Metropole, in peeling wicker chairs, she drinking coffee and gazing at her fingernails, Kate fiddling with her doll's clothes, waiting.

He got back two hours later. He had obviously had a trying time, for his manner was even more taut.

'Right,' he said, standing over them, hands in pockets as if in self-restraint. 'I think we should have some lunch and then head towards the station.'

'It was very good of you,' said Mrs Avery tensely, rising and brushing at her immaculate navy skirt. 'I'm sorry we're causing so much trouble.'

'Can't be helped,' he said. Kate noticed he didn't say they *weren't* causing trouble. She got up, her doll under her arm, and followed Mrs Avery towards the dining-room. She was tired, and slightly sick with the heat. Behind the lacquered reception desk a thin, hawk-faced African with pocked cheeks watched them impassively. There was a big choking lump in Kate's throat, so she scowled and pressed her lips together to force it down.

Suddenly she felt a hand on the back of her neck, and, glancing up with a jump, she saw Mr Kingsley looking down at her.

'Don't let it get you down, Ginger,' he said.

Kate closed her case with a snap. Jack would be in his office now – writing, telephoning, paying bills, but mostly worrying. Right from the start he'd done his best to be kind to her, he couldn't help being blunt, but she sensed some fundamental block to his complete acceptance of her. It was nothing to do with her personally, but simply something beyond her control. Had he not wanted a child at all? Or not a girl? Or was it that she was a European? But when she had arrived he and Thea were Kenyans of only three years' standing. His attitude no longer caused her any anxiety, but she was curious.

A chatter of voices reached her, wafting round the side of the house from the back door. It was Thea's morning 'surgery'. She had provided this *ad hoc* service for the farm labourers for as long as Kate could remember. She removed jiggers and leeches, dressed cuts and bites, distributed quinine and aspirin, admired and examined babies. Injuries ranged from the trivial to the truly horrific, and sufferers from blank-eyed stoics to unashamed howlers, usually in inverse ratio to their complaints. Above the sound of the surgery, she could hear the crackle of Joe's wireless from his room along the corridor. That reminded her of her records, which she would not be able to take with her. She went over to the gramophone and riffled through the pile. Having made her selection she placed it on the felt-covered turntable and put a bright new needle in the stylus. Then she wound the handle and placed the needle on the faintly hissing rim of the record.

'What'll I do when you are far away, And I am blue, what'll I do . . . ?' sang the sweet, melancholy voice.

Kate sat down on the floor and hitched up her knees, clasping them tight and resting her forehead on them. She thought of England where, once she had done her duty by the Tennant family, she would be her own woman. There would be no need for pretence there, no one to whom she was responsible for her behaviour. She would start with a clean, empty slate, and write her own life on it. She had no specific ambition, her aspirations took a general, rather than a particular, form. She was full of eager energy, and had not the slightest doubt that a course of action would present itself once she was off on her own. The secretarial qualifications which she had acquired to please her parents, and of which Thea spoke so reassuringly, did not figure in her plans. She could not see herself as someone's efficient assistant, the smiling handmaiden of some businessman or editor. No, autonomy was what Kate craved, in all things. Her very lack of preparedness excited and stimulated her. She would be an opportunist and live on her wits.

She looked forward to the journey to England with the keenest anticipation. She was no longer the insular, incurious little girl who had boarded the train at Mombasa sixteen years before . . .

The drily nicknamed Lunatic Express, which ran between Mombasa and Nairobi, had been just another train to the five-year-old Kate. She had known nothing of its stirring history, of the thousands of Asians imported to build it, whose descendants were now an integral part of the Kenyan scene; of the slaughter of dozens of railway workers by man-eating lions at Tsavo; of the rigours of laying hundreds of miles of track across desert and through bush; of the dream it represented to those who believed East Africa to be White Man's Country.

In an exhausted trance she had been shepherded along the platform teeming with people of all colours and their assorted goods and chattels. Unfortunately Jack's brief display of sympathy had broken her hitherto iron control. She had not wept, but she did wilt, and by the time they reached their carriage, she had only the haziest memory of being hoisted aboard by Mr Kingsley and lain on the seat of a first-class compartment. She had felt the rough pile of the upholstery beneath her cheek, and the enveloping weight of something laid over her by one of the grown-ups. Then, finally, she heard the dragon-like hiss of steam from the burning eucalyptus logs as the great engine pulled away from the platform and towards Nairobi. After that, she slept.

The train was a microcosm of Kenyan life. First-class compartments were reserved for Europeans; second class for

Asians; and the most basic accommodation, with hard wooden benches, for Africans, who sat up all night chattering and eating from huge baskets of food they had brought for the journey.

Dinner for first-class passengers was served at the Asian-run dak bungalow, a halt on the line. Mr Kingsley woke Kate about half an hour beforehand. Outside the train window, the huge darkness was patterned with trundling clouds of smoke and handfuls of sparks. Kate felt stiff and dry-mouthed.

'Hungry?' asked Mr Kingsley. Until that moment she hadn't been, but now that hunger had been mentioned her stomach rumbled sonorously. 'Never mind, we reach the *dak* bungalow soon,' he told her. 'That's the place where we get down and have supper. It may not be very nice but it will fill us up.'

Mr Kingsley's prediction that supper might 'not be very nice' proved a rank euphemism: it was horrible. Kate's stomach, which had been rumbling so welcomingly, closed like a Venus flytrap on being confronted with tinned soup, tinned stew and tinned fruit, all tepid and sharing the same glutinous texture and unappetizing taste. The meal was accompanied, oddly, by tea and toast, two adjuncts which might have been thought proof against mishandling. But the tea was cool, with curds floating on its surface, and the huge doorstep of ready-spread toast had the consistency of a damp bathmat. Tanty, thought Kate, would have had a fit. The desirability of toast's remaining severely upright until the moment of consumption was part of her culinary creed, the only real rule of the elusive *'cuisine Anglaise'* which she had managed to pick up in Weemburlden.

Mr Kingsley despatched his supper without a murmur. Mrs Avery was frank: 'God, it's foul!' But she laughed and ate some anyway. Kate, overcome by the nastiness of the food, the strangeness of the *dak* bungalow, set down in the middle of apparently eternal darkness, and the snarlings and hissings of the engine, could only push her fork about, and got back on the train as hungry as she'd got off.

During their absence the African servant had laid out bedrolls neatly on the seats, Kate and Mrs Avery in one compartment, Mr Kingsley next door. Mrs Avery helped her off with her outer clothing and between the coarse sheets. Then she rummaged in her bag.

'Here, would you like one of these?' She proffered a screwed-up paper bag with a few barley sugars welded together in the bottom. Kate remembered she'd bought them on board ship one rough night when she'd felt queasy.

'Thank you.' She took one and sucked it gratefully. Mrs Avery seemed to be improving as the journey went on. 'What about my teeth?' she added, guiltily.

'They'll still be there in the morning. Night-night.'

In the brief interval between waking and sleeping, as she lay glooping the sinful barley sugar from one cheek to the other, she caught the tail end of an exchange between the two adults, who were standing just outside in the corridor, smoking.

'She should have eaten something,' Mr Kingsley was saying.

'. . . no, but it *was* disgusting.'

'She must get used to it . . .'

'But how could she?' Laughter from Mrs Avery. 'She's a Parisienne!'

Oh, thought Kate. So *that's* what I am.

When she woke at dawn the next day she felt better. The train was now only two hours out of Nairobi, nearing the end of its fifteen-hour run. Opposite her on the other seat Mrs Avery was still sound asleep, her back to Kate, the sheet pulled up over her pointed shoulder.

Kate gazed out of the window. For the first time she felt a leap of pure excitement. For there, separated from her by that one sheet of glass, was the Africa of her imagination. But for one thing – there was no jungle. In fact the landscape she saw was rolling and grassy, a great undulating gold and ochre plain, studded with the weather-warped figures of acacia and thorn trees, and with hills in the distance rising in remote, mysterious ranks.

She was fortunate in sitting on the northern side of the train as it puffed westward, for she was looking out on an area where all game was preserved. So the scene illuminated by the sun, which was just lifting above the horizon like a great copper gong, resembled a children's picture of Noah's Ark-land. It teemed with game. No longer perturbed by the passing of the roaring black train, Thompson's gazelle grazed so close to the track that she could see the black and white splashes on their tails, and their limpid eyes as they glanced up. Beyond them, a drifting, shifting shoal of thousands of wildebeest melted into the distance; she saw the occasional darting run of the hideous warthog, once followed by its ludicrous babies, tiny trotters twinkling, tails sticking straight up in the air like the burgees of yachts; two giraffes, tall and beautiful, moved with them for a moment with their ghostly, rocking gait; ostriches raced like scrawny maiden aunts in bustles; and once, incredibly, there were lions, lying not fifty yards from the track, between the train and the grazing gazelle.

'Lions!' squealed Kate, surprising even herself with the shrillness of her voice after so many weeks of near-silence. She craned her neck and pressed her cheek to the glass to keep them in view as long as possible. Mrs Avery moaned and huddled deeper under the bedclothes.

But Mr Kingsley, who must have been standing in the corridor outside, heard her and put his head round the door.

'What's up?'

'Lions,' she said again, feeling a little sheepish.

'You'll see plenty of those.' He entered, sliding the door shut behind him. 'May I come in?' He sat on the end of Kate's bed, nearest the door. The lower half of his face was shadowed with a faint stubble, and he wore no tie: both these factors made him appear more approachable. He fished with his finger and thumb in the breast pocket of his jacket and took out a packet of cigarettes, a short ebony holder and a box of Swan matches. He tapped the cigarette on the outside of the packet and then pointed with it at Mrs Avery.

'I wonder if she'd mind if I smoked?' Kate had no idea whether she would or not, and wasn't used to being consulted, so she shook her head.

'Good.' He lit the cigarette and drew on it voraciously.

For some minutes they sat in silence, while he finished his cigarette. Then he leaned across Kate to stub it out in the ashtray, and enquired: 'Do you want to wash, or anything?'

Kate did feel sticky, and she did want to go to the lavatory. She sensed that his 'or anything' was a euphemism for the latter. The habit of cleanliness and *regularité*, as Tanty put it, was deeply ingrained in her.

'Yes please, I'd better.'

For some reason, her reply made him smile. 'Oh, quite,' he said affably. He helped Kate find her washbag in her overnight case, looked away as she pulled her dress over her head and escorted her along the swaying corridor to the washroom. She carried her doll, Tanty, in one hand, its skirt dangling over its head to reveal broderie bloomers, in a posture that would have made its namesake blanch. The plain outside the window on the corridor side was vast and empty, and the early morning air was cool. Kate experienced another painful spasm of homesickness.

Mr Kingsley pushed open the washroom door. 'Can you manage?'

'Yes, thank you.'

'I'll be just here.'

Kate went in. It was noisier in this confined space and the floor of the train heaved and rattled beneath her feet. She couldn't get the heavy brass tap to work except in short spurts, so she made do by wiping her face, hands and teeth with a wet flannel. She spent a penny, found her brush, and looked at herself in the swaying mirror. Her hair, which she had at that time worn long, stuck out in a frizzy cloud on either side of her small, pale face, like the hair of Alice in the Tenniel drawings. In Paris Tanty had plaited it and Mrs Avery usually put it up in a ribbon. Kate didn't know what to do with it, so she wet the brush and scraped as much of the frizz behind her ears as she could. Then she picked up her washbag and let herself out into the corridor again.

Mr Kingsley was standing a few yards further down, leaning back, his feet braced against the side of the train, arms folded, apparently in a reverie. But he must have seen Kate, for as she approached he straightened up.

'All done?'

'Yes, thank you.'

'Shall we go and wake Mrs Avery then?' There was an unmistakably mischievous note in his voice as he made this suggestion which Kate did not fail to remark, but they were deprived of the pleasure, for when they reached their compartment the African servant was just leaving, having tidied Kate's bedroll and left a thermos of tea, presumably procured at the dak bungalow the night before.

'*Jambo bwana*,' he said to Jack, and '*Jambo* Missy' to Kate. His face was the colour of strong coffee, smooth and sculpted above his spotless white *kanzu*. In daylight and at close range he did not look quite so much as if he was carrying a dagger. Kate had been told his name was Njuma. 'I must go and make myself presentable,' said Mr Kingsley. 'I'll leave you to it.' And he did.

The record had long since ended and had continued to revolve for some minutes before running down. Kate got up and removed the needle. It was not like her to wallow in reminiscence, but it was as if she had to do so, to parcel up this piece of her life and set it aside. Just as the very old recall their youth with startling clarity, so she now remembered the start of her life here as if it were yesterday. There was a tap on the door, and Thea put her head round, the surgery finished. 'That's that for today. Need any help?'

'No, thanks. I've done most of it except the things I'll throw in tomorrow morning.'

'You're so efficient . . .' Thea came in, closing the door after her. 'It's Joe I worry about.' Joe was leaving with Kate. They would first have a few weeks' holiday with Thea's father and brother, and then Joe was bound for boarding school and Kate, she hoped, for a job in London.

Kate shrugged. 'He'll be all right.'

She knew she wasn't being as sympathetic as she might be. It was hard for Joe, and for Thea, who was losing half her family at a stroke. But Kate herself had been torn away from all she knew at the tender age of five, with very little in the way of explanation, understanding or sympathy, and she could never forget that. It was a big step for Joe, but she would be with him, and he carried love and security with him like a talisman, where she had had nothing.

As if reading her mind, Thea came and put an arm round her waist. 'Of course he will, he'll have you there.'

She withdrew her arm again, mindful of Kate's dislike of emotional scenes, and wandered over to the wardrobe, which still looked full. 'Heavens, darling, are you sure you've packed everything you'll need?'

'Yes, of course, I shall have to buy a lot of thicker things anyway.'

'It'll be summer there, remember.' Thea smiled teasingly at her.

'But it won't be like here.'

'No, that's true.' Thea went to the verandah door and stood looking out, hugging herself with crossed arms. 'It will be very green and damp, even in London, and the roses will be blooming and the grass will be growing at such a rate it will need mowing every few days –'

'Because of all the *rain*,' said Kate pointedly, squatting down by her bookcase and peering at the contents.

'Because of *some* rain,' corrected Thea. 'England has the best climate in the world.'

'And the worst weather,' responded Kate, and then looked up and they both laughed at, and with, each other.

'Oh look!' Thea suddenly pointed. 'The beastly thing!'

Kate bounced up and went to her side. Among the lilac blossom of a jacaranda tree about a hundred yards from the house they could make out the leggy, beruffed silhouette of the baboon.

'Right! I'm going to scare him off,' said Kate, opening the door, but Thea caught her shoulder.

'No, don't, he'll go away.'

'He won't. Why should he? He's an outcast and a trouble-maker –' Something about her own choice of words gave her pause. She changed her tack. 'Think of the puppies.'

'I am.' Thea sighed. 'All the same . . .'

'What?'

'Perhaps this afternoon, if he's still hanging around, Jack can do something.'

'Perhaps.'

Both women turned back into the room. Thea realized that her dread of her children's departure was extending to foolish softness over a dangerous animal. Kate knew that, for the same reason, she was becoming increasingly brusque and unfriendly.

Both felt lonely, each was inhibited by what she knew of the other's emotional make-up. They were silent.

Nairobi had not been the way Kate had imagined. If Mombasa was a port and Nairobi a capital she had expected the difference to be like that between Marseilles and Paris. Instead, the opposite had been true: Mombasa was an impressive, solid town with stone-built buildings and a presence rich with the patina of history. Whereas Nairobi turned out to be a rough frontier town, with dirt roads, few buildings of stature, shops, of which some were no more than covered stalls, and the endless bush stretching away on all sides. The much-vaunted (by Jack) Norfolk Hotel where they were to spend the night was a one-storey edifice fronted by a verandah and hitching rail like a wild west saloon. Riding horses and wagons were tethered out front, and a number of people with a rough and ready appearance were drinking in the shade when they arrived.

After a wash, a rest, and an early lunch – which Kate devoured ravenously – Mr Kingsley informed both of them that they were to come with him to Jacob's Department Store – not like any store Kate had ever been in, but certainly one of the more substantial in Nairobi – to be 'kitted out properly'. This, they found, entailed buying stout boots and socks, broad-brimmed hats, long serviceable linen skirts and baggy shirts and assorted phials of insect repellent and anti-sunburn cream. Mr Kingsley, it transpired, had ordered a vast quantity of goods of all kinds before leaving for the coast, and these were stacked in boxes for him to check, which he did assiduously and in minute detail while they waited patiently. Tinned food, paraffin, ropes, nets, clothing, lamps, and medical supplies, and goodness knows what else were painstakingly itemized, and it was clear that they would be taking all these purchases back with them the next day, though in what form of transport Kate could not imagine.

They were early to bed that night, and were up with the dawn. At breakfast Mr Kingsley presented himself having undergone a metamorphosis. Gone was the neat, suited English gentleman and in his place they saw a Kenyan farmer dressed in cool, loose but heavy-duty bags, shirt and jacket, with a hat similar to the ones they had bought but a great deal more greasy and battered. Along with his suit, he seemed to have discarded his crisp, formal manner and some of his reserve, and appeared more at ease.

'All set?' he enquired quite jovially.

'I can feel the pioneer spirit positively leaping in me,' remarked Mrs Avery with an ironic little smile. But she looked trim and scrubbed and somehow serviceable, as though she intended to give the adventure all she'd got.

Kate, too, felt better in her new tough clothes, and when they went outside her reflections as to the nature of their transport were answered. For there in the cool, golden early light was a large wagon with a hooped canvas cover. At the front, between the long shafts, were no fewer than six doe-eyed oxen the colour of honey (three span, Kate later learned to call this number). Among the piles of boxes and sacks from Jacob's Store in the back of the wagon, Kate could see their baggage, looking rather lost and incongruous. Seated on the tail-board was an African wearing cut-down army trousers, bare-chested except for a tie round his neck, swinging his thin black legs. There were one or two ramshackle cars parked opposite the Norfolk, in front of the row of Asian '*dukas*', or small shops, but they didn't look nearly as fine as the ox-cart. Kate was open-mouthed with wonder.

Mr Kingsley seemed conscious of the impression the wagon had made on them both, and with an air of almost boyish pride introduced them to the African. 'This is Jesus.'

Kate gawped. 'Not really?' whispered Mrs Avery. The African beamed.

'His name is Jesus,' repeated Mr Kingsley. And then, indicating the striped tie: 'An MCC member, too.'

This incomprehensible remark sent Mrs Avery into fits of delighted laughter so that she could scarcely climb up. And she was still shaking with laughter as they began to trundle forward, spreading a cloud of swirling dust, towards the bush.

The ox-cart had taken a full day to reach Gilgil. First they toiled up the escarpment out of Nairobi and rode along its crest through country that was almost Tyrolean, with thick dark forests, and glimpses of lush green, where the air was fresh and crisp. And then they had begun to descend, with the great shimmering umber plain of the Masai country to their left, and the flat, steely glitter of Lake Naivasha ahead, where some of the loveliest European houses had been built on the shores. But as they came down into the sweltering heat of the Rift Valley they turned away from Naivasha and north to Gilgil, keeping the great rampart of the Aberdare mountains always on their right.

And it was hot. So hot that once Mr Kingsley put both reins in one hand and with his free one lifted Kate's hair off her neck in a bunch and asked: 'Better, Ginger?'

Mrs Avery had taken the hint and made a plait, which she had popped under Kate's hat, so that her neck was cool.

But in spite of Mr Kingsley's increasing affability, and Mrs Avery's kindness, Kate felt herself dwindling once more as the journey went on, in the face of such a huge landscape. There were no reassuring landmarks to give a sense of scale, no proper roads, or villages, or streetlamps or buses or churches or telegraph poles – nothing. So that a mountain which looked close never got any closer, a lake that glittered in the sunlight floated like a teasing mirage, always the same distance away. She felt like a tiny pebble dropped into a vast red furnace.

When at last Mr Kingsley had said: 'There it is, that's our place' she looked where he pointed with a kind of dull fatalism – she was beyond surprise. Besides, it was just an ordinary grey stone bungalow with two brick chimneys. She could hear a dog barking faintly. Jesus jumped down and opened a gate for them, though there was no discernible difference between the land on this side of the gate, and on that. In those days, there was only the house, and the thousands of acres of land that went with it, which the previous owners had used to graze sheep. None of the outhouses had yet been built, there had been no garden to speak of, no paddock, little fencing and few trees. Between the ox-cart and the house was simply a bare tract of scrubby ground, with a stony, furrowed track traversing it. The late afternoon sun glittered on the two large oil drums which collected rain water from the roof for domestic consumption.

The setting for this undistinguished residence was fine

enough. Beyond it to the west loomed the truncated peak of the volcanic Mount Longenot, and the mysterious bulk of the Mau escarpment. Behind it, the Aberdares and beyond them, seen only occasionally, the miraculously snow-capped peak of Mount Kenya. What, beneath the crushing wheels of the wagon, was harsh, desiccated scrub, thorns and yellow grass, became in the distance a landscape of mystery and magic, vast and beautiful and tremulous in the heat.

But Gilgil had never rated high among the settlements of the White Highlands, nor were the Kingsleys among the true lotus-eaters of Happy Valley. Their friends, who congregated from time to time to play coarse polo at the Kingsley place, were serious and hard-working, farmers and soldier settlers rather than dispossessed younger sons and dilettante millionaires.

To Kate, the house was better than the mud-hut of her imaginings, but only just. With tiredness her sense of foreboding returned, overwhelmingly. About a quarter of a mile to the side of the house were a collection of huts and some small cultivated patches like allotments. Here one or two black figures appeared, waving and shouting. Jesus, grinning, waved and shouted back. Another figure came out of the house and began to walk to meet them. Jesus held the oxen, and Mrs Avery jumped down at once and ran over to embrace the woman, the two of them chattering and laughing and then walking on with linked arms. It must be Mrs Kingsley, thought Kate, and lowered her eyes. Mr Kingsley jumped down, pulled off his hat and beat out the red dust from it against the side of his leg. Then he replaced it, and held up his arms to Kate.

'Come on, Ginger.'

He lifted her down. She made herself ramrod-stiff. The women came over to them, Mrs Avery standing back a little.

'Hallo, darling,' said Thea Kingsley to her husband, and kissed him warmly. Kate hadn't looked at her yet, but she heard a voice that was light and vivacious, that seemed to contain laughter like an underground stream.

Jack Kingsley released his wife reluctantly and put a hand on Kate's shoulder. 'This is she,' he said.

Thea Kingsley dropped down on her knees in front of Kate,

taking her hands. 'Oh, Kate – Kate, we're so pleased to see you. It's so lovely to have you here, bless you.' She put her arms round Kate and squeezed her taut body. Then she released her, and tilted her face up with one hand. 'You must be worn out.'

Obliged now to look Thea Kingsley in the face, Kate saw that she was black-haired, brown-skinned and far, far prettier than Mrs Avery, though far, far less smart. She was smiling broadly but her dark eyes, mysteriously, were shining with tears. The two stared at each other.

'She travels remarkably well,' said Mr Kingsley. 'Doesn't she, Andrea?'

'She certainly does.'

'You both do,' he added gallantly. Kate could sense how pleased he was to be home and resentment boiled up in her again. It was all right for them. This was their home, their house, their dry, hot, dusty land. They had chosen to live here, she had not. She frowned.

Thea stood up and said something to Jesus, who nodded assent and hoisted down the cases from the back of the wagon. Five cases, two of them large, looked a fantastic load for one man but he managed it, and tottered off in the direction of the house. The four of them began to follow, the adults talking over Kate's head. She was slightly deafened by the long hours rattling and jolting on the cart, and their voices sounded distant and distorted. Mrs Kingsley's hand, encircling hers, felt firm and friendly, but she let hers lie in it as cold and clenched as a stone.

They went up steps on to the verandah and through a screen door into a cool, dark hallway. There was a faint, appetizing smell of fresh toast, all the more welcome to Kate for being so unexpected.

'Kate's coming with me,' said Mrs Kingsley. The other two went into a room on the left, and there was the familiar chink of decanters and glasses. Thea took Kate down the hall, round a corner, through another door and into a kitchen. It was a very large kitchen, but not well equipped – there seemed to be a lot of sacks and cartons and jars and drums standing about as if waiting to be unloaded, but the large deal table in the middle of the room looked permanent enough. A black man with fuzzy iron grey hair, and wearing a white apron, stood by the stove.

'Kate, this is Karanja, our cook,' said Mrs Kingsley.

'Hallo,' said Kate. The old black man grinned and nodded.

Thea pulled out a chair at the end of the table and sat Kate down in it. Karanja placed before her a large brown boiled egg in a wooden egg cup and a plate of hot, slightly charred, buttered toast.

'Thank you.'

Thea Kingsley cut the toast into soldiers, decapitated the egg and stuck a piece of toast in the top.

'There you are,' she said, and popped a kiss on Kate's head before sitting down next to her at the table. She did not watch Kate, but opened the table drawer and took out a dog-eared notebook and a stub of pencil and began to make some kind of list, occasionally conferring with Karanja in a mixture of English, and a mumbo-jumbo which Kate supposed was African.

Realizing with relief that she was not going to be watched over, Kate addressed herself to the egg. After the tasteless nursery food on board ship, the horrors of the *dak* bungalow, and the exigencies of Jesus's chop-box on the journey from Nairobi, the egg was welcome. She ate it all, and all the toast. Mrs Kingsley looked up as if she'd almost forgotten her presence, and smiled.

'Well done!' she said, as if Kate had done something wonderful. 'Now would you like some cake?'

Kate nodded, 'Yes, please.'

Karanja, beaming, got down a square green tin from a shelf, opened it, and cut a large wedge of madeira-like sponge.

'That looks huge,' said Mrs Kingsley. 'Still, you do your best. I've just remembered I've got something for you and I'm going to go and fetch it now. I'll be back in a minute.'

She almost ran from the room. She seemed to have lots of energy and enthusiasm, as if nothing would get her down. It was hard to be sulky with her. Kate tucked in to the cake, but she was no longer all that hungry and tiredness was beginning to get the better of her. Also, she was a little wary of Karanja, who kept on treating her to his wide, untidy grin.

Abruptly, she pushed back her chair and left the room, her

heart thumping. But without meaning to do so she had behaved quite suitably. Karanja cleared the table.

She went round the corner and up the hall. As she did so she heard the grown-ups' voices through the half-open door.

'. . . certainly doesn't give much away,' Mr Kingsley was saying about someone.

'But she must be quite overwhelmed – she's only five and half, bless her!' replied his wife. So it was her they were discussing.

'Well, *I'm* overwhelmed,' said Mrs Avery, 'and we won't bring my age into it!'

They all laughed. Then Mrs Kingsley said: 'We must make a big fuss of her. After all, she didn't ask to come here, this isn't her home, yet.'

Well, that was true.

'You know,' went on Mrs Avery in that spirited conversational tone that Kate knew so well, 'she's not like a child, she's like a little old lady.'

They laughed again, not unkindly, but Kate felt tears of mortification sting her eyes, and wiped them away with her knuckles.

'Anyway,' said Mrs Kingsley. She opened the door and added something over her shoulder to the others in a quieter voice. She carried something in her hand. When she looked round and saw Kate standing there she did not look guilty or embarrassed.

'Kate! I'm sorry, I didn't realize you'd finished. Come on in.'

She held the door for Kate, who marched into the centre of the room and treated all three of them to her most strafing glare. Mrs Kingsley came to her side and held out the gift, which was wrapped in brown paper.

'Someone told me you had a lovely doll,' she said. 'So I made her some new clothes – for the hot sun.'

Kate concentrated the glare on Thea. All her loneliness, her tiredness, her humiliation boiled up in her. Furiously, she dashed the parcel to the ground and stamped one booted foot down on top of it.

'I don't want it!' she yelled. 'I hate it here, and I hate you!'

*

The trouble was, they had none of them reacted as she'd hoped. Mrs Avery had smiled with a stupid, mock-fearful expression, Mr Kingsley had shaken his head and turned away, rubbing his face, and Mrs Kingsley had left the doll's clothes where they lay and crouched down next to her.

'Well, of course you hate it here,' she said with feeling, as if blaming herself for not having recognized the fact sooner. 'It's all so beastly and strange. I hated it at first — I still do sometimes —' she glanced at her husband with a smile, 'but you'll get used to it, because it will be home. And as for us — you'll have to be patient with us, Kate. We want you so much, even though you don't want us, so could you just try and put up with us for a bit? Then after a while, when you've got to know us better, you may get to like us. *Please* try, for all our sakes.'

Of course, not knowing Thea as she did now, Kate had not realized that all this was spoken from the heart and with the utmost sincerity. She had assumed it was more adult double-talk and trickery, an attempt to win her round by underhand means. She had shrugged off Thea's hand and covered her face, not to cry but to shut out the sight of these horrible, scheming people. And she became utterly determined to show them that she meant what she said.

She had not actually run away, because even she was doubtful of her ability to survive in the African bush. But her behaviour had been enough to drive ordinary people to murder. She had been perverse and hateful. The doll's clothes for Tanty had been on the end of her bed the first morning, but she had kicked them aside. She had refused to eat meals, and then pilfered from Karanja's kitchen. She had been silent, sometimes for days at a time. She had wet her bed, quite deliberately. And she had cut off her hair with a pair of nail scissors.

This was to spite Mr Kingsley, who professed to admire her hair. One day as she sat on the verandah with Tanty he'd come along, obviously wanting to be friendly, and said: 'Don't ever have that hair of yours cut, will you, Ginger?'

'Stop calling me that! I hate being called that!' she spat. It wasn't true. She had liked his nickname, it had been the first sign of friendship extended to her on foreign soil, it was like a little secret between them. But now, more than anything, she wanted to rebuff him, and she succeeded.

'Sorry,' he said, and walked away. He had never called her Ginger again, ever, but seemed unable to use her name, so from then on he had no name for her.

That day she'd cut the hair off. At lunch, Mr Kingsley had said: 'Good grief, what on earth have you done?'

But Thea had been more canny. 'Doesn't it look marvellous?' she exclaimed. 'And so much cooler — come here and I'll tidy it up for you.'

Kate's atrocities had a particular, as well as a general, purpose. She knew that Mrs Avery was only on holiday, and that she would be returning to the coast for embarkation to Europe in a few weeks' time. It was Kate's plan to have made herself so unacceptable by then that the Kingsleys would send her back at the same time. But no matter how badly she conducted herself they stubbornly refused to admit defeat.

On the last evening before Mrs Avery's departure she resorted to assault. When Mr Kingsley leaned across to pull her chair up to the table at supper she had bent down and bitten him on the forearm, drawing blood. A shambles had ensued. Mr Kingsley had yelled in pain and put her over his knee there and then, to administer corporal punishment, against a background of Mrs Avery's laughter and Thea's rigorous protests. Then Thea had tried to hug her and console her and she had kicked her on the shin, and several things had fallen with a clatter from the table to the astonishment of Karanja, who was looking on with a dish of potatoes in one hand. At last Mr Kingsley, a table napkin round his wound, had borne her thrashing and screaming from the room and dumped her unceremoniously on her bed with orders to stay there 'till she'd cooled off'. Lying there hot with shame and fury she had heard gales of laughter wafting from the dining room. And the next day they had still gone without her.

She was left alone with Thea. Physical violence having failed, she simply went on strike, refusing to get up in the morning and lying curled in bed as tight as a hedgehog and just as prickly. Thea tempted, wheedled and cajoled, in vain. When Thea eventually gave in and left Kate alone she would get up and go and demand breakfast from the luckless Karanja, only a fraction of which she would eat. She would then go back to bed and repeat the process.

She kept this up for three days. On the fourth day, when Thea came to say good-night, she brought something with her.

'Look,' she said, placing it on Kate's bedside table. 'Jack bought this in Nairobi when we first knew you were coming. We were going to save it till your birthday, but I think it might be handy for you now.' It was a brightly painted alarm clock. Kate peeked at it ungraciously from the corner of her eye, her face impassive.

'This is how you work the alarm,' explained Thea, undeterred. She demonstrated and the clock emitted its shrill, cheerful blast, fit to wake the dead, before she silenced it again.

'I'm going to leave it here,' she said. 'And then you can set it for whenever you want. I shan't bother you in the morning any more. Breakfast is at eight, but if you don't want it you don't have to have it. I think it's much better if you suit yourself. By the way —' A terrible thought suddenly struck her. 'Can you tell the time?'

'Yes!' Kate's vehemence betrayed her enthusiasm, but her expression was one of scowling rage.

Thea smiled. 'Night-night then, poppet.'

As soon as she'd gone Kate picked up the clock, turning it round and round in her hands, her eyes drinking in the painted smile, the sun, the clouds, the proud cockerel and the nodding chicken. It was beautiful.

The next day the alarm went at seven. Kate got up, got dressed, and had breakfast with Thea.

Kate, perched on the paddock fence, reflected on how astonishingly patient they had been. Had she been older she would have realized they *must* have wanted her to put up with so much. Anyone upon whom she had been merely foisted would have given up, or resorted to drastic measures.

Joe came up and leaned on the fence beside her. 'Shall we go for a ride?'

She shook her head. 'I was just saying good-bye to Sailor.'

'Dad said we could go out with him this afternoon — are you going?'

'Try and stop me.'

'Wouldn't dare.'

'I know.'

This exchange passed between them automatically, like rehearsed dialogue, a kind of spoken shorthand with which they confirmed their relationship. They were good friends these days, but it hadn't always been so. When Joe had arrived, Kate had loathed him.

She had been on the farm for two years, and was actually beginning to look on it as home, when Thea had begun to get fat and to take things more slowly than she used to. Both Thea and Jack explained that there was a baby on the way, but Kate had closed her ears and pretended it wouldn't happen.

The day of Joe's birth was scorching, but with a sky full of towering purple clouds. Things had been happening during the night, there had been noises and mutterings and the sound of a car. Jack breakfasted with Kate, his face white as a sheet, his hand shaking so much that the spoon jingled when he stirred his tea. The doctor, a Dutchman whose arrival Kate had dimly heard in the small hours, appeared and managed to eat several slices of toast and jam, and to make small talk, before returning to his task. As he left the room he put a hand on the back of Kate's neck and asked if she was looking forward to the new brother or sister whose arrival was imminent. She could still recall the heaviness of his large hand, his red face hovering in front of hers, his breath stale and smelling of stewed tea.

She had answered: 'No.' And he had roared with laughter as much as to say 'What an amusing child' but Jack had gone, if possible, even paler, knowing it was true.

After breakfast she had fled to the garden and hidden amongst some of the then plentiful scrub which Thea and the gardener had been laboriously clearing. She stayed there all day, sweating, scratched, stiff and hungry, but determined not to give in. At about twelve-thirty she heard Karanja calling her name. But he had not persisted — he was rather in awe of Kate — and she had not responded to the summons. At one, when the heat was becoming unbearable, she saw the doctor's ancient black Ford rattle away in a cloud of red dust. Shortly after that Jack had come down to where she was sitting. She saw his feet appear, but said nothing. She wasn't going to help him.

'Would you like to come and see the new baby?' he asked.

'No.' She knew instinctively how to hurt him. Sulky, cold-eyed indifference would be her weapon.

He sat down by her, with effort, scraping himself on the sharp twigs. 'He's rather nice,' he added.

So it was a 'he'. 'Oh,' said Kate.

'He was born about an hour ago,' went on Jack manfully. 'He's got black hair and weighed eight and a half pounds.'

Poor Jack, a father for the first time, tossed on a wild storm of elation and excitement, but having to keep it all hidden on account of jealous, mean-spirited little Kate.

'You really should come and take a look.'

'No, thanks.'

It was hard for Kate, this acting indifferent, for what she actually felt was a violent access of rage and loathing. Now they had their very own baby boy, why should they care about a sorry piece of human flotsam like herself?

She squatted like an African, her chin sunk between her scabby knees, scratching with one finger at the dust between her feet.

'Will you come?' She could tell from Jack's tone that he was beginning to lose interest in the task of persuading her. It was what she'd wanted, but now, sensing his urge to be gone, angry tears of self-pity welled into her eyes. She shrugged, lowering her head still more so that her fuzz of hair shaded her face. 'Well come if you want to. But I honestly wouldn't sit out here any more in this heat, you'll make yourself ill. All right?' He gripped her bony little shoulder and squeezed it encouragingly as he rose, glad that he'd done his bit and could now return to Thea and the intruder.

She'd remained there for another half an hour, both her mood and her stomach curdling and churning nastily in the broiling heat, oily crocodile tears of self-indulgent misery sliding down her cheeks, all the sensation leaving her legs because she'd squatted for so long. She thought that if one of them was watching her from the house, and they saw a movement, however slight, they would take it as a sign of weakness – and she couldn't bear that.

Suddenly there had been a crash of undergrowth and she had glanced up to see Baltazar, the gardener at that time, hacking at the edge of the scrub with a billhook. Baltazar was a tall Somali with a face like a falcon. He was muttering to himself as he worked, drawing closer with every swing of the wicked curved blade. Kate felt like a small animal about to be discovered and destroyed. The muttering grew louder. Black magic, Kate had no doubt, something about eviscerating little white girls and casting their entrails to the buzzards . . .

With a scream like a banshee she rose and shot out of the bushes past Baltazar's legs. The bewildered gardener caught a glimpse of a small white face with an expression of blood-chilling ferocity, and then she was pelting across the rock-hard lawn towards the house, half-expecting to see a long shadow overtaking hers before she reached safety.

Thea had been unsurprised when Kate burst in, fierce-eyed and jealous and perspiring. She had, after all, other things on her mind. But she did say: 'Kate, darling, where have you been? I was expecting you ages ago.'

Kate went over grudgingly and perched on the edge of the bed. Mercifully, she couldn't even see the baby, which was in a small wicker bassinet. There was a blood, sweat and tears smell in the room, overlaid with a faintly antiseptic odour. Thea looked exhausted, rinsed and wrung out but placid. Neither of them said much. Big drops of rain began to patter down outside. Thea said that was nice, they needed it, and asked Kate what she wanted for tea. And gradually, since the baby had not been mentioned, Kate sidled round the bed and peered distantly over the rim of the cradle. Inside lay, not a viper, nor a grinning, miniature edition of Thea, but an expanse of cream flannelette, a small blue-veined, downy head, and one tiny red hand curled like an unopened bracken frond. The baby looked passive, unthreatening, acceptable.

Thea leaned up on her elbow and looked in as well, one hand on Kate's shoulder as if to show how important she still was. 'Not bad, is he?' she said softly.

And so it turned out. Joe had not been bad at all. And when Kate had had her tea Jack had taken her by the hand and introduced her to Sailor, beautiful, beautiful Sailor, a pony of her own, the most wonderful possession a little girl could have. He was not a complete surprise, they had always promised her a pony, but the timing was perfect. Sailor had been specially brought over from a neighbour's farm that day to compensate Kate for Joe's arrival.

After that, there had been no more stumbling-blocks. Kate had not changed. She remained stubborn, touchy, intransigent and independent. But now all these qualities were ranged alongside, and not in opposition to, her foster family. Joe, though dark as a baby, had turned into a gentle, brown-haired little boy, more like his late Uncle Maurice, Thea said, than either her or Jack. If anything, Joe's advent had made her see that she was loved by her foster-parents for herself, uniquely, and that nothing could alter that.

That afternoon, Kate and Joe went out with Jack in the pick-up. He usually made a tour of inspection several times a week, but on this occasion they all knew it wasn't really work, but a kind of disguised farewell.

They drove away from the house, through a series of five-barred gates which Joe leapt out to open and close, past the acres of pyrethrum, now lush and leafy, and on towards the slopes where the sheep were grazed, and where the squatters had their shambas.

The Kingsleys had given up growing coffee during the world slump in the twenties. Now, the farm looked flourishing and even reasonably prosperous. No casual visitor could have guessed at the punishing toll of work, and disappointment, and trial and error which the place had exacted from the Kingsleys. Even now, in spite of its established air, it was precarious. A couple of bad seasons, no rain (or too much), a fall in world prices, and the whole enterprise could collapse like a card house.

Beyond the last gate they turned west on the murram road, towards the shambas, those areas given over to the Kikuyu labourers for their own cultivation. They were so densely packed and heavily cultivated that they looked like a patchwork quilt thrown over the hillside. They were picturesque, too, at a distance, with curls of smoke rising from the huts, women hoeing and digging among the plants and children playing. But proximity revealed the shambas as not entirely idyllic. There, still, were the well-built huts, the carefully-tended plots, the busy women and the skittering children. But between the huts lay a dead dog, stiff and bloated, seething with maggots and flies; nearby a pile of rotting rubbish, mostly vegetable matter, gave off a powerful stench, and this was overlaid with the unmistakable odour of open latrines. The air was hazy with woodsmoke, and dust, and heat, and the steam rising from the rubbish. People ran to meet them as they drove up, from the very old hobbling with the aid of sticks to the very young, as sleek and supple as black fish leaping round the truck; random, discoloured teeth – or no teeth at all – in young faces; hands covered in callouses and sores, but with elegant mauvish filbert nails, clutching the wing mirrors and the edges of the doors; the excitable rattle of Swahili rising from the bobbing sea of black heads like the cacophony of an orchestra tuning up; the glossy, nubile beauty of the unmarried girls, with their many strands of intricately-beaded jewellery and their fat, bouncing buttocks and breasts; and the married women, divided from their sisters by only a few years, but by a wealth of experience, their foreheads deeply gouged from the carrying-strap they used for transporting huge loads of wood, their private parts often painful and septic from the gross practice of female circumcision.

You either understood the African instinctively, or you did not. Thea didn't, and nor did Joe. They applied English reasoning, and English ideas of niceness and fairness, and were consequently put upon, not out of malice but through the African's logic – if a thing is easy, you might as well do it.

This particular ethic had been brought home to Kate one day a few years back when they had been driving up through the baking and thorny Northern Frontier District to visit friends at Eldoret. They had come across a village which had been subjected to a tribal raid. The raid had been some weeks earlier, for the village was deserted, but they had found numerous skeletons, all of women and small children, one so tiny that it was clearly no more than a foetus. The smaller skeletons were scattered about over the thorn bushes like bizarre decorations. African logic at its most lucid and brutal: the weak were disposed of first, and left for the vultures. That cleared the way for the serious fighting with the morans.

At the village Joe, then only eight, had been violently sick, and Thea had returned to the car and sat there white and shaking, while Kate and Jack examined the gruesome remains. Kate had found to her surprise that she was quite able to look at and talk about them dispassionately. It was dreadful, but it was a dreadfulness that was part of a culture, that had been applied consistently and rationally for thousands of years before the Europeans, with their delicate sensibilities, had arrived on the scene.

They left the shambas, with a diminishing escort of shouting hangers-on, and Jack went on a few miles into the bush, pushing the truck along game-trails and through ditches. Kate could remember a time when they'd seen a cheetah here, resting in the afternoon heat, all that speed and grace and power drooping in the fork of a tree like a discarded coat. Friends of theirs, the Dalhousies, had kept a cheetah as a pet, having reared it from a cub. It would prowl among the cane furniture and glass coffee tables, and lie on the verandah in its red collar with an expression of somnolent hauteur, like a bored chieftain. No one was allowed to touch it but Vera Dalhousie, and she used to wrestle with it on the lawn. Then one day heredity had proved more potent than environment, and the cheetah had killed the Dalhousies' two-year-old daughter, and eaten most of her, in an outhouse. So two lives were gone, the child's and the cheetah's, naturally. Jack had just said: 'Bloody fools.'

They didn't talk on their drive, but Jack concentrated on the driving, and Kate and Joe gazed and looked, and drank it all in so that they wouldn't forget. The country was a brownish green, like bronze, and the sky pale and cloudy in spite of the heat. Once Kate looked over her shoulder at Joe with a question on her face — are you all right? And he gave her a little close-lipped smile. He was suffering, time was running out.

They went back, past the shambas, down the winding murram road, through the interminable gates, and round to the side of the house. There was uproar and commotion. Jela was standing outside the back door shouting and stamping his feet. Meru was banging a water butt with a wooden spoon. Somewhere inside the house Cornet, shut in, was barking frantically. As they alighted from the truck Thea emerged from the kitchen, looking harassed.

'Thank God you're back — look, he's there again.'

Sure enough, among the lettuces and beans and sweetcorn they could see the strutting, lion-headed form of the baboon. Kate experienced again that wave of murderous hate. She picked up one of the whitewashed stones that edged the drive and shied it at the animal, but he was already making off and the stone landed short, amongst the vegetables.

'Mind my lettuces!' wailed Thea.

Jack said: 'Hang on —' and got his gun out from its canvas cover in the back of the truck. He tried to get a sight on the baboon, but it was rapidly disappearing among the over-shot cabbages at the far end of the plot. Running forward a few yards he aimed again, and fired a couple of shots in quick succession. The result was a kind of explosion: soil, small stones and plants flew into the air and there was a tremendous scurrying and crashing as the baboon made its getaway, becoming entangled in the bean canes as it went so that both rows collapsed. Thea groaned and covered her eyes with her hands. Jela and Meru, encouraged by the gun and its obvious efficacy, gave chase with much yelling and waving of arms.

'Damn!' said Kate. 'He's beaten us again.'

'I'm afraid so.' Jack reset the safety catch and replaced the gun behind the seat of the truck. Thea went over to inspect the damage to the vegetables. Jim appeared at her side, leaning his linked hands on the handle of a hoe.

They went back into the house. Kate called to Jela for tea, and the three of them went into the drawing-room, releasing Cornet from bondage in Thea's room as they passed. The sun had moved over the house and was pouring in at the drawing-room windows.

Jack and Joe sat down, Jack with a week-old copy of the London *Times*, Joe in a brown study. Kate wandered to the piano and stood by it, picking out a tune with a couple of fingers, idly, looking at the photographs that clustered on the gleaming lid. Some of them were just groups of snapshots which Thea had arranged in old frames. There was Thea's father, whom Thea was said to resemble but who in this picture looked black and irascible. Kate studied him with new interest, for she and Joe would be staying with him in Lewisham. Of course, he was an old man in his eighties now, and probably foul-tempered one by the look of him, she thought. Their other host would be Thea's brother Aubrey. There was a picture of him as a rather staid-looking youth in cricket clothes, with a bat under his arm and gloves in his hand. On either side of his wide, solemn face his ears stuck out beneath the cap like handles.

Next to Aubrey in the same frame was a photograph of Thea's cousin Maurice, who had died just after the war. He stood in the middle of a lawn, his feet together, his hands in his pockets, obviously ill-at-ease before the camera. He looked skinny, bespectacled, donnish, but Kate knew Thea had a special affection for him, and that in spite of his unheroic appearance he had been courageous in defence of his pacifist beliefs. Then there was Thea's beautiful mother, also now dead, a lovely Edwardian lady with flowers in her hair and a long fan in her hand.

Finally there was Dulcie, Thea's younger sister. Kate took a particular interest in the two photographs of Dulcie, for of the English branch of the family it was Dulcie who had taken the most interest in her as an individual. Right from the start she had sent little presents – or *cadeaux* as she called them, for she was given to French phrases. Kate, though grateful, had been mystified, but Thea had explained this behaviour by saying that Dulcie had always been something of a loner and a rebel, and probably saw her as a kindred spirit.

The first picture of Dulcie showed her and Thea when both girls must have been in their early teens. Thea, though serious and composed, looked a little wary. But Dulcie was beaming, curling one tendril of blonde hair round her finger, dimpling prettily.

The second picture was a newspaper cutting which Dulcie had sent about two years ago, with an inked-in arrow declaring 'This is me!' It showed a slightly older Dulcie, pretty and chic (though poorly reproduced in the paper) among a group of equally smart people in the Royal Enclosure at Ascot. The picture's caption said that it showed HRH The Prince of Wales 'studying form' as they put it, not without intentional *double entendre*, with friends among whom were . . . Dulcie's name was not mentioned.

Kate was sure she would meet her Aunt Dulcie while in London, but in spite of the presents she did not expect to like her. She sounded a vain and silly woman. She picked out 'Blue Moon' very softly. Cornet, lying on the sheepskin, moaned and yelped.

Joe said: 'Shut up, Sis, you're upsetting the dog.'

She let the tune peter out. The afternoon was turning into evening.

That night after supper they sat out on the verandah. Kate had put a record on and they could hear the debonair tones of The Master warbling about being 'World Weary', an unimaginable condition in the soft African night.

Joe sat on the steps, his chin on his knees, holding a book but not paying it much attention; Kate was leaning on the verandah rail; Thea and Jack were sitting on either side of a round wooden table. On the table stood an odd assortment of objects: Jack's whisky glass, and a china water jug covered with a small net, weighted with coloured beads, to keep insects out; a gardening book of Thea's, open, the place marked by the spectacles which she should have worn more often; a plate of Huntley and Palmer's mixed biscuits; and a mug containing half a dozen apostle teaspoons which Meru always provided with any kind of drink.

A hurricane lamp hung from the roof, surrounded by a flittering halo of moths and insects. In the soft, black sky a golden moon, large and low, hung like a second lantern. The air near the house was still, but beyond it in the night it shivered and vibrated with small sounds, the dark seething with nocturnal life.

Jim's lanky form crossed the far edge of the pool of light shed by the hurricane lamp. He had taken off the shorts and was swathed in the traditional red Masai blanket against the evening cold.

'Doesn't he look marvellous?' said Thea as Jim dissolved once more into darkness.

'Hm. What's he up to?' Jack had little admiration for the Masai, whom he regarded in the main as untrustworthy vagrants.

'Who cares?' said Thea.

She was leaning back in one canvas garden chair with her feet up on another. Her long, thin, brown legs protruded from the hem of her faded blue linen skirt, disappearing at the ankles into thick grey socks and rubber-soled boots. Beneath the bridge made by her legs sat Cornet, sheepishly protective of her even in such familiar company.

She turned to Kate. 'We're going to miss you so much,' she said, putting out a hand.

Kate clasped it briefly, embarrassed. Cornet, in sympathy with his owner's every mood, peered up at Kate mournfully, the hem of the skirt trailing over his brow like a monk's cowl.

'You won't forget to send me those photographs, will you?' asked Joe.

'Of course not.'

'And what about that other jacket I was supposed to have?'

'It's ordered from Daniel Neal's, darling. You should get it as soon as you arrive at school, and I've put extra Cash's names in your trunk so matron can do that for you right away.'

'Don't forget you're having a holiday first,' said Jack, a little forced, trying to lighten the mood. 'You're going to enjoy yourselves.'

'I can't wait,' said Kate, meaning it, though it was not the holiday she looked forward to. 'It's going to be terrific, I know it.'

She glanced at Joe. The book dangled from one hand. His face was averted, his left cheek resting on his knees. Abruptly, Thea put on her glasses, took a letter from inside the back cover of the gardening book, and read aloud: 'We are so looking forward to meeting them both, and just hope they won't find their elderly relations too dull . . .'

There was a long, humming pause.

'By the way, we should leave at five,' said Jack.

'Jack . . . !' Thea didn't like him to be so blunt and practical, but Kate found it helpful. She had to withdraw from them, and become once more the stern, reclusive determined little girl who had arrived in their home fifteen years before.

She didn't really belong to them, their blood wasn't in her veins, and now was the time to remind herself of that, so that she could be strong for both herself and Joe.

'I'll be ready,' she said.

She reflected on her foster-parents. People wondered at their apparent differences, but Kate knew that Jack's dryness was the flint that drew Thea's spark. For him, Thea had learned willingly, but often painfully, to care for Kenya. East Africa was his life, the dry red soil had his blood in it, every stick and stone of the farm was as it was because he had made it so, his body was battered and bruised with the effort of keeping it his. And, because she knew how much he cared, she had stuck with it, and with him, through the bad times — and there had been many — and never spoken of unhappiness or regret. The last time they had gone back to England had been ten years ago, for a couple of months, and Kate and little Joe had stayed with the Dalhousies for that time. But for Thea the tug of home was powerful and persistent.

Meru came on to the verandah. 'Tea, *Bibi*?' He addressed Thea.

'Tea, anyone . . . ? No, thank you, Meru.' Cornet growled a token shot. 'Naughty,' said Thea mildly, putting her hand on the dog's head.

'Blasted dog,' said Jack.

'What's that?' said Joe. He stood up, dropping *The Thirty-Nine Steps* on the ground. A dark shape was just visible in the middle of the grass. It was still now, but it must have advanced to its present position while they were talking, for it had not been there before. Joe took a step forward. Thea clasped Cornet's collar. Jack rose and went down quietly to the edge of the grass.

'Shut that dog in, would you,' he said. Thea opened the door and ushered Cornet in, drawing the curtains so that he would not bark.

Kate went down to join Jack. 'Can you see?' she asked.

'No. Well, whatever it is, it's not moving.'

They stood straining their eyes in the semi-darkness, watching the black shape for nearly a minute. It was motionless. Softly, Jack went forward until he stood over it. 'Well, I'll

be damned . . .' His voice sounded quite gentle. 'So I got the
old reprobate after all.'

The three of them went to join him. On the grass lay the
baboon. There was a gunshot wound, dark and sticky, clearly
to be seen amid the long coarse hair on his shoulders. The
wicked, strutting truculence that had so inflamed Kate had
gone. He looked now what he was — a beaten, broken old
animal, an outcast with no place to die but the territory of a
hostile species. His eyes were opaque slits. His small, delicate
front feet were curled in a prayerful attitude.

'How funny,' said Joe, 'that he came towards the house when
he knew he was going to die.'

'Yes, poor thing,' said Thea, forgetting Dora and the puppies
for a moment.

'I don't suppose he did any such thing,' said Kate, because
she felt rather the same way. 'You're just being fanciful.'

Very early next morning, a little before five, they set off. It was
cool, and the light was grey. Soon, the sun would rise steeply
over the horizon in the swift, brilliant, African dawn. Long
before they began to climb the escarpment, it would be
broiling.

Thea stood by the truck with her arms folded. It was loaded
with trunks and cases and Kate's and Joe's hand-baggage. At
the back rode Meru, as Jesus had done on that occasion many
years before, to help Jack pick up supplies in Nairobi. Only he
was grinning broadly, sitting on his hands and swinging his
dusty black legs as they made their farewells.

They were brief. No one could think of anything appropriate
to say, or they could think of too much and so remained silent.
A dawn hush presided over their quick hugs and whispers,
giving them an almost furtive air, as though their leaving was
a secret. And then the truck, with Kate in the front seat and
Joe squeezed in between her and Jack, moved bumpily towards
the first gate.

Thea waved vigorously, and smiled, the tears pouring down
her cheeks. Then she went back to the house and sat down on
the verandah chair she had occupied the night before. Cornet
came and sat by her knees. Infected by her mood, he whined.

The tears continued to trickle through her fingers, and to drop in dark spots on her cotton skirt. In a little while the crimson crescent of the sun slid over the horizon, and in an hour the skirt was dry and she went into the house to begin her day's work.

CHAPTER TWO

'I'm a little lamb who's lost in a wood:
I know I could
Always be good
To one who'll watch over me . . .'

'Someone to Watch Over Me'
George and Ira Gershwin, 1926

'CELINE!' Dulcie Tennant, dressed in a lace-trimmed petti-coat of eau-de-Nil satin, opened her bedroom door a chink. 'Celine! *Viens ici, s'il te plâit.*'

She went to her dressing-table, with its ranks of bottles reflected in the smoked-glass top. The many facets of her own pleasing reflection looked back at her from the elaborately arched mirror like the golden-haired angel in some sentimental Victorian triptych.

Her blue Persian cat, Fondant, jumped on her knee. 'Shoo!' cried Dulcie, but she cuddled him beneath her chin before placing him on the floor, where he began to wash fussily to conceal his chagrin.

'Madame?' Dulcie's French maid, Celine, appeared in the doorway, her overblown figure poured incongruously into a prim navy dress with white collar and cuffs.

'Celine, be a perfect angel and make sure the white dress is all right for this evening – I think it may need a stitch in the shoulder.'

'Certainly, Madame.'

Celine came into the room and stood admiringly behind Dulcie, who was powdering her throat. 'Your friend is coming for tea?'

'Yes!' Dulcie smiled brilliantly at her maid in the mirror,

cocking her head to put on tiny gold earrings. She was in excellent spirits. The two women presented an interesting contrast. In June 1936 Dulcie Tennant was approaching forty-one and her maid was a year younger. But whereas Dulcie might have passed for thirty, Celine looked her years. And where Dulcie was gamine, fair-haired and pale skinned, Celine was a stout, swarthy woman who still, after more than twenty years' service for Mlle Tennant, looked like the Corsican peasant she was, and whose short upper lip bore the shadow of a slight moustache.

Dulcie rose from the dressing-table and stepped into the dress she had lain ready over the end of the bed – a slub-silk shirtwaister in brown and white dogtooth checks, with a pleated skirt.

'What time will Mr Donati be calling?' asked Celine, as she removed the white evening dress from the wardrobe.

'Oh . . . about eight.' Dulcie twirled, so that her skirt fanned out round her slim legs in sheer stockings.

'I shall take the white dress to my room then,' said Celine. 'The tea trolley is ready in the kitchen.'

'Then – *allons-y*!' cried Dulcie, clapping her hands and clasping them together with an air of the warmest well-being.

She had two engagements which were out of the ordinary this weekend. This afternoon a woman friend was coming to tea. Tomorrow, Sunday, she was going south of the river (a journey which for Dulcie was akin to crossing the Styx) to spend the day with her father and brother in Lewisham. The first of these she looked forward to; the second she dreaded. Both were part of a secret life which the majority of her acquaintances would have found most curious – so she didn't bother to tell them. Dulcie was a woman with a great many secrets, and the keeping of them was second nature to her.

Now she put tomorrow from her mind and went through to her drawing-room which overlooked the street. Her flat was on the second floor of a tall, cream stucco house in Belgravia, whose colonnaded porch and lofty entrance hall gave no clue that it was not, like its neighbours, the private palace of some wealthy aristocrat, but contained the homes of several persons of more modest means. Dulcie liked her smart address. It meant a lot to her to be surrounded by the big guns of London high society. Only last year Sir Henry Channon had bought a magnificent house in nearby Belgrave Square, and though Dulcie never expected to be invited there she liked to think of Emerald Cunard, von Ribbentropp, Diana Cooper and other exalted beings flocking there of an evening to dine in Regency splendour and exchanging *bon mots* over the gulls' eggs.

Now she sat down in the window seat and gazed out, waiting for her visitor. Chesham Gardens, with its central island of leafy green enclosed by forbidding black spiked railings, bore a superficial resemblance to a street Dulcie had once lived in in Paris, but the difference between that and this reflected the upward curve of her fortunes in the intervening period. Or at least that was what she told herself. To question the assumption would have been to open up a veritable Pandora's box of fears.

Fondant came to sit by her and she stroked him with firm, quick strokes. She would have liked a cigarette, but she did not want her guest to find her smoking.

As the carriage clock on the mantelpiece struck four she saw her visitor pass between the pillars and mount the steps to the front door, and she herself left the drawing-room and hurried along the passage so as to be out on the landing when the lift came up.

She watched the ropes, hawsers and pulleys swing gently, and peered down between the wrought-iron bars of the outer door at the top of the lift as it rose, majestically, two floors. It stopped with a slight bounce and Dulcie's guest, after a short tussle with the stiff inner door, emerged.

'You're so beautifully punctual, Primmy,' said Dulcie, beaming.

'I do my best,' replied Primrose Dilkes. 'How are you keeping?' she added, as Dulcie closed the door of the flat after her.

'I'm extremely well,' said Dulcie, taking her friend's unseasonal navy coat and hanging it in the hall cupboard. 'And what about you?'

'I've no time to be anything else,' answered Primmy, straightening the cuffs of her good plain blouse, 'you know me.'

The trouble was that Dulcie was not at all sure she *did* know Primmy. Once, in another time and place, another world,

Primrose Dilkes had been the Tennant family's parlourmaid. Now she was a ward sister at St George's Hospital, only a short walk from where Dulcie lived. The circumstances of their meeting again, after an interval of many years, had not been propitious. It was 1922 and Dulcie had only been back in London a few months, living in stylish impoverishment in a mews flat lent her by a friend, Simon Garrick, and roaring through her meagre savings on a flood-tide of gin-and-it, pink champagne, couture clothes, Russian cigarettes and other basic essentials. No Bright Young Thing had been brighter, everyone agreed, than this beautiful girl with a past, newly arrived from Paris. She was 'taken up' in a big way by young men and women to whom money meant nothing and whose main purpose in life was to be gay, modern and amusing till four or five each morning. From the smoky, suggestive gloom of the Kit-Kat, the '43 or even once or twice from the plushier sanctum sanctorum of the Embassy, she would emerge with the rest of her set just before dawn, all of them intoxicated not just with bubbly but with dancing and laughter and their own glamour, and set off on treasure hunts that took them all over London, six to an open sports car, screeching and shouting and *parp-parping* down the deserted streets on a quest for drakes' feathers from St James's, or a guardsman's jacket button.

On the night in question Dulcie had simply fallen (it still made her cringe to think of it) out of the MG convertible in which she and five others were cruising round Hyde Park Corner, looking for an amenable bobby whose truncheon they might appropriate. Mercifully, because of the importance of the search, they had been in the outside lane and travelling slowly. Dulcie, fairy-like in silver and stephanotis, and as drunk as a lord, had leaned too heavily on the side door which she had in the first instance not closed properly. It had given way, and lo! she had been deposited almost at the feet of a constable, but in no state to take his truncheon. Grazed, bruised, soiled and very, very sick she had been escorted into the Emergency Department of St George's, there to spend a miserable half hour in the company of other, less pretty drunks, down-and-outs and accident victims pouring blood, before being attended to.

The ministering angel — firm, efficient and disapproving —

had been Primmy. If anything had been needed further to humiliate Dulcie, it was this. Each stinging dab of disinfectant, each wad of lint and tight-wrapped length of bandage, served to underline Primmy's practical value and her own uselessness. They had hardly exchanged a word, but next day Dulcie had sent flowers and a note, and from these unpromising beginnings their unlikely friendship had grown, at first haltingly but at last into something sturdy and real, though they met but rarely.

When they did, certain rituals were observed.

'I brought a cake,' Primmy said now, taking a round tin from the tartan shopping bag she had set down beside the cupboard. 'And I bought some muffins on the way,' she added, 'though how you keep body and soul together with the prices they charge round here, Lord alone knows.'

Dulcie ignored this last comment. 'Muffins, the utterest heaven. But in June . . . how decadent.'

They went into the tiny kitchen where Celine had laid the tea trolley. Primmy knew quite well that Dulcie employed a maid, and Dulcie knew that she knew, but it was part of the game that they never mentioned her. Primmy removed the cake carefully from the tin and laid it on a plate. It was a cherry cake, the top decorated with a mosaic of almonds in concentric circles. Dulcie watched her friend from the doorway. She herself was far from useless in the kitchen, but she lacked confidence there, feeling always that she might initiate some messy calamity. She was quite happy to look on.

Primmy made the tea, re-filled the kettle for extra hot water, turned off the grill and buttered the muffins.

'There we are.' She dusted her palms, executed one or two small manoeuvres which, miraculously, made the kitchen look tidier, and pushed the trolley back along the corridor to the drawing-room.

On more familiar territory Dulcie resumed the role of hostess, pouring the tea— stronger than she herself would have made it — into translucent Sèvres cups and proffering lump sugar with silver tongs (Primmy took three).

'Tell me all about your new flat,' she went on, 'are you pleased with it?' She knew Primmy had recently acquired a small flat of her own in Bethnal Green, having survived hitherto in a nurses' home, an environment whose ghastliness Dulcie could scarcely imagine.

'It's not at all bad,' replied Primmy, sipping her tea and balancing a plate with a muffin on the arm of her chair, 'though I say it myself . . .' and she proceeded to enlarge, speaking of spring-cleaning and a lick of paint, and a set of chairs at a knock-down price in the market, while Dulcie listened, fascinated.

As she listened she broke off a morsel of cake and gave it to Fondant, who sat at her feet. Primmy at once paused in her discourse to suck her teeth disapprovingly.

'I didn't make it for him, you know, he'll get fat.'

'What a thing to say! He *always* has a bit of what I'm having.' It pleased Dulcie to provoke Primmy a little.

Primmy sniffed, in a way that was very like her late mother. 'Cats never struck me as very friendly animals.'

'Oh but he is. He runs to meet me when I come home.'

'I daresay – he knows who feeds him.'

'Celine!' Dulcie laughed. 'Celine feeds him. But it's still me he loves.'

'Hm.' Dulcie had slipped up. Talk of Celine made Primmy feel awkward, raising as it did the spectre of her years in service. She relapsed into silence while Dulcie, anxious to cover up her slip, described how she had seen Gertie Lawrence at a recent party, not to talk to, of course, and what she had been wearing.

Primmy munched her muffin reflectively. In the far-off days when she had been the Tennants' employee she had never been discouraged from friendship with the daughters of the house, quite the reverse, in fact. But had she herself been disposed towards such friendship the youngest of the Tennants' three children would not have been her choice. The young Dulcie had been vain, selfish and lazy, and had been the centre of a scandal – Primmy had not known what, nor dreamed of investigating – the ripples from which had been felt throughout the family for several years thereafter. But worse than all this, from Primmy's point of view, Dulcie had been cruel to Maurice, the Tennant children's cousin, obliged with his mother to live at Mapleton House in the unenviable situation of a dependent relative.

It would not have been true to say that Primmy and Maurice had fallen in love. For one thing, their relative situations in the Tennant household militated against it, and for another their separate natures, in quite different ways, obstructed it. But during the war years Maurice's pacifism had given Primmy something to respect in him, and her nursing provided Maurice with yet more to admire in her. A tentative mutual attraction had grown. But though Maurice had found the courage to tell Primmy of his feelings she had resolutely kept hers hidden, denying them even to herself for reasons which seemed excellent at the time, until it was too late. Maurice had died only weeks after the war ended. Whatever fragile shoot of love had pushed its way to the surface of their odd relationship was prematurely nipped off.

But Dulcie, of all people, who had so incensed Primmy with her baiting and teasing of Maurice, had returned from Paris for his funeral. And Primmy, always fair, knew what that must have cost. So when Dulcie had turned up in Emergency four years later, bruised and bedraggled in silver and white like a fallen angel, Primmy had been disposed to magnanimity and touched, the following day, to receive a chastened note of thanks and ribbon-wrapped pink carnations. Dulcie was right in assuming that Primmy would intuit a good deal about her without being told, that she would guess that the intervening years had not all been a bed of roses, and give her the benefit of any doubt. Primmy admired resourcefulness and it was plain that it must have been present in large measure to see a vain, silly creature such as Dulcie had been through four years of war in a foreign city.

Added to this, both women were in their different ways solitary, Primmy mostly from choice, Dulcie from the strain of keeping so much of herself secret, even from her family. So it suited each of them to have this friendship which was quite outside their everyday lives and dealings.

But the delicate fabric of their relationship was composed of a warp and weft of tact and things left unsaid, and Dulcie had snagged it with her unthinking mention of Celine.

The phone rang in the tiny dining-room and Dulcie rose with relief to answer it. 'Excuse me a second.'

Primmy listened to her light, animated voice, punctuated

by laughter and exclamations. Primmy, though not entirely lacking a sense of humour, rarely laughed or exclaimed, so it was like eavesdropping on some foreign language.

'. . . But how extraordinary, I didn't know they knew each other . . . yes . . . yes . . . would that I'd been a fly on the wall! No, I'm dining with Rex tonight, but we shall be at the Chambers' on Tuesday . . . I don't know, is that what she said? I shall just wear what takes my fancy . . . yes, no . . . I'll see you then. Good-bye, Giles.'

The phone went down with a *tring* but Dulcie did not reappear immediately. Primmy guessed that she was writing something down in her diary.

Now she came back into the room briskly, with a smile. 'That was my friend Giles,' she announced, flinging herself down in her chair. 'I'm afraid he and I gossip like anything.'

'Do you now,' said Primmy.

The rest of their time together passed in peaceful small talk. When, at five-thirty, Primmy rose to leave, the two women engaged in another small ritual.

'You will take the rest of the cake with you?' asked Dulcie.

'Nonsense. It was a present.'

'The trouble is, I shall eat it.'

'So long as it's you and not that cat.'

'And it will make me fat.'

'You could do with a bit more weight.'

Primmy buttoned and buckled her gabardine coat, and skewered a little felt hat to her head. She still wore her brown hair long and scraped back in a bun, just as it had been all the years Dulcie had known her. She longed to tell Primmy how much prettier she would look with a shorter, fuller style, but such a recommendation would have fallen on very stony ground indeed.

Primmy's ankles were trim in dark stockings beneath the unfashionable long coat. She looked businesslike as she picked up her tartan bag. Hers was a life too busy and purposeful for frippery, reflected Dulcie a little wistfully.

'Keep in touch,' she said, as they waited on the landing for the lift to come.

'Of course I will,' replied Primmy. Dulcie knew she would, she was nothing if not sturdy and dependable.

The lift arrived, Primmy got in and closed the stiff door with a clank. Dulcie watched her thin, erect figure sink slowly out of sight, heard her brisk tread across the tiled hall, and the clunk of the heavy front door behind her.

In Dulcie's bedroom Celine had laid out the mended white evening dress, silver shoes, and tiny silver evening bag. Dulcie wore a lot of white, because it suited her and there were not many women of her age of whom that could be said. She stroked the dress. The sound of the bath running floated along the passage.

'Celine, you're an angel,' she called. She undressed in her room and wrapped herself in her white towelling bathrobe.

She had just closed the bathroom door behind her when the phone rang. 'Be a dear and answer that.'

She gazed at herself in the mirror, listening to Celine's distant voice; footsteps back along the passage; a knock at the door. 'Yes?'

'It was Mr Donati, Madame.'

Dulcie closed her eyes. 'I'll come.'

'No, Madame, he left a message.'

Dulcie opened her eyes and gazed down at the perfumed steam rising in clouds from the surface of the bath.

'Madame . . .?'

'Yes, go on Celine.'

'He wishes to go to a cocktail party first, in Cadogan Square. Please can you be ready at six-thirty.'

'Thank you, Celine.'

Dulcie removed her robe, stepped into the water and sank down, lying full-length and looking up at the ceiling. The bathroom was very Rex, stylish, modern, expensive, but strangely unluxurious. The ceiling upon which Dulcie now gazed was painted with overlapping geometric shapes in brown, black and cream. Now, she thought, I shall have to hurry, and still manage to appear calm when he arrives. He might even turn up before she was dressed, and shout at her through the bedroom door, a practice she detested, but had to endure for the sake of a quiet life. How like him just to leave a message and assume she would comply!

At six-fifteen, as she was putting on her shoes, she heard his key in the lock, and Celine's effusive welcome. She thought

Rex wonderful, even her accent became perceptibly richer when she addressed him. Listening to her, Dulcie smoothed her stocking a shade too vigorously, and laddered it.

'Blast!'

Rummaging in her drawer for a fresh pair, and once again removing her shoes, she heard the clink of glass in the drawing-room, Rex's sharp, snapping laugh, Celine's admiring giggle. Then a rap on the door.

'Buck up old girl, what's keeping you?'

'I've just laddered a stocking, shan't be long.'

'Get a move on, won't you, it's the Roth-Veseys.'

'You said half past six.'

He didn't reply. Just outside the door he was whistling softly: *Blue Skies*. She knew he would be leaning against the wall. The whole thing was a sham, since he had no respect for her privacy and would march in without knocking if he felt like it.

She replaced her stocking and shoes, sprayed scent on her wrists, throat and neck, fluffed her hair and went out to face him.

As soon as she emerged he bounced away from the wall and embraced her with the casual, proprietory air she so detested. At the same time his embrace served to remind her, forcibly, that he was only twenty-four years old, smooth skinned, lean-bodied and rapaciously sybaritic as only the very young and very rich can be.

'You look simply terrific,' he said. He kissed her. 'As usual.'

'Thank you!' She brushed her fingers across his cheek with just the faintest hint of motherliness, to keep him at bay. 'Do I have time for a drink before we go? To set me up?'

He drained his own glass. 'I can hardly refuse.'

In the drawing-room he poured her a Martini, and another gin and tonic for himself. 'I should tell you,' he said, handing her her glass, 'that the Roth-Veseys are buying a new house.'

'I see.'

'I'm fairly certain old Percy will ask me to do it. Tonight I want to make sure.'

'Oh, absolutely.'

So it was business, thought Dulcie wearily, and he's telling me to be on my best behaviour. When am I ever anything else with Rex?

Rex Donati, though possessed of a substantial private income, also ran an exclusive but flourishing interior design business. His talent was small, but his contacts in high society were legion and his vanity colossal. This last, rather than financial necessity or pride in his work, spurred him on to win commissions. The existence of his business also helped him to strike an artistic attitude among the socialites, and that of an insouciant dilettante among the intellectuals, thus he was never obliged to compete with either. He had no style of his own. Futuristic, romantic, Victorian, or oriental, he would provide it speedily and at such enormous cost that the customer was bound to consider it the best that money could buy, or himself a gullible fool. It was a case of the Emperor's new clothes.

Dulcie would have liked to discuss his work with him. She herself had a flair for the subject, but he regarded her as woolly-brained, and never consulted her. She sometimes regretted having missed the boat in the '20s, when many enterprising young women were setting up in boutiques, and hat shops, and home decorating and other small artistic endeavours. But she had been too busy enjoying herself at the time, and trying to drown the past under a tide of dissipation, to attempt anything so challenging and realistic.

'I shall be as good as gold,' she said.

At the cocktail party Dulcie moved from group to group, sometimes accompanied by Rex, sometimes not. She spoke to people she scarcely knew, operating on an automatic level, her smile brilliant, her manner animated and engaging, spouting small talk spiced with some wit and considerable charm, giving the impression she was a person of greater consequence than was actually (she thought) the case. When Rex was not beside her she could tell his whereabouts by the sound of his laugh, or the gleam of his fair head a couple of inches above everyone else's. But she did not seek him out, or feel abandoned if he was not at her side. She was his accessory, she completed the picture of Rex as a gay dog, the sort of fellow who could afford to keep a pretty, older woman as a *divertissement*. And it was as an accessory that he treated her — not badly, but casually. It wouldn't do for her to appear miffed because he abruptly left her to talk to another woman, and never came back. A flower in the buttonhole was no good if it wilted.

Their hosts at 23 Cadogan Square, Percy Roth-Vesey and his American-born wife, Una, were rich beyond the dreams of avarice; Percy because his family had been tyrannical and acquisitive landowners for generations and Una because her father had clawed his way up to become something huge in the automobile industry in Chicago. Dulcie was in the habit of referring to Percy and Una as friends, though she knew that in fact they were merely acquaintances. Una was professionally effusive and had raised social gushing to the level of an art form. Now she fell upon Dulcie.

'Dulcie, my lamb!'

'Hallo, Una.'

'You look quite, quite lovely. Every party should have at least one woman with your style. How on earth do you do it?'

'Just low cunning, I suppose,' said Dulcie sweetly.

Una hooted with laughter. Nearly all her utterances came out with a hoot. In a crowded nightclub it was always possible to locate the Roth-Veseys by means of Una's mooings and croonings. She was a smart, confident woman, whose day-time excursions were habitually taken in the company of a flotilla of hyper-thyroid chihuahuas. Dulcie, a cat person, dreaded encountering Una between the hours of midday and six because of the unpredictable yapping and snapping of these pets. Una's chief cachet, as a hostess, aside from her money, was her American blood, on account of which she claimed an understanding of the behaviour of the Simpson woman, whose existence was now grudgingly acknowledged by London high society.

'. . . and white is *so difficult* to wear,' she was saying now, 'I do have so much admiration for a mature woman who can wear white . . . Now *where* is the beautiful Rex . . .?' She set off, steering Dulcie by the elbow so that her champagne cocktail sloshed dangerously in its glass.

Rex was busy furthering his business interests with Percy Roth-Vesey. Dulcie could tell he was making headway by his animated gestures and frequent laughter, and by Percy's look of slightly confused agreement. Percy was in his late fifties, a good twenty years older than his wife, and might once have been handsome. Now he was increasingly red and wheezy and troll-like, and Dulcie quailed when she thought of Una's stick-insect figure submerged beneath that mountain of whiskery flesh.

Also in the group, listening to Rex's sales pitch with an air of polite and somewhat amused curiosity, was Louis Avery. Louis had been one of the young lions of the government during and just after the war, but had left politics with a flourish upon the formation of the National Government and had since become plump, sleek and bland on the huge profits from an advertising agency in which he was a partner. He would still, at the drop of a hat, air his political views with wit and verve in the quality dailies, but he was now generally regarded as a born advertising man who had gained political experience, rather than a retired politician turned advertiser. At Louis's side stood his wife Andrea, an old friend of Dulcie's sister Thea. Andrea was a left-wing intellectual, full of good works, and since childhood Dulcie had viewed her with a mixture of scorn and envy, the latter giving way to the former as the years had passed. Beside her husband's air of glossy, pomaded opulence Andrea, though impeccably groomed, looked severe.

'You've brought us Dulcie, how absolutely topping!' exclaimed Percy, perhaps glad to escape the hold of Rex's glittering eye.

Dulcie smiled and kissed and was kissed back as Una drifted, cooing, away.

'And looking like a fairy queen as usual,' added Louis, putting his arm across Dulcie's bare shoulders because he knew it irritated Rex.

'I'm not sure I know how to take that,' said Dulcie, laughing across at Andrea who was smoking a small cigar in a holder and looking non-committal. Andrea probably did not know the meaning of anything so base as jealousy, but one had to allow for it just the same.

'Dulcie . . . Dulcie . . .' Percy leaned over and tapped her forearm with his fingers. 'You must take it like a man!' He subsided into a rumbling, bubbling whistling spasm of laughter while the others smiled faintly.

'I was telling Percy how keen I am on this new all-white look,' said Rex to Dulcie, though he had never previously mentioned this predilection to her. 'Their new house is quite modern. Think how stunning it could be all in white, but with everything in different textures – silk, wicker, velvet, rattan. I'm certain Una would adore it.'

'I'm certain she would,' said Dulcie.

'And how are you keeping, Dulcie?' enquired Andrea, as Percy recovered and Rex resumed the attack. 'It's ages since I've seen you.'

'Yes – far too long,' agreed Dulcie, though with Louis's arm still hot and heavy on her shoulders, and Andrea's gimlet eyes on her face, it seemed not nearly long enough. 'I'm in the pink,' she went on, 'very idle of course, but then I always was.' She paused, laughing, and Andrea did not bother to deny it. 'Not like you, you're always so occupied – what are you doing at the moment?' She did not in the least want to hear, but anything was better than further enquiries about her own life.

'I'm working at a settlement in the East End,' replied Andrea, tapping her cheroot briskly into one of the solid silver ashtrays in the shape of a cadillac with which Una's father had endowed the Roth-Vesey household.

'You should come and see us some time when you have a moment,' she added, 'you'd be very welcome.'

When do I not have a moment? thought Dulcie wryly. 'Oh, I should just be in the way,' she said. 'You don't want silly unqualified people like me standing about and getting underfoot.'

'Who said anything about standing around?' Andrea raised neatly-plucked crescent eyebrows. 'There's plenty to do, I assure you.'

'Oh, well . . . I didn't mean . . . .' Dulcie was momentarily thrown. 'Of course I could help, but I'm no good at anything.'

'Any fool can wash up,' said Andrea.

So she is capable of jealousy, thought Dulcie, and buttoned her lip. She felt Percy's lecherous, rheumy eyes on her and flashed him a winning smile. It had the desired effect.

'Dulcie! Let me take you away from all this. You see this

fellow –' he slapped Rex in the midriff, 'all the time. There's a whole host of unfortunate people who haven't met you waiting out there, and I'm neglecting my duties as host. Come along now.'

He ushered her away, effecting his own escape as well as hers and leaving Rex and Andrea, who loathed each other, to make the best of it. I managed that well, thought Dulcie, I bet I could do more than wash-up.

Suddenly she spotted Giles Huxley standing alone near the door. A warm spring of delighted surprise leapt up in her. She waved. 'Giles!'

Percy followed her gaze. 'Someone you know?'

'Yes, Giles Huxley.'

'Means nothing to me, my dear, friend of Una's would he be?'

'Oh – probably.' She clasped Percy's arm in both hands and gazed meltingly into his face. 'May I go and talk to him if I promised to circulate like a Trojan afterwards?'

Percy chuckled and patted her hands. 'Of course, of course, just run along and enjoy yourself.'

She wended her way to Giles's side, coinciding with fresh supplies of champagne and helping herself.

'Heavens, it's good to see you, Giles!'

'That bad?' He kissed her hand and laid it fondly for a moment against his cheek. 'I didn't know when I called you this afternoon that you were going to be here. Or I shouldn't have bothered. Naturally,' he added, grinning at her.

'I didn't know I was going to be either. Rex rang at the very eleventh hour because he wants to do up the RV's new mansion. And as a matter of fact your call was very welcome, because it saved me from an embarrassment.'

'Good Lord, what can that have been?'

'I had put my foot in it – as usual. With someone whose feelings I'm usually most careful not to hurt.'

'In that case I'm glad I was of service.'

'You know Percy hasn't a clue who you are. Did Una invite you?'

'It was indeed the bold Una who summoned me. I suspect she leaves little gaps in her guest list for A. N. Intellectual, or in my case A. Playwright, and then invites any with whom she has a nodding acquaintance.'

Dulcie laughed and put her arm through his. 'What space do I fit into?'

'A. Trollope, of course.'

'Of course.'

Since the war, in which he had distinguished himself, and whose legacy he bore in the shape of a gammy leg, Giles Huxley had been first, belatedly, a student at Cambridge, then a schoolmaster, and was now a highly successful playwright in the new more thoughtful and political mode. His current work, *A Hornet's Nest*, was attracting large and enthusiastic audiences at the Haymarket. Its subject was the effect of a personally charming, but rabidly Marxist teacher on an English public school. It was the blackest of black comedy, and Dulcie, who had gone without Rex at Giles's invitation, had thought it magnificent. She thought Giles magnificent. In appearance he was of medium height, grey-haired and a little fleshy as many once-muscular men are prone to become in middle-age. His voice was deep and intense, almost an actor's voice, as though each word had been carefully considered for its absolute rightness. He was in almost every respect an attractive and accomplished man.

But Giles Huxley was homosexual. People knew about it, of course, it was part of his 'artistic' persona, but for him to display any evidence of his penchant would have been absolutely not on. And since his sexual proclivities were, in any case, illegal they necessarily found expression in clandestine promiscuity. So Giles, a man of vision, integrity and humour, and capable of great and unselfish affection, was obliged to lead an unsavoury double life.

'You know I could have introduced you to Gertie the other evening,' he said now. 'You'd have liked each other, she's enormous fun and absolutely unaffected.'

'I'm sure she is, Giles, but Rex wouldn't have liked it one little bit.'

'Why ever not?'

'He doesn't like theatre people, he feels upstaged by them.'

'Foolish boy.'

'He doesn't like you.'

'But for other less mentionable reasons, I suspect.'

'For every reason you can think of.'

'Imagine! What a hero I am to soldier on without the benefit of Rex's esteem.'

'You're good to keep a sense of humour about it.'

'It's easy, my dear, as far as young Rex is concerned, because I don't care a jot or a tittle for his opinion of me. Now if it were you who thought these harsh things, that would be a very different matter.'

'Bless you, Giles.'

They stood together for a moment in companionable silence. Then Dulcie caught sight of Rex craning imperiously over the heads of others, looking for her. She caught his eye and lifted a hand.

'I think I have to go. We're going out to dinner.'

'Good-bye then. Have a nice evening.'

'It'll be the same as usual, I expect.'

'Cheery-pip.' He raised his glass to her as she went.

Rex was scowling. 'What were you discussing with Huxley amid so much laughter and merriment?'

'Other people,' she said, half truthfully. 'They're so funny.'

'He's funny. He gives me the creeps.'

'Well never mind.' Safe in a social context, Dulcie was prepared to stand her ground. 'After all, I hardly have any friends of my own. I mean, that weren't originally your friends.'

'No, and if Huxley's anything to go by you display atrocious taste when left to your own devices.'

'Oh dear . . .' she kissed his cheek. 'Don't be cross. How did you get on with Percy?'

'Not half bad,' Rex brightened. 'I think it's in the bag. I mean Una is the go-ahead one and she will buy whatever I care to sell her, and he will want to indulge her so I think I've got it.'

'That's splendid – so we can make our dinner a celebration.'

They found their way to Una, like dutiful children after a Christmas party. She turned to them as though they had plunged a dagger into her heart.

'You're not *going*?'

'Table's booked, *c'est la vie*. But it was the most tremendous fun.'

Rex took her by her bony shoulders and kissed her on both cheeks. 'See you soon.' He raised his eyebrows quizzically.

'Oh, I'm sure of it.' She gave him a speaking look.

Deep inside Dulcie a hitherto sleeping snake of rebellion lifted its head and flickered its tongue.

The intimate dinner in a small French restaurant, and subsequent early return to Chesham Gardens which Rex had organized, were not the best treatment for Dulcie's quietly mutinous mood. A late night with a gay crowd — dinner, dancing, cabaret and yet more dancing — might have taken her out of herself and reminded her that life could be fun with Rex, and expensive fun at that. As it was he was at his most trying — lustful, overweening, contentious and petty. After three hours of putting up with his behaviour in the sort of dark, garlicky, candlelit atmosphere designed for romance rather than sniping, she felt worn to a nothing, a shadow. Her usual teasing, feminine acceptance came hard to her tonight, and her difficulties did not go unremarked.

'What the hell's the matter with you?' Rex asked peremptorily as they drove home in his Daimler Dart.

'Nothing! Why?'

'You know bloody well why. I don't mind other men flirting with you. I do object to your behaving like a tart.'

As they moved off again Dulcie folded her hands tightly in her lap and stared out of the window. She tried to work out why it was that when Giles called her a trollope it was all right, but when Rex used that word it made her stomach lurch with pain. After all, both terms were accurate, and both users knew it.

'. . . when you must have known I was talking business with Percy,' Rex was going on, working himself into a silly rage, 'and within two minutes you had everyone dancing attendance on you, and even succeeded in removing RV altogether. Really Dulcie, sometimes you are so bloody childish it leaves me speechless.'

She gave a hysterical little laugh and converted it into a cough. 'I'm sorry, I really am.'

'Hm.'

He relapsed into a sulky silence, broken only by occasional colourful vilification of other road-users.

For the remainder of the journey Dulcie allowed herself the dubious indulgence of self-analysis. She was of a certain age, a middle-class spinster with a chequered past, very little formal education and a single talent which could only deteriorate. Her position was precarious. When she looked about her, she concluded that this was because she had not served the right apprenticeship.

Take Una Roth-Vesey for instance (and many had). She compensated for a life of unbridled selfishness and immorality with an outward show of affluent respectability. She admitted to thirty-eight; had two strapping sons at Eton; a household in Mayfair and another in Norfolk (and now, apparently, a third); and that final, crucial asset to promiscuity, a husband. All of these constituted Una's passport to social acceptability. Una, unlike Dulcie, had laurels upon which to rest.

Dulcie, on the other hand, was a kept woman. It was ironic to think of the hours she had spent in her room as a girl, ignoring the appeals of Thea and Aubrey to go riding, swimming, cycling to the village. She had shut the door and dreamed of being a rich man's plaything, and now here she was. Of course in the beginning, in Paris, she had been her own mistress – what an odd expression that was – but gradually, almost imperceptibly, one thing had led to another until what had started as a brave show of independence had ended in this subtly demeaning form of luxurious slavery.

They turned into Chesham Gardens and drew up outside Number 6. Rex switched off the engine. 'Cheer up,' he said, 'for heaven's sake.' It was an order. He never assumed he had hurt her feelings or caused her unhappiness.

He opened the door of the flat with his own key while she stood by, his goods and his chattel.

Fondant trotted soundlessly across the carpet with a welcoming 'prrrp!' He writhed round Dulcie's ankles, then Rex's. Rex nudged him away and brushed the long, blue-grey hairs off his trousers.

Dulcie walked ahead of Rex into the drawing-room. Celine had, as usual, left everything ready and welcoming, and lit the two pink glass lamps which were Dulcie's pride and joy. The lamps had white silk hand-painted shades; she had bought them in Paris and had them shipped over at great expense when she had moved back to London.

They were the only items in the room which Dulcie had bought herself. There were a few gifts, notably a long Chinese wall-hanging depicting fighting cocks which Giles had given her, and a tall palm also from Giles, to stand in front of the hanging when Rex was present. The rest of the room, in shades of champagne, white and pink, had been put together to complement the French lamps, more or less to Dulcie's taste, but at Rex's expense.

She slipped off the red coat, her gloves and evening bag and dropped them on a chair. Then she went over to the bamboo and glass drinks trolley – 'very Raffles' Rex called it, but she thought it vulgar – where Celine had left ready glasses, ice and olives. And also an airmail letter, propped against the whisky decanter. It was from Thea. On the envelope, Celine had written in pencil: 'So sorry, Madame, it came this morning.'

Dulcie set it aside to read later.

'What's that?'

'A letter from my sister in Kenya.'

'Aren't you going to read it?'

'Not now. It'll be enormously long. I'll settle down to it when I've got plenty of time.'

She poured a Martini for herself and a whisky and soda for Rex. When she turned back he was lying on the champagne velvet sofa, his feet up on one end, well-groomed blond head on the other, one hand trailing knuckles-down on the floor.

Dulcie took him his drink and he lifted his hand languidly and held the glass balanced on his white shirt front. She curled up on the floor beside the sofa.

'Isn't this nice?' She took a cigarette from the onyx box on the coffee table, lit it and passed it to Rex. She helped herself to another, drawing on it voraciously.

'Giles –' Dulcie was going to say 'rang' but thought it wiser only to mention those exchanges of which Rex already knew, 'Giles said that on Tuesday Flavia Chambers wants us all to go as famous murderers.'

'Jesus wept.'

'I thought if we went as someone recent it need hardly mean dressing up at all.'

'I shall go as myself and murder Flavia when I get there.' He tapped the ash of his cigarette over the back of the sofa on to the white carpet.

He drained his glass and passed it to Dulcie to put on the table. He left his arm extended, making a little snapping motion with his fingers as you would to an animal. 'Come here.'

It was Fondant who padded over and nudged his head into Rex's palm.

'Infernal cat.'

Dulcie, glad of the diversion, laughed and scooped up her pet in her arms.

Rex thought how taking Dulcie looked, kneeling on the rug like a young girl, cuddling that bloody cat. It was scarcely decent for a woman of her age – he guessed she wouldn't see thirty-four again – to appear so youthful. Time and again he told himself to get shot of her, to find some pretty, well-connected young lady of whom his parents would approve, and marry her, instead of wasting time and money keeping middle-aged Dulcie Tennant in a manner to which she had readily become accustomed. But then he would be struck afresh, as now, by her luminous beauty, her exquisite elegance, and put off the evil day once more. Also, he was intrigued by the slightly quixotic air of mystery which surrounded her.

'Come here for God's sake.' He snapped his fingers again. She hitched herself along the floor to him, still holding Fondant. 'And get rid of that wretched animal.' She did so. 'What do you want to make a fuss of him for when you have me?'

She bent gracefully beneath the encircling pressure of his arm, smiling before she kissed his upturned face. 'You don't need a fuss made of you.'

'Do.' His voice became childish. It was often the prelude to their lovemaking.

'Don't.'

'I do. I need pampering.'

'You're pampered quite enough already.'

'Then pamper me more.' His voice was soft now. He

transferred his cigarette from one hand to the other behind her back and reached to drop the butt in the ashtray. 'Show me what little girls are made of.'

Dulcie lowered her face to his again, and his arms tightened about her bare shoulders. Across the room the rejected Fondant, sitting in state on a cream velvet armchair, watched them with drowsy detachment.

Dulcie woke next morning with a bad headache. In spite of many years' practice, heavy smoking and drinking were activities she could engage in with impunity only when she was in the right frame of mind. The previous evening at the restaurant she had drunk Chablis like lemonade in the hope that it would deaden the impact of Rex's rantings, and it had not. They had drunk again on their return, and yet more later, before he left in the small hours. (Since the withdrawal of Sir Hector and Lady Donati to Wiltshire, Rex had sole use of their opulent Park Lane establishment, but Dulcie rarely went there.) At three in the morning, when they had finished one bottle of champagne, he had begun criticizing her again, this time for certain sexual tactics which he had clearly enjoyed at the time, but which he now declared to be further evidence of her 'tartiness'. It was a line of attack she was well used to, but all the same she was so exhausted when he finally left that she poured herself a large whisky and finally went to sleep with her stomach churning and the room revolving sickeningly around her.

When Celine brought her tea and *croissants* at nine o'clock she moaned and waved a limp hand at the bedside table, saying, 'Just put it there, Celine, I can't face a thing.'

She lay on her side, listening to Celine move about the room, picking up things from the night before, tactfully reclaiming dirty glasses, drawing back the curtains.

'What's it like outside?'

'*Il fait très beau*, Madame.'

'*Merde.*' Dulcie pulled the bedclothes tighter. A lovely day, and she and her hangover had to trail all the way down to Lewisham to do her duty by her family. She turned her face into the pillow and made a determined effort to get back to sleep.

Half an hour later she was disturbed by the shrill note of the phone. Celine answered it and then came to her bedside, leaning over her solicitously and speaking in a low voice. 'It's Mr Donati. Do you want me to say . . .?'

'No, no, I'll come.'

Pulling on her towelling robe, she stumbled across the passage into the dining-room and picked up the receiver.

'All merry and bright?' Rex's voice fairly crackled across the line. Dulcie winced.

'Not exactly.'

'Parrots, is it? I've got just the thing for you. I rang the RVs this morning and they suggest we go down and look at the house. . . which obviously means I'm in. It's at Sunningdale, we could tootle down in the jalopy, see the house, have lunch at a watering hole . . . and so forth. What do you say?'

Her heart sank. 'Rex, darling, I did tell you, I have to go and visit my family today.'

'Put them off. We could walk by the river – go for dinner at Skindle's, even, it's ages since we did that.'

'I can't! I don't see them very often, and the date was fixed ages ago.'

There was a short, loaded silence. 'You're not honestly telling me that on a glorious day like this you would prefer the ghastly tedium of a day with your next of kin to a spin in the country with Yours Truly?'

'Not prefer, of course not, but duty calls.'

'What about your duty to me?' His tone was petulant, but she knew that he meant it. She felt frightened.

'You're not a duty, you're a pleasure.'

His laugh came over the wire like machine gun fire. Relief washed over her.

'Very well, abandon me in my hour of glory. Fly to the bosom of your boring family, but allow me to run you there.'

'Thank you.' She would much rather have gone on her own, but to refuse would have been to push her already over-strained luck. 'I have to be there for lunch.'

'See you at twelve, then.'

When, at ten past one, he roared and squealed to a halt

outside the Tennants' house in Mapleton Road, he leaned over and peered teasingly into her face.

'*Dulcie* — you're not honestly going, are you?'

'I *wish* I hadn't got to, but I must.' She bent to kiss him quickly, anxious in case the door should open and she should be caught in an awkward clash between her two worlds.

'Rubbish! Let's just drive on, and you can ring them from the other end with some absolutely spiffing excuse which we shall concoct on the way.'

'I simply can't.' The trouble was, she was tempted. Rex was a delight this morning, so good-humoured and carefree and persuasive. But she knew from experience that the sunny mood could break into a storm at any moment. She glanced nervously up at the house and saw the front door open and her brother Aubrey emerge to stand at the top of the steps.

Rex laughed and leaned across her to push the door open. 'Go on then, I know when I'm not wanted.'

'A drink, or something . . .?'

'Wouldn't dream of it old girl, and I'm late for my tryst with the RVs anyway.' He raised his arm in salute to Aubrey. 'Hail and farewell! Mustn't stop!' And with a roar and a clarion blast on the horn, the Dart shot away down Mapleton Road.

Dulcie went up to greet her brother, who was peering after the car suspiciously.

'Who the blazes was that?'

'Rex, he gave me a lift.'

'A dubious favour by the look of it, you took your life in your hands.' He kissed his sister's cheek and closed the door after her. The hall was high and dark and smelt faintly of mutton. Dulcie thought of Rex, and the Dart, and champagne in the sunshine.

'How come you answered the door, where's the girl?' she enquired as she removed the scarf from her head and bent to fluff her hair out in the hall mirror.

'I didn't "answer the door", I heard Donati's car fouling the atmosphere and came to investigate. Doreen has the second and fourth Sundays in the month off.'

'What, when you have guests?'

'You're not a guest, Dulcie, and we can't just move her day off when it suits us.'

'Celine is there whenever I want her.'

'Ah, Celine.' All Aubrey's considerable powers of caustic wit were contained in these three syllables. Dulcie followed him across the hall. He wore a whiskery tweed suit more appropriate to a grouse moor in November than Lewisham in June. But then she had never seen Aubrey dressed less than formally.

He opened the drawing-room door and walked in ahead of her, going directly to the mantelpiece for his pipe and settling it comfortably between his lips.

'Here's Dulcie.'

Ralph Tennant was sitting in a wing-backed chair to the right of the fireplace, his legs set squarely apart, his face obscured by a newspaper. Now he lowered the paper and glared at his daughter. 'You're late.'

Dulcie glanced at her tiny watch. 'Not very.' She went over and kissed his truculent, upturned face.

Ralph had always been a big man, and his particular development in old age had been to become somehow more massive, and gnarled like an ancient tree. His hair, though still dark, was now wiry and wild, and his moustache curved down over the corners of his mouth, giving the lower part of his face a threatening, piratical look. He had become cantankerous with no women to grace his life and only a bachelor son for company.

'Late, just the same,' he added accusingly, setting the paper aside with a swish and a smack, to indicate that now she was here she had better set about entertaining him.

'Well, I'm sorry.' Dulcie accepted a glass of sherry from Aubrey. It was an excellent brand, but she loathed sherry and they never offered her anything else. She took a sip and set her glass down precariously on top of the pile of periodicals which occupied the surface of the only occasional table.

'Here, I brought you a little something.' She took a prettily wrapped package from her handbag and handed it to him. He undid it, puffing and sighing. It was a small round box of French truffles. He turned it this way and that with a scowl, but his passion for sweets was unassuagable.

'Thank you, that was kind. Very kind. Thank you.'

'Don't have one till after luncheon,' she admonished.

'Why not, dammit? They're mine and I'll have one whenever

I please.' He put one in his mouth and ate with relish. They went through this routine, or variations on it, every time she came.

'You'll have no appetite, you're very naughty.' She handed a second package to Aubrey.

He removed his pipe from his mouth. 'For me?' He opened it. 'Good Lord, the pernicious weed, that's very civil of you.'

'You shouldn't encourage him,' rumbled Ralph through a truffle. 'It's a filthy habit and I have to live with it.'

'No filthier than eating truffles before luncheon,' remarked Aubrey equably.

Dulcie took another sip of her sherry, feeling the dreaded creeping paralysis of boredom taking a hold. 'So — what news?' she enquired brightly, perching on the arm of the sofa opposite Ralph and crossing her legs.

'We had a letter from Thea yesterday,' said Aubrey. 'Actually she said something about writing to you at the same time.'

Dulcie clapped her hand to her brow. 'Oh! How silly of me. Yes, a letter did arrive yesterday, and I told myself I'd read it when I had some peace and quiet . . . I just haven't got round to it.'

'Too occupied for reading family letters, eh?' said Ralph caustically, but she ignored him.

'What did she have to say?'

Aubrey went to the desk by the front window and fetched the letter, putting on his spectacles to peruse it.

'A lot of the usual sort of thing . . . Thea's writing is terrible . . . not enough rain . . . farm problems . . . some black fellow beaten up . . . ah here we are, about the children, Kate and Joe.'

'What about them?' Dulcie took a cigarette from the silver case in her bag, placed it in a short jade holder, and lit it. She drew deeply, and exhaled a smoke screen in front of her face. She was conscious of a tiny moving speck of anxiety, like an armed man on a distant horizon, getting nearer.

'They're coming over at last,' said Aubrey. 'Apparently the lad got a place at Hartfield House, down in Sussex, starting in September, and Kate will accompany him over and find a job in London . . .' He continued to scan the letter, turning the pages and muttering to himself. 'Nothing much else.'

Dulcie placed her feet, in navy high-heeled sandals, neatly together, to conceal the surely obvious fact that her heart was in them, trembling like a frightened rabbit. Carefully, she smoothed her stockings to calm the shaking of her legs. Her face felt icy cold, her whole body heavy. Kate was coming over . . . nothing much else. Briefly she closed her eyes, tried to steady herself.

Sitting up and reaching for her drink she asked: 'What about holidays? Where will they live? I mean — it all sounds a bit sudden.' And I, she thought, sound shrill and anxious. So she added: 'But how very nice.'

'Hm.' Aubrey glanced at her. 'I don't foresee any problem. They'll come here to begin with, at least, for a bit of a holiday.'

'When?' Again, she was sharp. She took another gulp of sherry. 'When will that be?'

Aubrey flapped the letter. 'Thea says they're hoping to book a passage in a couple of weeks' time, which would get them here about the middle of next month.'

'So soon! Lovely.'

'These truffles are top-hole,' remarked Ralph. Aubrey folded the letter twice and stuffed it into his jacket pocket, as if closing the conversation.

So, thought Dulcie, the blow which shatters your life is dealt casually, briefly, carelessly, between sherry and lunch. She felt she must do something in case they were both staring at her.

'Could I have another?' She held out her glass, conscious of Aubrey's disapproving look. But further infusions of Dutch courage were denied her by the reverberation of the gong in the hall.

'Luncheon!' cried Ralph, lurching ponderously to his feet, truffle papers showering from him like confetti. Aubrey took Dulcie's glass and set it, with a censorious air, on the mantelpiece. Dulcie, aware now that she was being waited for, rose unsteadily. Her hands and face were chill and damp. She felt awful. Please God just let me get through it, she prayed, with no great faith in her prayer being answered.

Ralph glared at her. 'What's the matter with you, you look even peakier than usual. Been burning the candle at both ends, I suppose.'

'I expect so.' She smiled faintly and followed him out of the drawing-room and across the hall. The slight figure of Mrs Duckham stood by the top of the back stairs, next to the gong.

'And what culinary delights have we today?' barked Ralph, rubbing his hands together, pretending he was back at Chilverton House when 'Old Duckie's' powers had been at their height.

'A nice leg of mutton sir.'

'Caper sauce?'

'Yes, sir.'

'Capital!'

The dining-room, even in midsummer, was cold and rather dark. The long sash window framed a view of the truncated plane trees which lined Mapleton Road, their bulbous arthritic branches barely softened by a meagre growth of green. The two central leaves had been removed from the dining table so that it looked forlorn in the middle of the worn Persian rug, the three places laid for lunch a dismal echo of what used to be.

Dulcie sat down with a sigh. The silver needed polishing. Aubrey went to the hatch in which the food arrived by pulley from Mrs Duckham's subterranean galleys. On the high-sided tray, when it appeared, was a large greyish leg of boiled mutton, a jug of caper sauce with an incipient film of skin, and two dishes of vegetables cooked to within an inch of extinction. Dulcie found herself breathing deeply, as if there was no air. She wished she had never come. She should have been out in the sunshine with Rex, enjoying one more day of gaiety and freedom before reading her letter.

'Only a *soupçon* for me,' she said, touching Aubrey's arm as he began to carve, 'I'm not all that hungry.'

After tea, which was taken in the long, walled garden, Dulcie declared that she must go, and Aubrey went into the house to summon a cab from the local rank.

'Unless, that is, you are returning with the death-defying Donati.'

'No.'

She stood up and glanced down at her father, who was dozing in the dusty sunshine. Sunk deep in a deckchair, heavily shod feet planted on the lawn, thunderous jowls resting on his chest, Ralph looked comical. She reached out her hand and laid it on his knee in a rare gesture of affection.

'What's that?' He peered up at her dazedly.

'I'm off, Father. Don't disturb yourself. And thank you for a nice day.'

'Nonsense, I'll come and see you off.' He leaned forward, his face suffusing with the effort of levering his bulk out of the chair, then sank back. 'Confound it. Anyway, take care of yourself and come and see us again soon.'

'I'll try.'

Already, his eyelids were drooping once more. A fly settled on the back of his large, thickly-veined hand and sat rubbing its feelers together. Incensed, Dulcie shooed it away.

In the hall she took her scarf from the peg and tied it loosely round her neck. From the open door of the dining-room drifted the smell of the plum duff they had eaten for pudding four hours ago. Aubrey put his hands on her shoulders and kissed her firmly on each cheek. Dulcie felt that he was stamping her, like a parcel, to remind her where she had come from.

'You know it might be a good thing for you to get to know young Kate Kingsley,' he said. 'She'll need some female company, I don't doubt, before she finds a place of her own. You could take her about a bit, show her the sights and that. Keep both of you out of mischief.'

'Don't treat me like a child, Aubrey.' She felt terribly weary.

'Just the same.'

He opened the front door for her. The cab was parked at the bottom of the steps, the engine idling, the shirtsleeved arm of the driver resting on the open window in the late afternoon sunshine. A small girl played hopscotch on the pavement.

'Good-bye then, and thank you.'

'Good-bye Dulcie. Take care of yourself.'

She ran down the steps, gave her address to the cabbie and climbed in. As the taxi drew away she waved gaily to Aubrey. Then she leaned back and closed her eyes with a long, trembling sigh.

When she arrived home it was to find Rex *in situ*, reading the

Sunday paper and drinking pink gin, his good humour apparently untarnished by a day deprived of her company. He had caught the sun, he looked burnished and healthy.

'Surprise!'

'I am surprised.'

'Libation? Why don't you help yourself.'

She went to the trolley and poured herself a drink. Then she slipped off her shoes and sat down in the window seat with her legs curled up beside her. She reflected that Rex could with very little trouble have given her a lift home, and that his failure to do so was her punishment for not going with him. He's just a selfish child, she thought. Celine had moved Thea's letter from the trolley to the mantelpiece, as a reminder.

'Since you're kind enough to ask,' Rex said, 'I am duly commissioned to revamp the Roth-Veseys' new house.'

'Well, that's simply wonderful,' she forced a smile. 'And you had a good day?'

'First-rate day.'

'I'm so sorry I couldn't be there.'

'Couldn't be helped. Tell you what though, I've got another surprise for you.' He came and sat down on the floor, so that his head was on a level with her knees. The evening sun fell brightly on his upturned face.

Dulcie's heart sank. 'Really? You're full of them today.'

'Aren't I just. And this is a corker.'

'Tell me.'

'How do you fancy a cruise in the Med?'

'I don't understand . . .' Rex went abroad quite often, to Venice and Monte Carlo and Le Touquet, but had never taken her before.

'It's perfectly simple, old girl. I'm the RVs' best boy at the moment, so they invited both of us to be guests on their yacht in a couple of weeks' time – to cement the contract and so forth. You know how old Percy lusts after you, your presence is the absolute *sina qua non* as far as that lecherous bugger is concerned.'

Dulcie saw, now, what it was all about. It was business again, or she would not have been invited.

'Don't look so wary, we'll go and buy you a few outrageous beach outfits.'

She thought, he's nearly twenty years younger than me, and yet just like Aubrey he assumes he can treat me like a child. 'No, you go,' she said, 'they don't really want me.'

'Don't fish for compliments, it doesn't suit you.' The cloud no bigger than a man's hand appeared in the hitherto clear sky of his mood. 'What on earth have you got against the idea anyway? I should have thought you'd have been tickled pink at the prospect of three weeks' unbridled luxury on the ocean wave at the RVs' expense.'

Three weeks. Suddenly Dulcie's mind began to race, to make calculations and see possibilities. An escape route, sunlit and fun-filled albeit temporary, opened before her. 'You're right,' she said. 'I'm just tired this evening, that's all. Of course I'd *love* to come.'

'Attagirl.' He reached up and took her hand. She put down her glass and allowed him to pull her down on top of him, 'I knew you'd come round.'

'I love you,' she whispered, perjuring herself for the umpteenth time.

He did not stay the night – he rarely did, anyway, and never on Sundays – and at ten o'clock she fetched Thea's letter and sat at her dressing-table to read it. In spite of her sister's careful wording, it had obviously been a delicate letter to write. Certain phrases jumped off the page at Dulcie. 'She's always felt the pull of England . . . I couldn't stop her, even if I'd wanted to . . . I'm certain everyone will fall for her, though of course you need no persuading of *that* . . . dear, dear Dulcie, we've been so lucky, and I think of you so much . . . it was bound to happen some time . . .'

Dulcie put the letter down. Her own reflection in the mirror startled her. Such a small person, such a shrunken white face, and thin arms and neck, such staring eyes, shadowed by too many late nights. It horrified her, it was like watching oneself disappear. A terrifying sense of unreality swept over her. At Mapleton Road she had felt that her true identity was with Rex. Here, alone, it seemed that she had been more herself with her family. The truth was, she thought, she was nothing and nobody. Her whole life had been constructed from deceit and pretence and downright lies. Even Primmy, who deserved better, did not know the half of it. She allowed Rex to feed on his prejudices and assumptions about her because she thought that was safer than the truth. And to her family, with the exception of Thea, who was thousands of miles away, she had lied so long and so skilfully that she could never undo the damage. There had only ever been one true and real thing in her life, and she had chosen to deny it.

But soon – postponed only by the holiday – she was going to have to confront that reality, that creation of hers from which there was no escape. She feared it would be too much for her, that the brittle, hollow thing she had become would be smashed to smithereens by the shock. She raised her hands and pushed her hair back roughly, revealing her face, stark and small and frightened.

'Look at you,' she said bitterly. 'You're not fit to be a mother.'

CHAPTER THREE

'I'm world weary, world weary,
Living in a great big town,
I find it so dreary, so dreary,
Everything looks grey all round . . .'

'World Weary'
Noel Coward

To meet his nephew and niece at Tilbury, Aubrey Tennant had set off at least an hour earlier than necessary, and wore his best dark suit and a bowler hat. Far from being hot this mid-July afternoon it was blustery and overcast, threatening rain. Aubrey had brought his umbrella, too.

He stood on the dock, as stocky and solid as a capstan, watching the HMS *Balmoral* bump into her moorings, the lowering of the gangplank, the arrival and departure of customs and immigration officials. Further up the quay, an army band was thumping out a medley from the popular shows. The ship's rail was thronged with people waving and shouting amongst whom, he supposed, were Thea's offspring, scanning the crowd for him.

What had they been told, he wondered, what were they looking out for? He would like to have been characterized as a successful businessman. His period at the helm of Tennant Enterprises in Southwark had been notable for high productivity, stability, expansion and good labour relations. In sharp contrast to the coalmines, steelworks and shipyards of the north, the light service industries of the south-east were flourishing.

Aubrey, though brusque in manner, was a kindly man. He felt for the suffering of the unemployed. But his duty, as he saw it (and duty was a prime force in his life) lay in those areas with which he was directly concerned, that was to say his family, and his family business. He couldn't understand the young left-wing intellectuals who aligned themselves with causes they could not possibly understand — hunger marches, the war in Spain — instead of getting out and adding to the country's wealth by doing a job of work.

He sighed. Whatever his talents as a businessman — and he was liked and admired by both his own work force and the heads of other companies with which he dealt — he doubted whether they bulked large in the picture that Thea had painted of him. Fond though she was of him, she would have given her children the impression that he was a dry stick, a stuffy old bachelor. All true, of course.

But he'd done his best. He had consulted, awkwardly, with Doreen, to make Kate's room a little prettier, with a new chintz bedspread and some roses from the garden which he had put in himself that morning. In the boy's room, he had placed a desk by the window and rooted out some of his own old books from the case in the basement. He felt sorry for the lad, coming all this way from home to face up to the rigours of an English public school.

Passengers began to trickle down the companionway, like a stream, into the waiting lake of friends and relatives. Aubrey pressed forward, craning his neck, looking out for a likely pair. The people who had been first off were already starting to walk away from the quay, so that he was moving against the tide. It would be too terrible if, in the confusion, he missed them.

'Uncle Aubrey? Aubrey Tennant?'

They were upon him. In the press, he had trouble for a moment deciding which of the sea of faces had spoken.

'Yes, that's me.' A tall, sharp-faced, red-haired girl.

'I'm Kate Kingsley, how do you do. And this is Joe.'

'How do you do, sir.' A quieter person, less emphatic.

'Well — welcome to you both!' He debated with himself whether to embrace either or both of them, but he was at best undemonstrative, and they were such complete strangers. They all shook hands. 'How did you know it was me?'

'A simple process of elimination,' said the girl. Aubrey wondered again what Thea had told them.

'Well, shall we go? The car's parked through there.'

They seemed to have an unconscionable amount of luggage. They toiled across the docks, with Aubrey carrying as much as he could manage, and breaking out in a heavy sweat. When he stopped to rest his arms Kate picked up one of the cases.

'This is ridiculous, let me have that back.'

'Really, I'm perfectly . . .' But she was already striding on, making light of the case. Aubrey caught the boy looking at him with a look of shy understanding.

'Oh well,' he said, and they set off again.

He regretted having brought the smaller of the two cars. He put the largest case on the roof of the Austin, with difficulty and his nephew's assistance, another two in the boot, and asked Joe if he would mind having the fourth on the back seat next to him.

'Not at all sir.' The boy resembled someone of Aubrey's acquaintance whom he could not at that moment call to mind.

As they got in, Kate said: 'Sorry about the luggage. There's more, as a matter of fact, but it's coming by road services.'

Aubrey hoped he hadn't seemed to be making heavy weather of the cases. 'That's perfectly all right. After all you're going to be with us for some time.'

This remark, intended to be reassuring, initiated an awkward silence. Aubrey sensed irritation on the girl's part, despondency on the boy's. The length of their proposed stay was obviously not a good topic to dwell on when they'd only just arrived.

They joined the queue of vehicles leaving the docks. There was a storm brewing, great purple-black clouds were piled over the rooftops, and some of the cars had headlamps on.

Kate turned her collar up. 'It's going to pour with rain.' She sounded almost pleased, as though she had been confirmed in her prejudices. Aubrey told himself to be patient.

'Looks like it. But the weather's been simply beautiful, so we're due for a bit.'

'What a funny thing to say!' She turned to Aubrey and grinned, as if to cancel out any rudeness of which she might have been suspected.

Aubrey was conscious of the grin, but did not take his eyes off the road. He would have felt a little more confident if he had actually known who she *was*, but in spite of all his good intentions the fact that she was adopted was a stumbling block.

Good Lord, she might say or do anything, she was a total stranger. Also, she seemed to be surrounded by a crackling forcefield of aggressive confidence and self-possession which he found most disconcerting. From the moment she had located him on the dockside she had effortlessly relieved him of the initiative. He began to wonder if the chintz bedspread and the flowers had been such a good idea after all.

At Mapleton Road Ralph was not in evidence and Aubrey showed Kate and Joe at once to their rooms 'to settle in' as he put it, telling them that tea would be in the drawing-room in half an hour. Kate was not sure what she was meant to do. Having been told that someone called Doreen would unpack for her if she left her cases out, there seemed little left to occupy her. So she unpacked the smaller case anyway, put her nightie under the pillow, and the chicken alarm clock on the bedside table with her book of Scott Fitzgerald short stories. She wound up the clock and the black chicken began pecking away, a solitary familiar sound in this strangely silent house.

She went to the long window and gazed out over the garden at the back of the house. A long narrow garden, bounded by high brick walls; on all sides a vista of other high houses, long gardens, forbidding walls; tall trees that craned for the light; rain, that awful rain that plummetted from the low, grey sky to the soggy ground and lay in dirty puddles on the black pavements. The view from her window was like a weight pressing on Kate's heart. She had been used to space, and light and heat, a landscape spread out in shimmering shades of umber and gold, stretching to a far-off but visible horizon. On board ship there had still been that space, that light, that sense of freedom. This sudden, terrible change was almost more than she could bear. She was going to hate it. After so many months of longing to be here, of dreaming of a new life where she would make her own way, she felt a terrible breathless fear that she would fail, simply because she could not live here. She turned abruptly from the window, and as she did so her arm caught the roses which stood in a china vase on the chest of drawers, and a few pink and white petals dropped with a tiny, dead sound on to the polished wood.

There was a faint knock on the door.

'Yes?'

Joe's head came round the door. 'It's me.'

'So it is. Come on in then.'

She went to the bed and flopped down on it, full-length on her back, her fingers laced behind her head, ankles crossed. Joe entered and closed the door carefully and quietly behind him. His excruciating politeness suddenly infuriated her.

'There's no need to creep about as if you were in church,' she said loudly. Joe sat down on the edge of the bed and gazed at her. Perhaps he was checking her out for signs of weakness. She braced herself.

'So. How are you?' she asked more brightly. 'Room all right?'

'Yes it's fine. A bit dark . . . but okay, you know.'

'I know.' She stretched out her hand and tapped his arm. 'Hey!' He looked at her. 'Chin up, it's going to be fine. Let's go and find some tea, I'm rattling.'

Ralph Tennant, putting on his jacket and fixing his collar with slow, heavy movements, heard the two sets of footsteps going down the stairs. He was apprehensive, and he knew he had been cowardly. Far from sleeping this afternoon, as he normally did between two and four, he had lain awake, tense and watchful and listening. There had been the sound of the car, the voices in the hall — theirs so high and penetrating after Aubrey's deep rumble — then the heavy clump as cases were carried upstairs, the doors of long unused rooms flung open, the voices nearer. New occupants for an old house, new ways, no doubt, to jar on their old ones, to uproot them from their dull, comfortable habits. He was unsettled. Also, though it had taken him all afternoon to admit it even to himself, he was suspicious of the girl. For Ralph, blood ties had a mystical, almost a heathen potency, he believed in them with stubborn ferocity. None of the vicissitudes of the Tennants' fortunes could shake his faith in them, nor quite conquer his mistrust of those he saw as interlopers. No matter what the boy was like, Ralph could accept him, for he knew that Thea's blood ran in his veins — Thea who had been his darling, his favourite, and whose loss to another man he could never quite forgive. But this girl, who was she? Some complete stranger masquerading as his granddaughter. How could it possibly be the same?

'Can't be. Can't be.' He growled to himself as he left his room and stumped along the passage to do battle.

'Father,' said Aubrey, coming to meet him at the drawing-room door, 'I'm sorry we weren't back before you took your rest.' This last was said pointedly, but the implied rebuke was lost on Ralph.

'Never mind that.' Ralph marched past his son into the centre of the room. 'Now then, who have we here?'

Joe sat on the sofa with a photograph album open on his knee. The girl was over by the window, a dark shape against the wan afternoon light.

'This is Joe.'

The boy stood up and advanced politely, hand extended. 'Hallo Grandpa.'

It was a heady moment for Ralph. He clasped the thin, brown hand in both his, squeezing it, and peered fiercely into his grandson's face. 'Hallo young man. You're the dead spit of your Uncle Maurice, did you know that?'

'As a matter of fact Mummy did mention . . .'

'Ain't he?' Ralph glanced mischievously at Aubrey.

'Not unlike, certainly.' Aubrey held out his arm to encircle Kate, who was advancing from the window. 'And this is Kate.'

'How do you do.'

The girl stopped short of Aubrey's extended arm. Ralph took her hand and kissed it, then her cheek. She was long, and thin and taut as a whippet, unyielding to the touch. And yet when he looked into her face, so unlike anyone else's in the family, Ralph experienced a lurch of recognition, a surge of some instinctive sympathy, too primitive to be affection, but disconcertingly powerful.

'Well my dear,' he said, 'I'm sorry I wasn't here to greet you both.'

She shrugged, standoffish. 'It doesn't matter in the least.'

'Tell me,' he took her stiff arm and led her back towards her brother, 'do you have a temper to match that hair of yours?'

'Certainly not.'

'Yes, she does.'

Kate and Joe spoke both at once, and all four laughed nervously, glad of a crack in the ice. Ralph lowered himself into his chair with a mighty wheeze.

'I *think*,' he said, putting his fingertips together and resting his chin on them, 'I think I am disposed to believe my grandson on that score.'

There was a knock and Aubrey opened the door to admit Doreen with the tea trolley. Ralph slapped his hands together gleefully.

'Aha! Chocolate cake, forsooth – you observe here, Aubrey, the advantages of having young relations to stay.' He leaned across to address Joe conspiratorially. 'I'm told I eat too many sweet things, but do you think it matters at my age?'

'Absolutely not.'

'Precisely!'

Aubrey poured tea and Joe handed round cups and cake. Ralph, having taken two enormous mouthfuls, waved his hand at the album which now lay beside Joe's chair and said, through crumbs: 'I see you've been taking a look at your relations.'

'Yes, I was.'

'What do you make of them? Not a bad looking bunch in the main, are they? Your mother was a good-looking girl, took after me of course.'

'What about Aunt Dulcie,' put in Kate. 'Who does she take after?'

'She looks like my late wife,' said Ralph shortly, with a marked emphasis on the second word of the sentence.

'Doesn't she live in London?' went on Kate. 'I half expected to see her here today.'

'No, no, no,' Aubrey shook his head vigorously. 'She lives up in town, we don't see all that much of her. As a matter of fact, we're having a few people in to dinner the day after tomorrow, your father's parents included, and I had hoped she might be able to come. But she'd been invited to take a holiday on somebody's yacht, and I suppose one doesn't turn down that kind of invitation. She'll be back in a couple of weeks' time.'

'Your aunt,' said Ralph, with heavy sarcasm, 'always has some damn lounge lizard or other dancing attendance on her.'

Kate soon realized that if time were not to hang very heavy indeed between now and Joe's going to school in September she would have to find something to occupy her. She was not a person who could take pleasure in idleness. What she really wanted was to become independent of her relations, but since a 'holiday' was the proposed order of the day, and it would be churlish to be seen to be over-eager to leave, she resolved to make the best of it. It was noticeable that Joe had far less difficulty in adapting himself to his surroundings than she did. This was in part because he shared some common ground with his uncle — an innate conservatism, a passion for cricket, a genuine interest in all things to do with the family. Aubrey had also pulled off something of a coup in striking up an acquaintance with people a few doors up who had a boy of Joe's age or thereabouts. William Treece was precocious and a swot, but he had a crystal set and a long holiday from Westminster to be endured, so a friendship was born.

Kate was not so lucky. She did not seem to share any of the preoccupations of this intransigently male household, and at the same time did not feel that Ralph and Aubrey were ready to accept her own. On her first morning she woke to a quiet house, and more rain. With Aubrey at the works — though he had announced that he would be taking time off the following week — and Joe having been summoned by the dutiful, and perhaps desperate, Treeces, she found herself utterly at a loose end, and retired upstairs to write home, a long letter of passionate gloom and heartfelt complaint about the awfulness of England, while the rain hissed and spattered on the window and on the leaves of the scrawny trees in the garden.

But it was the garden, whose aspect so depressed her when she gazed out of her bedroom window, which proved her ally. After lunch, for which Joe reappeared briefly, Ralph, clearly feeling he had neglected his responsibilities, remarked: 'Come outside and let me show you our roses — I take quite a pride in them.'

She glanced out of the window. It had stopped raining and a watery sun shone on a dripping, glistening world.

'Thank you, I'd like to.'

He took her along the hall, breathing wheezily, and through a back door into a room which an estate agent might have called a conservatory, for the roof and two sides were of glass. Now it was, as Ralph said, 'a glory-hole', piled with old wellington boots and sports equipment in various stages of dilapidation, rusty gardening tools, mackintoshes, seed trays and cardboard cartons stuffed with old periodicals. Ralph nudged the clutter aside with his foot, wincing.

'Sorry if I've seemed rude this morning,' he said in a tone more aggressive than apologetic. 'I suffer from gout, for my sins, and it's been playing me up like the dickins.'

'I'm sorry.'

'Not your fault.' He jerked open the door and held it open for her. They stepped out on to a kind of wooden platform, with a ricketty balustrade. From the platform a flight of slatted wooden steps ran down past the kitchen window to ground level. Ralph flapped an impatient hand at her.

'Go on, I'm slow.'

Kate preceded him down the steps, conscious of his puffing, painful progress behind her. Like Orpheus she felt that to look back would be fatal. Instead, on reaching the bottom she walked a little way into the centre of the sodden length of lawn, and waited for him to join her. He did not pause, but continued stumping up the cinder path past her, motioning peremptorily for her to follow. At the end of the garden he stopped, and lowered himself on to a green-painted seat, stretching out one leg before him.

'There it is.'

Kate left him and took herself for a walk round, strolling with her arms folded, peering at the borders, occasionally leaning down to pull up a weed. It was all in a mess, neglected and overgrown. She returned more purposefully and sat down at the other end of the bench with her hands beneath her, and her ankles crossed tucked under the seat. She gazed around thoughtfully.

'I bet I could sort out your garden for you,' she said.

Ralph shifted so that the bench groaned and heaved like a galleon on a high sea.

Kate went on, without looking at him: 'I rather like gardening, I help Thea a lot at home in far less rewarding conditions. I've got time on my hands, I could lick this into shape.'

'I daresay you could.' There was an unfamiliar inflection in Ralph's voice which she only belatedly recognized as embarrassment. 'But it hardly seems the right way for me to be entertaining my granddaughter.'

Surprised and amused, she turned to look at him, but his head was averted. One large hand massaged the knee of his gouty leg.

'I don't want to be "entertained" as you put it,' she said. 'We're family aren't we, Joe and me? We just want to be part of the operation.'

'What an odd way you have of putting things.'

She didn't want to be forced back into their old relationship after such a promising new development.

'I shall start with weeding,' she said, standing up and stretching. Ralph observed that she was a fidget, that if she had nothing to do she engaged in a lot of unnecessary animal movement. The garden was probably just what she needed.

'I'm afraid the tools are rather the worse for wear,' he said threateningly, creaking painfully to his feet. 'You'll just have to see what you can find up in the glory hole.'

'I'll manage. In fact I'll start by sorting *that* out.'

She strode briskly across the grass and went up the wooden stairs two at a time. She wore trousers and a boyish-looking striped shirt. Ralph puffed across to the foot of the steps and stood there with his hand on the bannister, looking up. The door stood open, and sounds of enthusiastic reorganization emerged from within. Ralph took a deep breath and made his way up the steps, with frequent pauses to ease his leg.

He reached the platform at the top and leaned back on the balustrade, breathing deeply. The doorway was already blocked by two old doormats rolled and tied with garden twine.

'Now just steady on,' he admonished with as much force as he could muster.

'Might I come through?'

'Yes, of course.' She moved the doormats aside. She had rolled her shirtsleeves up, her arms looked thin and muscular and boyish.

'You're all right then, I take it?' he enquired caustically, his hand on the doorhandle.

She was running her thumb down a pile of old motoring magazines, and did not look up. 'Of course.'

'I'll leave you to it then.'

He closed the door behind him, shaking his head, muttering.

'You all right sir?' It was Doreen, crossing the hall to the back stairs.

'Perfectly thank you, Doreen.'

'Only you look a bit puffed.'

More blasted women. Where had they sprung from all of a sudden? Ralph stumped past Doreen without another word and went into the drawing-room. When he and Aubrey had been here on their own with Doreen and Mrs Duckham he had never noticed the presence of the domestics other than as cogs in the machine that kept Mapleton Road running smoothly. Now, with Kate's arrival, they seemed suddenly more positive. He noticed their high voices, their critical looks, the way they walked.

'Where will it all end?' he asked himself aloud, sitting down in his chair and picking up his book. But though he only admitted to irritation, he was not entirely displeased with the turn of events.

Ralph was not the only one who had felt the need to amuse his young relations during the course of that first afternoon. It was plain to Aubrey that if seven weeks of each other's company were to be endured without recourse to petty sniping — an aspect of family life which he loathed — some outside activity would have to be organized.

He had for some time, long before the proposed visit of the Kingsley children, been cherishing an ambition to attend the Olympic Games in Berlin. A great sporting and ideological spectacle, the sort of holiday that he and Ralph, both congenital non-holiday-makers, could really enjoy, the days fully and thrillingly engaged in watching sport, the evenings passed pleasantly in some top-class hotel in Berlin, a city which Aubrey had long wished to visit. No irksome social obligations, no need to be frivolous and idle, the perfect break for a couple of gentlemen fond of their comfort and set in their ways.

Until now Aubrey had regarded this notion pretty much as pie in the sky. There was no financial impediment to their departure. He and Ralph were extremely well off, in spite of their frugal lifestyle. But he could not appear so self-indulgent as to go on his own and doubted that his father would agree to accompany him. Ralph had turned mean in his old age, his attitude would be 'What do we need a holiday for?' and Aubrey would feel bad for suggesting it.

But now Aubrey reclaimed the idea from the back of his mind, dusted it off and reassessed it. In the light of this new situation it seemed once more to be an excellent idea. And the notion of taking the young Kingsleys, giving them a treat, showing them a bit of Europe, would appeal to Ralph as a very right and proper thing to do, whether or not he actually wished to go himself. If they went for, say, a week, to include the opening ceremony, it would break up the long stretch of holiday very nicely and afford much innocent interest and amusement. He liked the idea of giving his nephew and niece a complete surprise, especially that rather over-confident young woman. Show her he wasn't just an old fuddy-duddy. The other factor to be considered was that Ralph would be prepared to spend more if they were taking the Kingsleys. Mean he might be, but he would certainly not want to appear tight-fisted before Thea's children. So they would stay in the best hotel, travel first class and have good seats in the stadium. Aubrey could hardly contain his excitement. So swept away was he with his scheme that he got his secretary, Mrs Cliffe, to telephone Thomas Cook and elicit prices, times and travel details so that it might be expedited forthwith, and was rewarded by her look of surprise and admiration. Oh yes, there was a lot more to him than met the eye.

He got home an hour earlier than usual, borne on wings of enthusiasm, and was a little crestfallen to discover the house deserted. Doreen was laying up for supper in the dining-room, and he poked his head round the door.

'Doreen — where is everybody? It's like the grave.'

'Mr Tennant's upstairs changing, the young man won't be back from up the road till five-thirty, and Miss Kate's out in the garden.'

'Out in the garden?'

'Gardening.'

'Oh, I see.' Aubrey did not see. 'Right. I'll go and see what she's up to.'

He left his briefcase in the hall, and went out through the conservatory. To his astonishment, it seemed almost empty, with everything stacked neatly at the sides, and the gardening tools arranged in a tidy row. The floor had been swept and the glass was patterned with damp arcs where it had been recently washed. The far door stood open and he went out on to the platform. His niece was down on her hands and knees in the flowerbed to the left of the cinder path, the one they had been accustomed to call the shrubbery before it became a sadly overgrown mess. She was wearing trousers tucked into wellington boots, a shirt with the sleeves rolled up, and some kind of bandanna tied round her head to keep her hair out of her eyes. Behind her on the path stood a cardboard box overflowing with weeds. She was tugging and forking, wholly absorbed.

'Hallo down there!'

She looked up, and waved the small fork she was holding aloft, careless of the soil which sprinkled over her shirt from its prongs.

'What are you up to?' he asked, beginning to go down the steps.

'Enjoying myself.'

He came to stand behind her on the path. It was a fine afternoon now, the sun was warm on his back, the air was heavy with the scent of damp grass, and soil rich with rain, and wet greenery.

'You've been doing sterling work,' he remarked, surveying the border. She had already made an appreciable difference, the various flowering shrubs now had room to breathe, the soil was dark and loose and free of weeds and stones, she had hoed the edges and cut back some of the woody dead growth on the giant clematis that covered the wall at the back.

'I like to have things to do,' she said, standing up and wiping her hands on her trousers. She wore no gloves, her hands were filthy, and her face smudged with earth where she had pushed her hair out of the way with her wrist. But Aubrey could see that the gardening had done her good, she was bright-eyed and more relaxed and pleased with her handiwork. He saw that her sense of her own usefulness had defused much of that spikiness which had so unnerved him the day before.

'You've done wonders,' he said. 'Now wouldn't you like a cold drink or something? You must be exhausted.'

'Well — I might in a moment, I'll just finish this bit. Then I suppose I should have a bath, I'm absolutely caked.'

'Have a bath, by all means.' He was pleased that she spoke so freely of having a bath, that she seemed so much more at home than he could have hoped. Something occurred to him.

'I hope young Joe is all right along there with the Treeces.'

She grinned. 'He's happy as Larry, it's nice for him. They came along in the middle of the afternoon and he said they'd offered him tea. He'll be back soon. It was good of you to arrange all that.'

'Good heavens . . . the very least I could do . . .' Aubrey thrust his hands into his trouser pockets and stared down at his toecaps. 'I just hope he doesn't feel pushed out. It's only his first day here, he might think—'

She smiled out loud. 'You are funny.'

He smiled, confused, and then remembered his plan. 'When we're all together, I have an announcement to make.'

'How exciting!' The shadow of the laugh was still in her voice. She was teasing him, but he found he didn't mind.

'Yes. I think so.'

They stood side by side for a moment and then he said: 'Right, I shall go and see what Father's up to.'

'I'll be in soon,' she called after him as he went up the steps, and he waved a hand. He felt happy.

When they were all assembled in the drawing-room at a quarter to seven he put forward his proposal for the trip to Berlin. He was overtaken by nerves at the last moment — what if they laughed at him, thought the idea entirely ludicrous? But he needn't have worried. To a man, their reaction was one of surprise and delight, and even Ralph's slight demur was largely, Aubrey thought, because he wished he had thought of it himself.

'So I take it we're all in favour?' Aubrey beamed, and poured himself more amontillado.

'I think it's absolutely tremendous,' said Kate.

Aubrey smiled genially at her. If he had been a winker, he would have winked at her, such was his elation. As it was he did something equally out of character, and raised his glass aloft.

'To Berlin!'

And Kate responded with a flourish. 'Adventure!'

By the following evening, the night of the dinner party, the trip had been arranged. Aubrey was still in the grip of a self-satisfaction he had not known for years. He was sure that the organization and anticipation of the holiday would draw them all together. Why, it had already made him feel like an uncle to those two of Thea's, and not just a stranger, and he was sure they felt the same. And though he had some misgivings over his father making such a journey at his age, he was sure that he could be made comfortable, and that the change would do him the world of good. He propped their tickets on the mantelpiece in a conspicuous position.

There was, however, the dinner party to be negotiated first, and Aubrey had underestimated the awkwardness of such an occasion for Kate and Joe.

Joe called on his sister during the hour set aside for changing. 'Sis – what ought I to wear?'

She gave him an exasperated look. 'Try trousers, jacket and shirt.'

'Very helpful. I mean, will I be all right in a soft collar and so on?'

'Good Lord, how should I know?' It was the sort of needless fussing that annoyed her, Joe's passion for correctness was one of his most irritating qualities. She was sitting on her bed in her petticoat, continuing her letter to Thea. Seeing his wild look she put down her pen.

'Look, it's only a small affair, the other grandparents and these Averys, it won't be smart. Just make sure you're clean and respectable – what more could anyone ask?'

He continued to look doubtful. 'What are you wearing?'

She sighed and closed her eyes. 'A string of beads and a loincloth. Buzz off.' He still hovered. 'Look, if you're still worried go and ask your uncle.'

'I'd feel a chump.' He caught her threatening look. 'It's okay, I'm sure you're right.'

Unfortunately, Joe's instinct in the matter had been a good deal surer than his sister's. When they foregathered in the drawing-room at seven, neither of them was appropriately dressed. Both Aubrey and Ralph were in dinner jackets and waistcoats, and unfamiliar cut-crystal sherry glasses and decanter were much in evidence on a silver salver. Kate's heart sank. She had on a white linen shirtwaister with tab pockets and a wide belt. Joe looked neat but far from formal in a sports jacket and flannels with a grey soft-collared shirt and his prep school tie.

She avoided his eye and came straight to the point. 'Look, I'm sorry, we're not dressed right, we'll nip up and change before they come.'

'Nonsense, nonsense, you're perfectly all right, don't think of it,' Aubrey cut in, cursing himself for not having primed them properly. He himself would have been far happier and more comfortable in an ordinary suit, but Ralph saw tonight's dinner as an important occasion, and knew of only one way to approach it.

'Let them change if they want to,' Ralph said now. 'Might be the best thing.'

'I'm quite sure it would. Come,' Kate began to lead Joe from the room, but the bell rang. 'Damn, now what?'

'Don't give it another thought, it's of no importance whatever. You both look splendid.'

So they'd had to endure it, the conspicuousness of their novelty underlined by the conspicuousness of their ignorance. Neither of them could fail to notice the momentary surprise at their appearance which registered on the otherwise beatific faces of their paternal grandparents. Robert and Daphne were dressed in a kind of genteel faded grandeur, he in a tailcoat the bottom half of which rose when he bent forward so that he resembled an ancient blackbird, she in a long brocade dress and beaded stole. Kate inwardly cringed with mortification, but this was not apparent from her manner, which became brusque in direct ratio to her anxiety.

'My dears . . .' there were tears in Daphne's eyes as she kissed them, 'I simply can't tell you how much we've been looking forward to meeting you. And look how you have to lean down to me, Kate, she's even taller than Thea, isn't she, Robert?'

'Yes, and a very modern lass too, by the look of her,' said Robert, pressing his cool, wrinkled cheek to hers.

'Yes, I'm sorry about that,' said Kate. 'We're not dressed right. We were going to change when you arrived.' She realized that she did not sound apologetic, but slightly hostile, and anyway they behaved as if they hadn't heard her. She realized too that she had simply made matters worse — and felt ridiculous.

In the drawing-room Robert, who had a heart condition, sat down on the sofa, and patted the seat next to him as an indication to Joe to do the same. Kate sipped her sherry and looked at the two of them together, the boy and his grandfather. Robert leaned towards Joe as he spoke to him, stared into his face. His bumpy, freckled, old man's hand gestured uncertainly in the air, came to rest lightly on Joe's shoulder, his knee, his hair; his moist, old man's eyes were bright with love as they rested on Joe. Kate found that she was squeezing her glass so tightly she was in danger of crushing it. She was jealous. Daphne touched her arm. 'Kate?'

'I'm sorry, I was miles away.'

'In Gilgil, perhaps?'

'Oh — No, actually, not just then.' She looked down briefly into her empty glass, dredging her mind for something to say. Daphne patted her hand.

She was an astute woman. 'Aren't men funny,' she said, 'they find common ground so quickly. No wonder they all belong to clubs.'

Kate gave her a quick, sidelong smile of gratitude. 'You're probably right.'

'I know I am. Now tell me how your parents are, and all about your plans.'

Kate told her. Daphne sat in the big armchair and she perched on the arm and talked about Thea and Jack and the farm and getting a job and a flat. But though Daphne was a good listener Kate was still conscious of the two on the sofa, the old man and the boy and their absorption in one another, and deep inside she felt like the same furious, resentful little girl who had sulked among the bushes on the day Joe was born. Because there it was, lighting an old man's eyes, animating his arthritic hands, loosening his tongue — the incontrovertible evidence that Joe was flesh and blood, and she just an outsider.

The other guests were late, and Ralph began complaining with increasing vehemence about their bad manners and lack of consideration.

When the bell finally rang and Aubrey went out into the hall Kate at once recognized the crisp, animated voice, the bright laugh and the poised, intelligent manner which made of lateness a mere bagatelle. When Andrea Avery entered the room the interval of fifteen years seemed no more than the same number of days. Apart from such alterations in style as had been dictated by fashion, she was the same woman — slight and wiry and erect, her rather thin sandy hair neatly coiffed, her brows finely arched, her clothes expensive and elegant but not showy, her composure complete.

She greeted everyone with graceful apologies, accepted a mere half-glass of sherry because they had already delayed dinner and did not wish to do so any further, and then crossed at once to Kate.

'Kate! Let me look at you. I can scarcely believe it. That solemn, grim-faced little girl that I was so scared of.'

Kate could not withhold a snort of sceptical laughter. 'Scared?'

'But of course.' Andrea smiled down at Daphne Kingsley, eliciting her understanding. 'Remember, I wasn't used to children. I'm still not, but don't let's worry about that. You were a complete enigma to me Kate, I had absolutely no idea how to treat you.'

'I don't think I was typical,' said Kate guardedly. 'I was fairly beastly.'

'Fairly? You were atrocious.'

Kate thawed a little. 'I couldn't help it.'

'Tell me — did I do everything wrong?'

Kate looked into Andrea's bright brown eyes. 'Almost everything.'

'As I thought. And you've hated me ever since.'

'I haven't thought of you that much.'

'Ha!' Andrea's husband joined them. 'Do I perceive the demon honesty rearing its ugly head?'

Andrea, laughing, turned slightly towards Louis, her hand on his shoulder. As she did so Daphne Kingsley rose from her chair and excused herself to go and talk to Ralph.

'Kate – this is my husband, Louis. This is Kate, darling, whom I've told you so much about.'

Kate's hand was swept up and kissed with a flourish, her chin tilted for inspection, her plain dress scrutinized with amusement.

'Just as I suspected, one of the new women.'

'Don't be ridiculous, Louis. Take no notice of him, Kate.'

Kate's overwhelming impression of Louis was of a smooth, cuddly richness, like plush velvet. He was a sleek, dark, plump man with bright, appraising eyes and an unctuous mouth. His hands were soft and warm, his clothes expensive, his scent fragrant rather than masculine. Kate's mistrust of Louis Avery was instant and powerful. She withdrew her hand from his as if scalded.

'I apologize for not being appropriately dressed,' she said.

'You look charming.'

'I mean, you called me a "new woman" whatever that is, and I suspect you thought I was deliberately under-dressed.'

'Nothing could have been further from my thoughts.'

Doreen, prettified for her evening's work in a navy dress and goffered cap and apron, appeared to announce that dinner was ready, and they drifted across the hall to the dining-room, Kate still with Louis in close attendance, Andrea between Aubrey and Ralph, Joe with the Kingsleys.

With the table extended, the silver cleaned, the best glasses in use and roses in a silver bowl, the gloomy dining-room looked almost festive. Aubrey took up a position at the head of the table, and directed the others according to his pre-arranged seating plan. This involved putting Kate at the far end, in the position of hostess, with Robert Kingsley on her right, and Louis on her left.

Louis leaned across her, before they sat down. 'A rose between two thorns, is she not?' he said to Robert.

'Certainly, certainly.' Robert Kingsley had once been a gay dog, with a fruity, caddish voice, a high complexion and a jovially flirtatious manner with young women. But with the infirmity of old age all the juice and the hot air had gone out of him, so that he was stooped and wrinkled and diffident. He viewed Ralph's continued peppery ebullience with dismay — how did he do it? Now, seated next to his granddaughter, he was alarmed, and had not the least idea what to say to amuse her during dinner. So he decided not to try, and turned instead to Joe, who was on his right.

'When are you coming down to visit us, then?' he asked.

'Whenever you like – I mean, that would be super.'

'Very soon then, we must make it very soon.'

'We'd like that. We've heard all about Long Lake.'

'We? Ah yes?' For some reason Robert had not envisaged Kate as part of this particular plan. He saw himself walking with his grandson around the house, the grounds, the lake, the woods, showing him Jack's old room, the stables, the garage where one of Jack's pre-war cars still stood . . . Neither his estimable wife nor his prickly granddaughter were present in his dream. He sighed as Doreen placed consommé before him, her thumb red on the white and gold rim of the Crown Derby soup plate.

'So,' said Louis to Kate, flicking his napkin out to one side and laying it over his knee, 'how do you find us all?'

She picked up her spoon. 'I've hardly had time to get to know you,' she said guardedly.

'Quite true. Though of course you've met Andrea before.'

'Simply ages ago.'

'She is a formidable woman, my wife.'

'I'm sure she is. I remember her as being – formidable.' She glanced uneasily to where Andrea sat beyond Joe on Ralph's left, but she seemed deep in conversation with Aubrey opposite her, across Ralph who drank soup with noisy, rapid relish.

Louis patted his mouth with his napkin. 'Bossy, some would say.'

Kate was appalled that he should say such things about Andrea to her, whom he hardly knew. She sensed that he was not thick-skinned or stupid, that he knew very well what game he was playing, testing her for her reaction. With a superhuman effort she decided not to argue or to make herself vulnerable by losing her temper, but to change the subject. She remembered something Thea had told her. 'Aren't you in politics?' she enquired.

'I was. I'm an advertising man now.' He smiled at her, waiting for her comment.

'What an odd transition.'

'Ha!' He tipped his head back. 'Not in the least, my dear. It's all selling.'

'That's terribly cynical.'

'You think me cynical? I'm deeply wounded.' He laid down his soup spoon and rested his elbows on the table, his fingers laced in front of him. 'Now let me see, how can I convince you that I'm no cynic . . .'

Kate stared desperately past him at Daphne, but she had now joined the discussion with Aubrey, Andrea and Ralph — who had finished his soup and was glaring impatiently at the others. On the other side Robert was describing something to Joe, using his pudding spoon and fork as markers. No escape.

'Here's something for you,' said Louis with an air of triumph. 'I used to be in love with your mother.'

Kate gathered the crumbs on her sideplate into a bunch and squeezed them into a pellet. 'Oh really? I imagine lots of people must have been.'

He did not appear cast down by this opinion. 'Yes, a woman like Thea might have been the making of me.'

'You seem to have managed,' she said coldly and quietly, hoping against hope that Andrea could not hear.

'She had a quality of innocence — still has, I'll be bound. A rare and attractive thing in a woman.'

'I wouldn't know.'

'Now you,' he said, 'I suspect that you see yourself as a very worldly-wise young lady, but that's not how I see you.'

'I'm not interested — honestly.'

'I believe that you also are an innocent beneath that combative exterior. It's a most piquant combination, take my word for it.'

As he spoke the last words he laid his hand lightly on her

arm. Her sleeves were elbow length, and the over-warm, confiding pressure on the bare skin of her forearm seemed to light the touchpaper of her suppressed anger. In a spasmodic reflex action she jerked her arm upwards, shaking off his hand, but unfortunately having the same effect on her side plate and soup bowl, which hurtled from the table. The side plate fell to the ground and shattered. The soup dish's fall was broken by her lap, where it paused long enough to deposit a lake of tepid consommé before it struck the carpet and rolled in a wide arc to the skirting board, where it finally came to rest with a series of diminishing thuds.

'Oh God, I'm so sorry.' She closed her eyes for a minute, the soup trickling through her skirt and petticoat and on to her legs above her stocking tops. It felt disgusting. She stood, pushing her chair back violently, so that the legs caught on the broken china and she had to catch it to stop it, too, crashing to the ground. She stared about her wildly.

'I'll clear up the mess!' she announced, and realized she was shouting. She took in various reactions, directed upwards at her from around the table like spotlights – Robert's mild bafflement, Joe's scarlet-faced embarrassment, Andrea's intelligent concern, Ralph's amusement. Both Aubrey and Daphne rose, Daphne to come to her assistance, Aubrey to ring for Doreen.

She bent to begin picking up the pieces of plate and on the way down caught Louis Avery's bright, wide-eyed look of interest, as if she had just produced some new pattern of behaviour which made his picture of her complete. Her eyes stung and her face burned with fury and humiliation. She began scrabbling amongst the debris and promptly cut her finger.

Daphne patted her shoulder. 'Come on, my dear, Doreen can cope with that. You pop along upstairs and change out of the wet dress.'

'I must do *something*,' Kate growled. 'How could I be so stupid?'

'She blames herself,' said Louis to Daphne, 'isn't it silly? This sort of thing can happen to anyone.'

Doreen appeared, armed with dustpan and brush and cloth, and Kate allowed herself to be ushered from the room by

Daphne. Conversation, temporarily halted, began to burble on again.

'Quick as you can now,' said Daphne, 'or we'll miss you.'

Upstairs, still shaking with mortification, Kate put on an emerald green silk dress and opened the window. She leaned out, breathing deeply, nerving herself for the stares that would greet her when she re-entered the dining-room.

But their manners were perfect. She slid into her re-laid place, with a plate of rare beef put ready, without so much as a head turning. Doreen handed green peas, roast potatoes, gravy, marrow, all without mishap. Louis was talking to Daphne about civil aviation. She caught Ralph's eye, briefly, and he gave a little sideways jerk of his head as if to encourage her. Robert Kingsley, much taken with the change in her appearance, turned to her.

'You look well in that colour, my dear, it suits you.'

'Thank you.'

'I have been saying to your young brother here how much we look forward to having you to stay at Long Lake.'

'Thank you . . .' She was suddenly debilitated and perilously emotional. 'Thank you very much.'

She endured the remainder of the evening in what was, to her, a totally foreign attitude of quiet attentiveness. Over coffee and liqueurs Aubrey made his Berlin announcement and everyone reacted with suitable amazement. He passed round the tickets, which were duly admired. Joe was advised to go to bed, demurred politely and was allowed to remain. Kenya was much asked-after, and Kate told them what it was like, though the thought of evenings at the farm, and Thea and Jack and Cornet and African voices, was almost more than she could bear. The homesickness was like a vice around her throat, making her voice small and tight and her words dull, with no possibility of conveying how she really felt about what she had left behind. She could scarcely breathe, and she was suddenly so bone-tired that her whole body ached.

When they did eventually go, with promises of early meetings and enjoyable get-togethers 'after Berlin', she felt only relief at their departure.

Ralph and Joe went at once to bed. Exhausted, she flopped down on the sofa and prised off each shoe in turn with the toes of the other foot. She put her hands to her face and pressed her fingers over her eyes until colours danced on the dark of her eyelids. When she lowered them Aubrey was standing in front of her, holding out a glass of something.

She looked at it. 'What's that?'

'Whisky. I'm having one.'

She took it. 'I've never drunk spirits in my life.'

'I'm not trying to make you. I just thought you'd like a nightcap.'

'Thank you.'

She sipped it. Aubrey took his own glass to the mantelpiece and began filling his pipe.

'I'm sorry,' she said, shaking her head. 'I was a disaster.'

He raised his eyebrows. 'I never heard such nonsense.'

'Spilling that wretched soup . . .'

'Oh that,' he laughed. 'Just what the party needed.'

She smiled ruefully. 'Do you want me to be honest?'

'I can't imagine that you are often anything else.'

'It was Louis Avery. He unsettled me.'

Aubrey sat down in Ralph's fireside chair and crossed his legs. 'Delighted to hear it. I can't stand the fellow.'

'Oh can't you?' She looked at him with delight. 'Neither could I.'

'So that's got that out of the way.'

She took another sip of the whisky, and made a face. 'I'm sorry, I don't really care for this.'

'Here –' He held out his hand and she gave him the glass. 'Why don't you go to bed? You look whacked.'

'I'm not usually so pathetic. I don't know what's the matter with me.'

'You've come halfway round the world to meet a bunch of people you're not at all sure you like. That's what's the matter.'

'You must think me hideously ungrateful.'

'Gratitude doesn't come into it.' He was gruff. 'You're family.'

She rose, tall and slim, her shoes hanging from one hand. Aubrey, looking up at her, thought her not unattractive, though she was not pretty. Her colouring, with the green dress, was most fetching and she had a kind of athletic style and vibrancy which no amount of social gaffes could quench.

'Good-night then.'

'Good-night. And by the way—'

She turned in the doorway.

'You're doing splendidly,' he said.

As the door closed after her and he heard her footsteps on the stairs he wondered again where she had come from, this changeling child of his sister's.

CHAPTER FOUR

'It's a Barnum and Bailey world
Just as phoney as it can be,
But it wouldn't be make believe
If you believed in me.'

'It's Only a Paper Moon'
Rose, Harburg and Arlen, 1933

DULCIE and Rex returned to London during the last week in July, only four days before the other members of the family were due to leave for Berlin.

The holiday had not been an unqualified success. An oceangoing yacht resort-hopping round the Mediterranean was not a setting designed to display Dulcie to her best advantage. It was a time when the fashionable woman was active and sporty, able to hold her own on the golf links and tennis court, buoyant in the water and masterful on horseback. Also, since to be well-travelled was evidence of a healthy bank account and plenty of time on one's hands, it was chic to have a suntan. Poor Dulcie had no eye for a ball, was scared of horses and could not swim. Her skin was so pale and delicate that it never bronzed, and the few freckles which had been fetching at eighteen looked ludicrous, she thought, on a woman in her forties. Una Roth-Vesey, on the other hand, tanned like a Red Indian and swam like a fish. She also played excellent golf and creditable tennis. She left Dulcie with no alternative but to take on the role of decorative spectator.

Things had got off to a bad start due to a patch of unseasonal weather off the north-west coast of France. The *Brantus* had lurched and bucked through mountainous seas, and the Martinis which Dulcie swallowed to bolster her courage quickly found their way into the heaving bosom of the ocean. No one else suffered. On the contrary, they all took to behaving like old salts, swapping tales of previous voyages whilst doing justice to the Philippino cook's seafood extravaganzas. Dulcie could not even bear to watch the *moûles*, *crevettes* and *langoustines* disappearing down their throats, but languished in her cabin while meals were taken, appearing later to a chorus of badinage that was only just short of mockery. She knew that she was letting Rex down by her shaming weakness, so she bore the humiliation with a good grace and swore, as she retched miserably into her peach-pink basin, that she would never go to sea again.

After this inauspicious start things might reasonably have been expected to improve, but it was not to be. Percy, who became redder and more troll-like by the day as they approached sunnier climes, reinforced Dulcie's sense of inadequacy by constantly referring to her and to himself as a pair, as 'we two spectators' and 'those of us who like to take things quietly'. The pattern was set. She was not an avid reader, and could not sunbathe, so all that was left to her other than the doubtful pleasure of playing Percy like a grouper on a line, was to drink, which she did with a kind of lack-lustre determination. She began to feel liverish and suspected she was putting on weight. She found herself worrying, in what she considered a most old-maidish way, about the flat, and whether Celine was feeding Fondant properly. The prospect of her meeting with Kate was so terrible that she kept it locked away at the back of her mind, not even removing it to worry over. In fact, her disproportionate concern over small things was a kind of smoke screen put up by herself to distract her from the real problem.

The hot, trying days rolled by, and at last they turned the corner and were on the homeward voyage. They alighted in the Algarve, to spend two days and nights at the Portuguese villa of friends of the Roth-Veseys' in order, Una told them, 'to get their land legs back' before their return to England. This she meant more literally than Dulcie could have imagined. The Porters, though wealthy and hospitable, had a passion for games which caused Dulcie's discontent to plummet to new depths. Palely, she languished among the shady, aromatic pines gazing out at Una, Rex and their hosts playing badminton and miniature golf in the brilliant sun, as if on a stage. Gloomily, she accepted one cocktail after another from the delighted Percy, and daily nursed a sick hangover which lasted till luncheon.

Rex, who was enjoying himself, became testy. 'Come on, old girl, chin up for Christ's sake.'

'I'm sorry.' Why should she apologize? Why didn't he stay at her side, look after her, protect her from Percy? 'I am trying but I feel so inadequate. I can't do anything.'

'You can look beautiful, that's what you're good at. But you're not beautiful when you're sulking.'

Dulcie could remember her childhood nanny making just such an observation. She smarted.

'That's a terribly patronizing remark, Rex.'

'True, though.' And he sprinted away, golden haired and tawny skinned like a young Apollo. The Porters' Portuguese manservant came gliding between the trees, bearing a glass of Pimms and a dish of olives. He glanced after Rex, who was now shouting gaily to Una. Dulcie was sure the manservant laughed up his sleeve at her. As he set the drink and the olives on the table she returned his ingratiating smile with a look of pure vitriol.

'I think I'm a winter person,' she told Rex as he put on his dressing gown to return to his room that night. 'I'm a moth, not a butterfly, I need artificial light, not bright sunshine.'

'That's very good,' said Rex, 'very well put.' He had partaken of the final pleasure in the long round of pleasures that his day afforded, and was ready for bed. He leaned over her and kissed her bitingly on the mouth. 'See you in the morning, ready to embark once more.'

'Oh God.'

When he had gone she rolled on to her side and lay staring at the moonlit white wall, barred by the striped shadow of the half-closed shutter. When they got back to London, Kate would already be there, at Mapleton Road, so she would return not to relax into the rhythm of her old life, but to face new and momentous challenges.

In spite of the unsatisfactory holiday, or perhaps because of it,

Dulcie decided to contact her family at once on her return. She was in a mood to grasp the nettle. If she waited she would simply give herself time to build up a greater burden of dread.

Ralph answered the telephone.

'Hallo, Father, it's Dulcie.'

'What can we do for you?' His telephone manner did not improve with age.

'Are the Kingsley children with you?'

'Not at this moment, if that's what you mean. Aubrey's taken the lad to a cricket match, and the young woman has gone to the Tate Gallery.'

'I didn't mean at this moment. What are they like?'

'He is like your cousin Maurice and she is a beanpole with red hair.'

'Oh . . .' Dulcie faltered. The hard, bright detail of reality forced itself upon her. 'Obviously I'd like to meet them.'

'Obviously.' Did she detect a note of sarcasm?

'Well, perhaps Kate could telephone me this evening?'

'I'll tell her you called.'

'Or do you think she would rather I called again, as she doesn't know me?'

There was a short pause, punctuated by Ralph's sterterous breathing. She was fiddling about, annoying him. He said: 'She's no shrinking violet.'

'Very well then, ask her to ring me. Then perhaps they could both come up to town and have lunch with me.'

'Possibly. Anyway I'll give her your message.'

Dulcie found that she was shaking with frustration as she put down the receiver. Nobody understood her, nobody even came halfway to meet her, she was forever swimming against the tide. The knowledge that it was her own fault, that years of careful deception had placed her in this position, made her more, not less, angry. She rang Giles Huxley at the Albany. He was working and sounded a little distant at the other end.

'Huxley.'

'Giles, I'm sorry, you're busy.'

'Not too busy to speak to you my dear.'

'Are you free at lunch time?'

'I can be.'

'Please don't put off anything important on account of me.'

'You knew perfectly well I'd put off almost anything for you. And it's not important anyway. Just say when and where.'

When Dulcie arrived at the Savoy Grill at one-fifteen Giles was already there, sitting at a corner table reading a book, with a glass of iced soda water in front of him. He had an ulcer and was obliged to be careful in his eating and drinking habits. She slipped in beside him and picked up the menu.

'Hallo there!' He kissed her cheek and closed the book, placing a marker neatly between the pages. 'How were the ocean-going yacht set?'

'*Très sportif*,' said Dulcie. 'I was miserable.'

'It sounds ghastly. Still, if you will mix with these frightful people.'

'Don't start telling me to mend my ways.' She touched his cheek lightly with her hand. 'Let's order, I intend to make a pig of myself.' She smiled brilliantly at the waiter, and they placed their order.

When Dulcie had been furnished with a Martini, and the waiter had departed, Giles said: 'It's very nice to have you back, I've missed you.'

'Don't be silly, it's not as if we see that much of each other.'

'It's quality, not quantity, that counts. I see you only a little, but take enormous pleasure from our meetings. Whereas you and Rex —' he sighed expressively.

'Giles, I don't want to talk about Rex.'

'Nor me neither.'

'It's Kate, she's over here. She's here, *now*.'

Giles sat back, with folded arms. 'Go on.'

'She'll be ringing me this evening.' She fixed her friend with a look of such pitiful desperation that he covered her hand with his own, almost laughing.

'Worse things happen at sea. As you know.'

'But . . .' she snatched her hand from beneath his, began rummaging in her bag for cigarettes and lighter, 'what on earth shall I do?'

'Nothing, just be yourself, act naturally —'

'*Naturally* — my God!'

'I mean it. Presumably she's not expecting any drama, so don't give her any. Be her Aunt Dulcie, be her friend, she'll probably love you for it.'

'Oh Giles, help me!'

Food arrived, whitebait for Dulcie, melon for Giles, but neither of them began to eat.

'For one thing,' said Giles, 'you must stop behaving as if she were a dragon. Remind yourself why you took the course of action you did, and how well it has all worked out. Everyone's happy. Enjoy the girl's company, be content.'

'But it's all the deceit, the not telling, it's going to kill me.'

'Highly unlikely. After all, you don't *want* to tell her, do you?'

'No, but that's different to not telling *anyone*.'

'You can always talk about it to me.'

'You're a saint.' Dulcie speared two whitebait with her fork and plunged them into her mouth as if taking poison. 'What shall I suggest – when she rings?'

'What had you thought of?'

'Well . . . lunch somewhere not too smart. Joe will be there too, you see. I thought if we met on neutral ground, so to speak . . .'

'There you go again, using bellicose terminology. Anyone would think you were talking about battle tactics instead of lunch with a couple of youngsters. How would it be if I came along to help out? If you let me know where you're going I could turn up accidentally on purpose and oil the social wheels a little? Anyway, I should like it, it does me good to meet the young,' he added wryly.

'It's so sweet of you.' Dulcie laid down her fork beside the half-eaten whitebait. 'But no, I can't let you. I have to do it on my own.'

That evening the telephone rang at six, as Dulcie was pouring herself a drink. Rex was due at any moment, she felt jittery and unprepared. Stiffening the drink she ran and relieved Celine of the receiver.

'Hallo?'

'Is that Belgravia two six three nine?'

'Yes — is that Kate?'

'Aunt Dulcie?'

Dulcie felt a shock to hear her name — with such an improbably august title — pronounced in such clipped, cool tones by this youthful stranger.

'That does make me sound grand,' she said, and thought: And *that* makes me sound silly.

'They said you asked me to call.'

The occupants of Mapleton Road came across like recalcitrant hotel staff. Kate also gave the impression that she would not have called at all had 'they' not told her to. Dulcie felt at a disadvantage.

'Hallo? Are you still there?'

'I'm sorry,' said Dulcie, 'I was looking at my diary.' Lying, in small matters as in large, was so natural to her that she did not have to consider it. 'Look, I was wondering if you and Joe would be my guests for lunch one day.'

'We leave for Berlin on Friday.'

'Berlin?' Dulcie was taken aback. 'Good heavens! Then how about Wednesday?'

'Fine, I should think.'

'Shall we meet at Fortnum and Mason's in Piccadilly and have lunch there?'

'Why not?' Casual, restrained, slightly imperial. Dulcie could have given her a thousand reasons why not.

'About one?'

'I'll write it down.'

There was a pause, during which the receiver was put down at the other end, and there were some muted rustlings and scratchings. Dulcie tried to picture Kate in the dark, high-ceilinged drawing-room at Mapleton Road. Was she on her own? Or was Aubrey standing by the fireplace filling his pipe, drinking sherry? How odd that this young woman was probably already more at home in that house than she had ever been.

Because she had been there in spirit, she jumped when Rex arrived and put his arms round her.

'Who are you talking to?' he said, into her neck.

'Sssh. Family.'

'God, I'm for a drink.' He left, and Kate came back on the line.

'Sorry I couldn't find a pencil. We'll see you at Fortnum's on Wednesday, then. We'll look forward to it.'

Again that mixture of breezy curtness and formality. She doesn't like me, thought Dulcie. She's never met me, and she doesn't like me, it's not fair. A thought struck her. 'Do you know how to get there?'

'Yes, thank you.'

'*Alors — à tout à l'heure.*'

'Good-bye.'

Dulcie put the phone down and drained her drink. She was ashamed to find that the hand which had held the receiver was damp with sweat, and her head was beginning to ache. She went through to join Rex in the sitting-room.

On Tuesday Kate and Joe went up to the West End on their own, via train and bus. They went to Daniel Neal's to check on the supply of the remaining items of Joe's school uniform, walked in St James's Park and over Westminster Bridge, took a boat to Greenwich and back, and established the whereabouts of Fortnum and Mason's. By the end of the day, Joe was shivering and complaining of a sore throat.

At Mapleton Road that evening Aubrey took his nephew's temperature and found it to be a hundred and two. The doctor, when called in, pronounced it 'flu, and prescribed bed-rest and a high fluid intake for the next couple of days at least.

'You will have to lunch with Dulcie on your own, I'm afraid,' said Aubrey over dinner. 'I shan't be able to come.'

'You're not invited,' replied Kate, with no slight intended. Ralph gave a great bellow of laughter, subsiding into a protracted, hiccuping wheeze.

'She's got you there! Fair and square.'

'I only meant,' said Kate, 'that I shall be perfectly all right going on my own.'

'Of course, of course,' said Aubrey hastily. 'I see no reason why the pair of you shouldn't get on famously.'

Ralph emitted another roar of laughter. Kate reflected that Aubrey was protesting a little too much.

The following day it rained. Kate took this to be an omen. She put on a short-sleeved seersucker dress, then realized she had no mac, and took it off again. She would have to go shopping. After sorting through her other clothes she realized the short-sleeved dress remained her best option, and put it back on with the addition of a linen jacket. If the rain was too heavy she would have to resort to a taxi, a practice she despised as gutless. She like the jacket, which was long and loose with patch pockets, but was not sure about combining it with the dress. Dulcie, after all, was an arbiter of fashion. Tentatively, she added a necklace of wooden beads, and went down to breakfast.

Surprisingly, both Ralph and Aubrey were at the table: it was late by Aubrey's standards and early by Ralph's. They both looked up as she entered, and Ralph remarked: 'Ah, dressed to kill I see.'

Aubrey left and she used the paper as an excuse not to converse. When she had consumed kipper, tea and toast she excused herself and went back to her room. She envied Joe, staying in bed with a good book. She collected her handbag, and the envelope containing her few photographs of the farm and her foster-parents, and went downstairs.

Ralph was in the drawing-room, standing at the bay window gazing out at Mapleton Road through the rain. Doreen was on her knees at the hearth, lighting a fire. A fire in July, thought Kate. Still, he was old. And he looked his age, too, this morning. His big shoulders drooped, and his head hung slightly, like a tortoise's from beneath its shell. His hands were loosely clasped behind his back, but every now and then he squeezed them together, as if to remind himself that he could still do so. Kate felt a pang of sympathy. It must be hard for him, who had once, according to Thea, been so powerful and energetic, to be trapped beneath the net of old age, with so little to do, and needed by no one.

She took a few steps into the room, taking a deep breath. 'Grandfather?' It was the first time she'd called him that.

He did not react at once. When he did, it was with an expression of amusement and accusation in about equal parts. 'You were addressing me?'

'Yes.' She was rather defiant. She hoped he wasn't just going to make her feel foolish, standing there with her small olive branch, as it were, in her hand.

'You're off then.' He stumped back into the centre of the room and stood there, feet apart, shoulders pulled back, looking down his nose at her.

'Soon.' Kate stood aside to allow Doreen out of the room with the fire-box. The newly-lit fire flickered palely, and crackled with smoke from the damp kindling. 'I have to buy some clothes for this awful weather.'

To her surprise he did not retaliate, but went with a humph to his chair by the fireplace and sat down.

'Are you all right for money?' he asked.

'Yes, thank you. Jack gave me an allowance to last me for a couple of months, till I get a job.'

'Well . . .' He looked down at his heavy, shiny shoes, 'I believe there is still an account at Swan and Edgars. Get yourself a little something extra, something you don't need. Present from your grandfather.' He flashed her a fierce, not altogether mocking smile.

She was confused and touched. 'Thank you, that's kind. I will.'

He stared into the fire. His eyes were rheumy, and vacant. Depression emanated from him like a London smog. When he spoke again, it made Kate start, because he had seemed so far away.

'What job will you get?'

'I'm a trained secretary. I did a postal course. I'm sure I should be able to find something.'

'Probably, probably. But don't just rush into any damn fool arrangement for the sake of being shot of us.'

She had to laugh. 'I won't! Anyway, I shan't do anything until after Joe's at school. If, that is, you can put up with me for that long.'

He grunted. 'You'll do.'

Dulcie took one look at the weather and decided to remain in bed until the last possible moment. She wanted, anyway, to push her meeting with Kate as far away as possible. She did not succeed in this. Lying there, sipping her coffee, with Fondant purring on the bedspread next to her, and the rain beating on the window, she found herself inexorably treading the Via

Dolorosa of long-suppressed memory. She saw the Casse-Croute where she had so often dined with Simon Garrick, and with David Reed. She heard the lilting piano, and saw the soft light of the red candles, and the round tables with their pink cloths brushing the ground. She smelt the aromatic Parisian food and felt David's hand on hers, always so eager, so impatient, so hot, so passionate. And how she had loved to make him wait. He had been her favourite, though at the time she had claimed to have no favourites. She loved him for his importunate arrogance, his certainty that she could no more wait for him than he could for her; for his thin, white body that was so supple and strong, claiming and holding her like ivy; his determination – no, his assurance – that the day would come when she would give up all the others for him. But she'd always teased him, a girl has to make a living, she'd say, and laugh at his rage. Then one night, after six weeks of feeling unaccountably tired and sick, she had nearly passed out at the Casse-Croute, and it had been David who had taken her home. She knew, of course, what it was, and he had been triumphant – it's mine, of course, he'd said, it's mine, and now you will be too. But ill as she was, she had shouted at him that the father could be any one of a dozen men, and why didn't he leave her alone? He had. And within weeks he had been dead, at Passchendaele.

She had been serious about getting rid of the baby, but there was one problem: she was terrified of pain. Even a tiny cut made her feel ill, and the thought of voluntarily and in cold blood doing her body a violence was anathema to her. So she had carried on, pretending all was well, feeling terrible, longing and longing for David, who would never come back. Until it was too late to do anything. She had told Simon Garrick – dependable, handsome, stalwart Simon, whom she had so loved to goad into arguments with David – crying, as she always did, what shall I do, oh what shall I do? And he had been stern and fatherly and told her that all her friends would see her right, and she must be a sensible girl and see it through.

For the final months of her pregnancy she had lived like a hermit, loathing her fatness, her incapacity, the pity and understanding from men who had once admired and desired her. They were faithful, they found time on their thirty-six-hour leaves to come to her apartment and leave little notes and presents; those who didn't remained absent only because they were dead. But she had doggedly refused to see anyone, sending Celine out to shop, feeling like a tragic fairytale heroine immured in a tower not of stone, but of bloated flesh. She had become sluggish and sluttish, dragging herself from room to room in a dressing-gown, eating and drinking too much, indulging, in fact, in an orgy of idleness and self-pity while refusing to face up to what was to be the product of this nine months' purdah.

Eventually it had been Celine, with peasant phlegm and common sense, who had located an elderly – and sceptical – local midwife, and only just in time. The baby was three weeks early. There should have been no problems with the birth: Dulcie had been young and healthy, but because of her small build, and more importantly her profound resistance to the whole enterprise, the labour was protracted. She was stiff, tense and furious throughout. In vain did Celine and her poker-faced handmaiden exhort her to breathe deeply, to push, to place her legs so, to think of the baby – for a day and a night Dulcie had raged and screamed and wept and bled, and felt rushes of disgusting fluid ruining her beautiful sheets, and those parts of her which had brought her the most pleasure (and profit) being stretched and torn by this creature whom she did not want and had never wanted.

At last the baby had arrived, and been placed on her breast, still attached by a slippery, purplish cord. It was even more dreadful than Dulcie had imagined. She gazed, bruised and bleeding, and with exhausted distaste, at a female infant with a cowlick of damp red hair, a yelling tunnel of a mouth, and fists like tiny mauve hammers. Dulcie had been appalled, not just by the baby itself, but by the barren vista of drudgery and loneliness which its yelling conjured up. She had pushed it away, averting her face, sobbing in self-pity and terror. Celine, sensibly having foreseen such a contingency, and having failed to persuade her mistress to put the child to her breast, prepared a bottle, paid off the grumbling old woman, and settled down happily to act *in loco parentis*.

Dulcie had lain on her back, cried herself to sleep, and slept for twelve hours.

For two days Celine, in her element, had cared for and doted on the baby, while Dulcie rested. Unlike her mistress, Celine had never been interested in sex, but she had always wanted a child. Now it appeared she had everything: secure employment, a vicariously glamorous existence through Dulcie, a kitchen to work in and a baby to bring up. She was ecstatic.

But on the third day Dulcie had emerged, cold-eyed and determined, and told Celine of her intention to have the child looked after elsewhere. It was the closest they ever came to parting company. Celine had sobbed, pleaded, clasped the baby, promised that she would do everything, anything, but Dulcie had been adamant. The baby would go. She did not want to see it, nor to recognize its existence. She was willing, nay grateful, for Celine to care for it until the situation was resolved. But that was all. Celine, poor thing, had held the infant out — look how lovely she was, such a good baby, thriving, already putting on weight. But Dulcie had turned her back. She did not love it, had not wanted it, did not want to hear any more on the subject.

Against the background of a most uncharacteristic attack of the vapours on Celine's part Dulcie had sat by the phone, then realized she had no one to ring. They always came to her. She could only wait.

It was Simon Garrick, as ever, who had come up with the solution. About a month afterwards he had been passing through Paris on his way home for extended leave in England, and had come to visit her. Unlike Dulcie he had admired the baby, tickled and dandled it and complimented the ashen Celine on her skills. But he recognized at once that Dulcie was not to be swayed, and that the worst possible thing would be to leave the child with a mother who so patently abhorred motherhood.

Dulcie at the time had not been badly off. She had been doing well, saved a little, and had been left a sum of money by David Reed. Simon recollected that his married sister in Wimbledon had had a wonderful French nanny before the war, and had remained in touch with her. She sounded ideal. Simon's detective work while on leave enabled him, on his way back, to locate Mlle Paul living in spinsterly discomfort in one of the seedier *faubourgs* of the city. Simon went to see her. She had received excellent references from his sister, but had not worked since the start of the war. After voicing a few token objections about the clandestine nature of the work, she agreed. Simon and others clubbed together to assist in the acquisition of a small apartment in the Rue St Marc, and within a month the infant and Mlle Paul had been installed.

Relief warmed Dulcie like the spring after a long winter. Once more the windows of her life opened, light and air poured in, the scents and sounds of sweet freedom. She easily ignored Celine's pale and hangdog look, got her figure back, and began to see old friends and patrons once more. By mutual, tacit agreement the events of the past few months were never mentioned. Except by Simon, who no longer came to her as a lover, but only now as an adviser and, thought Dulcie, a rather stern one at that. His disapproval was evident, though he never criticized her outright. She felt that she had let him down in some way, or that he considered she had, and resentment at his attitude made her fuel it by behaving in a perverse and irresponsible way. If he dared to mention David Reed, whom he assumed (as she did, though she did not admit it) to be the child's father, she would accuse him of being maudlin and living in the past. This despite the fact that she missed David terribly.

On the whole, Simon treated her behaviour with grave tolerance. But on one matter he was firm: she must name the child, and soon. He would see to its registration and so on if she wouldn't, but she herself must name it. Very well, said Dulcie, I'll call her Kate. Sensible, downright, English Kate, who will live a sensible, downright, boring life and never be silly like her mother.

There followed an interval of about three years when life almost returned to normal. Dulcie's favoured friends continued to repay her favours handsomely, Celine stopped sulking, and in the winter of 1918, after one of the most violent bombardments the city had know, the war ended. In spite of Dulcie's lack of maternal instinct, she found herself surprisingly proprietary, it pleased her to know the child was there, safely parcelled up, maintained and cared for in the Rue St Marc. She harboured a fantasy that one day she would produce her daughter, like a rabbit from a hat, to confound those who would call her nothing but a butterfly, a ne'er do well. She too could have children, and here was the evidence to prove it! She went to the Rue St Marc from time to time, to look things over, and talk to Mlle Paul, and take little presents – a pretty dress, a toy. On these occasions she would steal a furtive peek at her daughter as she lay asleep. She had become an arresting, if not a pretty child, with a pale skin and a mop of red hair. Simon kept telling her to think of the future, that the arrangement with Mlle Paul would only work for the first two or three years, but Dulcie paid him no attention.

At the end of the war, still shaken and ill after the final assault on Paris, she had forced herself to return to England to attend Maurice's funeral.

When she had returned in the new year it was a different place. Although her own street and the Rue St Marc were intact, many parts of the city were wrecked. The feverish excitement of war had gone, along with the fear. People looked to the future now instead of living for the moment, their old lives and identities closed about them once more, they became sensible again now that they did not expect to die. Dulcie knew that her best time had gone. She became more French, for there were fewer Englishmen in Paris. On her return to England Ralph had made over to her, somewhat grudgingly, some of Venetia's jewellery that she had wanted Dulcie to have. She could have asked him why he had not given it to her sooner since that had been her mother's wish, but she did not. She accepted it, and sold those pieces which were now old-fashioned. She was intensely worried about money, about the upkeep of the child. In a matter of weeks she had sold the rest of the jewellery, for what she knew was a risible sum. She felt panicky.

Simon Garrick remained faithful, and visited her often, because his job in London took him to Paris every few weeks. He repeated his worries about Kate: she needed a family, contact with other children, security, education. Frantic, Dulcie pointed out that Mlle Paul taught the child a lot, that she had more security than most, that the arrangement worked beautifully. Simon was adamant. Why didn't she take the child back, go back to England, to the support of her family? She became hysterical. It was too late now, Thea had gone and she was the only one who would have understood . . . It was then, as she raved and wrung her hands and paced up and down, that the idea of the Kingsleys as adoptive parents first occurred to her.

Thea had had two miscarriages, and though her letters continued cheerful, Dulcie knew how much she had always wanted children, what a wonderful mother she would make. They lived far away, and were never likely to return; they were the very soul of integrity and discretion. The more she considered it as a possible solution, the more perfect it appeared to be. Kate was four and a half, she was a little girl, running about, asking questions, knocking on the door of Dulcie's life. Yes, she must and would do something.

She wrote to Thea. Even now she had found it impossible to be direct. She had reached the nub of the letter on the third page, after the usual news and pleasantries, most of it only partially true. Then:

'. . . Thea, do you still want a family? I've been so sad to hear of the bad time you've been having, you who always wanted children so much and would be so good with them. You see, I know of a dear little girl, a war orphan. She is four years old and has never known her parents. At the moment she lives all alone with a nanny, but she does so need a family — her name is Kate. I don't know her well, but I'm told she is bright and lively. She would so love a proper home, a new start, and you are just the person to provide it. But of course I'm just dreaming as usual, take no notice of me . . .' and she had gone prattling off at a tangent again for a paragraph or two, before returning to the subject. 'About Kate, though. Of course, it would be the utterest madness on your part to take on a child you know nothing about, what could I have been thinking of? Not another word, all my love, your distracted sister, Dulcie.' But there had been a PS: 'Of course, knowing you, you will have realized that she is mine. Oh please, please, help. D.'

Her deviousness astounded even Dulcie herself. Even over this most crucial of matters she could not be properly serious, or straightforward. She had to cast herself on someone's mercy and behave like a child herself, unable to take responsibility for asking for help, but forcing others to play guessing games. She hated her letter, but could not bring herself to rewrite it. In the weeks before she received a reply she was like a cat on hot bricks. Illogically she had succeeded in convincing herself that this and only this was the solution, that if Thea refused it would be the end of the world.

When the reply did arrive, it was not from Thea, but from Jack. When she recognized the handwriting Dulcie's heart plummetted. She turned the envelope over in her hands, nervously, as she sat before rapidly cooling croissants and coffee. A delightful day stretched before her, a day she had been looking forward to: a lunch party out of town, and the races, and dinner in the evening, all in the company of a rich, charming (and married) elderly Belgian, who paid her quite simply to enjoy herself. Now the day turned to dust and ashes. She tore open the envelope. The letter was typical of Jack, neatly written and carefully considered, ruthlessly to the point; quite unlike the effusion of understanding, sympathy and unqualified assent she had hoped for from her sister.

'Dear Dulcie,' he wrote, 'I hope you will forgive me for replying to a letter which was addressed to Thea. We agreed that I should do so, as you will appreciate it is hard for your sister to be objective over the matter you mention.' Matter? Mention! Dulcie pushed her chair back and walked up and down as she read. 'We talked long, hard, and often heatedly, on the subject. We had not until now considered adoption, since there is no reason, the doctors assure us, why Thea should not have a child of her own. However, the miscarriages have left her depressed, and she has been advised not to embark on another pregnancy just yet. We feel that on balance we would like to adopt your Kate (Thea's feelings about family loyalty weighed heavily in the argument) provided she, Kate, is happy with the arrangement. I mean, that she is happy with the arrangement once it is under way. I would hardly expect a four-year-old child to have views on the matter in advance. It will be a tremendous upheaval for her, and for this reason we think it is important that she sees her new life with us as complete and final. She should not be told who her real parents are, nor be encouraged to investigate. If a graft at such a late stage is to succeed, the wound must be allowed to heal and close without interference. Please realize that it is for the child's sake we insist on this, and not with any thought of estranging you from her. But we shall not treat you as her mother once she comes here (if she does). There will be no progress reports, or things of that nature. If you ever meet her in the future, it will be as her aunt. I gather from your letter, however, that you would be quite happy about this, since it is your chief wish that she be taken off your hands,' Dulcie put her hand to her mouth – did he have to hit so hard?

'So the short answer to your request is, yes.' They were agreeing. Then why did she feel so wretched, so mean and dirty and defeated? 'I suggest an interval of a few months for Kate to become acclimatized to the notion. We shall arrange for a friend (Andrea Avery, whom you may remember) to accompany Kate on the journey out. She will, of course, know nothing. I suggest that the more simple and immediate the arrangement, the better. You may keep this letter as a guarantee that we shall tell no one of Kate's real parentage. From the moment you agree to our terms she will become our child. And I hope that you will write soon with your assurances – for Kate's sake. Thea will be writing soon, she has things she wants to ask you. From here on I will hand over to her. With best wishes, Love, Jack.'

Dulcie re-read the letter. Its directness was a shock, as though she had thrown herself at a door she thought to be locked and it had burst open before her. It was perfectly clear that Jack had looked at the suggestion purely from his and Thea's point of view, and from Kate's, and not from that of her own anxiety and inconvenience. She knew it was the only criterion worth applying, but she was still resentful.

But the resentment didn't last. By the end of her day with Monsieur Leclerc the realization of her good fortune had fully dawned. Everything had sorted itself out beautifully. When, at the end of the week, Simon Garrick came to see her, she told him all about it – describing the Kingsleys as friends in Kenya.

He watched her solemnly as she enthused.

'I just hope you won't find it painful,' he said afterwards.

'Painful? My darling Simon, I'm ecstatic!'

'So I see,' he remarked drily. He reminded her of Aubrey. And she reacted to him as she had so often done to her brother when he had been sceptical.

'Don't be dreary! It's good news, and I think we should celebrate.'

'As you wish.'

At the Casse-Croute that night he told her he was engaged to be married. He showed her a photograph of Lady Davina Trevor, who was brown-haired and a little chinless, but with a good complexion, and Dulcie said 'she looks nice' and had ordered more wine. Because it was a shock, more of a shock than she would have thought possible.

The letters from Thea came, the questions, the sympathy and support and affection she had so wanted, and they were like a healing balm after Jack's abrasive directness. The travel arrangements were made, the assurances given, Mlle Paul informed. The day drew close. Dulcie had not seen Kate since before she had first written to the Kingsleys. It was not that she was afraid of weakening, there was no danger of that, but she wanted it all to be over, and at as great a distance as possible.

But Mlle Paul was continually on the telephone, fussing and flapping and asking the sort of questions which she herself was much better equipped to answer than Dulcie, questions about underwear and shoes and haircuts. 'Just see to it, Nanny!' Dulcie would shriek in despair. 'I trust you completely, do whatever you think fit!'

So it was hard to put Kate from her mind, try as she might. After these conversations she would sit by the phone in an agony of helplessness, wishing she did know more, that she could help, that she was not so useless, and hoping that Kate would not suffer irreparably from her lack of knowledge. And in the end, on that last, damp, early morning, when the child — her child — had left Paris, she had taken a taxi to the Rue St Marc, and stood in the doorway of the little *boulangerie* on the corner, her feet frozen in her fashionable shoes, her fur collar turned up, waiting.

She had seen the second taxi arrive, seen Andrea Avery run up the steps and ring the bell. Andrea Avery — plain, brainy, opinionated Andrea whom she had so envied and despised: how ironical. Dulcie experienced an urge to rush forward and make herself known, claim her daughter, shout defiance, and sweep off in the taxi. But she quickly overcame it, and stood there like a criminal in the cold drizzle, watching.

Mlle Paul had appeared, mopping her nose and eyes with a hankie, embracing the child. There had been an exchange between the brisk Andrea and the weeping Tanty. Beside them, as they talked, stood the stiff, upright, unbending figure of five-year-old Kate, in a double-breasted coat, gaiters, scarf and gloves, her red hair in a thick plait beneath a knitted tam-o'-shanter. She looked like an army officer. I would have dressed her more prettily, thought Dulcie. Nanny has dressed her sensibly and economically and serviceably, but I would have dressed her more prettily.

Before the adults had finished talking, Kate had marched down the steps and into the waiting taxi, like a martyr before a firing squad. No tears, Dulcie noticed, no fussing or fidgeting or seeking of attention. So grim and dry-eyed, and just five years old. She's magnificent, thought Dulcie.

Andrea had got into the back seat beside Kate, and said something to her, but the child had not turned. She kept her small, set white face averted, staring out of the window. But not seeing, thought Dulcie. She can't see me, and even if she could she wouldn't know who I was.

She watched as the taxi drew away, the little white face glaring grimly through the window. And when it was gone there remained Mlle Paul, sobbing into her hankie, trudging up the steps like an old woman; and not a hundred yards away, Dulcie, dry-eyed and staring, like her daughter.

Now, Dulcie stood just outside the main door of Fortnum's, sheltering beneath an umbrella. Because she was nervous, she had been early, and now had to experience the added strain of waiting. She did not want to be taken by surprise, so she scrutinized every passing female: she wanted to see before she was seen. She had fussed interminably over what to wear, and even now was not confident in her choice — she, to whom matters of style and appearance came as easily as breathing! And for what? she had asked herself, as she changed her blouse for the third time. For a twenty-year-old girl from the Styx, who was hardly likely to be critical of her dress sense, and whom she did not have to impress. In the end, anxious not to appear over-formal, she had opted for a pleated skirt, with a yellow shirt and a plain blue blazer – cheerful, casual, summery. Now, in the pouring rain, she felt ridiculous, the sort of woman who would rather be smart then sensible, the very opposite of what she had intended.

She peered up and down the street. Opposite, a newspaper seller with the first edition of the London evenings shouted about the war in Spain. Primmy was right, they just had to have a war. She sighed. War had been good to her, but it would never be so good again. She hoped there would not be another. Where were they? She felt a headache coming on.

At five to one, Kate emerged from Swan and Edgar's with two large carrier bags, and realized that she was either going to be late, or get soaked. She had no umbrella (and anyway, her hands were full) but everything in her protested that to hail a taxi for a few hundred yards to Fortnum's would be rank extravagance after a morning's unbridled spending. She hovered on the steps for a moment or two, hoping the rain would let up. The doorman came over to her.

'Taxi, miss?'

'No, thank you, I don't have far to go.'

'It doesn't need to be far in this.'

Kate thought he looked smug and self-satisfied in his uniform.

'I'll make a run for it,' she declared, and fled from his amused, avuncular look.

Dulcie saw the young woman dashing across the road, waiting with obvious impatience on the traffic island, putting her bags down for a moment to push her wet hair back off her face. Dulcie noticed her because she was tall, and ran like someone used to running, not with the splay-footed gait of most city women. Her legs were spattered with dirty water from the puddles, and she carried two Swan and Edgar bags, both of which were saturated – the corner of one was beginning to give way beneath the weight of its contents, Dulcie wondered if the girl knew. But as she darted forward for the second half of her journey across Piccadilly, the bag burst and several garments fell on to the road in the path of an oncoming bus. The bus, and several cabs and private cars, stopped politely.

The girl, managing to appear furious and determined rather than flustered and embarrassed, picked up the wet and dirty things, rolled them up in what was left of the bag, tucked them under her arm and strode on with head held high. Dulcie felt admiration for anyone who could appear so scornful and aloof after such a disaster. But where were Kate and Joe?

She was gazing down towards Green Park when a voice said: 'You wouldn't be Dulcie Tennant?'

Kate had spotted her aunt from the other side of the road. She had the advantage over Dulcie in being late — the elegant woman waiting in the rain could only be waiting for her. Besides, she was instantly recognizable, not so much from the poorly reproduced newspaper clipping, but from the childhood photograph which Kate had so often studied at home. There she was — slight, golden-haired, pretty — and apparently endowed with the gift of eternal youth. By the time Kate reached the traffic island she was beginning to curse her pigheadedness in not taking a taxi. Her feet in her good shoes and stockings were soaked, her collar was clammy and she had a suspicion that one of her bags was about to burst.

Halfway across the road it did so. Muttering furiously to herself and calling down a murrain on England and its weather, she scooped up her now soiled new things and stalked on. At the entrance to Fortnum's she confronted her aunt.

'Yes, that's me.' Dulcie turned to find the girl of the carrier-bag incident standing before her.

'I'm Kate. How do you do.'

Dulcie's hand was enclosed in a grip that, in spite of being cold and wet, was firm and confident. She leaned forward and kissed Kate's cheek which was smooth, and wet with rain. She had to reach up to do so, for the girl was a head taller than her.

'Hallo, Kate.'

'My God, what must I look like? Can we go in?'

'Of course!' Dulcie was glad of the rain at that moment, for she suspected there were tears in her eyes. This meeting was so long awaited, so dreaded, and yet somehow now unexpected, quite other than what she had imagined. This tall, courageous redhead, soaked to the skin, head tilted defiantly — was her daughter. Her little abandoned Kate. Dulcie's daughter. It was so wonderful that it took her breath away. She took her arm and led her through the door.

'You poor thing. I did feel so sorry for you when you dropped everything, but of course I didn't realize it was you.' Dulcie was on automatic pilot. 'I was looking for Joe as well — isn't he with you?'

'He couldn't come, he's got a cold — 'flu — he's got to spend a couple of days in bed.'

'Oh I'm so sorry.'

Dulcie was sorry. It meant she had Kate to herself and she was not sure she could cope; she reeled under the onslaught of powerful unfamiliar emotions. She wished she had allowed Giles to come as he had suggested. But she went on smoothly: 'Look, I'll show you where the Ladies is, and then you can tidy up and leave your shopping and that wet jacket. You must buy some more stockings, your feet look soaked. I know, I will buy you some — a present from your aunt.' How easily it came to her this monstrous deception, how trippingly it moved on her tongue.

'I really can't allow you to do that.'

'Nonsense, indulge me.'

Dulcie felt there must be a great spreading stain on her silk shirt, where her heart was bleeding, bleeding.

She bought Kate Kayser Bondor silk stockings, in the face of vociferous protest, and ushered her into the powder room. She sat on the pink chaise longue outside, staring at herself in the scrolled gilt mirror opposite, and occasionally at the smart lunch-time women tripping to and fro on the pile carpet in their high heels. Her face was calm, habit had organized her expression into one of refined detachment, but her emotions were in uproar.

Kate emerged after only a few minutes, her wet hair combed, dry stockings on, jacket removed. Her seersucker dress was creased, there was something waif-like in her clothes that was out of keeping with her manner. She looked so like David Reed that Dulcie was once again obliged to operate on an automatic level.

'Let's go and find something to eat. It's so heavenly to see you . . .'

As they walked together Dulcie was overwhelmed by Kate's presence, the powerful, individual reality of it after so much vague and unsatisfying speculation. Was this then the creature she had shuffled off, disowned, rejected, never wanted to see? Oh, if only she had known, if only someone had been able to tell her what it would be like. Never in her wildest dreams had she imagined the exaltation of knowing that she, vain, venial Dulcie as Ralph had once called her, had created this magnificent person.

They sat, and ordered *vichysoisse* and sole.

Kate, in her turn, found herself unprepared for Dulcie's beauty. Thea's enthusiastic praise and Jack's ambivalence had both led her to expect something bogus, all artifice and surface gloss. But here she knew was the genuine article. Dulcie Tennant was a beautiful woman, a woman who even in middle-age had kept that shining loveliness, that gold and silver colouring, that slim, graceful figure for which Thea said she (and her mother before her) had been famous. Dulcie's was not a beauty enhanced by age and experience, like Thea's, but seemed to be untouched by either. Kate supposed that Dulcie Tennant had led a cushioned and pampered existence, that her trials and tribulations must have been few compared with her sister's, that her time must be spent being flattered and feted by the 'boyfriends' of whom Aubrey had so scathingly spoken. She deferred judgement on her aunt.

'How are you settling in with Ralph and Aubrey?' Dulcie was asking.

'They're very kind to put up with us,' replied Kate. And added, to salve her conscience: 'Very kind.'

'Not at all!' Dulcie was vehement. 'You're family, Kate. There's been little enough anyone has been able to do with you all living so far away, it's good to be able to help. And for what it's worth I know Aubrey feels the same. It's so lovely to have you here.' She glanced down, brushing some imaginary particle from her skirt. When she looked up there was something brilliant and appealing in her smile. 'I expect you find them very trying.'

Kate looked down at the bowl of creamy soup which the waitress set before her, then back at Dulcie. The smile, which now contained a hint of something wicked, beguiled her. She grinned. 'I was going to say no, of course not. But Grandfather and I,' she made herself say it again, 'seem to irritate each other.'

'Snap!' Dulcie laughed. 'He misses Thea dreadfully you know.'

'Heavens!' Kate raised her eyebrows – her face was very mobile, like her father's – 'how he must hate me for coming here in her place.'

'No, I shouldn't think so,' said Dulcie, trying not to stare. 'That would be too subtle for Father. No, it's just that the stronger the character the more argumentative he gets. It's a compliment in its way.'

'I'll try to see it in that light.'

Dulcie ate about a quarter of her soup, with difficulty, in the time it took Kate to finish hers. She noticed that Kate's expression as she looked about her was frankly appraising, even critical. Dulcie saw the restaurant through her eyes: the patrons, herself included, a lot of foolish fashionable women with nothing better to do than spend money on food they didn't want. She must talk, keep the occasion light and amusing, beguile her daughter so that she would not have time to form unfavourable opinions.

'What have you been buying?' she asked as their fish arrived.

Kate grimaced. 'I needed some heavier clothes.'

'Yes, you must feel it terribly after Africa. Have you been frozen at Mapleton Road? You know those two have plenty of money but Ralph is so miserly these days –'

'I haven't been cold.' Kate felt again that she had been brusque, and added, 'he told me to buy something extra as a present, which was very decent of him.'

'Oh good.'

'So I got a suit, and a wool dress, and a coat, and a shirt. I spent twenty pounds. I feel a marked woman.'

This was familiar territory to Dulcie. 'You did well to spend so little, I can tell you. There are so many good ready-to-wear clothes from America in the shops these days, one doesn't have to spend a fortune.' Kate looked blankly at her. 'What's the suit like? Do tell.'

'Oh, I don't know, I've never owned a suit before and thought I ought to . . . It's sort of . . .' Kate made a gesture to indicate lapels and cuffs, 'not the sort of thing I'd normally wear, but I thought for taking Joe to school in September . . .'

'You must look the part, of course.'

'It's grey,' added Kate. 'I think it's quite smart.'

'I'm sure it is,' said Dulcie reassuringly, though Kate was the very last person she could imagine wearing a smart grey suit. It sounded horribly inappropriate, but she wasn't going to say so.

'As a matter of fact I don't like new clothes,' Kate was saying, as though in self-excuse, 'they're too stiff. I like things that have acquired character, old things, comfortable things that can be lumped together. But I realize that won't do at all over here.'

Dulcie laid her knife and fork together beside her almost untouched sole, and sat back. 'Do you know what I think?' she said lightly, charmingly. 'I think that style is the important thing. And you have that, Kate, a natural style of your own. If I were you I wouldn't bother with smart grey suits – which is a fine thing to say when you've been spending all that money! – just be yourself and you will be a *succes fou*.'

'Perhaps you're right.' Kate grinned.

Her hair, now that it was dry, was a mass of feathery curls, her eyes a speckled yellow, like a cat's. She looked so like David that Dulcie was obliged to fiddle with her bag. The strange momentousness of the occasion was once again borne upon her, and her head swam. How could she bear it? What had she done? What sort of monster was she, when all this life and youth and energy might have been hers to cherish and to vaunt? What status might have been hers in the eyes of family and friends, to stand a little aside and say: 'May I introduce my daughter, Kate?'

Kate was warming to Dulcie. She felt that ease and peace in her presence that we often do in the company of our opposites. She didn't need to be other than she was, they were two such different people that pretence would have been irrelevant. Also, Dulcie was fun, and friendly. An ally. Now she was staring away from her across the room, apparently in a reverie.

'Aunt —' said Kate.

'Oh please,' said Dulcie gaily, turning back to her with that brilliant smile, 'I wish you'd call me Dulcie.'

When they emerged from Fortnum's at half past two the rain had stopped, Kate had organized her purchases into the intact carrier bag, and they had chosen a box of chocolates for Joe. 'But don't let my father near them,' Dulcie had warned.

'The sun's come out for you,' she remarked now, 'isn't that nice?' She felt buoyantly happy, walking down gleaming, rainwashed Piccadilly with her daughter.

Kate was quiet, swinging loftily along beside her, so she added: 'I'm only sorry that I was away when you arrived, and that you're off again so soon. I might have been able to make your first couple of weeks a bit easier.'

'Oh, they were fine.' Kate dismissed these problems almost scornfully, and went on: 'In September when Joe's at school I must find a job.'

How capable she is, thought Dulcie, how firm and resourceful. Her Kate whose name had been chosen for its sensible plainness! Instead, she was a firebrand. She would never make terrible mistakes, reflected Dulcie, alight with parental pride, her life would progress onward and upward, straight as a die.

'Perhaps I could help?' she ventured. 'What sort of job were you thinking of?'

Kate frowned. 'That's the trouble, I don't know. I'm not fussy so long as I'm not trapped in an office wearing my best clothes every day at someone else's beck and call —' She caught sight of Dulcie's expression and laughed, loud and clear, so that people looked at her and smiled reflexively. 'Heavens, I've no idea what I want to do, and I'm certainly in no position to be choosy — I'll know when I find it!'

Dulcie was sure that she herself would not know it if it jumped up and punched her on the nose, so she did not press her offer of help.

At the tube station they kissed each other on the cheek and

it seemed the most natural thing in the world. And they parted each with that happy sensation of a good beginning having been made.

That evening, sitting in the window seat waiting for Rex to arrive, with Fondant warm and purring on her silk-clad lap, Dulcie thought about Kate as one might pore over a secret and wonderful treasure. Sadly, it was one she was forbidden to share. Faustus-like, she had forfeited the right to this most precious and rewarding of intimacies for the sake of a few years' silly, gilded freedom. And she knew now, if in the past she had ever doubted it, that she must never, ever tell.

CHAPTER FIVE

'I know my heart won't beat again,
Until the day we meet again . . .
Auf wiedersehen, auf wiedersehen, my dear . . .'

'Auf Wiedersehen My Dear'
Hoffman, Nelson, Goodhart and Ager, 1932

BILL Maguire alighted at the Bahnhof Friedrichstrasse at
midday on 31 July and felt that he had somehow been
transported not just the two miles from his apartment in
Charlottenburg, but back a decade in time as well. In the
gentle summer weather, with soft sunlight and smiling, cloud-
blossomed skies, Berlin had once again become the city that
had seduced him as a young man. On the hard, rattling
wooden seats of the Stadtbahn, beneath the glass canopy of the
station, on the noisy stone staircase leading to the turnstile and
now out on the Friedrichstrasse itself, carefree foreigners and
smiling Berliners thronged cheerfully together, caught up in
the same holiday spirit. Multi-coloured bunting and the flags
of many nations fluttered above the shopfronts, so that even
the crooked cross of the Third Reich seemed to take its place
graciously among its peers. Bill stood for a moment outside
the station, just breathing it in and allowing himself to take
pleasure in it all. With one hand he loosened and removed his
tie. He rolled the tie and put it in his pocket, then shrugged
off his jacket and slung it over his shoulder. The sun was warm
on his face and neck.

He went over to the news-stand, cosmopolitan and unex-
ceptionable as a result of Goebbels' public relations clean-up.
Julius Streicher's *Der Sturmer*, the most violent and vulgar of
the anti-semitic news-sheets, was nowhere to be seen. In the

slot normally reserved for it stood propped a sheaf of *Das Schwarze Korps*, the organ of the SS guards. Bill reflected that the substitution mirrored merely an editorial, not an ideological, improvement. He bought himself a two-day-old copy of the *Herald* to see what they had done to his copy on the Olympic village, and that morning's issue of *Der Angriff*. He glanced cursorily at the front page as he moved away from the news-stand. Traditionally *Der Angriff* was one of the most aggressive of the Nazi papers. Today it was all 'welcome to our overseas visitors' and 'Berlin plays host to the world'. He shook his head, rolled both newspapers tightly and thrust them into his jacket pocket along with the tie. Hostess, he thought, *I* should've said hostess.

At the end of the Friedrichstrasse he turned left into the Unter den Linden, heading for the Adlon Hotel. The loveliness of the most famous avenue in Berlin squeezed his heart a little as it always did, but especially now when it was almost like old times. He paused again, to allow himself the luxury of a glance over his shoulder, at the graceful vista leading down to the Brandenburg Tor. The double row of trees in a froth of summer green formed an arch over the wide gravel walk down the centre of the street – a dappled space for people to stroll and talk and drink and eat and take their civilized pleasures. And after too many bitter barren years the people were back, and the music. The Unter den Linden surged with the soft ebb and flow of humanity enjoying itself. Beyond the trees the triumphal arches of the great gate glittered in the sunshine.

As Bill walked on he recalled a recent editorial in *Der Angriff*: 'We must be more charming than the Parisians,' it had urged its readers, 'more easygoing than the Viennese, more vivacious than the Romans, more cosmopolitan than London and more practical than New York.'

Well, they had done it, the clever bastards. They'd covered their tracks and hidden their slogans, and put out the flags for the Olympic visitors. After the embarrassing *faux pas* of the winter games at Garmisch-Partenkirken where the politics of victimization had still been clearly on view, they were making everything all right again with this unrivalled display of summery goodwill.

He reached the Adlon. Opposite the pavilioned entrance,

on the space beneath the trees, a small crowd had gathered round some street entertainers. On the fringes of the crowd a clutch of lads in the light brown uniforms of the Youth Movement craned to get a better view. Just boys, with bare knees and tanned necks, standing on tip-toe to see a free show.

A little burst of laughter rose from the crowd. Bill glanced at his watch. Marty Wiseman could wait another minute or two. He ran across the road, weaving between the slow-moving close-packed traffic, lifting a hand in acknowledgement of not being run over. When he reached the other side, with the traffic noise behind him, he could hear a concertina playing *Let the moon shine bright on Charlie Chaplin*. He skirted the crowd until he was standing parallel with the entertainers. He scanned the faces of the spectators: almost all of them bore anticipatory smiles.

There were four players, three young men and a girl, all dressed in identical baggy dark suits, waistcoats, black boots and bowler hats in the style of the old silent film comics. One of the men stood to one side playing the accordion, the other three were engaged in an elaborate slapstick dumbshow. The two men were after the girl who was tiny and petite, but she was too clever for them – time and again they closed in on her, only to end up bumping into one another or flooring each other with wild punches intended for her. The routine was simple, but perfectly timed. When it ended the applause was noisy. The girl beamed, bowed low, and then moved aside with a grandiose gesture as the men pulled a cloth from a large object which had been standing behind them.

It was a life-size wooden model of Charlie Chaplin, set into a wooden block so that it stood securely upright. It was complete in every detail – the over-large shoes and clothes, the cane, the hankie, the large mournful eyes and the tiny moustache. All it lacked was a hat. The girl removed her own and set it on the model's head, and then took from one capacious pocket a tennis ball, holding it aloft and indicating with a flourish that someone in the audience might care to try and knock the hat off. The musician began playing and at once there was a queue of contestants, and one of the men had taken up a position behind the model as backstop. The girl marked a place in the gravel with her toe, and the first thrower took aim. But it wasn't to be as easy as it had first appeared. The accordionist placed one foot on a wooden pedal at the base of the model, and as he moved the foot in time to his tune, so the model swayed rhythmically from side to side. There was something almost eerie about the lugubrious face swinging in a wide arc, staring but lifeless.

Watching the increasingly hilarious members of the audience take their turn, Bill wondered if the choice of Chaplin as a target had been entirely random. There was no doubt that the similarity between this toothbrush moustache and that adorning another much-photographed face was not lost on the bystanders.

No one hit the hat. With each successive failure the girl whooped and turned a spectacular cartwheel, her tailcoat flopping down over her shoulders, her blonde hair brushing the ground. She became red in the face, she discarded the coat and mopped her brow with a spotted handkerchief. She displayed the palms of her hands, grazed from the continual contact with the hard ground. Who would be her champion? Who would dislodge the hat and save her from further cartwheels?

A young woman stepped forward from the far side, holding out her hand for the tennis ball. The man who was acting as fielder tossed it to her and she caught it effortlessly in one hand. Bill watched, amused. There had been a boy standing with her, perhaps a young brother or nephew, and he was now scarlet with embarrassment. From the blushing of the boy and the girl's air of sporty confidence, Bill guessed they might be British.

She stood at the mark and took aim, tall and leggy in trousers and shirt. When she threw the ball it was with a flick of the wrist that sent it humming through the air with deadly accuracy. There was a thump and the hat fell to the ground. The model stopped swaying, the crowd cheered delightedly. The girl grinned and executed a couple of bows. Then, quite unexpectedly, she took a short run and threw herself into a perfect cartwheel, her long legs scything through the air, her arms straight and strong. Bill found himself clapping. He even surprised himself by crying 'Encore!' and meaning it as she returned, grinning, to her place and her still blushing, but now gratified, young escort.

Kate heard the 'Encore' as she went back to her place, and when she turned she saw at once the man who had shouted it. Her eyes found his face as if she had already known just where he was standing, and when they met his she experienced a shock of something between recognition and a kind of thrilling fear. Those eyes, blue, and narrowed by a knowing intrusive smile, seemed to look right past her face and into her self. She felt, for that split second completely exposed and vulnerable. But then Joe was speaking to her, the crowd shifted, and the man had gone.

Bill crossed the road to the hotel entrance and paused on the busy pavement, before the aloof stare of the commissionaire, to replace his jacket and tie and comb his fingers through his hair. He tried to define what had been so attractive about the girl. Many would have called her plain. And yet real physical confidence was sensual, and there had been the assured, innocent vanity of that grin. He smiled to himself, remembering it, and went in to the Adlon to meet Marty Wiseman.

As press barons went, Wiseman was affability itself. But to Bill, who was becoming a sceptic, such relentless affability was in itself suspicious. If a man was always beaming and chuckling and shoulder-slapping, like some bon-vivant Santa Claus, you never knew where the hell you were with him. His loud, simplistic joviality, like his cigars, threw up a smokescreen. For Wiseman had a shrewd intelligence and a keen appreciation of the *Herald*'s place in the Fleet Street hierarchy. The *Herald*, when Wiseman bought it, had occupied the same special niche for years, as the opinionated, left of centre, thinking person's paper – humane and intelligent, its circulation unremarkable but steady.

Marty Wiseman had not changed any of that. But what he had done was subtly to underline its character, to point out that it was not solemn and pedagogic as it had appeared in the '20s, but up-to-date, liberal and informed like the responsible young intellectuals of the '30s. Its readership increased, not enough to worry the really big guns, but enough to give the paper cachet, and win it respect. Clever people with minds of their own read the *Herald*.

Bill had worked there for eight years now, and had now become regarded as both the paper's most valuable asset and its greatest liability.

Bill entered the lofty opulence of the hotel's cocktail bar. It chattered and hummed with the gaiety of the pre-prandial happy hour. Expensively dressed women and men with high complexions smoked, drank and talked with extraordinary vivacity. Bill wondered at them, as he cast about for Marty Wiseman.

He was not hard to spot, and true to form he had attracted company. Bill threaded his way across to the corner table where he sat, large, puce and benevolent behind a Scotch and dry ginger.

'Bill, you son of a gun!' Marty had spent time in the United States and liked to affect American mannerisms.

'Mr Wiseman.'

Bill's hand was enclosed and wrung in Marty's vast, humid paw as he said, 'Let me introduce these good people to you, Bill. This is Mr Ralph Tennant, and Mr Aubrey Tennant.'

'How do you do. No, please don't get up.' Bill shook the hand of a burly, square-jawed man in his forties; and then that of a glowering but magnificent-looking old gentleman with a gnarled, fierce beauty worthy of a Rembrandt or a Dürer. Father and son, he supposed. He sat, gave his order of whisky and soda to the hovering waiter, and turned to the younger man.

'Are you over here for the Games?'

'We are, yes.'

'Aren't we all?' bellowed Marty, making an expansive gesture with his cigar stub, to include everyone in the room.

'We flew in yesterday,' added Aubrey Tennant, with an air of quiet pride. Not an habitual traveller, Bill guessed.

'A good flight?'

'Excellent.'

'It may be quick but it's bloody uncomfortable.' This was the old gentleman. 'Indeed it would be hard to imagine a less natural form of transport.'

Bill smiled. 'Aha,' said Marty. 'The English would walk everywhere in stout boots if they could.'

'Not me,' said Aubrey drily. It struck Bill again that he was witnessing a basically conservative man in an adventurous mood. 'I can scarcely believe that at this time yesterday we were at Victoria Terminus, and yet by six we were having a drink in this very bar.' He turned to Bill. 'We only decided to come a couple of weeks ago.'

'Creatures of impulse,' said Bill.

'I suppose we must be!'

Marty leaned forward. His system was so permeated with cigar smoke and gourmet food and whisky that he seemed to seethe and bubble like a rich stew. 'If there's anything you good people want to know about Berlin,' he confided gutturally, 'Bill is your man. He knows this city like the back of his hand.'

'Is that so?' said Aubrey. 'You've been here some time have you?'

'A couple of years. And before, in my misspent youth.'

Ralph made a growling sound as though about to comment on this last remark, but he was prevented from doing so by the arrival of Bill's drink and, close on its heels, two more persons. Marty and Aubrey rose. Bill glanced over his shoulder and followed suit.

'This is my niece, Kate Kingsley,' said Aubrey, with a trace of pride, 'and my nephew, Joe.'

'Charmed!' said Marty. They all shook hands. The girl had a direct, appraising stare and a commanding handshake.

'Congratulations on your cartwheel,' said Bill.

'I thought it was you,' was her reply. In her rather pale, set face her eyes were yellow bright, like windows into a lighted room. Bill retained her cool hand for a moment so that he and she remained standing while the others sat.

'You stole the show, you realize.'

'Good gracious' – she removed her hand with unembarrassed firmness – 'I certainly didn't mean to do that.'

He was amused by something incongruously tight-arsed in her tone, but as they sat down she gave him the hint of a smile, eyes narrowed. Bill swallowed his drink, and stared at her with undisguised interest. In spite of the affected primness of her opening remark, he could readily picture being in bed with her, and perhaps his thought was apparent, for he detected a slight snub, now, in the way she lifted her chin and turned her head to join in the conversation. Bill enjoyed the snub, too.

'You two have met already?' enquired Marty of Kate.

'I wouldn't say that.' Sharp and fresh as a lemon.

'I *was* merely an admiring onlooker,' put in Bill affably, knowing it would annoy her.

'Could I have a drink?' she asked, looking round imperiously.

'Why, my dear young lady!' Bill watched delightedly as Marty, all gallant apology now, snapped his big fingers over his head like castanets to attract the waiter and ordered lemonade for Joe and dry sherry for Kate, and the same again for the rest of them. Furnished with another drink, Bill conceived a plan and proceeded at once to put it into action. He leaned forward and addressed Aubrey.

'You know, if you would like to go anywhere in particular, I'd be very glad to help out. I do know this town.'

'That's awfully good of you!' Aubrey, as Bill had recognized, was flushed with the success of the arrangements so far. 'Of course we shall be at the stadium tomorrow, for the opening ceremony, and after that —'

'What about tonight?' asked Bill. 'Any plans for this evening?'

'Now then, Bill!' Threateningly jocular, Marty turned away from his discussion with Ralph, thereby revealing that he had not been attending to what the old man was saying. 'Don't you go leading these good people astray!'

Bill shrugged ingenuously, as if to say, what, me? But in Aubrey he had a willing subject, and one who did not care to be patronized.

'We haven't arranged a thing,' said Aubrey firmly. 'But I must say it would be rather pleasant — why not?' He glanced at Kate who in turn stared levelly at Bill over the rim of her glass.

'It looks as if we're in your hands,' she said rather acidly.

'Splendid. Dinner and a club, then. I'll be here at eight.'

'Hm.' Marty sounded uneasy. 'And the best of British.' He rose from his chair like a great, florid cactus. 'I think we'd better get along to lunch and leave these people in peace,' he said in the tone of one removing a disobedient child. He paused beside Kate, one hand on her shoulder. 'I'm only sorry to be going just when an attractive young lady's arrived, but that's the story of my life.' Bill thought it was a pity Marty couldn't see Kate's face, which was a study in frosty distaste.

'See you tonight then.'

They shook hands and departed. From across the room Bill glanced back at the family group in time to see Kate idly lift his own empty glass, sniff it curiously, and set it down again. This, like other things about her, made him smile.

At lunch, over the menu, Marty remarked: 'That girl, what an oddity!'

'You thought so?'

'Bony and rigid like a hockey stick.'

'Ah, but you noticed her.'

'I could hardly avoid it, now, could I?'

'I thought she was attractive. Unusually so.'

'So.' Marty pointed a large, red finger at Bill's chest. 'Not such an altruistic guide, after all. For Christ sakes, Bill, go easy on them, you can see they're innocents abroad.'

'I'll have the fillet of veal *Holstein*,' said Bill, putting down the menu. He did not intend to get into an argument with Marty over the proposed evening out. Instead, he would keep his powder dry for the larger issues which waited in the wings. These made their entrance with the arrival of the main course.

'You know I never interfere on the editorial side,' said Marty, and it was true. 'I wouldn't want to' (false), 'but I just want to say: easy does it.'

'I see.' Bill adopted the time-honoured journalistic technique of leaving the obvious question unasked in the hope that his subject would unburden himself of more than was strictly necessary. But Marty, given enough rope, had no intention of hanging himself.

'That's all,' he said, and hung the wine bottle over Bill's glass.

The warning had been given, the summons delivered, the black spot passed on. But with such seeming innocence that the words themselves, if repeated, would convey nothing more than a gentle admonition to watch his health or temper his style.

Marty was waxing lyrical about Berlin. 'It's still a wonderful city, one of the best, and I've always maintained we British have more in common with the German people . . .'

Bill ate his veal, and nodded, and watched Marty, not really listening. He knew the score. Marty Wiseman had been in the city three days already. Bill had met him at Templehof, accompanied him to the hotel and then left him, the willing recipient of lavish pre-Games Nazi hospitality. Dinners, receptions, tours of the various Olympic sites, an extravagant all-day party at the *Schloss* of Hermann Goering, all to the soothing accompaniment of Goebbels' expert propaganda. Marty Wiseman was shrewd, but he was also as susceptible as the next man to the best endeavours of others. If Nazi top brass were putting on a good show and going to great lengths to make things pleasant for their distinguished guests, then one good turn deserved another. Like many powerful men, Marty was magnetically drawn to power in others.

'. . . they've even cleaned the city up. Did you see this leaflet they produced with information on all the known crooks, so that you and I and the good ladies can go about our business without our pockets being picked or our noses punched?'

'I saw it. But obviously it's just cosmetic.'

'But they try, Bill. And I admire them for that.'

'Everyone will.'

Kate, entering the hotel dining-room with her family, spotted Bill Maguire and Marty Wiseman at their table. An almost-empty wine bottle stood between them, a full one awaited their pleasure. Marty talked, Bill listened, but with an air of detachment. As if he could feel her eyes on him he suddenly glanced her way, lifting his glass and ducking his head slightly, smiling. Marty glanced rather irritably over his shoulder, ignored her, and continued his harangue. Bill transferred his attention back to Marty with studied politeness.

The waiter had already drawn back her chair — Kate sat down hurriedly. She found, with mixed feelings, that her place at the table afforded her a direct view of Bill Maguire. What she saw affected her in a way that was unfamiliar and unsettling. Certainly, he was no beauty. Like his clothes, which were notable for a slight fraying of the cuffs and curling of the collar, his appearance was one of disorder, one thing at odds with another. His face was dominated by the perspicacious blue eyes and a broken nose. A redoubtable jaw was emphasized by a cleft chin, but balanced by a wide, sensitive mouth. His hair was prematurely grey, but abundant, curly, and untidy. His tie seemed to have been knotted without the aid of a mirror. She thought — he doesn't care what impression he makes on other people. And she liked him for it.

More than anything she remembered the way he'd looked at her, as much as to say: you don't fool me. And she realized, rather to her own surprise, that it was delightful to be singled out in that way, to be seen for what she was, uniquely and specially herself.

Aubrey, menu aloft, looked at her over his spectacles. 'And now, if Kate would tear herself away from the gentleman of the third estate, perhaps she'd let us know what she's going to eat.'

'Scruffy blighter,' said Ralph, breaking his bread roll and reaching for the butter. 'As for me, I'll have the herrings in sour cream to start and then the roast pork. And if I were pressed I'd take the black cherry strudel to follow. With a bottle of Piesporter, of course.' He smacked his lips noisily.

'And complain of your stomach all afternoon, no doubt,' said Aubrey, but quite mildly.

'I don't know — someone choose for me . . .' said Kate, whose mind was for some reason not on the meal.

'Ha!' Ralph seemed hugely satisfied about something. He popped a chunk of bread into his mouth, nudged Kate, and said, between munching: 'I wish you joy of your night on the town. By heaven I do!'

At two-fifteen Bill left Marty and made his way to the old building in the centre of Berlin, now re-modelled as the Olympic Games Press Headquarters. Devotedly pursuing its policy of pampering reporters, the Third Reich had equipped the Headquarters with three hundred desks, plentiful free paper and publicity shots, secretarial assistance and dark rooms. With the opening ceremony only a day away, the place now hummed with the international gentlemen of the press, their satisfaction with the facilities tarnished by the complex procedure for obtaining the necessary press cards.

Bill gathered a sheaf of the latest fulsome press releases which he dismissed as the usual junk, and an instructive map showing the route of the procession the following day, and the consequent redirection of traffic. On his way out he met Les Smedley, chief sports correspondent of the *Herald*. Les was thin, stooping and mournful, bowed down by years of enforced spectatorship, depressed by the constant reminder of what the human body could be like when released from the slavery of nicotine and alcohol. But Bill liked Les and his lugubrious humour.

'How's it going?' he asked. 'Got your card?'

'At long last and with difficulty. You must be hellishly glad you don't have two weeks of this in front of you.'

'I quite envy you. It's a straightforward job for you boys.'

'Ah . . .' Les gave him a sympathetic look. 'You've been with Wiseman, I dare say.'

'The same.'

'And he overcame his distaste for interference just enough . . .'

'Let's say he's been availing himself of the hospitality.'

'Yes.' Les glanced about him. 'They're buggers, aren't they?' he added admiringly.

In spite of his remark to Les, Bill did recapture his earlier, holiday mood as he stepped out of the Press Headquarters into the balmy afternoon sunshine. In a cavalier spirit he took all the press releases with the exception of the map, tore them in half and dropped them in a litter bin. As Berlin correspondent he had a wide brief. Apart from hard news, he selected his own material and gave it his own treatment. Now that the Games were actually about to begin, their sporting content was not his pigeon. While Les sweltered and scribbled in the stadium press box, he'd be content to roam around picking up unconsidered trifles. Only tomorrow he would be there, for the opening ceremony.

By bus, and then on foot, he made his way north-east from the centre of the city to the insalubrious suburb where Ilse Bauer lived. Going to visit Ilse always induced pleasant feelings of nostalgia. Looking out of the bus he saw that they

were crossing the square where the communist headquarters
had once been, a focal point for national socialist gatherings
prior to Hitler's election victory. He remembered standing on
the edge of one such meeting on a dark, freezing January
afternoon on the way back from the bread shop. He recalled
Israel's Department Store, long since in Nazi hands, where he
had gone to buy Ilse a bottle of scent for Christmas.

In the scruffy Hollman Strasse he alighted to walk the
remaining half mile or so to the tenement block where Ilse
lived. He stopped at a small grocer's and bought a bag of fresh
ground coffee, some cigarettes and chocolate as presents.
Somewhere near here had been the Jewish delicatessen they
used to frequent when they had the cash. He'd seen it the day
the Nazis had put up their notice on the door. Outside the
little shop, stern and even rather ludicrous before a background
of loaves and bagels and rollmop herrings, a young soldier had
stood at ease, his eyes wary beneath the rim of his helmet. As
Bill had crossed the road there had been a splintering crash and
he had turned to see a jagged hole in the shop window, the
soldier looking at it in vague dismay, his gleaming boots now
standing in a puddle of pickling fluid.

They none of them thought it would last. Along with
many other sophisticated Berliners they'd laughed up their
sleeves at the storm troopers and devised endless mocking jokes
at the expense of their screaming, gesticulating Führer. A bad
miscalculation.

The barren squalor of the Hollman Strasse did not bother
him. He supposed his empathy with such areas stemmed from
having spent so much time in them, when both he and the
century had been in their twenties. In these surroundings,
tough offal, watery lung soup and rancid horsemeat had sped
down their gullets while they inveighed against starvation and
dreamed of champagne and caviar. Thugs, crooks and tarts of
both sexes had plied their trades beneath their window as they
discussed Art and The Novel. After stuffy, smoky afternoons reflecting the human predicament and the possibility of true
love, they had repaired to stuffy, smoky clubs where sexual
gratification of all kinds was to be had for cash. Talk had been
their food, their drink, their exercise, their air. On summer
weekends in the afternoon they had gone by bus to the

Grünewald or the Wannsee, and sat among the tussocky dunes between the woods and the beach, discussing life and smoking cheap cigarettes while others swam, sailed and sunbathed.

The only area in which they had been undeniably active, and where their participation was not merely imagined or vicarious, was sex. They had copulated all the time, with each other, with Ilse whom they knew too well, and with strangers whom they knew not at all. The only punctuation to the endless merry-go-round of screwing had been periodic bouts of gonorrhoea and pubic lice.

Bill waited on the corner of the Hollmanplatz for a chance to cross. A tram hummed and rattled on its tracks through the cobble-stones. Cars, bikes and vans revved and hooted in a noisy shambles – Berliners' driving was no better than it had ever been. An army staff car with a couple of outriders on motorbikes nudged its way effortlessly through the mêlée, the two crisply uniformed officers in the back seat regally impassive. A shabby little man with a string shopping bag hawked and spat noisily after the car.

Bill crossed the square, weaving between the stationary vehicles, dodging the moving ones. On the far side he went down the Baustrasse for fifty yards, then turned left into the Metzallee, to be admitted into another world.

It was absolutely familiar to him, this hinterland of alleys and tenements and courts which lay behind the main roads of Berlin. Although he came now as a professional man, with money in his pocket and presents in his hand, he felt perfectly at home.

He doubted whether there were many party members here. Life was too hard for an ideology which stated 'Arbeit Macht Frei'. These people worked just to exist, freedom was a concept for people with money. Though, of course – Bill dodged a small boy kicking a ball – Hitler encouraged the workers in areas where they scarcely needed encouragement. Even unmarried mothers, of the right sort, were patted on the back. Ilse Bauer, fat, feckless and fifty, was suddenly some kind of heroine with her three (or so) children born on the wrong side of the sheets. Though Bill was satisfied none of the children was his, he was the only one from the old days who continued to see Ilse. They owed her a debt. She had been so wonderfully big, in every sense, there had been room for all of them in Ilse's heart, and between her coarse sheets, and in the warm, inviting recesses of her luxuriously fat body. In spite of their frenzied promiscuity, Bill and his friends had been insecure young men, afraid of life and anxious about the future. Ilse was a comfort. She reached a seismic orgasm with each and every one of them, no matter how many times she obliged in the course of a day. At the time, they had affected to despise her a little; they liked to think they were men of the world and that Ilse was their camp follower. But really it was they who had followed her, thought Bill, whimpering at her gargantuan breasts for comfort, sinking into her warm mattress of flesh like babies.

He turned left under the arch which led to Ilse's apartment, and crossed a yard in which, incredibly, a few tussocks of grass and a scattering of spindly marguerites craned towards the rectangle of light between the rooftops. Around the sides of the yard were, variously, five overflowing dustbins with a ginger cat in attendance; bicycles in a tangled, rusty row like dead insects; two small, pale children playing ball against the wall; and a very old man sitting on a hard chair, both hands resting on his stick, staring straight ahead with his mind's eye. From a high window on one side hung a swastika flag, and lower down a banner proclaiming Strength Through Joy. On the other side, in weary opposition in this most secluded of settings, the hammer and sickle hung flat and drab in the lifeless air.

On the far side of the yard was another arch. Bill passed beneath it into a short, dark stone-flagged tunnel, and took the second flight of stairs on the left. He ran up the two flights to Ilse's door. As he knocked he could hear her wireless, a present from him and her greatest luxury, playing martial music.

Knowing she wouldn't hear the knock, he let himself in and went through to the living room. The apartment had high ceilings that disappeared in a miasma of dusty cobwebs and damp stains. Ilse was sitting with her feet up on a very small cheap sofa. She seemed to ooze dangerously over the edges. Her legs, now swollen and knobby with varicose veins, stuck straight out in front of her like a doll's. Hearing him close the door she turned, her broad face, powdered like a floured cottage loaf, now lit by a brilliant smile of welcome.

'Willi! Willi *liebchen* . . .' She struggled to get up but he came over and restrained her with a hand on her shoulder and a kiss on her forehead. She smelt of plain soap and recent sweat. Though she was dilapidated now, as well as fat, there was still something about her, something a truly sexual woman never loses. She made him want to cry.

'Hallo, Ilse.'

She would not release his hand so he put his packages on the floor and crouched down next to her. She stroked his hair. 'What are you doing all this time, naughty boy, it's so long since you are here.'

'Too long, I'm sorry. It's these Games, they keep us busy.'

'Olympic Games — wonderful!' Ilse was passionately devoted to crowds, and bands, and uniforms and spectacle. 'And tomorrow you watch.'

'Yes, I'll be there.' He found he didn't want to talk about it. Instead he put the parcels on her lap. 'Here, I brought you one or two things.'

'Willi, Willi —' she tore off the paper bags, thrilled, 'why are you so good to your fat Ilse?'

She was neither complaining nor fishing for compliments. He smiled as she undid the chocolate and began munching. He knew she would systematically eat the lot.

'You?' She waved it at him.

He shook his head. 'No, but do you mind if I brew some of the coffee?'

'Please, you know, you carry on . . .'

He went through to the kitchen and put the kettle on the stove. 'How's work?' he called. Ilse was a waitress at a café on the Ku'damm, it did her bad legs no good.

'Okay,' she replied.

'And Tomas, how's he?' He referred to Ilse's fifteen-year-old son, the only one of her children to have remained with her.

'Tomas is a good boy, and so handsome — many hearts will be broken.'

Bill waited until steam began to emerge from the kettle spout, at first drifting, then in a jet. He removed it from the stove and poured the boiling water on to the coffee grounds in the jug. It was not Tomas's undoubted good looks that concerned him but the boy's enthusiastic politics. He poured his coffee and took it through.

'Still busy in the youth movement, is he?' He sat down in the only other chair, its spindly legs creaked under him.

'Yes, of course, very busy. He is going to be a leader. Tomorrow he is there, and in September, at the rally. Always he's chosen.'

'That's fine.' Bill wondered how long the owner of the hammer and sickle would be left in peace with youthful zealots like Tomas in and out of the building all the time, and whether Ilse herself was careful enough in her everyday dealings. She was the most incautious, unsuspicious of beings, and a political innocent. He changed the subject, asking her about her health, her finances, her job. Hers was a sanguine nature – everything was 'okay'. But her answers were a delight, full of inconsequential anecdotes and graphic description. After three-quarters of an hour she had finished the chocolate, and he rose to leave.

'You're not going so soon, Willi?' She looked up at him reproachfully, holding out her hands.

'Sorry, I must.' He clasped her hands and she used his grip to pull herself up. 'Tell you what, though. The day after tomorrow I'll give myself a day off. Why don't we go out to the Wannsee and have a picnic, like we used to? Everyone will be in town, there'll be nobody there.'

She enfolded him in a huge, soft embrace, speaking rapidly in German now, in her excitement. 'I can't think of anything nicer! I'll try and change my shift and we could be there for lunch, couldn't we? What fun, just like old times – how I love you, Willi!'

He patted her warm back. Her hair against his face was frizzy and brittle from too many cheap perms. Holding her like that Bill felt there was something valedictory in their clinging together. A chapter was ending, there was a threat in the air. He squeezed her tightly.

'So I'll see you then. I'll come and pick you up, at eleven-thirty.'

Beaming, she preceded him stiffly across the living room and into the dark, narrow hall. At the door they heard someone coming up the stairs. It was Tomas, home from school. Seeing them there he ignored Bill and kissed his mother perfunctorily.

He was taller than both of them, and broad, with fine, regular features which were strangely blank and passionless. Bill extended his hand.

'Tomas, good to see you again, how's school?'

'Not so bad. Thank you.' The boy spoke as though the last two words would choke him. He despises her, and hates me, thought Bill. At an age when I thought of nothing but rugger and girls, he's a full-blown Nazi.

Tomas turned to Ilse and spoke in German. 'I'm going out this evening. Did you press my shirt?'

'Not yet, I'll do it now, in a minute.' She tweaked his cheek with a plump hand which he brushed away in irritation, frowning.

'*Aber schnell!*' he snapped. 'Excuse me.' He went into the flat, pulling the door to behind him.

'You shouldn't let him speak to you like that,' said Bill.

'Ach . . .' She made a flapping gesture of dismissal. 'Young boys are always in a hurry, and there's no father to tell him this and that. The Führer is his father.' She chuckled, highly satisfied with this notion. 'He does so much for the young people.'

'*Auf wiedersehen.*' He bent to kiss her. 'I must get back and do some work.'

'Bye, bye, Willi.' She gave him an indulgent little push, sending him on his way. She admires me as she admires Tomas, thought Bill, she likes us men to have our important jobs, and assumes they're all noble and worthwhile. He felt momentarily annoyed by her, but her warmth and simplicity were so genuine that the annoyance did not last. He ran away from her down the stone staircase, passing a door which closed hastily as he went by.

'Shall I lead the way?' enquired Bill urbanely. 'They know me here.' Entering the throbbing twilight of the Klub Dalilah on the Motzstrasse, Bill found himself caught in a weird clash between past and present. The Dalilah was one of the few *Tanzbars* to have retained its peculiar character, it was still substantially the same as it had been when he'd come here in the '20s.

They left their coats in the lobby, with a pretty girl pale, fluffy and nocturnal as a moth. Then they went through curtains, down stairs, through more curtains, and were in the *Klub* itself, a small room, crammed with tables round a tiny dance floor. In this time warp even the people appeared like the ghosts of a past Berlin — pale faces and dark eyes in the half-light, turning and nodding and grinning and laughing with eerie vivacity, accompanied by the skeletal clink of bottles and glasses, the continuous pulse of music like a heartbeat. The room's décor was approximately Middle-Eastern but identifiably Berlinese. Waiters and waitresses were dressed identically in skimpy embroidered waist-coats and diaphanous harem trousers, their hair slicked back, faces made up with startling definition — dark lips, high arched brows, and doll-like, spikey-lashed eyes. The effect was exotic and confusing, calculated to disorientate the unwary punter.

Bill was subject to neither confusion nor disorientation, but he was gratified to see his guests' expressions of bewilderment, Aubrey's saucer-eyed, Kate's more wary.

The head waiter, Erich, bore down on them, disconcertingly androgynous in purple and gold, his richly waxed black moustache at odds with the soft, pouchy whiteness of his naked torso and plump hips.

'*Wilkommen!* Herr Maguire — and friends, how nice.'

'I booked a table.'

'Of course!'

Erich led the way, followed by Bill, then Kate, head high, and Aubrey, leaving a trail of bumped chairs in his perturbation. They sat down, Aubrey hurriedly, perspiring in his agitation, glad to be less conspicuous. Kate, waiting while Erich fussed with her chair, raked the Dalilah's polyglot clientele with a typically disparaging look. Bill was enjoying himself.

'Champagne, my chickens?' enquired Erich, with all the tender solicitude of a vampire bat surveying a fat cow.

'Why not?' It was Kate, in combative mood. All three men looked at her, Erich speculatively, Bill with frank interest, Aubrey with the direst trepidation.

'Why not?' echoed Bill. 'The best.'

'You must let me . . .' put in Aubrey diffidently, but he was ignored.

'The last word, isn't he?' said Bill, jerking his head after Erich's receding backside. 'Been here for donkey's years and hasn't changed one iota.'

'What's he supposed to be,' asked Aubrey. 'I mean, the get-up?'

'Certainly not Samson,' said Kate.

'Palace eunuch, that kind of thing.' Bill took out his cigarettes, offered the packet, was refused, and lit one himself. 'Type casting.' He saw Aubrey fingering the stem of his pipe which peeped from his jacket pocket. 'Do smoke that if you want to,' he said. 'It's the very least of the noxious substances being ingested in this place, I promise you.'

'Perhaps I will,' replied Aubrey, and lit up with a trembling hand.

The three of them had enjoyed a pleasant, civilized dinner at a restaurant in the Unter den Linden, not far from the hotel, the bill for which had been picked up by the *Herald*, on Marty Wiseman's insistence. This generous gesture had sprung out of Marty's awareness of the indignities likely to be visited on all concerned later in the evening. Aubrey, keen to appear no slouch at the art of good living, had matched Bill drink for drink, and ended up squiffy. Kate had been more circumspect but Bill saw that she too was a shade flushed.

Erich sashayed up with the champagne, popped the cork with a flourish and poured the foaming golden stream into their three glasses held in one hand, like a posy. 'Piss of the gods,' he observed. 'You are here for the Games?'

'That's right,' said Aubrey, glad of a more straightforward turn to the conversation, but it was not to be.

'Much bedder games here, my chickens!' cried Erich archly, patting Aubrey's fiery cheek. 'You stay under your Uncle Erich's wing, you have bedder games . . .'

Bill sat and smoked, smiling, letting Aubrey get out of that one on his own. He watched Kate who was, in his opinion, a feast for the eye in a sheath of apricot silk. The dress was soft and clinging, it wrapped itself round her long, slender body and thighs like water running down a vine. She wore a necklace made up of something which looked to Bill like lumps of half-eaten barley sugar but which he assumed must be amber. The chunky necklace was quite wrong for the dress, but the whole ensemble perfectly suited its wearer. Her hair was newly washed, a coppery cloud in which he imagined burying his face as they danced, later. Now she sat erect and aloof, sipping champagne. Erich waltzed off, leaving Aubrey snorting and stuttering.

'Good God, did you hear the fellow?'

Bill tore his eyes away from Kate. 'Being a bit saucy was he?'

'That would be an understatement!'

'Naughty Erich.'

'Good God,' said Aubrey again.

Bill knew Aubrey was on the horns of a dilemma and had not the least intention of prising him off. The man must decide which mattered to him most, propriety or adventure. In the hotel at midday he had been playing the devil-may-care traveller. Now let him prove it. This was unfair, of course, since Bill also knew Aubrey was far too good-mannered to renegue on an evening where he was the guest, anyway.

There was a roll on the drums. Bill finished his champagne, topped up the glasses, and waved the now-empty bottle at Erich for more.

'Here we go!' He stubbed out his cigarette and felt in the packet for another. '*Amusierkabarett!*'

The Klub Dalilah had long enjoyed a reputation for adventurous entertainment and tonight it didn't disappoint. A string of a dozen buxom Aryan lovelies swung in from the side of the dance floor, naked except for chiffon yashmaks and G-strings. Their entrance made, they cast aside their veils, tossing them on to the nearest tables, and got down to the serious business of pleasing the customers. In the old days, Bill recalled, the girls of the Dalilah had been half-castes, with wonderful, gleaming black ringlets bouncing on soft, coffee-coloured flesh, dark nipples standing out like organ stops, those provocatively jutting arses . . . he sighed. Such foreign delights were in short supply in Nazi Berlin.

The girls twirled and primped and wiggled, breasts and buttocks trembling tantalizingly a shade behind the beat. Bill glanced first at Kate, who wore the expression of someone waiting to be impressed — well, let her wait — and then at

Aubrey, who was smiling now, more at ease in these better-charted heterosexual waters.

Bill leaned over to Aubrey. 'What do you think?'

Aubrey chuckled, man-to-man. 'They're not wearing much!'

'I've seen them in less,' Bill assured him. He looked again at Kate. He had an idea that she knew he was inspecting her, and was determinedly resisting the impulse to return his stare.

The tempo of the music changed. Enter Danni, thought Bill, the moment he'd been looking forward to.

Long red curtains to the right of the band were parted by unseen hands to reveal the star of the show in all her considerable glory. The pretty, home-town girls of the chorus line were instantly outclassed by this vision of sexual allure, nearly six-feet tall, platinum haired, statuesque as a Valkyrie, her sooty, smouldering eyes sweeping the room, her dead white face split by a mouth red and moist as crushed strawberries. Long white hands tipped with gleaming crimson nails held her gold lamé cloak out like wings on either side of her clinging white evening dress. Her left shoulder was bare. Spiralling down the dress from the right shoulder to the left ankle was embroidered a golden serpent with glittering eyes.

As Danni walked to the front of the floor she drew an admiring gasp from newcomers, a welcoming cheer from regulars and old hands. Bill put his cigarette between his lips and clapped, squinting through the smoke at Kate to see her reaction. She too was clapping, smiling, impressed – beginning to enjoy herself.

The girls of the chorus line formed a tableau, and were now put literally in the shade as a white spotlight picked out Danni. She began to sing in her distinctive, booming voice, with its slight tremor:

'*Ich hab noch eine Koffer in Berlin* . . .'

They all fell silent under the spell of that wistful, world-weary song. Yes, it was true, thought Bill. Everyone who loved Berlin kept a suitcase here as the song had it. They all left a part of themselves, hostage to the past, in the shade of the linden trees or the sun-filled cafés of the Tiergarten or even here in the smoky snugness of the clubs and *Tanzbars*. for better or worse you couldn't shake off this sultry, irrepressible whore of a town. Even now, crushed under the joyless rule of national socialism she had not surrendered and one day, he had no doubt, she'd spring up again as bright and as gorgeous as ever. For him the song had added piquancy because Danni, like Erich, had been one of the attractions of the Dalilah for many years. Her looks belied her age. She was a trouper: she covered the lines with make-up, put more dye on her hair, wore more and yet more fabulous gowns to distract attention from the loosening skin of her neck, and carried the whole thing off by the sledgehammer force of her personality. When she finished the song the applause was enthusiastic and a scattering of small gifts – ties and scarves, brooches and cigarettes – were thrown on to the floor by her feet. She bowed graciously and one of the girls trotted forward to pick up the offerings. Aubrey leaned towards Bill; and spoke loudly into his ear.

'Unusual voice – rather a fascinating sort of woman.'

'Yes, isn't she?' Bill put out his hand and touched Kate's bare arm where it rested on the table. She jumped slightly, as if she'd been in a world of her own.

'More champagne?'

'No thanks.'

'Enjoying it?'

'Yes –' She looked as if she would say more, but simply added: 'Yes, I am.'

Now the music changed again and became sly and rhythmic. The pianist grinned, the girls swayed, and Danni came among the tables, towering over her admirers. She had discarded the cloak, leaving it lying in a shimmering golden pool on the dance floor, and now she began to remove her jewellery, dropping it bit by bit into glasses and ashtrays with queenly disdain. Bill knew it was only junk, the sort of thing young girls bought with their pocket money at the Kaufhof in order to look like their mothers. On Danni they glittered like the real thing, but once discarded they were just so much plastic and paste.

The chorus girls concluded some silly, suggestive song about the price of love, and Danni came to their table.

Bill held up his arms welcomingly and she leaned into his embrace.

'It's quite a while since you were here,' she boomed, tousling his hair. *'Du bist schrecklich.'*

'Yes, but look what I've brought.' Bill indicated Aubrey, smiling nervously round his pipe, and Kate who looked guarded.

'Ah . . .' Danni undulated round to Aubrey and bent over him. 'You're having a good time?'

'Yes, thank you,' said Aubrey.

'Good.' Danni positioned herself behind Aubrey and placed one magnificent leg over his right shoulder. She then cupped his jaw in her hands, tipped his head back and kissed him voraciously on the mouth. Then, without releasing him, she picked up his pipe from the ashtray where he had courteously laid it on her arrival, and jammed it unceremoniously back between his lips. Only then did she let him go, giving his head a little push.

Bill slapped Aubrey on the shoulder as, scarlet-faced, he combed his fingers through his disarranged hair.

'Don't worry, it's all in the evening's work. Nothing personal.'

'I dare say . . .' Aubrey took out a large white hankie and mopped his brow. 'Just the same – I'll have another if you don't mind.'

'That's the spirit.'

Bill topped up Aubrey's glass and watched as Danni turned her attention to Kate, as he had known she would. Danni had always had an unerring eye for a good subject, and once she had reached their table without playing her *pièce de résistance*, there was little doubt whom she would select.

'What a beautiful lady!' she boomed huskily, surveying Kate from her great height. 'Such beautiful ladies not allowed in this club!'

Bill had heard Danni's routine dozens of times but he still liked it. He observed that Kate retained her composure in the spotlight's glare, staring levelly at a point just below Danni's majestic bosom.

Danni placed a forefinger beneath Kate's chin and tilted her face up to look into hers.

'Around here, pretty girls are eaten for breakfast,' she said, and a ripple of expectant laughter went round the audience. 'But first I shall let you into a little tiny secret . . .'

Kate raised her eyebrows coolly. She was doing well so far, thought Bill, though that careful coolness might be her undoing, for if it wavered at all the day would indeed be Danni's. People at the other tables were craning and grinning now, eager and curious to see what would happen.

Danni leaned forward so that her thick, curling lashes almost brushed Kate's face. 'You want to know the secret, red-haired girl?' she asked in a stage whisper.

Kate shrugged. She did not blink, or draw back by as much as a hair's breadth.

'Yes or no? *Ja oder nein?*' She was threatening as well as wheedling, she wanted to make Kate speak because a reaction — any reaction — could be the first step to victory.

'Whatever you like,' said Kate, her voice startlingly loud and clear.

'Aaah!' Danni flung wide her arms, turned to the audience, then back to Kate, smiling benignly. 'Very well, I show you what Danni likes!' With this she parted the side of her long skirt, which was split from hip to ankle, took Kate's hand and thrust it underneath.

As realization dawned on Kate's face, so a broad and beatific grin spread over Danni's.

'That's what I like . . . !' she crooned, lowering her lids and rotating her hips extravagantly. 'That's what I like . . . !'

Beneath Kate's cool, motionless hand, Danni's little secret pulsed and became larger. The audience applauded and shouted their affectionate appreciation.

Kate removed her hand. She sat very still. Then suddenly, with the cheers still ringing round, and Danni preening and bowing she rose and took his arm. He glanced at her, real surprise showing now in his eyes. With great deliberation she reached up and kissed him on his smooth, powdered cheek. 'I'm sorry for you,' she said.

Still grinning, the onlookers transferred their attention to her, sensing, perhaps, a finale to the show.

Kate turned back to the table. Aubrey had risen, horribly flustered and embarrassed. He watched with foreboding as his niece lifted the champagne bottle.

'I'm just coming,' she said. 'We'll go in a minute.' She looked down at Bill with splendid contempt. 'I feel sorry for him,' she said, raising the bottle on high. 'And disappointed in you, Herr Maguire.'

With that she emptied the remaining champagne over Bill's head, dropped the empty bottle in his lap and stalked from the room with Aubrey in tow to enthusiastic applause.

The following day at his place in the press box Bill still smiled to himself, remembering it. What an exit! His brief chagrin had been quickly overcome by admiration. Her style, her élan, her steady hand with the champagne bottle – he could still feel the icy cold stream splashing on the crown of his head with perfect accuracy – all had exceeded his expectations.

She had even succeeded in making him feel, if not ashamed, at least regretful. She had read him right – he had been trying to discomfort them both, and to get a reaction from her in particular. Now, since she had risen so magnificently to the occasion, his behaviour appeared base and even puerile. He had enjoyed his evening, even in its wetter moments, but at their expense. And Aubrey was such a decent, civil fellow, far less able to cope than his niece.

So Bill had gone to the Adlon on his way to the Stadium that morning and left flowers for Kate, and a note of apology addressed to them both. Now he was trying unsuccessfully to put her from his mind, not because he believed the incident to have queered his pitch with her, but because it seemed highly unlikely he would see her again. The city was in a fever of excitement, the crowds were huge and Wiseman, his other contact at the Adlon, returned next day. He himself would be working till all hours tonight. No, only a very lucky chance, a chance in a million, would bring them together again.

All the same he felt elated. The powerful excitement of a great occasion gripped him in spite of himself. At that moment he would not have wished to be anywhere else in the world.

Of course, he had been to the *Reichssportfeld* before. He had toured the main stadium, the stands, the hockey pitch, the swimming pool and the equestrian park. He had been force-fed statistics until his head reeled, he had been told again and again that this was the greatest sports complex ever built. He had looked on it with a cynic's eye, admitting its size but immune to its grandeur. Today was a different story. The huge crowds had breathed life into the *Olympiastadion*. The spine-tingling reverberative drone of thousands of voices shuddered round the stands like thunder. It was a warm day, but overcast, threatening rain, and the closeness of the atmosphere deepened the sense of suppressed, feverish excitement. Enclosed by the shimmering banks of spectators, the perfect red oval of the track and the smooth emerald green of the central field were like the single painted eye on some strange totem, staring impassively up at the pale sky. Occasional slow clouds trailed their shadows across the stadium and stands, but the rows of standards hung utterly still in here, where there was no movement of the air.

The press seats were immediately above the official box. Below the undistinguished suits and macs and jackets of his colleagues, Bill could make out a brighter border of elegant hats, colourful dresses and uniforms. But the front row of the box was still empty, awaiting the arrival of the Tribune of Honour.

Bill felt a tap on his arm. It was Les Smedley, leaning forward from a couple of rows in front, brandishing his rolled up programme. 'Ready to be assaulted on all fronts?'

'The atmosphere is extraordinary.'

Les grimaced. 'Atmosphere's more in your line than mine. I'm not interested in all this hooey, I'll be glad when the real stuff starts.'

'I think this may prove to be the "real stuff" as you put it.'

'What's that?'

'All this —' Les cocked his head, putting a hand to his ear. Bill smiled. 'Forget it. See you later.'

He sat back, glancing at his watch. Three-thirty, still at least half an hour before anything was due to happen. And yet many of the 110,000-strong crowd had been on their concrete benches since early this morning. Their enthusiasm made him think of Ilse, and how she would love to be here. But at this moment she would be getting herself ready to go and catch the tram for the tea and dinner shift at the Kaffee Wein, probably listening to a commentary on her wireless, her throat already constricted with emotion. And she would be proud of her handsome Tomas, out there standing to attention with thousands upon thousands of other true Nazis, Stormtroopers, guard corpsmen, members of the Hitler Youth, all lining the flag-bedecked and garlanded 'Via Triumphalis' from the city centre to the *Reichssportfeld*. And there, too, the crowds would be twenty or thirty deep: the biggest captive audience in the world.

He glanced up at the sky. The audience would be even bigger than the one gathered here, for above the stadium, alongside the great hovering bulk of the airship *Hindenburg* with its Olympic flag, like a pilot fish attending a shark, was the Zeppelin containing one of Leni Riefenstahl's film crews. Her movie-men had swarmed all over the city for weeks – in the air, on booms, in vans, on foot, their whirring cameras feeding like voracious buzzing flies on every aspect of the city in preparation. He could easily imagine what they would make of the Games proper. Bill had seen Riefenstahl's *The Triumph of the Will* and had found it magnificent, clever, terrifying. She had endowed the monstrous engine of the Nuremburg rally with a fierce glamour, a Wagnerian romanticism that burned with a cold fire. And now, with her army of prying eyes, she would do the same for the XIth Olympiad.

And the German people were ripe for that glamour. He thought again of Ilse, whose heart was in the right place and who had not a cruel bone in her body, moist-eyed as she ironed Tomas's shirt and polished his belt. Only a few weeks back he had taken her out of the city for the day. They had gone on the motorbike to a little village on the Spree, a few miles east of Berlin. But, anticipating a day of idyllic rural peace and quiet, they had arrived to find themselves preceded by the Olympia-Zug. This phenomenon, a huge caravan of lorries and trailers fitted out to provide a mobile exhibition, covering all aspects of the Olympic Games through the ages and with particular reference to the Aryan ideal, was drawn up in a circle in the small cobbled village square. Bill had been appalled, Ilse thrilled to bits. To him it was just more heavy-handed ramming home of the point: to her, further evidence of the Reich's concern for the ordinary folk who would not be able to attend the Games. As they went round the exhibition he had become silent and depressed. It had driven a wedge between them and ruined their day.

He looked west, towards the *Marathontor* where the official party would make their entrance. Already the line of black Mercedes would be on their way, gliding through the sea of wildly cheering spectators.

Beyond the *Marathontor*, to the far left of the *Maifeld*, stood the 243-foot *Glockenturm*, or bell-tower, the tallest structure in the Olympic complex. The great steel bell, weighing over sixteen tons, had been transported from Bochum, in the Rhineland, to Berlin, over a period of months, moving majestically northward on its giant trailer, never attaining a speed of more than twelve miles an hour, attracting bigger and more thrilling receptions at each step along the way. It had reached the Prussian royal city of Potsdam on the birthday of Frederick the Great. Thousands of Hitler Youth, Tomas among them, had lined the bell's route through Berlin and band after band had played solemn, moving marches. Ilse had wept happily — 'Wonderful, wonderful!' — and Bill had witnessed again the power of empty ceremony to move a nation.

'Hi, pleased to meet you.'

Bill turned to see a plump, perspiring young man in shirtsleeves, his hair crew-cut to within an inch of its life, his face round and Bunterish beneath a peaked cap.

'Hallo. Bill Maguire, *London Herald*.'

'Danny Todd, *Chicago Clarion*. I sure cut that a bit fine.'

'Trouble getting here?'

Todd took a large handkerchief from his trouser pocket and mopped his brow and the back of his neck. 'You could say that. But hey —' he made an expansive gesture with the hankie, 'how about this, isn't it something?'

'It's something all right.'

Todd smacked his lips and settled back in his seat, still wiping his neck. 'It makes me nervous, you know? I could throw up.'

'Yes. I know.'

As four o'clock approached, Bill reminded himself he would have to write something. He folded back the cover of his notebook, took a pencil from his breast pocket and wrote a heading. The small, white oblong of lined paper looked ludicrously inadequate. Beneath the heading he scribbled idly: 'Extras in a cast of thousands.'

Sitting no more than forty yards from Bill Maguire, Kate did not share his fond memory of the previous evening though she had broken off one of the long-stemmed roses he'd sent and tucked it in her buttonhole. From the moment they had arrived at the *Reichssportfeld* the atmosphere here had driven everything else out of her head.

She shivered. The stadium was spotlit by that peculiarly livid light that comes with threatening clouds. Around the still centre of the amphitheatre the banks of watchers muttered and murmured like an approaching storm. Then, like the first breath of a cold wind from the north, an anticipatory sigh ran round the tiers. The sense of an orchestration more grand and more sinister than she could imagine made Kate's stomach turn over. Somewhere outside the stadium the official party had arrived. It was about to begin.

Suddenly, the still, muggy air was ripped by the electrically amplified snarl of thirty trumpets in a martial fanfare. The sound galvanized the crowd. Kate felt herself break out in a sweat, the hair on her neck rose and her throat tightened with shock. She glanced along at Ralph, and saw that his face was loose and pale. Next to him, Joe's cheeks were very flushed, his eyes wide and enthralled. She felt a touch on her other arm and looked at Aubrey. He was pointing, and his lips formed the words: 'There he is.'

They were seated between the press box and the *Marathontor*. She looked towards the dark mouth of the underpass leading from the *Maifeld* into the main stadium. From it, a dwarfed, scattered column of men emerged, moving almost nonchalantly, it seemed at this distance, out of the darkness into the bright red and green eye of the stadium. Great waves of sound rolled forward from the stands to greet them, crashing and rebounding so that Kate felt she was drowning in a boiling cauldron of voices, 'Heil Hitler . . . Heil Hitler . . . Heil Hitler . . .'

The cool weight of Aubrey's binoculars was pressed into her hand, she felt his mouth against her ear: 'Take a look.'

She lifted the binoculars and focused on the group of men. Some were in uniform, some in suits, some in morning dress as for a wedding, decked out with the extravagant gold chains of Olympic office.

At their head, Hitler strolled, smiling, hands behind his back. In sharp contrast to the others he wore the drab, unadorned brown uniform of a storm trooper. He appeared relaxed and benign. And he was rather larger than Kate had thought – perhaps that Chaplinesque moustache had fooled them all into imagining a diminutive comic figure, not to be taken too seriously by the lordly and dignified British. But here she saw a substantial man, with a long stride, dressed plainly to attract attention as only the supremely confident can do. And as he walked forward there rose from the thunderous sea of greeting a mighty swell of singing, the triumphant assertion of the German national anthem.

She lowered the glasses and handed them back to Aubrey. Looking again at Ralph, she saw that his eyes were closed. She reached across Joe and touched his hand. It was cold. But his eyes snapped open at her touch.

'Are you all right?' she mouthed.

But he stared back at her, a very old man, baffled and deafened and disturbed, and could not answer.

As she withdrew her hand and returned her attention to the ceremony she heard Joe say: 'Crikey, it's terrific!' and gave him a sharp, reproving glance, though she could not have said what prompted her to do so, and it was quite lost on him.

The singing swelled. Bill could feel his heart thumping, the blood pounding in his head while, beside him, fat Danny Todd mopped and muttered and shifted his plump backside on the hard seat.

He's so clever, thought Bill, he's fixed everything so he'll come out of it smelling of roses . . . He's presenting himself as some kind of new Messiah, gathering the nations to him. On the great bell were inscribed the words: *'Ich rufe das Jugend der Welt'* – 'I summon the youth of the world'. It was a quotation from Schiller, but in the Olympic literature it was used as a caption beneath a photograph of Hitler, implying that it was he who summoned, who presided, he who had given the

Games a new meaning and magnificence. And now, like a Messiah, he walked among his followers plainly dressed.

He paused. A little fair-haired girl stepped forward, dainty in a blue dress and a glint of white pinny. She hesitated. Hitler bent forward encouragingly. The child advanced again, proffering a posy. She was the five-year-old daughter of the Games organizer, Dr Carl Diem. Hitler took the posy, smelt it, leant and kissed the little girl, ushered her back to her place with almost paternal gentleness. The crowd sighed, touched.

'Get a load of that crap,' observed Todd under his breath, and Bill warmed to him. He found himself straining to see what Hitler would do with the posy. For a few yards he carried the flowers behind his back, held tightly in his left hand. Then he turned to the small figure of Goebbels, just behind him, as if eliciting admiration for the posy, and passed it on to him. Bill was satisfied that he had read the man correctly. He was excitable, and he enjoyed a theatrical moment, but he did not have the patience to carry a child's posy as far as his seat in the box.

As the official party mounted the steps to their seats, the singing ended. The details of their appearance were suddenly clear to Bill in the moments before they sat down: the cadaverous pop-eyed face of Joseph Goebbels, once a farmer, now white-suited like a Hollywood star; the massive, thick-necked bully's profile of Hermann Goering, the heavy figure encased in a sky-blue uniform encrusted with gold braid and unearned honours; the dignified, slightly ill-at-ease Olympic officials, many of them wearing their chains of office as though they were manacles; and Hitler, austere and acute and elated. As he glanced about him before taking his seat, his eye seemed to catch Bill's for a second, though it must have been impossible in that sea of faces. Bill experienced the usual body-blow of that overweening ambition and the greedy energy powerful enough to realize it.

Dan Todd fanned his face with his programme. 'He looked at me like he knew my granny's name was Levenson, for Chrissakes,' he said.

In the hot, heavy silence after the singing ended, the sonorous chime of the great bell began to sound from the

Glockenturm. The vibrations of one chime had only just begun to die away in the thirty seconds before the next rang out. *'Ich rufe das Jugend der Welt'*. Bill closed his eyes for a moment, the sound of the chimes thundering and shuddering in his head. Let them beware, he prayed, the youth of the world.

But when he opened his eyes once more, there they were, answering the summons, the flower of many nations beginning to march into the stadium with heads high and backs straight. And he realized almost at once that even this steady-flowing river of humanity was not immune to the cross-currents of politics. For where many of the teams used the long-neglected Olympic salute, with the arm extended, palm-down, to the side, only a few inches difference in the angle of the arm turned this gesture of unity and peace into one of Nazi loyalty to the leader in the Tribune of Honour. This fact was not lost on the teams, or on the crowd, who reacted instantly to each small variation. The Austrians' salute was certainly a *Heil*, and so was that of the tiny group of Bulgarians, who strutted past the Tribune in a goose-step, their standard dipped so low that it dragged in the red cinders, to the wild applause of the crowd.

Dan Todd whistled. 'Will you look at that?'

'Don't take it too seriously,' said Bill. 'Their king's in the box, it's him they're saluting, not Hitler.'

The teams continued to pass, some with the Nazi salute, some with the Olympic, some, like the dapper straw-hatted British, with no more than a civil eyes-right. But all with flags dipped. Until the entry of the huge team from the United States, nearly four hundred strong — the stars and stripes remained aloft. A small trickle of American applause, almost more damning than silence, filtered down from the stands. Bill glanced at his neighbour quizzically.

'Well, well . . . ?'

'You know what? That makes me proud.'

'It should do.'

But the slight, whether intended or no, by the American team, was immediately trumped by the arrival in the stadium of the Germans, dressed in pure white, marching to the strains of *Deutschland Uber Alles* and the *Horst Wesselleid*. No doubt about their salute.

With the whole concourse of athletes assembled, there

followed a rambling speech announcing the imminent lighting of the Olympic flame. Dr Lewald's voice crackled and blared over the amplifying system.

Joe nudged Kate. 'What's he saying?'

'How should I know? Declaring the fête open, I suppose.'

Aubrey leaned over to Joe. 'The flame will be lit soon.'

'Oh.' Joe glanced at Ralph. 'Grandpa's asleep.'

'No, he's not.' Ralph opened his eyes and glowered threateningly at them from beneath lowering brows. 'He's thinking.'

'Sorry, Grandpa.' Ralph gave Joe a quirky little smile and closed his eyes. It occurred to Kate, not for the first time, that her grandfather was slightly mad.

As Dr Lewald concluded his interminable speech, several things happened at once in a wonderful flowering of theatricality that made the crowd gasp. In the infield, a party of sailors sent up the huge Olympic flag, while simultaneously there rose, like flowers around the lip of the bowl, the banners of all the competing nations, bright against the skyline. The trumpeters sounded a flourish, and as the blast of sound died the far-off thunder of a twenty-one-gun salute could be heard in the distance. And, finally, the boys of the Hitler Youth ranged round the edges of the arena opened the cages beneath the stands and released twenty thousand doves.

As the singing of the Olympic hymn began, Bill tilted his head back to watch the white birds fly away. His eyes were smarting: it was a spectacularly beautiful sight. Like an inverted snowstorm the doves began their ascent in a rush, and then slowed, to move upwards in drifting, meandering spirals into the cloudy afternoon sky, wings glinting as they turned, the soft rushing of their flight making a sound like wind in the windless arena.

'Birds of peace,' said Bill, his voice drowned by the singing, but Danny Todd had heard him.

'You must be kidding.'

The singing ended. Suddenly Kate put her hand on Joe's shoulder and exclaimed, 'There he is – look!'

Aubrey lifted the binoculars. 'You're right.'

'Tell Grandfather.'

Joe put his hand on Ralph's arm and gave it a little shake. 'Grandpa – they're going to light the flame!'

Ralph opened his eyes, staring straight ahead. He'd been truthful when he'd said he was not asleep. He felt perfectly alert, but detached. A terrible loneliness had taken hold of him. For the first time in years he felt the pain of Venetia's death as if he'd held her in his arms that morning. It was as if this great adventure so late in life, these huge crowds, this breathtaking spectacle, had forced open doors in his mind that had been closed for two decades, and pushed him back through them so that now he crouched, alone, in a private place of darkness and misery while all these people round him gasped, and cheered, and pointed and exclaimed.

He patted the hand that lay lightly on his arm, and felt it withdrawn. Whose hand? Strangers touched and jostled him, and spoke in his ear.

Kate snatched the field-glasses from her uncle. 'Let's have a look.'

At the eastern end of the stadium, at the top of the *Olympisches Tor*, a slender white-clad figure had appeared, holding aloft a torch from which the faint, flickering plume of precious fire and smoke barely leaned in the sultry air.

Every face was turned towards the young athlete, everyone was under his spell. And as if he realized this, he paused for a spine-tingling moment, gazing the length of the stadium, before moving on.

Kate passed the binoculars to Joe. It was odd, she thought, that even now with the naked eye she could see that single figure so clearly, almost return his calm stare, while the banks of spectators on either side of him were at this distance no more than a mosaic of coloured blobs. The boy's very solitariness cast its own spotlight.

He ran down the steps from the Olympisches Tor and turned left, beginning the half-circuit of the track which would take him to the west end of the stadium. As he ran with long, easy strides, the wisp of grey smoke streamed back from the torch in his right hand. When he reached the *Marathontor* he ran effortlessly, like a young winged god, up the curving flight of stairs to the dais.

Near the giant tripod and brazier he stopped – then stepped

forward, paused again. The crowd sighed. He's playing on us like a professional, thought Kate, and resented it.

The smoking torch stayed aloft for a telling moment, then dipped slowly towards the brazier. When it rose once more, it was above the fluttering ring of fire that marked the start of the XIth Olympiad. And like a bush-fire the crowd shuddered and roared in response, alight with excitement.

Suddenly Kate couldn't take any more. Her own excitement had turned cold, she could taste its sour dregs in her mouth like an over-rich dish that had made her sick.

She glanced wildly at Joe and Aubrey. Both wore enthralled expressions. She leaned past her brother and pulled Ralph's sleeve. 'Grandfather – I have to get out. Do you want to come?'

He turned his head slowly, to stare at her. She said again: 'Do you want to stretch your legs?'

In reply he rose ponderously from the bench. Those sitting round them craned and peered and complained impatiently. Aubrey looked at the pair of them in bewilderment.

'We're going out for a moment,' she said curtly. 'Sorry. Excuse us.' She began to ease her way past his legs.

'But hang on – where shall we meet?'

'Oh – by the entrance to this block.'

'Very well. Are you all right? Is Father . . . ?'

'We're both fine.'

As they pushed their way laboriously to the entrance her need for escape became more and more urgent. Her breath was short. She looked over her shoulder and saw her panic mirrored on the old man's face. She stretched her arm back and grasped his hand. It was so cold. She realized, with a shock, that she was terribly afraid.

Bill saw Kate and the old man leaving. As they turned on to the ramp leading to the exit, he was struck by their manner, like a couple of mountaineers, linked together, with a grim and fearful common purpose. The girl's face was stern and white and the old man had a look of stumbling, dreamy dissociation like a circus elephant. Bill saw that they were holding hands, she pulling him along, rescuing him. Here, surely, was fate taking a hand.

He rose, saying to Danny Todd: 'I'm going out for a second.'
'You okay?'
'I just saw someone I know.'

Down below, the rich voice of Rudolf Ismayr, the German weight-lifting champion, boomed over the microphone, reading the Olympic oath. As Bill left the light of the stadium for the cool dark of the exit tunnel, the orchestra and chorus struck up with the '*Allelujah Chorus*'.

With the singing still ringing in his ears, the scene outside the stadium came as a surprise. Bill had somehow imagined that all the world was there in that crowded oval space, that all eyes focused on the ceremony, that the rest of the world had stopped in acknowledgement. But here it was, going about its business. Kiosks and stalls selling papers, programmes, snacks and drinks; families picnicking on the grass or round the boots of cars; children running, people sitting and listening, or just talking, enjoying the sense of occasion but not paying much attention.

He looked round for Kate and the old man. He was outside the Sudtor, and the westering sun, uncovered at this moment by clouds, cast the shadows of the tall flagpoles across the *Platz*. Bill turned to his right and began to walk round the south-west corner of the stadium, in the direction of the *Maifeld*. He stopped at one of the many bars, deserted at the moment, the attendant reading a paper, and bought himself a drink, swallowing it down like medicine. Dutch courage? Surely not.

Then he saw them. Up ahead there was a sloping grass verge between the *Platz* and the concrete walkway that ran along the side of the *Maifeld*. There were a few stone benches placed along the top of the bank, and on one of them they sat, side by side, not touching, and apparently not talking.

With a sense of relief he went over to them. She was wearing one of the yellow roses.

'Hallo again. Is everything all right?'

She seemed to accept his arrival as a matter of course, glancing up at him without surprise, or hostility and saying: 'God I hated it in there.'

Bill sensed that she was afraid, but her expression and tone were angry. She radiated nervous energy.

'But you're not ill – you didn't feel faint, or anything?'

She gave him a withering look. 'I don't faint.'

'What about you, Mr Tennant?' He tried to catch the old man's eye. 'Anything I can get for you? It was terribly stuffy in there – overpowering.'

'I shall be all right,' said Ralph, in an odd, measured way, as though asserting some general truth rather than commenting on his present condition.

Bill said: 'In that case I should go back and do my job.'

'I'm sure you should.'

'And by the way, I apologize.'

'Yes, we got your note.' She wasn't conceding anything.

'Okay. Enjoy the rest of the Games.' He began to walk away, but his last remark seemed to have unsettled her.

She rose from the bench. 'Perhaps I will get us both a cold drink. Will you be all right?'

The old man raised a hand and then let it fall again on to his knee. He already looked better than when Bill had watched them leaving the stadium, but seemed profoundly unhappy. Kate put her hand on his shoulder. 'Don't budge, I shan't be a moment.'

Bill walked with her to the cold drinks stand and bought two bottles of orangeade. But as he turned to hand them to her she exclaimed: 'Oh look!' and ran away from him towards the dark area beneath the stands. People glanced at her, some stopped and stared quite openly. Bill followed her, carrying the two bottles. From inside the stadium a great burst of applause reminded him that he should be back in his seat.

As he approached he could see that she was kneeling, cradling something in her hands. She rose, still looking down at what she was holding, and said: 'Poor thing.'

It was a white dove, one of the thousands that had been released not half an hour before. Now it was quite dead, but unmarked and still beautiful. It lay on its back in Kate's hands, claws curled, its head drooping back over her fingers. Bill found himself transfixed by this image: the girl's hands – long, thin, capable hands with pronounced veins on the back, and slightly chapped knuckles – cupping the silken, limp body of the white dove. The image was intensely erotic, and when Kate stroked the bird's smooth breast with one finger he could not believe that she was not aware of its eroticism. He set the drinks down on the ground and reached out his own hands to cover hers. 'Here, let me . . .'

There was a moment, a fraction of a second, when his hand seemed soldered to hers, as if by an electric current. But then she said, 'That's all right.'

As if snubbing him, grinding that electric moment beneath her heel, she went to the nearest litter bin, took out a paper bag and dropped the dove into it. Then she twisted the top of the bag and pushed it back into the bin.

He picked up the bottles, and she dusted her palms together briskly before relieving him of them. 'Thanks.'

'My pleasure. My regards to your grandfather. Perhaps we'll meet again — here at the Games, I mean,' he added hastily.

She cocked her head on one side appraisingly. 'I doubt it, let's be honest.'

He laughed outright, and lifted a hand in a gesture of surrender and farewell, moving away from her. '*Auf wiedersehen.*'

'Good-bye.'

Before he entered the tunnel he glanced back at the two of them, apparently so different but oddly the same, companionable in their shared unease. He experienced a demeaning wrench of jealousy for that sick old man.

Kate sat down and passed Ralph his drink. 'There you are.'

'Thank you. He's not a bad sort of chap, that journalist,' he added. He knew nothing of the previous evening, for Kate and Aubrey had tacitly agreed to keep it to themselves.

'No,' she agreed. She was overcome with regret. She had messed things up again. 'No, he isn't.'

Surprisingly, he said: 'Takes your fancy, does he?'

'Good Lord no!' Too quick, too shrill. Too false. 'Whatever makes you think that?'

'Just a notion.' Ralph shrugged his big shoulders. 'You seem to have taken his.' He let that sink in, and then added, 'Typical scrum-half, and the nose to go with it.'

This remark closed the subject.

*

By the time Bill arrived at the block in the Metzallee to pick up Ilse the following day he was punch-drunk with exhaustion. Though the ceremony had been virtually over by the time he regained his seat – he had apparently missed the presentation to Hitler of Spiridon Loues, the Greek hero of the 1896 Games, clad in fustanelle, and bearing a sprig of olive from Mount Olympus – the excitement had continued at fever-pitch through the rest of the afternoon and far into the night. Between the ending of the opening ceremony, and the evening's scheduled Pageant of Youth, nearly two million Germans had blocked the *Via Triumphalis* to catch a glimpse of the *Führer*.

As they'd filed from the stadium, Danny Todd had remarked: 'What can you say about these guys?' and he'd shrugged – what indeed?

When he'd finally got back to his apartment, well after midnight, there was nothing in his notebook, but his brain teemed with ideas. And in the end, when he'd left for the Press Headquarters at eight o'clock to telephone his piece to London, he knew he'd burned his boats, but it felt good. A sense of freedom and release combined with his extreme weariness to make him quite light-headed. He bought the basic items for a picnic and rode the motorbike somewhat recklessly through the heavy traffic. For months he'd been a good company man, he'd been conscientious and informative and tried to let the facts speak, and kept his opinions to himself. Many of the American journalists had been far more outspoken than he, but he'd kept his powder dry. He knew there'd been bad reasons for his caution – his attachment to Berlin, the city of his heart, a desire not to exacerbate by rash words an already worsening situation, a fondness for Germans in general and Ilse in particular. Soft, unprofessional reasons, but they'd weighed heavily with Bill. Now, suddenly, they were reasons not for holding back, but for speaking out. And if Wiseman considered, as he clearly did, that he had been too frank in the past, he had seen nothing yet.

Ilse was waiting for him, all dolled up in a cotton dress printed with baskets of flowers and a pink cardigan, and a tulle scarf over her hair, and stockings to cover her bad legs, and cheap, smart shoes to make them worse. But her face was alight with pleasure, and he jumped off the bike to kiss her and say: 'You look nice. Will you be okay in the sidecar?'

In response she hitched up her skirt and got in as he held the door for her, tightened her headscarf beneath her chin, fastened the buttons of her cardigan and folded her arms. '*Also!*'

They drove out of the city, with a warm wind blowing in their faces, the noise and vibration of the motorbike engendering in them a kind of childish excitement, so that they revelled and sang. It was a better day, the sky had lifted and lightened, there was bright sun and a fresh breeze. Bill thought of Les Smedley and Danny Todd and the rest, packed into the *Olympiastadion* and thanked God he wasn't there. Though there was Kate, of course.

That evening, when he'd taken Ilse back to her apartment to change, and then on to the café in the Kurfurstendamm, Bill called briefly at the Press Headquarters, to glean the news of the day and see if there were any messages. The former mostly concerned the trial heats in the track and field events – no records broken yet – but there was a phone message from Marty Wiseman.

'Call hotel after six,' it read. 'Urgent matter.'

And as he was leaving the building one of the German secretarial staff ran after him. His editor was on the line from London.

Bill returned to the editorial room and went to phone booth No 6. Trevor sounded wary.

'Bill?'

'Speaking. I was expecting to hear from you.'

'Yes, well. I like it, Bill, and I'm sure you're right, but the Old Man's not so keen.'

'I know. I have to call him in half an hour's time.'

'I've already had a word on your behalf, just don't foul things up after all my efforts. Be polite at least.'

Bill closed his eyes and prayed for patience. 'I'll be polite, Trevor. I'm always polite.'

'Mm.' There was a pause, during which Bill could imagine Trevor staring through his grimy window, tapping and turning his pencil on the cluttered surface of his desk. 'I think we'll be seeing you back in London.'

'I think so too.'

'As long as you're being sensible about it. I'd rather you worked for us than for someone else.'

'Well, thanks.'

'Bye.'

'Good-bye, Trevor.'

Bill went out once more into the golden early evening sunshine. He would go back to his apartment, open the windows, clear his desk, light a cigarette and go down to the pay phone in the dark hall to do battle with Wiseman.

CHAPTER SIX

'You came along from out of nowhere,
You took my heart and found it free.
Wonderful dreams, wonderful schemes from nowhere
Made every hour sweet as a flower for me . . .'

'Out of Nowhere'
Edward Hayman and John W. Green, 1931

ON the afternoon of 8 September, when she had seen Joe on to the school train at Victoria, Kate went to meet Andrea Avery for tea at the National Gallery. The arrangement had been quite deliberate on her part. She had expected to feel flat and depressed after seeing her brother off, and she was right. The depression was caused not least by her own feelings of inadequacy. Confronted by Joe's stiff, white-faced anxiety, his sudden smallness in slightly over-large and crisply new school uniform, she had been quite unable to strike the right note, or even to know what the right note was to strike. On all sides, confident, well-dressed parents had spoken in loud voices about tuck and kit and half-term while she had stood awkwardly with Joe, neither one thing nor the other, neither mother nor chum nor even (she felt it again) a proper sister. She had no idea how to comfort him or, failing that, how to distract him from his misery. The other boys, noisy, pink-cheeked and privileged, seemed a heartless lot.

She could visualize how Thea would have acted under these circumstances, and suffered by the imagined comparison.

Still, she comforted herself, as she alighted from the bus and began to walk across Trafalgar Square in the soft late afternoon sunshine, perhaps her manner had been better for Joe than too much sympathy and artificial smiling. He had been reserved and dignified, very like his father, in fact, as he had finally boarded the train and taken his seat. She had felt proud of him.

She glanced at her watch. Andrea had said four-thirty. She was a little early, and didn't want to be there first and appear over-keen. So she sat down by the fountains and watched the pigeons pecking and rustling round her feet. She had on the dreaded grey suit, concerning which Dulcie had been right, and in which she felt quite out of place. In an attempt to modify its severity she wore it with her favourite purple shirt, large wooden beads and a jaunty black beret. The effect was stylish and witty, but not elegant. She resembled an Apache dancer who had collected the wrong clothes from the cleaners. Knowing this had done nothing for her confidence among the well-heeled county mothers at the school train and had probably embarrassed Joe, too. She felt glum.

On the other hand, the four weeks since their return from Berlin had seen a marked improvement in family relations on all fronts. On the neutral territory of Berlin the four of them had shaken down together, and Aubrey had been glad of her energy and her flair for organization. She had enjoyed the Games, and had not suffered again from the claustrophobic panic of the opening ceremony. By the end of the week they were looking forward to having dinner together in the evening, making scurrilous remarks about the hotel's other patrons and discussing the events of the day. There had been much to discuss, for they had all in their different ways been conscious of witnessing history in the making, and it had sharpened their perceptions and given a special dramatic quality to the great individual athletic performances.

Kate got up from the wall and began to make her way in the direction of the National Gallery. As the awkwardness of Joe's departure receded a little, so her mood brightened. Her life was now her own, she could move forward at last.

In the National Gallery tea room Andrea Avery sat waiting at a corner table. The first thing that Kate noticed as she sat down opposite her was that Andrea looked plain, and tired.

'How went the family farewells?' asked Andrea, when they'd ordered a pot of tea and some cake.

'Ghastly, I was hopeless.'

'It's not a test, there are no prizes for correct behaviour.'

'That's not how it felt.'

Tea arrived and Kate fell on a jam doughnut while Andrea poured. Andrea thought her companion seemed much younger than her years, worlds apart from the average London girl of twenty. And yet it was only sophistication that she lacked, and ease of manner. Of other good things – confidence, intelligence, energy, drive – there was an abundance. Andrea felt peculiarly protective towards Kate. She was glad that she had a positive suggestion to make.

'How is the rest of the family?' she asked. 'You're the first one I've seen since your trip to Berlin. Did the old fire-eater get on all right?'

Kate licked sugar from her fingers. 'He was splendid. He had a bit of a gloomy turn on the first day, I expect he was tired, but after that he was terrific. He's got tremendous spunk.'

'Oh he has, he has.' Andrea recalled many pitched verbal battles over the dinner table at Chilverton House when she had been Thea's upstart blue-stocking schoolfriend, and no quarter given.

'And you all enjoyed yourselves?'

'We were all impressed. It was very exciting.'

Andrea realized that Kate's answer deliberately begged the question. 'So what now? The holiday's over, Joe's at school, what are your plans?'

Kate frowned. 'To be honest, I don't know. Since I came here I've felt so useless, so cooped up . . .' Her voice tailed away and she stared into her tea. Then she seemed to rally, and said almost truculently, 'The whole point of my coming here was to work, and make an independent life for myself. I love the farm but I can't go on battening on Jack and Thea for ever.'

Andrea raised her eyebrows. 'Battening? You're their daughter.'

'Not their actual daughter as you very well know. And don't say it doesn't make any difference, because it does. It does to me, anyway.'

'It shouldn't.'

'I can't help the way I am.'

Andrea reached down for her bag and took out a packet of her small cigars, and a lighter. She offered one to Kate, who refused, and lit one for herself with obvious pleasure.

'No, you can't,' she said, adding, 'I've got a proposition to put to you.'

'Oh?' Kate was instantly on the defensive.

'Yes, let me explain.' Andrea looked her straight in the eye, giving as good as she got. 'I do voluntary work at the Ross Institute off the Commercial Road in Whitechapel. Do you know anything about the city settlements?'

'Good work among the poor and underprivileged – that kind of thing,' said Kate, a little ungraciously, her attitude having been unconsciously influenced by Dulcie's less charitable sallies.

Andrea did not smile. 'Exactly that sort of thing. And the work is good, and hard, too. You said I looked tired, well I'm damn tired. I've been helping organize a baby and toddler clinic all day, and I've been wetted and sicked on, and screamed at and complained to until I feel like a dirty dishcloth.'

'I'm sorry.' Kate *was* sorry. She remembered the brittle, glittering Mrs Avery of the voyage to Mombasa, and how readily she had given way to the spare, practical adventurous lady of the overland ox-wagon. Andrea Avery was no empty, silly woman.

'Go on,' she prompted.

'If I sound as if I'm whining, I don't mean to. I work at the Ross because I love it, and because at the end of the day I can come back and be Louis's cocktail party hostess, knowing I've put my back into something worthwhile.'

'I see that.'

'Now. Nearly all the work at the Institute is voluntary, my own included. Bobby Hollis, the Anglican priest who runs it, is paid, but that's it. However, there is a crying need for someone to help with the paperwork, and we did agree at the last management meeting that we'd be prepared to pay a small retainer to the right person. I happen to think you are the right person, Kate.'

Kate stared at her, and found her stare met steadily. She who was so blunt herself, was somewhat taken aback by the straightforwardness of this approach. And suspicious of it. 'You don't have to do me any favours,' she said coolly.

'I'm not.'

'I've never done good works before, I've never done any work at all, so how can you possibly know whether I'm suited or not?' she said, a shade disparagingly.

Andrea leaned forward, prepared now to pursue her advantage to its conclusion.

'I'm a fairly good judge of character, Kate. When I said we'd pay the right person, that's what I meant. Don't be misled by the word paperwork, we're not looking for a high-powered secretary. What we want is a capable, resourceful, energetic person with some secretarial ability. You'd probably spend as much time helping out generally as you would pounding a typewriter. It would be exhausting and chaotic and often infuriating, but I think you'd find it exhilarating, too. I wouldn't even have mentioned it, but I'm sure you'd be ideal.'

'Can I think about it?'

'Not just that, you must come down and see the Ross. Tomorrow, perhaps. And then let us know. You're needed Kate, so don't be too long thinking.'

'I won't,' said Kate. In fact, she had already done her thinking. It had taken about five seconds. It was the phrase 'you're needed' that had done it. It was music to her ears. She would go to the Ross Institute and everyone would be glad that she, Kate Kingsley, and nobody else, was there to help them out. She felt suddenly that she was expanding, growing, literally rising to the challenge of this call on her special qualities.

Andrea noticed the brightening in her young companion's face. She decided to leave her suggestion there to do its own work. 'More tea?' she enquired.

Their conversation moved on to more general topics. Kate had consumed a second doughnut and Andrea's cigar was almost finished, when a heavy hand came down on the back of each chair and a sleek dark head interposed itself between theirs.

'Now, now ladies, hen parties are so unhealthy. Can a chap get a cup of tea, or what?'

It was Louis. Kate stiffened at once, sat back, resumed the defensive glare she had only recently shed.

Andrea said, 'Hallo, darling,' and indicated to the elderly waitress that a third cup was needed.

Louis pulled up a spare chair from the next door table and sat down, a little nearer Kate than his wife. And it was Kate he addressed.

'I hope you don't mind me breaking into your womanly tête-à-tête like this, my dear, but I happened to escape my office early, and remembered Andrea saying she was meeting you here. So I came on the off chance, and here I am!' He beamed at her. Kate thought his smile like the Cheshire Cat's — large, mocking, ever-present, meaningless.

She shrugged. 'I don't mind in the least.' She glanced pointedly at her watch. 'I must go soon anyway.'

'Ah, the cocktail hour chez Tennant, what a seductress it is,' sighed Louis. Andrea passed him his tea.

'I think Kate may come to work for us down at the Ross,' she said.

Louis, who had never taken his eyes off Kate's face, raised his eyebrows.

'Splendid! Of course, Kate, I was hoping you might bring your talents to Avery Associates, but I had forgotten that good works run in the family. There was no holding dear Thea once the war was under way. Like a battle charger she got the whiff of carnage in her nostrils and was off to do her bit.'

Kate ignored the last part of this remark. 'I should loathe to work in advertising.'

Louis tipped his head back in a silent laugh. 'But we have the Mason's gravy powder account, think what you could have done with that!'

'Stop it, Louis,' said Andrea. 'Drink your tea and then we can all go together and you can give Kate a lift to the station.'

'I don't want a lift,' said Kate, 'I'll go from Charing Cross.'

'She doesn't want a lift,' said Louis, taking sugar. Suddenly he turned to his wife for the first time. 'How are things,' he asked, 'among the underprivileged?'

And then Kate witnessed an interesting thing. Until that instant Andrea's attitude to her husband had been guarded, and even a little reproving. But now that his eyes rested on her face, and his concern, however slight and temporary, was for her, she unfolded like a flower. Her taut, pale face softened in a smile, her thin body leaned towards his, her eyes brightened, her hand rested gently as a bird on his arm. She loves him, thought Kate in astonishment, and not just that she's *in love* with him. She disapproves of his work and his manners and his morals, but she'd follow him through hell-fire. Kate regretted having been so rude to Louis, and resolved to do better, though as they came down the steps from the main entrance she suffered in stiff misery the avuncular yet suggestive hand he placed beneath her elbow.

It had clouded over while they'd been inside, not enough to threaten rain, but enough to cast a drab, neutral greyness over the scene. There seemed to be some kind of gathering in Trafalgar Square, a ragged, shuffling assembly of quiet men, and they too had a grey appearance, drab jackets and heavy caps that shadowed their faces. Some stood in little groups, others had sat down on the ground, all seemed listless. Against one of the great stone lions a cluster of placards leaned like dead flowers.

'Who are they?' asked Kate.

'Hunger marchers,' responded Louis. 'Stopping here to rally themselves before going on to Parliament.'

They were standing at the foot of the steps, looking across the road towards the square. Just behind them a pavement artist scraped and scrubbed with his coloured chalks, perfecting a lakeland view.

'But where do they come from?'

'Up north. They've got no work and no money.' Louis sounded matter-of-fact.

'It's another world,' said Andrea. They crossed the road and began to walk round the corner of the square in the direction of Charing Cross. The presence of the hunger marchers, a grey, reproachful assembly on their right, cast a blight on conversation. Kate stopped.

'It's terrible,' she said. 'They're like ghosts.'

A group of four men was sitting on the ground just beneath the wall where they stood. Three of them were almost asleep, in attitudes of exhaustion, their heads resting on their knees. The fourth, sitting cross-legged, had removed his cap and was turning it round and round in slow, old man's hands. Indeed Kate had thought them all elderly, but she saw now with a shock that this was a young man, in his late twenties or early thirties, but prematurely aged, his pale face lined with weariness and a pinched kind of stoicism. His hair lay flat and greasy on his narrow skull. His jacket, trousers and heavy laced boots were covered in a film of dust. His hands were black-nailed and creased with dirt.

As Kate stared he must have felt her eyes on him for he suddenly looked up, his eyes piercingly bright in that tight face. And his voice when he spoke was surprisingly loud and lusty. 'Know us next time, will yer?'

She was appalled, guilty, shocked.

'I'm sorry,' she said. As she began to catch up with the Averys, who were walking slowly on, she heard several voices raised in a not unkind chuckle at her expense.

'God, how awful,' she said, coming alongside Andrea.

'What's that?'

'I was staring — like some child in a zoo — and he noticed.'

'He doesn't care. Why should he care? He came a long way to be stared at.'

'How far will they have marched to get here?'

'Oh, several hundred miles.' This was Louis. 'But you shouldn't worry about that. These marches are very well organized, with proper scheduled stops along the way, and town bands to help them swing along. And they'll get a fair hearing at the House.'

'You make it sound like a Sunday School picnic,' said Kate.

'Did I? I didn't mean to. I have nothing but sympathy for these men's plight. I'm just saying that they are on the whole sensible enough to organize their protests properly.'

Kate had to be satisfied with this, but she noticed that Louis had hardly spared the marchers a glance. And it seemed to her that he looked the other way not out of indifference, nor even out of guilt, but from a kind of supercilious embarrassment, like a woman whose own house is in order but who perches on the very edge of a chair in the home of a less fastidious friend. She thought, he blames them for their poverty, their roughness, their despair, he thinks they should have done better. And while she could well see why Andrea needed to work at the settlement, it was less and less clear to her what Andrea could possibly find to love in Louis Avery.

That evening as she sat at the desk writing her first letter to Joe, the phone rang and it was Andrea arranging for her to visit the Ross Institute the following day. She returned to her letter excited, and quite involuntarily continued with it in a way which implied she already had the job.

Her trip to Whitechapel, therefore, was made in a more than receptive frame of mind, and it took only a quarter of an hour to convince her that she had found a place where she wanted to work.

The Ross Institute was the creation of a philanthropic Edwardian business tycoon who had brought it into being with the stated intention of providing 'an example, aid and provision for the poor and needy of the area, a door always standing open to those in need of shelter, a place of Christian charity and humble good fellowship for the spiritually destitute.' In the less paternalistic atmosphere of the '30s, Bobby Hollis was more concerned with the welfare of bodies than the uplifting of souls, though he himself was the very embodiment of practical Christianity.

'Hallo, hallo and a thousand welcomes, young friend of Andrea's,' was how he greeted Kate, wringing her hand in both his. He was a small, wispy balding man in his late forties, with a *distrait* staccato manner reminiscent of a village scoutmaster, but which masked formidable energy and perception. He was dressed in moth-eaten grey flannels and a pullover, topped with an artist's smock on the front of which some wit had daubed the words 'SAINTS ALIVE!'

'The lads and I are refurbishing the games room,' he explained, catching Kate's eyes on the smock, 'so you must excuse my appearance.'

'You look nice,' said Kate with a grin. 'I don't want to keep you from what you're doing.'

'Well I tell you *what*,' said Bobby. 'I shall let Andrea show you around, and then bring you along to my humble office in twenty minutes or so for a little talk. How does that strike you?'

Accordingly, Andrea led Kate away on a tour of inspection. The Ross was not an old building, having been built by Alfred Ross expressly for his noble purpose in 1902, but in accordance with its founder's stern religious principles it had a spartan, forbidding air, with small windows mostly too high to see out of, stone-flagged passages in which the mildest tread sounded like that of a bullying jailer, and a huge, monkish refectory set with long trestle tables and benches in which Kate could readily imagine the luckless Oliver Twist asking for more.

'Pretty grim, eh?' said Andrea, 'but there isn't a lot going on this morning. The place gets busier as the day goes on. What you see at the moment is mostly helpers and a few worthies who come in all the time for what they can do rather than what they can get.'

In the refectory a handful of shuffling elderly men were being served tea from a huge urn. At the opposite end of the room from the urn was an ancient upright piano upon which a lady with white-blonde hair was offering a lusty rendition of *Yes, We Have No Bananas*, her warbling nasal voice echoing in the vast space.

'That's Merle,' said Andrea. 'Guess how old she is.'

Kate could only make out the dazzling hair, and hear the strident voice. 'Forty?'

'She's seventy-eight, and completely destitute.'

'I hope I can sing like that when I'm seventy-eight.'

They both laughed. In the proposed games room Bobby Hollis was painting the walls yellow with the assistance of three lads of between fourteen and eighteen. Though they were generally pallid and thin, they all dwarfed the priest and were in appearance so villainously sullen that Kate experienced a moment's concern for his safety. But as they closed the door behind them, Andrea said, 'They look a bit surly, I know, but they're all here because they want to be, and they think the world of Bobby.'

In the Institute's chapel, with its daisy-stitched altar-cloth and one coloured window depicting, oddly, the wedding at Canaan, the pews were bulging, not with worshippers, but with boxes of old clothing. Two middle-aged women in printed wrap-around pinnies were sorting through them with great speed, and looked up only to smile and wave.

'It's all been handed in and collected,' said Andrea. 'We get masses of old clothing every week and we see to it that it all goes to people who need it, though a lot of it needs fumigating. Sometimes you see two or three generations of children wearing the same shirt and pullover that keeps being handed back here.'

The first floor consisted mainly of two dormitories, men's and women's, a small sanatorium and first-aid room, a 'nursery' on which valiant effort had been expended to provide brightness and warmth, and a vast store-room for dry goods of all kinds from powdered soup to floorcloths.

Already, as they returned to the ground floor and went down the passage to Bobby's office, the air was tinged with a faint aroma of food cooking, not unappetising, but plain and institutional, shepherd's pie or mutton stew, cabbage and potatoes. In the entrance hall stood some new arrivals, one or two old hands were talking, others, shy and awkward, were holding themselves apart. A woman whom Kate recognized as one of those from the chapel was greeting them.

'First sitting for dinner,' said Andrea, and Kate noted her quite unself-conscious use of the word 'dinner' for the meal which at home she would have referred to as lunch.

'Do they get it free?'

'No, they pay a nominal charge for as much as they can eat, unless we know they genuinely *can't* pay, in which case they don't.'

'Aren't you always being taken for a ride?' Kate was incredulous.

'You'd be surprised. Trust repays trust.'

She knocked on the door of Bobby's office and pushed it open in response to the shouted: 'Come!'

The tiny office, with its one window overlooking the dustbins at the back of the building, was so cluttered that none of the furniture was at first glance visible. Bobby Hollis sat behind what Kate assumed was a desk, attending to some kind of ledger, and smoking a Woodbine, the ash from which he occasionally tapped off into the half-eaten plate of stew that lay next to the ledger. By the window she saw an enormous birdcage in which a small, white, crested parrot hung upside down from its perch.

The parrot was the first to speak, though Kate didn't immediately realize that the salty east London voice was coming from the birdcage. 'Carrots!' it remarked. 'Boiled beef and carrots!'

Kate burst out laughing. 'They used to call me that at school!'

'No, no, no, no, wretched fowl—' Bobby leapt up and flung a newspaper over the cage. 'It has absolutely nothing to do with you, I assure you, Merle taught it to him, it looms large in her repertoire. Come, come, sit down . . .' He bustled round and cleared two chairs. 'Now then.' The telephone rang. 'Excuse me.' He lifted the receiver, dislodging a pile of books with the flex as he did so, and grimacing as Kate darted forward to pick them up.

'Hallo? Bishop, good-day to you . . .' he put a hand over the mouthpiece. 'My bishop, wouldn't you know it?' He removed the hand. 'Yes, we soldier on, we fight the good fight. Shall we be privileged to see you down at the Ross one day soon?'

During the bishop's evidently lengthy reply he put his hand once more over the mouthpiece and leaned towards Kate. 'When do you join us?' he asked.

'Join us! Carrots!' echoed the parrot.

Some time later, when Kate and Andrea had long since left to catch the bus in the Commercial Road, Ernest Marx left Pear Tree Court, Golden Row, bound for the same bus stop. His crisply laundered waiter's jacket and polished shoes were in a small suitcase, and he walked fast because this evening's function was at the home of some arty-farty types up in the Muswell Hill area, and that was a long journey.

As he walked past the back of the Ross Institute he glanced scornfully at the grimy lighted window of Bobby Hollis's office, at the overflowing dustbins, and the parrot cage. And heard with distaste the sound of a sing-song, a thumping discordant piano and warbling old voices. Ernest hated everything the Ross Institute stood for: middle class patronage and Christian charity. They made him sick. He had been furious when on one occasion he had found out that his mother had been getting dinner there, and had half frightened her to death with his rantings about hand-outs and pride and do-gooders.

Ernest was twenty-two years old, handsome, intelligent, vain and somewhat humourless. So much of his considerable energy was consumed in loathing and contempt for various sections of society that it was a wonder he had any left over for the day-to-day practicalities of life. Now, if looks could destroy, the Ross Institute would have been reduced to a pile of rapidly cooling ash.

Giles Huxley and Dulcie Tennant were not as late as they might otherwise have been for Clara Southgate's 'literary' party in the uncharted wastes of Muswell Hill, because they fully intended to depart early. In spite of their shared lack of enthusiasm for Clara's brand of hospitality they were in high spirits, Giles because he had Dulcie's delightful company, and Dulcie because Rex was out of town at the Roth-Veseys' Sunningdale house and she was increasingly glad to be free of his clutches. Also, Kate had rung while she and Giles had been enjoying a stiffener before leaving, and told her about going to work at the Ross Institute. The fierce propietory admiration she felt for Kate was somewhat tempered by a gnawing jealousy of Andrea.

'Be pleased for Kate,' Giles had said, lifting his glass, 'and don't concern yourself with Andrea. You're not in competition with her or anyone else.'

Privately, Giles considered that Dulcie's role as 'aunt' was ideal, however much she might complain about the strain of concealing her identity. This way, she could have influence, intimacy, friendship and affection, all without responsibility. He also recognized that Dulcie would no longer rely on him to the same extent now that Kate, however slightly, relied on her. He gazed fondly at Dulcie as their taxi drew up outside the tall Edwardian house (not unlike Mapleton Road, though bigger) where the Southgates lived.

They walked arm in arm up the flight of cracked stone steps that led to the front door. Donald Southgate was an inventor and the porch of the house was crowded with potentially useful scrap — bits of old bicycles, planks, piping and plastic, which the locals had been invited to dump there for a small remuneration. Beneath Dulcie's grey kid sandals, the red tiles of the porch were spattered with oil and gobbets of mud.

Their ring on the bell was greeted by a volley of hysterical barking. A door slammed, the barking became fainter, and Clara herself admitted them.

'Greetings!' she boomed. Clara was a large, raw-boned woman whose appearance seemed always to be slightly out of her control. Now she wore a long skirt, with a lace blouse and a darned cardigan. Her straight, wispy brown hair had been assembled in a bun on the nape of her neck, from which most of it had already escaped and hung in Medusa-like strands about her face. But she was utterly without malice, and it was to her credit that she treated everyone with the same enthusiastic soulfulness.

'Tonight,' she said, as she walked between them to the drawing-room, 'I want both your opinions on my new book.'

'Of course,' said Giles politely, though harbouring a secret dread. Clara was not, in his opinion, a very good novelist.

'It's a children's book,' she added, 'with illustrations.'

'How simply lovely!' cried Dulcie. 'Did you do the pictures yourself?'

'Sadly no,' replied Clara, opening the drawing-room door, 'I have no talent in that direction.'

Just as they were about to enter, she drew the door shut again, as if about to divulge some shameful but necessary information. 'We have caterers this evening, by the way — much against Donald's principles, and mine too, but it does leave me free to enjoy my own gathering. I hope you don't think it too dreadfully lazy of me.'

'Not at all, of course not!'

Giles's heart leapt, and he exchanged a look of delight with Dulcie as they helped themselves to champagne. Clara's own catering generally ran to rough red wine, nut cutlets, pumpernickel and borsch, all of which played havoc with Giles's duodenum.

There were plenty of people already at the Southgates' party, including Clara's children (Giles never knew how many) who, in tartan dressing-gowns, were grappling noisily on the floor in the centre of the room, ideally placed to break the ankle of the unwary guest.

'Come, children, mind,' admonished Clara, stepping over them, and turning to beam at Dulcie and Giles. 'Just like puppies, aren't they . . . ?'

Giles, who in general liked children and would have liked some of his own, could think of many other forms of life which his hostess's offspring resembled, but refrained from mentioning them. Dulcie sidestepped the scrum with an expression of anxious politeness.

Faces turned towards them, patently glad of moral support. 'Now who knows who, I wonder?' said Clara.

In the Southgates' basement kitchen Ernest Marx, waiter with Franconi's Superior Catering, surveyed the conditions with distaste. These people had ordered the most expensive buffet menu – with one or two strange provisos such as all brown bread and no red meat – and yet they lived like pigs. The large kitchen was untidy and far from clean. The resident help (she did not seem to be anything as authoritative as a cook) was a red-eyed foreign girl with a bad skin who watched with an air of helpless despondency as Ernest and Mae, the waitress, began to remove the food and set it out on Franconi's community plate serving dishes.

Mae leant across to the girl. 'Could you make us a cuppa tea, love? Put the kettle on –' she pointed, *'comprendi?'*

The girl went to fill the kettle and Mae shook her head. 'Bit dozy, isn't she?'

Ernest placed a sprig of parsley beside shrimp vol-au-vents. 'What would you expect in a set-up like this?'

Milo Franconi bustled in. He was a plump, ingratiating third generation Sicilian immigrant. In the presence of clients, he assumed an exaggerated Latin accent beneath which his more natural tones (those of Walthamstow) struggled to get out. But this was an affectation he did not bother to inflict on his staff.

'What's going on down here, all getting organized? Ernest, you were late, I don't need that. I don't like lateness.'

'Don't worry about it,' said Ernest in a soothing voice. His manner towards his employer stopped only a whisker short of rudeness. The job was so far within his capabilities he could have done it with his eyes shut, a few minutes' lateness were neither here nor there and Milo Franconi knew it. Ernest Marx was an asset with his Italianate good looks (he looked far more

Latin than Milo himself), his well-spoken voice and suave manners, and he was a good worker, too. So Milo pretended not to notice his cheek.

When he'd gone, and the girl had given them both a cup of weak tea, Mae said to Ernest, 'Too good for this job, intcher, eh?' She looked at him cheekily, like a starling. 'Too clever by half. Eaten up by it, you are.'

'What's that?' Ernest took a small comb from his breast pocket and stood to adjust his smooth black hair, using his reflection in the kitchen window.

'Envy, doll, the old green-eye. You'll go on despising this lot —' she jerked her chin and rolled her eyes upward, 'till the day you get the chance to join 'em, then zoom! You'll be off up there, swilling the bubbly and puffing the cigars with the best of 'em.'

She sipped her tea complacently, watching him. He replaced the comb in his pocket and came back to sit by her. They both ignored the foreign girl who stood by the sink, gazing miserably at them.

'I've got my pride, if that's what you mean,' said Ernest.

'Oh, don't I know it!'

Mae had the brassy, well turned-out glamour of a chorus girl, a swanky figure and bedroom eyes. Ernest was immune to her sexual appeal, but he and Mae got on well. He felt flattered that she could so easily picture him swilling and puffing with the rich. Her view of him, though not intended to be complimentary, bore out the pride he had just mentioned.

'Wotcher Valentino,' she would say some evenings when they met. He would give her what he hoped was a look of glacial hauteur, but she wasn't fooled. He *was* vain about his sleek dark hair, and his pale oval face with its heavy-lidded brown eyes and the mouth with the pouting underlip.

Now he lowered his voice, with a meaningful glance at the unfortunate foreign girl. 'Not that you'd want to be in with this lot tonight,' he said. 'The arty set.'

'Yeah,' agreed Mae. 'That explains the dirty kitchen.'

Upstairs in the Southgates' lofty, down-at-heel drawing-room Dulcie was thinking much the same thing. She and Giles had been placed firmly in a group with three others, all, as Clara put it, from 'the world of letters' so Dulcie had ample time for reflection. Clara had a private income. Indeed, she was a wealthy woman. Before her marriage to the lugubrious Donald she had been Lady Clara Marchant, and both Southgates now lived on her money. And yet they lived in a tatty bohemian style which Dulcie thought just plain mean. They would not employ a large staff, claiming that it was against their principles (and choosing to ignore the unemployment figures) but were patently unable to keep an orderly home under their own steam. It was the worst of all possible worlds, thought Dulcie, who liked above all to be in pleasant surroundings.

She glanced affectionately across at Giles, so stylish and impeccable with his waistcoat and watch-chain and flowing silk handkerchief.

The young woman standing by her suddenly addressed her. 'Have you read Clara's children's book?'

Dulcie was not abreast of the conversation. 'No, no I haven't.'

'You must.' The young woman's pointed nose was sharp, like an Afghan hound's, between her drooping wings of hair. 'It's perfectly enchanting, and Edgar Morrissey has done some Beardsleyesque woodcuts to accompany each chapter heading.'

Dulcie looked at her with an expression of bright interest, and her mind a total blank, hoping someone would come to her rescue.

A red-faced man with whiskery nostrils obliged. She had come across him before, he was a theatre critic, hated by Giles. 'My feeling is it'll be wasted on the little beggars,' he said caustically. 'Whose children is she thinking of, for God's sake?'

Dulcie felt a fleeting sympathy with whisker nostrils, and saw from Giles's face that he did, too.

Just then Clara reappeared, frog-marching a late arrival through the throng. 'Here's someone you must all meet,' she said. 'May I introduce Bill Maguire of the *Herald*?'

Everyone murmured politely and Giles said: 'Actually, we've met, have we not?'

'Yes indeed, good to see you again.'

Clara beamed. 'Excellent. I'm sure those of us who read the

Herald couldn't fail to have been stirred by that wonderful piece on the Olympic ceremony.'

'Thank you.'

'Now I shall leave Giles to look after you for a little while.' She moved away, and the group broke, and re-formed, leaving Giles and Dulcie with the newcomer.

'This is a very dear friend, Dulcie Tennant,' said Giles.

Dulcie held out her hand. 'Will you speak to me again if I say I don't read the *Herald*?' she said, with her most bewitching smile.

Bill, saying something ungallant about not giving a damn what paper anyone read, thought Dulcie Tennant one of the loveliest women he'd ever seen. He also suspected that the flirtatious smile and the self-deprecating remark were part of a carefully maintained pose. Why otherwise would she be at a do like this with a chap like Giles Huxley whom Bill liked and admired but knew to be homosexual?

'. . . surprised you're still in Wiseman's employ,' Giles was saying now, 'after that blistering broadside on the National Socialists.'

'They promoted me sideways,' replied Bill. 'Not wanting to appear cowardly. I'm based in London now. I'm their columnist without portfolio.'

'You don't feel hard done by?'

'Not really. There's no fun left in Berlin for those of us who love her.'

'You talk about the city as if it's a woman,' commented Dulcie.

'Everyone does, don't they?' He looked at her. She had blue eyes and golden hair, a cliché, he reflected, but somehow she embodied the attraction of every fairytale princess cruelly immured, ripe for rescue.

'If you want to extend the metaphor,' he went on, because it gave him an excuse to continue staring at her, 'London is my mother, the city I was born to and take for granted. Berlin is my mistress, the city I chose, the one I feel passionate about.'

'And which do you prefer?'

He spread his hands. 'Invidious to make a choice. Everyone's somebody's child, that's continuity. But when we grow up and find someone new to love, that's growth.' He laughed, glancing at Giles. 'Is anyone taking all this down?'

But his remarks, which he now felt to have been pompous, seemed to have given her pause for thought.

An elderly waiter brought champagne on an old high-sided butler's tray.

'We were so delighted to find this at Clara's,' said Dulcie *sotto voce*, raising her glass. 'Now what do you think we're going to have to eat?'

'Why don't I go and investigate,' said Giles. 'Excuse me for a moment.'

He left them, making his way across the room, exchanging smiles and waves and pleasantries with various acquaintances, until he reached the door, and went out into the high, narrow hall, in search of the food. The Southgates' dining-room was usually requisitioned as a children's playroom – would that the children confined themselves to it, thought Giles – but tonight it had been dragged kicking and screaming back into its original role. The reversal had been achieved by the simple and speedy expedient of pushing the mountains of tattered books and broken toys to the sides of the room, and placing a huge, dusty rubber plant on a wrought-iron jardinière just inside the door.

On the far side of the room, like a faithful acolyte at the altar of a neglected church, a dark-haired waiter in a spotless white jacket was laying out cutlery on the table. The table had been covered with a gleaming damask cloth – surely not Clara's – and was set with several still-covered dishes of food, plates, napkins and a huge centrepiece of fresh fruit.

'That looks appetising,' remarked Giles.

The waiter turned, holding a silver ladle and the cloth with which he had been rubbing it. As he moved his shiny shoe crunched on a wax crayon. He lifted his foot delicately, like a cat's paw, and examined the sole. Then he crouched and began to pick up the minute particles of crayon in his finger and thumb, transferring them into the cupped palm of his other hand. Failing to find anywhere else to put them, he dropped them in his pocket.

'Good evening sir. Yes, it's our best menu. I'm hoping it will be safe.' He glanced about him with a faint air of mistrust which amused Giles. His voice was soft and precise, with a slight London accent.

'The whole place is alive with animals and children,' agreed Giles, colluding.

'I shall keep the door closed, sir, until the guests come through.'

'A sound idea.'

The waiter turned, with his fingertips neatly together, and surveyed the table. Then, with the cloth over his arm, he walked to the door and paused politely.

'I imagine this is a little different from your usual venues,' said Giles, in the mood to talk, and finding this young man droll with his graceful air of well-modulated disdain.

'A little, sir. But then it takes all sorts.'

'How true.' Giles realized he was being waited for. 'I'm sorry.'

'That's quite all right, sir.'

As the waiter closed the door after them a small girl appeared in the hall. Fat, ringleted, with an air of sullen precocity, this was the Southgates' seven-year-old daughter Zinnia. She wore a plaid dressing-gown and fluffy slippers.

'What's in there?' she demanded, pointing a stubby, imperious finger at the closed door of the dining-room. 'That's our playroom'

'Not tonight,' replied the waiter in an authoritative tone. 'Tonight it's for the grown-ups.'

'This is my house,' Zinnia retaliated threateningly.

'It's your mummy and daddy's house,' said the waiter, his stock rising ever higher in Giles's eyes. 'And I'm in charge of their party.'

'I'm going to look in there —' Zinnia charged with fearful energy towards them, hell-bent on storming her way back into the playroom.

Giles sidestepped hastily, knowing when he was beaten, but before she could reach the door his companion had shot out one hand and caught her by the collar. Carried by her own considerable momentum she spun round, unbalanced, and the young man crouched down to face her, with a chilly smile.

'Now then young lady, you don't want to spoil the grown-ups' party, do you? And I don't want to have to complain to anyone about you. So off you go and be a good girl, right?' The cockney in his voice became more marked as the sentences were spoken, giving his veiled threat an added dimension of menace which was not wasted on Zinnia. He gave her a not entirely gentle push and she stumbled away up the stairs, casting a look of mixed outrage and respect over her shoulder.

Giles was filled with admiration. 'Congratulations. I was scared out of my wits.'

The waiter raised his eyebrows slightly in polite reproof. 'You surprise me, sir.'

With that he excused himself and disappeared through the door that led to the back stairs. Giles re-entered the drawing-room, but just inside he collided, literally, with Clara, who announced that she had been looking for him everywhere, and there was just time before supper to show him the book. At least, he reflected, as he was ushered into her study, to look at the book now would assist an early departure after supper.

In the drawing-room, sitting on the lumpy horsehair sofa with Bill Maguire, Dulcie was a little drunk. She could tell, because everything she said seemed especially witty and vivacious and yet she was sufficiently detached to know from experience that she was not really being that amusing.

'I'm a bit tiddly!' she confided in Bill.

'I know.' He straightened her glass which hovered at a forty-five degree angle above his sleeve.

'Do you ever drink a little more than is good for you?' she asked him earnestly.

'Frequently.'

'I can't imagine it . . .' She took another deep draught and sighed. 'I sometimes think everyone is in control of their lives except me.'

'That's nonsense, I'm sure. Cigarette?'

She took one. 'That's one more I have.'

'What, brand?'

'No. Vice.' She gave him a look that could only be described as brazen, he thought, as he lit her cigarette. She was a curious and amusing mixture and he was surprisingly content just to be with her. He usually disliked parties, especially these self-conscious gatherings of the litterati. He was tired of answering questions about himself, and feeling obliged to ask others similar questions to which he did not wish to know the answers. Dulcie Tennant did not seem especially interested in his work, or his reputation. It was restful to have his remarks go unchallenged, to be accepted completely. And of course she was beautiful.

Clara swept by, arms aloft, calling like a she-elephant, exhilarated by Giles's carefully worded compliments on her book. 'Food everyone! Food in the dining-room!'

They rose and followed her obediently, Dulcie staggering a little and catching his hand.

'Whoops.'

'Are you all right?'

'Perfectly, your honour.'

He laughed and she smiled back at him, pleased by her little joke. Bill suspected the existence of another woman, tougher, secretive, more complex, beneath this bright and child-like exterior.

Giles, first in the queue, encountered Donald Southgate by the Wendy house. He was a stringy man with a wispy beard, who never put in an appearance at his wife's gatherings until at least halfway through. Now he stared gloomily at the buffet. 'Do you have any idea what all this cost?'

'It looks awfully good,' said Giles.

Donald sighed heavily. 'It's exactly the kind of conspicuous consumption I've always fought against.'

'I know, I know.' Giles tried to sound sympathetic. 'But look how it's liberated Clara to talk to her guests.'

The young waiter and a waitress with unnaturally golden hair stood behind the table, poised to serve. Giles asked Ernest for turbot in *chaud-froid* sauce and green peas, and then leaned across and enquired, *sotto voce*: 'Everything untouched? No sabotage?'

'Oh no, sir.' The waitress glanced at him and giggled.

'Splendid, well done,' said Giles. 'I must say I thought you handled that marauding child magnificently.'

'Thank you sir — *pommes de terre?*'

Giles found this affectation enchanting. He patted his waistcoat. '*Non merci — je dois regarder la ligne.*'

Smiling to himself he moved on, in high spirits, to rejoin the mournful Donald.

*

Some time later, as they stacked dishes in the kitchen, Mae gave Ernest a dig in the ribs, saying, 'Hey Valentino — got yourself a new admirer, aintcher?'

Ernest scowled. 'How's that?'

Mae wiped her finger round the lip of a cream jug, glancing slyly at him. 'That old bloke with the nice voice, he fancies you.'

Ernest tweaked his cuffs. 'Shut it, Mae.'

Ernest reached home at one-fifteen, having made the journey by Franconi's van, the last bus, and on foot. Pear Tree Court, Golden Row, was not aptly named. There was nothing either leafy or golden about it, but like a death on a sunny day its pretty name emphasized its grim, arid squalor. The eponymous pear tree may once have existed, but now there was no green to be seen at all unless you counted the one or two window boxes that some brave soul had tried to cultivate. It lacked even the moth-eaten grandeur of Ilse Bauer's apartment block in Berlin. Pear Tree Court was mean. Its meanness showed in small windows like tiny close-together eyes; in a central court that was a waste of gritty concrete and whose focal point was an open drain, frequently blocked; and in a bleak, cheapskate architecture into which the working class families had been herded row on row like pigeons in a hutch. In appearance it was almost indistinguishable from the Routon House a hundred yards up the street. And at night its warren of poky, fetid rooms, like those of the Routon House, sighed and seethed and creaked with the trials and ailments of impoverishment.

As Ernest crossed the corner of the court towards his staircase he could hear the sounds of a marital fight being conducted in one of the ground floor flats: a man's enraged, bullying shouts, followed by a woman's scream, sharp and aggrieved, and a crash. Another black eye and a thick lip on show in the morning, reflected Ernest, another mothers' meeting at the bottom of the stairs.

He went up to the fourth floor and let himself in. As he entered, he heard his mother coughing, a husky wisp of sound, and then her voice floated through the semi-darkness to greet him.

'Ernest? That you love?'

'Yes.'

'Glad you're back.'

'I'll come and see you in a minute.'

Ernest went through the small living-room to the cooking alcove — kitchen would have been too grand a word — lit one of the two gas rings and placed on it the kettle which he had earlier filled at the communal tap in the corridor. Then he went back into the living-room, which doubled as a bedroom for himself and Tony, his eleven-year-old brother. Tony was already asleep on the sagging foldaway bed in the corner, and Ernest went over to tweak the blanket up over his shoulder. He stood looking down at him for a moment. Funny the way kids slept so deep and so sound. Tony's face — unwashed, Ernest noticed, he would tear him off a strip in the morning — was tranquil and contented, like the richest lad in London cushioned on a goosefeather mattress. His rough black hair stood out in spikes on the greasy ticking of the uncovered pillow.

Ernest struck a match and turned up the gas mantle. Tony lurched over, dragging the blanket with him, turning his back to the light. The kettle whistled, and when Ernest had made a pot he put it on a tin tray embellished with a picture of spaniel puppies, added two cups and saucers and a small jug of milk, and carried it through to the bedroom.

Maria Marx was sitting up in bed, her red crocheted shawl wrapped tight round her thin shoulders, a Woodbine in one hand. As Ernest came in she began to cough, putting her free hand to her throat in an incongruously genteel gesture of self-excuse which did not fool Ernest.

'Where'd you get that?' he enquired brusquely, putting down the tray on the end of the bed and indicating the cigarette with a curt nod of his head.

'Hallo, love. What, this? Doris gave me a couple.'

'Hm.' Ernest began to pour. 'They don't do your chest any good.'

'And they couldn't make it much worse, either!' retorted his mother cheerfully, maddeningly. Ernest passed her a cup of tea. 'Thanks, duck.'

'So how you been keeping?' Ernest glared at her, his bedside manner was poor. Every time he looked at his mother's emaciated form, or heard her cough, he was reminded of the disadvantages of poverty.

'I been fine.' Maria smacked her lips. 'Ah . . . that's good.' She leaned back with her cup, the cigarette resting in the saucer. Ernest watched her in amazement. She had absolutely nothing to be happy about. Since her husband had died ten years ago, his body having never fully recovered from the depredations of the war, and of the Spanish 'flu just afterwards, she had been always poor, usually ill, and often lonely — and yet she had a capacity for enjoyment which many a healthier, wealthier person might have envied. Not pluck in the face of adversity, but honest to goodness enjoyment, a robust relish for the few — and they were very few — good things which came her way. She didn't know the meaning of jealousy, though God knows he did. It nagged at him day and night like the tuberculosis that chewed at her lungs.

Now she asked, without a trace of rancour, 'Good do, was it?'

He shook his head. 'Tatty. The arty crowd, up in Muswell Hill. They get right on my wick, that lot.'

'Any band?'

'No, you couldn't've heard a band for all the talking.'

'I like music, myself,' said Maria. She started to hum in her throaty voice: 'Down Sunnyside Lane . . .'

Her sparkiness irritated Ernest — where was her sense of outrage? She was still a young woman, only forty-two, and even now you could see how pretty she had once been, her hair was still black and her eyes luminously bright in her haggard little face.

She made conversation. 'Doris said they had one of them fascist meetings this afternoon, in Lucknow Park up near the Institute. Quite a crowd, she said, getting quite ugly.' She didn't sound perturbed.

Ernest leaned forward on the creaky bed, peering into her face. 'You just keep out of that sort of talk, understand?'

She laughed, patting his cheek. 'Where do I ever go, love?'

'And make sure young Tony stays away, too. He's a right tearaway, he'll get into all sorts of trouble.'

'I do my best, but he's bigger than me!' She chuckled again.

She was impossible in this mood. 'He says with a name like Marx the trouble'll come to us.'

'He doesn't know what he's talking about, he's always looking for a fight, I'll sort him out in the morning.'

'Now, Ernest —'

'Did you eat that dinner?' He had left some mutton and potatoes on the stove.

'Yes,' she lied.

Later, lying on his made-up bed on the old settee, Ernest could hear her whistly breathing and little mutterings, like the feet of mice, as she dreamed.

Dulcie sat with Bill Maguire in his car outside her front door in Chesham Gardens. They had dropped Giles at the Albany about half an hour ago. The peculiar feeling of freedom and exhilaration engendered by Rex's absence, and which had caused her to succumb so quickly to the effects of the Southgates' champagne, had left her. What she wanted, more than anything, was to invite Bill Maguire to come up with her, and for them to make love. But it was so long since she had wanted, or dared, to do this with anyone but Rex, that her own temerity frightened her. So she sat there with him in the dark interior of the car like an awkward girl, uncertain what to do, torn between guilt and desire. And he sat by her, quietly, not expectantly, but attentively. There was certainly nothing presumptuous in his sitting there with her; indeed she would have found it companionable had she not wanted him so much. How ironic, she thought, I've lost all those little skills which used to make this kind of thing easy. And then she thought, angrily, it's Rex's fault.

'Cigarette?' he held out the packet.

'Thank you.' She took one, and got her small holder out of her bag. He struck a match and lit hers, then his.

'Would you like to go somewhere else?' he suggested. 'A nightclub, or something? Or just for a drive?'

'No . . .' She glanced at him. 'I suppose you must wonder why I'm still sitting here.'

He shook his head. 'I'm not looking a gift horse in the mouth.' There was a short silence, then he said: 'This is the first car I've owned in years. In Berlin I used to ride a motorbike. I miss it.'

'You left it there.'

'Oh yes, I sold it, it wasn't worth bringing it back. But I shall probably get another. You're insulated from the exhilaration of speed in a car.'

'A friend of mine has a Daimler Dart,' she said, as if by mentioning Rex, and his car, she could somehow break down the awkwardness. 'And in fine weather we go along with the top rolled back, so I can imagine how you feel about the bike.'

'A Dart is a nice car,' he said.

She could feel her heartbeat drumming in her ears, in a minute she would take the plunge. She glanced up at the windows of her flat. There was a dim light behind the half-drawn curtains of the drawing-room, Celine always left one lamp on. And Rex had been quite clear about not being back until tomorrow.

The pounding in her ears became a roaring, as if a floodgate had burst in her brain.

She turned to him. 'Would you . . .?'

'I thought you'd never ask,' he said.

Inside the flat she led the way into the drawing-room and went to the drinks trolley, but he was close behind her, and took her arm. 'No, don't let's bother with the others.'

She turned towards him, already surrendering. 'What others?'

'Vices . . .' He grinned at her, echoing her earlier remark.

Dulcie gave up. His arms, warm and strong, were around her, his still-smiling mouth enclosed hers. She was almost faint with desire. His body, larger and heavier than Rex's, less teasing and more forthright, overwhelmed her; she gave herself up to it, relaxing against him and letting her head fall back beneath the hungry force of his kiss. She linked her hands behind his neck and he placed both hands under her buttocks, pushing up her skirt, lifting her against him so that she moaned and wrapped her legs round his waist, kicking off her shoes, grasping his rough grey hair and pulling his face against her breasts. He dropped to his knees on the ground. She was nearly frantic now with impatience, dragging at her dress as he fiddled clumsily with the small buttons at the back, longing to feel his mouth and hands on her bare skin. For the first time in years she was more concerned with her own pleasure than with someone else's. As she dragged her dress off over her head he grasped her breasts, pushing them together, fondling the rigid nipples with his thumbs, sucking and kissing. She gave a little scream and reached down with her hands, pushing at her pants, then his, feeling for his penis, cradling its warm, pulsing weight, savouring the sublime anticipation, but only for a moment.

'Do it! Do it!'

He poured himself into her with a soft growl of appreciation and at once she held him close with her legs, lifting her pelvis and moving so tightly with him that it seemed he was carrying her, and every movement caused her a shockwave of almost agonizing pleasure so that she wanted it to last for ever, but knew it was too piercingly sweet to be anything but short-lived. His arms rested on the floor on either side of her head and his lips moved over her face, kissing and murmuring, then gasping as she pushed her hands down in between their bodies and held him as they came, gloriously together.

Fondant, the cat, sat impassively watching them. As they fell apart, breathless, still joined at the hips like Siamese twins, he began to purr, sensing return to normality and perhaps a share of his mistress's attention.

But Dulcie had eyes only for Bill. As if testing his substance and reality she reached out and ran her hand over his face, round his head and neck, feeling his ears and his nose, parting his lips. When she did this he grabbed her wrist, kissed it, and pulled her closer again.

'Christ!'

'What?'

'I thought that was supposed to take twenty minutes . . .'

She laughed. 'That's for amateurs.'

'It was rape, woman.'

'If you don't like it . . .' Teasingly, she moved away, but he snatched her back against him. She could feel him swelling again inside her.

'Don't go – I don't want you to go,' he said softly.

'Give in?' Slowly, wanting his pleasure now, she placed her hands on his chest and eased herself on top of him, sitting astride and leaning forward so that her breasts just touched his chest.

'I give in.' He raised his arms and laid them over his face in an attitude of surrender, but inside her he was huge, a tree of desire growing and towering, so that it took all her self-control to be slow and languorous. But she did it, and his head turned aside in ecstasy as she made love to him, and at her climax tears started from her eyes, not tears of grief, but of wonder and relief, like the juices of love itself.

At five-thirty, before Celine was up, she saw him out, whispering and touching and promising on the dark landing as the birds began to twitter in the trees in Chesham Gardens.

When she'd watched him go, disappearing down the spiral staircase, she went back into the flat, closing the door softly so as not to disturb Celine, and ran through to look out of the drawing-room. On the pavement below, in the still-dim early morning, he looked up and blew her a kiss. She sat there and watched as his car pulled away. Then she went to the kitchen to make tea, Fondant trotting after her, tail aloft, in expectation of a saucer of milk. On the way she caught sight of herself in the mirror and paused. She looked pink and dishevelled. Inside the warm cocoon of her white dressing-gown her body felt not weary and used, as it did after a night with Rex, but purposeful and renewed. Had she been already dressed, and not mindful of Celine's reaction, she would have gone out for a walk. She gave Fondant his milk and took her cup of tea back to her room, sitting on the bed with her knees drawn up, watching the sun come up outside the window.

In bed, they had lain wrapped in each other's arms, laughing and murmuring, and Fondant had come to lie at their feet, with his paws tucked under his chest like a furry, humming teapot, and had not been thrown off.

Dulcie had had many far more handsome men than Bill Maguire in her bed. Beside Rex's slender, youthful, patrician beauty his face and form would have appeared coarse-grained. And yet everything about him filled her with an unreasoning delight. He touched her in the same way that he talked to her, as though he instinctively knew the person she really was, as though there were no need for any pretence or fencing between them, no need for anything but their marvellous proximity. They had talked long and inconsequentially, not ready yet to exchange important confidences. Dulcie did not tell him about Rex. She fully intended to, of course, but another time. Instead she had made enough glancing references to other 'friends' to ensure that he appreciated the many demands on her time, and it was agreed that he would telephone her soon, preferably during the morning, to arrange another meeting.

Now, when she tried to analyse her immense feeling of well-being, she concluded that it was because she no longer felt alone. There was someone on her side, someone from whom she did not have to conceal things, or justify herself in any way. If Bill Maguire considered her a person of consequence and value, then she owed it to herself to think the same.

When Rex dropped in at lunchtime he found her gay, teasing and wholly irresistible, though more inclined to go out to eat than to go to bed with him. Mentally, he shrugged this off. She was delightful company today. And there would be other times.

CHAPTER SEVEN

'For all we know
This may only be a dream;
We come and go
Like a ripple on a stream;
So love me tonight,
Tomorrow was made for some;
Tomorrow may never come,
For all we know . . .'

'For All We Know'
Sam Lewis and Fred Coots, 1934

Bᵧ early October, when she had been working at the Ross Institute for three weeks, Kate already felt that her life had moved into a new phase. The feeling sprang from the fact that she was in demand, in a quite specific and challenging way, and because of this sense of her own usefulness, and the fact that there was no longer any need to prove it, she was able to regard her family with greater equanimity, and to write to Thea with complete honesty for the first time: '. . . at last I'm beginning to feel part of things. Even at Mapleton Road I seem to be less of a square peg in a round hole and am no longer quite so anxious to find a place of my own. How's that for a victory?'

What she still shied away from telling her foster-mother was that Ralph's health was deteriorating. His gradual decline seemed to date from their visit to Berlin and seemed to Kate to be psychological rather than physical. He had lost interest – in food, in company, in argument, in life. His mental processes were still active and acute, but were turned inward on that other remembered world which he seemed increasingly to inhabit. One night when she took him his nightcap in bed he inexplicably mistook her for someone else. The early autumn day had been overcast and wet, and a fire was glowing in the small black grate. The room was hot. Ralph's bedside light was on, but he was lying back on his pillows with his eyes shut, his huge gnarled hand resting heavily on the wrinkled pages of his open book.

'Grandfather?'

He did not stir. His massive, almost monumental stillness was unnerving. Kate put the whisky and lemon on the bedside table, went to the window and reached between the half-drawn curtains to open it a little. It was stiff, and eventually moved with a rasping sound.

'What the dickens are you doing?'

She jumped, almost guiltily. The light from the lamp was behind Ralph, his face was dark on the pillow.

'It's awfully stuffy in here . . .'

'Perhaps you'd let me be the judge of that, seeing as it's my room.' He sounded almost like his old self, but when she drew the curtains over the still-open window he did not notice her small deception.

She stood at a distance, her arms folded, and said, 'Your drink's there.'

Still he stared at her. 'Women like you,' he said, in the same provoking tone, 'should be content to be ornamental, and not tell other people what to do.'

Kate laughed incredulously. 'Ornamental?'

'Run along now, Dulcie, and let a chap get some peace.'

In the dark passage outside she almost bumped into Aubrey. 'Hey, don't trample me underfoot! What's up? You look as if you'd seen a ghost,' he exclaimed.

She shook her head. 'Not me. But I think he has.'

When she mentioned this incident to Dulcie, thinking her aunt might find it curious, Kate was surprised to find her entirely uninterested. But she was accustomed by now to Dulcie's enigmatic patches, and so did not press it.

As it turned out, Dulcie had some enthralling news of her

own to pass on, the coincidental nature of which caused Kate to exclaim: 'I don't believe it! The *enfant terrible* of the *Herald*?'

Dulcie shrugged. 'I suppose he must be.'

'I've met him – we met him in Berlin. It's so extraordinary that you and he are –' she paused. She assumed Dulcie and Bill were lovers, but the word for some reason stuck in her throat. So she finished lamely: 'seeing each other'. She went on to describe the meeting, the visit to the Klub Dalilah (making much of Aubrey's reactions and little of her own), and the subsequent encounter at the stadium. Dulcie listened, fascinated. All this was proof, surely, that she and Bill were meant to be.

'He makes me so happy, Kate,' she confided. 'And I haven't always been happy, you know.'

It was a Saturday afternoon and they were having tea in her flat. She sat on the sofa, and Kate was on the window seat with her feet up, Fondant leaning snugly against her chest. Outside in Chesham Gardens the trees at window-level were beginning to yellow, and the five o'clock light to hint at earlier evenings.

Kate, conscious of her own ambivalence in this matter, determined to be philosophical. 'You owe it to yourself to be happy,' was her reply.

Dulcie smiled. 'But it's not something you can be to order.' Then daringly she added: 'There is something I should tell you.'

Kate scratched Fondant's chin. 'What's that?'

'This flat isn't mine. I mean I don't pay for it, and I hardly own any of the contents, either. The whole thing – including me – is owned by Rex Donati.'

'You're not owned unless you want to be,' said Kate.

'Well –' Dulcie lit a cigarette and blew smoke over her shoulder as though spitting out a cherry stone, 'I suppose in the beginning I *did* want to be. I'd had my good time, or that's what I thought. I'd alienated myself from my family and I had no money and no job. So Rex's offer of an arrangement seemed heaven-sent.' She fiddled with her rings. 'He can be very persuasive.'

'How old is he?'

Dulcie hesitated. But having now committed herself to

honesty she felt Kate deserved as much as she could muster. 'Not much older than you.'

'And he's terribly handsome and you're financially dependent on him.'

How bleak she made it sound. 'That's about it.'

Kate put her arms round her knees and looked out of the window with a little shrug of her shoulders. 'It doesn't sound so terrible.' She wanted to help Dulcie, to be sympathetic as Thea might have been, but she was not at all sure what she was being asked to sympathize with.

Dulcie struggled manfully on, horribly aware of the possibility of alienating Kate with all this squalid confession. But she had an idea, rightly as it happened, that Kate would like her the better for telling the truth, no matter how unpalatable that truth might be.

'It is terrible now, Kate. Because I'm frightened by Rex, and because for the first time in ages I've met a man I actually like . . .' Kate continued to look out of the window. 'Bill makes me feel that I do have it in me to be free again, that there are good things in me after all,' she laughed nervously, 'though not many and I keep them well hidden.'

'I liked you right away,' said Kate gruffly.

'Oh Kate . . .' Dulcie was quite *bouleversée* by the niceness of this remark. 'Me too,' she added lamely.

'Anyway,' said Kate, swinging her legs down off the window seat and standing with her hands in her pockets. 'What's stopping you? Going, I mean?'

Dulcie shook her head. 'Everything, Kate, absolutely everything, though it would seem like nothing to you. I don't have any money and he has a lot. He's paid for everything for about three years now, and what he pays for –' she waved a hand '– is the best. What would I do if I left?'

'But surely Bill –'

'No, Kate. In spite of what I said, I don't see him all that often. I can't, because of Rex. He's my dark secret. And we're certainly not going to get married, I mean I wouldn't want to. If I were to walk out on Rex it might look as if I was casting myself on his mercy, which is the last thing I want. It looks as though the only way I can keep him is to stay with Rex.' She laughed brightly, stubbing out her cigarette. 'What a dilemma!'

Kate saw how her eyes shone. 'I won't have that sort of talk. Only a moment ago you were full of your newfound self-respect.'

'Oh that . . . that doesn't last long.'

Suddenly Kate crouched down on her heels, a hand on either side of Dulcie. She felt particularly strong and clear-headed. 'Look — I can't tell you what to do, because I don't have any experience in — well, in matters of the heart. But I stick by what I said. You're so famously pretty and sought after,' Dulcie allowed herself a wry little smile, 'all this nonsense with Rex is beneath you. You *don't* need to depend on someone like that!'

'Do you really think so?'

Kate pounded her fist on the sofa cushion. 'I wouldn't say so if I didn't!' She glanced at her watch. 'And now I must go.' She knew Dulcie liked time to discard one face and put on another, for Rex's benefit. But as she put on her coat in the hall, she added: 'I'll tell you another thing. You may think you've alienated your family, but blood's thicker than water. I wish I could put my hand on my heart and say I truly belonged to Thea and Jack. If I make mistakes there's always a chance they might say "oh well, only to be expected, after all we don't know where she came from". But you *know* who your family are, and they'd be there for you if you really wanted them. So there.' She planted a kiss on Dulcie's cheek and left.

There were no easy tears to make Dulcie feel better when the door had closed. She was ashamed that she had not even had the decency to say to Kate that there were no circumstances under which Thea and Jack would think or say any such thing. She had made no attempt to redeem them. The slightest supposed fault in them as parents was a comfort to her, even when she knew it was untrue. Dry-eyed and robot-like, she prepared to attend a charity ball with Rex.

At the station, as she thought of Dulcie and Bill, Kate saw a French magazine with a photograph of the King and Mrs Wallis Simpson on the cover. They wore beach clothes and were smiling in a carefree way. She was surprised to find that her reaction was one of warm sympathy, even envy. She decided that of all the people she did not understand she understood herself least.

But this was not true at the Institute. There, the things she knew she was good at came into their own. A complete dearth of directives as to the nature of her job stimulated rather than worried her. Her first day was spent clearing a path through the almost impenetrable shambles of Bobby Hollis's office, against a background of highly-coloured verbal abuse from Nelson the parrot. Bobby's response to queries about his business affairs was habitually evasive.

'What shall I do with this bill?' Kate would enquire from time to time in that brief period before she learned that such enquiries were pointless.

'Just remove it from my sight, my dear, take it as far from me as possible.'

'It's from the fuel merchants.' The Institute was heated by means of a huge and temperamental coke boiler in the cellar, a monster with a cavernous appetite.

'Yes . . .' Bobby would always be abstracted, doing something else, 'they do require paying from time to time.'

'Well, shall I then — pay them?'

'Pay them some of it, my dear, if you want to.' He treated the paying of tradesmen as a kind of whimsical eccentricity.

'Only some?'

'And then some more when they ask for it.'

'Ask for carrots!' Nelson would sign off in some characteristically insulting way and Bobby would end the exchange by hurling a cloth over the cage in a manner that suggested it contained importunate fuel merchants.

Like a frail but surprisingly effective Canute, Bobby Hollis outfaced the rising tide of problems and forced it back a little at a time, not always without getting his feet wet. Kate soon abandoned all attempts to reform him, and took up a position between him and his creditors in a frequently turbulent buffer zone. She stopped asking him what to do, and just went ahead in her own way, taking responsibility for any mistakes she might make. She kept his office ruthlessly tidy in the face of his constant complaints that he couldn't find anything. Like the garden at Mapleton Road, she licked it into shape, and it became her preserve.

This part of her job — what might loosely be termed the secretarial part — took only half the day. In the afternoons she helped with the practical side of things — baby clinics, old folks' afternoons, cooking, cleaning, the collection of old clothes and cheap food donated by local shopkeepers. Three nights a week the Ross provided a free soup kitchen for down-and-outs, and Kate generally helped at one of them. She was happy in her work.

But if Kate was not daunted by her tasks in Whitechapel, poor Dulcie felt like a frail boat on a stormy sea, positively buffeted by unpleasant surprises, and all of them on her own front doorstep, if such a phrase was not inappropriate. After Kate's departure on the evening of the charity ball she took refuge from depression, as usual, in a most careful and lavish toilette. The better her appearance, the better she could make herself feel. By the time she heard Celine admit Rex she was largely restored to good spirits and even quite looking forward to a night on the town in the knowledge that tomorrow Rex would be in Sunningdale and she would be lunching with Bill.

When she came out, in her blue chiffon dress, to find Bill standing there, her instinctive delight at seeing him was quickly superseded by a shameful, childish panic. 'Bill — but I'm just going out!'

'I thought you would be.' He stood there in his mac and scarf, staring at her warmly. She suspected she was blushing. Celine, with a look of waspish disapproval, went into her room and closed the door. She considered that Dulcie had acted badly in allowing this scruffy interloper regular access to the flat bought for her by the elegant and dashing Mr Donati.

With Celine gone Bill came over and cupped her face in his hands. 'Don't look so wild-eyed, I shan't stay.' He ran his thumbs over her mouth. 'And may I say you look like a zephyr?'

She wanted to melt, to cry, to give up the unequal struggle and beg for help, but years of keeping deception in running order were too powerful for her now, and she stepped back from him as he leaned to kiss her, her cobwebby skirt clinging to his legs, trailing from him with the reluctance she was too scared to show.

'You must go! Rex will be here in a minute.'

'Do him good, I'm bored with sharing you.' She looked at him in terror, but saw that he was joking. His long maroon scarf (knitted for him by Ilse) was beaded with raindrops, and his hair was damp, too. She loved him. She wanted to unwind the scarf and rub his hair with it, to chafe his hands and lick the rain from his beloved face. But all she could do was stand apart from him, fussing.

'It's all right.' He was laughing at her, and she could have screamed. 'I'm not looking for trouble, but I wanted to tell you I can't make tomorrow.' He saw her look of anguish. 'I'm sorry, Dulcie, but I must go down to this big fascist meeting in the East End. It is important.'

'Of course,' she said in a small, unconvinced voice. And then, with more emphasis, 'Of course it is. You must go. I shall have a quiet day and play house.'

'Bless you.' He moved towards the door. Relief, gratitude, love, washed over her. Tomorrow she would plan the rest of her life and get everything straightened out. Tomorrow.

But as she opened the door it was to be confronted by a key, poised for the lock, pointing at her heart like an assassin's gun.

'Would it be quite out of the question,' asked Rex, 'for me to be introduced?'

The moment he saw Rex, Bill experienced a feeling of fierce protectiveness towards Dulcie, and of defensiveness on his own account. For Rex was the epitome of every self-confident young blade who had sneered at a failure, or ruined a reputation, or snatched an older man's job, or his wife. A repellent air of casual brutality hung about him like an animal's scent.

But, for Dulcie, Bill held out his hand. 'How do you do, I'm Bill Maguire.'

Rex looked at the hand, and then away, stepping forward to embrace Dulcie and kiss her on the lips, saying, 'Time we were off, are you ready?'

Bill watched as Dulcie went to her room to fetch her things. He supposed he should have gone, but he felt stubborn. The two men stood quite close to each other in the narrow hall, but neither touching, nor speaking, nor even looking at one another. Hatred and suspicion stood between them like an invisible wall.

Finally, Rex said: 'Where exactly were you going, Maguire?'

'Home.'

'May one ask when?'

His rudeness, Bill told himself, was at least partly justified. After all, in Rex's eyes, he was the interloper. He had known of Rex's existence, but Rex had obviously not known of his. Perhaps Rex was even behaving with admirable restraint, though he somehow doubted it. Someone would get it in the neck, probably Dulcie. Just looking at young Mr Donati certain things about Dulcie were made crystal clear to Bill. Here, dressed in immaculate white tie and tails, like Lucifer in evening dress, was the root and cause of her anxiety, her secretiveness, her peculiar lack of confidence and her bouts of unwise drinking.

So in answer to Rex's question Bill simply remained where he was. He hitched up his mac and took cigarettes and lighter from his trouser pocket, lighting up with hands that shook slightly. His hands always shook, but now he felt Rex's eyes resting on their involuntary trembling with scorn.

Dulcie returned, in a dark blue velvet cape and long white gloves, a pearl-encrusted white evening bag in one hand. She looked beautiful and petrified, like a graveyard angel. Bill scarcely knew her. Rex held out his arm for her and she took it, not looking at Bill.

Celine emerged, a little flustered, saw them out and closed the door after them. On the landing as they waited for the lift Rex said, 'Look, Maguire, run along would you?'

'I was simply waiting —'

'Don't bother, there's a good chap.'

Bill looked at Dulcie, that white, expressionless, doll-like beauty, a ghastly parody of the real woman.

' 'Bye for now.' He held out his hand to her, his right to her left, to clasp in friendship rather than to shake in farewell. But her gloved hand was stiff and unresponsive.

'Go away, Bill.'

Quickly and quietly he went, running down the stairs as he always did, while they entered the lift. On the second floor he caught sight of her white face staring out, trapped in the small cage with Rex, and he was filled with tenderness and rage, both of them helpless.

Later, when he'd let himself into his basement flat in Warwick Avenue, he did not at once turn on the light, but went to the window and stared up past the area steps. He didn't much care for his domestic surroundings, but he liked to be an invisible watcher of the outside world. It was going to be a cold night, people were hurrying home. Leaves spiralled and skittered down on to the pavement, moving through the yellow glow of the streetlamp like fish in a tank.

Bill thought of Dulcie, dancing with Rex, light as a zephyr in her blue chiffon dress. And he knew that even if she refused to ask for help, even if she sent him packing, he owed it to her to be consistent.

Dulcie and Rex returned to Chesham Gardens several hours after Bill had done some reading and gone to sleep. In spite of the ghastly meeting between Rex and Bill, Dulcie felt that the evening had not gone too badly. She had made a special effort to please, and she thought she had succeeded. They were both a little drunk, Rex still carried a half-full bottle of Moet et Chandon. She supposed that now they were back he would raise the subject of Bill and possibly hector her a little, but she was confident, now, of her ability to defuse the situation. He made an appealing drunk — rumpled, boyish, even a little waiflike, an uncharacteristic Rex. He was very young, after all.

'Coming?' He stood before her, the champagne bottle hanging from his right hand. A lock of blond hair fell over his eyes and he blew it upwards ineffectively.

In answer she put her hand in his and allowed herself to be led into the bedroom. It would be a poor show if she couldn't handle him tonight, poor tousled, confused boy that he was.

As she closed the door, leaving the indignant Fondant on the landing, Rex flopped down on the bed on his back. He drained the last of the champagne and cradled the empty bottle on his chest like a lily in the hands of a corpse. With a contented smile, he closed his eyes.

Dulcie undressed, laying her clothes meticulously over the back of her chair, finishing with her silk stockings and coffee

lace suspender belt. Then she went over to the bed and lay
down beside Rex. His eyes were still closed. She undid his tie
and slipped it off, and then tried to remove the bottle in order
to unfasten his stiff shirt front but his hands instinctively
tightened their grip, like a sleeping child with a favourite
teddy. Gently she removed his shoes and socks and unbuttoned
the waistband of his trousers. He rolled his head towards her
on the pillow, opening one eye drowsily.

She propped her chin on her hand and smiled down at him.
'Are you going to.let me get that horrible stiff shirt off?'

He spread his arms. 'All yours.'

The moment she had removed it he was on top of her. She
laughed teasingly. 'And I thought you were half asleep!'

'That only goes to show,' he murmured, the bottle still in
his right hand, his left reaching down to his fly, 'how wrong
you can be.'

He lay heavily on her, she felt his arms moving in some
awkward, uncomfortable way. She was suddenly frightened.
'What are you up to?'

He was wide awake now. His face was so close to hers that
she could smell his champagne-stained breath and see the tiny
markings on the irises of his narrowed eyes. 'You silly bitch,'
he said, caressingly. 'I'll teach you to play fast and loose with
me.'

As he spoke Dulcie felt the cold hard mouth of glass entering
her body. She did not make a sound, but closed her eyes,
relaxed, made her mind a blank. She was not a brave person
but she could stay silent.

He finished with the bottle and made a mess over her sheets.
Then he got up and began adjusting his clothes and hair,
looking at his reflection in her dressing-table mirror.

Dulcie no longer felt obliged to stay silent. She felt for the
edge of the sheet and dragged it over herself, disgusted by the
sight of her body — spreadeagled, abused, immobilized by pain
and shock like a butterfly in a collector's case.

'Are you proud of yourself?' she asked. 'Does it make you
feel big to have punished me?'

'Don't talk rot.' He sat on the stool to replace his shoes.
Already he was forgetting, moving on. His callousness was
breathtaking.

Dulcie propped herself up on one elbow. 'Shall I tell you something, Rex?'

'Hm?'

'I've had more lovers than you've had hot dinners.'

'Oh yes?' He didn't believe her, or if he did he didn't care. Her sense of outrage was complete.

She lied in her teeth. 'It might interest you to know that you're the only one I've had to pretend with. You simply haven't satisfied me, Rex. Until tonight, that is.'

Now he looked at her. With an effort she was careful not to show she turned away from him, on to her side, and closed her eyes, snuggling her shoulders in feigned contentment.

'So thanks,' she said, and yawned.

She waited for him to strike her, or to abuse her, but he did neither. Instead he left. She heard him in the hall, telling Celine she was not to be disturbed, and then the front door closed after him. The sense of triumph worked on Dulcie like an analgesic, and within a few minutes, in spite of her discomfort, she was asleep.

CHAPTER EIGHT

'Somewhere the sun is shining,
So honey don't you cry,
We'll find a silver lining,
The clouds will soon roll by . . .'

'The Clouds Will Soon Roll By'
Harry Woods and George Brown, 1932

DURING the day Ernest Marx worked for a firm of fur importers in Robertson Road, near the docks. He was as discontented here as he was working for Milo Franconi in the evening. The furs themselves, destined as they were for the backs of the wealthy, disgusted him. In his fertile imagination, the analogy of exploitation and death which they provided was carried to horrific extremes: the champagne drinkers became bloodsuckers, the furs hanging in the warehouse became the scalps of the underprivileged. This did not alter the fact that Ernest wished not to improve the lot of the prey, but to become himself a predator.

The job of grader and sorter was so far within his capacity he could have done it blindfold. But it was physically exhausting because of the cold and the dark and the smell, and the dragging weight of the bundles of pelts which had to be carted about. Ernest was slightly asthmatic and would finish the day red-eyed and tight-chested. His mother would say: 'You ought to pack in that rotten job, Ernest,' but he would treat her to his most withering look (and it was extremely withering) and ask her what she supposed they would all do if he were to pack it in, with her poorly and Tony still at school? He found it annoying that his mother so disliked his work for Zelinski's, when she considered his white-jacketed nocturnal slavery a glamorous occupation, conducted in glittering halls to the accompaniment of romantic music. Her cheerful and undisguised envy of the better-endowed portions of society provided an uncomfortable satire on Ernest's own venomous jealousy.

Ernest got to the warehouse at eight-thirty in the morning, and left around five. In the interim he would return home for what amounted to about half an hour in the middle of the day to see to Mrs Marx's dinner.

On the corner of Golden Row stood the Jewish grocer's, Aronsohn's. At midday on Friday, October 2nd, Ben Aronsohn was sweeping the floor of his shop, and the door stood open. As Ernest went by Ben appeared in the doorway, ushering a small pile of dust out into the street.

'Good day, Ernest! How's your mother keeping? I haven't seen her in months.'

'No, well she doesn't get out these days, her health's bad.'

'It's a damn shame,' said Ben, shaking his head. 'She's a lovely woman, Maria. Beauty that shone out, she used to have.'

'She keeps cheerful.'

'She would do.' Ben held his broom in front of him, with both hands clasped on top of the stick in the manner of a sentry at ease. 'I have great respect for a woman like that. And the young lad?'

Ernest made a face. 'He fights too much.'

'M-hm. Trouble at school?'

'Nothing he couldn't stay out of if he tried.'

Ben sighed. 'You can't blame the boys, Ernest, they're hot-blooded. I haven't had no trouble to speak of. A few remarks, a few looks –' he made a rocking motion with his hand – 'nothing to worry about.' He propped the broom against the door and took a blue and white duster from his overall pocket, flicking it along the top of the already gleaming counter. 'I can't complain.'

Ernest watched him, spruce and businesslike in his long alpaca overall over neat striped shirt and black trousers. Beyond his busy figure, on the shelves of his well-stocked shop, rows of jars glistened, trays of bagels, dishes of herrings, sacks of pulses, packets and cartons and tins all neatly stacked and displayed, all fresh and in good condition, nothing tatty or past it. Ernest experienced a surge of impatience with Ben's clean, thrifty, self-effacing shopkeeper's mentality.

'I must be off,' he said curtly. 'I have to see Mother eats.'

'You're a good son, Ernest,' was Ben's reply as he waved him good-bye.

Maria Marx was in the living-room when Ernest got back, standing by the grimy little window, staring out. She turned at once when she heard him come in, her haggard face lit by its incongruously radiant smile.

'Hallo, love!'

'What can I get you?' he asked, embarrassed as usual by her warmth, turning into the kitchen as if he hadn't noticed her outstretched hands.

'I'm not hungry.' There was a laugh in her voice.

'You have to eat.'

'I don't know . . .' He knew she was making her way painfully across the room towards the kitchen, using the backs of chairs for support, pausing and panting. He clattered the lid of the kettle to cover up for her. When he'd got it on the gas he turned and saw her in the doorway, a little stooped, and breathing heavily, but smiling. 'I wish you wouldn't bother, Ernest,' she said. But seeing his exasperated expression she added: 'Very well, I'll have some bread and cheese. Anything to oblige.'

He glared at her. 'Go and sit down,' he ordered, 'and I'll bring it to you.'

Chuckling, she shuffled back to the living-room. Ernest found the cheese, sniffed it thoughtfully and then placed it, with a slice of bread and marge, on a plate. Then he put the plate, and a glass of water, on a tray and took it through to Maria. With a waiter's flourish, he placed it on her lap.

'Thanks, doll.' She laid her hand on his sleeve as he withdrew, her face still struggling with laughter. 'Give us a kiss.' He bent and kissed her cheek, stiffly.

'What about you?' she asked, dutifully enfolding the cheese in the bread and lifting the sandwich to her lips. It looked enormous, a great doorstep of unmanageable food. 'You not having anything?'

'I'll have a cup of tea in a minute, I'm in a hurry.'

She struggled with a mouthful, munching and gulping, her thin throat working furiously. 'You shouldn't come back here every day, it's not necessary.'

'It's no trouble.'

'See Tony?'

'Yes.'

'How was he? Minding his p's and q's?'

Ernest made a series of lightning decisions. 'Yes.'

To avoid further talk of Tony he went into the kitchen and made the tea. There was silence for a few minutes while he did so, during which Maria managed another three mouthfuls of bread and cheese. Feeling she'd earned a respite, she put the tray on the floor and gratefully accepted the cup of tea he brought. As she sipped it she surveyed him perspicaciously where he sat on the edge of the put-you-up, dark browed and tense.

'You know your trouble,' she said. 'You work too hard.'

Ernest loathed this affectionate litany of hers. 'For crying out loud, Mum—'

'Look at you . . .' she felt in her skirt pocket for fags and matches and lit one under his disapproving gaze, '. . . you're so handsome, Ernest, you're a real eyeful, but do I ever see you with a girl? You want to get out and enjoy yourself, love, before it's too late.'

'Too late? I'm twenty.'

'Twenty and you act forty,' commented Maria with spirit. 'It's not right. You don't want to worry about me, I'm perfectly happy.'

The trouble was, he knew it was true. She would actually rather die, pottering about the flat at Pear Tree Court, singing and whistling and dreaming and living on tea and fags, than have an extra year or two of life bought by his stern, dutiful attentions. She was a realist, in a way, and a fatalist. But she was happy, and he was not, so where did that leave them? This kind of conversation with his mother always confused him.

'I go to the pictures, don't I?' he reminded her. The cinema was his one indulgence, his other life, the weekly shot of intoxicating glamour that made everything else bearable. The wall by his bed was plastered with pictures of his heroes —

Edward G. Robinson, Clark Gable, Johnny Weissmuller, Errol Flynn.

'Yes, you do, love, you do,' said Maria.

He caught the pity on the edge of her remark and stood up, shaking it off like a bluebottle. 'I got to be going,' he said.

On the way back to Zelinski's, Ernest thought about his father. A second generation London Jew, the cause of all the trouble in Ernest's opinion. Maria was given to characterizing him as a gay dog, but Ernest's memories of him were of a man mentally and physically ruined by war, nervous, tense and choleric. His 'miraculous' recovery from a stomach wound sustained at Vimy had left him with a legacy of pain and tiredness which affected his whole life. Before the war he had been a saxophonist with a dance band, *that* was the gay dog of Maria's memory. But afterwards the unsocial hours and heavy drinking of a bandsman's life had not suited him. He had got a position in a musicshop, but his fits of pain-induced rudeness and his jealousy of his colleagues soon got him the sack. He had taken a caretaking job, and managed to keep it because he worked alone. Maria had to watch her prince of romance become a pinched, ill-humoured drudge.

But all this pain and unhappiness had only lasted a few years and in late '25, soon after Tony's birth, he had died, leaving his family more or less destitute. Ernest had done a paper round, Maria a cleaning job, and their income had been augmented by a series of uncles. Ernest had never had to have the role of the uncles explained to him, and he had not resented them, or felt hostile towards his mother. She had managed her second job quite gracefully and without the loss of a natural carefreeness which was her special characteristic. Somehow they had survived, with Tony crawling around, and the uncles in and out, and a great deal of borrowing and making do, until Ernest left school and began work.

That had marked the beginning of Maria's decline. During her husband's last years, and those just after his death, the necessity to 'keep the show on the road', as she put it, had kept her going like a pain-killing drug. But with Tony at school and a regular wage coming in again she at last opened the door and let her illness step inside. The stairs to the flat made her so breathless that she stopped going out, and she became so thin and weak that the demands of the flat itself, let alone those of the uncles, were quite beyond her. She faced up to the fact. 'Sorry, love, no can do' became a regular remark of hers. Since then their roles in relation to each other had become well established. Ernest was a dutiful dark horse; Maria a cheery optimist; and Tony represented hot-blooded youth, of whom little was expected.

As Ernest passed Ben Aronsohn's shop he noticed that it was shut, the closed sign hanging at an angle behind the glass, against the brown blind, the upstairs curtains drawn. He could not remember that Ben normally closed over the dinner hour, but possibly he was stock-taking.

Golden Row was very quiet, as though the occupants had all gone somewhere else, but Ernest could hear a distant hubbub. He did not bother to ask himself what might be going on that he was missing; he willingly absented himself from the preoccupations of the herd. He pushed his hands into the pockets of his neatly buttoned jacket and walked down the middle of the road.

But that evening after work the same road presented a very different picture. There was a crowd outside Aronsohn's, a crowd from which angry shouting and argument rose like black smoke from a bonfire. On the fringes of the crowd a dog ran back and forth, barking in agitation.

Ernest realized at once what had happened. They were all behaving perfectly in character. As he walked by someone left the crowd and ran over to him, plucking his sleeve. It was Tony.

'Ernest! They bloody nearly killed 'im! They wrecked the shop and bloody nearly killed 'im!'

'Don't swear,' said Ernest automatically.

'Didn't you hear—'

'I heard. Terrible thing, but it's no concern of ours.'

'What?' Tony looked as though he might burst. He was scarlet, and shaking. 'But it was Ben, and he's Jewish like us!'

'Now then, Tone,' admonished Ernest, 'you want to keep your distance.'

'I don't! I want to smash them like they smashed Ben.'

He burst into a noisy flood of childish tears. Ernest squeezed his shoulder. 'Come on, Sunny Jim, let's go home to tea.'

'Piss off!' Tony wrenched away from him, wiping his nose on the sleeve of his jacket.

'That's enough of that,' said Ernest, passing him a handkerchief and beginning to propel him forward.

There were people all along Golden Row, in little clusters on the pavement, round doors and windows, passing the gruesome tale round and round. Ben was a widower with no children, there had been no one to run for help. Ernest wondered how he was going to tell his mother about it.

But when they got back he found he didn't need to do so. The omniscient Doris had been up already, the gleeful bearer of dreadful tidings.

Maria looked wan and frightened. 'I don't understand,' she kept saying, 'Ben never harmed a living soul . . .'

Tony lay down on the put-you-up with his back to them, and sulked.

Ernest felt the old irritation with both of them — so foolish and ineffectual.

That night, two more Jewish shops, just up the road from Zelinski's, were set alight; and a whole row of terraced houses belonging to Jewish families had their front windows broken, and a big sign like a flash of white lightning daubed on their front doors. There had been a gathering on the corner of St George's Street and Ezra Road, from which marauding groups of men had departed intoxicated, not with alcohol, but with hate, and feelings of power they did not really have.

Next day was Saturday, and Doris called round in the morning, bringing a packet of cigarettes for Maria and gossiping up a storm. 'I heard what was said, you know,' she confided, perching on the arm of the ricketty settee, a cigarette cocked in one podgy hand. 'And I don't mind telling you . . .'

No, she never minded telling them, thought Ernest darkly as he ironed his white jacket (Mr and Mrs Victor Carew at home, Hans Crescent, 6 pm). She didn't mind telling them at all. She didn't care that they had a Jewish surname. Unfortunately Maria was a pathetically ready listener, and captive one, always there and waiting for these juicy titbits from the outside world.

Ernest glanced with distaste at Doris as she sat there,

prattling on. Her vast bottom sagged down on either side of the narrow settee arm so that it was all but concealed in the bulging folds of flesh. There were moons of dark sweat in the armpits of her tight dress, surrounded by yellowish ripples where previous stains had not washed out. Her hair was like a scouring pad and she had lipstick on her teeth. She was good-natured and kind, so there was no denying her right to politeness from Ernest, but he knew why she came so often — no one else would have her. Doris's common-law husband, George, was a drunk, and she was a slut, their noisy altercations forever echoed up and down the stone staircase of Pear Tree Court and the sight and sound and smell of their excesses were inflicted on all who lived there. No one could have called the occupants of the Court precious, or over-sensitive, but Doris and George were a bad lot. It was a measure of Maria's decline, in Ernest's view, that she was so pathetically grateful for Doris's company.

'. . . making the country fit to bring up children in, he said,' she rattled on, 'cutting out the sores and the bad bits, making it clean and whole, you know? You can't really argue with it, can you? It's just the way they go about things that get's people's backs up, isn't it?'

'Yes,' said Maria. They neither of them, thought Ernest, slipping the now immaculate jacket on to a hanger and hanging it on the kitchen door, have any idea what they're talking about. His craving for escape was so strong it nearly choked him. He knew he had to make it happen, though he had no idea how.

That evening after the Carews' cocktail party he was free by nine and, declining Milo's offer of a lift in the van, he set out to walk as far as Vauxhall Bridge, intending to pick up a bus on the far side. But it was a fine evening, with a sky full of stars and a milky, dappled moon, so when he got to the bridge he did not cross it but turned, impulsively, right along the Embankment. The black satin water lapped the wall below the parapet; one or two couples strolled like him, enjoying the evening air; cabs and cars purred along the road. Ernest knew that this was where he belonged, on this side of town, with the smart men and the lovely girls in the taxi cabs. He could outshine the lot of them. He'd watched and he knew how it was done. All he needed was a chance.

He stopped, and leaned on the parapet, lighting himself a cigarette. He rarely smoked, it was an affectation. Now, in his imagination, the cigarette was not a Woodbine but a Sobranie in an ivory holder, his baggy gabardine mac was the choicest of camel-hair trenchcoats, his cap a snap-brimmed fedora. He was not Ernest Marx, waiter, but George Raft, Al Bowley, the Jack the Lad of the small hours set. It was a moment of the purest magic.

Giles Huxley had been enjoying a rare evening in, with a good book. He took much pleasure in his own company, for he was permitted so little of it since his plays had become successful.

Normally, left to his own devices of an evening, he would simply have read till about ten, had a bath, gone to bed and written his diary, and been asleep by eleven. But it was an especially beautiful night; the sky from his window was vast and starry over London. So at nine-thirty he set aside his book, turned out all the lights except one, put on his coat, and left the seclusion of the Albany for a walk. He crossed Piccadilly, stepping out briskly, and headed for the river.

In about fifteen minutes he reached the Embankment, by Charing Cross. Beneath the arches dark shapes whispered and scrabbled and coughed. There was a clink of a bottle, the hawk and slap of someone spitting, the scrape of a match followed by a short, guttering light. Somebody said something in a sharp, whining voice and the pale disc of a face moved towards him out of the darkness. Giles turned away quickly, his heart thudding. He was ashamed — the great war hero scared by a cadging down-and-out! It was because of what he was. They might know, they might be able to smell it on him as a tiger smells fear on its prey.

He walked swiftly for a few minutes, breathing deeply until his composure was fully restored. He began to reflect content-edly on the disparate elements that made up his life — the exuberant, sentimental gregariousness of the theatre, the quiet satisfaction of writing in the comfort of the Albany, the treasured company of real friends, like Dulcie (though he didn't see quite so much of her these days, for excellent reasons). Giles felt that he had much to be grateful for. With the stars above him and the river below on this tranquil October night he even dared admit to being a happy man.

So engrossed was he in these thoughts, and walking so fast, that he literally bumped into the young man.

'Oh I say, I'm sorry.' Giles put his hands for a second on the other's shoulders, to steady them both, and at once recognized – but could not place – the face that looked out at him from beneath the flat cap. 'I was far away I'm afraid,' he continued, 'I do apologize.'

And he began to walk on, not bothering to try and place the face. He met so many people at parties, and first nights, and lunches, he must have dozens of glancing acquaintances whose names he could not recall. He was surprised, therefore, when he felt a touch on his sleeve.

'Hey, what's the hurry?'

There was something stylized about this remark. Intrigued, Giles turned. The young man was holding out a packet of cigarettes.

'Cigarette?' Again the slightly artificial note, which Giles now defined as vaguely transatlantic.

'I don't, thank you all the same.'

The young man lit one for himself with something of a flourish, striking a match along the top of the parapet, and drawing deeply, with narrowed eyes. 'Nice evening.'

'Yes, it is.' Giles stepped alongside him at the wall, prepared to be companionable. 'I hate to be trite, but I seem to know your face.'

The young man treated him to a magnificently sardonic smile. It suddenly dawned on Giles that he was speaking to someone in the grip of a potent fantasy. Their conversation was taking place on two quite different levels. This realization he found both fascinating, and strangely touching. It was like watching the mimicry of a precocious child who apes the mannerisms of a particular adult with no understanding of what those mannerisms denote.

Giles smiled back and asked, amiably: 'Now where might we have met?'

'I know where.' Again the carefully contrived hint of

mystery. Beneath the peak of his cap the youth's face was pale and oval, full-lipped and shadowy-eyed.

Giles felt a rush of tenderness. 'Tell me then, I want to know.'

'At a party.'

'You're an actor!'

The young man smiled enigmatically and shook his head. In the monochrome of streetlamps and darkness he needed only the frame of the cinema screen to complete his performance.

'You look like an actor,' said Giles. It was the truth but he felt himself slipping, slipping.

Suddenly his companion removed the cap and held it flat on his palm at shoulder level, his head tilted in the merest hint of polite enquiry. The dumbshow was so excellent that Giles remembered at once where they had met, but he did not wish to spoil things for the young man by mentioning his work.

'Of course — it was at that awful party in Muswell Hill.'

'Got it in one.'

'You impressed me enormously with your handling of the terrible child.'

'Flipping kids.' The mask dropped, the illusion fell away. All at once the young man's voice was flat and ordinary, his luminous poetic pallor faded into the undernourished pastiness of the East End. Giles noticed the frayed cuffs of his mackintosh, and the battered suitcase on the ground by his feet. He took a last drag on his cigarette butt, now held like a dart between finger and thumb, and shied it over the parapet, a tiny red spark to be doused in the black water.

Though Giles thought Ernest's return to normality an involuntary thing, it was not. Ernest was profoundly, instinctively aware of the value of tension and surprise. Once embarked on his course he was in an exhilarating state of heightened consciousness, intoxicated with the knowledge of his power. He was in control.

'Not working tonight, though?' observed Giles.

'I have been,' said Ernest. He put on a voice. ' "Only a cockers-p, dear," ' he said, his face sulky.

Giles laughed aloud in genuine delight. 'That's most unkind! Still —' he gazed about him, stretching his arms, 'it's a lovely night for a walk. Where were you heading?'

'Nowhere special.' The young man rolled the cap and stuffed it in his mackintosh pocket. His black hair was very well greased and brushed.

'Shall we walk a little way together, then?' suggested Giles. He was disposed to behave in an unguarded, outgoing way, he felt no anxiety.

In reply the young man picked up his scruffy suitcase and they fell in step together heading east, with the windows of the Savoy like a wedding cake of lights on their left.

The case, though it only contained Ernest's work clothes, seemed symbolic. It placed a stamp of finality on events, which may have caused Giles to ask, when they had walked almost up to Blackfriars Bridge: 'Would you care to come and have a drink, or some coffee at my flat? Do you have time?'

'Plenty of time, thank you.'

They picked up a cab on the bridge. In the intimacy of the back seat, Giles asked, 'Where do you live, by the way?'

'In Whitechapel.' Ernest watched Giles's face to read his reaction, but there was none beyond polite interest.

'And of course – forgive me – I don't even know your name.'

Ernest hesitated for a second. What was the smart thing to do, use an alias? But he was too vain for deception tonight. 'Ernest. Ernest Marx.'

'And I'm Giles Huxley. How do you do.'

They shook hands. Ernest could not believe it was this easy. He had had no plan when he came out tonight, but the moment he had seen this Huxley fellow coming dot-and-carry-one towards him Mae's words had sounded in his head like a revelation: 'That old bloke . . . he fancies you!' And that had been that. It occurred briefly to Ernest that he might have misconstrued the whole thing and that Giles Huxley might be taking *him* for a mug, but he quickly dismissed the idea. Ernest had had no sexual experience of any kind but he did not feel, or act, like a virgin. He saw that Giles was the vulnerable one, the one who had something to lose and who had put his reputation in jeopardy by inviting a strange young man back to his flat.

Ernest stole a glance at Giles. He could have done a lot worse. Giles was not young, but then no one sufficiently well-heeled for his purposes would have been. And he was nice looking, clean and smart (Ernest set considerable store by a good turn-out) with a pleasant, educated voice. He wondered what he did for a living, and then asked, 'What's your line of country?'

'Me? Oh, I'm a scribbler.'

'What do you write? Books?' Ernest asked hopefully. An author would be very good news.

'Plays, actually.'

Ernest remembered that he had been taken for an actor, and was flattered. Something occurred to him. 'Do you write film scripts?'

'No, I never have. It's something I should like to try, though.'

'I'm mad about films,' said Ernest, though Giles had already guessed that this was the case.

Everything about Giles's flat impressed Ernest: its sedate luxury and comfortable good taste; the hundreds of books; the well-chosen paintings; the *objets trouvés*; and its serene orderliness. All these things spoke of a cultured as well as a wealthy occupant. He sat down on a brown velvet chesterfield and looked about him.

'What can I offer you,' said Giles. 'Coffee? Tea? Or something stronger.'

Clearly the best thing now, thought Ernest, was to let Huxley make the running. 'I'll have whatever you have,' he said.

Giles poured two cups of coffee and two brandies and brought them on a tray. Like Ernest, he had a sense of events running on their predestined course. It was rare for him to bring a man back here to the Albany, and he had done so on this occasion because his attraction to Ernest Marx was only partly physical. He actually wanted this young man to stay, to talk, to put their eventual and inevitable coupling into the context of a friendship, however slight and transient.

He sat down near Ernest on the chesterfield. The curtains were not drawn, and outside the long window the rooftops were rugged and romantic against the clear night sky, and fringed with an orange glow like phosphorous from millions of streetlamps. The faintest drone of traffic was audible, like the humming of bees.

'This is very nice,' remarked Ernest.

'Tell me,' said Giles, 'do you enjoy your work as a waiter?' He was genuinely interested. He well remembered Ernest's look of scornful detachment at Clara Southgate's party. Another of his poses, or did he really hate his job?

'I hate it,' said Ernest, as if echoing Giles's thoughts. 'There's nothing I wouldn't do to change my life.'

And with this he turned on Giles the most penetrating, the most pleading, the most alluring look that Giles had ever seen. His senses reeled under the onslaught of that look. At once he put out his hand and laid it on Ernest's shoulder, stroking his pale cheek with one finger.

'Perhaps I could help a little,' he said.

About an hour later, Ernest swung his legs out of bed and began pulling on his socks and underpants. He was strangely unmoved, both physically and emotionally by this, his first sexual adventure. The flame of desire burnt low in Ernest at the best of times. On the very few occasions when, out of a sense of duty, he had embraced a girl, he had been disgusted. The human body with all its bulges and blemishes, its scents and secretions, seemed to Ernest an unlovely thing beside its idealized representation on the silver screen. What he craved was the drama, glamour and romance peddled twice nightly at the Astoria, the women filmed through gauze, the men unbelievably tough and heroic, the cars fast and the drink strong, the background music rising and falling like the sound of the sea, carrying the whole thing along. Sex was not part of his fantasy, but he had known instinctively that it might be a means of realizing it. He had not been particularly surprised at what had been expected of him in bed, since he had always believed sex to be an awkward, uncomfortable business. And at least Giles was a tender and considerate lover, touched by Ernest's ignorance, and had managed to imbue the act with some traces of dignity. Now, looking around him, Ernest considered it to have been a small price to pay for admission into this delightful new world. He was light-headed with success.

The bedside lamp was on. It had a red shade so that it cast

a glow like firelight. The bedroom was decorated in dark shades of red and brown and terracotta, with heavy fringed curtains and two Persian rugs, the walls crowded with more pictures. The bedside table with its tooled leather top bore, in addition to the lamp, a pile of books, a second telephone, and a brown leather diary with a gold lock and gold propelling pencil. Why, thought Ernest, you could do anything if you lived in a place like this, you were a king in your own palace. He wriggled his stockinged toes on the rug.

Giles was leaning back on the pillows, his hands linked behind his head. The bedhead was rosewood, carved in the shape of an enormous scallop shell. Ernest smiled, at the bedhead as much as at Giles, and stood to pull up his trousers and tuck in his shirt. He hoisted his braces up over his angular shoulders and released them with a snap. He rather liked an audience. As he sat once more to put on his shoes he nodded his head at the diary on the bedside table. 'What do you write in that?'

'I write my life in it,' said Giles, 'and I keep the key well hidden.'

'What, everything you do, everything that happens?'

'Oh, everything,' confirmed Giles. 'Don't worry, you'll be there.'

'I'm not worried,' said Ernest, a shade huffily. He tweaked at the laces on his shoes and Giles observed how well-polished they were.

'What family do you have, Ernest?' he asked gently.

Ernest realized that in this department nothing could serve him half so well as the truth. 'There's just me, and my mother – she's an invalid – and my young brother.'

'So you're the breadwinner.'

'I have to be. I do the catering job in the evenings and work in a fur warehouse during the day.'

'That's a big load for young shoulders,' said Giles.

Ernest smiled at him, cheerful and plucky now, a working class hero. 'I'm used to it.'

'How tiresome you must find us idle partygoers.'

'Yes, I do.' Giles raised his eyebrows. Ernest added: 'I'd like to be one of you, though.' He shrugged on his jacket.

Giles laughed. 'You'd have them by the ears, Ernest!' Seeing that Ernest was now fully dressed and anxious, he thought, to be gone, he slipped on his dressing-gown and walked through to the drawing-room.

'You must get back to your mother,' he said. Ernest thought it a pretty funny remark under the circumstances. Giles took his wallet from the jacket he had discarded earlier. 'And I want you to accept a gift because I've enjoyed your company so much. Make sure you get a taxi home.'

'Thank you.' Ernest's hand moved slightly towards the neatly folded banknotes.

'On one condition. Perhaps we could meet again. You have an evening job, you must often have to pass this way on your way home. You know where I am, you could come and have a drink and a talk any time, and then take a taxi. I should truly like that.'

I bet you would, thought Ernest. 'Of course I will.' He took the money — clean crisp notes, and several of them, in a wad.

'Good. Now don't forget. I shall be looking forward to our next meeting.'

'I won't forget.'

In the hall, Giles took Ernest's face between his hands. 'I'd like to help in any way I can,' he said.

'Thank you,' said Ernest.

The following morning Maria Marx woke a little later than usual to the realization that Ernest, incredibly, was still asleep, breathing deeply on his bed in the corner. Even on Sundays it was unheard of for her dutiful son to indulge in a lie-in. From the living-room she could hear Tony's light snore.

Painfully she pulled herself up on to her elbow, and it was then that she spotted the money on her bedside table, just lying there as if casually thrown down, and with it a little note scribbled on a scrap of paper.

She picked up the note. It was from Ernest, and it was brief. 'Your worries are over,' it read. 'Plenty more where this came from, and all above board, love Ernest.'

Incredulously she looked down at the cash. Ten pounds in singles and ten bob notes. She leaned back, closing her eyes and holding the money to her face, breathing in its fresh, papery smell. Downstairs a toddler screamed and screamed and was smacked, which made it scream even more. But Maria lay quietly, breathing in the banknotes and smiling.

Having left his flat at about eight that Sunday morning, Bill Maguire headed towards Tower Bridge. Contingents of Blackshirts were due to foregather at nearby Royal Mint Street, thence to march in four groups to meetings in Limehouse, Shoreditch, Bow and Bethnal Green.

As the ghostly emptiness of the City began to give way to the wharves and warehouses of the East End dockland, so the streets and pavements became more crowded. In spite of urgent dissuasion by the national press, anti-fascist rallies were planned for nearby Cable Street in the afternoon, and at Shoreditch Town Hall in the evening, and already there were signs of huge crowds gathering. Bill parked the car in Thomas More Street alongside Western Dock. As he got out he could hear the blare of a loudspeaker van, and as he began to walk up towards Royal Mint Street a man on the corner broke away from his companions to run down and press a leaflet into his hands.

'Stay with us brother – fight the fascist threat!'

Bill lifted a hand in acknowledgement and glanced down at the leaflet as the young man ran back to join his friends. All standard stuff: he pushed it into his pocket. And that young fellow had been no son of the downtrodden proletariat, but an Oxbridge idealist unless he was much mistaken, getting it all out of his system. In moderate Britain the fascists and communists needed their mutual vilification to give them a stature which they would otherwise lack.

At the top of Thomas More Street he found himself placed almost exactly between the two opposing armies. It was still only nine-thirty, but when he looked to his right, in the direction of Cable Street and the East End, behind a line of policemen ranged like a picket fence across the road stood a crowd already numbering several hundred, and bristling with banners and placards. The tinny, strident sound of a loudspeaker could be heard above the rumble of voices.

On the left, towards Tower Bridge, Bill could make out the darker, more orderly mass of the fascist troops, and hear the thud of a band in the middle distance. The stretch of road separating the two factions was no more than a quarter of a mile long, but was occupied by a veritable army of police — over 6,000 overall had been drafted into the area for the day — both on foot and on horseback. It was raining slightly and a faint, acrid smell rose from the damp rubber capes of the men and the steaming coats of the horses. The officers on foot carried batons at the ready. All the men wore that look of phlegmatic preparedness that Bill had seen on the faces of police everywhere.

The anti-fascist crowd seemed to be increasing both in size and confidence by the minute, the narrow line of police delegated to hold them back bulged and leaned dangerously, strained to near breaking point by the explosive pressure of so many angry bodies. Bill turned right, his intention first to speak to the police, and then get into the crowd behind the cordon for the point of view of the protesters. A few intrepid commercial vehicles — baker's and newsagent's delivery vans, and a horse-drawn milk float — had entered Royal Mint Street from the north side, and belligerent drivers, determined not to be cowed by the situation, bellowed abuse at the police and both political factions. Blaring horns, revving engines and the panicky whinnying of horses combined with the mounting clamour on both sides to create a deafening din.

Suddenly, a boy darted from the crowd in Cable Street, ducking beneath the linked arms of the police, and hurled something into the middle of the road. The firecracker skittered and fizzled for about thirty yards before exploding in a series of sharp reports and a plume of sulphurous yellow smoke. The reports, so like gunfire, galvanized the police. The boy was overwhelmed in a moment, the firecracker kicked aside, but not before the horse pulling the milk float had shied violently, its hooves clattering and skidding on the wet road. The float lurched, and a crate tipped off the far side, sending shards of glass, borne on a widening river of milk, flowing across the road towards the gutter. Unsettled, one of the police horses reared and then side-stepped rapidly, mounting the pavement opposite Bill, its head, wild-eyed, snapping up and down, its massive hindquarters bunched beneath it.

Bill flattened himself against the wall of the warehouse, but still it kept coming until its enormous flank buffeted him, winding him, and the flailing boot of its rider grazed his cheek as he fell. As the officer regained proper control, his shout of apology caused the horse to kick out one last time with its hind leg, as if in retaliation, catching Bill a painful blow on the point of the elbow. For a moment he was nauseous with pain, and sat slumped against the wall with his head bent forward. He was shocked, the sense of freedom and exhilaration that had been his only a minute ago had been completely knocked out of him, along with his breath. To his right, opposite the warehouse doorway, there was no kerb, and a river of milk, now grey with dirt, washed around him.

He began to struggle up, his head still swimming. Hands grabbed his arms and hauled him, a voice shouted in his ear: 'Not a good place to be, sir, if I may say so, why don't you cut along home?' There were policemen on either side of him, anxious to remove him as soon as possible. Bill ran his hands through his hair and felt in his breast pocket for his press card.

'Thanks. Sorry I'm in your way. I'm press.' The big sergeant gave his card a cursory and disparaging glance.

'We've got our work cut out here, sir.'

He moved off towards Cable Street, but as he did so the crowd suddenly and violently broke through the police cordon, with an effect like a dam bursting. The street was filled with a torrent of yelling men, some brandishing their placards like spears, others clutching an assortment of missiles ranging from stones to tin cans and coins. Oblivious once more to everything but the excitement, Bill turned and keeping level with them ran back the fifty yards or so to the top of Thomas More Street. Ahead of the mob about a hundred police had formed into a phalanx and were preparing to counter-charge. The drivers of the various vehicles abandoned their posts with alacrity as a volley of missiles, thrown without any apparent hope of reaching their target, rattled and ricocheted off their roofs.

The police battalion moved steadily and purposefully forward, and reinforcements could be seen advancing in every side street. Outnumbered and out-organized, at any rate for the moment, the first and most excitable of the protesters fell back; some were arrested and dragged off, a few diehards engaged in undignified and unsuccessful fisticuffs with individual police officers. The first wave had been beaten off, but if the sergeant's estimate of the crowd's size were anything like correct, Bill guessed it could only be a holding operation.

Still feeling a little giddy, and his arm now throbbing dully, he continued along Royal Mint Street. The atmosphere as he approached Tower Bridge changed almost palpably. In Cable Street there had been frustration and fury. Here there was discipline and arrogance and implacable resolve. Three thousand or so Blackshirts were now assembled, and almost as many spectators and supporters, but the gathering was quiet. There seemed to be some kind of parade or inspection going on to the martial beat of a drum. Bill pushed his way through the throng, and round to one side so that he could look along the ranks of men who stood so smartly to attention. Momentarily he glimpsed the coldly handsome face of the leader inspecting his troops. All he had to do was show up, thought Bill, and the opposition was fatally tempted into an affray. He could abide in every particular by the letter, if not the spirit, of the law, and then march away smelling of roses, leaving a chaos of damage and injury behind him.

The man standing next to Bill must have misconstrued his reflective expression, for he nudged him and said: 'Does you good to look at them, doesn't it?'

Bill turned to him. He was a neat, dapper little man, the sort you'd see behind the counter at a bank.

'Does it?' asked Bill.

'Men with a bit of pride, a bit of spit and polish. Men who care about their country and want to see Britain great again.' Bill had the impression he was listening to a litany carefully learned from fascist literature. 'It gets me here,' said the little man, thumping his chest in the general area of his heart.

Bill moved away, pushing his way through the crowd, deciding to look elsewhere for his story.

These days Primmy generally enjoyed her outing to church on off-duty Sundays. She had never in the past been a great devotee of organized religion, taking the view that God had a pretty funny way of showing that all men were equal in his sight. But now she liked the feeling of being part of this, her adopted community. And she enjoyed the walk to and from church, with its opportunity to watch less Godly East-Enders going about their business. She saw the little old men trundling their barrel organs away from the local depot, with the odd curly-tailed dog or chattering monkey in attendance; the Indian toffee-seller with his cardboard box tray slung around his neck; 'Seppi, the Italian ice-cream man, trailing a wake of children behind his barrow, his pork-pie hat at a Runyonesque angle on the back of his head; and the commonest sight on a Sunday morning, the hand-pushed police ambulance bearing away drunks to the local nick.

But today she hadn't even made it as far as the church. Globe Road was only the hinterland of the riot, but it was seething with people, and crowds filled Primmy with panic. There was an unpredictability about a crowd, especially one that was predominantly male, a bubbling potential for violence which reminded her of her father. She recalled all too vividly the queerness of his behaviour late on Friday nights, a terrifying mixture of mawkishness and cruelty, quite unlike his real self. Those nights had taught her the value of control. Whatever you did with your life it had to be your own conscious, rational decision and carried out in the perfect knowledge that it was your responsibility. Today, out on the streets, she saw men and youths borne along on a tide of mad, undirected anger.

When she reached the corner, and had just decided that she must go back, she spotted some lads arguing vociferously, tugging and swiping at one another. They were very young, eleven and twelve year olds, and when she saw that one of their number was dabbing at a large cut on his forehead, Primmy decided to intervene. She went over to them and caught the nearest boy by his shirt sleeve.

He rounded on her. 'Hey! Wotcher doing? Piss off!'

'Less of the language, young man. Now what are you boys up to? What's the matter here?'

Impressed by her naturally authoritative tone, they fell back and she went up to the boy with the cut head. 'How did you do this?'

'Mind yer own business,' growled Tony.

'It is my business, I'm a nurse.'

'Oh yeah?'

'Yes. Tell me how you did it.'

' 'Orse kicked me.'

'Pardon?'

'Bleedin' 'orse kicked me!'

'I see.' Primmy examined the cut. 'That's what you get for getting under horses' feet. Your elders aren't always your betters, you know, there are some around today you'd do better not to copy.'

'What about 'is 'ead miss?' asked another of the boys, genuinely disturbed by the sight of so much blood.

'He'll live. You get him round to the Institute, it'll be quieter over there, and they'll patch him up. Do you know it?'

They mumbled and grumbled, yes they did.

'Go on then, quick sharp! And then cut along home, the lot of you!'

They were rebellious, but frightened too. And Tony looked terrible with his bluey-white face all sticky with half-dried blood. So they moved away, contenting themselves with glaring over their shoulders at Primmy as they went.

When Bill reached the Ross Institute he at once saw signs that the ripples from the Cable Street affray had reached this far. There was coloured glass on the pavement from one of the chapel windows, and the main doors stood open, allowing the sound of a noisy confrontation to spill into the street.

As he approached, two or three boys backed out of the doorway nervously, almost bumping into him, clearly anxious to put some distance between themselves and whatever altercation was being conducted *con brio* inside.

'Steady!'

'Sorry, guv . . .'

'What's going on – trouble from Cable Street?'

'No, nothing like that.'

The lad seemed almost surprised at his suggestion. Bill indicated the broken glass. 'But there has been trouble.'

'Yeah, most likely.'

With this the boys scuttled off. From half a mile away behind him the noise of the fracas suddenly swelled, and there was the tinny braying of a voice through a megaphone and the shrill whinnying of horses. Things were getting no better, then, and he was suffering considerable pain from his elbow, which was swollen and throbbing. He was damp and dirty from his fall in Cable Street and he could feel the dried blood on his forehead. He must look like a prime suspect, he reflected ruefully, any eager young bobby worth his salt would snap him up as soon as look at him. He decided to kill two birds with one stone and nip into the Institute, where he might at any rate unearth some interesting inside views and perhaps get a cup of tea and a sticking plaster on the side.

There was still a tremendous racket going on in the hall, and when Bill first entered he couldn't make out, in the sudden gloom, who the combatants were. Then one of them, a young woman, suddenly came towards him, clearly not seeing him, one long arm extended, pointing towards the street. He had an impression of a white face, blazing eyes and a wild mop of red hair. A familiar voice yelled: 'Would you please get out of here, I've had about as much as I can take!'

He thought at first she was shouting at him, but as his eyes grew accustomed to the dimness he saw the others. There was a dark-haired young man, with a cold, contemptuous appearance, a miserable, sick-looking boy holding a wad of bloody cotton wool to his head and a skinny, wild-haired chap in a dog-collar, carrying a dustpan and brush. They presented such an odd picture that Bill was at a loss to think what they might be arguing about. The nature of the dispute was clearly personal rather than political. He edged further in and listened.

'I just wish you do-gooders would mind your own business, instead of fart-arsing around with other people's!' snarled the young man.

'And I wish you'd taken better care of your young brother in the first place so that he didn't get mixed up with police horses! You've got a nerve sailing in here now when we're picking up the pieces and telling us not to interfere!'

'I just want to get him home where he belongs. Is that too much to ask?'

'It is when I'm just in the middle of trying to patch him up – do you want him to pass out cold in the street?' Kate made a theatrical gesture in the direction of the boy, who looked as if he might pre-empt her threat by fainting right then and there.

The wispy cleric intervened. 'Come now one and all, it's the boy's welfare we're concerned with, we're all on the same side here . . .' He took Tony's elbow and helped him to sit down on a bench.

'Well you could've damn well fooled me!' snapped Kate. Turning, she suddenly spotted Bill. 'And what in heaven's name are you doing here, this is not a casualty department, you know! Oh, it's you,' she added shortly as if she'd seen him five minutes ago. She glared at him. 'Make yourself useful and chuck him out, would you?'

Bill looked over her shoulder at the young man, then back at her. 'Why don't you let the boy go?'

'What!' She was so incredulous her voice rose to a squeak. 'Oh, get out of my way!'

She went back to Tony. 'Come with me.'

Bill pushed himself off the wall and arrested Ernest just as he was, apparently, going to leap on Kate and throttle her. 'Tell me — sorry, Bill Maguire, *Herald* — do you live round here?'

'Yes, I do.'

'Could you spare me five minutes, I'm trying to form a picture of the background to all this.'

The young man hesitated, but Bill knew vanity when he saw it. 'Okay.'

Bill turned to Bobby Hollis, saying, 'Is there somewhere we could talk?'

Bobby was grateful. 'Chapel might be best, the refectory's packed out with locals.'

'Perhaps I could have a word with a few of them later . . . ?'

'Of course, anything! Diabolical business.'

Later that morning, in Bobby's office, they heard on the wireless that Sir Oswald Moseley had agreed to call off his march in response to a plea from Sir Philip Game, and had paraded west instead, along the Embankment.

'There's a relief,' was Bobby's comment.

Bill left, reasonably satisfied, having obtained story, tea and sticking plaster, and in the knowledge that he had averted a further confrontation between Kate and Ernest.

He met her in the corridor on his way out. She wore a greasy overall and was carrying a large enamel dish containing shepherd's pie.

'Hallo again,' he said, casually, taking his tone from her earlier one, 'is the boy recovered now?'

'Oh yes,' she said, 'nothing I couldn't patch up — given the chance.'

He was intrigued as always by her, and loath to move on. 'Good. Well —' he nodded at the shepherd's pie — 'I'd better let you get on. Things seem to have quietened down now.'

Another woman, passing by, smiled at both of them and relieved Kate of the dish.

'Thanks.' She wiped her hands on the overall. 'I might as well see you out. By the way, are you all right?'

He touched the sticking plaster on his face. 'This is nothing, but I do have an extremely sore elbow — not my drinking arm, fortunately, so I shall be able to take medicinal measures almost at once.'

As he had hoped, for it was not her sympathy he sought, but her touch, she reached out and took his arm at the wrist and elbow, flexing and bending it firmly but gently, with an air of expert concentration. He was excited by the feel of her hands, but he still winced.

She glanced up at him. 'That hurts?'

'Yes!'

'I don't think anything's broken, but you should really take yourself up the infirmary and get it looked at.'

'If nothing's broken it'll sort itself out, I can't be bothered.'

'Typical,' she said shortly.

At the door, when they stopped to say good-bye, she added, equally tersely, 'I haven't said thank you, have I?'

'For what?'

'For getting the brother off my back.'

Bill made a gesture of dismissal. 'Self-interest. I came in here to get a story, and I got one.'

'Oh.' She eyed him. He thought, though perhaps it was wishful thinking, that she was disappointed. 'Fine.'

He held out his hand. 'Good-bye again, then. Or perhaps I should say *auf wiedersehen*, since we seem destined to bump into each other.'

She took his hand and shook it firmly. 'We certainly shall now. I think you know my aunt, Dulcie Tennant.'

'Good God!' Bill laughed out loud. 'Of course – she said her niece was working at a settlement, her niece called Kate – but I never put two and two together.'

She shrugged. 'Why should you? But of course when she mentioned you I knew at once who you were.' She was a shade waspish.

'Someone who frequents seamy clubs . . .'

Now she grinned, and it was like the sun breaking through. 'Sorry about that, but I did enjoy it.'

'And I enjoyed it – enjoyed deserving it, I mean.'

Suddenly more relaxed, she stepped out into the street, pushing her hands into her hair and lifting her face to the sun, eyes closed.

'I'll see you soon then,' he said, admiring her as she stood there.

'Yes!' She seemed to come back to earth. 'And take care of that elbow.'

'I'll do my best.'

As he walked away, Bill was suddenly aware of cross-currents in his life which had not been there before, and which might presage storms.

The weekend of 11 October was not one on which Kate had to be at the Ross, and for once she was glad to be away from it. The aftermath of the previous Sunday's unrest had spread a stain over the intervening week, with the locals in a volatile, frightened mood, and damage to be repaired, and endless stories to be listened to. Quite a few of Bobby's lads had presented a battered, hangdog appearance and the elderly had been too scared to leave their homes for their usual get-togethers at the Institute and had to be visited. She had only spoken to Dulcie on the phone, and her aunt had sounded rather listless and out of sorts, not as intrigued as she might have been by Kate's meeting with Bill.

All in all, by Friday Kate was glad that this weekend had been set aside for a visit to the Kingsleys at Long Lake.

*

She went down to Joe's school by train, and the pair of them were picked up from there in Robert Kingsley's chauffeur-driven Bentley.

The Saturday was given over to much walking round the house and grounds, the visiting of old haunts and the rooting-out of numerous old (and obviously treasured) possessions of Jack's, many of which were pressed on Joe. On the Sunday morning there was church, and a sherry party at which the grandchildren were ceremoniously presented to friends and neighbours, mostly of a great age and rather hard of hearing. But on Sunday afternoon Kate got the opportunity she had been waiting for. Joe had been offered a driving lesson by Sumpter, the chauffeur, the Kingsleys were comatose after the pre-prandial sherry, and Kate announced that she would go for a bike ride. Sumpter provided her with an ordnance survey map and an ancient but well-maintained black bike from the garage and she set off. She reckoned her objective was about five miles away, just right for an afternoon's excursion with a bit of exploring the other end, and home by five.

Kate hadn't ridden a bike since her 'Carrots' Kingsley days at the Sacred Heart Convent in Nairobi, but after a certain amount of initial wobbling and swerving she began to enjoy herself. It was delightful to be footloose, fancy-free and alone in the countryside and for the first time she could see around her the soft, chequered green landscape, in all its textured variety, that Thea missed so keenly. The Weald of Kent was hazy and golden, the smoke of bonfires trickling upward from autumn gardens, tractors trudging over the plough with a sparkling wake of gulls, the hedges beginning to show their bones, but bright with hips and haws. Kate pedalled vigorously, feeling the sharp fresh air washing her face like spring water. At one point, she paused to catch her breath on the long up-hill slog, she saw a hunt streaming across open country, hounds singing like bells, horses rippling over a grassy bank, the pink of the huntsmen brilliant in the soft afternoon light. She stood still astride the bike, with one foot braced against a gate, to watch as the riders galloped along the valley and up across the hillface opposite with the horn sounding in the still air. She had seen hunts organized by the Happy Valley set at home, all stirrup cups and hairnets in the broiling heat, and thought them ludicrous affairs. Not until now, in this place, had she felt their atavistic magic.

As she began the descent, she saw her objective, rising above its protective cloak of trees in the valley below. She had not told the Kingsleys she was going to Chilverton House because she sensed a reticence on the subject, that the house represented 'old, unhappy, far-off things, and battles long ago'. But just the same she had wanted to come, for Thea's sake. She wanted to write and say '. . . went over to Chilverton House and it was just the way you described it', that would be a sort of present she could give.

And it was, just as Thea had described it. Its chimneys rose solid and straight and somehow stern like a group of formidable elderly relatives. Kate felt a little involuntary quickening of excitement as the wheels hummed down the hill; she let out a whoop as she sped along and her hair was whipped back from her face.

Checking, she squeezed the brake lever and felt the tyres respond, so she released it again and allowed the bike to gather speed and momentum. The house disappeared from view as she came down below the level of the trees but the hedge on her left became a high wall and she braked again. To her horror there was no response, she was travelling at tremendous speed and quite unable to stop. About fifteen yards in front of her there appeared a couple of tall brick gateposts topped by stone pineapples, and flanked by a large sign: CHILVERTON HOUSE NURSING HOME.

Kate squeezed the brake again – nothing. Wildly she stuck out her left arm and turned between the gateposts, praying fervently that there was nothing coming in the opposite direction. There wasn't, but the bicycle wheels skidded on the gravel of the drive and shot sideways, depositing her painfully on the ground, the tilted handlebars gouging her leg, the pedals spinning gently.

'Damn and blast.' She struggled to her feet, rubbing her leg and righting the bike, which didn't seem to be damaged. Then she saw that the chain had been dislodged. 'Oh –!' She shook her head in frustration, then pushed the machine a little further up the drive and propped it against a tree trunk. She was on the incoming curve of a horseshoe, on the apex of which was Chilverton House's main entrance, with its rounded shallow steps and ornate stone-canopied porch. Set symmetrically around the front door like numerals on a clock face, long windows glinted in the afternoon sun. A figure in a light blue nurse's uniform appeared momentarily in the stair window just above the door, but didn't pause to look out.

Kate set about reinstating the chain. A large gleaming car swept past at speed, narrowly missing her and spraying up gravel, and then another, not quite so flashy. But she was concentrating on her task and it was a moment or two before she noticed that the second car had parked just beyond her and its driver was standing in her light. It was this added annoyance which made her look up, with obvious exasperation.

'Need a hand?'

'No thanks, but if you could just –'

'Sorry.'

As the dark silhouette moved to one side and crouched down next to her she saw a young man with an eager, amiable expression. Just the sort of expression she could have done without, right at that moment. 'You'll be filthy,' he remarked. 'Let me.'

'Then *you'll* be filthy.'

'Gentleman's prerogative.'

She ignored this sally as beneath her and continued with the chain while he watched. She found his continued unasked for attendance irritating but she would not be put off by it.

After another couple of minutes she sat back on her heels. 'That's that, I think.'

'Bravo. Here, have a hanky.'

She glanced at her oil-stained fingers, and at the pristine acreage of white cotton which he held out. 'I couldn't.'

'Please, you must. It's the least I can do.'

Thinking that to comply might be to get rid of him she wiped her hands and handed back the now sadly-blackened handkerchief, saying, 'Thanks.'

They got to their feet, Kate wincing and rubbing her thigh. Thank God she'd been wearing trousers, she'd have a lump tomorrow.

'Come off did you?' enquired the young man. 'Are you all right?'

'It was my own stupid fault, I was going far too fast down the hill and the brakes went on me.'

He nodded sympathetically. 'Bad luck. Were you on your way to visit someone here?'

'No.' She realized she was probably being offensively monosyllabic, but to explain further might be to encourage him.

'My mother's in here now,' he said chattily. 'She broke her hip.'

'I'm sorry to hear that,' muttered Kate. 'Don't let me keep you from her.'

'No hurry.' Another car swooshed past and he hunched his shoulders in exaggerated fear. 'I think we're dicing with death standing here. Do you want to put your bike in the shed? Sunday, you see, everyone's doing their duty by their grannies.'

Taking charge he began pushing her bicycle round the drive, and took it beneath a tall arch into what she saw must have been the stableyard. A lean-to cycle shed had been erected against one wall. On the other side of the arch was an old green pump, encrusted with rust. She was interested in spite of herself.

'No horses here now, I suppose,' she said, almost to herself, but he at once answered.

'Not for years, I shouldn't think. By the way, I never did catch the reason for your visit.'

'I didn't say.'

'Ask a silly question.' He was unfailingly pleasant. She felt suddenly ashamed of her ungraciousness in the face of his continued kindness and civility. She also saw, for the first time, that he had a charming, mobile face, thin and unlined, with particularly large bright eyes. These eyes, along with the wide smile which seemed his natural expression, and the rather shaggy straight fair hair which flopped on to his forehead, gave him the air of a delightful pedigree dog. Kate reminded herself that he had been quite unusually solicitous, and that she had been surly to a degree.

'I'm nosey-parkering,' she said, in a more agreeable tone. 'This used to be my foster mother's family home when she was a girl, so I thought I'd come and take a look on her behalf. She lives in Kenya now, she'd like to hear that I'd been.'

'She was a Tennant, was she?'

Kate looked at him in surprise. 'How on earth did you know that?'

'We've lived in the Ewehurst area for years. My mother's a great one for good works and one of her charitable outlets was an old bird called Mrs Maxwell, who was Ralph Tennant's sister. Dead now of course.'

'That would be Great Aunt Sophie. I never met her myself — I never met any of them until recently.'

He leaned an elbow on the rusty arm of the pump. He had what Kate now thought an attractive air of wanting to do nothing but talk to her all afternoon.

'You didn't miss much in her case,' he said. 'She was a crusty old girl, as cross as two sticks and not a good word to say for her brother. She claimed he threw her out.'

'Well . . .' Kate reflected. 'It wouldn't surprise me.'

'No indeed. Bit of a lad your grandfather, by all accounts.'

Kate was still unable to let this pass. 'Not my *real* grandfather.'

He either had not heard or was uninterested. 'Look, I've got an idea. I know the layout quite well. Why don't I just nip in and have a word with matron, you hang on here, and then I can show you round a bit.'

'What about your mother?'

'She's hardly going to go anywhere, is she? I've been at a different time every day since I've been on leave, so I'm not expected. Yes?'

'I mustn't be too long, I've got five miles to cycle back.'

'A potted tour let it be, then. Don't go away.'

He ran across the drive and in at the front door, a tall, thin, rangy figure in a frayed jumper, baggy cords and tennis shoes. On leave from what?

After a couple of minutes he re-emerged, bounding across to her with his right hand extended. 'By the way, how do you do, I'm Lawrence Drake.'

'Kate Kingsley, hallo.'

'This way.'

'On leave from what?' she asked, following him out of the stableyard and round the side of the house.

'Regular army.'

She was surprised, because she had taken him for a student, hardly more than a schoolboy, certainly no older than her. But then if he had been that young he might have been easier to snub.

'Now here before you,' he went on, 'is the back garden. My knowledge is encyclopaedic, isn't it? How would you have known that without me to tell you?' She smiled. 'Regard the terrace, the lawn, the magnificent rhododendrons. And down the middle the elm walk, a notable feature.'

A handsome double colonnade of tall elms led away from the far side of the lawn. The ground on either side of the elm walk was rather more rough, as if it had once been open park, or grazing land. Away to the north of the garden rose the steep wooded hill down which she had so rashly sped half an hour ago.

'Madam, will you walk?'

'Why not?'

They walked across the moss-covered terrace with its tubs of well-ordered but now dying geraniums and petunias, and on to the lawn where one or two bath chairs stood, their occupants well wrapped up against the early autumn chill. Lawrence raised a hand to the nearest of them. 'Afternoon, sir!'

They walked down between the trees, layer upon layer of yellowing leaves rising on either side of them like a mackerel sky. A rabbit darted out of the long grass and zig-zagged away in front of them, its white scut bobbing, before disappearing again. When Kate glanced back over her shoulder at the house it was as though a thin veil had dropped in front of it to conceal its present role as a nursing home. It looked like a family home, and the nurse walking across the terrace like an Edwardian tweeny maid, pert in her uniform.

Lawrence had not turned, but he said, as if reading her thoughts, 'You can picture them all with their cucumber sandwiches and croquet mallets, can't you?'

'Yes, you can.'

He strode on. He had a long, purposeful stride with a slight bounce in it, and now that she knew what he did she could picture him in uniform with a swagger stick beneath his arm. She could also imagine that he would be spontaneously liked and respected.

'There's a lychgate at the bottom here,' he was saying now, 'and a path from there across the field to the parish church. I suppose in the old days it was some kind of manorial right – the private path to God of the rich and well-born.'

She glanced at him. 'Do I detect a note of rancour?'

'Who me?' He beamed at her. His smile was so infectious that she smiled back as though its brilliance were reflected on her face. They came to the gate, and leaned on it, surveying the outlook. Before them the ground fell away in a tussocky meadow, rough with molehills and thistles. In one corner stood a tractor with a tarpaulin over it. In the centre of the field the grass grew slightly thinner, marking some scar on the earth.

'Was there a cottage there?' She pointed.

He shook his head. 'I believe that's where they had the bonfire on Armistice night.'

'Heavens.' She stared respectfully. 'It must have been some bonfire.'

On the far side of the field a five-barred gate marked the boundary between it and the churchyard. The stubby Norman tower with its needle of flagpole looked trim, but the churchyard was a tangle of yellowing grass, so that the gravestones appeared to be drowning.

Lawrence put his hand on the gate. 'Shall we?'

She demurred. 'I don't know . . . I haven't really the time.' She was torn. She was intrigued in spite of herself, she did want to go on, to explore the overgrown graveyard and go into the echoey hush of the little church. But she had to get back, too, or Joe would be late.

He was sensitive to her dilemma. 'I'll tell you what. Let's go down and take a look, then I can run you home. We can tie your bike on the roof of the barouche.'

'That is kind. But your mother –'

'Will still be here when I get back. And she's an incorrigible gossip, she'll enjoy hearing about you'

'Well – thanks.'

They went through the gate and down across the field, picking their way between the spiny thistles. She stopped for a moment in the circle where the bonfire had been, and shivered. In the churchyard she began at once to examine the graves, parting the long grass and crouching to decipher writing blurred by weather and lichen. As before he joined her, squatting down at her shoulder, peering with every evidence of keen interest at the inscriptions.

'Looking for anything special?'

'Oh – things for my foster mother. I think her mother's buried here, that would be Venetia Tennant. And I think Thea's cousin Maurice is here too, he was a conscientious objector during the war –'

She stopped abruptly, she who was not normally careful about her effect on others, in case she had offended him. But he was already proceeding with the search, and his only comment was, 'Brave chap.'

'He was the son of your crusty old Mrs Maxwell.'

'No wonder she never mentioned him. I didn't know she had a son.'

They soon found the two graves. Venetia's had been kept tidy, and the small stone vase at the foot of the plot contained some rosehips and copper beech.

' "Beloved wife and companion of Ralph",' Lawrence read aloud.

'It sounds so desperately pious,' said Kate, 'and he's not at all a pious old man.'

'My mother usually characterizes him as a kind of stylish ruffian. She didn't know him personally, of course, but she must have seen him about and I suspect he fluttered her heart a bit.'

'I must tell him, he'd love that.'

Maurice's grave was neglected. Kate remembered Thea's photograph of the shy, bespectacled young man, and her book of poems so lovingly inscribed, and was indignant. She began to tear away the dandelions and ground elder that covered the grave. Lawrence helped her and in a few minutes they had effected a considerable improvement. It was just a simple grassy mound with a stocky stone cross at the head. On the cross were the words: 'There's no discouragement, shall make him once relent'.

Lawrence sang: 'His first, avowed intent, to be a pilgrim!' The sound of his clear, light tenor voice hung in the still air.

'I don't like to think of it being overgrown like that,' said

Kate, in a voice that was sharp and angry because she had felt perilously emotional. 'Thea would hate it.'

'Don't worry.' He put his hand on her arm, and it was extraordinarily warm, as though the blood coursed more quickly in his veins than other people's. 'I'll ask the churchwarden about it if you like.'

'Would you? That would be kind. I'd like to be able to write and tell her that everything was in good order.'

'Of course.'

By tacit, mutual consent they did not go into the church but stood there in reflective silence for a moment before starting back the way they had come. It was becoming cooler and Kate folded her arms tightly as she walked. Lawrence talked, and pointed, as they went up the elm walk.

'That bottom left-hand part of the house was destroyed by fire and then rebuilt. Some mental lad that Ralph Tennant took in after his wife died, apparently – just put a match to the place, talk about biting the hand. Then I believe the dining-room and library were on the right as we look at it, and the long window in the middle is on the staircase. It must have been an impressive outfit in its heyday.'

'Yes.' She was suddenly tired. 'It's very decent of you to have spared me all this time.'

'Nonsense. I've enjoyed it, you don't know how much.'

'I really don't think I should let you give me this lift –'

He raised a hand and silenced her. 'Lifts, stranded ladies for the use of, a speciality.'

They continued in silence. As they drew near the house it seemed deserted, for the elderly patients had been wheeled in off the lawn and the low sunlight striking on the windows prevented them from seeing any movement inside. Kate felt a violent and unexpected surge of familiarity with this place. It was almost as if she had walked up this path before; as if, were she to open a door and go in, she would know her way about, and find people that she knew sitting by a fire. There was a brackish stain of woodsmoke in the cold air from some nearby bonfire and she could hear horses – perhaps returning from the hunt – clattering down the lane towards the village.

She shook her head. 'It's funny,' she said, 'I think Thea's

talked about this place so often it feels as though I've been here before.'

'I know what you mean. It must be eery for you. And how do you greet it – as a friend or an enemy?'

She thought that that was fanciful of him, but not unreasonably so. 'Certainly not as an enemy. But there is something suffocating about these big old English houses. They're so *definite*. If you ask me to make it a person I'd call it a kind of starchy, formidable aunt.' She thought of Dulcie and laughed. 'Actually I do have an aunt and she's neither of those things.'

Back in the drive he took a coil of rope from the boot of the battered Morris and together they hoisted her bike aloft and lashed it down as best they could. When the juddering engine started up the rattling of the bike was like a hailstorm on the roof. What with this and the trouble the Morris had getting up the hill, conversation was virtually impossible. Kate confined herself to wondering whether she would have to invite him in at Long Lake. A drink was the very least she owed him, but she did not know what her grandparents would make of her returning with a strange young man on her very first solo sortie from their house. They would probably take a very dim view of such forwardness.

However, the issue was decided for her when they reached the gateway to Long Lake, for Joe and Sumpter, with Joe at the wheel, were advancing down the drive at a speed that was less that judicious considering the age of the car – an old Austin of Jack's – and Joe's inexperience. Lawrence, having just braked, reversed hastily.

'My God, what's that?'

She laughed. 'I'm sorry, it's my young brother having a driving lesson.'

'Say no more. I suggest you get out here to avoid a brush with death, and cycle up to the house, but be careful!'

'I will.'

Together they unlashed the bike from the roof. While they did this the Austin passed them in a downhill direction.

Lawrence looked after it. 'Can he turn corners?'

'I don't suppose so.'

'They'll just drive on till he drops off the edge at Dover.'

'I expect they're going to the crossroads where he can do a U-turn.'

Lawrence closed his eyes. 'U-turn at a crossroads . . . Lord save us.'

'Sumpter knows what he's doing.'

'He'll need to.'

'Won't you come up for a drink or something?'

'No thanks. Mother, remember.'

'Yes, of course.'

There was a pause, which was very slightly awkward, because Kate knew that all she had to do was go. But he cast a different light on this pause by saying reflectively, as though he had been pondering the matter: 'I could take a night in London before I go back next Sunday. Shall we do something?'

It never occurred to her to say anything other than 'yes', but his face lit up with delight.

'Splendid! I'll book dinner somewhere nice and be the envy of every fellow in the place.'

She laughed, for his compliment contrived to sound both casual and wholly sincere.

'What are you laughing at?' he was laughing too.

'No one has ever said that kind of thing to me before.'

'Really? I can't imagine why not. Here –' he turned and rummaged for a moment on the shelf beneath the Morris's dashboard, emerging with a brown paper bag and a stub of pencil. 'Give me your telephone number.'

She did so, and he read it over to her before pushing it into his pocket, saying, 'I can't tell you how I shall look forward to that.'

He held out his hand. Taking it, and looking into his face, Kate realized that she felt exactly the same.

CHAPTER NINE

'Blue Moon – you saw me standing alone,
   Without a dream in my heart,
   Without a love of my own . . .'

'Blue Moon'
Lorenz Hart and Richard Rodgers, 1934

THE intervening week dragged its heels. Not that Kate was entirely happy with this new state of affairs. For the first half of the week she felt slightly disgruntled and sheepish, as though she had made some careless and indefensible blunder. Looking back on the events of Sunday afternoon, she scarcely recognized herself in them. Had she really been so easily sweet-talked by a complete stranger, had she allowed her solitary pil-grimage on Thea's behalf to be so invaded, then almost entirely orchestrated, by a bumptious young English army officer? And even more extraordinarily, had she been so flattered by his casual gallantry that she had not demurred for one instant when a second meeting was proposed? Good Lord, she had not even mentioned a diary, let alone the likelihood of its being spattered with choice engagements for the following weekend – she had just stood there with a silly smile on her face and said 'yes'! She quite seriously entertained the idea of being frosty with Lawrence when he rang, or at least postponing their next encounter on the grounds of previously overlooking prior commitments.

'Is that Kate?'
'Oh – hallo.'
'I'm looking forward to Saturday. Are you still on for that?'
'Yes, of course.'
'I've booked us a table at Bilbow's, do you know it?'
'No.'

'I'm sure you'll like it. Look I can't stop, stern daughter of the voice of God and so forth . . . I'll pick you up at, what? Seven-thirty?'

'Fine.'

'I can't wait. See you then.'

'Yes.'

' 'Bye, Kate.'

'Good-bye.'

So much for her steely resolve and haughty prevarication, Kate thought ruefully as she put down the receiver. It had taken only a few seconds, just the time it took for Lawrence to utter his first three words, for her to be reduced, or exalted, to a state of beaming, biddable acquiescence. Only now did she remember his presumption in having already booked a table – but then how was he to know she had planned a base change of tactics? The fact was, she had to admit it, she wanted to go and she wanted to see Lawrence Drake again. It was not a matter of rational choice or even of will. For once in her life Kate was the slave of her emotions.

'Who was that?' This was Aubrey, who had returned from work as she was talking on the phone, and was now in the drawing-room, winding the clock on the mantelpiece.

She sauntered in and flopped down on the sofa, linking her hands behind her head. 'Someone I met recently – he's invited me out to dinner on Saturday evening.'

'Really?' She sensed her uncle's keen interest, though he finished winding the clock, closed the back and replaced it in its exact position before turning to look at her. 'Who is he?'

'He's called Lawrence Drake, I met him down in Ewehurst when I cycled over there last weekend. He's in the army, but his mother lives in the village.'

'Drake . . . Drake . . .' Aubrey frowned his brow. 'Can't say the name means anything to me, but then . . . ah, Father.'

Ralph came into the room, breathing heavily from having recently negotiated the steps from the back garden. He wore a panama hat and a magnificently shapeless and threadbare beige cardigan, the front corners of which drooped almost to his knees. 'Good evening to you both.' With a great gusty exhalation of breath he lowered himself into his chair, removed the hat and began to fan himself with it.

'Father,' said Aubrey, 'do you remember a family named Drake, down in Ewehurst?'

'I do.'

They stared at him expectantly for a moment, and then Aubrey said, 'Only Kate has been invited out by a young man named Lawrence Drake who was brought up there, and whose mother still lives there, apparently.'

Kate smiled inwardly at this 'apparently', as though anything she might say required immediate verification from a more reliable source.

Ralph rummaged in his trouser pocket for a handkerchief and blew his nose with a series of explosive honking sounds.

'Loelia Drake I remember,' he said. 'Rather pretty young woman, but officious, always wanting to start things up and organize things. Didn't know her socially though,' he added, with an old man's disregard for how this might sound.

'I expect that was Lawrence's mother,' said Kate, but did not add that this pretty, officious woman with whom the Tennants had not mixed socially was at present convalescing in their old house.

From this point on, Kate little doubted that she would enjoy herself. On Friday she claimed a rare half-day off and went up to the West End to buy herself a dress. She had arranged to meet Dulcie for tea at Fortnum's — the venue had become something of an affectionate joke to both of them since it was the site of their first meeting — there to show off her purchase, but in the end she failed utterly to find anything to her taste or that suited her. She concluded that she must be a freak — too thin, too tall, oddly coloured, hard to please.

In this frame of mind she was hardly delighted to find Bill Maguire sitting at the white-clothed table with her aunt, smoking as usual, a rolled up copy of the *Herald* sticking out of his jacket pocket, tie askew. Why can't he smarten himself up? was her reaction as she sat down between them, and exchanged a kiss with Dulcie.

'Hope you don't mind me tagging along,' he said, with a grin, squinting at her over his cigarette in that uniquely maddening way he had, as though her secret pretensions and aspirations were an open book to him.

'No, why should I?' she replied, as offhandedly as she could without hurting Dulcie's feelings.

'Well,' said Dulcie, 'let's see — what did you get?'

'Nothing. It was awful, a complete waste of time, I couldn't find a thing I liked, or that liked me.'

'Oh dear, what a *pity*!' cried Dulcie. 'If you'd waited till tomorrow I could have come with you. I'm awfully good at spending other people's money.'

Kate shrugged. 'Can't be helped.'

The waitress arrived with tea, cakes and small sandwiches garnished with florets of parsley.

'The cup that cheers!' announced Bill. 'Shall I be mother while you two sort out the dress problem?' There was something satirical in his whole demeanour which annoyed and unsettled Kate. She wished he would be more *appropriate*.

'Was it for something special?' asked Dulcie.

'Oh, I'm going out tomorrow night — no, not really.' Suddenly, with Bill there, she did not feel inclined to share her pleasant feelings of anticipation.

Bill poured and distributed tea, helped himself to a tomato sandwich and popped it in his mouth whole, munching with relish, swallowing, and taking another one within a matter of seconds.

'Thanks for enquiring, my arm is better,' he said.

'I'm glad to hear it.'

'I was horrified to hear you'd been down at the settlement with that dreadful riot raging all round,' said Dulcie. 'And on a Sunday — surely they can't need you on a Sunday.'

'We're open seven days a week,' replied Kate, 'and I do one Sunday in three. It was my Sunday on. Anyway we had very little trouble, it was mainly a question of mopping up the casualties.'

'Yes,' agreed Bill, 'and she does it so nicely.'

The look Kate gave him must have told him he'd been facetious enough, for he now abruptly and easily altered his manner and became the amiable host, treating Kate with a sort of brotherly niceness entirely suited to the young female relative of one's lover. For some reason Kate found this equally infuriating, but realized she was being perverse, and put this down to the frustrations of the abortive shopping expedition.

Half an hour later the three of them emerged into Piccadilly, and Bill suggested: 'Why don't we go and take something a little more stimulating at the Ritz?' He put his arm round Dulcie, but looked at Kate. 'What do you say?'

Kate shook her head firmly. 'I won't, thanks very much. It's Friday night and the trains will be awful, I must be on my way.'

'You know I'd love to, Bill,' said Dulcie, looking up at him almost pleadingly, 'but I did tell you I had something on this evening.'

He looked at Dulcie now, for the first time properly, Kate saw, as if deliberately re-focusing his attention, and gave her a quick, gentle kiss.

'Yes, you did. Only trying.' His eyes rested, with rueful tenderness on Dulcie's face. How he must hate Rex, Kate thought, what a stupid, cruel, hopeless situation. Dulcie's expression was so full of love, and anxiety, that Kate could look no longer. She felt that she was witnessing her aunt in a state of almost unbearable vulnerability.

'I'll be off, then,' she announced stiffly. 'Thanks for tea, I'll see you soon.'

Because Dulcie still stood in the circle of Bill's arm she did not, as she would usually have done, kiss her, but simply raised her hand in an awkward little wave.

'Just one thing — Kate!' Bill's voice stopped her as she began to walk away.

'Yes?'

'You couldn't do better than that dress you wore in Berlin — that sort of orange, slippery number. You were an absolute knock-out in that.'

There was nothing jokey, or sly, in his tone, but something about this remark, coming from Bill, who stood with Dulcie, and upon whom Dulcie still gazed with such obvious and intense love, threw Kate into confusion. Something was wrong, and though she could neither pinpoint nor define it she sensed that she herself was at least partly the cause, and that she must go.

'Oh that,' she growled. 'I suppose I might. It doesn't matter anyway.'

*

'I have to tell you, Kate,' said Lawrence, 'that you look absolutely terrific. That is the most lovely dress.'

'Thank you. It's quite old, actually.'

'I daresay, but then, you've probably kept it for ages and worn it a lot because you like it. Because it's so absolutely you.'

They were sitting in Bilbow's restaurant, over coffee, and Kate had rarely been happier. From the moment Lawrence had picked her up at Mapleton Road – discreetly but discernibly 'sirring' Ralph, and listening with intelligent attention to Aubrey's dissertation on the problems of British industry – he had made it plain that her pleasure was his main concern and wish. Without in the least affecting the manners of a lady's man he had charmed her to pieces. His gift to her at the start of the evening, a nicety which she had never expected and of which she was not a little suspicious, turned out to be a cutting taken from the passion flower at Chilverton House – 'don't worry, I asked first' – planted in an attractive terracotta pot.

'I hope you won't mind my giving this to Kate,' he had said, addressing both Ralph and Aubrey, but chiefly the former. 'Only I know how interested she is in the old house, and she might plant it here, in your garden. I could get you more if you like.'

'Well. I don't know. Have to see.' Ralph was gruff, ambushed by emotion.

Aubrey stepped in. 'It's a kind thought. And Kate's our horticultural expert, anyway.'

'We can over-winter it in the conservatory,' Kate said, gazing down at the brave little green shoot. 'I think it's a lovely idea.'

He had quite simply not put a foot wrong, and she had found herself carried along on a warm tide of beneficence, blossoming in the light of his interest and admiration, and leaning towards that light, pulled by an instinctive natural attraction which she was powerless to counteract even had she wanted to.

Situated in the V between Long Acre and Monmouth Street, Bilbow's had turned out to be not, as she had once or twice feared, a terrifically smart night spot patronized by off-duty officers and their debutante girlfriends, but a noisy, homely restaurant, with its own tiny dance floor and band, and a bohemian ambience; men playing chess at a table in the corner, people talking animatedly not just with their immediate companions but with friends and acquaintances at other tables, so that there was an agreeable hubbub of general conversation and laughter. Of the Bilbow's patrons, a smattering were dressed up to the nines, obviously slumming it for an American cocktail before a night on the town; most were dressed for comfort rather than for show; and a few were scruffy as only the supremely confident, or creative, can be. This cross-section meant that Kate — in her orange, slippery number — felt that she had made a felicitous choice. Or had it made for her.

During the meal — which was domestic French, aromatic, richly textured, plentiful and delicious — their talk consisted mainly of the mutual exchange of information concerning themselves. Nothing intimate or revealing was disclosed, each was painting in the background, with broad strokes, against which the personal and revealing portrait would later be placed. Lawrence said his father had been a flier, shot down in the last year of the war when he himself had been a prep school boy of ten. Yes, he remembered him with perfect clarity but the loss, so cataclysmic at the time, was too long ago now to be more than a memory. He had always wanted to go into the army, and had entered Sandhurst straight after school. He was now a captain, and for the past week had been on leave from camp near Salisbury. He spoke of 'soldiering' as he called it with an enthusiasm which tinted even Kate's uninterested, and previously even somewhat hostile, view in a rosier shade. He managed to convey both a boyish romanticism, the longing for action and adventure, and a sturdy idealism — that the army protected peace rather than fostered war. And indeed it would have been hard to imagine anyone less warlike; Kate's abiding impression of Lawrence was one of benevolence and harmony, of a man whose first instinct was to think the best of the other fellow, or woman.

He laughed delightedly when she passed on to him Ralph's comments regarding his mother. 'Yes, I can see how she might appear like that. But I must tell her — she'd be awfully flattered that Ralph remembered her at all. I think they may have been rather alike. As a child it struck me she wasn't much like other boys' mothers — she tore about those lanes in Kent in a car, especially during the war, trying to get people to join things, and do things, and be practical. The one thing she couldn't stand was apathy and indifference.' He added, confidingly: 'It was probably an excellent thing that she was the way she was – or is – because I'm an only child and if I'd been left to the mercies of a smothering maternal influence after the pater died I should probably have turned out like Little Lord Fauntleroy.'

Kate laughed. 'What a thought!'

'And now . . .' he leaned back in his chair and surveyed her, 'you can tell me all about you.' Spotting the beginnings of a shrug he held up his hand to arrest it. 'And don't tell me there's nothing to tell, or that I shouldn't be interested, because I shall be the judge of that.'

'All right!' She was bright, and amenable, even quite relishing the prospect. It was the effect he had on her, this sense that she was infinitely more interesting, more *likeable* than she had ever previously imagined. 'Where shall I start?'

More coffee arrived, and was poured, and Lawrence ordered two brandies. Then he said to her, 'Wherever you like. Let's begin with what I already know, that your family once lived at Chilverton House.'

She realized there was a misunderstanding here which, for her own peace of mind, she could not allow to continue. 'They're not really my family,' she said, hastily. And immediately wondered, not for the first time, why she was so eager to disown them. She behaved as though the different blood that ran in her veins denoted some shameful dependence.

Lawrence raised his eyebrows. 'What does that mean?'

'It means I'm adopted. I've never been there – to Chilverton House – before in my life. I just know it from Thea talking about it.'

'And so?' He opened one hand in an expressive, almost Gallic gesture. 'What's the difference? I mean, do you know who your natural parents were?'

'No. They were killed in the war. I think they may have been French. I spent the first five years of my life in Paris, being brought up by a nanny. She was paid by some philanthropic lady or other, presumably a friend of my parents, but I never met her. No one really wanted to know. I was a kind of left-over.' She realized that she was voicing feelings which she had never before expressed in so many words to another person. It was a relief, in a way, but at the same time she did not want these shadows from the past to fall across the bright tranquillity of her evening with Lawrence.

'Do you want to talk about all that?' he asked, with gentle concern.

She shook her head vigorously. 'No. At least, I don't know — I don't want to spoil our evening.'

'But it has to come out some time.' He was agreeing with her, giving a voice to the other side of her dilemma.

'Yes.'

'Well then, we have all the time in the world. There'll be another day for that.'

She did not, as she might have done with anyone else, find this remark presumptuous or complacent, but comforting.

'It occurs to me, though . . . perhaps . . .' he was tentative, the very embodiment of tact. 'Perhaps one way of looking at it is that your parents chose you — you're the product, as it were of conscious, rather than natural, selection. Which must be rather delightful . . .'

She looked down at her cup. She was suddenly flooded by memories, so painfully vivid that for a moment she couldn't speak. A memory of Tanty telling her how lucky she was to have, at last, *'une vraie famille'* . . . of arriving in a lonely, foreign place where strange adults murmured about her behind her back . . . of feeling not like a person at all but like a small, featureless grey stone in the shimmering hot wilderness of Kenya.

'I'm not sure it was like that,' she said at last, quietly.

'I'm sorry.'

'Please don't tell me I'm lucky — please *don't*.' She looked up at him with a fierce, pleading expression. 'I do love my parents — Thea and Jack — and I owe them more than I can possibly repay. But that doesn't help me to know who I am. There's so much I haven't worked out, I really can't bear to be told how I should feel!'

He did not seem taken aback in the face of this outburst, but said quite matter-of-factly: 'Very well. I won't.'

He allowed a small pause, as if giving her confused

impressions time to settle, and then asked, 'And what are you doing now? I mean, how is your time taken up?'

'I work, of course!' She was amused by his careful phrasing, and by whatever picture he might have of how she 'took up her time' — petit point, perhaps? Or flower arranging? 'I work at a settlement in the East End, the Ross Institute.'

'Now that,' said Lawrence, 'sounds very much the type of thing of which my mother would wholeheartedly approve, and about which I myself know next to nothing. You'll have to tell me exactly what it is you do there, so I can picture you in your setting.'

She told him, and he shook his head admiringly. 'It sounds exhausting.'

'But *I*'m not exhausted by it,' she explained. 'What exhausts me is being shut in, or just sitting around. Or it would do if I let it. I thought I'd die when we first arrived!' Here I go again, she thought, letting it all pour out, I must be boring him. But his expression told her so plainly that she was not, that she carried on: 'I looked out of the window of that house and it was as if there was no escape, no space or light or air. I simply could not imagine what I was going to do. I came over with such high hopes — and yet here I was in this tall dark house with these two stuffy men who weren't really anything to do with me, and the rain pouring down outside — oh God it was *ghastly*!'

'It must have been.' He was not being facetious. 'But you remained there, at your grandfather's. You haven't felt tempted to move out?'

'Yes, of course I was *tempted*,' her dismissive scorn was almost comical to Lawrence. 'I was desperate! But I knew that if I had no job, some awful poky flat would be even more depressing than Mapleton Road, so I just used them, I suppose. And then when I did get the job — it was only a few weeks ago — I felt so much better about everything that the urgency seemed to wear off. Besides, Ralph is old, and not all that well now, and I enjoy doing their garden for them . . . it's a case of the devil you know.' She pulled a self-deprecating grimace. 'That sounds awful. They couldn't have been kinder, I'm fond of them. And I think they actually like having me there.'

'Astonishing. Truly astounding.' Now he was teasing her, but she didn't in the least mind. She took a gulp of her brandy.

'Well it is in its way – after all, I don't suppose they were predisposed to like me any more than I was to like them. I'm the cuckoo in the nest after all. Ralph particularly must have resented me, since Thea and he were so close.'

'Do you call him Ralph?' Lawrence asked, out of real curiosity, but also to prevent her becoming once more bogged down in questions of identity, or the lack of it.

'No. I sometimes call him Grandfather. Not often. But Joe Grandpa's him enough for two.

'Ah yes, Joe. He's at school now,' he recapped, 'and then there are your other grandparents, the ones you were staying with last weekend –'

'The Kingsleys, that's right.'

'And then I seem to remember you mentioning an aunt – a young aunt.'

'She's not all that young,' declared Kate emphatically, causing Lawrence to smile. 'But we have become good friends. She's always been the black sheep of the family, the prodigal daughter, so we're a couple of outsiders.'

'Whatever did she do?'

Kate was aware of the rattle of spilling beans, but was enjoying herself so hugely that she did nothing to check them. 'She was very beautiful, and still is, and she's got by on her looks and her wits.'

'Not so very dreadful, then, her crimes.'

'Absolutely not – it's all so stupid, because the only person to suffer because of it is Dulcie herself. She's in a kind of trap of her own making and she feels it's too late to change.'

'And is it?'

'No! I told her so – she *must* change. There is someone now, a man that she really loves, but she's so dependent on this other, awful person that she can't break free!'

Suddenly, Kate was conscious of having said too much, too loudly, and for too long. Her fine flow of confidences and opinions was suddenly stemmed by a wall of embarrassment.

'I'm going on. Sorry.'

'What for? It's all the most fascinating stuff.' He reached out and touched her shoulder very lightly with the tips of his fingers as if to reassure her of his continued interest. She smiled, sheepishly. 'And what of your followers,' he asked, 'left behind in the bush?'

She looked blank. 'My what?'

'Followers — admirers? Boyfriends?'

'Oh I see,' she sounded almost bored, as if her mind were still elsewhere. 'I don't have any.'

'Didn't,' he corrected. 'Didn't have any. And anyway I don't believe you.'

Because she was now a little discomforted by the abruptness of her own denial, she became abrasive. 'You'll have to! It's true.'

'Wait a second.' He leaned forward on the table and peered, smiling and quizzical, into her face, reading it as a palmist would a hand. 'Let me give you my version. I put it to you, Kate Kingsley, that plenty of fellows admired you, but an awful lot were scared too —'

'Oh *really* . . .!' She tossed her head.

'Don't scoff. A lot were scared, and only one or two were bold enough to make advances. But when they reached out to touch —' he stretched out his hand, just brushing her cheek with his fingers — 'Ouch!' He withdrew it sharply, as though stung. 'Prickles, a sharp and painful deflation.' He cocked his head on one side. 'Am I right?'

'Well — perhaps partly,' she admitted grudgingly. 'But you make it sound as if I was choosy, and I wasn't, I didn't have a chance to be. Hardly anyone *tried* to touch, as you put it. And I didn't care.' She lifted her chin scornfully. 'I hated those young idiots.'

'You despised them for qualities they couldn't help — their youth, their clumsiness, their inexperience, their unattractiveness. You didn't know them well enough to hate them.'

'Very well, I despised them for all that, and I frightened them off. But they couldn't have been that keen, could they, or they would have persisted? So they were feeble, too.'

This made him laugh and cover his eyes momentarily with his hand in an attitude of pity for the spurned swains of Gilgil.

'Poor chaps! Really, Kate, you overestimate the toughness of the youthful male ego. Rejection and contempt are very bitter pills indeed and it's safer either not to risk them or, once having had them rammed down one's throat, not to try again. Why do you think boys so often choose cheerful, homely, even tomboyish girls rather than beautiful, exciting, challenging ones? Because they're safer.'

'That's just a theory.'

'But you see,' he went on amiably, as though she hadn't spoken, 'you're up against sterner stuff now.'

Glancing at him, she realized it was true. She sensed beneath his boyish, charming exterior something more formidable, a confidence no less resolute for being mild-mannered. Effortlessly he had won her over and she — she scarcely recognized herself — had given up without a struggle.

She hastily mustered her small remaining store of suspicion. 'What about you?'

'What about me?'

'It's time I asked you some personal questions.'

'Ask away.'

Kate was unpractised in the arts of coquetry. She came straight to the point without regard for her own dignity. 'Tell me about your followers,' she said. 'And how old you are,' she added as an afterthought.

'I'm twenty-eight. And I like women very much, funny thing, always have done.'

She was not to be deflected. 'Yes, but do they like you?'

He laughed uproariously. He was a good laugher, full of forthright delight, people at other tables looked at him and smiled when he laughed.

'Umm . . .' he composed himself. 'Let's just say it's been possible, up till now, to overcome any resistance without causing bloodshed on either side.'

'I see.' She felt a shade crestfallen and wished now that she had not been quite so quick to admit her own lack of experience in this department. In spite of his amused and apparently guileless evasions it was plain that his social life had teemed, and probably teemed still, with pretty, lively, amenable girls.

He must have caught her expression for he added, more softly, 'That's not to say that I can't be as discerning as the next man. I know a good thing when I see it, and I'm tenacious in pursuit.'

'I'm sure you are.' She stared down into her glass, avoiding his eyes.

'Kate? Hey —' He held out his hand, and rose. 'Would you like to dance?'

'Yes. Thank you.'

The music was lilting and sweet, a foxtrot played on a tinkling piano and a crooning saxophone, the rhythmic susurration of drums playing catchily with the beat.

' "Even educated fleas do it . . ." ' hummed Lawrence, taking her in his arms and spinning her round as they stepped on to the floor. To her delight, he danced exceptionally well, so that their steps fell in together effortlessly. Kate was a natural, if an untaught dancer, but always before she had felt awkward with her partners — too tall, too dominant, ill-at-ease in the arms of some perspiring youth or young farmer whom she knew instinctively was no dancer, but whom she had out of politeness to follow as he shunted her round the perimeter of the floor. Lawrence was good enough to be free and easy, he hardly seemed to lead her at all. They were truly partners, moving as one.

It was such a lovely feeling such a pure, simple delight to dance with him, that she was quite surprised to hear his voice in her ear, saying: 'You're a wonderful dancer, Kate, as I'm sure you're aware — or is that something else they omitted to tell you?' And though she didn't answer, his hand on her back exerted the lightest pressure, inviting rather than obliging her to come closer: an invitation she willingly accepted.

So that it was like a splash of icy water, full in the face, awakening her brutally from a voluptuous dream, when she saw Bill Maguire.

She spotted him instantly, over Lawrence's shoulder, as he entered the restaurant. He was with a group of others, three women and two men, they might have been a party of friends, or perhaps colleagues, they were very at ease with each other, casual, vociferous, laughing. They were also apparently regulars at Bilbow's, for they went straight to a table in the corner and one of the women paused for an amicable exchange with the head waiter, her hand on his arm, clearly on a relaxed and everyday footing with him.

She lost sight of them for a minute or two beyond the crush

of dancing couples as she and Lawrence moved to the far side of the crowded floor, but when she spotted them again they were seated, and laughing uproariously. Bill was pouring wine, telling a good story, his arm casually around the shoulders of one of the young women. It was not this last fact, but something in his general demeanour which made Kate think, or rather feel, instinctively: 'He's not in love with Dulcie.'

This realization was neither judgement nor criticism, but fact. She knew it in her bones as she saw the tilt of his head, the amused gleam in his eye, the rapid, stylish way he talked, his hand gesturing animatedly above the girl's shoulder; and the girl's face turned towards him with friendly, smiling attention, on the verge of a giggle. Kate could imagine that he had told Dulcie 'I'm working', and it had been true. But it hadn't ended there, he had preferred to come out and eat and drink and dance and talk with these casual friends than to seek out Dulcie with all the contingent complications of Rex, and of love. No, thought Kate, he doesn't love her. And even though Dulcie herself had admitted the inequality of the relationship, Kate found herself wondering if her aunt knew what she was up against.

Kate's evening was spoilt. She did not wish to be in the same room as Bill Maguire, now of all times. She closed her eyes for a second and rested her cheek against Lawrence's, to try and recapture the bliss of a few minutes before, but it was impossible.

He sensed it, and held her away from him a little to look into her face. 'Is anything the matter?'

'Not really.'

'You mean, I wouldn't understand.'

They stood still, the other couples twirling and bobbing round them, and she looked into his face. He probably would understand, but she had given away enough for one evening.

She smiled briefly, apologetically. 'I'm sorry, it's a long story.'

'Shall we have another brandy, and continue the cross examination?'

'I'd rather leave, if you don't mind.'

'Of course.'

He was always just a little unexpected, surprisingly sensitive to her mood. He had not teased her, nor demurred over her wish to go. 'I'll fetch your coat.'

Lawrence went ahead, towards the door, and Kate returned to collect her bag from their table. But as she followed him, as quickly as she could, keeping her eyes straight ahead, she was suddenly aware that two couples were advancing from a corner table in the direction of the dance floor, and that one of the four was Bill. Since her intention was to appear not to have seen him she could do nothing but press on, and hope he wouldn't speak to her.

But somehow she knew she would not fool him. Even as she made her way between the tables, her eyes fixed on Lawrence's back view where he stood near the door, settling up, she could feel Bill looking at her with amused surprise, and that peculiarly perspicacious way of his which so unsettled her.

He did not greet her, nor stop her, but as she walked within yards of him she distinctly heard him say, over the heads of four people at an intervening table: 'I see you took my advice about the dress.'

She pretended not to have heard and, in her ludicrous agitation, almost ran the last few steps, arriving at Lawrence's side in record time and in a mild sweat.

He put her coat round her shoulders. 'Okay? Are you sure you feel quite well?'

'Yes, thank you. Come on.'

Her last glimpse of Bill was of him dancing, his arms loosely linked round his partner's waist, and hers round his neck, the pair of them deep in conversation.

Enraged, though unjustifiably she knew, Kate burst out into the street, gulping air as if she'd been deprived of it, and set off at a brisk pace.

'Hey!' Lawrence shouted after her. 'Wrong way!'

Mortified she went back to his side. 'Sorry.'

'You're in the dickens of a hurry. Slow down, take deep breaths.' He possessed himself of her hand and tucked it firmly into the crook of his arm, forcing her to adjust to his more measured pace.

After a little while he said: 'Better?' and she nodded. He made no further enquiries, and they walked back in silence to where the Morris was parked in Monmouth Street. Though she appreciated his delicacy, it left her with her thoughts, which were not comfortable. She could not divine, or would not admit, why she had been so unwilling to acknowledge Bill. After all, nothing had passed between them at their earlier encounters to make such a meeting difficult. Any protective feelings she might have towards Dulcie were surely misplaced – romantic and sexual entanglements were her aunt's stock-in-trade, after all. And it was unreasonable to brand Bill as a heartless two-timer, for his affection for Dulcie was obviously real, and he had promised nothing. At the same time she had feared – actually feared – meeting him this evening, as though she herself might be the catalyst for some terrible disaster which would affect them all. But like someone suddenly plunged into darkness she could make out no pattern, no landmarks or clues to assist her.

This anxiety-ridden confusion was the absolute antithesis of the sunny contentment she had enjoyed for the most part of the evening, and its abrupt descent made her caustic with Lawrence because it now seemed that her contentment had been no more than foolish, gullible weakness.

'Shall I see you again?' he asked, when they were about halfway back to Lewisham.

'I don't know.'

'Perhaps I should phrase it differently – may I see you again? Say next weekend?'

She looked out of the window at the massed ranks of suburbia, cosy squares and oblongs of muted light, and neat triangular rooftops against the orange-tinted night sky, a woman taking her dog for its bed-time constitutional.

'If you like,' she said listlessly.

He did not reply, and after a while she turned to look at him. Only then did he say: 'I'd like, or I wouldn't be asking. But would you?'

She felt as if she were made of wood, she couldn't respond to him. His very generosity brought out the worst in her at that moment. For she could not free herself of the sensation of being watched by someone – not Lawrence – who knew her too well for comfort, someone it would be better not to know.

'I'll have to check,' she said.

'Fine. You check, and I'll get in touch during the week.'

Back at Mapleton Road he saw her up the steps to the door. The stained glass fanlight glowed dimly with the light from the hall, but the rest of the house was in darkness. In the twilight intimacy of the porch, and with the whole of night-time London between her and the source of her discomfort, Kate felt calmer. She suddenly seemed to see Lawrence again, and to remember just how much she had enjoyed most of their evening together. And there was the simple fact of his proximity. She remembered the feeling of being in his arms, as they danced, and wanted to be there again. That would, and could, make things right, she knew it.

'I'm sorry, Lawrence,' she said, and meant it. 'I behaved badly.'

'It doesn't matter.' He did not contradict her.

'I will try and explain some time but if I tried now it would sound too complicated, and silly.'

'You don't have to explain. So long as I may see you again soon.'

'Yes – yes, I'd truly like that. Please ring.'

'I was going to anyway. I'm fairly thick-skinned.'

'And thank you for a lovely time.'

Was it her imagination or did he incline his head a fraction towards hers? She felt that he was going to kiss her, she wanted him to kiss her, her eyelids drooped, she could almost feel the magnetic attraction between their two tentative, enquiring, longing mouths. There was a voluptuous downward-sucking, draining pull on her body so that she was rooted to the spot with craving. Kiss me, Lawrence, make it all right, show me that I don't spoil everything, oh, kiss me . . .

But he didn't. Instead he just said: 'Good-night, Kate, and take care. See you soon.'

Then he was gone, too quickly, disappearing down the dark steps, reappearing briefly in the yellow glow of the streetlight as he got into the car, and waved from the window. Then there was nothing but the sound of the engine puttering and fading round the corner at the start of the long, lonely drive back to Wiltshire. The thought of that drive, and what Lawrence might be thinking, what conclusions he might reach, left Kate in an agony of frustration. And she was not a little alarmed by the strength of certain feelings which had left her weak at the knees and trembling.

'Are you going to come in?' asked a voice, and there was Aubrey, magisterial in his brocade dressing-gown, holding the door open.

'Yes. Thank you.' She stepped in and he closed the door after her and shot various bolts in his meticulous way. As he did so she caught sight of herself in the hall mirror — white face, red hair, glaring eyes — an image so intense and uncompromising that it shocked her and she was glad to look away.

'Did you have a good time?' asked Aubrey.

'Very good, thanks.'

'Seems like a nice chap, your officer. Personable, too.'

'Yes, he is.' Suddenly Kate noticed something distinctly speculative in her uncle's face. Good Lord, he was matchmaking, and on such a slim pretext!

'He's nice enough,' she added airily as she went up the stairs, 'but I don't know if I'll see him again . . .'

Aubrey was not a man of the world in the sexual sense, but even he could see through the transparent deceit of this remark, and smiled to himself as he turned out the hall light.

Just as inevitably as the soft, coppery London autumn faded and hardened into iron-grey winter, Kate fell in love with Lawrence Drake. It was very easy for her to do so. The process was instinctive and bore an almost pre-ordained quality, like the coming together in nature of two different and complementary organisms which is both random and accidental, and part of a grander pattern.

Around them, everything conspired to make that autumn of 1936 a special time, as if the very air of London anticipated great and cataclysmic changes and was soothing the population into a false sense of security. Kate, busy now with her job, and with her free time happily monopolized by Lawrence, saw less of Dulcie, but when she did she found her aunt gay and cheerful, apparently keeping the disparate currents in her life flowing along smoothly and separately. Since their earlier conversation on the subject, Kate knew that all was not sunshine and light, that the problems were horrendous and insurmountable, but the mere fact that Dulcie was bearing up so well was a tribute to the effect Bill had on her, so she did not probe deeper. She felt the presence of Rex Donati – whom she had never met – permanently in the background like some lurking evil spirit; but she had said her piece on that subject and did not want to rock the boat any more. Only once was Bill Maguire in evidence, and there had been nothing even implicit in his behaviour to which she could possibly take exception: he did not mention having seen her with Lawrence, he was attentive and warm towards Dulcie and perfectly civil towards herself. He conducted himself, in short, like a man with nothing whatever to hide, and though Kate was profoundly unsettled in his company she had to be content with that.

The day after Kate had introduced Lawrence to Dulcie, her aunt's verdict had been: 'He's a freak of nature.'

'Oh! Why do you say that?'

'He's a naturally faithful man. And if that's not a freak, I don't know what is.'

An uncharacteristic note of cynicism in Dulcie's voice made Kate wary. 'So what are you saying – that I should be pleased? Or the opposite?'

Dulcie gave her a rueful look and shrugged: 'My darling, that's up to you. He's lovely, a charmer, but once he's made up his mind he'll stick, and that's a responsibility that I for one couldn't have coped with at your age.'

'But we haven't reached that stage yet,' said Kate, without conviction. 'I mean, he hasn't made up his mind – and neither have I.'

'That's all right then,' was Dulcie's reply, giving Kate at least the option of feeling she'd had the last word on the subject. Still, she was glad they'd liked each other. At last the disparate pieces of her world seemed to be fitting together smoothly to make a harmonious whole. Everyone liked Lawrence, and because it was she who had introduced him she basked in the reflected glow of his popularity.

She was a little uncertain how to tell Thea and Jack. For one thing she was not sure *what* it was she must tell them. She balked at committing the word 'love' to paper, when she had not even fully admitted it to herself. The thought of appearing even a little over-enthusiastic and so provoking Thea's fond surprise and delight, frankly embarrassed her. It might look as though she had tamely forfeited her dream of sturdy and spirited independence, capitulating to the first practised charmer to come her way. And there was certainly nothing more concrete to report – no hint of engagement or marriage, nor had Lawrence 'declared himself' as Ralph might have put it.

So she simply slipped Lawrence's name into her letters without explanation – we went here, he took me there – and took care not to vouchsafe an opinion.

Others, though, had clearly not been so cautious, and Thea's letters back were in a quite different vein.

'. . . darling, I'm so glad about your Lawrence. Dulcie – and even Aubrey! – seems to think he's an absolute poppet, and Dulcie says he's terrifically good-looking. It's so *nice* to think of you having a good time and being fêted by someone; you deserve it, there was really nothing for you over here. So be happy together and enjoy yourselves, you're only young once as the saying goes . . .' And there was more in the same style. So, Kate reflected ruefully, it appeared she was quite transparent, she had not needed to say anything to anyone, for they could read it in her face and hear it in her voice. It was fruitless to deny that Lawrence had brought about a change in her, and equally fruitless to fight it.

On Tuesday 3 November Lawrence and Kate attended the wedding, in Wiltshire, of one of Lawrence's closest friends, Josh Maloney, and Beth Warrington-Taylor. The Warrington-Taylors were gentleman farmers in the village of Studham Wyngate near Devizes and had, at very short notice, planned a classic English country wedding insofar as the exigencies of late autumn would allow. But the weather was awful. King Edward VIII, opening his first Parliament in pouring rain, cancelled the state procession on the grounds that there was no more dismal sight than 'a dripping cortège splashing down a half-empty street' (as he would later write), and drove to Westminster in a closed Daimler. Observers couldn't help but notice that the traditional 'Royal weather' had so signally deserted him, and also Edward's uncharacteristic disregard for the few stalwarts who had turned out and waited in the rain for hours just for a glimpse of him.

In the church of St Peter and St Paul in Studham Wyngate the ladies shivered in their Sunday best, and only the officers in uniform and the vicar in his cassock were reasonably warm. The bride in all her filmy white nuptial splendour glowed prettily, but the four bridesmaids — two kindergarten and two lumpishly adolescent — displayed mauvish forearms stippled with goose pimples, and grim faces, teeth firmly clenched to prevent them chattering.

It was the first occasion of its sort that Kate had ever attended, and it interested her both for its curiosity value and the dimension it added to her picture of Lawrence. She had never seen him in uniform before, and this alone served to bring him into sharper focus, reminding her of how short a time she had known him, that he had other preoccupations and allegiances besides herself. Also, he was Josh's best man; she realized how many friends he had, and how general was his popularity. The army was another world, a world in which he spent most of his time and sank most of his energies, and she so far had existed only on the periphery of it.

Under these circumstances she might once have felt defensive and an outsider, but she was simply not allowed to. Except when his social duties took him away Lawrence was at her side. She enjoyed for the first time in her life the pleasure of being generally praised, and teased, and flirted with in that atmosphere of fraternal affection generated by Lawrence and his friends. So complete was their acceptance of her, and so great her pleasure in that acceptance, that Kate almost forgot that she and Lawrence were not themselves 'those whom God hath joined together'. Never had marriage seemed so romantic nor the phrase 'happily ever after' so apposite. Kenya, London, the Institute, Dulcie and her affairs — all seemed unbelievably remote, and her anxieties and frustrations things of the past, belonging to a different person.

Just before the newly-weds went up to change, when Lawrence had run out in the pouring rain to fetch the car from a nearby barn, Beth came over to Kate. After such a good day Kate was quite prepared to concede that the new Mrs Maloney was one of the prettiest girls she'd ever seen, smooth, plump and appetising as a peach, thick brown hair coiled up beneath a length of antique Honiton lace, and caught with two hothouse gardenias, like a Thomas Hardy heroine.

Kate had been temporarily deserted by her entourage of subalterns, who had gone after Lawrence to perpetrate atrocities on the bridal car. She sat in the windowseat of the farmhouse's big drawing-room, with her cup of tea and half-eaten wedding cake. The Warrington-Taylors' black labrador, Jester, sat soulfully before her, drooling with cake-induced cupboard love, eyes misty with greed. Beyond the uncovered lead-paned window the smooth, bleak Wiltshire fields were almost forbidding in the gathering dusk, blurred by the cold driving rain.

Beth moved a couple of glasses and sat down by her, saying, 'Hallo — may I rest my feet a minute?'

'Yes, do, it must be like being royalty, all that tooling around being polite to people.'

'They're all nice people though,' said Beth, 'so it's no hardship.' She pushed Jester with one small, white satin-covered foot. 'Isn't he disgusting, you'd think he was never fed. Where's Lawrence?'

'Gone to fetch your car.'

'Oh God, yes, I should be getting changed. You know . . .' she suddenly, impulsively, laid a hand over Kate's, a hand on which the Tudor rose cluster of superior diamonds glittered brilliantly, 'you know, I feel as if I know you. Do you mind my saying that?'

'Not at all.' Kate wasn't sure whether she did or not.

'He's in love with you, you realize that. Absolutely. Head over heels, gone for broke, up the spout — in love.'

'Really?' In the dreamlike contentment of the moment Kate was not surprised. It all seemed so entirely appropriate, she accepted this revelation as her due. 'How do you know?'

'Oh, I know all right. Partly because I've been in love with him in my time, oh my goodness, yes. Just about every girl who meets Lawrence falls for him, to a greater or lesser extent. He doesn't even have to try — does he?' Kate shook her head. 'He's one of the few men I've ever met who is really a gentle man, in the true sense. He simply wouldn't make a promise he couldn't keep, or even say something he didn't mean. And he hasn't stopped talking about you since the day you showed up. You can have no idea how bursting with curiosity we all were, you damn nearly stole my show.'

'I'm sorry . . . I had no idea.' Rather dazedly, Kate fed Jester the remains of her cake. 'He hasn't said anything to me.'

Beth stood up. 'I must go. That's because he has all these old-fashioned notions about integrity and honour – watch out!' Kate glanced up, but Beth giggled, as if conscious of having been too serious. Now she unfastened one of the gardenias and handed it to Kate. 'There you are – just in case you don't catch the bouquet . . .' She rustled away. The rain rattled like handfuls of gravel on the glass behind Kate as she stared down at the single, gorgeous flower, its waxy white petals both bridal and voluptuous, pure but full of promise.

As she tucked it into her buttonhole she heard a firmer knock amid the hammering rain and turned to see Lawrence grinning at her from the darkness outside, his collar up, his hair plastered to his wet face. He enacted a brief dumb-show, pointing to the flower, and placing one hand with a fluttering motion over the region of his heart.

She laughed at him and waved him away, but as she rose to go out to the hall, to say good-bye to the honeymooners, the rich fragrance of the gardenia was strong in her nostrils, heady with expectation.

'We could go to the Hart and Trumpet.'

'Where is it?'

'Close. Twenty minutes in the car.'

'Will it be all right, I mean will they –'

'It's known locally as the Fart and Strumpet. They're discreet.'

'Then let's go, Lawrence. Let's *go*!'

'You've no objection to such an unromantic hostelry, then?'

'We're not going there to be romantic. We're going there to –'

'Yes. We are.'

'I don't make a habit of this, you know. In fact I've never done it before.'

'I'm flattered. Come on.'

It had been as simple as that. As Beth and Josh had left, and everyone had stood in the hallway, waving them good-bye as they disappeared beyond a screen of rain, she had turned to him and held his head and kissed him with all the longing and love which she had not spoken. 'Lawrence . . . can't we go somewhere too? For a honeymoon.'

And she had known then that what Beth had said was true. He had pulled her into the dining-room, where the wedding presents lay displayed in starchy splendour on the long refectory table, and closed the door after them. For a long time afterwards, and especially in those black moments when she hated herself, she would remember the sigh he gave before he took her in his arms. It was no mooning, romantic exhalation but a great gasp of love and desire and triumph, like a knight who sees the holy grail, or a lone explorer in sight, at last, of his legendary objective. She had never suspected this ardent strength, which crushed her so that she felt the wet receptive-ness of her mouth and, between her legs, the juice of a most unvirginal lust.

'Please . . .' she said, against his lips. 'Please, oh, please . . .' And it had been her body's pleading for something her mind could not yet even imagine, yearning for a strange, dangerous, mysterious prize. And with their distorted reflection gleaming in the untouched surfaces of Beth's kettles, and silver teapot, and inscribed salver, and with someone's voice shouting, 'Where's Lawrence?' in the crowded hall outside, her hungry open mouth had stifled his 'Yes!'

There had been few words left. They had simply arranged what they would do, and somehow got through the remaining hour or two before they could decently leave, not touching each other, holding off, waiting, saving. They had helped clear up, and had another drink, and jollied along the slightly tremulous mother of the bride, and congratulated the scarlet-faced father, and opened yet another bottle and said good-bye to the bridesmaids, and explained to everyone that they were going to have a quiet dinner somewhere. And, finally, left.

It was a measure of Lawrence's standing with Aubrey and

Ralph, acquired in so short a time, that there had been no quibbling over his request to put Kate up somewhere for the night following the wedding. The idea was for the two of them to spend one night in Devizes — with Kate appropriately accommodated in some local hotel — and then to drive up to Kent, there to spend two days with Lawrence's mother, before Lawrence brought Kate home on the night of the fifth, and himself returned to camp. They had never had so much time together in the short while they'd known each other; it was a kind of test of their feelings which they were both aware of.

And this, Kate thought, as they drove through the hissing rain, in silence, was the greatest test. She felt no anxiety, she was impatient, she pictured her body as some kind of ripe, soft fruit, so *ready*, so perfect, so available that it ached to be taken, and bitten. The phrase 'to give oneself' crossed her mind, a phrase which, when she had read it in novels, had had a prim, even a patronizing ring to it, but which now seemed exactly apt. She had so much to give, she had the feeling of ecstatic anticipation experienced by a child who has spent all her pocket money on some wildly extravagant and special gift for a friend. Just wait, she thought, just *wait* . . .

And the waiting seemed to be spun out almost interminably, first hour by hour, at the house, then minute by minute as the little car puttered through the rain-lashed darkness, then second by second as Lawrence booked the room, lied like a good 'un in the register, followed the elderly porter up the stairs, carrying her case, thanked him, tipped him, closed the door.

He was quiet, tense, purposeful. She stood, her body seeming to hum with excitement, as he turned down the bed, lit the lamp, drew the curtains and came over to her, unbuttoning the high collar of his tunic. His face was stark, bright white against the dark blue material, his hair silkily fair, a military angel, a St Michael — she did not wait, but wound her arms around him, devouring that burning pale face with kisses, moaning with excitement as his long, beautiful hands clasped her bottom and she was spread against him, lusciously receptive. She was speared on a delicious narcissism, feeling his urgency and her readiness, a piercing awareness of the beauty he saw in her, a sense of pride, and triumph, and luxurious vanity.

They undressed each other with more speed than grace – his thick, tight uniform trousers were a source of the most exquisite frustration – and then fell, clasped together, on to the bed. The room was unheated and bitterly cold, the sheets glacially laundered, they were like two warm, moist seals rolling on the ice. This contrast added an exquisite piquancy to their first embrace that almost took Kate's breath away – the cold sheets, the snow-soft fall of his hair on her breast, the fiery pull of his lips on her nipples, the sultry, silky warmth of his body which she had so often recently imagined – it was as if each texture, each temperature was separately imprinted on her so that she was a mosaic of vivid sensation, almost fearfully transcended.

With the spine-tingling, careful passion of an expert lover he lifted, then left her, brought her along so far then abandoned her momentarily for his own pleasure, carried and released her until they were bathed in sweat in the dim, draughty room. When he at last entered her there was a moment's shock, a small discomfort which she almost embraced, impaling herself on him with masochistic glee and then giving herself up rapturously to the ebb and flow which seemed to drag and suck on her like a spring tide. And then he could go no longer, and with a great shout – 'I love you' – he reared up for a moment above her, and then drooped, sank, spent, on her breast, his wet hair trailing on her throat, his hands clasping her shoulders like a dying man. And in that quiet moment before he left her body she, too, reached her climax, and shuddered before the force of it, gripping him in near fury, that it could not go on for ever.

But it couldn't, and only afterwards was she able to embrace him with real tenderness, cradling his head, kissing his face and neck, whispering her delight, flattering him with silly names, nestling and cuddling, cherishing and mothering him. She found time to notice, and to remark on, the solid, bound strength of his body which she might not have guessed from its dressed appearance of coltish grace. Although Kate had been surrounded by black male nudity from an early age, she had never till now suspected that such voluptuously heavy fruit could hang on a slender white man's body. Avoiding her eager, curious fingers Lawrence knelt up and reached for her jacket which lay across the end of the bed.

'Come here . . .' he pulled the gardenia from the buttonhole, and pushed the stalk behind her left ear. Then he fluffed out her hair around her face and sat back to survey her. The glossy white flower, and Kate's slender body were delectably at variance with her springing red hair and brilliant eyes.

'How do I look?' she asked him. For probably the first time in her life Kate was actually conscious not just of how she looked, but on the effect she was having. She, too, was kneeling now, on her heels, her back straight, her hands on her knees in a demure, almost a geisha-like pose. But under his admiring gaze she slowly lifted her hands and linked them on the top of her head, at the same time very slightly tilting her face to one side.

'How do I look?' she asked again.

'Wonderful. Terrifyingly wonderful.'

'Why terrifying, don't you like it?'

'I love it. I love you, Kate. That's why it scares me.'

'Don't!' She reached out, suddenly sorry for playing on his feelings. 'You were so beautiful, so splendid. Don't turn meek on me, will you?' She sat astride his lap, smothering his face and ears with kisses, her fingers clutching his hair. He put his arms round her waist and pulled her down on top of him, grasping her so tightly she could scarcely breathe.

'Oh, so it's meek now, is it?' he whispered fiercely. 'We'll see about meek!'

It rained all that night, and the wind reached near gale-force proportions. The ill-fitting windows of the Fart and Strumpet whined and rattled before its onslaught, the curtains bellied in the draught. The sounds of the country hotel evening marked the passing of the hours as surely as any bell – the jovial hubbub of the public bar at six; the civilized chat of voices in the hall as patrons crossed to the dining-room for dinner between eight and ten; the hiss of tyres in the car park; the shouts and laughter and slamming doors of chucking out time, the trickle of more muted voices as the residential guests came up to bed. Downstairs in the bar there was the faint rumble of a few favoured after-hours drinkers, and the more metallic tones of a wireless, crackling and bleeping as the wind played havoc with reception. Kate supposed she must have slept, sporadically, but the night passed in a kind of wakeful limbo of erotic exploration. The wild autumn night outside and the anonymous seclusion of the little old-fashioned hotel room emphasized their delicious intimacy. Kate was glad of the long November night, she never wanted it to end, she was greedy and grasping, tender and seductive by turns, all was pleasure. The bed became warm and damp like a swamp and they like two slippery, undulant entwined creatures rolling in it, oblivious to everything but their own gratification.

But as the rectangle of curtained window became grey with the first light she did sleep, and only awoke when Lawrence shook her gently. He was sitting on the edge of the bed in pants and shirt, his hair in disarray, smiling down at her. Outside it was still raining, but more quietly and steadily, the weather reflecting their mood.

'Are you for breakfast?' he asked.

'Yes!' She stretched, cat-like, and then reached for him, but he evaded her.

'Give over, you're insatiable.'

'Do you mind?'

'No, I don't.' He leaned over now and kissed her four times — on the brow, on either cheek and finally on the lips — with great deliberation. 'I love you, Kate.'

'Get back in then.'

'I want my breakfast, and then we should be going. I have to call on Beth's parents, and then we have a long drive to Kent.'

He got up and began pulling on trousers and pullover. She noticed that his blues were immaculately folded, ready to be packed, his cap lying on top. There was something poignant about this neat little pile, like a dead man's effects.

'I'm coming,' she said, 'just wait for me.'

Kate was to remember that day for its quality of dream-like serenity. They were both a little tired, besotted, surfeited, coasting along in the aftermath of their first lovemaking, happily anticipating the second, so close they didn't really need to speak, but needed to touch. As they drove through the steady grey rain Kate laid her hand either on Lawrence's knee, or on the back of his neck. When they stopped at Beth's parents' house Kate could not believe that the tremendous change in her was not visible, written across her forehead in letters of fire. The completeness of the secret, and its ambrosian sweetness, made her quite lightheaded as she sat drinking coffee, watching Lawrence confer with the Wyngate-Taylors about the bestowal of the wedding presents.

She took a possessive delight in observing Lawrence — the movement of his hands which had played on her till she sang out . . . his expressive, quick-moving mouth as he discussed mundane matters . . . his ready and engaging smile, which seemed quite the most natural expression for his facial muscles, as though he relaxed into happiness as a matter of course. He amazed her with his ability to shift so quickly into this different gear; while she was still engorged with lust and love he stepped into his busy, sociable, practical best man's role with absolute ease — he was decisive, agreeable, reassuring, she could almost see the tired and slightly depressed parents of the bride reviving under his ministrations. From this it was quite a short imaginative leap to envisaging him rallying troops in the field, and for the first time she made the mental connection between the perpetual ominous rumblings about war with Germany, and Lawrence's job. This idea, coming as it did now that they were part of each other, seemed almost unbearably cruel, like the severing in half of a single living organism.

It still hung over her like a threatening storm cloud when they got back into the car for the long drive to Ewehurst, and she flung her arms round him, holding him in an embrace of frantic strength.

'Kate? What's the matter? My darling —' He kissed her. 'Tell me.'

'There won't be a war, surely?'

He hesitated. Minutely, but she noticed it. 'I couldn't say.'

'*God* — you mean yes.'

'I mean it's quite likely, but it could be averted.'

She was furious, her anger almost choked her, she pulled away from him, clenching her fists together on her lap. 'Don't say it like that! I don't want to hear!'

'But you asked, you raised it,' he reminded her gently. 'I'm just being truthful as far as I can.'

'But you sound as though you don't care whether there is or not – as if we all just have to accept it and be good and polite and uncomplaining.'

He started up the car. The windscreen wipers hissed and clicked to and fro like twin metronomes.

'I care, Kate. No one in his right mind wants a war, least of all me in spite of my calling. But as to accepting it, if it happens we shall all have to. It'll be started by the few and fought by the many, as usual.'

'I see.' She was clipped. A crack, black and jagged, had suddenly slithered snake-like across the calm of the day, a crack beneath which she sensed there was a roaring black void. 'We won't talk about it any more,' she said.

'Very well.' She sensed him glancing at her, but she stared straight ahead, battling with herself.

The day and the night they spent with Mrs Loelia Drake in her cottage on the edge of Ewehurst was again instructive for Kate, and also marked by an almost unbearable sexual tension. After that moment of panic in the car she wanted more than anything to make love with Lawrence again, to heal the rift and drown the doubts with physical contact, to express with her body what she found so hard to express in words – her need, her desire, her fear. But in this most domestic of settings such a solution was unthinkable.

Not that Lawrence's mother was the crippled, doting old lady she had imagined. On the contrary she turned out to be a handsome, astute, whisky-tippling merry widow, upright and sprightly in spite of walking with a stick. Her gaze, when it rested on Kate, had a distinctly knowing light, but seemed also to carry a tacit approval.

'I hope you realize you have a reputation to live up to,' she said to Kate over drinks before dinner on their first evening. She placed a cigarette in a holder and held it to her lips for Lawrence to light, but her eyes remained on Kate as he did so. 'I've heard a great deal about you, you know.'

'Have you? All good, I hope.' Kate realized that this was the second person in twenty-four hours to say how much Lawrence talked about her. She could think of nobody of her acquaintance – not even Dulcie – who could have made a similar observation on her behalf to Lawrence. This apparent inequality made her feel, if not nervous, at least wary.

'Oh, pretty good, pretty good . . .' said Mrs Drake, 'you have nothing to worry about.'

'I'm not a great worrier,' said Kate, piqued, 'and certainly not about my reputation, as you put it.' She looked at Lawrence, who was sitting on the opposite end of the sofa to his mother, but he seemed perfectly at ease.

'Fighting talk!' laughed Mrs Drake. 'Now one thing this fellow has not described adequately is your work at the Ross, I am looking forward to your telling me all about that a little later. I'd like to have done something along those lines myself when I was younger, but in those days you just became somebody's wife and that was that. I came down here and turned into a rabid committee woman.'

Kate smiled, remembering Ralph's verbal sketch of Mrs Drake. 'My job's nothing special, I'm a kind of glorified skivvy but I love it.'

Loelia leaned forward theatrically. 'So, my dear, are a great many wives glorified skivvies, and they get no money and precious little appreciation.'

'*Mother* . . .' Lawrence interrupted, 'do stop making speeches.'

'No, I like it,' said Kate truthfully.

'He's right, of course,' confided Loelia with mock ruefulness. 'I'm a street orator *manquée* among other things, and always have been.'

'Anyway, supper's on the table,' said Lawrence, rising and beaming at the pink-faced village girl who appeared in the dining-room door. 'Thank you, Maureen. How are you by the way?'

'Very well, thank you, sir.'

'Rob still playing for the cricket team?'

'Yes, sir. Made fifty last match of the season.' She blushed scarlet.

'Did he, by heck – give him a slap on the back from me, will you?'

'Yes, sir . . .' Maureen looked across at Loelia who was listening to this exchange with an air of slightly jaded *déjà entendu*, waiting for it to finish. 'Supper's on the table, Mrs Drake.'

'Thank you, Maureen, we shall come.'

Kate was conscious of being the audience for a kind of double act, comprising Lawrence and his mother, in which the role of each participant was so well understood by the other that it functioned in a kind of emotional and verbal shorthand to which she was not, as yet, privy. She liked Loelia enormously, and more as time went on, and admired her too for having remained so much an individual, so quirky and forceful and amusing, when her life now must be rather dull, enlivened only by nagging physical pain and Lawrence's visits. Kate saw that it was no surprise that Lawrence was so sympathetic, so easy to like. During his formative years he had been brought up by this woman on her own, without brothers and sisters to modify her influence. Loelia had somehow fostered charm without smugness or vanity, gentleness without weakness, and that most feminine of qualities, intuition, with nothing effeminate about it.

But unfortunately her liking for the mother did nothing to dampen Kate's raging and importunate ardour for the son which reduced her to a fidgety gadfly of seething frustration. Indeed, it actually exacerbated it, for she and Loelia seemed always to be keeping one another company while Lawrence launched himself into a succession of filial chores. Kate stared rapaciously out of the window as he strode about the garden in shirtsleeves with the wheelbarrow full of leaves, and methodically raked the grass, his hair flopping over his eyes, and chopped wood, and climbed up ladders to clear autumn debris out of the roof guttering, and stood by the bonfire he'd made, waving at her through the curling blue smoke. She could literally have screamed; he was going back tonight and here she was trapped in the house while he literally paraded his charms back and forth outside.

'Go on,' said Loelia. 'Go out and see the bonfire. I shall do the crossword and read what the King had to say yesterday.'

Kate was suddenly hot with embarrassment — had she been

so very obvious? But Loelia was already picking up the paper, and putting on her spectacles.

'Thank you. Perhaps I will,' she said. And fled.

The smoke wafted round them, wrapping them in its acrid, evocative smell, shifting and crackling like a sleeping animal by their feet, the small floating flakes of black catching in their hair. Kate wrapped her arms tightly round him, feeling the sturdy rhythm of his heart in his chest, in its cage of bone covered with smooth skin that she wanted to touch.

'Oh God, I want to do it again,' she said. 'I could eat you up right here and now, it's killing me.' She felt his mouth against her hair, and his body shaking a little as he laughed.

'Don't laugh at me — is there something wrong with me?'

'Of *course* not . . . I'm delighted you feel like that.'

'And do you?' She stared up at him, scowling, almost accusing. 'Do you feel the same?'

'Oh, yes.'

'What are we going to do?'

'Do?' He laughed again, and this time she was infected by it, and joined in, grabbing the front of his shirt and shaking him in her comical frustration, so that he overbalanced and fell to the ground, and she with him. She glanced over her shoulder, suddenly guilty.

'It's all right,' said Lawrence, 'she's changed chairs.'

And indeed Loelia was now sitting with her back to the window, the soul of discretion. They picked themselves up and Lawrence began to rake the remaining leaves on to the fire.

'I'll tell you what we're going to do,' he said. 'Since you're so keen on bonfires we'll leave an hour early and I'll take you to the village fireworks up at Chilverton House.'

The Ewehurst bonfire was built annually in the field that lay between the gardens of Chilverton House and the parish church of St Catherine's, on the site of the great Armistice fire which had been lit there nearly twenty years earlier.

When Kate and Lawrence arrived the blaze was already well under way, fuelled by piles of old motor tyres from the village garage, and tons of junk which had been carried there by local people over the past fortnight — boxes of newspapers, broken toys, old furniture, planks and beams from defunct garden sheds, branches of trees and tattered mattresses — a rag-bag microcosm of village life.

It was six o'clock, a cold, blustery wind had got up. The tall flames leaned to the west, hurling armfuls of sparks into the turbulent black air, grey smoke swirling like wild witches' hair above them. The guy, his tragi-comic face painted starkly on a white dinner plate, sat on a broken deckchair atop the conflagration. His angular, lopsided broomstick arms reached out in mournful supplication as the pyre roared and crackled beneath him. Finally the deckchair began to burn, the canvas seat flaring like a struck match, and the guy toppled over and sank into the shivering red abyss.

Kate, who had never witnessed this particular British ritual before, was fascinated. 'It's primitive,' she said to Lawrence. 'Burning effigies, and encouraging children to join in.'

He looked down at her. 'But you like it.'

'Yes — it's exciting.'

'We all need our pagan rites. And what better setting than this —' he swept his arm from Chilverton House in the north, to the church in the south '— between God and mammon. A no-man's land for us to indulge in our primitive pursuits.'

Kate looked around, and felt that it was true. In the grounds of the big house a few lamps had been strung along the elm walk, to light the way for anyone who wished to walk down to see the fireworks. But it was a fitful light, flickering and bobbing as the branches tossed in the wind. Beyond the trees a few of the house lights were on and in some of the windows black silhouetted figures stood like icons. These figures had a timeless quality, the watchers at the window who were always there, looking on at the great fires that marked invasion, or peace, beginnings and endings, fires that were both destructive and purifying, funereal or celebratory: fire, the consumer and the life force. Kate felt its fierce magic as the heat flapped at her face, and the glittering sparks poured into the night sky.

Children scampered round the fire's edge, daring and unafraid, whirling sparklers, shouting, darting forward to retrieve potatoes and chestnuts from the embers. The faces of parents and grandparents, looking on, glowed in the red light and were beautiful. Young men from the village replenished the blaze, hurling branches and planks on to the flames, yelling and cheering, exhilarated by their own strength and the roaring energy of the fire.

The fireworks began, swooping and bursting in the dark, inscribing great arcs of brilliant unnatural colour in the blackness, showering fountains of vivid artificial stars, and plumes of lurid smoke.

Kate shivered. Beside her Lawrence stood, holding her close, wearing his uniform because he was due back tonight. His face, rapt and smiling beneath the peak of his officer's cap, was lit fitfully by the bursting rockets. Kate was suddenly fearful. Instead of fireworks she heard the whine and crash of shells, the rattle of gunfire, the boom of explosives, and saw the blinding flash and sickly glow of man-made light in this no-man's-land, and the whoops and sighs of the onlookers were like the cries of the dying. She was stiff, paralysed by this sudden fear, unable to communicate it to Lawrence who stood there like the eternal sacrifice in his uniform, as quiet and fatalistic as the guy they'd consigned to the flames. The setting, with its echoes of a powerful, unremembered past, confused her, she was conscious of a blurring between past and present, a fusion at once nostalgic and premonitory, a mixture of pride and dread. On this very spot the fire had burned which marked the ending of that other war which had so affected her adopted family, and she felt, piercingly, the presence of that family as they might have been twenty-five years ago before the Fall, before she was born – the laughing girls, the gallant men, the proud parents, the loyal retainers. She was conscious for a split second, and blindingly, of something she had never believed in – destiny.

She still looked at Lawrence, and he must have felt the intensity of that look for he turned towards her. He seemed just about to ask her something, but she spoke first.

'I love you,' she said. 'I do love you so.'

'And I love you,' he said simply. 'Are you going to marry me?'

Even his phrasing of the question seemed to echo her feelings of predestination, as though the answer were already written in the wind.

'I'm scared,' she said. Beyond them the flames, caught in a

sudden uprush of turbulence, scudded and snarled, the children darted back.

He pulled her towards him and held her tight, her arms at her sides as one might hold a bird to prevent it from flying. 'That's not one of your words, Kate. It doesn't suit you. Marry me.'

'I'm scared for all of us!' She looked into his eyes desperately, intensely, trying to convey the complexity of what she felt. 'It's this place, the fire — there's going to be a war — and nothing we can do —'

'We shall be all right, you and I, Kate.'

'And I'm scared of *myself*! I don't know who I am, or what I might do. I love you but I can't . . .' She ran out of words, her panic threatened to consume her, burn her up and scatter her on the wind like the sparks which flittered past them. But Lawrence's arms were still tight about her, holding her to his heart, securing her.

'I know who you are,' he said. 'You're the woman I love. Don't be scared, Kate, I'm not. Just allow yourself to be happy and I promise you happiness.'

'Oh . . .!' She sobbed, bending her head against his chest, pounding her fists against her sides. 'That's too much to promise!'

'Nevertheless.'

'I love you, I love you!'

'I know . . .' He stroked her hair. 'Marry me.'

And now Dulcie's words came back to her: '. . . a naturally faithful man, a freak of nature . . . what a responsibility . . .' She was on the rack. 'I don't know, I can't — there's so much future, and we don't know what might be lying in wait for us . . . if I'm a liability even to myself how can I ask you to take me on?'

'I asked you.'

'And I have to have time!'

He put his arm about her shoulders and began to walk her away from the fire. 'Come with me.'

As the last few rockets shrieked and fizzed in pink aerial fountains, and the final catherine wheel trailed its whirring white arms, he led Kate down the hill towards the church.

Away from the scorching glow of the dying bonfire and the

huddle of families around it Kate felt her terrible isolation. No one could help her but herself. The wind, colder all the time now, whipped round them, ragged clouds streamed across the dappled half-moon, it was dark and she had no sense of direction, she couldn't see her way. Together they stumbled over the bumpy field, and through the lychgate which squawked rustily on its hinges and was tugged from their hands by the wind, to bang and crack on its frame. Kate clung to Lawrence. He knew this place, he belonged here, and his knowledge gave him strength like a tree with its roots deep in the soil, the absolute and perfect product of its environment. Unlike her, so rootless, so frantic and uncertain, fretfully battering herself against walls of incomprehension like a bird trapped in a room. For Kate at that moment Lawrence was quite literally an anchor, mooring her to reality, keeping her safe.

A spattering of chilly rain flew in their faces as they walked round the church tower and out of the lee of the building, and Lawrence led her into the porch. Parish notices on a board snapped and fluttered in the draught, and dead brown leaves skittered across the flagstones.

'Would you like to go in?' he asked. 'We didn't before. And it's raining.'

'Yes.'

He grasped the black iron ring on the door, turned it and pushed. The door swung open silently, too heavy to be affected by the wind. They were admitted into that special, dense hush of all churches, the almost palpable silence laid down layer on layer by centuries of dutiful reverence and organized worship that is both formal and public, and deeply secret. Lawrence closed the door and flicked the switch which turned on the three aisle lights. The sound of the wind outside was now muted, clamorous and fretful like an angry child in a distant room, unable to claim their attention. The church smelt cool, of musty hymn books and Brasso and polish. There were no flowers tonight, but the empty vases stood clustered round the font, which was filled with copper beech, sprays of rowan, hips and haws and amber-gold chrysanthemums.

Lawrence took off his cap and walked away from Kate, looking about him and combing his fingers back through his hair. The still brightly-new roll of honour of the Great War

shone smooth and cold from the rear wall, near the belfry —
'David Roach, Samuel Rodway, George Rowles . . .' on and
on, a list of twenty from this tiny place. Lawrence walked up
the centre aisle. His hair was pale beneath the hanging
lamps, his slow reflective gait in his heavy greatcoat was
somehow ghostly. Kate's earlier vision of him as a sacrifice
returned more strongly. She suddenly, irrationally, feared that
when he reached the carved rood screen and the darkness
beyond he might melt away, be swallowed up and taken from
her, the victim of her selfish procrastination.

'Lawrence!' Her voice was harsh and sharp in the brooding
silence.

He turned, smiling as she ran to him, breathless with panic.
'I'm here.'

'I thought — I don't know what I thought, I spooked myself.'

'I like it here.' He turned on another light, in the chancel,
and in the sudden pool of brightness a little brown mouse was
caught in the act of scuttling across the threadbare and faded
strip of red carpet between the facing choir stalls. It paused for
a second, blinded and terrified, whiskers trembling, and then
darted on its way, disappearing between the hand-embroidered
hassocks on the far side.

Together they walked up to the altar rail. One or two dry
leaves, fallen from some earlier arrangement, lay on the white
cloth, giving the altar an air of desolation.

'When you decide to marry me,' said Lawrence, 'we must be
married in a church.'

'Why? That doesn't matter to me.'

'Well, it does to me.'

'Let's just leave things as they are : . .'

'You'll decide, in time, you know you will.'

'I'm not religious.' She spoke loudly, defiantly, pushing her
hands down into her pockets.

He grinned at her broadly. 'I know. And no more am I, in
any formal sense. But I think the more memorable you make
something, the more durable it is. No hole in the corner stuff.'

She tossed her head and began to walk away from him. 'It's
just frills.'

He followed her, turning off the lights, and finally opening
the door and coming out with her into the porch.

He closed the door and replaced his cap. She put her arms round his neck and kissed him hungrily, and he folded the sides of his coat about her so that they stood like one person, a breathing statue animated by love.

CHAPTER TEN

'Love is the greatest thing,
The oldest, yet the latest thing,
I only hope that Fate may bring
Love's story to you . . .'

'Love is the Sweetest Thing'
Roy Noble, 1932

'*Adeste fideles, laeti triumphantes. . . . !*' When Lawrence sang it, thought Kate, he seemed so joyful and triumphant that even the unfaithful would have found him irresistible. They were in the chapel of Joe's school, Hartfield House, at the annual carol service. Because she was suddenly and powerfully overwhelmed by a warmth of feeling which had a few weeks ago been unfamiliar, but which was now as natural to her as breathing, she tucked her gloved hand into the crook of his arm, the one which held his hymn book aloft, and squeezed it.

'*Venite adoremus, dominum!*' He covered her hand with his free one and they stood like that as the choir filed out to the continued pealing and thunder of the organ. She caught Joe's eye — he was still, to his slight embarrassment, a treble — and winked, but his face was aloof beneath gleaming slicked-down hair and there was no smile.

When the choir had gone the congregation sat down to allow the rest of the school to leave before the visitors. Kate huddled into her coat, and Lawrence put his arm across her shoulders.

'Okay?'

She nodded. 'Just frozen.'

'It is a bit parky. Only a fraction warmer than the dormitories, I suspect.'

'Oh God . . .' She chafed her hands together to restore the circulation. 'How does he stand it?'

'He has to. All part of the character-forming process of the English public school.'

She looked at him in horror, but saw that he was smiling.

'Your nose is red,' he said, and lowered his face to hers just near enough for her to feel his warm breath and the tickle of his eyelashes. At once, beneath her thick coat, her whole body lit up in a most un-Godly way, and she was no longer cold but hot. She had the uncomfortable idea that she might be glowing like a beacon, quite literally a scarlet woman, sending shock waves of heat through the chilly and proper furs, and pearls and pin-stripes in the surrounding pews.

'Stop it!' she said in a furious whisper, nudging him away with her elbow.

'What did I do?'

'Just —' She tried not to look at him, but she was laughing in spite of herself. 'Don't!'

They were representing the family at the service because Ralph was too poorly to come, and the Kingsleys were nursing a bad head cold. Since Joe had been up to Mapleton Road the previous weekend Aubrey had opted to remain behind on this occasion and keep his father company. It was Sunday, 6 December, only nine days till the end of term, so the boys were not to be taken out after the carols. Instead, tea and cakes were on offer for boys and their visitors, in the 'prom' or main hall of the school. There had not been the slightest awkwardness about Kate's bringing Lawrence. On the half-dozen or so occasions that he had met members of her family, since their first encounter two months ago, he had completely disarmed them. Even Joe, to whom in his new rather pompous public school *persona* the merest whiff of sentiment was anathema, was prepared to admit that Lawrence was a good sort.

Now she felt his arm tighten round her shoulders. 'Come on.'

They rose and joined the slow-moving queue down the central aisle. Outside in the crisp, wintry twilight there was a whiff of constitutional crisis in the air, along with the Arpège and cigarette smoke. These people who had refused to countenance the dreadful possibility that an English king might marry a social-climbing American divorcee, had now to accept that it was not just possible, but certain, and imminent. Elegantly hatted heads shook slowly in well-bred despair, veiled and powdered faces drifted together in cool kisses of sad understanding.

Lawrence and Kate crossed the quad from the chapel to the main school building. In the entrance hall a huge Christmas tree, studded with lights, stood before the panels which bore the names of past head boys.

A very small boy in spectacles stepped forward to greet them. 'Visitors' tea in the prom, to your right,' he announced, in a high, clear, self-confident tone.

'Thank you,' said Lawrence, and added in his characteristically conversational tone, 'can you recommend the tea, will it be any good?'

'I believe so, sir,' replied the small boy, rather loftily.

Lawrence laughed. 'I shall hold you responsible if I choke my last on stale fruit cake.'

The tea was, in fact, sumptuous, the featherlight bridge rolls topped with salmon, egg and anchovies, the fruit cake richly dark, the shortbread crumbly and melting. Tea, both China and Indian, flowed from silver pots into bone china cups and sugar was handed with tongs by fourth year boys with an air of studied dignity. Joe was waiting for them just inside the door, but Kate knew better than to kiss him these days. Instead, while Lawrence shook his hand she said: 'Hallo. It was lovely.'

'Glad you liked it. Shall we get some scoff before it all goes?'

When they were all three furnished with plates of food and cups of tea Joe took them to the far end of the prom, so that they could sit on the edge of the stage.

'Shouldn't we be circulating?' asked Kate doubtfully. 'I mean they didn't provide any chairs.'

'No, well, you can't eat properly standing up,' said Joe with his mouth full.

'Tell me,' said Lawrence, 'which one is the head?'

'The one with the big nose,' said Joe unhelpfully. Kate caught Lawrence's eye over her brother's head. He made a grimace that exactly caught the kind of fond exasperation that she felt herself.

'I saw Mrs Treece,' she volunteered. 'She's hoping you'll be able to get together with William again over the Christmas holidays.' God, she thought, I sound like one of these awful mothers.

Joe scowled. 'I don't know about Treece.'

'How do you mean?' She was baffled.

'Just that there's a limit to the amount of time a chap wants to spend mucking about with a crystal set with a fellow like Treece,' replied Joe, which took Kate no further along the road to comprehension.

When he had consumed his tea, and the remainder of theirs, and taken them on a brief tour of the school buildings, they departed.

As the Morris chugged through the dark lanes towards the London road, Lawrence explained: 'He's in a bit of a no-man's-land at the moment. He'll come round, don't you worry.'

'But he's so pompous, it's ghastly! And in the summer he got along so well with William, in fact I don't know what he'd have done without him. And now —'

'But, darling Kate, you've just put your finger on the problem. He was friends with the young Mr Treece when he was a bit desperate, and he's very anxious to show that he's not desperate any more. A few days at Mapleton Road and he'll be right as rain. You'll just have to bear with him.'

'I hope you're right.'

There was a short silence. Then Lawrence said, 'I'd take him out and about a bit myself over Christmas, but I don't know how much longer I'll be here for.'

'What?' She hadn't heard him properly, or couldn't believe that she had.

'We're due for a posting, and I think it'll come before Christmas.'

'You mean — abroad?' She was aware that she sounded obtuse, but she couldn't encompass the idea of his absence. In a few weeks he had become so much part of her life, and of her, that the prospect of being without him was like a death sentence.

'Abroad, yes,' he said. He took his left hand off the wheel and laid it over the two of hers which were clenched in a tight knot in her lap. 'Beastly, horrible, abroad.'

'Where?' She heard the hectoring note that crept unbidden into her voice when she was afraid.

'The Middle East, I suspect. The Jews are pouring into Palestine from Germany.'

'But —' she snatched her hands away from his and put them to the sides of her head, clenched, trying to make herself comprehend, 'but that's halfway back to Kenya!' The irony made her feel quite ill with rage.

'I suppose it is.'

'Damn the army! Why must you all play soldiers and go dashing off all over the world rattling your sabres, when there isn't even a war on!'

To her surprise, he stopped the car, and switched off the engine. When he turned to her, even in the dark of the car, she could sense that this was the most serious he'd ever been with her.

'Don't be silly, Kate. There's no sabre-rattling, we're going to do a job. And as for a war, you may get one of those a lot sooner than you think.'

'Don't patronize me!' She was shouting, she was angry with him, with everything.

'I'm a professional soldier, and if there's a war I shall be asked to do what I've been trained for. I shan't relish it, but I shan't hang back, either. Anyway, it's beside the point. All I meant to tell you is that I shall almost certainly be posted by the end of the month.' He started up the engine. 'And now I've told you.'

'And what am I supposed to do, just sit here and be meek and accepting till you come back again?'

He shook his head, and when he spoke she could hear that he was smiling. 'You couldn't if you tried, Kate.'

'And don't laugh at me!'

'I wasn't. You're behaving as though no one will mind about our separation but you. You're an extremely self-centred young woman.'

'And you're a prig.'

'I shall be a very lonely one.'

'Don't be glib!' She was ranting on and she knew it, pushing him as far as she dared, blustering to hide her misery. 'You have everything so easily, everyone falls for you, everyone loves

Lawrence, he's such a brick. Well, I'm sick and tired of being patted and soothed and flattered by you, I'm sick and tired of it!'

The car stopped again, this time with a violent jerk, and she bounced back in her seat.

'Is that better? And now do you want to hear what I'm sick of? I'm tired of being told that you're adopted, that you're an outsider, that nobody understands you. I understand you, Kate, and you'd better learn to live with it. And I love you, so if you don't like it you'd better go away. Go on —' He leaned across her and opened the door. 'If you can't put up with being loved by a patronizing prig like me, you can get out and walk.'

It was not for nothing that Kate had been able to embark on, and steadfastly maintain, a hunger and silence strike at the age of five. She got out of the car without demur, slammed the door and marched away from him up the lane, out of the range of the headlamps' beam. In a minute she was caught again in the funnel of light, then drowned in darkness as he drove past her.

She was so angry that she did not to begin with notice the cold, and she was walking so fast, fuelled by rage, that she kept stumbling and tripping in potholes in the road. It was pitch-dark and she had not the remotest idea where she was. Doubt began to erode her fine fury after about five minutes and after another five it took a still firmer hold when her right foot slipped into a ditch so that she was soaked to the knee in icy water. Cursing, she emptied out her shoe, hopping about on one leg in the middle of the road and staring wildly about her. Not a single car had passed her, other than Lawrence's, in either direction, it was truly a God-forsaken area. She contemplated heading back in the opposite direction, towards the school, but the thought of presenting herself at the main entrance of Hartfield House, bedraggled and alone, was more than she could stomach.

Wretched, frozen, her anger compounded by humiliation, she continued walking. Curiously, she felt a sneaking admiration for Lawrence, for driving off in such fine style. He had called her bluff good and proper. But at the same time she realized, when she saw the Morris parked beneath the white arms of a signpost, that she had never really expected him to abandon her, and even at the nadir of her pigheadedness she had never wanted him to.

He must have been looking in the mirror, for as she approached the door on the driver's side opened, and he stepped out. At first he walked slowly towards her, but then he was running, and they met with a wild collision, their arms so tightly about each other that to begin with there was no breath left for anything as inessential as talk. Wonderfully, in the icy cold, his mouth was hot, and his whole body warm against her, melting away her stubborn rage. His hasty, greedy, desirous hands made her thin, taut body magically pliant and yielding, and his breathless, loving words were like water on her barren pride, making it soften and blossom.

'Oh, Kate,' he said, 'don't ever, whatever you do, be meek and accepting. Keep swinging so that I'll always love you, but for God's sake be on my side! I'm stuck on you, Kate, and you'll have to get used to it!'

They reached Mapleton Road at nine o'clock, and as they got out of the car Aubrey opened the door at the top of the steps and stood waiting for them. He looked rumpled and tired and Kate felt affectionate towards him. He must have sensed an unusual warmth in her kiss, for he looked surprised.

'Hallo there, carols duly sung? Lawrence, you'll come in and sit by the fire for a few minutes, or do you have to rush off?'

'Thanks, Aubrey, just a few minutes, certainly.'

They went through into the drawing-room and Aubrey poured a whisky for Lawrence and himself and offered one to Kate, which she refused.

'Has Mrs Duckham gone up? I think I'll make myself some tea.'

'No, no, you sit tight, I think she's still around.' He left the room and returned in a moment. 'All fixed. So how was it?'

'A lovely service,' said Kate. 'But Joe was obnoxious.'

'Oh dear,' said Aubrey.

'She exaggerates,' said Lawrence. 'He's finding his feet, that's all. He's a nice boy, your Joe, absolutely nothing to worry about.'

'Good, good,' Aubrey looked relieved. Kate decided not to add to his anxiety by mentioning her brother's change of heart concerning the Treeces.

'How's Mr Tennant?' asked Lawrence.

'Not too good I'm afraid. He wanted to be here to see you when you got back, but he succumbed.' Aubrey sighed heavily 'He'd never have done that two months ago. Mind you,' he laid his hand on the Sunday paper which lay beside him on the sofa, 'this business with the King and that American female is cheering him up a bit. It's always gratifying to be proved right.'

Lawrence picked up the paper and scanned the front page. 'Only a matter of time, then.'

'Days, I should say.'

There was silence while Lawrence read on and Aubrey stared gloomily into the fire.

Kate stood up. 'I'll go and see him.'

Aubrey glanced at her. 'He may be asleep.'

'Then I won't stay.'

When she came down, Lawrence was standing in the hall. She came down the stairs slowly, her hand trailing down the bannister.

'Your tea's there,' he said, 'how is he?'

She shook her head. She felt utterly exhausted. Going close to Lawrence she lowered her forehead on to his shoulder and leaned against him, her arms hanging at her sides. In a small voice, she said: 'Perhaps I should give up the Institute and make myself useful around here.'

'Doing what?'

'I don't know . . . looking after him . . .' She saw herself how unlikely that was even before he laughed at her.

'That, Kate, is how to hasten the old chap into his grave. You know as well as I do that the pair of you would be at each other's throats in no time. Go on keeping him company from time to time, take him out of himself. You're a much better therapy for him the way you are.' He kissed her again. 'And for all of us.'

Aubrey came into the hall. 'Are you off then?'

'Yes, I must.'

The two men shook hands and then Kate went out of the front door and down the steps to see Lawrence off.

'If it's nice next weekend why don't you come down to Kent again,' he said. 'Mother would like to see you.'

Kate knew that what Lawrence was doing now was orchestrating their farewell.

'We'll see, shall we,' she said.

On Tuesday, 8 December, the headline on the front of the *Daily Express* read: 'End of Crisis'. Under this somewhat surprising announcement was a short statement from Mrs Wallis Simpson, in Cannes. 'Mrs Simpson,' ran the statement, 'throughout the last few weeks, has invariably wished to avoid any action or proposal which would hurt or damage His Majesty or the Throne. Today her attitude is unchanged, and she is willing, if such action would solve the problem, to withdraw from a situation that has been rendered both unhappy and untenable.'

'Too late, of course,' remarked Rex, heading west out of London in the Dart. 'And she knows it. It's just a calculated move on her part to win a bit of public sympathy. The woman has no idea.'

'Perhaps not. I mean, I don't know . . .' Dulcie was meek because she was drained of energy. She felt that if she were to become involved in an altercation with Rex today she would simply crack and crumble and be reduced to a little heap of scented dust on the floor. So she was going to concentrate on getting through the day as peacefully as possible, and not annoying him.

She sensed that he was building up to something, that it was not only she who was reviewing her life and finding it lacking. For the past few weeks she had seen much less of him, and because she had been frightened to see Bill she had been much alone. She had become jumpy and morbid. When Bill had turned up on her doorstep only the day before, telling her to snap out of it, she had become quite hysterical, screaming at him to stop ruining her life, to go away, to mind his own business. Celine had stood in the hall staring at her in astonishment as she slammed the door and then collapsed against it, crying noisily. Celine had tried to admit Bill, but then had started on her, telling her that she was interfering where she had no business and that her services were no longer required (an order Celine prudently chose to ignore).

Just remembering the scene made her close her eyes and shudder. She thought she might be going mad. Bill had rung her several times since then, once in the middle of the night, but when she'd heard his voice she'd hung up. She'd burnt her boats now. There was surely no way she could count on his love after the way she'd behaved.

This morning Rex had arrived unannounced and apparently in a good humour. The Roth-Vesey job was almost done, he declared, he would take her down there this very day to look over his handiwork, and they could all drink champagne in the elegant new rooms. Dulcie could think of few prospects she relished less than being exposed to Percy's wheezy importuning and Una's veiled bitchiness in her present vulnerable state, but there was no arguing with Rex. She decided to dress as simply as possible, like a penitent, almost, in a plain black dress with a high collar, because that was how she felt. Also, it would enable her to sidestep any possible competition with Una who was always done up to the nines. For some reason the black dress had amused Rex.

'Are poverty-stricken governesses all the go, then?' he asked as he helped her on with her fur coat.

'Don't you like it?'

'I do rather, as a matter of fact. You look – Garboesque.'

'Oh do I? Thank you.'

The house was called Links Lodge, because its two well-manicured acres backed on to a golf course. How like Una, thought Dulcie, as they swept up the drive between rhododendrons. It was large and gracious with white shutters and a vast garage.

'Lovely, lovely Rex and Dulcie – Dulcie, how *dramatic* you look – we are all going to have a celebration and ignore all this beastly business in the newspapers. Come in, come in . . .' Una, mooing, ushered them in at the front door and across an echoing hall to the ballroom-sized drawing-room at the back of the house, where Percy awaited them with champagne cocktails.

The predominantly white décor which Rex had chosen for the house was hard to appreciate in view of the 'teething problems', as Percy described it, which were affecting the central heating. Dulcie bitterly regretted having given up her coat in the hall, and even Rex chafed his hands together vigorously. The whiteness of everything, combined with the sub-zero temperature, made them feel that they were sipping champagne in the wastes of Antarctica.

'Don't you love my Christmas tree?' cooed Una. But the chic white and silver of her decorations made the tree, too, look frozen. A small coal fire burned in the marble grate, and they huddled round it.

Percy came close to Dulcie. 'Your young fella's done a good job, wouldn't you say? Sorry if it's a bit nippy. Shall I warm you up?' And with a chuckle he put his arm about her and rubbed enthusiastically.

'It's stunning,' she said, avoiding Rex's eye.

'And of course it's such a *wonderful* position,' Una was saying, 'I shall be able to improve my handicap no end.' Dulcie supposed she was referring to golf.

'There's a pool,' she went on. 'In the summer I plan to have huge, wonderful, alfresco parties the way we do in the States. Now!' She put her glass down on the mantelpiece with a purposeful air. 'I just have a couple of things I want to finalize with our creative genius here, so I'm going to take him away from you for a little moment.' She took Rex's hand and drew him from the room.

The couple of minutes became five, then ten. Dulcie accepted a second and third drink, and was shown the conservatory which was even colder than the drawing-room, and from which one could see the bleak, frosty wastes of the garden and the golf course beyond. Her feet and hands were numb and she was getting hungry. Also, she felt deserted. The very least Rex might have done after dragging her down here was to stay with her. It was like the yacht all over again, but without sunshine.

When Percy patted the plump white sofa cushion next to him, and suggested she keep him company, she could stand it no longer. She thought how nice it would be to be sitting by the fire in some cosy London pub, with Bill, eating shepherd's pie and laughing. Such a modest wish, such simple pleasures – she must be getting old.

'I must just go and powder my nose before lunch,' she said.

'Aha! Ladies' room upstairs and on your right, shall I get the girl to show you?'

'No, I can find it.'

'Don't be long now!'

Dulcie assured him that she would not be long and went once more out into the huge hall and up the graceful curved staircase. Everything was light, and white, and quiet and very cold. Silent as a shadow she walked along the thick pile carpet of the landing. In the guest bathroom the towels were white and blue, the bottles of bath salts crystal, the pale blue basin was supported by a single slender dryad, the soft swish of her diaphanous robe frozen in Italian marble.

As she returned across the landing she heard low voices and saw Una and Rex in a bedroom on the far side of the stairwell. The door was wide open, but they seemed to have no expectation of being surprised. The long windows behind them filled the room with a pale, clinical north light. Rex had his arms about Una's waist and her hands rested on his shoulders. Her head was tilted back, and her red, smiling, mouth was open.

Dulcie did not stop to stare. She continued along the landing, past the top of the stairs and the two closed doors, to the room where they were. She felt not astonished, or hurt, or vindictive, but clear-headed and calm. She realized she had known all along. When she appeared in the doorway she was triumphantly conscious of the picture she made – a small black figure in that pale room. Suddenly she was strong.

'Darling?'

Her voice was light, but the effect on them was electric. They moved apart sharply, Una's face was a study in shock. Rex, on the other hand, wore a self-satisfied expression. Dulcie suspected he had stage managed the whole thing. Smiling sweetly she walked up to him, ignoring Una, turning so that her back was to the other woman. 'Darling, I'm too cold, take me home would you?' She pressed against him, reached up her face to his.

'Of course.'

'You've done wonders with the house,' she went on, taking his arm and moving towards the door. 'But thank heaven you're not going to incarcerate *me* in a place like this!' She laughed her silvery laugh as they went out on to the landing. She had not so much as glanced at Una, but she could feel her gaze like a hand pressed on her back. She laughed again.

'They'll simply have to get their little heating problem sorted out before I come here again,' she said. 'I don't know how they'll coax all their smart friends down here, they'll all catch their deaths. I can see Una will have to find solace with a golf professional.'

'Dulcie!'

Till now he had been so astonished by her composure, so carried along by her confidence, that he had not even attempted an explanation. She stopped and looked at him with a bright, enquiring air. 'Yes?'

'We were finished, you must know that. Una and I –'

'Sh!' She place a finger lightly on his lips. She could as easily and happily have slit his throat. 'Not another word. Poor little Rex, you are in a muddle. But don't worry, you have the rest of your life to do just as you please with Una.' For the first time she looked over his shoulder and beyond at Una, who still stood rooted to the spot, her mouth a crimson 'O' in her white face. 'But Una dearest you'll have to keep a pair of warm pyjamas here for him. I simply don't know how he'll function in these kinds of temperatures.'

She ran, laughing, down the stairs. Rex hovered, muttered something apologetic to Una, and followed. In the drawing-room she bade Percy good-bye with such warmth and charm that he was rendered quite speechless.

Rex said something about getting a taxi, but she wasn't going to let him off that easily. Percy upbraided him for lack of gallantry and she clung to his arm until he was obliged to leave with her. It was the first time she had seen him so thoroughly discomforted. She was enormously pleased with herself. All the way back to London she hummed and chuckled and deflected his irate attempts to make a serious issue out of it all.

At Chesham Gardens she asked: 'Are you coming in? It is your flat after all.'

'Dulcie, you can keep it if you like.'

'Keep it? But what on earth would I *do* with it?'

She got out and slammed the door. '*Au revoir!*' she called as she ran to the house. 'I'll be gone tomorrow.'

In the event, she didn't even wait that long. What for? Suddenly, going was no problem at all. There was nothing to organize, no arrangements to make. The only possession she wanted to take with her was Fondant. She packed a small case while Celine watched, wailing miserably.

'But, Madame, where are you going? What do you want me to do? You cannot just leave me here. *Qu'est ce que je ferai toute seule? O mon dieu . . . !*'

'I'm not going to, Celine.' Dulcie patted her maid's shoulder. 'I'll call you tomorrow and let you know what I'm going to do. Then you can come and join me. Now go and order me a taxi, there's a dear.' She was afraid that if she did not keep going now she might weaken. It was late afternoon, grey and foggy and beginning to get dark. The flat was bright and cosy. It would be very easy to stay, just a little while longer. Fondant scraped and heaved in his cat basket and emitted heart-rending yowls.

She took a last look round the pretty pink champagne drawing-room and on an impulse unplugged and removed one of the two glass lamps. Then, unable to tolerate any more of Celine's mopping and moving she left, to wait for the taxi in the hall.

She was hopelessly overburdened with case, handbag, cat basket and lamp, and realized how unused she was to carrying anything for herself these days. She could have wept with frustration when the lift door closed on her suitcase, and again when she got out at the bottom and nearly tripped herself on the lamp flex which had come unwound and was trailing on the floor.

But the cab driver was masterful, relieving her of all her encumbrances and stowing them securely, then handing her in and slamming the door with a flourish. She sat in the cosy, purring darkness of the passenger seat, only half-listening as he regaled her with his views on the King's love-life, all the way to Maida Vale.

Bill had not been home long himself when the bell rang. He

had had a wearisome day trying to make overwrought, but stubborn, persons at the House and at Buckingham Palace admit the inevitable, to no effect. He had spent the latter part of the afternoon at the *Herald*, where everyone had been in a contentious mood because of the strain of filling the paper with stories which could be verified, when there was only one thing on everyone's mind. He had gone over the road to the pub with Trevor Parrish and Les Smedley and watched the latter become lugubriously drunk because, he claimed, this was the time of year when he missed his ex-wife who had run off with a jockey. Apart from Les's morbid ramblings, the whole atmosphere of the pub with its moth-eaten Christmas decorations and its smell and the seedy second-rate bonhomie of its Fleet Street patrons had depressed him unutterably. He wished he had been in Berlin where he could have gone to some place where there was music, and decent food and a wonderful array of run-down, glamorous eccentrics.

He was also concerned about Dulcie. She was a woman of the world, he could hardly break down her door and carry her off if she did not wish it, and on his last and ill-fated visit she had made that perfectly clear. He missed her lovely and amusing companionship, tonight of all nights he would have like her curled up beside him, sleek and scented and full of laughter, golden and bubbly as a glass of champagne, cheering up his life.

So when he heard the doorbell, and answered it to find her standing there, he could do nothing but open his arms and welcome her. She was loaded down like a travelling tinker.

'What is all this? What on earth are you doing?' He put the case and the lamp and the lurching cat basket to one side and removed her coat. She looked heroic in a plain black dress, her face pale, her eyes wide and excited.

'I've done it,' she said. 'I've left.'

He was incredulous. 'What?'

She began to laugh, her shoulders shaking, tears in her eyes, a hand over her mouth. 'I've left him – I just packed my case, and brought Fondant and walked out. He was having an affair with Una Roth-Vesey, it made it all so easy –'

The laughter became tears and she sank against him, shuddering with tiredness. Gently he led her along to the sitting room and sat her down on a chair by the purring gas fire. He crouched down before her and let her cry, wiping her cheeks with his hands, and stroking the hair back from her forehead. When her sobs began to subside, he said: 'You know, you've nothing to cry about. What you've done is absolutely splendid.'

She gazed at him tremulously. 'But here I am, messing up your life, I won't be any good for you, you know, and I don't have any money. Please can I stay here just for a little while, just until –'

'Darling, darling Dulcie.' He put his arms round her. 'You can stay here till you're old and grey. I've never been more pleased to see anyone in my life.' It was the truth.

'Really?' She was not being flirtatious. He had never heard her sound less confident. She put her hands on his shoulders and stared into his face with reddened eyes.

'Honestly.'

'Oh Bill –' She began kissing him all over his face, the feel of her lips like a shower of warm, damp rose petals falling on his skin. 'I want you so much I could die.'

The voice of Sir John Reith announced: 'This is Windsor Castle, His Royal Highness, Prince Edward.'

And now that other voice spoke, like a voice in a dream that we know to be familiar and yet which still in our dream sounds strange.

'At long last I am able to say a few words of my own. I have never wanted to withhold anything, but until now it has not been constitutionally possible for me to speak. A few hours ago I discharged my last duty as King and Emperor, and now that I have been succeeded by my brother, the Duke of York, my first words must be to declare my allegiance to him. This I do with all my heart . . .'

Dulcie felt tears spring to her eyes. She sat encircled by Bill's arm, with Fondant on her lap. The cat had not pined, but made himself instantly at home in the basement flat. There was no light apart from the glow from the gas fire. Out in the tiny second bedroom she could hear Celine coughing and sneezing plaintively — she had not found the adjustment so easy. The voice went on, with awful composure:

'. . . you must believe me when I tell you that I have found it impossible to carry the heavy burden of responsibility and to discharge my duties as King as I would wish to do without the help and support of the woman I love . . .'

Dulcie pressed her lips to Bill's cheek. 'I think that's wonderful,' she said. 'I admire him for saying that.'

Bill stared at the shivering violet flames of the fire. Dulcie had scarcely been out for two days. She still wore the same black dress that she had arrived in. She had cooked supper and scalded her wrist. Yet she seemed happy.

'So the world is well lost for love, then?' he asked drily.

'Oh yes —' she kissed him again. 'I know it is.'

'And I want you to know that the decision I have made has been mine and mine alone. This was a thing I had to judge entirely for myself . . . I have made this, the most serious decision of my life, upon a single thought of what would in the end be best for all . . .'

Ernest, standing behind the buffet paid for by Barnfields Publishing at the Connaught Rooms, reflected that the same was true in his own case. A momentous decision had been taken, he'd struck out on his own and there would be nothing more to hold him back. Tonight when he got home he would tell his mother that he had taken a job as secretary to a well-known playwright, that he would be living up west and making good money. He could hardly wait to see the look on her face. And first thing, he'd get her out of that rat-hole in Pear Tree Court and see her and Tony settled somewhere a bit more decent. All his own doing, achieved by his own efforts and initiative. From where he stood he could see Giles, standing silently, glass in hand, listening with the others to the broadcast. It was amusing to both of them to come across each other at these dos from time to time, and to play guest and waiter, hiding their secret like a couple of children with a forbidden cache of food.

Ernest saw that a few women were in tears, listening to the voice on the wireless. He couldn't understand it, everyone had seen it coming. Experimentally, he broke off a succulent morsel from the side of poached Scotch salmon that lay on the serving dish before him, and popped it in his mouth. Not a soul noticed, so he took another, and this time chased it down with a swig of champagne from an abandoned glass.

'. . . my brother, with his long training in the public affairs of this country and with his fine qualities, will be able to take my place forthwith, without interruption or injury to the life or progress of the Empire. And he has one matchless blessing, enjoyed by so many of you and not bestowed on me — a happy home with wife and children.'

Primmy, on duty on Women's Surgical, decided at this point that she had heard quite enough. She left the wireless on for the patients and returned to her office at the end of the ward. A young staff nurse was in the sluice, washing out bedpans and sobbing.

'Nurse Peach?'

'Sorry, Sister.'

'Pull yourself together now and get on with your work, that's quite enough of that.' Primmy watched her mop her eyes and sniff. 'And if I were you I should keep your sympathy for the new King who has a job of work to do like the rest of us.'

'Yes, Sister.'

'It's those who are left who have to pick up the pieces, Nurse Peach, make no mistake about it. Now no more silliness, if you please.'

'. . . I now quit altogether public affairs, and I lay down my burden. It may be some time before I return to my native land, but I shall always follow the fortunes of the British race and Empire with profound interest, and if at any time in the future I can be of service to His Majesty in a private station, I shall not fail.

'And now we all have a new King. I wish him, and you, his people, happiness and prosperity with all my heart. God bless you all. God save the King.'

'So there it is.' Aubrey rose and turned off the wireless. Mrs

Duckham, who had been sitting on a hard chair near the door, left the room quickly, closing the door after her.

Kate looked at Lawrence and saw that he was moved. His eyes shone, and though he did not look at her he opened his hand to receive hers, and squeezed it.

Ralph, wrapped in a tartan rug in his fireside chair, was exhilarated, his cheeks pink, his hair standing on end. 'And not a moment too soon! He's managed to do the decent thing at last and make way for someone with some sensible ideas. The American harpy is welcome to him.'

'Father,' Aubrey reprimanded him wearily. 'Don't be so hard on him. He did very well, I thought.'

'But of course, of course!' Ralph leaned forward, wagging a finger, 'of course he did well. He's always been good at the frippery side of things, at the talking and the shaking hands and the making friends.'

'Grandfather, he's *abdicated!*' Kate's patience was tried beyond endurance. 'You can hardly call that frippery.'

'Frippery reasons, though,' retaliated Ralph.

'I don't think they were to him,' said Lawrence gently. 'I think he might have made an excellent king under the right circumstances.'

'A nightclub king,' said Ralph.

'He's always been a good ambassador,' persisted Lawrence. 'You shouldn't underestimate the power of his popularity. After all, a king has no real power, so to be liked is important.'

'Young man,' said Ralph, threateningly. 'Don't make me think the less of you by speaking up for that damned lounge lizard.'

'Oh shut up!' Kate could stand no more. She stood up and towered over Ralph. Lawrence had driven from Aldershot that night to see her, and to hear the broadcast with them. He looked tired, and serious. She knew what he'd come to tell her. And yet they had not had one moment so far to themselves. Ralph, suddenly revitalized by the powerful whiff of drama and crisis, was being obnoxious. 'Really, you're being impossible!' she shouted. 'He's going now, can't you find a good word to say for him?'

'Why should I?' Ralph was truculent.

Lawrence stood up and took Kate's arm. 'Why don't we take a turn outside, Kate? We all need to cool off.'

'Oh very well!' She flounced out into the hall and hauled on her coat, rejecting Lawrence's efforts to help. He was in uniform, she resented the austere, professional look that this gave him, and the natural elegance with which he wore it. She resented its power, making him belong to others and not to her. She was angry. Out in the street she tried to walk quickly, but he linked his arm through hers and slowed her down.

'It's Palestine,' he said, holding her arm very tight. 'And we leave at the end of next week.'

'Thank you for telling me.' Her voice was tight and hard.

'I hate to tell you. And I dread being away from you.'

'But your country needs you, of course.'

He paused, keeping his temper. 'Yes.'

'Anyway, I shall be busy,' she went on in the same hatefully sarcastic tone, 'with my work, and I want a place of my own, and to see Europe, what with one thing and another —'

'Why don't you come to Palestine?'

She didn't reply for a moment. He repeated the question.

'What is there to see? People getting killed?'

'Come to Palestine, if it's possible. And marry me.'

Finally, she ran out of rage, and out of steam, and stood still, facing him. 'I'm not ready to get married, I'd be a terrible wife, surely you can see that, I'm nobody's idea of a wife —'

'You're my idea of the woman I love, and that I want beside me.' He took her face between his cold hands, and kissed her, and she put up her own hands to cover his and make the kiss last, because it was so very sweet and she could not face his awkward questions. But at last he stepped back and said: 'Well?'

'I don't know . . .'

'I love you, Kate. But I have a job to do, for which I've been trained, and unlike him . . .' he nodded his head back in the direction of the house, 'I can't give it up. I'm not asking you to be some kind of meek, well-dressed consort, the captain's lady, any of that. I want you there to share my life, just the way you are. I don't want to cramp your style, I want to show it off.' He linked his arm through hers again and began walking back. 'Don't say anything now, I won't press you. Think about it and let me know. But remember I'm dying a bit every minute that you keep me waiting.'

On the steps he kissed her again, and by the door, and she clung and kissed him back, hoping that her strength and her desire would show him what her words always failed to do — that she loved him, and wanted him, but was terribly afraid that he asked too much of her.

Inside, Ralph had gone to bed, and Aubrey was smoking a last reflective pipe by the fire. He looked up as they came in. 'Heads cleared? Good.' They were becoming used to his little rhetorical questions. 'Lawrence, why don't you stay in the spare room tonight? I say spare room, it's Joe's room, the bed's made up. You could make an early start in the morning.'

Lawrence glanced at Kate. 'Yes, that's kind of you, I might take you up on that. Thanks, Aubrey.'

'I'm sorry my father was in such a provoking mood. He can be very trying.'

'Don't mention it. He's a colossal age, he's entitled to hold strong views. It was good to see him so lively.'

They went up and Kate showed Lawrence into Joe's room, with its cricketing postcards under the glass of the chest of drawers. They passed Ralph's room. The door was ajar, but for once he was not snoring. Kate closed the door quietly. 'He's sleeping well tonight,' she said, 'arguing is good for him.'

'You're awfully like him, you know,' said Lawrence.

'That's hardly a compliment.'

'You could do a lot worse.'

'Good-night then.' She left him there, frightened to stay another minute, needing to think. And the picture of him that she took to bed with her was of him standing with one hand in his pocket, quite at home with the desk, and the postcards, and the model aeroplane and the threadbare counterpane, more at home in the setting he had occupied for two minutes than she would be anywhere, in her whole life.

In about an hour she crept out of bed and across the landing. She didn't knock, but entered softly. He was staring at her, he lifted the bedclothes and enfolded her in his arms as she slipped in beside him.

'We shouldn't . . .'

'I don't care. I'm a stray cat, take me in.'

They made love closely and quietly, in delicious clandestine discomfort, Joe's narrow upright bedstead seemed rigid with disapproval. And afterwards they remained joined, whispering and nuzzling in the darkness.

'You ought to go back to your room.'

'In a moment.'

'Think, if we were married —'

'Don't start.' She stopped his mouth with a kiss. 'I can't answer, you know I can't, you'll have to be patient.'

'I am. I know it's a case of "when", not "if".'

'You're unbearably smug.'

'It's self-protection. I'd wither away if I let myself believe anything else.'

'Oh, Lawrence, I love you. Don't leave me.'

He did not answer, but began once again to move inside her so that she softened, sighed and forgot herself.

The next morning she woke early, as usual. She had to leave for the Institute at eight, she told herself, but her real reason was that she needed a little while to get used to the idea of saying good-bye to Lawrence. She was shocked to find that he had already had breakfast and was bidding farewell to Aubrey down in the hall.

'You're not off already?' She heard an accusing note in her voice, and checked it. 'It's not seven-thirty yet.'

'He's not, but I am,' said Aubrey. He picked up his attaché case from the chair beneath the hall mirror. 'He's been telling me that he's off to Palestine next week. We're going to miss you,' he said, holding out his hand to Lawrence. 'But you will keep in touch, won't you?'

'Of course.'

When the door had closed behind Aubrey, Kate said: 'Please don't rush away.'

'I must go in another half hour or so.'

'We'll leave together. I'm just going to take Grandfather his tea.'

She collected the tray from the kitchen, and as she came

back through the hall, Lawrence picked something up from the ground. 'There's a letter for him.' He propped it against the milk jug.

She glanced at the envelope. 'It's from Thea. He'll like that.' She went upstairs, and nudged Ralph's door open with her shoulder. 'Tea . . .' Though the heavy curtains were still drawn, and it was dark, she knew at once that he had died. The stillness in the room was not peaceful, but forbidding. She put the tray on the chest of drawers and pulled the curtains a few inches apart. He lay on his side with his back to her, his shoulders even at his age bulking large beneath the blankets. She went over and looked into his face. She was not repelled, she had seen death before. And now her grandfather looked rested, tranquil, handsome. She remembered 'Venetia, beloved wife and companion of Ralph', and reflected that at least he would be seeing her again.

She remembered the letter and rose to fetch it from the tray. Then she sat on the edge of the bed, comfortably, with one hand on his shoulder, and read it aloud in a quiet, conversational voice.

'. . . I think they're holding out on me,' went the last paragraph, 'I have the feeling you're not at all well, and you won't admit it and Aubrey and Kate don't like to tell me the whole truth. Please say, I do have a right to worry, you know, I want to worry. I might even come over, there's an incentive! It hasn't been a bad year here, we could just about afford my fare and then I could see the children, as well. Thank you both for looking after them so well, and I'm more pleased than I can say that you've grown so fond of Kate. She's very special to us, but finds it so hard to accept love from other people. You jolly well teach her! And don't, don't forget to write, even just a line, to say how you *really are*. Why am I so far away from everyone? I'd better go before I start in earnest. So very much love to all of you, and don't scowl like that – love again, Thea.'

Kate lowered the letter slowly to her knee. The room was suddenly full of Thea, her voice and her laugh invaded the drab winter morning, they touched, and made good what was hurt and fractured. Kate replaced the letter in its envelope and slipped it under Ralph's pillow. Then she bent and kissed his cheek. 'He's not scowling any more,' she said.

She went down, carrying the tray, and entered the drawing-room. Lawrence stood by the window with the paper, Doreen was clearing the grate.

'Doreen, would you take this back to the kitchen please?' She waited until the girl had gone out, and then closed the door.

Lawrence came over to her and she went straight into his arms.

'He's gone,' she said, but her voice was calm.

'Oh my darling.'

'I read him his letter. They doted on each other.'

'That was nice.'

'She said —' her voice broke a little and she cleared her throat — 'she said I had to be taught to accept love, and that he was to teach me, but he's gone now.'

'Yes.'

'So I shall have to rely on you.'

'You will, yes.'

They moved apart, but she felt still their closeness. For the first time she had admitted weakness and asked for help, and incredibly she felt not weak and ashamed, but stronger because of it.

'Don't worry,' said Lawrence. He went to the phone. 'I'll make the arrangements and call Aubrey. You go and tell them downstairs.'

She went into the hall and paused for a moment at the foot of the stairs, her hand on the newel post. Outside in Mapleton Road there was the mundane clink of milk bottles. A king had gone, a new king reigned, men had died in the night. But milk bottles arrived, life went on.

She turned her head and saw Lawrence looking after her, the receiver in his hand.

'I'll marry you,' she said.

'I know,' he replied.

PART TWO
1939–41

CHAPTER ELEVEN

> 'Some day we'll build a home
> On a hill top high
> You and I,
> Shiny and new,
> A cottage that two can fill;
> And we'll be pleased to be called
> The folks who live on the hill . . .'

> 'The Folks Who Live On the Hill'
> Oscar Hammerstein II and Jerome Kern, 1937

KATE crawled through the small door of the hut on her hands and knees. The hut was made of corrugated iron, like a makeshift oven and just ahead of her the fire snarled and clamoured in the enclosed space. The heat was intense.

She'd been ordered to put on a pair of men's overalls over her own shirt and trousers, and a pair of wellington boots instead of the plimsolls she'd been wearing. Both were several sizes too large, and she felt heavy and awkward. To add to her discomfort, the dilapidated tweed fishing hat which she had borrowed from Aubrey for just this purpose, and into which she had stuffed her hair, kept slipping over her already streaming eyes.

'Push on!'

She scrambled forward. As she drew nearer the shuddering red tentacles of the fire the skin of her face felt as if it were being flayed from her skull. Though she knew the building to be no more than a few yards across, she could not see the far side for the thick smoke. She paused, shaking her head like an animal.

'Get a move on, you can't hang about!'

Stung, she crawled forward again. There was hardly any air now; when she gasped and gulped it was to swallow a scorching torrent of unfriendly smoke.

'On your feet! Stand up!'

She could no longer tell where the voice was coming from, she was completely disorientated. Shambling and bear-like in her heavy clothes, she staggered to her feet and at once the heat was even fiercer, she held up her arms in front of her as if to ward it off.

'All right, on your way, let's be having you!'

Where? she thought. Where do I go?

'Run, double quick!'

She lurched forward and as she did so a hand reached through the smoke and yanked the sleeve of her overalls. Following the pull, she was suddenly bursting through a tiny narrow doorway, barking her elbows painfully on the sides.

She coughed violently, gulping and snatching at the soft, fresh September air. She raised her hands to rub her smarting eyes, but was restrained. A firm, woman's voice said: 'Don't do that, my dear, your hands are all gritty. Here.'

A cool damp sponge was pressed into her right hand. Gratefully she dragged off the tweed hat and applied the sponge to her eyes, face and neck, squeezing little rivulets of water over her scorched skin. When she'd finished, and could see, she noticed that the sponge was competely black.

Behind her she heard a great hiss like a steam engine as the fire was doused with a bucket of water. It had only been that small a fire. She felt ashamed of her panic and clumsiness. But the ARP instructor, emerging from the hut with a galvanized iron bucket, slapped her heartily between the shoulder blades. 'Not bad, not bad.'

She smiled a little sheepishly at the handful of other women who had been through the smoke room before her, and who were now flopped down on the smooth lawn of the Convent of St Cross in Lancaster Gate. No one returned her smile: they were demoralized. One of them blew her nose vigorously and studied the sooty black stain on her handkerchief as if it were a substance from another planet. Before Kate stood one of the holy sisters, her little nubbly Rembrandt face smiling from the crisp white frame of her coif, large black rubber boots peeping incongruously from beneath the hem of her habit.

'All right now dear? You did very well.'

'Did I?' Kate grimaced disbelievingly. 'I don't know. How on earth would I have managed in a real fire – I couldn't have lasted another second.'

'Ah, but . . .' the nun raised a finger, '. . . supposing you had been going to rescue someone. I think you'd surprise yourself.'

'I certainly hope so.'

'Right, ladies!' The instructor clapped his hands. 'If you're all recovered, shall we proceed?'

'Your trials are not yet over,' said the sister.

'Oh God – I mean, I'm sorry –'

'That's all right, my dear. Just don't expect Him to help with training. He'll be along for the real thing.'

Kate joined the other women and the instructor, who had gathered on a further part of the lawn. To the right was a lovingly tended herbaceous border, over which presided a white stone madonna with demurely downcast eyes and a disapproving mouth. One languid, tapering hand rested on the folds of her robe as if to prevent it being soiled. To the left was a prefabricated wall, about eight feet high and ten feet long; beyond that, a length of concrete pipe a couple of feet in diameter and several yards long; finally a large tarpaulin secured with tent pegs.

'I'm going to put you over an obstacle course,' announced the instructor, not without a little amiable relish.

As he pointed and explained, Kate's attention wandered. She caught sight of a procession of nuns moving along the cloister at the side of the main convent building, in the direction of the chapel. None of them returned her stare, but glided on their way like swans, perfectly composed and incurious. Wisps of smoke and wandering black flakes of ash from the corrugated iron hut drifted past them. Unhurriedly they disappeared behind the rampart of sandbags which protected the outer wall of the chapel.

'Mrs Drake . . . are you with us?'

'I'm sorry.' She turned back guiltily to the instructor.

'Now this is what I want you to do.'

He rose on his toes, took a short, bouncing run, hauled himself up the wall, ran along the top and jumped down lightly; dashed to the pipe and wriggled along it; a final sprint and under the tarpaulin.

He returned to them, dusting his hands together. 'Now you. Think you can do that?'

He was answered by a faint, despairing chorus. Heads were shaken, hands raised to faces in attitudes of dejection.

'Now *then*.' He adopted a wheedling tone. 'Don't let's be downhearted. Is there anyone who'll give it a go?'

'Yes, I will.' Kate walked to the front.

'Attagirl, Mrs Drake!'

'Can I take these boots off and put my plimsolls back on?'

'Of course.'

Someone threw her her white plimsolls and she sat on the grass to change into them. The instructor said, over her head: 'Perhaps the rest of you'll feel braver when Mrs Drake has proved it can be done.' A mournful silence greeted this sally. Kate squared up to the wall. The instructor took up a position at its base, holding out one arm encouragingly — and a little patronizingly, Kate considered — in her direction. From the chapel came the soft lilt of plainsong.

'Ready when you are, Mrs Drake.'

Kate charged at the wall. So great was her determination after the humiliation of the smoke-hut that, assisted by her natural athleticism and the instructor's boosting palm beneath her backside, she almost flew right over the top. She teetered, got her balance and ran, half-crouching, to the end. Down with a bounce, on to the pipe, into the cold, stony darkness aiming for the circle of light at the end, elbows, knees, toes. Out into the sun, dash for the tarpaulin, a brief scramble beneath its warm stifling weight, and she'd done it.

Elated, she ran back to the others, to be met by a gratifying ripple of applause.

'There you are, you see!' said the instructor, 'it can be done. That was very good, Mrs Drake.'

The morning wore on, very hot. All the women went over the obstacles eventually, several times, with varying degrees of assistance. Even the most timid and unco-ordinated among them became too hot and tired to worry. No one disgraced herself. At twelve-thirty the instructor called a halt, and reminded them that next week they would be given a lecture on the use of the stirrup pump and different types of gases, and the week after that they would have a chance (he made it sound like a special treat) to go through the gas room, and pay a visit to a Gas Cleansing Station.

'That's it for today then, ladies, off you go.'

They trudged back over the lawns, carrying their boots and shoes, letting their feet enjoy the springy grass. War was hell, they agreed, beginning to see the funny side now that the class was over.

It was ten days since Kate and Lawrence had sat by the wireless in their flat above the chemist in Craven Road, Paddington, and listened to Chamberlain make his grim, though not unexpected, announcement. And within minutes the howl of the siren had risen like a grey sword of sound that carved the word WAR on the sunny sky over London. And people had bustled in off the streets into the public shelters, smiling nervously at each other, even laughing, relieved that the waiting was over, but not really knowing what had begun.

Now the women from the ARP class, most of whom were of an age to have been the daughters of one war generation, and now the wives and girlfriends of another, went into the Convent to get changed. ' *"Oh, it's only a phoney war . . ."* ' carolled a young secretary as she straightened the seams of her stockings, and the others laughed at the Americanism.

Kate left alone and walked over the road to eat her meat paste sandwiches in the Italian gardens by the Serpentine. She was no more than a quarter of a mile from home, but she much preferred to be out of doors.

She leaned on the wall, munching, and watched the faithful, monogamous Serpentine swans patrolling the bank with their flotilla of gauche grey cygnets.

When, on the grey December morning of Ralph's death, Kate had told Lawrence that she would marry him, she had meant it as a prophecy rather than a promise. Both knew that they would be together, that it would happen, but that Kate needed time to grapple with the idea. Within days, Lawrence had departed for the Middle East. Thea had come back to help settle Ralph's affairs, to be part of the old order again for a while, to mourn as a daughter. And during the time that she was over, Daphne Kingsley — cheerful, practical, sympathetic Daphne, who'd never had a day's illness in her life — had died, and the ailing Robert had been settled, not without much heart-searching, in a residential home for gentlefolk at Thorpness, near the boating lake.

It had been a strange time, and to enhance its strangeness, Dulcie had joined them. Not literally, at Mapleton Road — she would never live there again — but the three of them spent long hours together. In spite of everything it had been a serene and happy interlude, when the three women had felt close and affectionate; they had talked all night, and offered up confidences, and laughed and drunk and seen each other in a new and tender light. But every so often, at quite unexpected moments, the ghost of some ancient battle, a little malign shade which Kate knew had always haunted the relationship of these two sisters, would suddenly appear, in a look or a chance remark. And then the idyll ended. She would see the two of them back off like wild animals who won't fight in earnest in case real and lasting wounds are inflicted. And Kate would be forcibly reminded of how little she really knew of those whom she was pleased to call her family.

Thea's visit was short, and taken up with family duties. After a month she returned to Kenya, leaving Kate with a mild sense of relief which she did not bother to analyse. Though they had talked about Lawrence she had not mentioned his proposal, nor her acceptance of it, but hugged it somewhat selfishly to herself, a hostage to fate.

If anything, Lawrence dominated her thoughts more in his absence than he had ever done before. And it was no simple emotional deprivation that she suffered, but an awful physical craving that made her try to simulate his touch when she got into bed at night, until she was taut and damp with desire. When at last she fell asleep, exhausted and unrelaxed, she would dream the same thing all over again, and awake in the morning and unrefreshed. She grew thinner, and was short-tempered both at the Institute and at home. She lived for his letters, but when they came, bringing with them the sound of his voice and the look of him as he spoke, she was left feeling still more frustrated.

She wrote back: 'Please, *please* can I come now?' but as if to pay her back for her earlier procrastination she had to wait an agonizing three months. It was not as simple as that, the situation in Palestine was delicate and fraught, things had to be arranged. Kate felt the Army like an obdurate wall between herself and the gratification of her dearest wish.

During this difficult and stressful period of waiting she did a strange thing. She wrote Thea and Jack a quite brief and formal letter, saying that Lawrence had asked her to marry him, and that she had accepted and would be joining him as soon as possible. She was cool, almost as if emphasizing that she did not need their permission (she had now turned twenty-one), or require their approval. It was only some weeks later, when Thea replied, that Kate discovered that Lawrence himself had written a long and warmly affectionate letter to her parents, requesting their blessing and expatiating in no uncertain terms on his feelings for her.

But though she may have been less than just to the Kingsleys, she felt compelled to seek out Dulcie. They walked in Hyde Park, among the crowded early spring daffodils. Or at least Dulcie walked in a collected manner while Kate paced and circled, now walking backwards in front of her, now stopping dead, covering ten yards to Dulcie's two.

'I think you should do what will make you happy,' was Dulcie's measured response.

'He does make me happy. And I do love him.'

'That's all right then. Go ahead and marry him.'

Something in her aunt's choice of words provoked Kate into grabbing her arm and halting her.

'But what would you do in my place?'

'Oh, Kate . . .' Dulcie shook her head. She wore a double-breasted grey coat with a white cotton broderie blouse beneath it and a little grey felt cloche hat pulled down over her hair. She looked like a particularly bewitching and expensively turned-out nanny. 'How can I possibly put myself in your shoes? We're so completely different, you and I.'

'But I don't think we are!' Kate almost shouted at Dulcie. She had come straight from the Ross and was at her most eccentrically untidy. 'I don't think we are, I think we're alike!'

One or two passers-by glanced nervously at the two women,

perhaps thinking that the more elegant of the two was being harangued by a mad woman, or female tramp.

'Oh, no.' Dulcie walked on briskly. 'No, no. You're wrong.'

'Yes!' Kate chased after her. 'Just because we look different and have different manners — that doesn't mean anything. There's something deeper than that, as if we both grew in the same soil.'

'Poppycock,' said Dulcie lightly. She stooped to pick a daffodil and tucked it into the lapel of her coat. 'I'm a European, through and through.'

'But I was five before I went to Kenya!' declared Kate triumphantly, too carried away with the discussion to notice the whitening of her aunt's cheeks.

'Look, you wanted my advice — my opinion — about Lawrence,' said Dulcie with dangerous firmness. 'And you don't really need either because you have already accepted him. You just want your decision approved.'

'All right, I do! Yes, I do, I want it approved by you, though heaven knows why.'

Dulcie tucked her arm through Kate's. 'I'm glad you do — glad, and touched. I told you I think Lawrence is one in a million. But you're planting love in bedrock there, it won't easily shake loose. So just be very, very sure, for both your sakes.'

Kate replied, carefully, aware that her aunt had spoken from the heart: 'I do realize that. You know I refused him, several times —'

'Did you? Why?' Dulcie looked at her sharply.

'For the reasons you said, and because I was afraid of so much future, all that forever-ness, and afraid of the strength of his love, of perhaps hurting him or letting him down. But now, since he's been away I've been in agony, Dulcie, it's been torture, you don't know . . .'

'Yes, I do, poor Kate.'

'So I thought — this proves it. I'm meant to be with him.'

They walked for a moment in silence. Below them the Serpentine, dotted with cruising ducks, glinted in the spring sunlight. Suddenly Dulcie put her hand on Kate's shoulder and kissed her cheek. 'Then I'm sure you are. And I wish you all the luck and happiness in the world.'

*

The weeks dragged by. In her vulnerable condition the coronation of the new king in May moved Kate, if not to tears, at least to an incapacitating lump in the throat. She was filled with admiration and affection for that shy, stammering man, and his lovely, loving wife, and their two wide-eyed small daughters, all four of them thrust so abruptly into the full glare of regal limelight, and facing up to it with such dignity. Kate felt for the first time like one of the British people, because she had seen one king go, and another come, and it had touched her in spite of herself.

At last everything was arranged. In the space of a few weeks she had packed, left, and was married to Lawrence Drake in the hideous Anglican church in Haifa – she in a white tailored suit and a snap-brimmed hat with a feather, he dashing in uniform and sword. Armed soldiers among the orange trees and in the street by the church, on the look-out for snipers . . . the guard of honour, smiling young faces running with sweat beneath glinting swords . . . an armoured car trailing a plume of yellow dust all the way to the officers' mess for the reception . . . men who kissed her, and called Lawrence lucky, but whose names she didn't know . . . and Lawrence. In this hot, arid country, he was like something minted by the sun, golden and brown and smiling. That night in the best hotel in Haifa they fell on each other like greedy children at a party, without finesse or care or concentration, gorging themselves and coming back for more until they were exhausted. There was whisky and soda on a table by the balcony door and Lawrence had fetched the siphon and played the jet all over her bare back . . .

'Now, she stuffed her half-eaten apple back into its paper bag and set off in the direction of the tube station. She was bound for the Ross Institute.

They'd had a year in Palestine, a strange year of uncertain partings, and heat, and wild weekends of swimming and drinking and love-making, and long dusty days of boredom and loneliness. To her surprise and delight she found herself popular, and admired, both with Lawrence's friends and their wives. She even made a particular friend of Beth Maloney. Beth was gorgeous, frothy, flighty and incompetent. She wore lovely, unsuitable clothes, delicious hats and lots of immaculate make-up. In short, Beth was everything Kate was not, it was the basis of their friendship. Each quickly got to know just how much in the other was real, and how much a handy façade.

But at the end of that one year, in late summer 1938, Lawrence had been recalled for a post in Personnel at the War Office, much to his disgust, and it had been back to London and the flat in Craven Road.

Kate missed the life in Palestine, and she missed Beth. But the pattern of her life in London soon began to reassert herself. She took up her old job at the Ross Institute and rediscovered her close friendship with Dulcie.

Bill Maguire was now 'fixtures and fittings', as Aubrey put it, in her aunt's life, so it seemed that Kate's premonitions of disaster had been false. She herself was still not at ease in his presence, but Lawrence liked him, and since the four of them were in each other's company a fair amount she had to suppress this uneasiness. She felt all the time that the two of them functioned on a separate and secret wavelength, so that each involuntary gesture and unconsidered, innocent remark of the one was at once interpreted on a baser level by the other. It was as though they were so transparent to each other that discretion was futile and politeness a waste of time – it was extremely uncomfortable. And if he touched her, however casually and accidentally, she positively jangled with shock as if she had been subjected to the most intimate stolen caress. But all these things were secret, she scarcely admitted them to herself, let alone to anyone else. She swept them under the carpet like so much emotional clutter.

Another call on Kate's energies was Joe. During the Drakes' year abroad, Aubrey had stood stalwartly *in loco parentis*, but now that they were back Kate felt her responsibilities in this regard weighing heavily upon her. It was virtually impossible for him to get back to Kenya for holidays, and at fourteen he was becoming pompous and aloof. Kate had endured his company for half the summer holidays just gone – the other three weeks having been divided between the cricket-loving Aubrey and a schoolfriend in Sussex – and he had driven her nearly to distraction. She could nowhere recognize in this lazy, greedy, supercilious stranger the boy with whom she had willingly shared hours of her time on the farm in Gilgil. She had found herself thanking her lucky stars that she was not *really* of the same flesh and blood, then loathing herself for resorting to that when she'd always sworn she never would. His public-school armour was all the more impregnable for being newly acquired. Only once had a chink appeared in it.

At half-term they had gone to visit Robert Kingsley up in Thorpness. Lawrence had been away for the week on a course at Camberley and Kate had piled a protesting Joe – 'for heaven's sake, he won't know us from Adam!' – into the car and driven out through the austere East Anglian countryside in perfect summer weather. Robert had been frail, faded, and all too heartbreakingly aware of who they were. It was almost as if the strength of his pleasure at seeing them might prove too much for his weakened frame and cause it to collapse altogether. They had sat in the trim, antiseptic garden of the home, in a row on a slatted green garden seat, and the niggling east coast breeze had lifted Robert's few remaining strands of lank grey hair off his freckled scalp. Two pink spots had appeared on his soft, sunken cheeks, and tiny specks of foam at the corners of his seamed mouth, because of his excitement at having these two young visitors, proof of his past and of his substance.

Matron came to tell them there would be tea in the lounge if they wanted it, and they had moved in out of the sunshine to eat cherry cake and scones, and drink strong brown tea dispensed by a young woman with bright, patronizing manners: 'All you want, Mr Kingsley? There we are, that's the style!'

Robert asked a lot of questions, some of them many times over. He listened to their answers with rapt attention. His tea got cold, though he stirred it often. His cake and scone were left untouched. Kate dreaded the moment when they must say good-bye. But when that moment came he showed a surprising sprightly fortitude, insisting on coming out to the drive with them, wavering breathlessly across the parquet in the front hall, and down the steps, one at a time, prodding each with his stick first.

By the car, he had taken Joe's hand in his and pressed a ten-shilling note into his cupped palm with bent, careful fingers. Then he had patted his grandson's shoulder, saying, 'Good-bye, old man,' and kissed Kate with just a trace of the rakish fellow he had once been, but which she had come on the scene too late to recognize.

As they drove away he had stood there with his stick raised above his head in salute, leaning back a little from the waist in a way that showed how his trousers hung loose from his braces around his shrunken waist.

Kate glanced at Joe. 'He was glad to seé us.'

'Yes.' His head was averted. The tendons in his neck looked taut and stiff.

'He particularly liked seeing you,' she added.

'I daresay.'

His cool tone infuriated her. 'For God's sake, Joe, couldn't you manage to do these things with better grace? It's over now, you've done your bit, it wasn't so terrible – you even managed to get ten bob out of it –'

She at once regretted the unworthiness of that remark, but it was too late. He turned to look at her, his face distorted with anger and misery, the eyes brimming with tears.

'Shut up, Sis! Just put a sock in it, can't you?'

Two of the tears spilled over, and he dashed them away with the cuff of his blazer, sniffing hugely.

In bed that night she thought about the two old men, Ralph and Robert. She realized that in her mind's eye the former, dead now for nearly three years, retained more substance and vitality than the living, whom they had seen only a few hours ago.

And, in an indirect way, some good had come of Ralph's death. Aubrey Tennant, freed at last from the inhibiting presence of his more forceful parent, had blossomed. He had been undismayed by the departure of Mrs Duckham (who had been knocked for six by Ralph's death) after thirty years in the Tennants' employ. He had received quite a number of applicants for the advertised post of cook/housekeeper and had selected from their ranks Mrs Iris Pargiter, a trim, sprightly widow in her fifties.

Kate and Dulcie had given this arrangement a fortnight at most. Aubrey was no judge of character and on the face of it this looked like his worst error to date. Garrulous and managing, Mrs Pargiter seemed expressly designed by the Almighty to reduce Aubrey's bachelor nerves to tatters in record time. But astonishingly, the reverse was the case. Iris (as she very soon became known) took Mapleton Road and its incumbent in hand, and made herself indispensable. Aubrey became her devoted slave. She had rooms redecorated, furnishings 'seen to' (a favourite euphemism of hers covering everything from a darn to wholesale burnings), and soon found a willing lad to keep the garden down now that Kate was no longer around.

Iris it was, after only eight weeks in residence, who organized a slap-up buffet on the occasion of the Coronation, and actually persuaded Aubrey to hire a television set so that his family and friends might watch the historic occasion as it happened! Kate and Dulcie, in their baser moments, were given to covert gigglings and speculation as to when Aubrey might make an honest woman of Iris Pargiter. But she had won their liking and respect, and everyone else's, by sheer hard work. Neither did she take advantage of her success. Publicly at least she was scrupulously proper, calling Aubrey 'Mr Tennant' and never remaining present at a social occasion unless specifically invited to do so — which she usually was. Her manner was cheerful and friendly but not over-familiar. She was, in short, a treasure.

But while Iris Pargiter held a steady course, onlookers were treated to the extraordinary spectacle of Aubrey beaming and purring like a Cheshire cat, buying new lightweight suits and going to see musical shows.

'That woman's got him on toast,' remarked Dulcie to Bill Maguire one evening when they had been to supper at Mapleton Road. 'Do you think she's a gold-digger?'

Bill laughed aloud. 'You're lucky you can afford to be so hard on people. If you were plain I'd accuse you of bitchiness.'

'Don't you dare.'

After the somewhat chaotic and undignified manner of her arrival at his flat Dulcie had sensibly and to Bill's enormous relief asserted her independence. Her father had left her some money and she had got a place of her own not too far away on the fringes of St John's Wood. Not only that, she had found herself a job. It was quite humble, an assistant in a smart dress shop, but she had done well in it, and was now a kind of submanageress, and did some impromptu mannequinning, too. Dulcie took a pride and delight in it that he would not have believed possible, wore the required plain black frock and pearls day after day without a murmur of protest, and talked about it with warm enthusiasm. In spite of Aubrey's gloomy mutterings that it was 'hardly the thing' Bill saw that, on the contrary, it was precisely the thing. The job provided an outlet for Dulcie's style and taste and her ability to cultivate those things in others. She was surrounded by beautiful clothes and wealthy, elegant people. Her classiness and her obviously honest, but tactful opinions, won her a clientele all her own, who would be served by none but her.

The acid test had been the arrival one morning of Una Roth-Vesey. When Dulcie had reported the incident to Bill she had described it as 'hilarious', adding that she had sold Una the most expensive cocktail dress in the shop. That had convinced Bill that Dulcie had turned the corner. Wonderfully, incredibly, she made only those demands on him which he was able to supply. He could not believe his luck. He found himself wondering just what it was in her past that had given her such a talent for compromise, and then realizing he'd never know.

From the Commercial Road Kate turned down one of the side-streets, between the weekday market stalls. It was two o'clock and hazily hot. The smells of the market hung in the air – frying onions, and fish turning in the heat, and rotting vegetation from the discarded hulls of cabbages and cauliflowers that lay beneath the trestles.

The little man at the end stall knew Kate. Either she or Andrea usually called to pick up a box of leftovers to make soup for the Institute's supper patrons. The stallholder was a small, rickety man, his face pasty white, shadowed only by the peak of his cap above and the stubble on his chin below. He had no teeth, which added emphasis to his nutcracker profile.

'Afternoon, princess.' He flicked his fingers to the edge of his cap.

'Afternoon, Stan. Warm enough for you?'

'Struth –' he wiped his brow with the corner of his brown cardigan, 'don't talk to me about it. If the Nazis come this afternoon, they can 'ave me and welcome.'

Kate glanced up at the clear blue sky. 'You're out of luck, Stan. Anything for me?'

He heaved a potato sack round the side of the stall, and opened the top for her inspection. 'I put a few decent spuds in and some onions. If you come back later there'll be more.'

'Thanks.' She twisted and knotted the neck of the sack and carted it with her. Although strictly speaking the Institute came as a beggar, only asking for things which might otherwise be thrown away, Stan could generally be relied upon to 'chuck in' one or two good items. All the market men knew people who'd had cause to thank the Institute from time to time.

At present, their most pressing task was to liaise with the WVS and the local schools in the evacuation of children from the area. Many thousands had reached pre-arranged reception centres in Wales, Yorkshire and the West Country within hours of the declaration of war, but the process was still continuing. It was not a job Kate relished, but this afternoon she had been detailed to accompany a group of evacuees to Paddington and see them on to the four o'clock train.

Toting her sack, she went round to the back of the Institute and in at the kitchen door. As she crossed the small yard by the dustbins she was apostrophized by the parrot: 'Boiled beef and carrots! Carrots!'

'Boil your head, you horrible fowl!'

She left the sack of vegetables in the kitchen and went along the corridor to the front hall.

There were a dozen children assembled, standing silently in the dusty shafts of sunshine that came through the fanlight over the door. The bitter smell of old clothes and unwashed hair warred with the mutton-stew ghost of weekday dinner. Voices off, from the direction of Bobby Hollis's office, told her that the woman who had brought the children was in there, with Bobby and Andrea.

'Hallo,' said Kate.

One or two muttered "allo, Miss' but the majority didn't spare her a glance, let alone a word. Their heavy, hangdog silence was the backdrop against which buzzed a small cloud of insect-like sounds – the creaking of heavy boots on the wooden floor, the scratching of heads, the rasp of jacket sleeves on snotty upper lips, the rustle of awkward parcels of personal belongings.

'You can sit down,' suggested Kate, 'and rest your legs. If you want to.'

Nobody did so. But someone, with the first glimmerings of social know-how, said, ' 'Sorlright, Miss.'

'Does anyone need anything? Does anyone need to go to the lavatory?' This enquiry, as usual, brought a response, a bit of ungentle tweaking and urgent interrogation by older brothers and sisters of smaller fry. A tiny figure was pushed forward, bundled up in a heavy overcoat. In spite of the heat all the children were accoutred like Napoleon's army on the retreat from Moscow, in a motley assortment of winter clothes — jumpers, coats, mufflers and even hats — piled on by well-meaning urban mothers fearful of the rigours of country life.

''E wants the toilet, Miss,' said someone from the back row.

'All right, come along.' She held out her hand. The child put his hand in hers — it felt hard and calloused, like a little paw. He still carried his parcel, which dragged heavily beside him from its loop of whiskery string, and his gas mask slung round his neck in its box.

'You can leave those,' said Kate. She moved to lift off the gas mask, but he shrank away, glaring at her. A larger boy came forward with much sucking of teeth, removed parcel and gas mask and pushed the urchin's ear with scaly knuckles. 'Get a bloody move on or you'll wet yerself!'

Kate looked at the small boy's identification label, tied round the top button of his coat. 'Come on then, Archie.'

She led her charge briskly round the corner and down the corridor to the cloakroom. From his size she guessed he might be five, but experience had shown that children from this neighbourhood were often small for their age, with skinny immature bodies housing brains of quite staggering guile and deviousness.

In the lavatory she helped Archie locate the necessary outlet beneath coat, pullover, shirt, vest and incongruously flowered girl's pants. He then confounded her by turning and sitting down. Discreetly she withdrew, pulling the door to.

With a loud 'Oy, wotcher doing?' he yanked it open again, almost falling off with the effort of doing so. Kate reflected that someone somewhere was going to find Archie's mistrust of privacy a problem. He slid off, and Kate arrested the upward rush of pants and cut-down grey flannel trousers.

'Bend over.' She tipped him forward and availed herself of some of Bobby Hollis's old correspondence that hung from a nail. Besmirching for ever the signature of the bishop, she pulled the chain, and helped Archie with his clothes while the cistern went through agonies of clanking, belching and hissing before parting with its disappointingly small store of rusty water.

Back in the front hall she found Andrea, and a spruce, grey-haired lady in the green uniform of the WVS, who was taking a register. Andrea greeted Kate. 'All set?'

'I hate it. By the way, Stan said there'd be some more stuff to pick up later in the afternoon.'

'I'll go.'

Looking at Andrea, Kate wondered how she'd manage to carry a large sack of vegetables from the market to the Institute, a good half mile. She was thin and pale. She looked now what she had never looked before, a plain, tired, middle-aged woman with a philandering husband, who poured her energies into good works in order not to confront her problems. She was at the Institute more, she spoke of Louis less. Her clothes were still of good quality, but not so well cared for. She smoked, and coughed a lot, lighting each cigarette from the stub of the one before.

Now she touched Kate's arm: 'How's Lawrence?'

'He's fine. You must come round again.' They'd had the Averys to dinner with Dulcie and Bill, but it had been disastrous. Louis had been at his most extravagantly affected and ingratiating and Andrea had said nothing but sat with a set, white face and nervous eyes. The love which Kate had remarked that afternoon in the National Gallery seemed finally to have gone, crushed and squeezed out of her by the monstrous steam roller of Louis's vanity.

Andrea shook her head. 'I don't know, my dear. Louis is so busy, and I'm down here, what with one thing . . .'

'I know how it is.' Kate stopped her embarrassed catechism of excuse.

'I say, isn't that the Parfitts?'

Andrea brightened. 'Yes, I meant to tell you, they caught up with her at last!'

Mona Parfitt, though not many people's idea of a perfect mother, had been surprisingly loth to let her four offspring be removed to the safety of the Devon countryside. The system had been for all children to attend school each day ready for evacuation, clothes packed, sandwiches wrapped, heartrending farewells duly said. This dreadful note of preparation was designed to confuse the unscrupulous Hun so that he would not be able to divine on which day or on which train the flower of Bethnal Green and Whitechapel was leaving for its bucolic haven. No matter that not a single German plane had been seen in the cloudless summer skies over London, the fear of fifth columnists was rampant.

So most of the children whom Kate, Andrea and others had escorted to the big London rail termini had been through the painful business of leaving home at least three or four times before the real thing happened, and were too confused to care.

Mona Parfitt alone would have none of it. Day after day from the truly dreadful squalor of the Parfitt establishment in Empire Road she had sent forth Donald, Clara, Clark and Bobby quite unprepared. All approaches from kindly school-masters and welfare workers were met with squawks of: 'They stays with me!'

But today the Parfitts were there. Scruffy, sullen, charmless, but present.

Andrea turned slightly so that her face could not be seen by the children. 'I think Mona Parfitt has a new swain, and he has persuaded her that while the kittens are away — you take my point.'

Kate nodded. 'I do.'

The WVS lady bustled over, rustling papers. 'Excuse me, dear, could I borrow Mrs Avery for a second?'

Kate went over to Donald Parfitt, the eldest of the four at eleven. He had a cold sore on his upper lip, which he was picking with grubby fingers. Kate took his hand from his face and said: 'Hallo, Donald, so you're going at last. I'm sure it's for the best.'

'Suppose so.'

'Will we be all together, Miss?' asked Clara Parfitt. She was ten, and had all the makings of a pretty girl, fair and slim.

'I couldn't say. They do try —'

'I bloody 'ope not,' said Clara. ' 'E dreams all the time. *And* wets.'

Donald aimed a ferocious clout at his sister, which Kate checked. Clark and Bobby looked on with signs of animation at this more familiar interchange. Kate's sympathies were with Clara, who had been sharing not just a room, but a bed, with all three brothers for as long as she could remember. Continual intimate exposure to the noisy pubescence of Donald Parfitt would nip the hardiest libido in the bud.

'You'll probably have a terrific time,' said Kate, 'and your mum will be able to come and visit.'

'I bloody 'ope not,' said Clara again.

'Right!' carolled the WVS lady, waving her sheaf of papers aloft. 'Now, boys and girls, Mrs er —' she smiled distractedly at Kate, 'and I are going to take you to Paddington Station in the bus, and see you safely on to your train. You haven't a thing to worry about. You'll be met the other end and taken to the reception centre, and by tonight you'll be in nice new homes out of the danger zone, and well looked after by those very kind people who've agreed to take you in.'

During this homily Kate and Andrea gazed sympathetically at the group of small, sullen figures, swamped by their packages and heavy clothes. Kate thought: not a thing to worry about? The trouble was they had everything to worry about, but they didn't know it. She remembered all too well what it was like to be uprooted and packed off, to be told to be appreciative of the kindness of total strangers. And *she* had met with nothing but love, trust and understanding. Some of the 'kind people' that these children were going to were taking Hobson's choice.

And with the evacuees would come other, even less welcome visitors — lice, fleas, scabies, afflictions of the ears, nose, and throat too numerous to mention; eczema and impetigo, warts and verrucas, dirt in all its many shades and varieties from the recent and superficial to the habitual and ingrained. And lack of social training — Kate shuddered when she considered the shocks soon to be inflicted on the cleanly housewives of Babbacombe and Sidmouth when they were confronted with children who ate with their fingers, who had never seen a green vegetable, who wet and soiled the bed every night, who scratched and swore, who (some of them) had never slept in a bed, nor been in total darkness. Perhaps she was being too pessimistic. Many, probably half, of the children now beginning to file despondently through the door of the Ross Institute were well loved and well cared for. They knew right from wrong, but it had been apparent to them from an early age that the dividing line could be blurred. Life was hard. Their shortcomings were only those engendered by poverty.

In the bus on the way to Paddington the WVS lady, whose name was Mrs Southcott, said *sotto voce* to Kate, 'Poor scraps. I hate it, don't you?'

'Yes,' said Kate. 'And I'm afraid they're in for more shocks than they can possibly imagine.'

'Well – yes.' Mrs Southcott was not entirely sure whose side she was on. 'And so are the good people whose homes they are going to.'

'Quite.'

Mrs Southcott smiled brightly at Kate. 'Have you worked with the community for long?'

'For three years, on and off.'

'Ah, so you know the score. The first thing *I* would do with these children would be to take every stitch of clothing they possess and burn it.'

'Oh, would you?' said Kate, turning to study her companion with frosty interest. Mrs Southcott, abashed by the look and the astringent tone that accompanied it, murmured something about a figure of speech and gazed out of the window.

They alighted from the bus and the two women led their troupe back up the stairs, along the road, and down into Paddington Station. Mrs Southcott at the front, spruce and managerial; Kate bringing up the rear. In the middle, the children, less definite somehow now that departure was near, dwarfed by the hugeness of the station concourse. Little, pale, grim faces bobbed above bulky, overdressed bodies weighed down with packages and gas masks. High above, pigeons clattered and darted between the grimy glass roof and the drifting smoke. Two evacuee trains were due to leave, and shuffling queues of children were lined up at the barrier, with animated, organizing adults in attendance. A whole crowd of sailors, their kitbags over their shoulders, got a cheer from the crowd; they were so much more heartening than the unattractive children.

Kate waited with the group from the Institute while Mrs Southcott went to determine which platform they should go to. Standing there she felt the anxious questions, which they could not properly put into words, advancing from their set faces towards her like little chill draughts from beneath closed doors. She felt something at her side and saw that it was Archie. He was crying, his nose was running. She got out her handkerchief and stemmed the flow and then stood, one arm across his heaving shoulders, pressing him to her side and gazing at the others as if to include them in the embrace.

Two well-dressed women following a laden porter turned their heads, took note, exchanged remarks with an air of supercilious pity. Kate despised them.

Mrs Southcott returned. 'We're fine here,' she announced. 'Platform Six is us, and they'll let us on in about five minutes.'

'When will we be back?' asked Clara Parfitt suddenly.

Kate looked at her in surprise. Clara's pretty, pointed face defied her to fob her off. 'I don't know,' she said. 'When the danger's over.'

'Could be ages, couldn't it?'

'It could be quite a while.' Their silent stares pressed on her, willing her to say something encouraging. 'But your mother will be able —'

'Yes, you said.'

Archie cried and cried, more noisily now.

'Oh *dear*, oh dear,' said Mrs Southcott.

The barrier was opened and they filed through. Mrs Southcott marched bouncily to the front of the train, pointing out the engine to the indifferent children and enquiring well-meaningly whether they found it exciting. Kate, on the other hand, could think of nothing to say that was neither too brutal nor an insult to their intelligence. She felt that familiar, involuntary clenching of her heart, a tightening of its muscles against embarrassing, useless emotion. What good would it do any of them for her to be soft and sympathetic now? Firmly and calmly she checked them as they climbed the steps, securing knots on labels and parcels, securing unruly hair with kirby grips, pulling belts through buckles, wiping noses. In the train corridor Mrs Southcott corralled the children in their compartments like sheep where they sat down five to a side, just as they were, coats, hats and mufflers on, parcels on their knees, gas mask boxes sticking out every which way. They were uncomfortable, but too confused to sort themselves out and there wasn't time for her and Mrs Southcott to do it.

Kate put Archie on board last. In spite of his noisy tears and the hissing of the engine there was something she *had* to say to him. Taking his face between her hands she glared into his reddened eyes and shouted above the din: 'Archie! You'll never get into trouble if you *shut the door* of the lav when you're in there! Do you understand? Shut it!' Then he was whisked away from her.

Mrs Southcott lowered her well-upholstered form on to the platform, slammed the door, adjusted her hat. There was a flash of green, the shriek of a whistle. The engine snorted and heaved like a shire horse, and the train began to move. Kate raised one arm stiffly. The children's faces were just blobs beyond the two sheets of glass, with her own reflection superimposed on them.

'Good-bye! Good luck!' She wished Lawrence were here beside her, he would have known what to do or say, something gay and appropriate to cut through the fog of inarticulate misery in the train. But they were gone now, other faces rattled by, a miasma of steam came between her and the hastening carriages.

Ernest Marx had seen the evacuees boarding the bus in the Commercial Road as he alighted from a taxi on the other side, and had averted his eyes in distaste. Had *he* ever been that ugly and uncouth? He hoped not. That was the trouble with poverty, it was so unsightly.

He avoided the market where he might bump into people he knew, and turned up Globe Road. Number 121 was where his mother and Tony now lived, in a second floor flat indirectly paid for by Giles Huxley. He had not been able to persuade Maria to move any further away from the area where she'd always lived. In return for giving in to her on that score she had agreed to his paying for someone to live in, now that Tony was out at work all day. The someone was Doris, who had been only too delighted to oblige, her husband having finally flown the nest. Doris had been travelling up west every day, leaving at six, to do a succession of charring jobs. Living in a nice little local flat with the agreeable Maria was paradise by comparison. Ernest was by no means sure how conscientious Doris was, but she was affable and good-hearted and his mother liked her, so he was not about to rock the boat. He had also impressed upon Maria the importance of changing her name. She was to introduce herself to anyone she didn't know as Mrs Marker. Though she was as cockney as jellied eels, that name wasn't, and in the East End a foreign name could very quickly get you a label you'd rather not have, like spy, alien, fifth columnist.

As he walked along he was conscious of people glancing at him, in his tailor-made suit and gleaming soft leather shoes. He always had to brace himself for these filial visits, they were a terrible strain. But today Giles was off organizing some lunch-time show or other, so that theatre-mad Londoners could have their daily dose in spite of the black-out, and he'd been presented with a convenient free hour or two. He liked to come during the day because then Tony was out. With Tony elsewhere Ernest arrived at Globe Road like a conquering hero — smart, worldly, successful, the great provider. With Tony there he was subjected to bitter unspoken accusations — prodigal, class traitor, show-off, hypocrite. Ernest always felt that Tony had guessed about Giles, or guessed near enough — yet how could he have done? He arrived at No. 121, automatically glanced round like a fugitive, and let himself in.

Primmy saw him arrive from her first-floor window. She was on night duty at present and had just got up and made herself poached egg on toast. She was a bit of an insomniac these days, especially when it was a case of sleeping in the daylight. She would often wake now, after two or three hours, have something to eat and then try to go off again till five or so, when she would get up and get ready. Life was tiring physically, it was a long way up to St George's in the black-out, and the number of patients had been swelled in recent weeks not by the war, but by the black-out itself — accidents and pregnancies. And over thirty-three fatalities a week!

She was intrigued by her upstairs neighbours. You couldn't work in hospital all your life without becoming a judge of character, no matter how incurious you were. She saw the fat, wheezy, dyed-blonde woman coming and going, and sometimes exchanged a few words with her on the stairs. But Primmy knew it was the little black-and-tan cockney sparrow, the semi-invalid who never went out, who was the centre of things, and the mother of the two lads. On the three or four occasions when the siren had gone over the past few days Primmy had helped Doris to assist Maria down into the hall and they'd all sat there, them and the old couple from the ground floor, passing round sweets and chatting. Primmy saw at once that Mrs Marker was tubercular, yet she smoked like a chimney, and Doris encouraged her. Primmy didn't think much of that, but didn't want to interfere. She did, however, let it be known that she was a nurse — no harm in keeping Doris on her toes.

The younger boy, Tony, a lad of fourteen who worked as a delivery boy at Price's, she liked. To be sure he was no charmer, but he was a decent, straightforward lad who worked hard, and she quite often used to slip him some Pontefract cakes or Bluebird toffees when he passed her door on the way in from work.

The tones in which Maria Marker referred to her older son, 'my boy Ernest' conveyed the impression that he was only a little lower than the angels. But paragon though his mother thought him, he visited seldom.

This afternoon Primmy saw his glistening, black, brilliantined head pass beneath her window and heard the light tap of his soft shoes on the stairs. After he left, the tang of some after-shave lotion that he wore would linger on the dark landings. Once she had come face to face with him as he was leaving. 'Good afternoon,' he'd said, smooth as you please, and moved past her almost gingerly with one hand on the lapel of his camel coat, as if he suspected he might pick up something from her.

Primmy hoped Ernest Marker would notice that she and

Tony had taped and blacked-out the skylight in his mother's kitchen. Doris would never have done it, she was too fat to stand on a chair and she hadn't noticed, anyway.

'Where's Doris?' enquired Ernest when he had kissed his mother. Automatically, rather than sitting down to talk to her, he removed his jacket and gold cufflinks, rolled up his sleeves, and set about tidying up.

'She went shopping to the market,' said Maria. 'She'll be ever so sorry she missed you, love.'

'She won't be gone long, will she?' asked Ernest, washing the fat red half-moons of Doris's lipstick off a tea cup.

'No, no, I don't suppose so.'

'She shouldn't be gone long. I don't pay her to leave you here sitting on your own—'

'She doesn't, Ernest, honest. She'll probably be back any minute.'

Ernest came into the sitting room with a cloth and began wiping over the red oilcloth on the table. 'She doesn't exactly do a lot of cleaning either,' he said. 'Still, I see she did the business with that kitchen skylight. It's been bothering me, that. I'd have done it myself this afternoon.'

'Oh yes —' Maria looked as if she might be going to add something, but then simply said again: 'Yes.'

Ernest went to the window and wiped round the frame. Then he took the cloth back to the kitchen, wrung it out and hung it over the tap. He glanced in the cupboard, thought it a bit sparse, and then remembered that Doris was shopping. He was constantly trying to catch Doris out, but it was just for his own satisfaction. The last thing he wanted was to get rid of her; she was cheap and uncomplaining and she got on with his mother. He didn't want the bother of finding someone else. As he came back into the room the cold wail of the siren rose over Globe Road.

'Don't let's bother,' said Maria. 'It'll be another false alarm.'

'Don't let's bother!' Ernest was appalled. 'Is that what Doris says?'

'No . . .' Maria laughed wheezily. 'It's just I don't see you that often. I mean if Hitler drops a bomb on us, at least we'll be together.'

'That's just daft.' She watched in amusement as he replaced his jacket and cufflinks. 'Come on.'

Primmy had debated whether to go up the Markers' place when the siren went, because she knew Doris was out. But the Great and Wonderful Ernest was there, so she decided he could cope, and went down to the hall.

Mr and Mrs Denny were already installed. After only ten days they were old hands.

'Here we are, here we are, here we are again . . .' carolled Mr Denny, a veteran of the trenches. 'Afternoon, Miss Dilkes!' They arranged old mattresses and pillows against the Dennys' door and the front door, and sat down in the stairwell. After a couple of minutes Ernest and Maria came down. They made an odd couple, Maria in shawl and carpet slippers, Ernest like a film star.

'Hallo, dear!' said Mr Denny, 'Oh, I see you got your boy with you this afternoon, that's nice.'

'Probably just another fuss about nothing,' remarked his wife, 'but better safe than sorry.'

Primmy helped Mrs Marker spread out her rug, and got her settled on it. The effort of the stairs had made her breathing strained and wheezy, but she smiled. 'I could do with a fag, Ernest.'

Ernest took out a silver cigarette case and lighter. Primmy watched disapprovingly. There was thunderous knocking on the door and she got up, heaved aside the mattress and opened it. It was Tony Marker, still in his brown apron, and out of breath. His delivery bike with the metal basket lay on the pavement, pedals spinning.

'Sorry, can I come in?'

'I should think so.' She admitted him and replaced the mattress.

'I came to see if you was all right,' he said to his mother.

'There's a good boy,' said Maria. 'You shoulda looked after yourself, love. I'm snug as a bug in a rug.'

'Oh,' said Tony. 'I see *you're* 'ere.'

Primmy went back to her seat in the corner, Tony sat down by the Dennys, opposite his mother and brother. Primmy took out her knitting, to keep her eyes and attention occupied – it was none of her business.

'Hallo, Tone – all right?'

'Not bad. What brings you down, then?'

'Visiting.'

'Oh – *visiting*!'

Primmy finished a row and glanced up. She saw that Tony Marker was looking at his older brother with pure hatred.

Half an hour and nary a bomb later the 'All Clear' went and the occupants of 121 Globe Road dispersed. Tony went back to Price's, Primmy to finish the sleeve of the jumper for her sister Lisbeth's girl – she'd never get back to sleep now – and Ernest took Maria back upstairs and made her a cup of tea.

He sat opposite her while she drank it, and dunked a biscuit but he was not relaxed. Maria, looking at him, thought it was a pity Ernest was not a more cheerful lad. Even now, with all his advantages, a desk job with a writer, rooms in town, money to play with – even with all this to make him happy, his handsome features had a sulky set, he rarely laughed or smiled, he was forever tweaking his cuffs and stroking his hair and brushing his trousers – forever making sure.

She sighed. 'You'll be wanting to be off, love.'

He rose, glancing at his Swiss watch (a present from Giles). 'Where's Doris?'

'She'll be back, never you mind. There was a warning, remember?'

'I suppose you're right. Okay then.' He bent and kissed her, placing his hands on her thin shoulders to prevent her getting up. Her hand on his cheek was cold and dry and insubstantial, like a dead leaf.

'Now look,' he said. 'I've put Doris's money on the mantelpiece. You take care now. I'll be down again soon.'

They both knew that wasn't true. ' 'Course you will,' said Maria.

Primmy heard Ernest's footsteps going downstairs, quicker than when he'd come up. The funny thing was, although she disliked Ernest, the dislike was tinged with a queer sort of sadness which she couldn't account for. It was as if she felt *sorry* for him, and sorry for herself, too, though they surely had nothing in common.

In Globe Road Ernest met Doris, puffing back with a tartan shopping bag full of groceries. He was relieved to see her, and to observe the bulging bag, but as she came up to him and greeted him with her usual effusiveness he smelt beer on her breath. She'd been to the boozer.

' 'Allo, Ernie — sight for sore eyes, intcher? Sorry I wasn't there, it was queues, queues this afternoon. I got yer mum a meat tea, spam and salad and Battenburg cake, she likes that.'

'Glad to hear it,' he said coldly. 'I left your cash on the mantelpiece.'

'Thanks ever so, Ernie, you're a good son to that mother of yours, wish I'd got a son like you.'

'What would she have done in the air raid if I hadn't've been there?' asked Ernest. He did not mention Tony's arrival on the scene.

'I know, I'm sorry about that, but what could I do? Mr 'Itler doesn't tell me when he's going to bomb the living daylights out of us, does 'e? Anyway —' she grinned. ' 'E didn't! So no 'arm done, eh?'

As they parted company and Doris waddled away, Ernest heard the unmistakable clink of bottles from the depths of the tartan shopping bag.

Lawrence Drake got a lift with a departmental colleague from the War Office as far as the Dorchester and then, in view of the weather, walked across the corner of Hyde Park and over the Serpentine Bridge, turning right in the direction of the Bayswater Road.

Though Lawrence chafed at being stuck in a desk job when most of his battalion were still in the Middle East, there were advantages. Moments like this, Hyde Park at the turn of the year, with the faintest bronze tarnish appearing on the tired green of summer, gardeners replacing petunias and geraniums with bulbs and wallflowers, tweed-jacketed children riding fat ponies in Rotten Row. He felt a special affection for London because he knew in his bones that this eerie almost-normality could not last for long. And neither could the dull desk job in

Whitehall which kept him so preciously close to Kate. His was an optimistic nature, and these thoughts made him enjoy his walk all the more.

The war had so far not chucked anything at London from outside. The only visible effects were eruptions thrown up on the face of the capital from within – air-raid shelters, and jeeps in the park, and mounds of sandbags bolstering up Eros and Boadicea.

Walking along the west side of the Serpentine he passed a school crocodile, little boys in gabardine macs and red caps. The elderly teacher bringing up the rear of the crocodile cast Lawrence an indulgent look, and he raised his cap, smiling. He was used to the look: females of all ages had been casting it in his direction since he was a child. The only woman who had been slow in bestowing it was the one who was now his wife. He paused by the statue of Peter Pan, watching a nanny ushering her velvet-collared charge up the steps to count the bronze fairies.

'Mind the officer, Violet,' said the nanny, glancing up at him with something approaching coyness.

Lawrence liked children. He crouched down, pointing at the statue with his stick. 'Show me a snail, Violet,' he said.

Violet beamed. She stumped up the remaining step, found the snail and stood with one gloved hand resting on it like a Victorian explorer.

'Jolly well done, you are clever! How old is she, Nanny?'

'She's only two and a half.'

'Two and a half. I call that splendid.'

'She's forward for her age.'

'I got crusts,' announced Violet cryptically, but Lawrence caught her drift.

'I bet the ducks enjoy those. You'd better not keep them waiting.' He rose. 'And I must go home for *my* crusts. Bye, Violet. Nanny.'

'Good afternoon, sir.' Nanny was quite pink from all this unwarranted attention.

Lawrence walked on, more briskly now, eager to get home to Kate, still elated after two years of marriage that she was actually there, and his.

Or at least *with* him. Not his; Kate could never be quite

that. She was her own person first and last and always, it was what he loved most in her. It gave him the sense of having a tiger by the tail, of having been charged with the care of some wild and special creature, so that he was at once privileged and just a little endangered. He adored her. He was not vain, but he had always known that he could charm women, most of them right into marriage if he wanted to. It was Kate's fierce lack of susceptibility, her wariness, her prickliness that had lured him on, hacking through the scratchy thickets of her stubborn toughness, sweeping aside protestations here and insults there till he'd won his objective. And he had not been disappointed.

She'd once told him that her foster-father used to call her Ginger, and at school she'd been known as Carrots. He thought both these nicknames hopelessly inappropriate, and told her so. If she had to be called after a plant, then let it be chilis or red peppers, something strange and hot and spicy.

Or better still — he smiled to himself as he opened his front door — a tiger lily, part animal, part flower, slender and freckled and flame-coloured. He must tell her that, he thought. Lawrence Drake was a romantic.

As he closed the door behind him he heard nothing. A breathing, ticking silence. But he was sure she was in.

'Kate!'

No reply. He hung up his cap and put his case and stick down in the corner of the hall.

'Kate? Oh, there you are.'

He went into the living room with its too-small furnished-let furniture. His wife was sitting cross-legged on the floor in an attitude of the utmost dejection: elbows on knees, head resting on her hands, her unruly red hair sprouting between her long, outspread fingers.

'Darling? What's up.'

He sat down on the sofa next to her, and put his hand on the back of her neck. It was so thin he could almost have encircled it. She shook her head without looking at him.

'It's no good,' she muttered.

'What isn't?'

'It's those wretched children.' She heaved a long, shivering sigh. 'I honestly can't take much more of that.'

'You mean evacuees?'

She nodded. 'I felt like an executioner.'

'Well, you're not. You're doing a very necessary job. They'll be okay. Think of the scions of the upper classes packed off to boarding school. I was. Your brother is. No different.'

'It is.' She looked up now. Her face was pale, a little grubby where she'd rubbed it. Some hair at the front had escaped from Aubrey's hat and been frizzled by the fire that morning.

'They'll be safe,' he reassured her.

'Safe!' She threw up her hands. 'Safe and miserable. Hell!' she fell into his arms.

'Poor Kate.' He could smell the East End on her skin, and smoke in her hair. 'You're kippered.'

'I went through the smoke room,' she said in a muffled voice, into his shoulder. He could feel every bone in her long, thin, coltish body, her small breasts like buds on a twig, her hair a mass of individual coppery wires, each with its own determined life. He pushed her back a little to study her face. Her yellowy cat's eyes glared into his – passionate and challenging though her mouth was set. He thought those eyes were like the open doors of a furnace, a glimpse of all the fire that swirled around in there.

'What's for supper?' he asked.

'God knows.'

'Good.' He held her face and kissed her. Her eyes closed now, shutting in the fire, though he could feel it burning through her pale, sun-freckled skin.

He stood, taking her with him. They both staggered a little because they were still kissing. 'Come on,' he said.

It was an awful bedroom, made bearable only by their love-making. It was decorated in deadly shades of mushroom and mustard, the bed draped in a heavy quilt the colour of tarnished brass. There was a wardrobe which looked as if it might contain several skeletons, with a full-length mirror spattered with black flecks. On the mantelpiece were two green onyx candlesticks. Kate would have put them away, but on their first night there Lawrence had pointed and said: 'There you are, a shrine to love,' so they had been a joke, and stayed.

And a shrine to love it had become, albeit a hideous one. Now the creaking complaints of the old bed sounded to them like a voluptuous sigh of welcome, the threadbare quilt undulated gently like a warm sea and rustled like palms. And their reflection in the speckled mirror showed some wild, forgotten creature of erotic mythology – rising, falling, rolling in a bronze surf of undisturbed ecstasy.

And like sea creatures damp and smooth they lay entwined afterwards, with their breaths mingling and the juices and streams of love trickling languidly on their skin, and lying in warm pools and drops in the folds of their joined bodies.

Eventually they sat up, pulling the lumpy pillows up between their backs and the bedhead, Kate's tangle of red hair resting on Lawrence's left shoulder. Watching their reflection she lifted her right hand and stroked his fair moustache. 'You're so beautiful.'

He laughed. 'I'm supposed to say that.'

'What's stopping you then?' She nudged his chest with her elbow.

'It's not good enough for you.' He meant it.

'But you are, why are you? I ought to hate you for being so beautiful and nice and popular –'

'God knows why I waste my time with you.'

She turned to face him, leaning up on his chest and gazing into his face. 'Look at you, it's disgusting.'

Lawrence threaded his fingers through her hair and held her head like that, moving it a little from side to side as he spoke. 'I hope,' he said gently, 'that nothing ever happens to us.'

'It won't.'

He kissed her. 'I'm a possessive swine, you know.'

She crawled up to him, smothering his face with her thin, cat-like body.

'Show me then,' she said.

CHAPTER TWELVE

'The war correspondent has his stake — his
life — in his own hands, and he can put it
on this horse or that horse or he can put it
back in his pocket at the very last minute.'

Robert Capa, war correspondent

ON the evening of Thursday, 9 May 1940, Bill Maguire and
his colleague Mike Philpott of *The Recorder* signed in at
an inn in the small town of Bethel near Maubeuge in northern
France, about ten miles south-west of the Belgian border. They
had become separated from the other pressmen, but it no
longer seemed to matter, since there was little to report, and
had been little for the best part of eight months.

All journalists with the BEF were obliged to wear a pseudo-
military uniform, with a cap like an officer's bearing the letter
'C' (for correspondent, though more than one army wit had
suggested prefixing a 'W') — but Bill and Mike Philpott had at
least escaped being herded together under the control of the
Army's 'conducting officers'. This was due to their relative
seniority and, therefore, their supposed trustworthiness — all
journalists being regarded as only marginally better than spies.
As the long months of the phoney war dragged on into 1940
the conducting officers — most of them veterans of the first war
— began to outnumber the journalists they were supposed to
conduct, and also to prove that on most occasions they could
drink them under the table. The reporters were force-fed
communiqués at one end and had their articles censored to the
point of extinction at the other.

There was no story. The senior journalists at first dispersed
to see what they could unearth and, when they found that a

humdrum façade concealed more of the same, took themselves off in search of more rewarding assignments. The job of reporting on the BEF in France and Belgium had deteriorated into that of file-clerk, processing official handouts. Bill had grown a beard, and then shaved it off. He had learned to play golf, he had vastly improved his French, and he had enjoyed some first-class meals. He had put on weight and he was bored and edgy. He and Mike were on their way back to the so-called combat units dug in near Tournai. If the order of the day was still No Story he did not intend to remain.

The inn was quiet, only them and a couple of locals at supper in the small dining room. There was a Supply Corps unit billeted on the northern side of the town near the railway station, but none of the men had found their way down here. Mike Philpott drank a bottle of wine with his meal and struck up an animated discussion with the locals, and the *patron*. Bill did not think he could stand another evening on the sidelines of an Anglo-Gallic argument fuelled by alcohol and ending with mawkish protestations of lasting friendship.

He refused coffee and rose from the table. The two locals were already preparing to move their chairs to join Mike.

'Excuse me. I think I'll go out for a bit.'

'Don't go, for God's sake, we're just getting started here!'

'That's what I mean.' Bill smiled, not wanting to appear rude, and made way for the two Frenchmen. He liked Mike — a thin, bookish, witty man — but tonight he wanted his own company more.

'Very well, *mon brave*,' said Mike, lifting his calvados in Bill's direction. 'See you later.'

'In the morning, I should think.'

Bill went out. As he turned along the street he saw a bicycle in the yard at the side of the *pension*, leaning up beneath the kitchen window. He went to the window and hailed Madame, who was washing up, indicating that he'd like to borrow the bike.

'*Bien sûr, M'sieur. Prenez garde — c'est assez vieille!*'

'*Merci, Madame.*'

The early summer evening was soft and clear, and Bill's spirits rose a little as he bumped along on the ancient bike. Certainly no one could have called Bethel a beauty spot. At the turn of the century it had been a tiny village, but had grown into a sprawling town as a result of a nearby rail junction constructed during the last war. Crewe with garlic, thought Bill. With so many undistinguished private and commercial buildings erected during the last thirty years the skyline of Bethel was low, the streets of uniform width, not broad enough to be boulevards or narrow enough to be lanes. The only relief was the old village church, perched on a hill in the centre of the town with houses of the same vintage gathered round it like chicks round a mother hen.

Bill headed towards the railway station. The RASC had a massive fuel dump out there near the sidings. He had a mind to talk to soldiers, to people directly involved in this *'drôle de guerre'* as the French called it.

The town began to thin out and give way to ugly, low railway buildings like broken teeth, engine sheds and goods bays, the grass in between gritty and blackened with coal dust. He pedalled past the station in the direction of the sidings. The fuel dump was huge and obvious – thousands of cans stacked up like the foundation of a pyramid. Away to the right were a collection of army vehicles, lorries and trucks. He thought he could make out a couple of men in the front of one of them. At first he thought there was no one at the dump itself. He circumnavigated the dump, rattling over the bumpy ground. Not until he was well round on the far side did he see the soldier, sitting on a can, enjoying the evening sun and reading a magazine. A rifle lay beside him on the ground.

When he heard the crunch of the bicycle tyres he jumped up, more from a kind of schoolboy guilt than military alertness. The old, dog-eared copy of *Tit-Bits* floated to the ground.

'Stand easy, soldier. Bill Maguire, *Daily Herald*.'

The man mopped his brow. 'I'll go to the foot of our stairs!'

'Thought I was an advance party of the Werhrmacht?'

''Course not – sorry. World of my own for a moment there. Sorry, chum.'

He got a tattered packet of Park Drive out of the breast pocket of his battledress, helped himself and offered the packet to Bill.

He would have liked a cigarette, but – he indicated the cans. 'Should we?'

'Cripes.' The man replaced the cigarette in the packet and put it away hastily. 'You had me going there for a moment. Sorry again!'

Bill waved aside his apologies. 'I didn't suppose you chain-smoked next door to this lot, don't worry.' He laid the bike on the ground and pushed his hands in his pockets. 'I dropped by for a chat, that's all . . . you here on your own?'

'At the present. Night guard. By the way,' he stuck out a hand, 'Pete Whitworth, Private, RASC.'

'Pleased to meet you. Tell me, how much of this stuff is there here — I take it it's motor fuel oil?'

'About three million gallons.' Whitworth turned and looked the cans up and down as though verifying the estimate. 'Yup, about three million.'

'Good God,' said Bill.

'We keep it out in the open like this,' went on Whitworth, waxing important, 'it makes for easier distribution.'

'I see. No anti-aircraft gun?' Bill glanced round.

'No. Mind you,' he grinned confidentially at Bill, 'we've not exactly been bombed to bits over here. More likely to die of boredom. I've had more adventures on the road.'

'On the road?'

'I'm a commercial traveller.' Bill noted the present tense. 'Confectionery's my line — butterscotch, toffees, sherbet drops — you got kiddies, Mr Maguire?'

'I don't even have a wife.'

'I love kiddies.' Whitworth sighed. 'But I got none neither. Bachelor gay, I am. Sometimes —' his face puckered cheerily as he reminisced, 'if I park the car somewhere, go into a pub, something like that, I come back and find all these kiddies staring in the windows — they can hardly believe their little eyes, it's like Santa's cave!' He chuckled. 'I love 'em.'

'A pleasant job,' agreed Bill. There was a short silence, then he pointed to the rifle. 'Had to use that yet?'

'Not yet, I'm happy to say. But I could if I had to.' He picked up the rifle and made a few aiming motions taking in Bill and the fuel cans. Bill moved discreetly to one side. 'I spent near three days on the firing range, so just let anyone try any monkey business!'

'How do you mean, monkey business?'

'Pilfering, Mr Maguire. The Froggies been short of petrol quite a while, same as us. Might go to their heads seeing this lot.'

'I suppose it might.'

Bill felt that he was having one of those bad dreams in which one is fully aware that it is a dream but equally unable to stop participating in it and adding to its awfulness.

'Tell me, Pete,' he said conversationally. 'If a German plane came over, taking a look, what would you do? Fire at it with that thing?'

'My sainted aunt, no!' Whitworth mocked Bill's ignorance. 'Can't do that – that'd give away our position.'

It was light until ten-thirty in France at that time of year. When Bill got back to the *pension* he replaced Madame's bike beneath the kitchen window and went straight up to his room. He could hear Mike and the three Frenchmen still hard at it, in the bar now, approaching the lasting friendship stage. He crept past the half-open door.

Upstairs he lay for a while fully clothed on his bed, watching the grey sky darken over the unromantic rooftops of Bethel. He was trying to pull that marvellous well-rounded nugget of sense from the collection of impressions buzzing in his brain. He thought he might have a story – a feature – the kind of thing that would speak worlds about this fools' war and still get past the censor. He felt extremely interested, and sharp, his professional energies were fully engaged for the first time in months.

At around midnight he had still not undressed, but fell into a deep sleep.

At five o'clock something woke him up. He caught the last chimes of the church clock, and the crowing of Madame's bantam cock in the kitchen yard, but he knew it had been neither of those. The sky outside the window was a tranquil, expectant grey. The sound, when he caught it again, was almost part of that greyness, quivering in the air over the town, drawing nearer like the dawn. He swung his legs off the bed and went to the window, pulling up the bottom half and leaning out. For a moment he saw nothing. The sound itself faded. Perhaps he had imagined it.

Then he saw it — quite close, suddenly, taking him by surprise — a single German plane, circling arrogantly low, having a good look.

'God in heaven!'

The plane moved out of sight behind the roof of the inn. North, in the direction of the station. Its hum hung in the air. Bill dragged on his jacket and ran from the room. He could hear Madame moving about in the kitchen below. Outside, the cock crowed again like some ghastly biblical parody.

He flew down the stairs and burst into the kitchen. Madame stood, astonished, in flannel nightie and clogs, her hair in two incongruously girlish pigtails.

'*Monsieur! Qu'est ce qui se passe?*'

'*Je m'excuse, Madame* —' he foundered. His French, usually so reliable these days, failed him. He pointed to the window. 'Can I borrow your bicycle again?'

'*Mais oui, allez vous en, mais pourquoi . . .?*'

He was out of the back door, and on the bike, pedalling furiously along the route he had taken the previous evening. He felt an enormous exhilaration — it was almost as if he'd made it happen. He couldn't see the plane now, with the houses all round, but he could hear it. And other sounds — distant shouts, engines revving, the crack of a rifle — someone breaking the rules. For a split second the plane's engine seemed to cut out. There was a tiny hiatus, like the intake of breath before a child's tantrum. Then there was the granddaddy of of an explosion. The shock-wave jolted Bill right off his bike.

When he lifted his head the sky above the rooftops ahead of him was rushing upwards in a torrent of boiling black smoke, shot with flame. The heat beat at his face. He took out his handkerchief and tied it over his nose and mouth. Then he remounted the bike, put his head down and carried on. He soon found himself part of a general movement of troops, heading from their comfortable billets in the town to the scene of the disaster. There was a good deal of yelling and gesticulating — he suspected he was being told to bugger off — but the noise of the conflagration drowned everything, and he kept going.

The fuel dump was an inferno. There was nothing anyone could do. The wretched men of the Supply Corps careered round the sidelines like over-excited children at a bonfire party. A young soldier shouted something at Bill. He inclined his ear to catch the words.

'What's that?'

'Bally fantastic sight!' yelled the soldier.

'Yes!' bellowed Bill. It was about all you could say.

Taking a wide berth, he cycled round to the far side of the blazing dump. He could feel the intense heat stripping the hairs on the backs of his hands, and his head, even in his nostrils. But the wind was blowing from the north, and on the far side he was in its shadow, the great billowing column of dense black smoke was leaning away from him. A man in officer's uniform was struggling to move something that lay on the ground about a hundred yards away. Catching sight of Bill he shouted: 'Hey you! Give me a hand!'

Bill pedalled over and dropped the bike. The officer glanced at him and said with quite inappropriate formality, 'Sorry — not militia?'

'Correspondent. What shall I do?'

It was the horribly burned body of a man. They improvised a stretcher from their jackets, with the sleeves tied together, and rolled him on to it. Then they ran, half-crouching with their awkward burden, into the lee of a brick coal bunker.

The officer, who was very young, blew out his cheeks and wiped his brow. 'Thanks. The MO is coming. I simply dare not move the poor chap any more, what do you think?' He spoke with a rather tight-jawed public school delivery.

'I think you're right,' said Bill.

It was Pete Whitworth, sweetie salesman, bachelor gay, every kid's favourite uncle. The scourge of Froggy pilferers, now a blackened, bloated puppet.

'Surely,' Bill said, 'he must be dead?'

The officer cleared his throat. ''Fraid not.'

Bill stared down at Whitworth's scorched, cracked face. His eyes watered in sympathy.

One small plane. One bomb. Three million gallons of fuel oil. And no more phoney war.

*

On the afternoon of Saturday 11 May Aubrey Tennant was up a step-ladder in the dining-room of Mapleton Road, hanging a small watercolour which he and Iris had purchased that morning. Aubrey was an earth-bound creature with no head for heights, so Iris's high-pitched call made him teeter dangerously. 'Aubrey! Au – bree!'

With one hand holding the painting on its hook, he grabbed the top of the ladder with the other. In this hunched position he felt – and looked – like a circus elephant perched on a stool.

'What is it?'

'Aubrey, on the wireless . . . .' Iris Pargiter appeared in the doorway. She had come straight from the kitchen, but had omitted to remove her apron, a sure sign of her intense agitation.

'Mr Chamberlain's resigned. Churchill's forming a new government, a coalition.' It was typical of Iris that this news concerning Chamberlain, whom she admired as a true gentleman, the victim of cruel circumstance, had upset her more than the cataclysmic events of the previous day. Here was evidence indeed that times were out of joint.

Aubrey settled the picture on its hook and backed cautiously down the ladder.

'It's no surprise really, my dear,' he said. 'He's only been hanging on by the skin of his teeth since the Norwegian fiasco.'

He held out his arm. Iris automatically removed her apron now and laid it over the back of a dining chair before coming to his side. He squeezed her shoulders. 'Is that straight?'

'Yes, I should say so. It could do with a wipe over, you've put finger marks all over the glass.'

'I'll do it.'

'Aubrey.' An uncharacteristic falter in Iris's voice made him look down at her. She was a short woman, he could only see the top of her well-coiffed head.

'Yes?'

'We're really into this war now, aren't we?'

Aubrey had never been a man to dish-out half truths just to spare people's anxiety. 'I'm afraid so.'

They stood there gazing up at their precious painting, which now seemed a foolish extravagance.

'Anyway,' he went on ponderously, 'it's an ill wind. I'm

convinced that under the circumstances we shouldn't waste any time in regularizing the situation.'

'I beg your pardon?' She glanced up at him in her old, brisk way.

'Would you consider marrying me?' said Aubrey. 'I suggest 10 June – your birthday.'

At last Lawrence had his posting. He felt like a long-term prisoner released from jail as he went home that evening. Since the beginning of the month it had been evident that the days of the uneasy half-war were numbered, and with this realization his frustration had increased. The Nazi *blitzkrieg*, fanning out from Germany north and west across Europe, was bringing Hitler a series of the most rapid and assured victories since Napoleon won his empire, and there would be more to come. Lawrence and his colleagues at the War Office were all too painfully aware of how ill-equipped the BEF was to make any kind of stand against the swift, professional panzer divisions of Guderian and Hoepner, or the dazzling skills of the pampered Luftwaffe. In fact, the realization was dawning on politicians and service chiefs alike that they could be staring defeat in the face with hardly a shot fired.

It was clear from the newspapers that the British public were to be spared this unpleasant possibility. Lawrence knew from talking to Bill Maguire just how tight the press censorship was, but over the past few weeks, until today, he reckoned that Bill's frustration was as nothing beside his own.

The violence of his desire to be in action surprised him. In his day-to-day life Lawrence was the most peaceable of fellows, who scarcely even raised his voice in anger. He hated to see people in pain or distress, and he had no desire to rob any individual *Frau* of her son, or *Fraulein* of her lover. It was simply that he was idealistic about his country. Britain, for all its faults, possessed many qualities which Lawrence held dear, and had he been asked he would have freely admitted that he considered his life a small price to pay for the preservation of those qualities and the freedom which nurtured them. The minute British protectorate of Malta, a mere gnat-bite of rock in the middle of what the Italians in their overweening vanity called the *Mare nostrum*, might not be a major theatre of war, but it had housed a British garrison, and afforded unrivalled safety for the British fleet, for one hundred and forty years. For Lawrence, it represented a return to what he considered his proper job. Malta would do.

When he got home, he did not at once tell Kate. She was in the bath, listening to the wireless turned up loud in the sitting room. The equable voice of the BBC reported the continuing advance through Holland and Belgium.

Typically, she was incensed. As he unbuttoned his tunic and removed his tie she emerged from the bathroom, her hair dripping, swathed in a large towel, exclaiming, 'They make it sound as if no one tried to stop them!'

'I'm not sure they could have done, that's the trouble. They're outflanking us all the time.'

She marched over, switched off the wireless, and planted a damp, distracted kiss on Lawrence's cheek. 'But I thought we'd been over there for months just watching and waiting for something like this.'

'Well —' He sat down on the sofa and linked his hands behind his head. It amused him when she began to run the war. 'We have been, but the hiatus has gone on for too long — we'd got soft and complacent. And they've got the largest, most professional army in the world.'

She picked up one of the corners of the towel and began to rub her hair. 'Then why don't we make sure that we can match them? I mean, what earthly good is it going over there knowing we're not good enough?'

'Not much, I agree, but you see the British always believe they can win, because of their innate superiority — more character, better class of chap, that sort of thing . . .'

She peered at him from beneath the towel. 'Now you're joking.'

'Who, me?'

'I've had enough of this, I'm going to get an apple!' She pulled the towel round her and went into the kitchen.

'You look like Bud Flanagan!' he shouted after her.

There was a brief pause. She reappeared in the doorway. 'Do you want one?' She shied an apple at Lawrence. It whistled through the air but he caught it, one-handed.

'Thanks, don't mind if I do.' He bit into it. 'And not even bruised, thanks to your rotten aim. Here,' he held out one arm. 'Come and sit by me, I've got something to tell you.'

She came and perched on the sofa, but not too close, she was still somewhat argumentative. She sat sideways, with one leg folded beneath her, her elbow resting on the back.

'You're changing the subject.'

'No, I'm not really.'

'It had better be good.'

'It is. I'm rejoining the battalion, in Malta.'

He was gratified by her expression of complete surprise, and then of wide-eyed, open-mouthed delight. 'Lawrence! That's wonderful!'

'I told you you'd like it.'

'I'm so *pleased!*' She put her warm, damp arms round his neck. 'We'll see everyone again, and it'll be like when we were first married.'

'I hope so.' He didn't want to spoil her excitement by any grimmer prognostications. Instead he turned within her encircling arms and kissed her mouth, which flowered softly beneath his, reminding him that there were factors in his life more powerful than patriotism, for which it would be worth remaining alive.

On Sunday afternoon Lawrence had work to do, so Kate telephoned Dulcie and they went to a matinée at the ABC Edgware Road. The film was fine – Dulcie said Kate was like Lauren Bacall – but their enjoyment was marred by the Pathe News which preceded it, containing film footage of German tanks carrying all before them in Europe.

Afterwards, rather than disturb Lawrence, they went back to Dulcie's flat. The increasingly sullen and mutinous Celine was out, so all pretence at good behaviour was cast aside, and at five o'clock the gin and tonic joined the teapot on the table. Braced by a stiff drink, Kate delivered the news about Malta and received, as she had expected, a carefully modulated response.

'You're going to miss your job, aren't you?' Dulcie asked, in a tone of polite enquiry.

Kate shrugged. 'Not really. I'm not sure how useful I am down there any more, and I'm sick of London.'

'Oh.' Dulcie scratched Fondant beneath his chin.

'You know me, I feel claustrophobic in that flat and then I go down to Whitechapel and feel claustrophobic there, so I lose my temper and – oh, just the old story. They'll be glad to be shot of me.'

'I'm sure that's not true.'

'Even the refugees have come back!' said Kate. She caught Dulcie's look of disbelief. 'It's true. Half the little devils have turned up like bad pennies, because no bombs dropped while they were away.'

Dulcie smiled. 'It's ridiculous.'

'The Parfitts didn't last three months, I bumped into them in the market in January.' Dulcie stifled a laugh. 'After all the tears of blood I shed . . .'

They both laughed now, friends again on safer ground. Fondant showed his displeasure at all this unwarranted hilarity by jumping off Dulcie's lap and sitting with his back to her, like a bookend, his fat tail wound neatly about his feet. Fondant was not as young as he had been, and even in his youth he had not been one of those tile-prowling feline Lotharios who made the nights unholy with their fights and flirtations. He had always been a pampered pet. And now, suddenly, in his middle years, Dulcie had taken to leaving him on his own all day at the mercy of a bolshy Celine, who was quite likely to forget his meals and who, when he reminded her, would nudge him peremptorily out of the way with her foot in a manner that was perilously close to a kick.

'Poor Fondant,' said Dulcie. 'He's not talking to me.' And she picked up her cat and cuddled him extravagantly, to conceal her fears.

When she had fled to Bill after leaving Rex, that had been a bad time. Her defences were down, and she'd done something she'd never done with any other man – she'd cast herself on his mercy, the poor darling. She cringed now when she remembered the tears, the clinging, the declarations of love. Of course he had responded as she might have expected him to – he had taken her in and kissed her better. But as the months had gone by and she'd recovered, so her old *sagesse* had returned, and she had known that the best way to keep Bill was to leave him. Within a week she had found the little flat in St John's Wood and gone. Her eyes had stung a bit as she packed her case and bullied the recalcitrant Celine, but that was all.

Something told her that whatever it was between her and Bill, it depended for its continuance on her intuitiveness.

To add to her contentment, there was Kate. When she remembered how she had dreaded and feared her daughter's arrival she wondered at herself. Wise Giles had been right when he'd told her to relax and be herself and all would be well. Now that she could do those things her friendship with Kate was deep, and easy, miraculous to Dulcie. She did not in the least want to change things now. How could they ever be such wonderful friends again if the truth came out? She had Kate's confidence, her love, her company, in a measure that many an ordinary mother might have envied. No, Dulcie would say nothing.

That Sunday evening when Kate left, she sat down at the table to write another chapter in her long weekly letter to Bill. She had no idea whether the letters ever caught up with him, but she took her grass widowhood very seriously. In the pretty, curling handwriting in which she had once informed her family (indirectly, of course) of her intention to take up prostitution, she now told Bill Maguire that she had been to see a good film with her niece.

On Monday 12 May Ernest received his call-up papers, telling him to report to the depot in Maidstone at his earliest convenience. He might as well have been handed the black spot. Speechless with shock he sat on the edge of the bed with the letter trembling in his hand.

Giles put his coffee on the bedside table. 'Is something the matter?'

Dumbly Ernest handed him the letter.

Giles read it. 'It was bound to come, my dear. After all, you registered, didn't you?'

'Yes, but that was ages – I mean, I never thought –' he turned with pleading eyes. 'Giles, I can't, not now!'

Giles could read that look. It was not cowardice so much as

a powerful dread of losing everything. Giles did not delude himself about his lover. This was a young man who, even if Giles had not taken him up, would have found some way into the pleasure garden. And now here was the harsh voice of Authority telling him to leave it all, to exchange the elegance and comfort and nice clothes for khaki and heavy boots, to be once more no better than Joe Bloggs.

Giles put out his hand and rested it on Ernest's shoulder. 'I don't see how you can avoid it.'

'Get off!' Ernest shook him off with a snarl of rage. 'The big war hero!' he chided, his lips curling, his eyes cold. 'You make me sick!'

'I'm sorry.'

'We're not all cut out to say yes, sir, no, sir, I'll die for my country, sir.'

'I know that, Ernest.'

Ernest was winding himself up. 'You can sit there in bed with your gammy leg and tell me to go away, because you're all right, you've done your bit, everyone admires you – they don't know the half of it!'

'Excuse me.' Quietly and deliberately, Giles got out of bed and put on his dressing gown and slippers. He went out of the bedroom and Ernest heard the sound of taps in the bathroom. The sound enraged him: how dare the old bastard stroll off and take a bath at a time like this?

He ran across the landing and threw open the bathroom door violently. Giles had discarded the dressing gown and stood there naked in the eddying steam from the taps.

'I'd like my bath, Ernest,' he said gently. The voice which could so thrill Ernest now infuriated him – so well bloody modulated, never a word out of place.

'You think I care about that!' Ernest leaned forward and turned the taps off. Giles took his towel from the rail and wound it round his waist. He was actually managing to be dignified, which did nothing to pacify Ernest.

'Look,' he said now, 'why don't you just cool off for a few minutes. Have some coffee. I'll take a bath and then we can talk about it calmly.'

'Calmly? Ha!' Ernest threw his head back. Giles reflected that he was a terrible ham. 'I think you want to get rid of me.

I'm an embarrassment to you, aren't I, not quite *quite*, not *absolutely*, a bit of a rough diamond. Your life would be nice and clean and tidy again without me, wouldn't it?'

'I don't want to lose you.'

'Who knows?' Ernest's voice rose to a scream. 'I might even do you a real favour and get myself killed!'

Giles hit him so hard that he reeled, ricocheted off the side of the door and fell back with a thump on the Persian rug. It had been an open-handed blow to the side of the head, a kind of cuff round the ear writ large, but Giles was a powerfully-built man who rarely lost his temper. When he did, he made it count. 'Go away, Ernest,' he said, 'and let me have a bath in peace.' He closed the door and shot the bolt. The taps were turned back on.

Ernest fled once more to the bedroom and cast himself down on the bed, grinding his fists into his eyes. His head throbbed, but his pride hurt more. Just then he would have done anything to pay Giles back — carved his initials on Giles's face with razor-blades, thrown his typewriter out of the window and his papers on the fire, shouted from the rooftops that he was a rotten old pansy with a taste for rough trade.

But panic rapidly superseded vengeance in Ernest's over-wrought brain. The papers were still there, lying on the bedside table, his tantrums had left him no better off. On the contrary, they had probably sealed his fate. The things he had said about Giles weren't true, he had wanted to hurt him — but maybe they *were* true now. Behind that locked door Giles might at this moment be reconsidering their unequal relationship and finding it sadly lacking. Ernest sobbed. His breath was beginning to come short, he was panting. He realized that this was not just a symptom of his guilt and fear, but something beyond his control, taking him over. His panic at this realization simply made it worse. He struggled to the window and heaved at it, but it had always been stiff and he couldn't budge it. He sank to the ground, weeping.

He knew this feeling, though it was years since he'd experienced it. He remembered his mother sitting by him, stroking him, making him inhale the steam from a kettle. The bellows of his lungs were pressed flat, shut, he couldn't inflate them. Distractedly he thought: 'It's a punishment. I'm going to die in here, in Giles's flat, and it's the first time he's ever locked the bathroom door . . .'

The roar of his breath, being forced through what he now pictured as a narrower and narrower aperture, thundered in his ears. He felt faint. He was more terrified than he'd been in his life. Suddenly Giles was there. He wore his dressing gown, but he was still wet, his hair dripped on Ernest's face.

'My poor boy, what in God's name's the matter?'

He rose and pushed up the bottom of the window with ease. Fresh air and sunshine poured in, and the civilized hum of traffic in Regent Street and Piccadilly. Ernest gasped helplessly, his eyes and nose were running with fear and distress, his chest laboured and heaved. His wretchedness was mirrored on Giles's face.

Giles knelt down, cradling his head, stroking his hair, speaking softly. 'I'm sorry, I'm so sorry, I had no idea. I came to say I was sorry, how could I stay in there after what I did? Take it easy, Ernest, don't fight for air, there's plenty of air, I'm here, you're all right . . . my poor, poor Ernest . . .'

Giles's words were Ernest's best medicine. Gradually his gasping subsided. But even in his debilitated state he could not allow Giles to think that all this carry-on was just the result of a blue funk.

'I had one of my turns . . .' he wheezed.

Giles helped him on to the bed, propping him up on the pillows and sitting down by him. He took Ernest's hand, separating the fingers and massaging each one gently, as if putting on imaginary gloves.

'One of your turns?'

'I used to have them when I was a youngster.'

'Ah — you're asthmatic.' It was a statement.

'That's it.' Ernest rolled his head from side to side on the pillow, feeling much revived. 'I was scared, Giles . . .'

'Don't be.' Giles gave the back of his hand a little tap. There was a note of amused satisfaction in his voice.

Ernest glanced at him. 'How's that?'

'I said don't worry.' Giles lifted Ernest's hand, kissed it, and returned it to its owner's heaving breast. 'You won't be joining any army, Ernest. And now I must go and get dry.'

*

On 15 May Dulcie arrived at Zoe Modes with a heavy heart. The news was all bad, and there was still none from Bill, though she religiously took the *Herald* and read his column. Yesterday Rotterdam had surrendered after terrible bombing, and German tanks had swept across the Meuse. The new Secretary for War, Anthony Eden, had broadcast, appealing to all able-bodied men to join something called the Local Defence Volunteers, in case the enemy should attempt a parachute landing. She could not believe things had come to this! And now, this morning, Holland had surrendered – the French army, advancing to her aid, had never even made contact with the Dutch!

She stood gazing miserably out of the window of Zoe Modes. She could see that even this would be taken away from her. Clothes rationing was to be introduced, it would soon be fashionable to make do and mend. Places like Zoe Modes would die a patriotic death. She would lose this little bit of usefulness, Bill might be crushed by one of those great, rolling tanks – she shuddered. At that moment she saw that someone was waving to her from the pavement outside, trying to catch her attention. She reorganized her face into an expression of bright welcome.

It was Una Roth-Vesey. Una undulated through the door, hips first, in a cloud of the sort of scent Dulcie could no longer afford. She wore a red silk shift, with a red and navy scarf at the neck and diamond earrings.

Her arrival was the cue for Madame Zoe herself to emerge from her lair at the back of the shop, drawn by the scent, and the sparkle of diamonds and Dulcie's murmured greeting was drowned by Madame Zoe's more effusive one.

'Mrs Roth-Vesey, what a pleasure to see you – we saw your photograph in the *Tatler*, charming, charming!'

Una could be cutting when she chose. She agreed that it was a pleasure for Madame Zoe to see her, and that she had been shown to advantage in the *Tatler*. 'But I'm simply dying for a word with my friend here, Madame, would you mind?' Though Dulcie herself would not have described Una as a friend, she was well aware that this raised her still higher in Madame's estimation. Madame Zoe withdrew, with an indulgent smile.

'Dearest,' crooned Una. 'I saw Rex playing tennis at Queens and he looked simply *shot at*, I thought you'd like to know.'

'I can't imagine that.' In the face of Una's crowing bitchiness Dulcie was disposed to be charitable. 'One thing about Rex, he always looked wonderful.'

'He's aged, though. Too much of the demon drink makes Jack a dull boy, hmm . . . ?'

Una's dalliance with Rex Donati had not lasted long. Both parties were entirely self-interested, so their interests necessarily clashed. Since the first, ghastly embarrassment of their meeting in the shop, Una and Dulcie had re-established a cautious acquaintanceship. Neither any longer posed a threat to the other.

'We were down in Norfolk at the weekend,' moaned Una, 'and frankly I'm thinking of selling up. The place is a wreck, and I should imagine that half the staff will be joining this Local Defence thingummy and will henceforth think of nothing but spearing the Hun on their pitchforks. Anyway I've always abhorred the country as I'm sure you know –'

'What can we do for you, Una?'

'Well *actually* I just had to drop by as I was passing – say, did you hear the news last night?'

'Only the early one.'

'Well, normally I should have been out,' said Una hastily, 'but RV was at his club, so . . . anyway, it seems that we have to register *The Brantus*.'

The mere mention of the Roth-Veseys' yacht made Dulcie's stomach churn.

'Why?' she asked dutifully.

Una's eyebrows disappeared behind her dark, smooth fringe. 'In case she's needed, Dulcie! In case we seafaring folk are called upon to go and patrol the coasts or something. Imagine!'

Dulcie could not imagine, but her stomach swirled again, this time with anxiety. 'But didn't they say on the news why you had to register?'

'Well of course not, it's all far too hush hush . . .' Una tilted back her head and gave a hoot of mirth. 'Can you picture RV manning the cannon or whatever against the German invader?'

'No,' said Dulcie truthfully.

Una brushed aside an imaginary tear with one glossily manicured finger. 'Oh my gosh I'm a wreck.'

'Hardly, Una.'

'*And* I must fly. G'bye, Dulcie.' She opened the door wide, and paused theatrically. Dulcie was bored by her. 'And watch this space for further instalments!'

When she had left, Dulcie found she had a splitting headache.

On the same day that Dulcie and Una wondered what such strange goings-on at home might mean, the entry in the Ninth Army War Diary read as follows: 'No information – communications cut – liaison unworkable – back areas blocked by convoys and wrecked columns – petrol trains in flames – wholesale chaos.'

It was a rout. The BEF were driven and harried before the panzers like sheep in the charge of a quick, intelligent sheepdog. And like sheep they lost all initiative and sense of direction, columns of men frequently converged at cross-roads heading in opposite directions, orders became garbled in transit or lost altogether. Because of the impossibility of getting any clear directives, either from editors at home or officers on the spot, Bill and Mike Philpott had little alternative but to allow themselves to be swept along like civilian flotsam on the surging tide of soldiery. Lord Gort's first act after the invasion of Belgium and Holland on the tenth had been to move HQ, with all its staff, including the Director of Military Intelligence, out of range of the journalists he was supposed to serve.

To begin with there had at least been a plan, the same plan that had existed before the invasion: British troops would advance into Belgium and co-ordinate a defence of the country with the Belgian and French armies. Accordingly, on the morning of the tenth the RASC unit had moved out of Bethel, north-east for the Belgian frontier. Bill, jolting along in a lorry near the rear, was amazed at their cheerfulness. In spite of the appalling loss of fuel, and, subsequently, of a man's life (Pete Whitworth had died), in spite of clear evidence of a swift, efficient and deadly German attack on several fronts, there was an almost holiday atmosphere.

'We're going to hang out the washing on the Siegfried Line, have you any dirty washing, mother dear . . . ?' they sang, sure that they were heading for a famous victory, sure that they could win this cruel modern war by dogged strength of character and cheery optimism.

Only a few kilometres from the border the singing was drowned by a wave of Heinkels roaring overhead. There was no time to do anything but pray as the road shuddered beneath the trucks and rubble rained down like gigantic hail on the roofs. In less than a minute they'd gone. When the men got down into the road they assessed the damage. Three vehicles of the dozen were a write-off, a couple listed drunkenly and could be got on their feet. The occupants of one of the shattered trucks had been blasted right into a field, and all were dead except one, who would be soon. There was a bitter smell, and much shouting, smoke gushed across the road like sea mist, the stricken lorries flared and crackled.

It was over a week later, when they'd long since been reduced to footslogging that Bill spotted a lorry called *Kate* rumbling down the road towards them. He decided it was an omen. Mike was ill and couldn't walk much further. With as much energy as he could muster he flagged it down.

The driver leaned out. 'Full up, mate.'

'Look, we're correspondents, we got stranded. My colleague's not a young man, and he's not at all well. I'm asking for a favour, a bit of floor space, anything.' He produced his card, but the driver waved it away.

'Bring him over.'

The lorry was named after Katherine Hepburn, there was a painting of her on the side, flashing that rather wolfish grin, all those immaculate teeth.

Somehow they squeezed into the back of *Kate*, which was already jam-packed. The men made space for Mike on a seat along the side, where he sat, lolling but upright, literally supported by the crush of people on either side. Bill sat on the floor with his knees under his chin, his back against Mike's legs to prevent him falling forwards as the lorry roared and bounced towards Dunkirk.

Many of them slept, but Bill couldn't. He would have liked to talk to someone, but even the men who were awake didn't seem disposed to conversation. He stared out of the back. His stomach cramped with hunger. In one field he saw a group of men, tattered and blackened like tinkers, crouched round a small smoking fire, cooking dampers on sticks. At one cross-roads the lorry was held up for five minutes by a herd of cows commandeered by troops. The cows milled around, lowing frantically, their udders full to bursting. The men were actually riding on some of the cows, congratulating themselves on having solved two problems — food as well as transport. They knew they were nearing Dunkirk because there was smoke in the air, and a peculiar rancid smell. On a playing field on the edge of town they were halted. There was some kind of heated exchange between the driver and a sergeant. Bill got out.

The football field was an extraordinary sight — a kind of mechanical graveyard. Army lorries and trucks were being systematically destroyed to prevent them falling into the hands of the advancing Germans. Round the edge of the field soldiers attacked the task with hammers, rifle butts, anything they could lay their hands on. In the centre, almost ritually placed equidistant from both goal posts, burned a vast funeral pyre of vehicles, crackling and roaring.

The driver walked over to Bill, his expression bleak. 'Sorry cock, you and your mate'll have to walk from here on. I got to break her up.'

With ruthless, tight-lipped energy the driver got on with his job, helped by *Kate*'s other army passengers. Mike lay down on the grass, foetus-like, his legs trembling, and Bill crouched by him, taking advantage of the warmth from the fire.

He saw the driver's face as *Kate* was dismantled and pushed over to the vast bonfire. Just a machine, but one this man had cared for, and bullied and cajoled and fed with hard-come-by petrol, all this way. In return she'd got him here, damn nearly home, just to be repaid like this. The burly driver's face in the flickering light was a mask of misery. Bill looked away.

He couldn't budge Mike, so they spent the night there. Early the next morning a young *curé* from a nearby church came round, accompanied by two gentle nuns. They were in a van, and brought strong coffee and bread rolls. They were besieged by near-starving soldiers, but Bill managed to get some for Mike, and sat him up and made him eat it. Watching the *curé* and the sisters dispensing their manna with smiles and kind words, Bill wondered if they realized that the BEF were here not to defend their town, but to desert it.

When they'd eaten, Bill bullied Mike to his feet and they joined the tide of men heading through the town. It was a slow and painful progress, but Bill could find it in his heart to be glad his friend wasn't well enough to notice much.

Hitler had said that Dunkirk was the Luftwaffe's job, and the Luftwaffe was performing with its usual efficiency. Unfortunately, with only one telephone line left open there had been an error in interpreting orders, resulting in the deliberate destruction of over a hundred anti-aircraft guns, and leaving the town with no defence against the bombers. Thousands of incendiaries and tons of high explosives had already rained down on Dunkirk. Acres of docks, warehouses and quays had been pounded to a smoking, featureless rubble. For more than three days there had been no water supply. Civilian morale had been reduced to the point where French housewives and bank clerks jostled British soldiers to grab what they could from wrecked shops. Over a thousand corpses remained unburied. This model bourgeois French town was now like a hell conceived in the imagination of some wild and vengeful prophet. Flames licked up through torn roofs and leaned like beckoning hands from gaping windows. Overhead, through a sky churning with thick black smoke from the burning oil refineries at St Pol, the Stuka dive-bombers wheeled and screamed like vultures at a kill.

The streets were crowded not just with the living, but with the dead, and full of their sickening smell. On one corner Bill saw the rotting body of a British officer standing bizarrely upright, supported by a fallen joist which protruded like a swagger stick from his left armpit. But not all officers had remained so steadfast – in one alleyway a cigarette case and silver hip flask remained in evidence of one leader's undignified flight. And where the leaders failed, the troops had run wild. One group had raided a bombed-out bar. Reeling drunk, they had dressed the corpse of a corporal in a feather boa and straw hat. The gash of arterial blood across the corpse's face passed admirably for lipstick. The men lifted the arms of the corpse and moved them from side to side so that the body swayed and danced.

In the centre of the town a *gendarme* stood in a small cobbled square, directing the traffic. Beside him lay two former colleagues, dead, killed where they stood.

The harbour, they were told, was unusable. They must head for the undulating sandy beaches east of the town. To help keep them going they were told there was drinking water there. But when they reached the beach it was clear to Bill that the chances of locating the drinking water, or any other amenity, were remote. The grey dunes were black with troops, like some grim parody of Blackpool on a bank holiday weekend. It was early afternoon, but many of them looked as if they had been here since yesterday.

Bill scraped a hole in the sand for Mike, settled him in it and covered him up saying, 'I'm just going to take a look around.'

He saw a couple of naval officers down near the water's edge, apparently trying to organize the milling throng of men into squads. Far out on the horizon sat a couple of large ships, cruisers or destroyers. Four lifeboats were plying the intervening mile between ships and shore with nightmare slowness. An enterprising army cook had rigged up a field kitchen about halfway down the beach. Bill passed two officers lapping hot baked beans straight out of their cupped hands, like dogs. Some men were sleeping like babies in their funk-holes, others were hysterical with fear, still others just numb. But there were so many of them. Bill could not envisage how, at the present rate of progress, he was going to get Mike to a ship before this time tomorrow.

As he came down the beach, one of the navy men ran up to meet him, presumably taking him for an officer.

'Could I ask for your assistance?'

'You could, but I came to ask for yours. I'm a journalist, my colleague's very ill. Is there the remotest chance of getting him on a boat sooner rather than later?'

'Look –' the naval officer was harassed almost to breaking point. 'I'm trying to impose some order here. If you get your friend down here I'll do my best – but at the moment that's not much.'

Bill toiled back up to the dunes, dug Mike out and hauled him down as far as the wet sand where the tide was receding. The Stukas were concentrating their efforts on the town and harbour, but as wave after wave passed overhead from the Luftwaffe's VIII Flying Corps HQ near St Pol, so they sprayed the beach with bombs. Both planes and bombs were fitted with whistles, and the unearthly screaming as they dived added to the panic on the beach, but Bill could see no point in lying down — Mike would never get up again. A football sized lump of meat was washed in by a wave and rolled at Bill's feet. For a terrible moment he thought it was a human head, until a group of men fell on it, hacking it apart with bayonets and wolfing it down. It was a fourteen-pound chunk of corned beef, oil-soaked but still edible.

Gallantry and respect were of no use to anyone here. When the next boat came in Bill hoisted Mike over his shoulder and waded out, stumbling and thrashing in the shallows. He knew people were shouting at him, cursing him. As he reached the side of the boat someone pulled him from behind and he almost fell. He bellowed at one of the men rowing: 'This man is very ill!' But they weren't interested; their faces were blank. It was just numbers, first come first served. They dragged Bill and Mike on board. Bill said again: 'He's ill, he'll die if he stays here.' They didn't care. The lifeboatmen were rowing machines, already taxed beyond endurance. The soldiers in the water hated him for being there. As the boat moved off on the swell, wallowing under her huge load, he watched their faces crumple from fury into despair.

Alongside the boat a bloated corpse bobbed like a cork and, as the tide went out, seemed to keep pace with them like a bird of ill omen, until, at six in the evening, they reached the grey ramparts of His Majesty's cruiser *Beowulf*. Crammed on the narrow decks with two hundred others Bill Maguire, for the first and only time in his life, said a small prayer for forgiveness.

CHAPTER THIRTEEN

'Military intelligence is a
contradiction in terms' – Groucho Marx

'They asked me how I knew
My true love was true;
I of course replied,
"Something here inside,
Cannot be denied . . ."'!

'Smoke Gets In Your Eyes'
Otto Harback & Jerome Kern, 1933

DULCIE was just preparing for bed at eleven-thirty on the night of 27 May when there was a knock on the door. She was not nervous, because her flat in St John's Wood was in the secluded fastnesses of a huge mansion block. She had one or two elderly neighbours who had turned insomniac since the start of the war and quite often called at odd hours just for a chat.

'Coming!' she called. Fondant, always restless till she went to bed and he could curl up at her feet without fear of interruption, prowled after her as she went to the front door, and opened it a chink.

She did not at first recognize the figure standing on the well-lit landing.

'Who is it?'

'Who do you think?'

'Bill!'

'Can I come in, or what?'

Feeling shy – almost frightened – she opened the door wide and stood back to let him enter. For that moment he was a stranger, his damp, dirty, unshaven bulk seemed to carry the war right into her cosy hall. A smell that she preferred not to analyse hung round him.

All these things prevented her going to him. She stood tense, with her back to the door, staring.

Solemnly he said: 'Sorry I haven't shaved.'

'That's all right. Anyway, it suits you.'

He tilted his head back in a silent laugh. 'Oh, Dulcie, Dulcie, they threw away the mould . . . would you kiss me if I asked you nicely?'

She rushed into his arms, pressing her warm mouth to his cold, stubbly face, slipping her arms tightly round him beneath his jacket. He was here, he was back, at last. If she could have dissolved and been absorbed right into him, through his skin, she would have done so. She even, in the warm, breathing seclusion of his embrace, allowed herself a few luxurious tears. But only a very few, and by the time she drew back to look at him again they had gone.

'What do you want?'

He combed his fingers back through his hair. 'I suspect I shall only get what I want by having a bath first.'

'Of course!' Now she was all concern and activity. She helped him off with his jacket, flew to the bathroom to turn on the taps, to the kitchen to fill the kettle, to close the door of Celine's bedroom so that they shouldn't disturb her.

She made the tea, with plenty of sugar, and took a cup into the bathroom, fastidiously pushing aside his dirty clothes with her foot. He was lying back in the steaming water with an expression of the utmost contentment.

He held out a hand. 'I must be in heaven.'

She passed him the cup, and sat down on the uncomfortable white wicker bathroom chair, feasting her eyes on him. As he pulled himself more upright to drink the tea the water streamed off his shoulders. He'd washed his hair and it clung in slick black points to his forehead and neck. His pale skin was blotched with small scars and abrasions, reddening in the hot water.

'Shall I soap your back?'

'That would be a kindness.'

She picked up the flannel and soap and went to kneel at the end of the bath while he sipped his tea. Methodically, with voluptuous slowness, she lathered and rubbed and rinsed, and then put her arms right round him and pressed against him. 'When are you going to tell me what you've been doing?' she whispered. 'I thought you were dead.'

He chuckled, put down the tea and leaned back, holding her arms round his neck, so that the sleeves of her dressing-gown trailed in the water.

'Oh ye of little faith.' He pulled her head down and kissed her. 'Sorry about your sleeves.'

She curled up, her chin resting on the side of the bath, gazing at him. 'The news has been awful. Kate and I went to the cinema —'

'How is Kate?'

'She's fine. Lawrence has been posted to Malta, by the way, they go on Monday.'

'Do they indeed? I dare say he's pleased about that.' He glanced at her. 'But you're going to miss Kate.'

Dulcie shrugged. 'I'm used to missing people. I was going to say that there was this terrible film on the Pathe News, showing the German tanks — I just hoped it was only propaganda.'

'No, it's true. Just propaganda in the sense that they make sure we see it in our cinemas. Like everything else, when they do a thing, they do it properly. They certainly are sweeping all before them, most particularly the British army, who are even at this moment leaving France.'

'Leaving?' she didn't understand. 'For where?'

'For here.'

She leaned her forehead on the bath, and closed her eyes, trying to take in the implications of this information. But now that Bill was back she had no real interest in the war.

'I don't think I want to talk about it.'

'Suits me.'

'It only matters that you're back.'

She watched him as he pulled out the plug, and stepped out of the bath, rubbing himself vigorously with her fluffy white towel. Well before he was properly dry she rose and put her arms round him, closing her eyes and luxuriating in his powerful, solid nearness after the weeks of loneliness. She felt the resolute thud of his heart in its strong cage of flesh and bone, his skin still steamy from the bath, his body quickening against hers. He was all she needed.

Later, when he slept, she gazed at him, trying to read him. Perhaps with all that he had been through he had missed her too, and in missing her had realized that he loved her. This was such a delightful idea that she fell asleep nursing it in her heart, and awoke almost believing it to be true. Bill was already up, moving purposefully about the room. Blearily she glanced at the clock.

'Heavens, Bill, what are you doing? It's only six-thirty.'

'I must get back to Maida Vale and shave and get clean clothes and then get into the office.'

'Surely after everything, couldn't you just . . .?'

'Not really. I've got something to write about at last, Dulcie.' He rummaged in the chest of drawers. She kept a change of underwear and shirt for him, always. 'Got an egg?'

'Yes.' She climbed out of bed, dislodging Fondant. 'But be quiet.'

He followed her to the kitchen in his stockinged feet, buttoning his shirt. 'You let that battleaxe rule your life these days,' he said, referring to Celine.

'No, I don't.' She poured milk into Fondant's saucer. 'And she's seen me through a lot of bad times.'

'Exactly. It's because of that she's tyrannical now.'

Dulcie put an egg in a saucepan of water on the stove. 'No she's not, she's just a bit temperamental, that's all.'

She folded her arms and lifted her chin slightly. Bill liked the way she did that, it was an unconscious gesture, born of pretending to be braver than she was. And after all, wasn't that real courage, being scared to death and not showing it? Impulsively he embraced her. 'You're a softie.'

She pushed him off. 'And your face is like a doormat.'

While the egg bubbled she went into the living room and came back with an invitation card.

'Look – Aubrey's getting married!'

He glanced at it. 'Good for him. She's a nice woman.'

She realized that he couldn't really know just how momentous and amazing the news was. 'I *never* thought he would. If ever there was a confirmed bachelor, it was Aubrey. I used to hate him, you know.'

'Perhaps it was mutual.'

'Oh, I'm sure it was. But this —' she took the card back and gazed at it intently, 'it's just like a complete change of character, it makes him human. Oh well, I shall buy myself a hat, coupons or no coupons.'

As he sat at the little table, eating the egg with a slice of toast, Dulcie sat opposite him sipping tea. Conversationally she said: 'Una Roth-Vesey came into the shop the other day.'

'Oh yes?' Bill only knew Una as part of the Rex set-up, a figure from the bad old days. 'What did she have to say for herself?'

'Quite a bit actually. She'd seen Rex, she was horrible about him.'

'That's rich, coming from you!'

'Not at all. She's so cheap and bitchy, she was gloating because he looked awful.'

Bill turned his empty eggshell upside down and stuck his spoon through it. 'I shouldn't waste your sympathy on that bugger.'

'Anyway . . .' Dulcie didn't like him in this hard, unforgiving vein, 'she was all excited because they had to register their yacht, *The Brantus* — you know, the one I had that ghastly holiday on —'

'Yes, I know. Now that is interesting.'

Dulcie went on, 'There was something on the wireless apparently, I didn't hear it. She was full of herself.'

'I'm sure.' Bill leaned his elbows on the table. 'Keen sailors are they, the Roth-Veseys?'

Dulcie laughed. 'Hardly! They're just disgustingly rich people who own a yacht because it's the thing to do. They don't sail it, they have a crew. They literally have so much money they don't —'

'I'm glad you told me that.' He pushed back his chair, still holding his half-eaten toast in one hand. 'I must get going, thank you for breakfast.'

She followed him dejectedly into the hall. He shrugged on his army tunic and embraced her, but the tunic smelt, reminding her that he was heading back into a man's world where important things happened. She was stiff in his arms. As he released her Celine appeared from her room, fully dressed and with a pained expression.

'*Bonjour, Celine!*' said Bill cheerfully, popping in the last mouthful of toast.

'Good morning, Mr Maguire.'

'Hope we didn't disturb you – I'm just going.' Unabashed by Celine's hostile stare, he kissed Dulcie. 'I'll be in touch. Good-bye.'

He left. Dulcie was marooned standing uneasily between the warm receding tide of his departure and the icy waters of Celine's disapproval. The icy waters closed round her. She turned with a sigh to face her maid.

By mid-morning Bill had been back to Maida Vale, shaved, put on a clean suit and done some writing (none of which stood a snowball's chance with the army censor). He then went into the offices of the *Herald*.

Trevor greeted him as if he had just slipped out to post a letter. 'By the way, since you're back, an edict has gone out to all BEF correspondents to report to the Berkeley Hotel at midday.'

'Any idea why?'

'Mason MacFarlane wants a word.'

'I bet he does.' Major General Mason MacFarlane was the Director of Military Intelligence. So that was where he'd got to. Bill reflected that this briefing would have come in handy a couple of weeks ago.

'What the hell's been going on?' asked Trevor.

'I'm not sure you're going to believe it. Anyway,' Bill rose, 'I'll see what MM's got to say for himself first, and then give you my version. See you later.'

Before leaving for the Berkeley, Bill went to his desk and rang the Philpotts' number in Finchley. He'd dropped Mike off from a cab the previous night, without much ceremony, and it was on his conscience.

Mrs Philpott was strained, polite, accusing. Her tone implied that her husband's condition was somehow Bill's fault, as if they'd been pub-crawling together instead of caught up in a war. He wondered if Mike had been well enough to tell her anything. But after he put the phone down he realized that he had said nothing to Dulcie, no word about what it had been like, and she typically had not pressed him. Pub-crawl or war, he reflected, we hang on to our male preserves.

Feeling happy and energetic, he left for the Berkeley.

Mason MacFarlane began by saying that what he was about to tell them was strictly off the record. Bill reckoned that in that case it was probably true. Surreptitiously he undid his shoelaces – his feet were still painful – in order to give the Director of Intelligence his full attention.

The French, of course, were blamed. 'It is now no secret that on several fronts the French failed to withstand the assault . . . the result of these failures was disastrous from the point of view of the BEF, and led directly to the critical situation with which it is now faced.' He seemed quite to ignore the fact, well known by every man in the room, that the French army was still fighting for its life, and its country, while the BEF was doing its damnedest to get back across the Channel.

The major general cleared his throat noisily. 'In fairness to the British Army and its commanders, it cannot be too highly emphasized that it is the Allied High Command that has been outmanoeuvred, and the armies of the French that have been outfought – not the BEF.'

Now there was an interesting angle – Bill glanced down at his notes. The big noises were prepared to shoulder most of the blame as far as the BEF was concerned, in order to keep alive in the public imagination the picture of the dogged, plucky British Tommy who fought till he dropped. Bill had a good deal of respect for the rank and file of the British army, but on this occasion the only reason that it could be said they had not been outfought was that they had scarcely fought at all, nor been given a chance to do so. The leaderless drunks in the streets of Dunkirk were still fresh in his memory.

'I'm afraid,' Mason MacFarlane went on, 'that there is going to be a considerable shock for the British public.' He glared round at the journalists. 'It is your duty to act as shock-absorbers, so I have prepared with my counterpart at the War

Office, a statement which can be published, subject to censorship . . .'

When it was all over Bill encountered Lawrence in the hotel foyer.

'Bill! Good to see you, thank God you got back all right, it sounds a fiasco over there.'

Bill shook his head. 'You could say that. Dulcie's told me your news – you must be delighted.'

'I can't wait.' Lawrence smiled a little shamefacedly. 'But look, we're off Monday, Lord knows when we'll see you again – why don't you and Dulcie come round and have pot-luck tonight? I've got to go down to Sussex tomorrow for a couple of days, to help organize buses and billets and whatnot for the men arriving. Tonight though . . . you could give us the unexpurgated version.'

'That sounds fine, thanks.'

Lawrence glanced up the stairs. 'Old man's coming, I'd better go. We'll see you this evening then?'

'Look forward to it.'

Bill felt energetic, almost lightheadedly so. Apart from his feet he seemed to have suffered no ill-effects from his journey home. On the contrary he felt thinner, fitter, more alert, than he had done in months.

After the Berkeley he skipped lunch and went straight back to the office and spent an hour regurgitating Mason Mac-Farlane's statement in a suitable form for tomorrow's paper. Then he sought out the diary editor, Miles Lucas. The information he needed he could as easily have obtained from Dulcie, but he did not want to attract her inevitable questions.

Miles was a bland, round-faced Etonian, a fitter-in.

'Ask away, my dear fellow.'

'Do you know some people called Roth-Vesey? He's blue-blooded and she's American and rich.'

Miles nodded, and lit a cigarette with a reflective air. 'Certainly do. To say they're rich is the understatement of the year, they're abso-bloody-lutely rolling in it. She used to set herself up as a bit of a Simpson-ite pre '36, which didn't endear her to anyone much at the time. She gets precious few brownie points for it now, come to that. RV is fat and ugly and used to dote and forgive but less so now.'

'Forgive?'

'The lovely lads, of whom there are a string.'

'Oh yes,' Bill couldn't resist. 'Didn't she have a thing with Sir Hector Donati's son?'

'Only a bit of a thing, she'd met her match there. Rex was in lower school when I was in Pop, and he was a cold little bastard even then. Hasn't changed.'

Bill laughed. 'Thanks. Very succinct, very helpful.'

'Not at all. I forgot one thing.'

'What's that?'

'The chihuahuas. Kind of canine piranha fish, Una Roth-Vesey keeps a fleet of the blighters. Don't say I didn't warn you.'

'I won't. Look, Miles – do you have an in with these people?'

'I have an in with Una. Anything in trousers and under forty does.' He peered over his desk at Bill, who had removed his shoes. 'That could even include you at a pinch.'

'I want a word with them – or him, anyway, though she'd be better than nothing –'

'Oh, she's certainly better than nothing.'

'Could you give me their phone number, and do you mind if I take your name in vain?'

'Do, do, everybody does.' Miles pushed back his chair and took a large, tattered address book out of a drawer. 'R . . . R . . . Roth-Vesey, there you are. Mayfair 3031. Be my guest.' There was no reply. 'I expect she's out lunching with one or two other society crones,' remarked Miles. 'Try again about three, she'll be in putting her feet up with the doggies.'

When Bill rang again at three-fifteen he was gratified to hear a man's voice on the other end – a soupy, caddish voice, ripe with port and cigar smoke. Percy Roth-Vesey had been at his club.

'Mr Roth-Vesey?'

'Speaking.'

'I'm calling on behalf of Miles Lucas, *Herald* diary page –' Bill glanced at Miles.

'You want my wife.'

'No, I'd like a word with you, if I may.'

'Go ahead.'

'I wonder if I might come round?'

There was a long pause, during which Bill could hear the rhythmic wheeze and burble of Percy's breathing as he considered the suggestion.

'I suppose so, provided you're not all day about it. What did you say your name was?'

'Bill Maguire. Thank you. I'll be with you in about half an hour.'

Their faces were a study.

'Do I understand you to say,' expostulated Percy, stabbing the air with his cigar, 'that you have come round here under false pretences to ask if you can take my yacht over the Channel to rescue the army?'

'No. I simply wondered, since you'd had the yacht registered, whether your crew might be taking her over, and if so, whether I could go along. Also, I'm not here entirely under false pretences. If your boat goes over, if the small craft *are* called on, the readers of the *Herald* will be the first to know.'

'Mr Maguire,' said Percy scathingly. 'We don't need publicity.'

'But you should take credit.'

Una came forward and slipped her arm through Percy's. It was clear her imagination had been fired by this exchange. 'Captain Hamilton is naval reserve, isn't he, darling?'

'I believe so.'

'He's bound to want to go. You wouldn't not let him take *The Brantus*, would you, if it's a matter of national importance, that wouldn't be at *all* your style . . .' She flashed Bill a conspiratorial smile.

She knew her subject. Percy whuffled and grunted, gratified at her picture of him as a sturdy patriot for whom no sacrifice was too great.

Bill pursued the advantage so skillfully gained by Una. 'I was with the BEF. I got a boat from the beach at Dunkirk just yesterday evening. By rights I should still be there, it was only because my colleague was ill that we left when we did.' Una gasped admiringly. 'I'm quite sure they're going to want the small boats there, the situation is hopeless at the moment. All

I'm asking is to tag along and make myself useful, if there's a chance.'

Una advanced, with a high-minded expression and took his hand in both of hers. 'Something tells me you're an idealist, Mr Maguire,' she cooed.

'Not especially. Quite self-interested as a matter of fact.'

Abruptly, Percy said: 'I'll contact my skipper Hamilton for you, Maguire. I think my wife's right, if they do want the small boats he'll be keen to go. I see no reason why you shouldn't be on board if he does.'

'That's extremely sporting of you. Thank you.'

'She's a bloody expensive toy, mind you!' snapped Percy. 'No unnecessary heroics.'

Bill thought there was no point in telling Percy that his yacht could well be blown to bits. He thanked them both again, made arrangements to call that evening, and left while the going was good.

'Any luck?' asked Miles when Bill returned to the office.

'Plenty.'

'May one ask?'

'One may, but one will not receive an answer.'

'Say no more.' Miles bowed. 'Just so long as the chihuahuas didn't get you.'

'They were not in evidence.'

Bill went in to see Trevor again. 'Can I take a day?' he asked. 'I think there's a chance of going over in a small boat to France, to help with the evacuation.'

Trevor stared at him in the vague, dispassionate way he had. 'Take a day? France? You've only just got back.'

'Yes.'

'Sucker for punishment, aren't you?'

'I suppose I must be.'

Trevor let his glasses drop from their perch on the top of his head, to the bridge of his nose. He waved Bill from the room with his pencil.

'I haven't seen you, I don't know where you are. I shall expect you back in the office the moment I see you.'

'I don't yet know —'

'Don't bother me with it, Bill.'

'Thanks.' He went to the door.

'And for Christ's sake be careful!'

By the time Bill and Dulcie got to the flat in Craven Road that evening, Bill had already spoken once more to Percy, and subsequently to Captain Ian Hamilton RNR, a smooth, practical Scotsman well used to dealing with the fads and foibles of the upper classes.

'If Mr Roth-Vesey is happy with the arrangement, then I am too, sir. This is a registered vessel and I'm naval reserve, I'll make myself useful if I can.'

'Will you contact me again if there's any word?'

'I'll certainly do that, sir. She's berthed near Sheerness where I live at the moment, it would be a case of my picking you up at Dover or Ramsgate.'

'Whatever you say.'

'I should tell you, Mr Maguire —' the quiet Scottish voice hesitated, 'we none of us have the slightest idea what to expect.'

'Don't worry,' said Bill. 'I have.'

He waited to drop his bombshell till the middle of supper, which was partly vanity, partly a cowardly device to protect him from Dulcie's dismay. It had been a rather strange evening anyway, the flat bare of those things of Kate's and Lawrence's which had redeemed its ugliness, as if they had already left in spirit. Kate was in garrulous, self-assertive form, Lawrence thoughtful. Privately Bill thought Kate rather splendid in this vein, it was like having a fire in the room, towards which everyone automatically turned.

But towards the end of the main course he claimed their attention. Dulcie put down her knife and fork neatly, side by side, and sat back.

'Why?' asked Kate. 'You've only just got here!'

He smiled at her. He could not look at Dulcie. 'Everyone keeps saying that.'

'Because it's true,' said Lawrence. 'But I don't blame you. I'd do the same.'

Bill turned to him enthusiastically. 'Then why don't you? Come along, we could do with a military man on board.'

Dulcie looked at them in astonishment – were they all mad?

Lawrence shook his head. 'I can't. I told you, I've got to go down to Easthaven for a couple of days to organize the dispersal of these chaps. You have no idea the administrative kerfuffle all this has caused –'

'Lawrence!' Kate was impatient. 'You sound like some wretched civil servant!'

'That's more or less what I am till we go, darling, like it or lump it.' He smiled at her amiably. For a second Bill found himself thinking that Kate pushed Lawrence too hard. He was such an incredibly nice chap, and so wholeheartedly devoted to his wife – a self-destructive combination.

Bill said, 'A very necessary job.'

Kate poured herself another glass of wine. 'If Lawrence won't come, I will.'

'Kate!' Dulcie saw no reason whatever why her stoical non-reaction should extend to her daughter. 'Have you gone completely mad?'

'Never saner!' Kate grinned at Bill. She was a little drunk, it had made her bolshy and contentious.

'Don't be ridiculous, Kate,' said Lawrence gently. 'It's out of the question and you know it.'

'I don't know any such thing! I'm probably a lot better qualified than he is –' she waved her glass at Bill, who laughed. 'I'm younger for one thing, for another I've sailed a lot, and I bet you haven't – have you?'

'No, I haven't. But it's a motor yacht and it has its own crew.'

'Never mind that,' she was hugely pleased with herself. 'Added to which I've done an ARP course, and coped with all kinds of emergencies at the Institute –'

'Shut up, Kate.' It was Lawrence, no longer amused.

She turned on him. 'Why should I? You think I'm joking, don't you?'

'No, it's not funny. It's just entirely inappropriate. You're not going and that's that.'

Dulcie said: 'I agree. Kate, darling –'

'Oh Dulcie stop behaving like a mother hen!' snapped Kate.

Cut to the quick, Dulcie relapsed into silence. Kate turned back to Lawrence. 'Go on – why?'

He shrugged. Bill thought that he was exerting enormous self-control, when Kate really needed slapping down.

'I love you, and I don't want you to go,' said Lawrence.

'If you love me, then *let* me go.'

'That's childish.'

'No more childish than your saying I mustn't.'

'Kate.' Bill intervened. 'Don't get me wrong, I'm not talking down to you, I know you're fit and able and raring to go. But I have been there, and it's pretty nasty.'

'I'm not squeamish. I was brought up in Africa, remember? We had a murder a month in the shambas, and they weren't done with guns.'

Dulcie blenched. 'If we're going to discuss disembowellings over the pudding . . .' she half-hoped that mention of pudding might remind her daughter that she had duties as a hostess as well, but Kate ignored her.

'I'm asking you, Bill, will you have me along?'

Bill looked at Kate – fiery, excited, determined – and then at Lawrence, who was pale and still, twiddling his empty wine glass between his finger and thumb.

He chose his words carefully. 'I'm not in a position to refuse valuable help from anyone who offers it,' he said. 'But you're both my friends and it's your quarrel. I'm not going to take sides. Is there any afters?'

'Damn you!' Kate pushed her chair back, and it fell with a crash to the floor behind her. 'You can get it yourselves and I hope you choke on it!'

She stormed from the room and Lawrence followed her, but she slammed the bedroom door so hard in his face that he actually staggered. He came back with slow, measured strides and sat down holding the edge of the table as if testing its strength. His face was white.

'Sorry about that. She'll cool off.'

'Shall I go?' offered Dulcie.

Bill was rather enjoying himself. 'No,' he said. 'Let her stew for a bit. Go and see what's for pud.'

'Kate . . . ?'

She twitched her shoulder, shaking off Lawrence's tentative hand.

'Kate, come on, we can't let the sun go down on our wrath like this. After all, what the hell are we arguing about?'

'If you don't know,' she muttered, 'I'm not going to tell you.'

'Look.' She felt him sit up, and knew he was rubbing his face in that way he had when he was pulling his thoughts together. 'You're a grown woman. Short of physically restraining you – come to think of it that might be fun . . .' She said nothing, so he went on. 'But I do ask you, if you love me as you always say you do, not to go. You heard what Bill said, he's been there he doesn't exaggerate.'

She turned on her back now and glared at him. Even in the dark he could feel that glare.

'You know perfectly well that if you were able to go and had the chance, you would. No matter what I said or how dangerous it was – you'd be very kind and understanding, but you'd *go!*'

With a lurch that rocked the bed she turned away again, huddling the eiderdown round her shoulders to shut him out.

The next day Lawrence left for Easthaven. He had not again tried to argue with her or to reconcile their differences.

In the face of his severe, she thought reproving, silence, Kate became more rebellious. She felt that she was being subjected to reasonable, loving, but powerful blackmail. A letter arrived from Joe, wondering if she could possibly forward him more pocket money before they left, as he was going away for the weekend. Incensed, she tore it up. There was no one to commiserate with her – Dulcie and Andrea would be at work, and she did not feel that her complaints were appropriate subjects for discussion with her less intimate army friends. So she sulked and chafed on her own.

At lunchtime Dulcie rang. She was cautious. 'Kate – I wanted to thank you for last night.'

'Don't be ridiculous, it was a disaster.'

'Not at all, these things happen. I was furious with Bill, especially when we don't have much time left to see you.'

This remark irritated Kate for some reason. 'Don't go chipping at him, it wasn't his fault.'

'Don't worry, I shan't have a chance,' retaliated Dulcie with a hint of sharpness. 'He's going down to Ramsgate this evening to meet up with the Roth-Veseys' boat.'

'Oh, is he?' said Kate.

'Yes. And not a word from me on the subject, I assure you.'

'Sorry.'

'Don't mention it. But, Kate, you did sort something out with Lawrence, didn't you? I hated to see you like that.'

Kate glanced at her watch. 'Don't worry, it's sorted out.'

'Good!' Dulcie's voice was warm with relief. 'Look, I must go, I'm ringing from the shop while Madame Zoe's out. Do you want to come over this evening? We could be grass widows together while we still have the chance.'

'That's kind of you, Dulcie,' said Kate, 'but I don't think I will, I'm a bit whacked, and I've got a sore throat . . .'

'It's all the fussing and feuding when you've been so busy,' Dulcie assured her. 'You're your own worst enemy sometimes.'

'I know,' said Kate. 'I'm sure you're right.'

The Brantus, a 65-foot motor yacht, set out from Ramsgate before dawn on Thursday 30 May. On board were the skipper, Captain Hamilton; the only other volunteer from Roth-Veseys' crew, their steward, Dick Eames; a retired Royal Navy engineer, Bertie Talbot; Bill Maguire; and Kate Drake. She had driven down to Ramsgate early on the Wednesday evening and reached the boat before Bill. By the time he arrived she had established herself, was on Christian name terms with the crew, had made tea and sandwiches in the galley and won praise from Ian Hamilton for having had the foresight to bring a pile of old sheets, towels and blankets from the Institute.

There was nothing Bill could do to dislodge her now, short of throwing her overboard. In a single hour, she had already contributed more to the voyage than he had, and he could see at a glance that she was in her element. All the restless energy that had made her belligerent the night before was now channelled into the task at hand. In the face of a *fait accompli* Bill opted for a note of quiet, practical acceptance.

'Well done. You seem to have made yourself indispensable in double quick time.'

'I want to be useful.' She was making up the bunks in one of the double cabins, smoothing, tucking, plumping up pillows at great speed. She wore a pair of her own tan trousers, wellington boots with a couple of pairs of Lawrence's socks, a sweater and a combat jacket (also Lawrence's) out of the pocket of which protruded a tweed hat (Aubrey's, the same that she had used on her ARP course). No one could have accused her of being dressed unserviceably, though Bill thought it a little hard on Lawrence that she had plundered his wardrobe so freely. He had no idea whether the two of them had agreed to this arrangement or not, and he did not intend to ask. He could only assume that she came with Lawrence's blessing.

Also, he admitted to himself, he did not want to be put in a position where it would have been his duty to dissuade her. She finished the bunks. 'Come and have some tea, and I'll introduce you to the others,' she said.

On the way to the galley she pushed open doors, pointing out cabins and storerooms. She had familiarized herself with the yacht's geography, he observed.

She was enthusiastic. 'Isn't it fantastic? They must be filthy rich.'

'They are. I think they view this jaunt with some trepidation, and rightly.'

'Nonsense!' She was gay. 'We shall bring her back ship-shape.'

Bill remembered the pall of oily black smoke, and the terrible stink of the rotting dead, and the teeming throng of starving, terrified men.

'We can try to,' he said.

Aside from the three double berths, and crew's cabin for four, *The Brantus* had a small, well-equipped galley, a partially glassed-in sundeck to stern, littered with fat, striped cushions, and a panelled and carpeted lounge with a teak cocktail bar at one end.

'Skip the tea,' said Bill. He went to the bar and found the whisky and a tumbler, and helped himself. 'You? Heroes' perks?'

'No, thanks.'

He lifted the glass in her direction. 'Here's to us.'

'Here's to us.'

Their eyes met, and the powerful, instinctive empathy which they usually had to suppress so rigorously found sudden expression. Each was electrified by it so that they stood like two statues on either side of the room, their eyes fixed on one another, rooted to the spot by a challenge they couldn't deny but were at a loss to meet. The words of their toast hung in the air, suddenly imbued with a new and thrilling meaning.

Kate spoke first. 'You should meet the others.'

He emptied his glass, looking at her over the rim. 'Should I?' Their voices were flat, drained of energy and expression. When Kate moved her legs felt like lead, but she knew that move she must, and break the spell. But as she passed Bill he grabbed her wrist. She tried to pull away but he held her in a viciously hard grip.

'I'm bloody glad you came, Kate.'

She didn't look at him, her heart was pounding and roaring like big guns in her head.

'Come on,' she said, in the same bleached voice.

He released her wrist roughly, almost throwing her hand back at her, and as she walked away Kate heard him put the glass down hard on top of the bar.

On deck, she introduced the crew. Dick Eames, the steward, was a spruce Londoner with thinning, but immaculately combed and Brylcreemed hair, and the spry, ageless charm of a monkey. He wore a gleaming white jacket.

'It might seem odd to you, sir,' he said, as he shook Bill by the hand, 'but I feel undressed aboard *The Brantus* without my white jacket. It's just a little foible of mine.'

In contrast to Dick Eames, Bertie Talbot was a large, shambling man whose clothes looked as though they'd found their way on to him and were clinging there by a thread. His trousers defied gravity beneath the vast, swaying overhang of his paunch, his shirt parted above it to reveal a grey, threadbare vest. Where Dick was sharp and garrulous, Bertie was vague and bumbling. A lifetime spent working amid the wordless noise of ships' engines had left him a little punch-drunk.

'In good order, is she?' enquired Bill, who knew nothing of such matters.

'Sweet as a nut,' replied Bertie, and shambled back to the engine room, exhausted after this effusion.

'Where's Captain Hamilton?'

'He's gone to the skippers' briefing,' said Kate. 'He'll be back soon.'

Hamiton returned in about half an hour.

'Well,' said Bill, 'what's the score?'

The briefing had been conducted by Commander Eric Wharton of the Small Vessels Pool at Sheerness. Hamilton's expression was dubious.

'He was none too precise. It was all tally-ho and steer for the sound of the guns. There are some out behind the port of Dunkirk itself, but he said they are trained on the harbour area and shouldn't give us any trouble.'

'And the big guns at Calais.' Calais had fallen two days earlier, as the Germans moved inexorably east along the coast of northern France.

'Indeed.' Hamilton nodded. 'They're in German hands now, and they have a huge range. We'll have to give them a wide berth.'

'Where precisely are we headed?' asked Kate. 'To Dunkirk itself?'

Hamilton shook his head. 'Apparently they've had a message that the harbour's unusable. We've to make for the beaches east of the town.'

Kate glanced at Bill. 'You know all about that.'

'Only from that side, not from this. I'd have thought we'd just have to get there and play it off the cuff, see what the best system is. If we go with a preconceived idea of our role we could be disappointed.' He looked round. 'It was a shambles two days ago.'

Hamilton removed his cap and smoothed his thick, yellow-white hair. 'It's a pity about the harbour,' he said. 'I understand the navy have got a system going over there, berthing against a kind of long breakwater they call the east mole. They've got shore parties marshalling the troops along the top of the breakwater in an orderly column – *The Brantus* would have been better suited to that, I suspect, than going into shallow inshore waters.'

'Hm.' Bill tried to remember. 'How much clearance does she need?'

'Twelve foot, minimum. I should say, we're to leave at five o'clock in the morning, and we should have a high tide.'

Bill focused on a mental picture of the *Beowulf*. 'The ship we got on to was big, a cruiser, and she was anchored a mile offshore at low tide.'

Hamilton pursed his lips. 'We could halve that, I reckon. At a pinch I suppose we could ground her for the duration and let the next tide float her off.'

'That would be a waste of hours of time,' said Kate.

'I'm afraid so.'

Bill said: 'You're the expert, but they were dive-bombing continuously a couple of days back. To be in a beached boat under those conditions would be pretty hairy.'

Hamilton smiled. 'Quite. We'll anchor. She has a dinghy.'

Bill thought of the floundering, panicking men, the shoving and skirmishing, the sudden dead weight of exhausted, water-logged bodies too tired to move out of the way of the others behind.

'Yes,' he said. 'It might come in handy, we'll just have to see.'

'At any rate, the weather conditions are good,' announced Hamilton, as if persuading himself that there was at least something to be grateful for. 'The sea's calm, there's a bit of mist and good cloud cover, which should deter Mr Hitler.'

The *Brantus* did not set out alone, she was part of a flotilla. Kate, standing on deck after four hours' sleep, her collar up and her hat pulled down round her ears, felt a swell of pride and excitement as she watched the motley armada pull away from the homely beaches of Ramsgate on their great adventure. Leading the way was a minesweeper, *The Faraway*, towing behind it a lighter loaded with supplies for the men on the other side; behind her, two tugs from the Thames estuary, the *Daisy B* and the *Georgiana*, ploughed sturdily over the swell; around and behind *The Brantus* were three more small craft — another yacht, *Sunbeam II*, skippered by her owner, a stock-broker, and his son, a boy scout in uniform; a brand-new motorboat with two lanky young men in city suits aboard; and a fishing boat, the *Molly Malone*, with a stocky figure in black oilskins sitting at the outboard motor.

The creamy wake of *The Brantus* fanned out over the grey water. Mewling gulls dipped and wheeled hopefully overhead. The air was salty and damp on Kate's face. Exhilarated, she waved to the boy scout, and he waved back, the brim of his hat standing up flat above his face in the sea breeze.

Bill came and stood by her. They stood side by side, but not touching, watching the English coast fade and disappear. Kate was in a nearly exalted state of excitement. She felt – she knew – that she was striking out not just across the Channel and into physical danger, but into the equally distant and dangerous reaches of her self. Everything and everybody grew faint and insubstantial, except the present, the narrow pitching decks of *The Brantus*, and herself and Bill. It was a kind of madness, but she had rarely been happier.

Their two hands found each other and held fast, and she began to sing, shouting into the wind: 'And we jolly sailor boys were up, were up aloft –'

'And the landlubbers lying down below, below, below,' Bill joined her.

'And the landlubbers lying down below!'

But already the rushing air that snatched away their chorus carried on its back the rumble of the big guns.

When the flotilla headed by *The Faraway* reached Dunkirk in just over two hours' time it had become spread out. *The Brantus* had overtaken the two tugs and now lay not far behind the minesweeper. Beyond the tugs it was just possible to make out *Sunbeam II*, but the smart motorboat and *Molly Malone* were no longer in sight. It was seven o'clock, and the town of Dunkirk was shrouded in a light fog. Above the mist against the flat, grey sky, the cloud of dark smoke still hung, but the mist gave the scene a deceptive tranquillity. Even allowing for what he knew, Bill found it hard to see why the harbour had been put out of bounds. The cloud cover and the mist would certainly deter bombers; the German guns at Fort Mardyck were silent (for lack of shells, though he did not know that); the water moved by no more than a gentle, breathing swell.

The two breakwaters that Hamilton had mentioned, the east and west moles, reached out to them through the mist, the one longer than the other like a lobster's claws. He could make out a thick, dark line running down the spine of the east mole – a column of waiting men, hundreds strong. As he looked, one or two arms were raised, hailing the ships. But orders were orders. The flotilla moved past.

They were heading for Bray Dunes, about halfway along the fifteen mile stretch of beaches between Dunkirk and La Panne, in Belgium, where the army had established its new GHQ. It was a good deal further east than the area where Bill had been, but as soon as they began to leave the port behind on their right he felt a fluttering in his stomach, a surge of horror so strong that he had to get moving and do something. He went to join Hamilton on the bridge and found Kate already there.

'How's it going?' he asked. He looked at Kate and saw that her face was bright and unclouded by fear.

Hamilton cleared his throat. 'It's no picnic along here, it's a mass of shoals and sandbanks. This chappie in front is making for the narrow water in between the sandbanks and the beach, he knows what he's doing.'

'Let's go out, I need air,' said Kate. 'Coming?'

They went on to the deck on the shore side of the bridge. Dick Eames was there, a donkey jacket over his white coat, leaning on the railings.

He hailed them. 'Take a dekko at that, sir – those ruddy great breakwaters aren't going to make things easier!'

'Those aren't breakwaters,' said Bill. He peered at the narrow black ridges stretching into the water. 'Those are men.'

In silence, as they inched in closer to the beach, they took in the enormity of their task. Half a mile away the grey sand rose, like solidified sea mist, in a series of waves and undulations, to a crest of wispy dunes. The dunes were a seething anthill of men, in their thousands. Not just here, but as far as the eye could see in both directions. What Dick Eames had mistaken for breakwaters were now clearly visible as huge queues of men, those in front standing shoulder-deep in the grey water, their guns above their heads, waiting. The water in between was a treacherous stretch of miscellaneous debris, coated with a scum of glinting oil.

Already they could hear frantic shouts. Some of the men were beginning to wade out, cumbersome in full kit, using their rifles (the one item of military equipment which they had been ordered to bring back) as punting poles.

Kate ran back to Hamilton. 'What shall we do? Can you take her any further in?'

He shook his head. 'A few yards at most. We'll have to use the dinghy.'

Kate went back on deck. 'The dinghy!'

'It's not big enough, they'll overturn it.'

'The captain says he can't go in any further — we need a ferry.'

Dick Eames came along stern. 'That little fishing boat's on its way — she'd be just the job.'

'Okay, get back there and hail her as soon as she's close enough.'

Helplessly, they stood at the rail. The men floundered about, shouting waving, falling over in the icy water and dragging themselves up again. Further on *The Faraway* had released the lighter with its load of provisions, to be carried in on the turning tide. Two lifeboats were already heading for the shore.

Kate was a frenzy of frustration and impatience. 'We can't just stand here. If we could get the dinghy to them, they could use it themselves, work a shift system, anything!'

'You're right.'

They pumped up the dinghy. As they got her back to the rail so the *Molly Malone* came alongside. The big man in oilskins shouted up to them, but his voice was lost in the dissonant jumble of sounds coming from the shore — men yelling, the keening of bagpipes, the frenzied braying of a jammed ambulance klaxon. And from the front of the nearest queue two men had taken the plunge, literally, and were beginning to swim, frantic and ungainly as dogs, heads thrown back to counteract the weight of their kit, arms and legs thrashing.

Bill said, 'I'm going down to join him. When I'm there, you and Eames get the inflatable over the side and we'll tow it in.'

She watched as he scrambled down the ladder, *The Brantus*'s engine idling in the sludgy, congested shallows. She and Dick heaved the dinghy over the side, and it bounced and jostled against the flank of the *Molly Malone*.

Bill shouted at the fisherman, 'Could you operate a ferry service for us, we can't get in any closer!'

'This one can, we'll do it.' He stuck out a great, cold, calloused red hand. 'Jim Daley.'

'Bill Maguire.'

'Let's go to it then.'

They began to pull away from *The Brantus*, Bill holding the dinghy's tow-rope. The wooden hull of the fishing boat seemed naked and dangerous after the high solidity of the yacht, the filthy water with its scum of human and mechanical debris slapped threateningly at her sides.

As they drew closer to the two swimmers they could hear one of them yelling and gasping, 'Help me! Help me!', and the other shouted, 'Can't you see he's drowning?' as if they were doing nothing about it.

Bill pushed the dinghy to them. 'You, the big one, paddle this out to the boat, then come back for a load, then let another bloke do the next run, understand? Don't let it go!'

The man pulled his exhausted companion on board and they continued, paddling erratically, on their way to *The Brantus*.

On shore the jammed klaxon yammered on and on. Now they could clearly see the harassed naval shore officers moving up and down the lines of men, bullying order out of chaos. But their influence ended at the water's edge. A rot of fear and impatience had set in, several men grabbed whatever junk looked as if it might float, and planks to paddle with, and set out to ferry themselves to the waiting craft. Two soldiers perched precariously on a lorry tyre washed up against the fishing boat and simply fell in, making her rock dangerously.

'Daft idiots,' said Jim Daley.

'How many should we take?' asked Bill.

'A dozen – and not one more!'

Now they had almost reached the waiting queue. Bill could make out the lone figure of the piper standing on the dunes, the slight movement of the ribbons on his bonnet emphasizing his proud, stubborn stillness.

Jim's dozen became seventeen — they had no choice, they were besieged. Men clambered aboard on all sides, sometimes actually hauling themselves over the backs of less agile comrades. The *Molly Malone* rocked and lurched under the onslaught. Makeshift rafts and coracles jostled among the men in the water, impeding their progress and plucking on nerves already stretched to breaking point.

While Jim held the little boat steady, Bill helped the men in, counting, organizing, trying to be fair, though that was a forlorn hope. When they could carry no more they turned for *The Brantus*. The men they had had to leave on this trip cursed them roundly, one even tried to hang on to the side, but he couldn't maintain his hold as she ploughed forward, and slipped back into the water, a picture of dejection.

On board *The Brantus*, Kate and Dick Eames, waiting to take over, realized just how long a haul it was going to be. From the time that Bill had gone down the ladder to the *Molly Malone*, to the moment when her stubby hull, scarcely clearing the water under its load, had nudged the side of the yacht, was a full twenty minutes. The two in the dinghy had not been much quicker, due to the ineptitude of the oarsman, but they had now left their first soldier on board, and the other had gone back for more, not with a very good grace.

It was eight o'clock. They were at anchor now. Captain Hamilton and Freddie Talbot were on deck, waiting to help get the exhausted men on board. For once aboard the *Molly Malone*, all the frantic impatience and anger went out of them, they subsided into a daze of utter weariness.

Like blind, sluggish creatures dredged up from the ocean depths they came down the narrow companionway into the lounge of *The Brantus*. Kate and Dick had made tea, and Kate had found a carton of several hundred of Una's expensive cigarettes. These they distributed, along with towels and blankets. Some of the towels had come from the chests beneath *The Brantus*'s bunks, they were luxuriously fluffy and mono-grammed with a satin 'RV'. Others she had purloined from the Institute, and were threadbare as butter muslin.

One or two of the men had minor injuries or were clearly feverish and these she settled in the cabins.

As they arrived, they all looked the same. For days this one hope had kept them going. Now that the hope was realized there was no energy left for anything but a smile of relief and gratitude. Most fell asleep at once.

So Kate was surprised when a well-bred voice remarked: 'You're a sight for sore eyes, I must say!'

She turned. A young man sitting on the floor at the foot of the steps was smiling up at her. His manner, his voice, his jauntily-held cigarette, all suddenly provided him with a history and character. She could picture him in a smart West End club, smiling at his glamorous companion in just this way.

'You're absolutely the last thing I expected to see,' he went on. 'Bully for you.'

She struck an attitude. 'Eat your heart out Greta Garbo.'

He laughed. 'I don't like her – too chilly.'

He continued to smoke, eyes half closed in exhaustion. In the galley Dick Eames prepared a plate of wads, with the same deftness that he applied to elegant smoked salmon sandwiches. The enclosed space of the lounge was full of the smell of the beaches and the deep breathing of much-needed sleep. One man dreamed, whimpering and twitching like a dog. Another, leaning up against the polished rosewood doors of the Roth-Veseys' bar, whistled tunelessly to himself, his eyes closed.

'I hope you won't think too badly of them,' said the young man. 'They're not cowards.'

Kate shrugged. 'I know that.' She thought of Bill, lurching and rocking in the *Molly Malone* in the unfriendly black water. 'But they shouldn't panic – not when we're trying to help.'

It was concern for Bill that had made her say it, rather than anything else, but the officer was on his feet at once.

'No, no!' He thrust his face into hers, desperate to make his point. A blackened crust of blood caked the hair above his forehead, the smell was overpowering. 'For four days they've done nothing but hang about on that God-forsaken beach, with next to no food or drinking water, and no cover. Half the blokes who dug holes for themselves were buried when the bombers came over. We've just had to sit there and take it, day after day – do you realize this is the first day the Stukas haven't come – a sitting target, day after day!' He was almost gibbering. 'Half of us have seen our oppos blown to bits, or drowned . . . just waiting . . .'

He suddenly ran out of steam and flopped back on to the floor, quaking with what Kate was sure, for him, was quite unaccustomed emotion. 'Sorry.'

'That's all right. I understand. I take it back.'

On the *Molly Malone*'s second trip, the tide was beginning to turn. The shore party had managed to contain the queue a little better, which meant going further in, so that the keel of the *Molly Malone* nudged the soggy sand. But as this was her stock in trade, she was easy enough to push off. Bill and the fitter of the men heaved her back on to the swell in a matter of seconds.

Further along the soldiers had got hold of the loaded lighter from the minesweeper *The Faraway* and had succeeded in beaching it. Men swarmed over the raft like ants, but to Bill's surprise they seemed careless of the food. They seemed engaged in a frantic search, and tins and cartons slid into the water, to be washed ashore, or carried out to sea. Tins of meat and baked beans, boxes containing tea and powdered milk, sausages and dried egg, bobbed among the kit-bags and corpses. The men in the *Molly Malone* stared aghast at this display of conspicuous waste.

'What the hell are they doing that for?' asked Bill. 'What are they after?'

The man next to him answered in a flat voice. 'Water, mate. There just isn't a drop of ruddy drinking water.'

'Water, water everywhere,' intoned somebody tritely.

Bill and the others rescued as many of the tins and cartons as they could fit on the boat. By the time they'd dropped the men and were returning, slowly, against the tide, the men from the lighter had got onboard *The Faraway*'s lifeboat, thereby jumping the queue. A brawl broke out in the water, with men wielding planks, tins of food, rifle butts, anything they could lay their hands on. Their fighting was petty and savage, no Queensberry rules here.

'Makes you ashamed, doesn't it?' said Jim Daley.

Bill could not find it in his heart to agree, and so didn't

answer. Jim Daley was the salt of the earth, English to the marrow of his bones, brave, dependable, straight as a die. No matter what he thought, he'd keep going with the *Molly Malone* till he dropped. But he didn't know what it was like on the beaches.

All morning and through into the early afternoon the *Molly Malone* plied back and forth. When *The Brantus* had nearly a hundred men on board Captain Hamilton steered her out through the shoals to the destroyer HMS *Dauntless*. By two o'clock they had repeated this exercise three times, packing the yacht slightly more tightly on each trip. The mist was beginning to clear, and with the pale sunshine came the threat of Stukas. On the boats and on the beaches people looked anxiously at the sky.

When the *Dauntless* was full, Hamilton told Kate to let the men in the fishing boat know that he intended to load up one last time, and head for home.

Below decks Kate and Dick had exhausted *The Brantus*'s supply of just about everything, except the wherewithal to make tea. The oyster-coloured carpet in the lounge was soaked and filthy, there was sand everywhere, the cabins smelt like dungeons. In the galley, which had seemed to grow smaller with each hour, there was not an inch of unoccupied space — cups, spoons, plates, saucers, clothes, buckets, were stacked everywhere, and mostly dirty. The little bathroom, Una's pride and joy, daunted even Kate, but Dick Eames was philosophical. 'At least these blokes haven't got much in their stomachs. You should see this place after one of 'er dinner parties when the Solent's choppy.'

Kate laughed. 'I'm glad I haven't.'

Dick sucked in his breath. 'My eye!'

Throughout, he had contrived to keep his white jacket remarkably clean. And though at first Kate had thought the jacket an affectation, she now saw it as a brave symbol of normality and order.

Aboard the *Molly Malone* the sensibilities of the rescuers had become blunted. Bill recalled the blank, unhelpful faces of the lifeboatmen who had picked him up, and knew how they felt.

He had come to resent the men he helped, to hate them for their sodden, selfish, weary ineptitude. He was sick of hearing that they'd been ordered to bring their space-consuming rifles, sick of their leaden inability to get a move on and squeeze up tight. One man, however, was able to restore their sense of purpose. When the lone piper's turn came he marched through the shallow waves almost to the boat, piping the lament *The Flowers of the Forest*, his kilt dragging in the water round his thighs so that he looked like some mythological mer-king returning to his kingdom.

By three-thirty, as they started on their last trip to the beach, they could see in the clear afternoon light the conflagration that was the town of Dunkirk, away to their right. Two million tons of oil burned, throwing up an umbrella of thick black smoke that seemed to rest on pillars of darting flame many hundreds of feet high. To the east, the stretches of beach with their black ant armies huddled in the dunes and on the water's edge, were now visible almost all the way to La Panne, ten kilometres away.

The bottom of the *Molly Malone* was by now awash, in spite of their efforts, with a stinking soup of seawater, blood, oil and urine. Bill felt sick. A soft breeze brought them the smells of Dunkirk itself, where the corpses remained unburied, and where the horses of the French cavalry were burning alive in the buildings where they had been stabled. After the dream-like, mist-protected morning, reality was returning with a vengeance.

But his last trip was assisted by the brilliant idea of one of the shore commanders. Some lorries which had been considered vital for the transport of men, weapons and field kitchens, still remained. The commander ordered their drivers to drive them down into the sea, in single file, a row of twenty or so to create a pier along which men could move to the hard-pressed boats. The lorries were lashed together, and planks tied transversely on top, forming a gangway which could support a column of men, two abreast. The benefits were threefold. Apart from saving time and energy for both troops and boatmen, it gave the soldiers something to do, something to save them from the fear which grew out of boredom; and since pushing and shoving caused the huge lorries to rock dangerously, it also imposed order.

But the plan which seemed to all concerned to be such a real and valuable step forward in terms of co-operation, was also instrumental in providing the crew of the *Molly Malone* with their worst moment.

A soldier lost his footing and fell from the lorry pier, beneath the stern of the boat. Jim Daley, sitting at the tiller, neither saw nor heard the accident, and the man's shout was drowned by the sound of the motor.

Bill turned from settling the last man in his place, to see the shouting faces and wildly pointing hands of the troops on the swaying roof of the lorry. He looked where they pointed, but as the white, clutching fingers of the fallen man came over the side of the boat, so Jim gave the engine more throttle and the propellor whirred to speed them on their way back, on their final trip.

The hands disappeared, and a fountain of blood sprayed from the water, spattering like dark, squally rain on Jim's oilskin jacket. For a second the man's face appeared, a white mask with black holes, turning and rolling in the reddened water, and then he was gone.

As if in retribution for their carelessness, the propellor was hopelessly fouled by the accident. The man must have been sheared clean in half by the spinning blades. One blade was bent and twisted, and the other clogged by thick, sodden material twisted into rope, and a clot of human tissue. Bill was violently sick. In stricken silence they jettisoned the outboard, fitted the rowlocks and pulled back to *The Brantus*, a man to each oar. They could feel the tired, accusing looks of their passengers. Hundreds saved, one lost. But it was one too many.

When they were all boarded, Jim Daley said flatly: 'I'll leave *Molly*.'

Bill knew it was all the man could do, but still felt he should say something.

'She's your livelihood, isn't she?'

'I've got another.'

'She did a magnificent job. And so did you.'

Jim said nothing. He took the tea that Kate gave him, and

went to sit among Una's elaborate cushions on the sun-deck. Abandoned, the rotund form of the *Molly Malone* took on a poignant, almost animate air, like some faithful, dependable pet deposited in a strange place and left without explanation. Everyone, except Jim, watched as she seemed to scurry after them on the ripples of their wake, and then to give up, and rock listlessly on the summery, bloodshot sea.

The Brantus toiled and floundered with her unaccustomed load. Half an hour out, Bill came down into the lounge, picking his way over the recumbent soldiers. Kate and Dick were restoring order in the galley.

'Mission accomplished then, eh sir?' said Dick, putting away what remained of the Roth-Veseys' tea service on its special rack. 'Cause for cautious optimism?'

'I think possibly.' Bill was looking at Kate. 'Do you want some air?'

'Air? What's that?'

He held out his hand and she took it. As they crossed the cabin he said, 'Christ, what a mess. We'll have to get a woman in,' and she laughed.

There was a man perched on the bottom step of the companionway, smoking a cigarette. He winked at them.

'You 'ang on to that one, mate,' he said to Bill. 'She's one in a million, your missus.'

On deck, Kate laughed again, she was exhilarated. 'Did you hear what he said?'

'Yes.'

'He married us off!' She pulled off the tweed fishing hat which she had been wearing all day to keep her hair out of her eyes, and hurled it over the side. Gulls appeared out of an empty sky to investigate, dipping and wheeling over the hat before it gradually sank.

Kate leaned on the rail, her eyes shut, letting the wind comb through her hair and fill her lungs. Bill joined her. All round them the soldiers lay, or sat, huddled on the deck. They could hear the thunder of the guns at Calais, but already *The Brantus*'s nose was pointing north, and homewards. They were on their way.

She looked at Bill. 'We did it,' she said softly. And then, louder: 'We did it!' And as once before her words seemed to take on a more personal meaning.

'Not yet,' he said, 'not by a long chalk,' and that brought home to him the disparity of their ages, she so buoyant and optimistic, he a sceptic.

To show that he was not simply being gloomy, he added, 'She's desperately overloaded, really wallowing. It would only take one good knock and she'd capsize. There's a long way to go.'

She didn't reply, and he knew that she was refusing to entertain the notion of failure after all they'd been through. He was stirred by her spirited faith in all of them, there was something gallant in her that made them feel like heroes.

'I could do it all again,' she said.

He smiled. 'I think not.'

At that point he should have reminded her of Lawrence, of her husband who must have been frantic with worry, if he even knew where she was. The suspicion that Lawrence was being duped had occurred to him more than once, and by his refusal to ask her outright he knew he was a party to the deception. Now by rights he should speak Lawrence's name, restore his status. But looking at her, he couldn't do it.

Instead, he took her filthy hand and kissed it, on the palm. 'Something's happened, hasn't it?' he said. 'You know it as well as I do.'

She turned to look at him, facing across the wind, her fluttering red hair streaked across her cheek. 'Nothing's happened.'

'Don't lie.'

'Nothing *new* has happened.' There was an almost scathing note to her honesty. 'We're like a couple of electric eels, every time we get too close — whoosh, a shock. It's terribly dangerous.'

'It may be. But you came. You courted the danger.'

'Yes, I did.'

'And what now? You're going to back off?' He was acidly sarcastic.

Her eyes blazed. 'I love Lawrence.'

'That has absolutely nothing to do with it. One's choice, the other's compulsion. I see no dutiful wife, I see a woman who does what she wants.'

'I want Lawrence.'

'Sod Lawrence!'

She drew back her arm and struck him backhandedly across the face, her wedding ring gouging a cut along his cheekbone, and nicking the bridge of his nose. There was a faint cheer from one of the few soldiers still awake. Shaking with fury she clasped her arms about herself and leaned on the rail, whispering savagely, 'Sod *you*, Bill Maguire, don't ever say that to me again!'

'You don't care for the truth, do you, it frightens you.'

'Nothing frightens me!'

'Prove it. Sleep with me tonight. You know you want to.'

She looked up at him. He had not touched the cuts she had inflicted: his face was grey-white, heavily scored with lines, utterly without tenderness. One was choice. The other compulsion. She made no decision, said nothing, but put up her hand and smeared it across the blood on his cheek. Then, cat-like, she licked her fingers.

She took him to their flat, into their bed, as though having betrayed Lawrence this far she might as well betray him utterly, roll in the mire of her betrayal, squeeze every drop of vileness from it, revel in her wickedness.

Once past the door they fell on each other at once with a ferocious and bitter passion that was more like hate than love. They didn't wash. They made no protestations of desire or admiration, but came together like animals, grunting and grappling, copulating on the floor. So far from rejoicing in his body, as she had that first time with Lawrence, Kate was fucked by Bill Maguire without even knowing what he looked like without his clothes. He was far too quick with her, she screamed and writhed with frustration when he slipped away. But the second time, on the bed, she reached an explosive climax, swearing at him and biting his shoulder, drawing blood for the second time that day.

'Look —' she pointed in the mirror. 'Look at that. That's us.'

From the mottled glass there stared back two creatures from

some painting by Hieronymus Bosch — tortured, stained, smeared, ugly with brute passion and guilt, beyond the pale of civilized morality and, for that moment, outside the realm of normal human affection.

'Yes,' he said. 'And don't say you don't recognize yourself. That's you all right, Kate, and that's me. Don't ever forget I was here.'

'Get out.' She said it not in anger but in utter exhaustion, and he went. She lay rigid, listening to him slapping cold water on his face in the bathroom, peeing a torrent, drinking from the tap. When she realized he was going without saying good-bye she got up stiffly and walked naked into the living-room. He was already by the door.

'Bill!' She realized as she pronounced his name that it was the first time she'd spoken it all day.

He turned and stared at her as she stood there, bare and spent and ugly, and she sensed the power that he had, and would always have, over her. She did not take one more step forward into the threatful no-man's-land between them.

'Don't ever,' she whispered, her voice no more than a snake-rustle of sound in the dark room, 'don't *ever* tell about us.'

'I won't, if you won't.' There was the merest sour taint of a laugh.

'We can't let it happen again.'

'We can't prevent it.'

'We must! We will!'

He opened the door and left, without looking at her. But as he left he threw one more provoking handful of words at her, like a child that jiggles a stick between the bars of a tiger's cage:

'Don't bet on it, Kate. Just don't bet on it.'

CHAPTER FOURTEEN

'You are my sunshine,
My only sunshine,
You make me happy,
When skies are grey;
You'll never know, dear
How much I love you,
Oh please don't take
My sunshine away . . .'

'You Are My Sunshine'
Jimmy Davis and Charles Mitchell, 1940.

EVEN if Lawrence had not been feeling depressed on account of his contretemps with Kate, Easthaven would have oppressed his soul. It was the kind of small seaside town that was neither port, resort, nor genteel retirement centre, and whose pathetic pretensions to be all three simply emphasized its dreary facelessness. On one side of the bleak promenade, grey shingle shelved away down to the sea; on the other, a row of tall houses and second-rate hotels, their foundations well below sea-level, seemed permanently to lean forward, riding the punches of the offshore wind. At the far, westerly end of the prom was a huge playing field, only separated from the sea by a bank of tar-spattered shingle. At the easterly end a small harbour lay alongside the protective shoulder of the South Downs. Lawrence's area of responsibility comprised Easthaven itself, the two sheltered bays between it and the nearby Newhaven, and the Kuckmere estuary on the other side.

It was expected that the small boats would return in a haphazard way at any and every point along the south coast. Troops and officers dumped by the boats would have to be billeted somewhere overnight or transported to the nearest railway station, depending on the time of day. There was no proper brief. To have been too organized about the retreat would have been tantamount to admitting defeat. So officers in charge of the reception and disposition of the returning troops were left to use their initiative like boy scouts.

The harbour at Easthaven was no more than an amenity for local weekend messers-about-in-boats and Lawrence, on his initial reconnoitre of the area, did not believe that a large number of men could be dropped there. As for the estuary and the two bays, they appeared to his untutored eye to be a dangerous proposition for anything more than a small rowing boat.

He had been allocated a staff car for the job, and his driver, Brotherton, was optimistic.

'Jammy number this, sir,' he volunteered as they drove about on the afternoon of the twenty-ninth. 'It's not Blackpool, but the seaside's the seaside, eh? I can't see the BEF landing in force at Easthaven, can you?'

'On the face of it, no. But since we don't know what to expect we'd best be prepared.'

Accordingly he had liaised with his opposite numbers at Newhaven and Eastbourne, to establish the numbers and times of special trains to London, and contacted the local Greenline Bus Service. Easthaven had its own branch of the WVS, and members were alerted to the possibility of there being a good many mouths to feed. An emergency hospital had been set up in the grounds of a tudor mansion on the nearby Alfriston Road, and ambulances were standing by to take the wounded.

Billets proved more of a problem, until Lawrence discovered, via one of the WVS ladies, that Easthaven abounded with boarding schools ('such a bracing spot, Captain'), most of which were beginning a half-term holiday.

Early on the Friday morning Brotherton drove him up Sutton Avenue to the largest of these, Easthaven Ladies' College. His arrival in the staff car caused a flurry at the upstairs windows and a good many muffed shots on the grass tennis courts which flanked the driveway. Lawrence lifted his cap to a couple of giggling fifth-formers and left Brotherton to sit it out. Over Amontillado in the head's drawing-room, he tried to explain the situation as gently as he could.

'We are only talking about a night or two, Miss Margerison,' he said. 'And of course I wasn't thinking of your pupils' own accommodation but large areas like say, the gym, the hall, the sports pavilion?'

Miss Margerison, in spite of the gentility of her establishment, was an iron woman, not easily buttered-up.

'Captain Drake, I hope it will never be said that I hung back when it came to helping His Majesty's forces in time of war, but this is a school, and my girls must come first.'

'I believe it's half-term?' Lawrence smiled engagingly and stroked Miss Margerison's fat corgi, which growled at him.

'Half term starts as from four o'clock this afternoon, but not all the girls go away. I have a considerable number of foreign pupils who remain here, and members of staff to look after them. I simply cannot have the school turned into a barracks. You must understand that.'

'I do understand, of course.' Lawrence became serious. 'But at the same time this is a national emergency, a crisis. I cannot believe that your girls' parents would want you to refuse accommodation to these chaps. I have spoken to the WVS, they could organize the feeding and so on in some corner of the grounds that would not cause inconvenience. There's no reason why you should be aware of the troops at all.' God forgive me, he thought.

An even knottier problem occurred to the headmistress. 'What about what I believe you military men call ablutions?'

'Well –' Lawrence was momentarily stumped. 'If you could make available one cloakroom, we would of course ensure –'

'The Slop.'

'I beg your pardon?'

'The girls call it the Slop – the games cloakroom. I very much doubt that it can suffer much at the hands of the militia that it hasn't already suffered from visiting lacrosse teams.'

Lawrence smiled once more. 'Very probably not.' He had won.

He had approached two other schools during the course of the day – St Alfric's Roman Catholic boys' preparatory school, and Easthaven Juniors, the local church primary school. Both had already started the half-term holiday and were prepared to make their buildings available. The nuns at St Alfric's were particularly obliging, offering to man the kitchens and the school's well-equipped sanatorium if the need arose. The three schools, combined with offers from various local boarding houses and small hotels should, Lawrence estimated, provide billets for about three hundred men if necessary.

In the late afternoon he returned to his own billet at the Esplanade Hotel, briefly, to make a telephone call. There was no reply. Brotherton was hanging about on the other side of the revolving door, waiting to take him along to the harbour. Guiltily he waited a few minutes and tried again. He glanced at his watch – four-thirty. Kate could be on her way back from the Institute, but she was normally home by now on a Friday unless she were on duty at the evening soup kitchen. Still no reply.

He rang Dulcie.

'Lawrence! How lovely to hear your voice, I was feeling a bit bereft.'

'I'm sorry to hear that. Look, Dulcie, I've only got a minute, I shouldn't really be doing this at all – have you had any contact with Kate?'

'Yes, just yesterday. Bill had gone off to do his bit and I was rather dismal – so I called her at home in the afternoon, to see if we could get together.'

'And did you?'

'No, she was off-colour, she didn't feel like it. We left it like that.' There was a pause. When Dulcie spoke again, Lawrence heard his own slight anxiety reflected in her voice. 'Is everything all right? She did say you'd sorted things out.'

Lawrence sighed. 'Is that what she said?'

'Yes. Why? Haven't you?'

'Not really. Anyway, it doesn't matter now, as long as you know she's there. She probably stayed later at the Ross this evening if she missed yesterday.'

'I wouldn't be surprised.' Dulcie sounded more cheerful.

'At any rate I'm sorry to have troubled you with our affairs when you must be worried about Bill. Perhaps I may even see him before you do!'

'He said they were leaving from Ramsgate.'

'In that case not, I'm in Sussex.' He glanced over his shoulder and caught Brotherton's eye. 'Look, Dulcie I must go. See you anon – yes?'

'Yes – good luck with everything.'

'Good-bye.'

Fortunately for Dulcie she was going out, so she firmly set aside any apprehensions about Kate aroused by Lawrence's phone call, ran herself a bath and concentrated on getting herself in the right frame of mind for supper with Giles and Ernest at the Albany.

She was always pleased to see Giles, and Ernest was an excellent cook, but their evenings together were not without friction. Though their friendship remained as strong as ever, she and Giles had other commitments now, they could no longer laugh and commiserate as before. When Bill came along it was easier, but when she was on her own, as tonight, she knew that Ernest's baleful, jealous glare would be upon her.

After her bath she poured herself a gin and tonic and lay on her bed for a bit, sipping her drink till it was time to get changed. There was a strange feeling of old times about it all, the getting ready to go out on her own, the determination to put a brave face on her fears and anxieties.

Celine bustled in and took her satin suit out of the wardrobe, stroking it with loving fingers. Dulcie, watching her, felt a sudden pang of remorse that she had unwittingly, all those years ago, hired a slave for life. Celine had been haughty with admirers in her youth – none of them could compare with Dulcie's dashing officers – had never cultivated female acquaintances and now, in middle age, was too plain and self-centred for the former and too reclusive for the latter. She had no friends, and no life outside Dulcie's life. And yet she spoke of leaving!

'Why don't you go out, Celine?' suggested Dulcie. 'You could get in touch with the woman you met in the shop the other day, the one you talked to about the food rationing? You liked her.'

Celine gave a slightly patronizing little smile. 'Oh no, Madame, I think not.' And that was that.

Just before leaving, Dulcie debated whether to telephone Kate, but recalled the 'mother hen' shaft and decided against it. She would keep herself to herself tonight as she used to do.

The evening went much as she had foreseen. Over dinner they'd talked about Giles's new play, and the concerts at the National Gallery, and the shop and whether it would survive, and the inconvenience of war generally. Dulcie drank a little more than she was accustomed to do these days and began to enjoy herself. Ernest became taciturn in direct ratio to her talkativeness, but she refused to allow that to bother her. Once she turned to him and asked: 'How are your family, Ernest?'

'My brother's well. My mother's an invalid, you know.' He looked at her accusingly.

'Do you see much of them these days?'

'Not as much as he should,' said Giles, who had Ernest's mother somewhat on his conscience.

'I go when I can. I don't fit in down there any more,' said Ernest, giving Giles a hostile look.

'That's a pity, isn't it?' said Dulcie. 'I mean, to be isolated from your family — it's a waste.'

'I don't see how you would know,' said Ernest icily, pushing aside his unfinished syllabub as though it disgusted him.

'I would, actually,' said Dulcie. 'I was completely cut off from my family for years, and I regret it now.'

'I'll wait till I'm forty then,' responded Ernest rather rudely, 'and repent at leisure, isn't that what they say?'

Giles poured more wine and said gently, 'You're very good to your mother, Ernest, I wish I'd been half as good to mine. But I'm sure she'd like to see more of you.'

'Perhaps she would, but it's none of your damn business, Giles!' Ernest got up from the table. 'Excuse me!'

Giles looked at Dulcie and smiled. 'He'll cool off. I should know better than to hand out avuncular advice, it's an irritating habit at the best of times.'

Ernest went into the bedroom, slipped off his shoes and sat

down on the bed. He was disgruntled. Pettishly he turned on the wireless so that he would not be able to hear the voices of the others. The programme was one of band music, Geraldo's outfit from the Savoy, playing the old Cole Porter number *You Do Something to Me*. As Ernest listened his lip curled cynically. The tune finished. He looked through the open door into Giles's study. A pile of manuscript papers stood by the typewriter: he could always do some work. He had refused Giles's offer of a typing course, the thought of being in a class with a gaggle of women appalled him. But he had set out to teach himself from a Pitman's handbook, and was now proficient. He enjoyed his work. He was just about to get up and go to the desk when he heard the announcer say something about a new young rising star, a name to watch and a voice to enjoy – Mae Irving!

Slowly Ernest sat down again, and turned the volume on the wireless up slightly. Mae's familiar voice, husky and true, with a slight warble, filled the room.

'Don't know why, there's no sun up in the sky, stormy weather . . .' He knew the voice so well, he had even heard her sing this song as she stacked plates and garnished canapes, but the whole performance was mystically enhanced and enriched by the music of the band, there was a gloss to it now. He sat bewitched, scarcely believing his ears.

'Can't go on, everything I had is gone, stormy weather . . .' sang Mae. Ernest felt the song might have been written for him. He was so sorry for himself he could have cried. Mae, of all people, singing at the Savoy, singing on the wireless! There were probably millions of people listening to her, humming along with the song. Mae had made it! And he, what had he achieved? Mae had always told him that he'd be 'up there' one day, 'swilling the bubbly and puffing the cigars' and here he was. But whatever ailed him had not been cured. He still despised them, most of them, he had no influence nor any real status in his new life.

As Mae's final note faded in a warm round of applause, he switched the wireless off. Dulcie's laugh rang out in the other room. Stupid cow. The trouble with all of them was that they couldn't face up to the truth about him and Giles, it wasn't nice, they couldn't quite picture what they got up to. And yet at the same time they didn't see him as Giles's secretary — which he was, and a good one, too — but as Giles's fancy boy. They couldn't allow that he was efficient and conscientious and imaginitive about his work, because the other thing, too dreadful to mention but too tantalizing to ignore, got in the way.

Ernest went back into the living room. Giles and Dulcie turned to look at him, smiling, holding their glasses of wine. They had been enjoying themselves, without him.

'I just heard someone I know on the wireless,' he said.

'Did you?' Giles handed him his glass and came to stand near him, as if confirming his allegiance. 'Who was that?'

'Mae Irving, she was a waitress with that catering company I worked for. She always wanted to be a singer — I just heard her, singing with Geraldo from the Savoy.'

'The Savoy! She has done well,' said Dulcie. She sensed, now, that Ernest needed gentle handling. She was sorry that she'd been instrumental in causing his earlier huff.

'Oh she wasn't Geraldo's regular singer,' he said now, hastily. 'She was introduced, you know — a rising star.'

'Here's to Mae, the rising star,' Giles lifted his glass, his eyes on Ernest's face. 'Not much of a life though, I'd have thought.'

'It's what she always wanted.'

'The more we dream about something,' said Giles, almost tenderly, 'the more of a disappointment it can turn out to be.'

'That's true,' murmured Dulcie, thinking of Rex. And thinking of him brought Bill back to the forefront of her thoughts, and she put down her glass.

'Yes, I know,' said Ernest. He tossed back the remains of his claret as if it were medicine. 'I'm going to do some work.'

Lawrence had intended to call Kate again later in the evening, but in the event there was no opportunity. Several small boats came in, both at Easthaven harbour and at the Kuckmere estuary, and by the time the hundred or so men from these had been safely bestowed, more were arriving. A car ferry that had limped home with its stern shot away anchored offshore and help had to be organized to get the men back. He was shocked by the size of the operation. If it was like this here, in a God-forsaken place like Easthaven, what must it be like in the major ports?

Neither did the men look like troops taking part in an organized retreat. Bits of uniform and kit had been abandoned, they were filthy, the wounded had been patched up in the most hurried and inadequate way. The resources of the WVS soup kitchen and the bus and ambulance services were soon strained to the limit. It was clear that the fitter and better equipped men would have to remain on the playing field overnight, sleeping rough, and it was raining slightly. The occupants of Easthaven, baffled but patriotic, offered spare rooms and outhouses, and those that had no room to spare brought bedding and tents and food in shopping bags.

Someone sitting on the grass near Lawrence said: 'Bizarre, isn't it?'

He glanced down. A man in his thirties whom Lawrence assumed from his voice must be an officer, was sitting massaging his cracked and raw feet.

'Yes, it is rather. You can get something for those you know, over there.'

'My dear chap, I'd never make it.' He put up a hand. 'Higgins, Sappers.'

'Lawrence Drake, Staff. I was thinking it's either a disaster, or a triumph of some kind.'

'Oh it's a disaster, a sodding great disaster,' said Higgins cheerfully. 'But give us time and we'll be able to make it look like something else. I'm perfectly confident I'll be able to tell my grandchildren that I took part in the miracle that was Dunkirk.'

At about the same time that Lawrence was talking to Major Higgins on the playing field at Easthaven, Aubrey Tennant and Iris Pargiter were arming it round their garden at Mapleton Road. The south coast showers had not yet reached London, the air was soft and gentle after a fine day, and even at nine o'clock in the evening there were patches of sunlight on the lawn. This walking round the garden of an evening, seeing how things were doing, picking off dead heads, pulling up the occasional weed, was one of the many simple pleasure that Iris had opened up in Aubrey's life.

A blackbird rustled down from the top of the wall on to the grass, and they stopped to watch it. On Iris's instructions Aubrey had put up a bird table in the middle of the lawn, and during the winter they had enjoyed watching the birds come and go, and fancied that they were always the same birds, a kind of feathered family, dependent on them.

Arm in arm with Iris, Aubrey felt perfectly content, secure in the knowledge that he, Aubrey Tennant, was exactly what Iris had been looking for since the death of her husband twenty-five years ago. For once he was not just a dull second or third best, dependable but easily forgotten. What Iris sought in a man, Aubrey could provide. And though she got her own way a lot of the time, she made it plain that she admired and respected him. Conscientiousness, loyalty, stability, a sense of duty – these were qualities she prized, and for the first time in his life Aubrey was cherished. Only one thing bothered him – his lack of experience in the intimate side of things. His relationship with Iris had so far been limited to a little innocent kissing and canoodling, but now that a date for the wedding was fixed, the challenge of taking things a step further could not be ignored. Aubrey looked forward to it – he was only human, and he had waited a long time – but he lacked confidence. Iris was an attractive, worldly woman, older than he, and had been married, so she must know something of these matters, and had at least one other man with whom to compare him. What if he forfeited her regard when she discovered his fumbling ignorance?

He picked a flame-coloured rose and handed it to her, saying, 'A rose for a rose.'

'Aubrey –' she smiled at him reprovingly as she tucked it in her lapel. 'Really!'

'Shall we always be this happy?' he asked musingly.

'Being happy is when you're not wondering if you're happy,' said Iris, a trifle tartly, but Aubrey loved to be kept in order like this, it made him feel quite a gay dog.

'I'm absolutely conscious of being happy at this moment,' he said, resting his cheek on the top of her head.

'It won't last then,' she said, but she gave him her quick bright smile to show him she didn't mean it.

Their wedding day, 10 June was a Monday, but since Aubrey had had no intention of inviting anyone — 'we're too long in the tooth for all that' — he didn't consider that mattered. Iris had been horrified. What, not invite anyone? What an old misery! Iris, who had no relations but an older, married sister in Weybridge, made no secret of the fact that she envied Aubrey his family. In the beginning she used to scold him for not appreciating them, for being too brusque, too critical, not sufficiently welcoming, and he had been making a real effort to correct these faults. But he suspected that people might laugh about him at his wedding, albeit behind their hands and quite kindly, and the thought horrified him. He did not say this to Iris, for fear of hurting her feelings.

'Of course you must invite family!' she had cried. 'And I shall invite Molly and Ted' (the Weybridge contingent), 'so that they can meet everyone. There's no need for a big fuss if you don't want it, we could make it twelve o'clock with a nice little buffet here afterwards, they can fit it in in their lunch hours if they want to. And as for being too long in the tooth —' she had pulled at the bottom of his waistcoat in a nannying way which never failed to cut him down to size. 'I never heard such tosh!'

So it was all arranged. It was a pity Lawrence and Kate wouldn't be there, Aubrey had been going to ask Lawrence to be his best man, but the army had claimed him. All the others had accepted. The die was cast.

At six o'clock on the morning of the 31st Kate heard the telephone ring. She had literally to drag herself up through a swamp of exhausted sleep to the point where she could get her feet on to the floor and stumble into the other room. She sank on to the sofa, taking the phone with her, and picked up the receiver.

'Kate! Darling — God it's nice to hear your voice!'

'Lawrence . . .' she fumbled round in the chaotic ragbag of her mind for some appropriate response, she was befuddled with tiredness. Her hand on the receiver felt heavy and useless as though it didn't belong to her. 'It's only six,' she said.

'Yes, I'm hellish sorry about that. I haven't been to bed all night, it's chaos down here, this is the first chance I've had — Kate?'

'I'm still here.'

'They just keep on coming, it has to be seen to be believed, everything Bill told us was true.'

'Yes.'

'What's that? Sorry, I'm ringing from a bus station, it's rather noisy, what did you say?'

'Poor you, poor darling.'

'Oh, I'm all right, doing a useful job I hope, which makes a change. Darling, I can't tell you how relieved I am that you're there — that you didn't go, or any damn fool thing like that. When I couldn't get you yesterday I began to imagine God knows what, I've been worried to death. I even spoke to Dulcie. She said you were off-colour, are you okay now?'

'Yes, it was just a kind of sore throat thing. But I shan't go to the Institute today.'

'Quite right, you take care of yourself. I'm sorry I was such a pig. It's because I love you too much for my own good.'

'I was a pig too, a worse one.'

'What? Look, I've got to go. But I'll be home tonight. We can — you know, kiss and make up, bill and coo. By the way, is Bill back?'

Kate hesitated for a second. 'I don't know, I've been a hermit.'

'Never mind, he's a resilient chap. Au revoir then, darling. Look after the throat, I love you.'

Carefully, precisely, she lowered the receiver. She no longer felt tired but elated and energetic, enchanted by the facility with which she had deceived him. Now and only now did she experience a delightful and sensuous post-coital languor as though this exquisite treachery were in itself a sexual climax. She took a bath, and changed the stained sheets on the bed.

And, perversely, hearing Lawrence's voice had made him real again, the painfully unprotected love in his voice did not excite guilt, but quieted it. She needed the warmth and light of that love, like the sun, to make her grow and blossom, to bring out the best in her. The two sides of her nature seemed at the moment to coexist in complete harmony like the two sides of a coin, the side uppermost glinting in the light, the other close, dark, secret, invisible, known only to her. And to Bill. But she knew with absolute certainty that he would not betray her. She would return to Lawrence, and he to Dulcie, all would be well. And in the same way that she would be her better self with Lawrence, so the Bill that embraced Dulcie that night would be a gentle and generous lover, full of understanding.

Later in the morning, as she worked through a pile of ironing, with the trunk standing open on the floor of the bedroom, the phone rang and it was Dulcie.

'Kate? How are you, are you better?'

'Better . . .?' She felt so cheerful now she had to make a positive effort to remember her deception. 'Oh yes, it was nothing. I've just been speaking to Lawrence on the phone, he'll be home this evening.'

'I am glad. You sounded so grim the other day, I didn't even like to call again unless I caused a relapse.'

'I'm sorry, Dulcie.' She couldn't resist adding: 'Any news of Bill?'

'No, as a matter of fact, but we live in hope. Anyway, I shall see you tomorrow at Aubrey's?'

Iris had arranged a farewell lunch for Lawrence and Kate. 'Of course. Good-bye for now.'

Poor Dulcie, thought Kate, but she won't have long to wait now.

Bill overslept next morning, but on waking he sent a telegram to Zoe Modes: 'Safe and sound. See you soon. Bill.' He then headed for the *Herald*, thinking with pleasurable anticipation of the conversation he would have with the Roth-Veseys, describing the events of yesterday, eliciting their comments, and finally telling them that Captain Hamilton and others intended making the trip again today.

In this morning's edition of the paper a small, carefully-worded paragraph referred to 'large numbers of men arriving at a south coast port'. So the official floodgates had eased a chink. Just wait till he added the gallon or two of on-the-spot copy which would finally burst them.

He ran up the steps at Ludgate Circus and emerged, whistling, into the morning sunshine.

At five o'clock that evening, Joe Kingsley and his friend and classmate Rupert Govan were waiting for a southbound train at Michaelmarsh Halt, a couple of miles from school. With them was Rupert's younger brother, Govan Minor, but the two fourteen-year-olds ignored him. Govan Minor was undisturbed by their attitude, it was all part of a pattern he understood. He kept at a distance of about six yards, sitting on his suitcase and reading a copy of *Film Fun*.

All three were bound for the Govans' family home in Sussex for half-term. To Joe's considerable relief it had been agreed not to alter the arrangement – which had existed for some weeks – on account of his sister's departure for Malta next week. It was better, Kate had said, that he should be with his friends and enjoying himself, rather than give up a perfectly good holiday just to wave them good-bye, and he had wholeheartedly agreed. Joe was fond of Kate, in spite of their altercations, and he liked and admired Lawrence, but the thought of obligatory family farewells in an emotionally-charged atmosphere made him cringe. So the Drakes had been down to take him out the previous weekend, and salutations exchanged in the safe neutral territory of the school drive. The boys could easily have been collected by car from Hartfield House, but Rupert was a railway buff and had asked if they might go down the line by train for ten miles or so, to be picked up at a station nearer home. Lady Govan had arranged it all with the boys' housemaster, Mr Birrell, who had brought them to Michaelmarsh Halt in his own car just a few minutes ago.

The only thing which marred Joe's friendship with Rupert Govan was the fear that one day he would have to return his hospitality. The thought of taking Rupert to Mapleton Road – especially now that the *infra-dig* Iris would be a fixture – was too horrible to contemplate, and the flat in Craven Road, though both its occupants had been acceptable, could never have competed with Coppham Chase, Lewes (the sum total of the Govan address). He felt himself to be a somewhat displaced person, and this increased both his sense of inferiority and his consequent anxious snobbery.

The train was late. Govan minor finished *Film Fun* and began wandering about. The two older boys stood together, jackets open, hands in pockets. On the opposite platform, on a green bench in the sunshine, sat an elderly stationmaster-cum-guard, eating some sandwiches out of a Huntley and Palmer's biscuit tin. The banks on either side of the platforms were cloudy with pink willowherb, threaded by the white trumpets of convulvulous; butterflies trembled and dipped over thistles like purple shaving brushes. Dandelions and campions had even forced their way through the cracked concrete of the platforms themselves, as if to prove that the railway was an insubstantial Johnny-come-lately compared with the rich Kent countryside in full bloom. Suddenly Govan Minor started posturing in a ridiculous way. 'Hey, you lot – look at this!' he yelled.

'What?' Rupert cast a slant-eyed look over his shoulder at his brother.

'They've painted over the sign, look.'

The two older boys sauntered over. Sure enough, the Michaelmarsh sign had been blotted out by a thick coat of green paint. A quick glance informed them that it was the same on the other side. Rupert went to the edge of the platform.

'Excuse me!'

'Yes sir!' The old man heaved himself up and obligingly came to the edge of the up platform, leaving his sandwich tin on the bench.

'Why have you covered the station sign, we wondered?'

The stationmaster leaned forward confidingly, reducing the gap of several yards between himself and Rupert by about four inches. 'It's against an invasion – if the Germans get over 'ere they won't know where they are.'

Joe was incredulous. 'Invasion? Surely there won't be any invasion with our chaps all over on the other side.'

The man shook his head. 'I don't know about that, sir. The

army's been coming back, the last few days . . . That's why your train's late, been kept in a siding to let the army go through.'

'I think the old boy's a bit barmy,' said Rupert out of the side of his mouth.

After about ten minutes they heard a train. But as the clacketty-clack grew closer, and the plume of smoke appeared against the hot, grey-blue sky, it was from the south. They stood there, holding their cases as it bustled round the curve in the line. It was not slowing down.

The dawning realization of the boys and the quiet satisfaction of the stationmaster were mercifully separated by the intervention of the train, which steamed straight through Michaelmarsh, bound for London. It was packed with soldiers. They crammed the compartments and corridors, leaning up against one another like stocks of corn, their cheeks and foreheads pressed against the smutty windows as they slept. A few were awake, and waved to the boys, but they were too astonished to wave back.

On Saturday afternoon Lawrence, Kate, Dulcie and Bill went for a walk in the park, because it was a beautiful day and the June sunshine seemed to diffuse the tension over imminent separation. It was Dulcie who had suggested Saturday for their last meeting because, she said, it would make their good-bye less final if she knew they were still there in London for another thirty-six hours. She could always cheat, and telephone Kate on Sunday.

They walked slowly along beside the Serpentine and then right, past the Albert Memorial and between the flowerbeds with their massed summer bedding plants, towards the bandstand in Kensington Gardens. Their conversation was desultory. As they moved along they separated and re-grouped, Kate usually at the front, Dulcie at the rear. Kate and Lawrence had no more preparations to make. Their things were packed, or put in store; one or two precious items had been put in the care of Aubrey and Iris at Mapleton Road when they had been to make their farewell visit; bills had been paid, and final letters written.

Kate had sent Joe five pounds, in a fit of somewhat remorseful affection. Perhaps she had been too hard on him, he was growing up fast, in worrying times, and with fewer and fewer of his family within hailing distance. She knew of Aubrey's good intentions, and those of his bride-to-be, but Kate wondered if their responsibilities towards a sulky adolescent boy would suddenly appear less appealing now that they had their life together to consider. When she and Lawrence had visited Joe last weekend she had impressed upon him the necessity of replying in the affirmative to his uncle's wedding invitation, and attending in a proper spirit. Lawrence had arranged for him to travel up to Lewisham in style, in a taxi with Mrs Drake. She had been sanguine about her ability to snap Joe out of it.

'By the time we get there we shall be the best of friends,' she had assured them over her whisky and soda. 'I don't allow boys of that age to mope all over me, as Lawrence well knows.' And Kate had had to take her assurances on trust.

She and Lawrence were to travel down to Southampton the following evening – by train, they'd sold the car – and embark on a troopship, *The Millamara*, early on Monday morning. This would take them as far as Gibraltar, and those continuing to Malta would complete the journey by plane. Lawrence had contacted Josh and they were to stay with the Maloneys for the first few nights, after which Josh had told them they would have no difficulty in finding a small house or flat.

It all seemed very far away that Saturday afternoon. They stood under the trees near the bandstand, where a Salvation Army band was rendering unwarlike Viennese waltzes with a rousing oom-pah-pah. There was quite a crowd, listening to the music – a lot of uniforms, a sprinkling of lovers, locals with dogs, nannies from the affluent fastnesses of Knightsbridge and Kensington, roosting in clusters like seagulls in their summer blue and grey and white. The plump, pristine infants of the rich gazed down from their coach-built perambulators at the *hoi polloi* in deckchairs and on the grass. By the round pond an old lady was feeding the ducks; they scurried over the calm surface towards her leaving little skeins of ripples like drawn threads on silk. On the far side two small boys steered a model yacht with a long boathook.

Dulcie said: 'Now which of you is going to fetch me a deckchair so that I can be idle in comfort?'

Lawrence went to get one, and opened it with a flourish.

'Thank you – aren't you good with deckchairs?'

'An absolute Houdini.' He flopped down next to her on the grass, leaning on his elbow. 'This is nice.'

Kate was restless. 'I'm going round the pond to look at the model boat.' She nudged Lawrence with her foot. 'Coming?'

'No. Far too energetic.'

Dulcie laid her head back and closed her eyes, as the band began to play *A Room With a View*.

Bill said: 'I'll come with you.'

She did not reply, but began to walk away with long strides, elegant and nautical in a blazer and white linen trews. On the far side of the pond she stopped, by the boys with the boat. It was a beautiful yacht, sleek and fleet as a gull, with two great white uplifted wings of sail.

They watched it with unnatural concentration, unbearably conscious of one another.

'Damn you,' she said. 'Go away.'

'I can't, and anyway you don't want me to.'

'You take a lot for granted.'

'That's right.' He lit a cigarette, and she glanced at him as he did so. There was still a dark line of scab on his cheek where she had struck him. Her stomach lurched, she reeled under a body blow of desire, and looked away again.

'We're going, anyway,' she said. 'So that will be that.'

'You think so.' The flat, harsh incredulity in his voice caught her on the raw. She began to walk on, and he followed.

'I don't know what you want me to say,' she spat at him. 'It happened, we couldn't help ourselves, it was – an aberration.'

'You know it wasn't. You know very well it was our mutual inclination given its head.'

'It was horrible.'

'Liar. It was bloody marvellous.'

She crossed the broad path to the west of the pond and went down the shallow steps into the rose garden. Here, in the scented shade of the trellises, she stopped and rounded on him.

'Just what is it –'

He snatched her towards him with such force that her head

snapped back. He kissed her bitingly, she could feel his bulging hardness against her, his fingers bruising her ribs. He still held the cigarette, a flake of hot ash fell on her leg and burned her; he was coarse and rough, she resented him and yet she was weak and wet with longing.

'Oh – please –' she gasped against his face. 'Other people –'

'There's no one here. We could do it right now.'

'God in heaven!' She struggled, but her struggles enflamed both of them and she lost her plea to the Almighty in his greedy, open mouth. The hand she had put against his chest to push him away slipped involuntarily, to the back of his neck, just to keep his mouth against hers for one moment longer –

'Kate! Bill!'

She wrenched away and fled from the garden into the sunlight. Lawrence and Dulcie were approaching from the direction of the bandstand.

Kate was drenched in sweat, she burned all over. 'Hallo!' her voice, silly and shrill, shook, but they appeared not to notice.

'There you are,' said Lawrence.

'Just looking at the roses.'

'We thought we'd lost you,' said Dulcie.

'Lost us?' Bill joined them, hands in pockets. 'You're martyrs to nerves, the pair of you.'

'And the roses were lovely, weren't they Kate?' he added.

CHAPTER FIFTEEN

'Gesu, Guzeppi, Marija,
Itfghu I-bombi fil-hamrija'

'Jesus, Mary and Joseph,
Make the bombs drop in soil'

Maltese prayer

KATE had thought she was beyond surprise where travel was concerned. Her twenty-five years had been punctuated by strange, foreign arrivals and abrupt departures, she had cultivated a kind of resistance to changes of scene so that she would not be unduly disconcerted by shock, anxiety, fear or delight.

The excitement she had felt over coming to Malta was born of a sense of escape — she and Lawrence would at last be somewhere where their lives would be their own once more and where she herself would be, so to speak, out of harm's way. After what had taken place between herself and Bill, she had wanted only to flee, to prove her loyalty to Lawrence, and let his love for her heal her unseen wounds. She could not deny Bill, but she could mercifully put a great distance between them and hope that separation and good intentions would cauterize the open wound of loss. She kept calling on the spirited, commonsense part of her as a general might call on local, trusted troops, to come to her rescue and summarily send packing her mutinous feelings. But it was no good. She suffered. And as the busy, crowded trappings of the journey began to fall away, and the cumbersome aircraft to lose height in what was apparently the middle of nowhere, she felt a dread of the new life she had so looked forward to. What if she failed the test, and gave herself away? What if others found out, or Lawrence could tell? She felt that her helpless duplicity must show in her face like a stigma.

'There she is,' said Lawrence. His face was near hers, his shoulder pressed her shoulder.

From 30,000 feet the island was a crenellated silvery leaf lying on the sheet of intense blue water. By the time the plane bumped and droned down to 20,000 feet it had become a grey, green and ochre plateau of rock, rising from the sea on ramparts of white limestone, its two satellite islands of Comino and Gozo hovering close to the north-west like whale calves invisibly tethered to their mother.

As they descended further, so the island's features threw it into scale. It was extremely small – just ninety square miles of arid soil, a patch the size of greater London, a whole country you could circumnavigate in a day.

Lawrence put his hand on her arm, and she was so tense she flinched.

'All right?'

'Yes.' She half-turned her head and gave a little smile without actually looking at him. 'Just taking it in.'

'It's going to be fine,' he said in a way that struck her as ambiguous. 'Did you know Malta actually asked to become part of the British Empire?'

So he was talking about the war. 'No, I didn't.'

'Oh yes. We're as welcome as the flowers in May here.'

As they circled the island waiting for landing clearance, they could clearly make out the criss-cross web of rough stone walls cast over the small, dry hills like a net; the deep, ragged inlet of Grand Harbour thrust into the side of the land like a spread hand into a protective gauntlet, and the five great forts that protected it – Tigne, Manoel, St Elmo, Ricasoli and St Angelo; the long narrow arms of Sliema Creek and Marsamxett Harbour; the broad bite of Marsaxlokk Bay to the south; the massed roofs and ramparts of Valletta itself like a city of white marble in the afternoon sun.

The plane moved inland and now they could see the scattered villages with their distinctive pattern – the handsome church with its fine tower pointing to heaven, the dwellings of a devout and hardworking laity clustered round below, as if kneeling. And now, as they came in to land, the strange serpentine configuration of the three adjoining airfields, Luca, Safi and Hal Far.

Lawrence nudged her. 'Seat-belt.'

But within minutes the plane bumped down on the runway at Hal Far, skated, skimmed and bounced uncomfortably over the uneven surface for a few hundred yards, before turning to taxi quietly towards the few humble, stone buildings that constituted the airport. As the thirty or so passengers — mainly army personnel, just one or two women — stepped down on to Maltese soil, they heard the sound of another aircraft overhead.

'Look at that, what a splendid sight,' said Lawrence, pointing. It was an ancient Gloster-Gladiator biplane in full fighting trim, the sun glinting on her four machine-guns. As she came immediately above the landing strip, she executed a swoop and went into a steep climb, as if saluting the new arrivals.

'I didn't know there were any of those things still operational,' remarked Lawrence to Kate. 'They used to come over Ewehurst from Biggin Hill when I was but a lad. I thought them the height of glamour in those days.'

He put his arm through hers. She knew his conversation was only a cover for what his body and heart wanted to say, but she couldn't answer in the way he wanted.

The heat was intense, the air full of pale dust. Around the aerodrome the land looked hard and white, a bleached bone of sun-baked rock in the wilderness of blue sea and sky. Kate thought: Let it be as hot as it likes, let the sun burn the feeling out of me so that I'm pure and sterile and empty.

Then they were in the sudden shadow and cool of the airport building and a voice shrilled, 'Kate! Lawrence and Kate! Over here!'

Beth and Josh Maloney had not changed. Beth fell on Kate first, and then Lawrence, with her usual extravagant kisses, enveloping them in a wave of scent and enthusiastic affection.

Kate beamed at her. 'Oh, Beth, it's so good to see you.'

'It certainly is.' Lawrence stepped back to admire. 'You look as pretty as a cold beer in a desert. Hallo, Josh.'

Josh shook hands with Lawrence, and pressed his smooth

cheek decorously to Kate's. 'Back where you belong at last,' he said. 'Come on, I've got the car.'

The Maloneys these days presented an interesting contrast. Beth's peachy, dimpled prettiness was at its zenith now, in her late twenties. She was never less than fashionable – even now her hair swung in a glossy brown pageboy bob, her lips and nails were crimson, her incredibly high-heeled red sandals caused her rounded bottom to bounce slightly beneath her white cotton sundress as she walked. She presented a picture of lush, desirable – but somehow innocent – availability which had caused many a ripple in the officers' mess, but never a storm: Beth was faithful to Josh.

No one who had fancied his chances with Beth could imagine why. Josh Maloney was a neat, moon-faced, dapper man, five years older than Lawrence, yet ageless. Even out of uniform, as now, his fair hair was neatly parted, almost in the centre, and brushed to a smooth, flat sheen, his shoes gleamed, the crease in his trousers was knife-sharp. Anyone who did not know the Maloneys might have supposed that Josh was his wife's stern, if loving, master. But Kate knew that he was Beth's teddy bear.

Beth put her arm about Kate's waist as they walked ahead of the men, out to the car.

'It's so *lovely* to *see* you after all this time, Kate,' she said in her light, breathy voice. 'I can't imagine why the brass have kept you hanging about in London for so long when we've needed you desperately out here!'

By the side of some stone shacks between the airstrip and the rough were parked a few cars and a couple of army trucks. Josh said, 'Here we are, hop in.'

He and Lawrence put the baggage in the boot and the four of them piled in, causing the car to bounce and groan beneath the unaccustomed weight. It had once been a conventional Austin 10 but had, during its succession of ownerships on Malta, been so cannibalized, modified and added to that it no longer resembled any other motor car in existence. Three of its doors, and that of the boot, had been taken from another model and were an imperfect fit, so that in motion the Austin made a noise like a tank. The brown seats were split and bursting, and Beth had replaced the defunct sun-roof with a kind of canopy of her own devising made from a tartan rug.

'I have to say, Josh,' remarked Lawrence, 'that your car makes the banger I had in England look like the winged victory.'

'It's actually only the bodywork that lets her down,' said Josh, as the Austin started obligingly, if noisily, first time. 'She goes like a bird, and we're extremely lucky to have her.'

'It's home from home,' said Kate, hanging on tight as they rattled over the rough ground towards the road.

'Speaking of which,' went on Lawrence, 'there was an incredible old Gladiator swooping around over the airstrip – this is the last place I expected to see one of those again.'

Reaching the road, Josh changed gears with a sound like a klaxon. 'There are three of them here – Faith, Hope and Charity we call them.'

Beth looked over her shoulder from the front seat. 'Go on, Lawrie, ask him what they're doing here, he's dying to be drawn out.'

'Go on then, Josh, what *are* they doing here?'

'Defending the island, old man, that's what!'

Lawrence laughed in disbelief. 'What, a kind of reserve force?'

'Not a bit of it – front line defence, every one of them.'

'And what else?' asked Kate.

'Nothing else. That's it. "Faith, Hope, Charity, these three . . ." '

'My God.'

Beth shrieked with laughter. 'I should pack up and go home – your face!'

'When the enemy arrives,' said Josh, chortling, 'they're going to go round and round in circles very fast so as to appear more than three –'

'And to make the Luftwaffe dizzy!' added Beth.

Lawrence and Kate looked at one another. It was impossible not to laugh in the face of the hilarity in the front seat.

'Anyway,' said Beth, dabbing her eyes with a tiny white handkerchief, 'you're to stay with us for as long as you like, or until we find you somewhere.'

'It's very kind of you,' said Kate. 'We'll do everything we can to get off your hands as soon as possible.'

'Don't do that,' said Josh. 'Lawrie and I will be back on airfield defence as of tomorrow night – Beth'd be glad of the company, wouldn't you, darling?'

Beth gave her friend a quick, sharp look. 'Yes, I shall set about cheering her up.'

Another of the Gladiators trundled across the sky in front of them, and Lawrence asked: 'Who's piloting those things?'

'Flying boat chappies – never fired a shot in anger in their lives.'

This time there was no laughter. Lawrence and Josh began to discuss the Duty Officer and Lawrence's likely responsibilities, and Kate stared out of the window.

She could feel a fine, dry film of dust forming over her face like a caul, reminding her of Kenya, but this was a very different landscape to the rolling green and gold hills of the Rift Valley with its pewter-coloured lakes and brick red soil. This country had a Biblical air. Stone walls and low, thorny hedges enclosed fields where small herds of goats grazed or clustered in the shade of olive and fig trees. Once they fell in behind a goatherd with his charges. The man looked over his shoulder at them, grinning cheerfully and doffing his black cloth cap, his swarthy, arch-nosed face both ruffianly and aristocratic, entirely amiable. He seemed perfectly aware of, and happy with, the continuing noisy presence of the car just behind his flock, but made no attempt to get out of the way until such time, a few hundred yards further on, as he turned off the road in the direction of his own village.

'We fall in with them, rather than the other way round,' explained Josh. 'Though I rather doubt it would be possible to do otherwise.'

They drove through a small village where the white, flat-roofed houses huddled together, closed and secretive in the baking sun. Built from the same rock on which they stood, they gave the appearance of having sprung or grown out of the ground rather than been constructed upon it. Here and there Kate could see the luminous yellow of pumpkins set to ripen on balconies or rooftops, and the bright gleam of lemons and oranges hung like small lanterns over tall, white walls. High above the narrow street the occasional string of washing hung still in the hot, secluded air – drooping vines laden with shirts, and pants and petticoats.

Women leaned over their small iron balconies, arms folded, watching incuriously as they drove by. Old men sat in groups by their doorways, dressed like the market men in Whitechapel in dark heavy trousers, waistcoats and caps, and collarless shirts. Through one window Kate saw a little old woman like a doll in the towering black *faldetta* headdress that had once been common, but was now only traditional. Sallow, doe-eyed, smiling children scampered by the car, laughing and peering, and Beth waved to them.

'They're lovely children,' she said.

'But fearsomely entrepreneurial,' added Josh. 'They'd persuade you to sell your granny's wedding ring one minute, and buy it back the next. Don't say I didn't warn you.'

'Are they very poor?' asked Kate. 'I suppose I mean – are they self-sufficient?'

Josh shrugged. 'Depends what you mean by poor. No, they can't feed themselves off the land, they live mainly on bread, and they don't grow wheat, so – of course there's hardly been a moment when they haven't had an occupation of some kind, which has provided work. Sixty per cent of them are illiterate, but those that aren't farmers get work at the barracks or the dockyards. We scratch their backs and hope like hell they'll scratch outs if the need arises . . .'

'Now then, Zemola's only a couple of miles up the road,' he went on. 'I'll drop you girls off there at the house and we might as well go straight into Valletta, Lawrie. I've got a couple of things I can usefully do while you see His Nibs. We could have a snort at the Union Club, and be back for supper.'

'That sounds fine.' Lawrence glanced at Kate, but she was staring out of the window. 'It's good of you to run us around like this. We'll have to see what we can do about a car.'

Beth made a face. 'You'll be lucky. We've been here a year and we only got this one through wheeling and dealing and lots of happy coincidences.'

'So how do we get about?' asked Kate.

'A bike's a good investment – and there's a bus service, but it's not reliable.'

'A bike sounds fine.'

Now she had to look at Lawrence, because she could feel his gaze so intently upon her, reminding her of how they'd met. She added: 'I have a history of bikes.'

Zemola was very like the village they had driven through, but bigger. It was perched on top of a gentle hill, on the far side of which the ground fell away towards the conurbation around Grand Harbour, five miles away. The main street of Zemola ran west—east, and was narrow, like a canyon with its terraces of tall shuttered houses on either side, without pavements or front gardens. Halfway along its length the street swelled into a cobbled square, in the centre of which was the impressive baroque church, its façade heavily adorned with garlands, cherubs and angels with Clara Bow lips.

Beyond the square the street became Strada Comina, where the Maloneys lived, and a few hundred yards beyond that it widened as the village dissolved and became once more the main Valletta road.

Josh pulled up outside one of the almost identical peeling wooden doors in the continuous wall of house-fronts.

'This is us.'

They got the cases out, and as they did so the door opened and a slim young girl in a faded print frock appeared.

'Antonina, this is Mrs Drake, Kate, this is Antonina, who works for us.'

'How do you do?' Kate held out her hand and it was shaken lightly, with the suggestion of a duck and a bob.

They got the cases into the hall, and Lawrence and Josh departed. Antonina stood watching them shyly. Kate guessed she must be seventeen or eighteen, but there was something childlike about her, her narrow feet in flat sandals, her thick dark hair pushed to one side in a red plastic slide. When she caught Kate's eye she smiled gently and lowered her eyes. Her lashes were so luxuriant they cast a shadow on her cheek.

'Would you like some tea, Mrs Loney?' she enquired.

Beth looked at Kate. 'Tea? Or something stronger?'

'Tea would be lovely, thank you.'

Antonina disappeared, silently, and Beth took Kate into the living-room, which was cool and barred with light and dark from the partly closed shutters on the window that overlooked the street. Though the room was small, the whole impression was one of airy space, white walls and a tiled floor with a couple of pale rugs, a big mirror, a sofa draped with a fringed shawl, a wooden table with a huge earthenware pot of yellow chrysanthemums, like a cluster of suns in the semi-darkness. In the far corner of the room was a deep, arched recess containing shelves with more pottery, and books, and a rattan table with bottles on a tray.

Beth folded back the shutters a little. 'What do you think?'

'It's lovely, Beth. You are clever.'

'Yes, I am actually,' said Beth wrily. 'It doesn't have much on its side when you come to think about it. Poky rooms, hardly any natural light, not exactly all mod cons – but we've got to like it.'

Kate sank down on the sofa and slipped off her shoes. 'I'm terribly glad we're here.'

'Was London so ghastly, then?'

'Not ghastly. Complicated, but not ghastly.'

Antonina came in with a tray and put it down on the table. When she had gone, Beth poured two cups and came to sit by Kate.

'What's the matter?'

'Oh –' Kate leaned her head back and closed her eyes for a minute. 'I don't know. Nothing, probably.'

'Probably?' Beth raised her eyebrows. 'That won't do, that's not good enough, I want to know the whole thing.'

Kate turned her head to look at her friend. Dear, pretty, affectionate loyal Beth. But it was too soon to tell her. Perhaps the right moment would never come, her confessions would sound at worst selfish and hypocritical, at best silly. She was tired. For the first time in years she wanted to cry, but she knew Beth's friendly concern would not allow her just to weep and not explain. She felt her unhappiness like a second skeleton inside her, black and inescapable, flapping and screaming nightmarishly with no outlet. Her life, which so recently had seemed to rise like a magic mountain before her, the future lost in mists of unimaginable wonder and excitement, had now taken on the aspect of a tunnel – a fearful, claustrophobic place in which she must stoop and struggle, instead of climbing high and free, with Lawrence. Deception did not suit her, but it had ambushed her with terrible suddenness. But no, she could not tell Beth.

'No,' she said wearily. 'I can't tell you.'

'I'll tell you something, then,' said Beth. 'I'm pregnant.'

Now, incredibly, Kate felt her eyes flood with hot, soothing tears. She hugged her friend, to hide them.

'Beth, that's marvellous. How long?'

'Oh Lor', ages. I only mention it in case you should think me ungracious at breakfast. I can't seem to face a crumb till midday, and from then on I'm ravenous.'

This news cast a happier light on their conversation, and Kate was glad to be no longer the focus of attention. They exchanged news and gossip, and the patch of sunlight moved across the wall behind them till the room was almost dark.

'Look,' said Beth. 'They'll be back soon, and you must want to wash and change — but come up on to our battlements first and see the sunset.'

'Battlements?'

'Come and see.'

Beyond the narrow hallway was a tiny back yard, overflowing with rampant vegetation — chrysanthemums, and tomatoes, and huge arum lilies like waxen trumpets in the fading light.

'Watch out for the slit trench,' said Beth as they made their way across it. 'If we ever have to take cover I shall feel like Ophelia under all this.'

On the side of the yard opposite the door was a high wall with a kind of ledge running along the inside, like a firestep. At one end were steps carved out of the limestone, and Beth led Kate up these.

'There you are.'

The air was plangent with bells, not the tumbling peal of the English Sunday countryside, but the sonorous clangour of many different tolls, each in its own voice, for a separate flock. A little up the hill from Strada Comina the church of Zemola clanged like a beating heart, and the people of the village moved through the narrow streets with gentle deliberation to evening worship.

To the west, the sky was a wash of reds, from translucent shell-pink to arterial crimson, on which the huge, molten sun seemed to float. From the sun more colour had bled on to the dry, bleached land so that the high ground glowed warmly, as if lit from within. To the east the distant roofs of Valletta were caught by the westering sun and took on the appearance of a city in a promised land, shining and hopeful.

As the lower rim of the sun melted on to the horizon, the two women turned and went back down the steps, into the yard that was already dark, the plants purple-black and secret, their thick scent washing against the high, grey walls.

That night Kate and Lawrence lay curved together like two spoons on the hard bed in the Maloneys' tiny spare room, her back against his front. Their closeness had a kind of desperation and though they barely slept they did not make love. She felt his body pushing at hers, his hands on her breasts, but he was not insistent, and it saddened her to think that she had somehow stifled that bright fountain of confidence and open lovingness.

At dawn he was finally, deeply asleep, but she could stay in bed no longer. Stiffly she slipped out of his arms and pulled on underwear, a cotton dress and some sandals. Before leaving the room she looked down at him. This evening he would be going up to the airfield at Luca, the pattern of army marriage would reassert itself, she would see him for a day here and there, that was all – and he would be leaving with this impression of her, cold and strange and ungiving. But his face on the pillow was tranquil, mouth slightly open, one hand beneath his cheek, the other flung across the bed where a few minutes before she had lay curled like an ammonite and just as secret. She bent over and kissed him and he turned away with a great lurch as if a fly had settled on his face.

Lawrence felt Kate's kiss, cool and light like a polite kiss of farewell. In his dream, he was saying good-bye to her, in some cold, grey, empty place – a deserted station or church – and now she left. Her departure in his dream was a kind of dwindling, he tried to stop her, to grab her, but there was no substance, she seemed to be already lost to him. And there was another figure in the dissembling twilight, standing statue-like and waiting for her. He could make out nothing about this other figure but he knew, with the absolute chilling certainty of the dreamer, two things. That Kate was leaving him for this watcher in the shadows. And that the watcher, so still and sure of her, was someone he knew.

Lawrence's eyes snapped open in terror, his body jolted as if he had fallen from a great height. He rolled over and reached for his wife, but she had gone. Abject misery engulfed him.

Kate went into the tiled hallway. There was a sound of voices in the street, the pattering of hooves, a man's voice louder than the others calling, *'Halib! . . . Halib!'* The front door was ajar, and leaning on the jamb in the oblong of yellow sunlight was Antonina, holding a large enamel jug, with another on the step at her feet. She turned when she heard Kate and smiled her gentle smile.

'Good morning, Mrs Drake.'

'Hallo, Antonina.'

'I get milk.'

She pushed the door wider, inviting Kate to look. An elderly man with a herd of four goats was advancing down the hill from the direction of the town square. Seeing Antonina, he crossed to her, the goats pattering round him, and took her jugs from her, exchanging some quick sentences in Maltese, and giving Kate a curt but not unfriendly nod. He then milked one of the goats direct into the jugs, hissing a little tune through his teeth as he did so, so that his thick moustache lifted slightly in the breeze. The goats stood round staring with wall-eyed curiosity, giving the occasional sharp bleat.

When the jugs were full he handed them back and went on his way. Antonina closed the door softly with her foot and held out the jugs as if to prove the contents were genuine. *'Halib,'* she said. 'Milk.'

As Antonina disappeared into the small kitchen, so the bell of the church began to toll again. Sunday morning. Kate went through into the yard, everyday and unmysterious now in the early sunshine, and up on to the battlements where she and Beth had stood the night before. The timelessness of it all – the old man and his goats, the secretive stone houses, the church bell's continuous protective call – they soothed Kate. If life for some could be this simple, this orderly, why must it be such a battle for her? Surely she could learn acceptance, and stoicism. Malta could teach her.

'Up early.' It was Josh, in a light blue shirt and cream trousers, smelling of soap. 'Did you have a bad night?'

She had, but not in the way that he meant. 'It was fine. But it was so bright, and I heard the goat man, so I got up.'

'Want some breakfast?' He glanced at his watch. 'I'm OC breakfast when we have guests these days, Beth can't look solid refreshment in the eye before lunch.'

Kate smiled. 'She told me – you must be delighted, Josh.'

'I worry, of course, about Beth, and having the baby out here.'

'I think she's tougher than she looks.'

'Oh certainly! Yes, she's no broken reed.'

They stood together, looking over the huddled flat roofs, golden in the early sun. Kate was glad it was Josh beside her, he was so stalwart and kindly, so utterly straightforward.

'Tell you what,' he said. 'Since you and I are the early birds, fancy a walk up to the church before breakfast? Then we can decently rouse the dullards when we get back.'

'That's a nice idea, I'd like to.'

They went back through the house and up the hill in the direction of the square, joining a gentle stream of people bound for the same place. It was eight o'clock, the sun was already hot on their backs.

Josh said conversationally, 'This should interest you. You asked if the people were poor, and they are by our standards. But you're about to see what goodwill, hard work and blind faith can achieve.' They went round the side of the church where the street was still in shadow, and up the shallow semi-circular steps to the main entrance. Josh indicated that she should cover her head, and she untied the kerchief she wore round her neck and put it over her hair, knotting it beneath her chin.

One side of the great double wooden door stood open, but a thick red curtain masked the inside of the church from the public gaze. Josh held this aside for her to enter, and they stood quietly, just inside the church, watching.

There were already perhaps a hundred people there, and in the music gallery above the main entrance another thirty – the Zemola town band and choir. High above the nave, light blazed from a gigantic branching chandelier, and on the raised high altar where the celebrant and servers moved in slow and reverend ritual, a wealth of handsome silver gleamed — candelabra, crucifix and chalice — on an altar cloth worked in gold and red. The morning sun struck directly through the tall stained glass window above the altar, throwing a kaleidoscope of colour on to the mosaic floor between the ornate, banked choir stalls. To one side of the altar stood a giant statue, resplendent in bishop's robes and a scarlet chasuble studded with stones. The pedestal on which the statue stood was almost concealed by a wash of fresh flowers, amongst which the tiny pale flames of candles flickered like hovering butterflies.

'Their local saint,' whispered Josh. 'Very important chap in the life of the village. When they have their *'festa'* he's paraded along every street . . .'

The tolling of the bell suddenly ceased. In the church there was a kind of humming silence, a deep quiet just resonating with the gentle sound of private prayer, rough cloth on wood, and the trickle of beads between careful, work-hard fingers. The congregation was plain, and dark. But their church rose around them in rich, gaudy magnificence, a testament to joyful faith. A faith which Kate wished, at that moment, she shared.

Josh took her arm. 'Better leave them to it.'

Quietly they withdrew, back into the sunlight which seemed pale and workaday by comparison. The call of the goat man could be heard far down the hill now, and to the west over the airfield the lumbering drone of a plane.

Later that morning Josh drove them all down into Valletta for a look around, and lunch at the Casino Maltese — 'We don't normally live the high life, but as it's your first day . . .' — the Austin rattling along at high speed, trailing a funnel of white dust like a windsock. Kate sat in the front seat with Josh because she was the only one who hadn't seen it before, and Lawrence and Beth in the back. Lawrence seemed in good spirits. Kate knew it was because he had work to do, an important role to fulfil, he was back where he felt at home, and no matter what his worries these things could solace him. He leaned on the back of her seat, with one hand on her shoulder, he was loving but he was drifting from her.

'You wait, darling,' he said. 'This place is going to knock you for six. It's extraordinary.'

Beth laughed shortly. 'You soon get used to it, it's a city with all a city's disadvantages.'

'But not like any other!' exclaimed Lawrence.

'No,' said Josh. 'It's certainly different.'

Kate had to agree. The process of enchantment, or hypnosis, begun that morning, was taken a step further now as she saw for the first time Valletta, a fortress city built like a fanfare in stone. When the Grand Master La Valette had built his city four hundred years earlier, during the rule of the Knights Templar, he had created a place like a mighty army on parade – gorgeously attired, intricately adorned – an outward display of fanciful magnificence disguising a dense, impregnable toughness. Curtains, bastions, demi-bastions, ramparts, cavaliers and counterguards, ravelins, gates and lunettes, every delicate refinement of military architecture was here displayed with breathtaking virtuosity. And over the centuries, like a wise, skilful, much-sought after courtesan, Valletta had accepted rule from those who could benefit her, and withstood those, no matter how strong, who posed a threat. Behind the tall ramparts that embraced the finest natural harbour in the world, where the Custom House steps rose like a staircase to heaven from the waterfront, Valletta lay with perfect confidence.

Magnificent auberges, churches and palaces seemed to bask in the sun, showy and superb in their tightly-wrought web of narrow streets. On the far side of the harbour, as they leaned on the ramparts, the Fort of St Angelo stood at the end of the long promontory of Vittoriosa, reaching across the water, sisterly and protective. Valletta, Vittoriosa, Floriana – women's names, thought Kate. She had a strong sense of this tiny country being female. Secretive, strong, adaptable, a frivolous man-made façade concealing a stern integrity: this analogy soothed her a little. Her surroundings, at least, were on her side, and would protect her.

Soon after their return to Zemola in the afternoon, Josh and Lawrence left – Josh for Company HQ where he was ADC, Lawrence for airfield defence duty at Luca. The four of them walked up to the town square and the men were picked up by the supply truck heading from the Barraccas in Valletta to the airfields inland. It was no sober Sunday evening – the town band played on the far side of the square in front of the Palladian town hall, and there were stalls along either side selling everything from nougat to necklaces. As the truck drew up a small crowd of children assembled, so it was a very public farewell, drowned by thumping music and the noise of the engine and the giggling and chattering of the children. Kate couldn't help feeling enormous relief: with Lawrence gone, she could be alone and quiet with Beth.

The two women walked slowly down the hill, the strident music of the band fading behind them. It reminded Kate of that last day in the park.

Beth said, 'I expect this sounds terrible to you, but I quite like the first evening when Josh has gone back – it's only for a few days, after all, and it's so peaceful and undemanding.'

'Yes, I know what you mean.'

'Do you?' Beth looked at her doubtfully. 'But Lawrence isn't like Josh. I always felt you two were under some kind of spell.'

'Nothing so mystical.'

A small boy ran up carrying a basket full of paper bags, their tops tied with coloured string.

'Ladies! Some nice homemade sweets?'

'No, thank you, Fredu,' said Beth.

'What about your friend?'

'No, thank you.'

The small boy walked with them for a while, grinning up at Kate as if to win her over in spite of her friend. But she had played this game before, in Kenya, and took her tone from Beth. In the end he said: 'Okay, ladies, not to worry!' and was off up the hill again, quite unabashed.

Beth grinned. 'They're awfully sweet but they can be an absolute menace, always trying to sell you something, or do a job for you whether you want it done or not.'

They sat alone in the house that evening. Even Antonina had gone up the hill to evening mass, the band and the stalls had dispersed, there was perfect quiet. They made a few plans for the next day, some swimming and a bike for Kate, but they were lethargic. That night Kate went to bed early and slept the sleep of the dead.

On Monday 10 June, while Kate and Beth drove to St Julian's Bay to swim, the wedding of Aubrey Tennant took place in the large, gloomy Victorian pile of St Jude's, Lewisham. This was the same church where his sister Thea had married Jack Kingsley over twenty years before.

The new, young, go-ahead vicar had allowed the back half of St Jude's to be taken over by the local Mothers' Union as a day centre for children whose mothers were involved in war work, or working extra hours on account of the war – no point in wasting God's good space, was his view.

This meant that the tiny congregation was not as swamped as it might otherwise have been by the size of the church, but it being a weekday, the service was punctuated by the sound of children on the other side of the barrier of screens. Iris looked charming in a lavender blue dress and hat, and Aubrey dapper in a light grey suit and silk tie. The Mothers' Union, finding out that there was to be a wedding, had put flowers on the altar and round the pulpit – quite humble things, lilac, stocks, and pansies from town gardens, but they made a great difference. The congregation comprised Dulcie and Bill, Lawrence's mother with Joe; Robert Kingsley, whom Iris had insisted on Aubrey fetching the previous day and who had spent last night at Mapleton Road in spite of his faint protests about the unorthodoxy of the arrangement; Andrea Avery, without Louis; Iris' sister Molly and her husband; and Primrose Dilkes.

In the normal run of things it would never have occurred to Aubrey to invite Primmy but he had met her, as he sometimes did, when visiting her brother Eddie at the mental hospital in Southwark where he was accommodated mainly at the Tennants' expense. Ralph Tennant had always felt a keen responsibility towards Eddie Dilkes, who had worked for him down at Chilverton House during the years when Aubrey had been a POW, and Aubrey had seen to it that this responsibility continued to be discharged. He had encountered Primmy in Asylum Road just a few days after his proposal to Iris and had blurted out, on a wave of pride and elation – 'We do hope you'll come to our wedding.' Though afterwards he'd entertained misgivings, Iris had none.

'Oh, Aubrey, I'm so pleased,' she'd said. 'I've always wanted to meet Miss Dilkes, and I'm sure it meant a lot to her to be asked.' And she had squeezed Aubrey's hand and gazed fondly upon him so that he'd walked ten feet tall for the rest of the evening.

It was typical of Iris that she referred to Primmy as Miss Dilkes, though Aubrey always spoke of her as Primmy. Propriety was a habit with Iris – a working woman on her own had to be always on her guard – and even without Robert Kingsley's presence she would have insisted on keeping to her top-floor housekeeper's room to the last moment, like any blushing bride.

'Oh perfect love,' they sang, 'all earthly loves excelling . . .'

Robert Kingsley was the only one there who remembered Thea's wedding. The only other guests on that occasion – Ralph, Maurice, his dear wife Daphne – were all dead. Sign of the times. Where had they all been, the others, then? Aubrey a prisoner of war, Dulcie (he pursed his lips) up to no good in Paris, Venetia cold in her grave. War then, war now, weddings and wars . . . he nodded to himself. Strange that he looked back on that other wedding as Thea's not Jack's, in spite of Jack being his only son. Robert had doted on Thea – still did. Even last time she'd come over, a middle-aged woman, after Ralph's death, she had still had that magic, she'd come to see him often, always a smile – a splendid girl. In a funny sort of way, Jack had been a stranger to him, such a close devil, so watchful and reserved, not like Robert himself when he'd been young . . . But then, still waters run deep. There had been that terrible Christmas. Robert closed his eyes for a moment and dabbed at his mouth with his handkerchief. It had been unquestionably one of the worst moments in his life. He could have forgiven Jack a little lapse, it showed there was blood in the fella's veins – but that Dulcie, just a slip of girl then, should have announced the fact to the entire family at breakfast . . . 'Thea caught Jack and me in flagrant whatever you call it.' Her very words. He flinched. He could see her pouting expression, the tilt of her head, as clearly as if it had been yesterday. His palms perspired with the remembered humiliation of it.

Joe, next to his grandfather (who fidgeted and twitched absent-mindedly the whole time, the way old people do) was excruciatingly embarrassed by the whole thing. He'd been fond of his Uncle Aubrey, but the sheer awfulness of his marrying his housekeeper, a woman who wore a flowered overall to do housework, who had been married before and who was not absolutely out of the top drawer, had temporarily dried up his fragile store of youthful affection. Also, the occasion suffered by comparison with his recent weekend at the Govans', where everything had been dreamlike in its perfection. Even Lady Govan's dealings with her squad of evacuees had epitomized the ethic of *noblesse oblige* – kindly, dignified, gentle, always a little detached. So absolutely *right*. Whereas all this – he raised his hymnbook higher in front of his face to blot it out – was so second-rate.

'I, Iris Mary, take thee, Aubrey George . . .' interesting that she spoke up clearly where Aubrey had mumbled, thought Andrea, and she warmed to Iris. She was one of nature's stalwarts, she would always stick by her husband 'from this day forward, for better, for worse, for richer for poorer' Iris would mean every word of it. Andrea coughed, her eyes watered, and she got out a hankie. She caught Dulcie looking at her sympathetically. God, she probably thought she was shedding a sentimental tear. Andrea put the hankie away again. Dulcie had dragged Bill along, he said he had no place there, but she wouldn't take no for an answer. He was not a good church-goer, he kept losing his place and sitting down at the wrong moment, and he didn't sing or say prayers. She did, not because she was religious, but because she had been brought up to do so when required, and could still feel the hard corner of her father's prayerbook pressing her between the shoulder blades if she lapsed. Of course, it was evidence of how she'd changed that she was here at all. Time was, not so long ago, when wild horses wouldn't have dragged her to this sort of obligatory family occasion. Today, with Bill at her side, she felt quite warm and benevolent towards Aubrey and his chosen bride. Good luck to them, she thought, they deserve their slice of the cake. And even Primmy had come along – and looking very smart indeed though she still evinced a consciousness of the old order, Dulcie noticed, by sitting right at the back.

Primmy had made sure she was well behind everyone else, not out of any feelings of deference, but because she could not sing and she had never liked the sensation of people listening to her, or watching her from behind. She stood very erect, mouthing the words of the hymns and staring straight ahead without idle curiosity. There was an elderly lady standing just one pew in front of her: a thin, attractive, humorous looking woman who walked painfully from osteoarthritis — Primmy could see her without turning her head, and she wasn't sure where she fitted in. But when the woman turned to pick up her bag for the Offertory she had given Primmy a little smile and lifted a hand as though she knew who she was. Primmy had bought herself a natty hat for the occasion — she had always had a sneaking liking for hats, but no opportunities to wear them — and she knew she had nothing to be ashamed of, with her tailored costume and high heels. Maurice, she thought, would have been proud of her. And to think that here was Aubrey — Aubrey who had punched Maurice on the nose for being a pacifist — here was Aubrey marrying his housekeeper! It was a funny old world, and she and Maurice had just been together in it at the wrong moment.

They sat down for the signing of the register. As the group disappeared and the organist began 'Sheep May Safely Graze' so the children behind the screens chanted discordantly: 'The farmer wants a wife, the farmer wants a wife . . .'

Iris had excelled herself with the buffet, and there were one or two jokes about the black market. The fact was that she was a good cook and a thrifty one, and could do much with unpromising ingredients. Bacon and egg tart, potato salad, a splendiferous ham from the communal pig, beans and peas from Aubrey's carefully tended plot, new potatoes glazed with the merest sheen of hoarded butter and sprinkled with parsley, treacle tart and rhubarb jelly and strawberry mousse, and Iris's knobby, fragrant home-made bread. Even Joe thawed a little at the sight of the spread, and she had thoughtfully laid on a flagon of ginger beer to which he was invited to help himself whenever he liked. Everyone became friendly on Aubrey's sparkling wine, and as the day was fine a few people went out into the garden and sat in the deck chairs which had been put out that morning.

Aubrey went straight to Ted and Molly, who were looking rather stiff. 'We're both so glad you could make it — it's very good of you to come all this way.'

Ted beamed. 'We'd do anything for Iris, she's a girl in a million. You're a lucky chap, Mr Tennant.'

'Aubrey, please,' said Aubrey.

'She looks a picture, doesn't she?' remarked Molly, who was fatter and greyer than Iris but in whom the family resemblance was otherwise quite marked.

'She does indeed,' agreed Aubrey. As Iris joined them, he put his arm round her. 'Ted and Molly have been telling me how lucky I am.'

'Have they now,' said Iris. 'I hope you've been agreeing!'

Mrs Drake and Primmy encountered one another near the buffet table.

'Now how shall I describe myself?' mused Mrs Drake rhetorically before Primmy's blank stare. 'I am Aubrey Tennant's niece's husband's mother.' She laughed, her eyes squinting above her cigarette holder. 'Make of that what you can.'

'I'm Primrose Dilkes, how do you do.'

'Ah!' Mrs Drake's face lit up with a sudden realization. 'You're Primmy!'

Primmy stiffened a little. 'Some people call me that.'

'Do forgive me, that sounded rude. It's just that I have heard about you — all of it good.'

'Oh. How?'

Mrs Drake tapped the side of her nose with her forefinger. 'I've lived in Ewehurst all my life, my dear, and I'm an incorrigible gossip.'

The look she gave Primmy was so thoroughly wicked, and such a direct invitation to wickedness in others, that Primmy was obliged to smile.

'I saw you in church,' she said. 'It was a nice service, wasn't it?'

*

Out in the garden Andrea and Dulcie stood near the bird-table. Dulcie felt that she must make a really positive friendly move towards Andrea, especially since she had come on her own and had clearly been moved by the ceremony. '. . . so I shouldn't think the shop will hold out much longer,' she was saying, anxious to emphasize that she had her problems, too. 'It looks as though I shall be a bottle-washer down at your Institute after all!'

'It's unpaid,' said Andrea, curtly, stubbing out a cigarette on the side of the bird-table and dropping it on the grass.

'How is Louis?' Dulcie persevered. 'I'm sorry he couldn't make it.' This was a lie, and Andrea knew it.

'Are you?'

'He knows us all, he should have been here.'

'Louis isn't anywhere that he should be these days,' said Andrea, and began to cry. Dulcie was truly horrified. One moment Andrea was her practical, dominant self. The next here she was, her face a contorted mask of misery, nose and eyes running, shoulders shuddering. She didn't sob, but cried quite silently, with just an occasional little squeaky intake of breath as though her emotions were rusty with disuse. Dulcie was paralysed with pity and embarrassment. From the corner of her eye she saw Bill advancing, and flapped a frantic hand at him to go away which he did with a 'saints-preserve-us' air.

'Andrea – Andrea, what is it? What can I do, would you like to go in?'

'No, no . . .' Andrea attacked her face with her handkerchief, mopping and scrubbing viciously, 'I shall be all right, no one will notice me out here.'

'It's Louis.'

'Yes, it's Louis. Or it's me and Louis.' Andrea sniffed hugely and shook her head. 'All my fault, I suspect.'

'Don't say that!' Dulcie was indignant. 'He's a swine and always has been, he takes advantage –'

'No, Dulcie, no. I'm not ready for all that.'

'I'm sorry.' Dulcie gazed at her – thin, pale, miserably unhappy. Andrea, who had always been in control, who'd known the score and made the best of things, who had made up for plainness with her wit and industry – that she should be standing here, crying, in front of other people! She could scarcely believe it, it frightened her. And then she considered Louis, sleek, self-satisfied, manipulative Louis, and she could cheerfully have killed him.

'Is there somebody else?' she asked, taking Andrea's arm and walking towards the roses at the end of the garden.

'Oh no.' Andrea shook her head. 'He just can't be bothered with me any more.'

'What will you do?'

Andrea pulled the head off a rose and picked at it, letting the waxy, boat-shaped petals float to the ground. 'Find some decent way of leaving him, I suppose,' she said flatly. 'Something'll come up.'

'I'm glad to hear you're a leg-break man,' Robert said to his grandson. 'There's always a place for a canny slow bowler in any side. Brains not brawn! That was your father's style, too.'

Joe peered over his grandfather's shoulder, seeking escape, but Robert was enjoying himself.

'Your glass is empty, fella-me-lad,' he said. 'Shall we get another of those? Spike it with a bit of your uncle's fizzy stuff? Come on, let's see what we can find.'

Stoopingly, he led Joe away for more ginger beer.

Andrea pulled herself together as quickly as she'd dissolved, and Dulcie left her discussing the work of the Institute with Loelia Drake, and sought out Bill. He was sitting near the now-deserted buffet table in the dining-room, staring out of the window.

He didn't look up as she came in, but he knew it was her, for he said, 'I ought to be going, I've got writing to do.'

'I don't want to go just yet.'

He rubbed his face impatiently. 'Okay, but soon.'

Dulcie perched on the windowsill and he was obliged to smile at her. Sitting like that, with her back to the afternoon light, her summery skirt diaphanous over her slim legs, she looked a picture.

She said: 'What a pity Kate and Lawrence couldn't be here. I wonder how they're getting on.'

'You miss her.' It was a statement.

'Yes, terribly.'

He wanted to say something, to exorcize Kate's ghost which stood between them, but he didn't know where to start.

They sat in separate silences for a few minutes and then she got up heavily and said, 'Come on then, let's make our farewells.' She walked from the room without looking at him again, assuming he would follow. Which, after a moment, he did.

At dusk, on the verandah of the farm in Gilgil, Thea toasted her brother and his bride with a glass of horrible sherry. She did so alone – the light had gone on in Jack's office and would remain on till after midnight – and she drank the sherry because Jack only drank whisky, and they could no longer afford to keep a selection of drinks. By the time she had finished the glass, it was pitch dark, and she thought yearningly of England at this time of year, with the long, light evenings full of the putter of lawn mowers, and outdoor voices, and piano practice drifting through open windows.

Cornet sat by her, his breathing wheezy. When Meru came out to light the hurricane lamp he growled, only a token salvo but Thea could see Meru's anxiously rolling eyes glint in the darkness.

'Bad dog, Cornet. *Asante sana* Meru.'

Beside her on the table, next to the cooking sherry which Meru had placed on a highly-polished regimental salver, lay an open atlas. She had been finding Malta on the map. Just seeing how tiny it was had made her cast down: It looked as if one decent bomb would dispose of it. It was simply miles from everywhere but Italy, and that was a dangerous unknown quantity. Still, it was closer to home, she consoled herself, maybe they would even be able to come and visit.

She had never even met her son-in-law – it was a sad reflection on the times – but she instinctively liked him. He wrote to them sometimes, instead of Kate, and she could almost hear his voice, the voice that went with that eager, smiling face. If she never saw Kate again, at least she knew she was in good hands.

Thea rubbed her eyes and yawned. More than anything, she wished Jack would leave his office, and his worrying, and come out and join her, but she didn't like to be a whining wife, asking for attention when he had so much on his mind. The problems were horrendous. The winter just gone had seen the worst drought in years, so that when food production should have gone up, to assist the war effort, it had slumped. As the result of the drought there had been plagues, like the plagues of Egypt, puff adders and ants, to add to their misery. They had decided to do the sensible thing, lease some of their vast acreage and try to raise animals on the remaining land. They'd got a herd of cattle established, at vast and mostly borrowed expense, but now in the last month the cows had contracted East Coast Fever and about a third had died.

And Jack would not let go. She longed to scream at him: 'Let's give up! Let's get out and leave someone else the problems, we don't have to slave and suffer and worry like this!' But she hadn't done so, because she knew that she had married the man, and in turn had married this patch of fierce, beautiful land. She doubted whether he ever thought of his children, not properly. All his energy, physical, mental and emotional, went into this capricious tract of red earth and prickly bush.

She poured more sherry, and heard the strains of *Lily Bolero* the theme of the BBC World Service news on the wireless. Two minutes later she heard the scrape of the chair in the office; the door opened and he came and stood by the table. She looked up at him, full of love. He was pared down to the very bone with worry and work, his brown hair was beginning to recede at the temples, accentuating his widow's peak.

He said softly: 'I was thinking about you. The news is on.'

'I know,' she replied, 'I heard the music.'

He sat down by her at the table, and flipped shut the atlas. Then he took her hand.

'What is it?' she asked.

'Italy's in the war.' He sighed heavily, rubbing the back of her hand with his thumb. 'So I suppose they'll try and move in on us from Somaliland, unless we pre-empt them. They've been sizing us up from our doorstep for far too long.'

'It's what we expected,' she said, trying to be philosophical. 'It's no surprise.'

'That's true.' He lifted her hand to his lips and then added: 'But I'm afraid it's out of the frying-pan into the fire for Ginger and that husband of hers.'

All through the night of the tenth Kate and Beth sat up in the little white-painted sitting-room, not knowing what to expect. An event which is anticipated is somehow no less shocking when it finally occurs and Kate, who had experienced the end of one phoney war already, felt the change less keenly than Beth, who had enjoyed a year of peace in all but name here on Malta. The evening had passed in a series of lulls and flurries, like little eddying hot winds before a storm. Soon after the news of Mussolini's declaration of war from the Palazzo Venezia in Rome they had tuned the wireless in to the local Rediffusion service to hear the very different voice of the Governor of Malta. Lieutenant General Sir William Dobbie was a Scot, a non-smoking, non-drinking Plymouth Brother, a man whose hallmark was a dour, unshowy integrity.

The two women had sat on the sofa, physically close but locked in their separate imaginings, trying to take in the implications of 'at war with England and consequently with Malta' and 'hard times ahead'. They could almost feel the small lump of rock shrinking round them, and the looming shadow of the heel of Italy, ready to grind them into the sea bed.

The Governor's tone was one of solemn warning, and exhortation to British and Maltese alike to seek God's help in the defence of their country, and His aid for their leaders, to perform their duties unflinchingly.

Little Antonina had appeared, red-eyed. Her father, a stevedore, was on the guns with Dockyard Defence at Grand Harbour. Her mother was alone at home in Floriana with five younger children and her own eighty-year-old mother. Could she go to them?

Beth and Kate had stowed her in the car without demur, and taken her to Floriana, which lay in the cleft between Valletta and the Hamrun road. Already, a thin but steady trickle of refugees was heading in the opposite direction, bound for the villages and the comforting security of family and old friends.

In the teeming panicky streets of Floriana itself they found Antonina's family — her mother, three brothers, two sisters, and spry, skinny grandmother — had miraculously got to the bottom of the ninety-odd steps leading from their top-floor flat to the street, and were preparing to head for the night to the disused railway tunnel, 'The Ditch', linking Floriana with Valetta. Beth offered them transport, but Antonina's mother refused, firmly. Everyone was walking, a car would hinder other pedestrians and just slow things up, she said. They had an ancient coach-built Marmet pram with a faded English crest on the side, holding provisions, pillows, blankets and some candles and matches (with two-year-old Censu perched on top to hold it all down).

Kate was impressed with their phlegm and their organization. Everyone, including the granny and the toddler, was carrying something, none of them appeared in the least flustered. They would not leave the city, they said, because their main family base was here, but since Antonina worked for Mrs Loney in Zemola, perhaps she might stay there for the moment, out of harm's way? This recommendation, given in her best interests, caused Antonina's chin to wobble, and her lustrous eyes to swim with tears. Beth engineered a compromise. They had brought Antonina down because she was concerned about her family and wanted to help them, like the good, loving, dutiful girl she was. Perhaps she could stay this night with them, and Beth would come back soon to see how they were all getting on, and bring her back if that was still what everyone wanted. This suggestion seemed acceptable, and they watched the small caravan, women and children, three generations, melt into the throng of people heading for shelter.

They made their way slowly home, moving alongside the straggle of families going out to the villages. During all this time, since the declaration of war, they had hardly spoken to one another, all their actions had been dictated by external pressures, they had voiced no feelings of their own at all.

In Zemola the streets were already nearly deserted. The people had gathered in the church, or in cellars, or simply in the homes of friends and relations to take safety in numbers.

Round Grand Harbour as darkness fell, the thick honeycomb of walls seethed with humanity. Tunnels, caves, catacombs, cellars, funnels in the dense rock which had never been intended for human habitation and whose original purpose was lost to memory, all now afforded protection from the baptism of fire which the Maltese fully anticipated. The night of 10 June saw the birth of a nation of troglodytes.

In the strange, expectant quiet of the little house in Strada Comina Beth asked Kate: 'Are you scared?'

Kate considered. 'No.'

'No, you wouldn't be . . .'

'I'm not brave,' said Kate. 'I'm just not scared.' She might have added that she was almost excited at the prospect of involvement in the war – here was something bigger than her and her shameful problems of conscience and loyalty. She could abandon herself to it.

'Drink?' asked Beth.

'Why not.'

They sat quietly with their drinks, no lights on, the gentle Maltese night washing round them in a soft tide. Outside they could hear the bark of a single agitated dog, the distant bray of a donkey, the occasional clattering order of an officious policeman or ARP warden. But the solitariness of these sounds in the night simply emphasized the deep and fearful silence.

'I wish I wasn't pregnant,' said Beth. 'Why on earth did I get pregnant?'

'Because you and Josh wanted a family,' volunteered Kate.

'Not really.' Beth shook her head. 'It was just to take things a step further, if you know what I mean. Shore up the cracks.'

Kate didn't take her up on this. It was dangerous ground. She herself felt too vulnerable to venture on to it. Instead, she said simply, 'You'll have a lovely baby, Beth. And you and Josh will be marvellous parents.'

'I wish I was so sure.' Beth swallowed the last of her drink. 'Another?'

'No thanks.' Kate remembered something. 'My uncle got married today in London.'

'Your uncle?' Beth looked puzzled. 'What sort of age is he?'

'I don't know . . . late forties. He's marrying his housekeeper, who's older than he is and a widow. They're blissfully happy.'

'I should think so too,' said Beth, 'it sounds as if they've waited long enough.'

Kate wondered if Bill had gone to the wedding, and whether he had thought of her then, or now, now that he knew she was in danger.

Abruptly she stood up. 'Is that slit trench in a usable condition?'

Beth gazed up at her over the rim of her glass. 'Of course it is, you know Josh.'

'There's something to put over the top?'

'Yes, an old door. And yes, I can get down into it without having a miscarriage. Kate, sit down.'

'I can't help it, I want to do something.'

'Humour me then, I need humouring.'

All night they sat, dozing from time to time, but never really falling asleep. By six in the morning the sun was climbing and no bombs had dropped. Beth was disgusted: 'We could have gone to bed!'

They opened the shutters and looked out into the street. Over the road the family Aquilina – Marco Aquilina was first trombone in the Zemola band club – were admitting a woman and three children with a bike and a handcart, relations of theirs from Cospicua.

'They must have been walking all night on the open road,' said Kate.

'Yes, and all those others we saw,' said Beth. 'But they won't have felt safe till they were back with their families, they're extraordinarily clannish.'

'It's nice for them, though – to have people to go to. I had a bit to do with evacuating children from danger zones in London, and it was harrowing packing them off into the unknown, away from all their friends and relations and everything they knew.'

'I don't know,' Beth shook her head. 'All this is going to cause a fearful headache for the food distribution people. There was an official evacuation plan at the start of the war, but none of them took the slightest bit of notice. And now there's a crisis they're just going wherever they please.'

'Look at that.'

A *carozzin* swayed past the window under a teetering load of domestic paraphernalia. At the front, the owner pulled the bony horse that pulled the *carozzin*. At the back, his wife and children pushed. All shouted at one another. A saucepan fell from the wagon and bounced and clanged down the hill, ricocheting off walls in its noisy progress until, near the bottom, a small child fielded it and took it into a house, the first spoils of war.

The people of Zemola, many of them, went about their business now that the night had passed, the women going up to mass, the men heading for the bus stop, to travel into work at the dockyard or barracks.

'*Halib . . . Halib . . . .!*' The goats' milk man appeared at the top of the hill near the church, where the clock on the tower showed half past six.

Kate made some coffee and toast and they took it into the yard and ate it sitting on the stone bench among the tomato plants and the arum lilies.

'Do you realize I'm eating breakfast?' remarked Beth. 'All this excitement must be doing me good.'

At a quarter to seven the goat man reached their door and Kate took the large jug from the kitchen and went through. In deference to the situation he had just two goats with him this morning. Neither he nor Kate paid much attention to the clock, and when they first heard the sound they thought it might be the start of the seven o'clock chimes. For a split second the two of them stood there, holding between them the half-full jug of milk, under the ruminative gaze of the lop-eared goats. But only for a split second. 'Air-raid warning!' said Kate. 'Come on in, we've got a trench.'

Calmly she admitted the man and his goats, bolted the door, and went through into the living-room to close the shutters and shut that door too. Then she put the milk jug in the kitchen and took the goat man and his charges through to the yard. Beth was standing in the trench, her head and shoulders peering over the surrounding vegetation like an anxious rabbit.

'Goodness,' she said, but without that much surprise. 'Good morning.'

'Morning to you,' said the goats' milk man. '*Marija*, what a time to choose.'

The goats began to munch happily on the yellow chrysanthemums.

The cold shriek of the siren filled the sunlit air. In the streets outside there was another sound, like a rushing wind in long grass, a rustle and furious agitation as people fled for cover. Kate, Beth and the goats' milk man sat in the stifling trench. Above them the sky was a broad rectangle of untroubled blue, framed by the high white walls. The man took out a string of black beads and began to thread and turn them in his seamed brown fingers.

As the siren died down, and there was silence, they could hear the click of the beads, and the munching of the goats.

In his position near the guns on the north-east tip of Luca aerodrome, Lawrence looked towards Grand Harbour, the very eye of the target area. To his left the tense faces of the anti-aircraft gun crew were trained on the innocent expanse of blue like searchlights, or telescopes, seeking out something still too distant to be visible to the naked eye. Everything was very hot and still. His field glasses, when he put them to his face, felt as if they were burning black rings round his eyes. He could make out the sharp glint of the sun striking on other gun emplacements as far away as Senglea and Marsamxett. In between, huddled farm buildings lay peacefully in the sun. He could just see the greenish white dome of the church tower at Zemola, three miles away.

And it was then that he heard the grumble of approaching planes, fluctuating, fading, swelling in the still-distant sky, as if to tease the nerves of those who waited on the island. Lawrence trained his field glasses on the sky to the north, and now, yes, there was a glitter like stars in the morning, and he could make out a formation of perhaps a dozen planes, flying cautiously at 20,000 feet, too high for the guns, and above the Savoia Marchetti bombers nine escorting fighters, Macchi 200s.

'Just down a bit, you buggers,' said one of the gun crew, but the planes were miles away over the docks and shipyards of Grand Harbour. Even as the man spoke there was a thud, and another, and a few defiant white puffs appeared in the sky beneath the planes, reminding Lawrence of a small terrier snapping at a mastiff. The men of Dockyard Defence were showing what they were made of.

When the first wave of bombs fell on the solid rock of Malta, the ground rippled beneath Lawrence's feet, and the barrel of the gun seemed to undulate before the shock waves, even at a distance of some six miles.

For a moment he closed his eyes and prayed that his wife would take care of herself.

For the whole of that first raid, which lasted for about ten minutes, Kate, Beth and the goats' milk man stood on the battlements. They had not remained in the slit trench for more than a minute – curiosity and claustrophobia had got the better of them and they had scrambled up and stood where they had a view. The wall they leaned on trembled and shuddered as the bombs fell, and down in Grand Harbour great spouts of water shot into the air, and puffs of pale dust spotted with debris that had been people's homes. The noise, even at this range, was awesome. The snarl of the planes, the shuddering crash and boom of the bombs hitting solid rock with pile-driver force, the thunderous response of the anti-aircraft battery, all combined in an enveloping tidal wave of sound that made speech, and even thought, impossible.

A few minutes into the raid there was an explosion of ear-splitting force, dominating all the others – the sound of the guns of HMS *Terror*, lying in Marsamxett Harbour, giving it all she'd got. On that first morning the fabric of Valletta suffered more damage from the blast of these guns than at the hands of the Regia Aeronautica. This was the noise that actually arrested, momentarily, the ceaseless browsing of the black goats in the yard. Looking around, Kate could see other people on their rooftops, some just watching, others shouting and gesticulating at the enemy in a futile but comforting show of hostility. Marco Aquilina from the house opposite was one of these, and she waved to him and shook her fist at the air.

After ten minutes there was a sudden, uneasy silence. The signal 'Raiders Passed' had not sounded, but people began to come out into the streets, and to join the foolhardy ones on the rooftops. A constable ran down Strada Comina upbraiding them and banging on doors, telling them to get back under cover, it wasn't over. But if they'd obeyed him they'd have missed the sight of the bombers moving north again, out of formation, heading for home. And on their trail like a couple of game old hounds, two Gloster-Gladiators, two-thirds of Malta's aerial defence, still sprightly and undamaged, chasing the Italians out of the sky.

Or that was what it looked like. A great cheer went up from the rooftops.

'Chase the bastards out of it!'

'Let 'em have it boys!'

'We showed them!'

Then the siren sounded 'Raiders Passed' and the streets, like veins which had been blocked, filled once more with the life-blood of people, pleased to see each other still alive, excited with relief, crossing themselves, embracing, talking, weeping. Kate and Beth went back into the house and Kate let the goat man out. In a moment or two they heard him call *'Halib . . .!'* plying his trade down Strada Comina as though nothing had interrupted him, though, as Beth remarked, 'that milk must be cream cheese by now!'

Kate went out, briefly, to the general store in the square, and on all sides there was an atmosphere almost of victory. Some people had run up the Union Jack outside the town hall and were singing 'God Save the King', and in the queue for the counter an elderly woman clasped her hand and said fervently, 'We do it together and with God!' News filtered back from Valetta, with the refugees. The Maltese artillery had shot down one plane and damaged another, Mussolini's bullies had been sent packing with their tails between their legs. But on the debit side, two workmen had been killed at Porte des Bombes in Floriana, and a married couple had been blasted to bits in their house near the new hospital of St Luke's. Six soldiers had been killed at Fort St Elmo, and another at French Creek. At Gzira, a cinema was hit. There had been relatively few fatalities, but many had been injured by flying debris.

When she got back, Kate told Beth about the strange atmosphere of optimism, and Beth shook her head. 'They've got no particular reason not to be. *They* don't know there are only three planes.'

In all, there were eight raids that first day, many of them abortive. Panic in the cities subsided, as the problem shifted to the reception areas in the inland towns and villages, where hard-pressed priests, officers and civilian volunteers struggled to match existing supplies and preparation to a situation which bore no relation to their original plan. In some tiny hamlets clans over a hundred strong congregated. In other, larger places the centres were half-empty. The ties of blood and tradition were stronger than any helpful suggestion written down in black and white. The Maltese evacuated themselves where and how they wished and waited with patience, stoicism and good humour, for arrangements to catch up with them.

The last raid of that first day came after dark, and it felt like the end of the world, attacking nerves that were already worn threadbare by thirteen hours of fear and attrition. Beth's system finally remembered its condition and made up for its lapse of the morning by keeping her retching miserably in the bathroom for over an hour, clasping the lavatory bowl like a long lost friend. When the siren wailed for the eighth time she waved Kate away, moaning, 'I don't care, I don't care, I'm going to die anyway . . .'

But when the bombers came over they were closer, or less accurate, than they had been before, and Kate hauled at Beth's elbow and made her stumble down the stairs and into the slit trench, clutching a pudding basin she'd found in the kitchen. The yard already had a bomb-blasted appearance, since the goats had eaten all the flowers, but this time they huddled down in the trench, beleaguered, the frail door over their heads, wondering when, if ever, it was going to end.

The whole island shuddered and jolted as if it might split into fragments at any moment. Several of the upstairs windows blew out in the blast, and though they couldn't hear the crash, Kate and Beth felt the fragments of glass pattering down on their shelter like crystallized rose petals. Crouching like burrowing animals in the fitful dark, they felt tiny handfuls of powdery soil trickle on to them as the earth moved.

That night, thirty civilians were killed and another hundred and twenty wounded. When the siren sounded 'Raiders Passed' Kate and Beth crawled up to bed and slept a sleep of near-death from which the last trump itself could not have woken them. While they slept, the authorities established that no important military objectives had been damaged. It appeared the Italian air force was acting on information given to them before the war. They were not aware that Hal Far aerodrome sported only three planes, that there were no torpedoes at the depot at Msida, nor any seaplanes at Kalafrana. Their erroneous view of Malta's strengths had, mercifully, helped conceal from them her manifold weaknesses.

In another couple of days, a pattern began to emerge, and it was not encouraging. There were raids every day, many times a day – at dawn, at dusk, during the hours of darkness and at any time in between. They were often heavy and widespread. Raids were to be a way of life.

This much established, the city Maltese set about adapting to it. The matriarchs of families moved into tunnels and cave-dwellings which had housed nothing but vermin for centuries, and set up house with determination. They laughed to scorn the Italian wireless broadcasts which suggested that Malta itself was Italian, and villified the island's Italians who were rounded up for internment.

Kate took Beth's car down to Floriana and retrieved Antonina, tearful, but sanguine that her family were safely installed in The Ditch, with a church close at hand for the sustaining of their souls. Her father had been one of those injured in raids on the dockyard on the first day, but he was patched up and back on his six-barrelled pom-pom gun now, determined to blast the hell out of the Eye-ties.

The wives and families of naval personnel were summarily evacuated but the army wives, given the option, and having it impressed on them that the greater the British presence, the higher the Maltese morale, elected to stay.

Lawrence came down on a borrowed motorbike on the third

night of the raids, ill-shaven, and filthy from having to fling himself into a ditch twice on the road between Luca and Zemola, but cheerful.

He had found his wife much revived, as though she had been given good news instead of subjected to continuous air raids. Their embrace was clinging and intense, the embrace of dangerous separation and joyful reunion, especially because it seemed that Kate might be returning from whatever dark and desolate place she had been inhabiting for the last two weeks.

And Lawrence had news for Beth, who had applied make-up, Je Reviens and her last decent pair of stockings in his honour.

'Josh can't get down till the weekend, but I went over there on my way, and he says perhaps you should leave, in view of — you know, the baby. You do have the option, and there'd be no disgrace in you taking it.'

'Oh, I don't think I will . . . .' murmured Beth, wandering in the direction of the drinks table. 'I can't face the thought of packing. Snifter, anyone?'

But it was an ill wind, and some good came of it for Kate and Lawrence. With the evacuation of naval families, a little house in Strada Forni, Bakery Street, just off Strada Comina, became vacant, and they went to look at it before Lawrence returned to Luca the next day.

It was very tiny, sandwiched between the eponymous bakery on one side and a small abbey of Dominican nuns on the other. This, as Lawrence pointed out, meant that they had the needs of both body and soul catered for on their doorstep.

The house looked unprepossessing. Its walls had a greying, leprous appearance from old age and this, along with the peeling closed shutters, gave it a blank, shut-eyed look. But when they opened the door they stepped straight into a garden of such beauty it almost took their breath away. The reason for its lushness was that the house had once been part of the abbey, and the garden was still cared for by the nuns. The house itself formed the other three walls of the garden, the front door was beneath an archway, so that they stood in shade, looking at all that light and colour like children at a magic lantern show.

Though the area of the garden was small, the vitality and colour were intense: the warm air was thick with the scent of flowers, tumbling bougainvillea, waxen lilies, fiery chrysanthemums, red hibiscus, blooms like trumpets, flames and stars, alight in the sharp white sunshine, or luminous in the black shadow of the wall. On the left, between the narrow arched windows of the abbey, a smiling, busty Madonna looked down benevolently like the good-hearted madam of some exclusive brothel. In the far corner trees, fig and olive, held gnarled, protective arms out over a small terrace. Tremulous freesias and bridal stephanotis frothed beside a foolish little paved path, like stepping stones from one side to the other.

The house itself was still, and cool and white. Austere almost, a little aloof from all that abandoned rioting in the garden, but kindly disposed towards Lawrence and Kate.

He put his arms round her and felt the enclosed warmth of her leaping like a flame in a lamp, the way it used to do.

'We can be happy here,' she said, and he noticed the note of determination in her voice.

'Yes,' he said. 'We can be, if they let us.' But he didn't know why he said that.

CHAPTER SIXTEEN

'Don't know why there's no sun up in the sky,
Stormy weather, since my man and I ain't together,
Keeps rainin' all the time . . .'

'Stormy Weather'
Ted Koehler and Harold Arlen 1933

WHILE Kate and Lawrence had been pitched headlong into what was to become among the most intense, if the smallest, theatres of war, their family and friends at home in England played an enforced waiting game.

Since the middle of May there had been an unpleasant whiff of inevitability about events in France. By early June, while the British celebrated the return of their army from beleaguered Dunkirk the French, bitter over what they could only see as a mass desertion, prepared to concede victory. By the time the evacuation had become officially a joint enterprise, it was too late. In spite of Churchill's heated protestations that British and French soldiers should leave together, 'bras dessous, bras dessus', the imbalance was already established: when the first German troops entered Dunkirk on 4 June, twice as many Britons had been taken off as Frenchmen. Left behind in the smoking dereliction of the port, a hundred and fifty thousand *poilus* tasted the sour ashes of surrender and were taken prisoner for the remainder of the war.

Even a confirmed Anglophile like Mlle Berthe Paul, a retired nanny who had spent some of her best years working in the pleasant London suburb of Wimbledon, found it hard to stomach this latest turn of events. Only a short while ago she had stumbled across a German station while tuning in her wireless. The voice with its dreadful accent had crowed: 'People of France, cease thinking the world is with you — it is overwhelmingly ours!' Strange, disjointed times, and Mlle Paul was quite alone in them. Since Italy had entered the war four days ago Parisians had been leaving the city in their tens of thousands, with Mlle Paul's employers, the Laines, among them. She was too old to leave, though they had offered to take her with them. Whatever happened, she was sure her age, and her ugliness and her spinster state would afford her some protection – of what possible interest could she be to anyone? She was in her seventies now, reaching the age when the distant past was more vivid than the events of yesterday, she could remember all her charges with great clarity.

She found herself thinking of the self-possessed, tight-lipped little English girl whom she had cared for during the last war. When the girl had been adopted Captain Garrick had found her another post with a family, much more what she was used to. From there she had moved on to the Laines and had looked after their two boys, Jean-Marie and Luc, for the past ten years until the summer before the war started. Then they had very kindly allowed her to remain in her little flat at the top of their house.

It was the middle of June now. When they'd gone, a few days ago, they had told her that the cleaning woman would be coming in from time to time, to keep things in order for their return. But Mlle Paul didn't seriously expect to see the Laines again. Paris was becoming a ghost town. The government had already transferred to the Prefecture at Tours. It was, she reflected, with a little grimace at the irony of it, rather peaceful. On the morning of 14 June the habit of a lifetime combined with the short, light sleep of old age, ensured that she was taking coffee in her chair by the window at six o'clock as usual. From this chair she had a view along the Rue Valpaise, and a glimpse of the Place de la Concorde. The flat was her world now, and she went out as seldom as she could.

Eight o'clock. Two hours she had been sitting there with only her thoughts for company, time she was up and about her chores. But just as she was about to rise from her chair, her eye was caught by a movement – a lone motor cyclist in the Place de la Concorde. Berthe was a little short-sighted these days, but something about the rider's silhouette made her reach for her spectacles.

'Ah . . .' She exhaled a little gasp of shock. '*Alors, ils sont arrivés.*'

Much later, the cleaning woman had arrived, with no intention of doing any cleaning. She was waiting to tell Berthe all that she had seen. The swastika was flying from the Arc de Triomphe but that was nothing, she said! It was also flying at the top of the Eiffel Tower. The fact that the lifts were not in use had not deterred the German soldiers, who had carted their flag up nearly two thousand steps to get it there. They meant business all right, she assured Berthe, who stared at her coldly. Later that morning, when the woman had gone and Berthe was sitting peacefully in her chair at the window, she saw two German officers enter the *Chaumerie*, and in a few moments they emerged, each lighting a French cigarette. Next to the tobacconist's window was a tattered poster which had been there since the optimistic days of February. '*Nous vainquerons parceque nous sommes les plus forts,*' it reads, its frayed edges hanging like dead skin. Berthe remained rooted to the spot. In spite of the midsummer weather she was cold, and moving about did not seem to help.

The scenes she witnessed in the Rue Valpaise were so bizarre, that she wondered if in fact she was asleep, and dreaming them. German officers stood in the middle of the road with cameras, taking photographs. Others strolled about munching chocolate and confectionery like children on an outing — not that any child for whom she had had responsibility would have been allowed to eat in the street. She could not reconcile in her mind the knowledge of defeat with these grinning, self-indulgent monkeys in uniform. She felt that her whole life had been a waste when Paris could be overrun in this way by men with no breeding or manners. A soldier — a mere *poilu* — stood on the street corner opposite eating butter from a packet with his fingers.

She grew stiffer and stiffer, so that she could no longer have moved even if she'd wanted to. She decided it didn't matter, she would just stay here, safe and snug in her hidey-hole where no one could get at her.

At last it began to get dark. Berthe was barely conscious now, but from the bistro a little way up the street from the Laines' house she could hear the insistent pulse of music, and bursts of jovial male laughter. She sat there, quite still, while the world changed round her. Two things bothered her, vaguely. Would Madame Laine remember to put bitter aloes on Luc's fingernails before he went to bed? They'd be chewed to the quick before morning . . . and where was that little red-haired English girl these days, the little girl who never smiled . . .? She had so many responsibilities, they wore her out.

Next day the Laines' cleaning woman called on Mlle Paul to tell her about the goings-on in the night, with Germans ordering kilo steaks in the cafés, and drunk as lords all over the place. But there was no reply to her knock, and the door had not been locked so she let herself in.

The old dear was dead, sitting bolt upright in her chair by the window, with a disapproving expression on her face. She must have had a massive stroke, for she was both wet and dirty. Still, it was a mercy, the woman told her friends. Paris was going to be a bad place for those like the elderly, who could not adapt.

If Ilse Bauer had been able, like Berthe, to watch the German soldiers gorging themselves on the affluent delights of Paris, she would have been less censorious.

Life in Berlin, too, was hard and hungry. Ilse and others like her were fed on news of glorious victories and German supremacy, to help them rise above their everyday privations, but it wasn't always quite enough. Ilse would have been pleased if the food shortages had caused her to lose weight, but it seemed that her bulk had hardened now, and become permanent. It was her energy that was sapped, those extra kilos were like a ball and chain. Thanks to the collusion of her colleagues at the Kafe Wein, she still had her job. They covered up for her slowness, and she was popular with the customers because of her good memory and cheerful disposition. She tried hard — the prospect of losing the job filled her with terror — but now it took every ounce of her failing energies to haul herself through the working day, and a full twenty minutes to get up the stone staircase to her apartment. Night shifts were the worst, with the black-out, but she didn't dare complain for fear of jeopardizing her position.

And beneath these personal problems, and the deprivations shared by all Berliners on a surface level, Ilse was conscious of deeper and more sinister shoals. Her Hungarian neighbours, the Rodeskas, had been evicted, or 'sent for rehousing' – that was what the guard said. This followed a period of several weeks during which the family had been obliged to wear a yellow badge on their sleeves, and were under strict curfew. Frau Rodeska had only been allowed to go shopping at certain times of the day, and her husband's departure and return from work was strictly monitored. She was a cheerful, loud-voiced woman with a shock of greasy black curls, and Herr Rodeska looked younger than her and was handsome in a swarthy, gypsy fashion. Their children had brought life to the Metzallee with their exuberant screeching and fighting, playing games that took them hurtling up and down the ringing stone staircase like a troop of monkeys in the jungle canopy. Some of the inhabitants had not cared for the racket, but Ilse liked the children and let them come in and out of her apartment when she was there.

Now the whole family had taken on a cowed, hunted look. Their footsteps scurried furtively across the court, their voices were lowered. Frau Rodeska cuffed and pulled at her brood, and spoke in a snarling whisper, and her handsome husband walked hunched over with his hands in his pockets. He used to whistle, a high, clear warbling note like an exotic bird, resounding gloriously from the grey walls, but he had stopped that now. Then one day they'd all been turned out into the courtyard – the man, his wife and the four children, bag and baggage – and left standing there, under guard. When Ilse got back from work they were still there. Finally they were allowed back in, and the guard went away. But the next day the same thing happened, and the next. At the end of the third day, with the normally ebullient Frau Rodeska like a white-faced spectre, and the youngest child weeping with tiredness and confusion, they had been marched away. The occupants of the tenement watched through their windows, doubtfully. It was good news, wasn't it, that the hard-up and overcrowded Rodeskas were to be rehoused?

And there were others, like Hermann Farbe, a regular of Ilse's at the Kafe. He'd been a saxophonist with Rudi Schichter's dance band; he always came in for coffee and rum baba between the tea-time and evening sessions at the Klub Madeline. He was a lovely gentleman, and sometimes the band was on the wireless, and Ilse would feel that she had a stake in the glamorous world of entertainment. But Herr Farbe had suddenly stopped coming in. Ilse had plucked up courage to enter the plush twilight of the Madeline to ask the bandleader about her friend, but he had been quite short with her, just said Farbe had been called away, and she'd had to be content with that. These disappearances were happening all over the place as if, in a room full of candles, certain candles were being snuffed out by an invisible hand, secretly and silently. Ilse did not look for trouble. She took things as she found them and made the best of them. She took other people at their face value. She had seen the posters and read the propaganda, but she had always assumed that anyone who was pleasant and kindly and doing no harm would be exempted. Herr Farbe had been nothing like the vulpine, sneering Jew of the Nazi publicity machine, you could not have asked for a nicer gentleman. Perhaps, she thought, he has gone to relations, perhaps someone in his family was sick.

If at any time a terrible surmise had pressed its hideous face to the windows of her mind, she very quickly drew the curtains over it and returned, as it were, to sit by the fire.

Ernest had persuaded Giles to accompany him to the club where Mae was appearing. The expedition had involved quite a bit of detective work, as Ernest did not want Mae to know that he was there expressly to see her. Lunching with Giles at the Savoy, he had asked the head waiter to find out from one of the band where the talented girl singer was working whom he had heard recently on the wireless. He was eaten up with envious curiosity.

The club itself, situated at the Oxford Street end of the Tottenham Court Road, was nothing to write home about, but Ernest recognized the types who frequented it — arty-fringe, journalists and cartoonists and music publishers, backstage people in the theatre. By the middle of the evening when Giles and Ernest arrived, the rest of the Crowsnest's clientele were feeling no pain whatsoever.

They asked for a table near the band and Giles ordered a bottle of champagne, without commenting on the price. They'd had to become members of the club to get in – this satisfaction of Ernest's curiosity was costing a bomb, but Giles's only wish at the moment was to make him happy. He felt tender, understanding, protective. Ernest was so young, his life had been hard, it was Giles's privilege to indulge him a little. He had in the first instance been against this jaunt, for he sensed there was a lot more to it than just looking up an old friend. But now that they were here he was determined to make a pleasant evening of it.

The champagne arrived, and was opened with a flourish. Giles lifted his glass. '*Santé*. Here's to the entertainment business.'

'Down the hatch.'

Giles took a sip, Ernest a swig.

'There are quite a few people here I know,' said Giles, looking about him in the gloom. 'Surprising what people get up to, isn't it?'

'Ssh!' said Ernest. 'It's her.'

Mae hadn't really changed, except that now everything about her was writ large. Her lips were vermilion, her hair platinum, her figure looked as if it had been moulded on a potter's wheel. She wore a mauve dress with a swathed bodice which gave her fine bust the appearance of a decorated dais. The dress had short, cuffed sleeves, which fitted tightly round her plump arms. Her skin was very white.

Her voice, too, was somehow bigger than Ernest remembered, swelling, confident. He looked around and saw that people were taking notice, they liked her. It was not just the voice, she had stage presence, she radiated warmth and confidence and a pleasant, unthreatening allure.

She sang for about fifteen minutes and then waved and bowed and withdrew. Ernest went to the side of the stage and presented himself.

'Ernie!' She cupped his face in her hands and wobbled his face from side to side. 'Get you!'

'Hallo, Mae. Fancy running into you here. Congratulations, you were really good.'

She smilingly accepted a drink from another patron. 'See you later, love . . . You telling me you never been to this place before?'

'No, never.'

She sipped her red cocktail, holding the cherry on the stick delicately between finger and thumb. Now that Ernest was close to her he could see that it had not all been easy. Mae was a good few years older than he was, her make-up was thick, though expertly applied, and the skin beneath her eyes and chin was beginning to get crêpey. But these things did not detract from her glamour, she exuded a cheery worldliness. He felt she could handle anything.

'Here with a girlfriend?' she enquired.

Ernest had never let on about Giles. 'With my boss. There were people here he wanted to meet,' he lied.

'Where is he?'

'Over there.' Ernest pointed out Giles, who had been joined by a theatrical impresario, Wally Buxton.

'That's him?' Mae made big eyes and a teasing, disbelieving mouth. 'Pull the other one, Valentino, it's got Big Ben on.'

'What do you mean?' Ernest had a horrible suspicion he was blushing.

She ignored this. 'Are you going to introduce me?'

'If you like.'

He took her elbow and led her across the room. He was aware that they made a striking couple. .

'Giles – excuse me, this is Mae Irving.'

The two older men stood up. Giles presented Wally Buxton and folded Mae's outstretched hand in both his, saying, 'I enjoyed your performance, Mae. You have a good voice there.'

'Thank you, glad you liked it.'

'Ernest heard you on the wireless a few weeks back,' went on Giles, oblivious to Ernest's embarrassed grimacing, 'we were all most impressed. And you used to work with Ernest, I believe?'

'That's right.' Mae glanced almost coquettishly at Ernest. 'Franconi's superior catering, that was us. Actually,' she looked back at Giles, 'I remember you.'

Wally Buxton laughed. 'Makes you look a bit ungallant, eh Giles?'

'I'm so sorry. We met, did we?'

'Oh, it was years ago,' said Mae affably. She leaned across to Wally. 'Didn't you put on *Holiday Mood* at the Waverley?'

'That's right, it was a dog.'

'I enjoyed it, there was some good stuff in that show.' Mae went on to tell Wally where he'd gone wrong. She was extraordinarily forthright and unabashed. Giles and Ernest followed the exchange respectfully.

Later, when they'd all had another drink and were the best of friends, and Wally had got Mae's agent's number, Ernest escorted her back to the band. She was quite queenly in a brassy way, acknowledging greetings and compliments, keeping her distance just nicely, warm but not familiar. Jealousy writhed within Ernest. She'd got it all sewn up, she was her own person.

Back beside the stage she turned to him and kissed his cheek with her glossy red mouth.

'He's alright, your bloke,' she said gently.

'He pays well,' said Ernest, wiping his cheek.

'Come off it, Ernie.' She put her head on one side, surveying him with affectionate concern. 'I wasn't born yesterday.'

The bandleader gave her a nod and she set her glass down. 'No peace for the wicked. Nice to see you, love, keep in touch, why don't you? Bye now.'

Ernest returned to Giles. He felt humiliated.

'I'm sick of this dump,' said Ernest. 'Let's go home.'

'Your friend's going to sing again.'

'I've listened to her for years,' snapped Ernest, raising his voice harshly to compete with Mae's opening sally in *Two Sleepy People*.

'Very well.' Giles swallowed the last of his drink and got up.

Ernest disliked the feeling of being given in to. If only Giles didn't always behave so well.

They left, going up the narrow red-carpeted stairs into the warm city darkness. The strains of Mae's rich voice wafted after them like expensive cigar smoke, but Ernest did not look back.

*

At the end of June it was more than two months since Maria Marx had seen her son Ernest. She was not resentful, but she did hope he'd come soon. She needed a little of the light of Ernest's countenance from time to time to cheer her up, like a shot of vitamins.

She was grateful, of course, to Tony and Doris, for looking after her, for these days she was conscious of being a dead weight. She couldn't manage even a few steps now without getting short of breath, but she wouldn't give up cigarettes, her one luxury. She remembered the awful asthma attacks Ernest had had as a boy — he was such a sensitive lad, even then. But apparently the asthma had meant he couldn't enlist, so it was an ill wind . . .

It was six o'clock when at last Doris came in, cheerful as ever and talking nineteen to the dozen.

'Hallo, love, bearing up? Sorry I'm late, I got a bit caught up with that woman along the end, whose boy was at Dunkirk — the stories, you wouldn't believe!'

As she nattered away she bent over Maria, tweaking at her cardigan, patting her shoulders, enveloping her in a brackish cloud of light ale.

'I got us a bit of a treat,' she said, winking. Doris was good on 'little treats', she often had milk stout and a packet of fags for Maria, perhaps some pork scratchings or pickled onions, though the flat might be dirty and the cupboard otherwise bare.

'Where's your Tone?' she asked now, pouring herself and Maria a glass of Guinness.

'It's orders night, he's got late deliveries.'

'That's right, no hurry for tea then,' said Doris comfortably.

It was already an hour past Maria's usual teatime, her stomach felt as though it were being pressed against her spine, it rumbled cavernously. She remembered fondly Ernest's passion for regular mealtimes, the way he used to rush back from Zelinski's to see that she put something away . . . she sighed.

'All right, dear?'

'Yes, fine.' If the worst came to the worst Tony could fetch something, even if it was only a bag of chips. She knew from Doris's manner that she had spent the afternoon in the pub and gossiping on the corner.

Maria was resolved to speak to Ernest about this problem, when next he came. She had had to brace herself, but she was determined. If he could just say something to Doris to the effect that she, Maria, needed sustenance, however simple, at regular hours — she didn't even mind if he made her out to be a pernicketty old nuisance provided it had the desired effect. Doris worshipped Ernest, she would listen to him.

As if she'd been reading her thoughts, Doris said: 'I wonder when we'll be seeing your Ernest again, it's been, what, over a month?'

'About that,' lied Maria. She sipped her stout and felt it washing acidly about inside her, sour and unsustaining. 'I expect he's busy.'

There was a clamour of footsteps on the stairs and Tony came in, looking hot and bothered. He kissed Maria perfunctorily, and ignored Doris. 'We didn't half have a lot of orders tonight. I'm starving, when's tea?'

'I'll get weaving on it now you're in, Tone,' said Doris good-humouredly. 'I'm not dead sure what there is, but I'll rustle up something . . .' She lurched up from her seat, her cigarette dangling precariously from pouting, prehensile lips, eyes screwed up against the smoke, glass slopping.

Tony scowled. 'I'm famished!'

'Tell you what,' said Maria, reaching for her purse, breathing heavily. 'Go along and get us a pie.'

'No I bloody won't!'

This open defiance arrested both women. Maria was astonished. 'Now, Tony, what kind of attitude is that?'

'I'm hungry, I been working all day. I want a proper tea.'

'Doris is going to get it,' said Maria. She felt the storm brewing, Tony's hot, youthful rage filled the room like steam from a kettle, confusing her. Doris, on the other hand, stood in the kitchen doorway with a stupid smile on her face, as if it was all a lot of nonsense. To Maria's horror, she came over and put a fat arm round Tony's shoulders.

'Come on, love, keep your hair on, you'll frighten your Mum and me to death! Now why don't you do as your Mum says and nip up the pie shop—'

'Because I don't want to!' Tony shook off her arm and yelled right in her face. 'Because I'm fed up of coming back and not getting any tea, and I'm fed up of you not doing your bleeding job!'

Doris's jaw dropped. Maria put her hand over her eyes.

'Now . . . Tony,' she said, with as much force as she could muster, 'that'll do. Doris is very good to us—'

'No she bloody isn't! She's on the hog's back here, isn't she? She takes his money' (Tony couldn't speak Ernest's name), 'and makes herself at home. What does she do for us, you tell me?'

'Tony, love, let's wait till we get a chance to talk to Ernest, and we can all—'

'Ernest!' Now that the hated name was forced out of him, Tony spat it out with all the pent-up venom at his command. 'Ernest! Do you think he gives a monkey's about us? There's only one person he cares about, and that's Ernest Marx!'

'You better face up to it, Mum,' he screeched cruelly. 'Your lovely wonderful Ernest don't just work up west. He's living with a fucking fancy man!'

Primmy heard all the bumping around and raised voices upstairs, and debated whether to go up. They were usually a quiet lot, there seemed to be few arguments. On this basis she decided against even discreet interference — everyone was entitled to a blow-up from time to time, and she was tired. She did think that she had heard Ernest's name taken in vain; he might well be the bone of contention, in which case it certainly wasn't her business. She wished, from time to time, that there was someone else whose business she could reasonably share, she had a great desire to be leaned on. There was her backward brother, Eddie, but he was so institutionalized now, she meant nothing to him. Her visits to the asylum were more to salve her own conscience than to cheer him up. And there was her sister Lisbeth's family, with whom she had settled down into a state of armed truce, but they didn't need her. Finally there was Dulcie, but that friendship had dissipated somewhat since the new man had entered Dulcie's life.

As ever, on these occasions, Primmy thought of Maurice. She wished she had one thing, one tiny memento of him, but there was nothing. No little trinket, no lock of hair, no letter, not even a dog-eared snapshot. So she had to rely on her small well-worn stock of memories. Even they were fading with age. And now as she got older and faced the absolute certainty of solitary (she never termed it lonely) old age, she wondered if those memories played her false. Could she honestly look another woman in the eye and say she had loved, and been loved? There had been so little to go on. She had told no one, and she was quite sure he had not, so there wasn't a soul she could go to for reassurance.

Abruptly, she pulled herself together. Of course she was right! She had never doubted it before, why was she doing so now? And in any case, there was no earthly good in crying over spilt milk.

On Tuesday 9 July Loelia Drake, Lawrence's mother, sat down in her garden to write letters. She was an enthusiastic correspondent, and took considerable trouble, even now with her gammy leg, to get herself properly organized before she began.

On this occasion she had taken a comfortable, light basket chair to her favourite corner by the pink hydrangea, and then gone back into the house for the rest of her letter-writing equipment. This comprised a shady hat; a wood and wicker lap-desk containing her paper, envelopes and pen; a jug of iced coffee; and her handbag, with spectacles, cigarettes, holder and lighter. Thus equipped, she was ready to begin, lowering herself into the chair with a sigh of relief, and propping her walking stick against the arm.

She wrote first to Joe Kingsley, inviting him to come and stay with her for a few days in his summer holidays. Her reading of the young man's frame of mind was exactly right. He might well not want to come, but on the other hand . . . once he was here she was sure she could give him a pleasant time. She had friends in the neighbourhood with nice children, or grandchildren, of the same age, and Ewehurst now boasted quite a decent small tennis club, and a quite respectable cricket team, always prepared to give a game to a promising schoolboy.

'. . . I think you might very well enjoy yourself,' she wrote, 'and of course it would be an indulgence for me to have someone young in the house again, like old times. Quite a few young things congregate down here in the summer, staying with their ancient relatives, so I think we could ensure you would not be bored. Shall I contact your Uncle Aubrey and say I have extended this invitation? Then you need not let me know till you get there . . .'

She very much hoped he would accept. At the bottom of the letter after her signature — Loelia Drake, she did not go in for spurious 'aunts' — she added, as an afterthought: 'You would be able to see the house your mother lived in as a girl. It's a nursing home now, full of ancient wrecks like myself, but it might still interest you — it was *very grand* in its heyday!' If she'd understood Joe right, this last was a master stroke.

Smiling to herself, she picked up a fresh piece of paper and began writing to Robert Kingsley. Seeing him at Aubrey's wedding had brought back memories — as a young married woman, she and her husband had often seen Robert and Daphne at parties and dances given by the local county. Unlike the Tennants, the Kingsleys had been very much part of the hunt ball set, and Robert always the life and soul, flirting with the girls, dancing every dance, his genial face glowing like a beacon. She had been saddened to see him so weak and old, and to hear about the home in Thorpness.

She considered for a moment, tapping her pen against her chin, and then began: 'Dear Robert, I hope you won't mind my writing out of the blue like this, but it was such a delight to see you at Aubrey Tennant's wedding, and I felt I must keep in touch. I have just written to ask your nice grandson if he would consider coming to stay with me for a few days in the summer holidays. A forlorn hope, I suspect, but you never know. What a likable boy he is, you must be very proud.'

She paused for a moment, considering again, and then went on: 'I have come to the conclusion I'm too old to take this war seriously, except as a lot of petty inconveniences. Only six ounces of marge a week, now, and a paltry two ounces of tea — how is a body to survive? As a "householder" I have received two leaflets, one telling me what to do if the invader comes, and the other called *Stay Where You Are*! As if I should do anything else with my funny hip! Have quite decided that if the German army comes to Ewehurst I shall sit quietly in my garden and be civil and dignified, it will be too late by then anyway. I can't help seeing the funny side of things. My jobbing gardener, who is at least as old as I am, is a member of the Local Defence, but at present he has neither uniform nor gun. What a threat to the Nazis . . .!'

Loelia continued in this vein for a couple of pages, smiling to herself, before exhorting Robert to 'brighten up her life' by writing back, and signing herself 'Yours affectionately, Loelia Drake.' She then began the final instalment of her latest letter to her son and daughter-in-law in Malta. From what she could glean from the news, they must be taking the most terrible pounding, and she didn't suppose for one moment that much mail got through, but it did her good to put her thoughts on paper. If the truth were known, any anxieties she had were more concerned with their emotional, than their physical, welfare. After all, where bombs were concerned, one had no alternative but to be fatalistic.

'. . . de Gaulle broadcast again the other evening,' she told them, 'appealing to the French to keep on with the struggle, and so on. He does have the most thrilling, melancholy delivery. I'm sure if I were French I would rally to his call — and much use I would be! My darlings, I want to know so much — do you have somewhere reasonable to live, do you see much of each other, are you able to be safe when the horrible Italians are doing their damnedest? It's very hard for us to imagine constant bombing when over here it *still* hasn't happened. I feel a complete fraud sitting here in my lovely garden, perfectly peaceful, with the birds twittering like anything. I don't expect you to write back. If the news were bad, I should no doubt hear from some official source. Just take the best care of yourselves that you can, all my love, Mama.'

She replaced the cap on her fountain pen and sat back, watching a blue brimstone butterfly twinkling around this year's particularly fine show of lupins.

Joe Kingsley went to the Govans for the last two weeks in August. He had enjoyed his holidays in spite of low expectations (or perhaps because of them) and approached his stay at Coppham Chase in a very much more confident frame of mind than in the past. His Aunt Iris had really smartened things up at Mapleton Road, Treece seemed to have improved, and they had gone off all over London together, as happy as Larry. Uncle Aubrey had taken him up to Thorpness for a weekend to visit his grandfather, but they had been swimming and boating, and it had been quite bearable. His few days in Ewehurst with Lawrence's mother had been nothing short of spiffing. He had gone as a duty, feeling he should give Aubrey and Iris a rest, but it had turned out wonderfully. She had lived there all her life and knew lots of people, he had enjoyed the entirely novel experience of being one of the local 'young set', and had even attended a tennis club dance and not found it abhorrent. His connections with the Tennant family and Chilverton House had given him a kind of instant status. He had been something of a man of mystery, which was gratifying, and for the first time he had consorted with girls of his own age and discovered the fringe benefits of female company.

Since Dunkirk, the south-east corner of Britain was the front line. Every hitherto sleepy village was in a state of battle-readiness, every genteel seaside town was garlanded in barbed wire, every look-out point was manned by the LDV – or Home Guard as Churchill had dubbed them in a recent broadcast – now resplendent in uniforms and armed with rifles.

Since Operation Eagle, the German air offensive, had been launched in earnest earlier in the month, Coppham Chase itself had entered the war effort, as a weekend retreat for off-duty pilots from the nearby airfields. These young men – though some of them were barely five years older than Rupert and Joe – appeared like gods to the schoolboys, and the Battle of Britain being fought in the summery blue skies over Sussex and Kent was like a magnificent show put on for their benefit. They would lie in the long grass in the deer park, or in one of their many tree houses, and watch aerial dog fights taking place almost overhead, cheering on their heroes and shouting advice. In the evening the butler, Makepiece, frequently had to go out with a trug on to the croquet lawn and collect up the spent machine-gun bullets which littered it, and these the boys would stow away with their rapidly growing collection in Rupert's bedroom.

The pervading atmosphere was one of good sportsmanship and pluck. In the Chase's market garden – recently enlarged by the addition of the tennis court, ploughed up and laid to root crops – gardeners and turbanned land girls took time off from their labours to waves their hoes and rakes in salute as a British squadron swept dashingly overhead, and a 'scoreboard' set out cricket-fashion near the main gate proclaimed the state of play between the RAF and the Luftwaffe with optimistic inaccuracy.

Lady Govan's pilots – all of whom, to a man, carried a torch for their patrician hostess – did little to dispel this unrealistic attitude. Rupert and Joe, hero-worshipping, fetching and carrying, eavesdropping, were not to know that the bibulous flash and dash bravado of the drawing-room was just a defence against ever-present fear. In spite of the staggering output of new planes from Beaverbrook's Ministry of Aircraft Production, there was an acute shortage of pilots to fly them. The training period of pilots, already reduced to one month, had been slashed again, this time to a mere two weeks. Many of the young men being catapulted into the aerial front line had done no more than twenty hours in Hurricanes and Spitfires, had never fired their guns, nor used a reflector light. They were not dashing air aces but courageous novices.

On 20 August Joe and the Govan boys listened, enraptured, to Churchill's stirring speech. To think that 'the few' – or a few of them at any rate – were here, in the same house! The pilots' jokes about mess bills and the paucity of the pay only served to burnish their already considerable lustre in the boys' eyes.

The following afternoon Rupert and Joe went for a bike ride, without Julian (as they called Govan Minor in the holidays) whose bike Joe borrowed. They went to a favourite place, a beech wood, where the footpath wound between waist-high bracken like a deep green sea. The great thing about this path was that having been all uphill for about a quarter of a mile it suddenly fell away, and it was possible to freewheel in whatever rash manner took your fancy – no hands, feet on handlebars, standing on the saddle – bumping over the springy ground with its soft cushion of leaf-mould, swerving round roots or bumping thrillingly over them, before bursting out into the field at the bottom and falling off in the long grass. The sensation of speed was heightened by the tree trunks flashing by on either side, and the tunnel-effect of rushing from darkness to light.

This afternoon, as they toiled up the hill through the green surf of bracken, they could hear the stutter and whine of an air-skirmish about a couple of miles away.

'Come on,' said Rupert, standing on his pedals for greater impetus, 'let's get over to the field and have a look!'

But as they began their hurtling descent on the other side, so the sound of a plane's engine came closer and closer until the screaming enveloped them, and the flickering dappled light was blotted out by a great spinning black shadow like a bird of prey above the leaf canopy. Rupert turned and shouted something at Joe, but his voice was lost.

The two bicycles burst into the meadow and deposited their riders unceremoniously in the ripening hay. The plane, a Stuka, careered over their heads out of control and already on fire, so close that it seemed it must crash on them. With a splintering sound, it decapitated the row of trees on the far side of the meadow and came down just beyond them in a field of bronze corn. Following the earth-shuddering noise of the crash there was a tiny pause, then a boom as the flames took hold. The two boys, still sitting in the grass like startled rabbits, felt the rush of heat smack their faces and ducked. When they peeped, a column of black smoke was billowing up behind the broken trees, which now looked like stumpy, imploring hands.

'Oh God,' said Joe. 'Oh crikey, look.'

The figure of a man, rimmed with fire, had appeared on the ridge of bank between the tree trunks. His movements were slow and heavy. He lifted his arms and waved, the flames rippling and licking from neck to wrist.

'How could he see us?' said Rupert.

Over the sound of the burning Stuka they could now hear the clang of the fire engine approaching on the Lewis road, and shouts, some of which might have been the pilot's. But now he crumpled bonelessly and sank to the ground.

The boys had not moved. Other people were running across the cornfield now, threading the drifting smoke, little pur-poseful black ant-men swarming to the scene of the disaster. They felt suddenly guilty, as if they had had some hand in the pilot's death. Times without number they had exhorted the British fliers to blast the Jerries out of the sky, but now they found no satisfaction in success. With one accord they grabbed their bikes and rushed back into the wood.

Up the hill they pedalled, like fugitives, puffing and sweating with the effort. They didn't slow down until they had reached the lane on the far side, by which time both were sweating with fatigue and fear. In the distance they could still hear the noises of the crashed plane, pursuing them.

Back at the house they were greeted by a wildly excited Julian who rushed out to the garage as they were putting their bikes away, yelling: 'Hey, you lot, we've shot down a Jerry just the other side of the beech wood – a Stuka! Shall we go and have a dekko?'

'Buzz off, tick,' said Rupert, but without venom, just dully and automatically. Julian watched, crushed, as the two older boys walked past him and into the house, with long faces like a pair of boring, kill-joy grown-ups.

On the afternoon of Saturday 7 September, Iris was entertaining her sister-in-law Dulcie to tea. It wasn't very jolly to be on your own at the weekend, Aubrey was on firewatching duty at the works in Southwark and Bill was working, so Iris had invited Dulcie down.

It had been a gloriously sunny day, and Iris had spent it gardening, hoeing the patriotic expanse of vegetable patch which had replaced two-thirds of the lawn. She wore serviceable navy slacks and jumper, and a capacious apron with a front pocket from which her gardening gloves protruded like a joey kangaroo from its mother's pouch. Dulcie, on the other hand, looked cool and elegant in a pale yellow blouse and skirt with a white leather belt and white shoes. When Iris complimented her on her outfit, Dulcie assured her it was old as the hills.

The war had been very much in evidence in the skies over London during the past month, but since there was nothing much they could do, the two women did not discuss it. Today had been mercifully quiet, and the sun was shining as they drank their pale, weak tea out on the neatly-mown patch of grass. Instead, they discussed Andrea Avery, whom Dulcie had met for lunch that week.

'How was she?' asked Iris sympathetically. 'I was so sorry she was low at our wedding.'

'She's better,' replied Dulcie. 'She's going abroad, to get away from Louis.'

'Abroad, but where abroad?' asked Iris. 'That sounds terribly drastic.'

'Not really, I believe she has a job, she didn't go into details.'

'Do they plan a divorce, then?' enquired Iris carefully, not apportioning blame.

Dulcie shook her head. 'I don't know, Iris. She wasn't confiding in me. I think she rather regretted her lapse at your wedding and was busy making up for it. She's a very independent sort.'

'Of course, of course,' Iris nodded. 'So anyway, let's hope she'll be happier overseas.'

They sat quietly, digesting these facts. A bumble bee droned over the tea tray. But Iris's hearing was acute, it was not only the bee she could hear, but another sound, which had become almost as much part of this fine summer as birdsong and butterflies. 'Here we go,' she said, putting on her spectacles. 'I didn't think we'd get off scot free.'

The two women stood up, shielding their eyes with their hands, scanning the sky.

'Yes—' said Dulcie. 'There, look.'

A formation of some sixty planes glittered in the sky, advancing from the south, heavy bombers below and an umbrella of escorting fighters above.

'I wonder where they're headed,' said Iris. 'Still, they'll get what's coming to them!' She knew that our boys were winning, giving back everything that was dished out to them, and with interest.

Dulcie shivered, in spite of the heat. 'I ought to be going.'

From the top floor of the *Herald* offices Bill Maguire, alone in the tall building, heard the air-raid warning at five o'clock, and chose to ignore it. But shortly afterwards his attention was caught by what appeared to be a huge, premature sunset in the east, over dockland. He got up stiffly from his desk and went to the window, just as two fire engines dashed down Fleet Street with a panicky clanging of bells. Even so he could scarcely take in what was happening. The sky behind St Paul's glowed a dull red, casting the streets into a lurid half-light. It looked as though the whole of the East End was on fire.

What Dulcie and Iris had seen from the garden in Mapleton Road was the first party of London-bound raiders from the Luftwaffe's Bomber Group 2, despatched by Goering to bring London to its knees in an estimated four days.

CHAPTER SEVENTEEN

'London pride has been handed down to us,
London pride is a flower that's free;
London pride means our own dear town to us,
And our pride it forever shall be . . .'

'London Pride'
Noel Coward, 1941

EN route to the United States, Andrea Avery was at peace. The gracious limbo of shipboard life had always pleased her. Now it recalled to mind the long-ago voyage with Kate, when life with Louis had still been good. What a delightful interlude that had been for her, because in that context she had been able to preen and show off and be altogether more frivolous and self-centred than her role within marriage permitted.

In a thousand subtle ways Louis had never allowed her to forget that theirs was a marriage of convenience, on his part anyway. From her he required not protestations of love, or tenderness, or even necessarily fidelity, so long as he was assured of her administrative talents, her business and political acumen, her energy and her good sense. These she was happy to supply, she did not disappoint him. They had been content, he with a satisfactory bargain struck, she simply glad to provide what he wanted. The knowledge that others, often people less discerning than her, disliked Louis, did not help. On the contrary it increased, perversely, her passion for him and her own self-loathing.

But on board ship, suspended between the old life and the new, she relaxed a little. As a Volunteer Escort for the Children's Overseas Reception Board she was in charge of four children, all from the same family, packed off to relations in Toronto for the duration of the war.

Alexander was six, and Sophia, Marian and Juliet seven, ten and thirteen respectively. Their well-bred restraint was almost painful. When the *City of Benares* had set sail from Liverpool on Friday 13 September, they had manfully gulped back tears, waving vigorously to their poor little mother on the dock, as the band played 'Wish Me Luck As You Wave Me Good-bye'. There had followed a day or two of stoical unhappiness, during which Andrea had done her best to be sympathetic but not intrusive. She badly wanted to be remembered kindly by the children, and in their well-brought-up way they sensed this, and responded accordingly.

Juliet, the eldest, was a plain, bespectacled, but basically jolly girl, rather weighed down by the responsibilities of the first-born. Sophia was pale and pretty and enigmatic, always writing out her times-tables in a little notebook and surrounding them with elaborate borders in coloured pencil. Maria was the most outgoing, the one who would come and press her well-padded hip against Andrea's shoulder when she sat in the second-class lounge, peering at whatever she was doing and asking questions in a voice redolent of boiled sweets. Alexander, of course, was the baby of the family, the only and much-wanted boy, a frail, dignified and myopic heir to the Gordon-Smith title and estates.

After the uneasy start, the children began, cautiously, to treat the voyage as a holiday. The *City of Benares* was flagship of the Ellerman Line, and formerly on the India run. For the children of straitened, wartime Britain it was a floating paradise, where lavish dollops of American ice-cream were served up by stately Lascar stewards in immaculate blue and white uniforms with brocade sashes. The summer just gone had seen rations for the average British family scaled down to eight ounces of sugar, four ounces of butter and tea, two ounces of bacon and one and tenpence-worth of meat per week. It was the height of a period of success which jubilant U-boat skippers dubbed *Die Glückliche Zeit* – the happy time. But the ninety or so children heading for safety aboard a cornucopia of unrationed goodies gave little thought to the U-boat menace.

Even the adults among the 300 or so passengers felt safe. They were not aware that a shortage of flotilla craft meant that the Royal Navy could not provide an anti-submarine escort more than 300 miles west of Ireland. By the evening of the seventeenth, Convoy OB 213, now reckoned to be in safe waters, had already been twenty-one hours without an escort. The nineteen ships ploughed along at a slow eight and a half knots, about half the speed the *Benares* was capable of. At twenty to ten, Andrea was in the lounge playing Halma with Juliet. Beside the table Sophia sat curled in an easy chair, laboriously tracing a woodcut illustration of a cow from her copy of *A Child's Garden of Verses*. Maria and Alexander had been banished to their cabin – the former complaining bitterly – about three-quarters of an hour earlier. During the course of the evening a Force Five gale had got up, and even the stable *Benares* was pitching and wallowing. The Halma men juddered and nudged each other on their red and black chequered board.

'Just what I wanted you to do!' said Juliet, taking one of her men and making eight hops which took her right into Andrea's camp.

'Ah, *but* –!' Andrea returned the compliment with a flourish. 'Pride goes before a fall.'

'Gosh, I hate you,' said Juliet affably, pushing her glasses up the bridge of her nose with her middle finger. 'That's the trouble with this game, it's always tit for tat.'

'The first rule of life.'

'What?'

'I beg your pardon.'

'I beg your pardon, then.'

'Nothing – come on, your go. You must go to bed at ten, whether there's a result or not.'

Sophia looked up, peering with one eye round the drooping wing of fair hair that had fallen over her face. 'Can I go now, and colour in my tracing in bed?'

'Yes, but don't get wax crayon on the sheets, there's a good girl. Do you want me to come?'

'No, of course not.' Sophia gave her a quelling look, then added in a more conciliatory tone: 'But come and say good-night when Juliet comes.'

'Right you are. If the others are still awake, tell them I'll be down in about –' she glanced at her watch – 'ten minutes, so no nonsense.' Quite fondly, Andrea watched Sophia walk away, her fine fair hair cut severely straight across her neck at the back, her book, tracing paper and wooden pencil box tucked beneath her arm.

'Go on then, I've been,' said Juliet impatiently. 'I'm moving in for the *coup de grâce*.'

'Hm.' Andrea surveyed the board. As she did so the table gave a slight jolt and the whole game slid on to the floor. A small puff of dust rose from the thick carpet.

'There you are,' said Andrea, as she and Juliet scooped up the pieces and returned them to the box. 'It looks as if the decision's been made for us – an honourable draw.'

Juliet made a face, then grinned her nice, toothy grin. 'Rotten – and I was winning.'

The steward came over to their table, bearing coffee pot and milk. 'More coffee, madam?'

'No, thank you.' Andrea got up. 'Come on, we must say good-night to the others.'

As they threaded their way across the lounge there appeared to have been one or two spillages – several ashtrays had landed upside down on the carpet, and a steward was mopping up spilt coffee by a table of wholly engrossed bridge players.

Andrea and Juliet were half way down the stairs, heading towards the children's cabins in the stern of the ship, when Juliet sniffed and remarked: 'Someone's had candles.'

'Surely not.' Andrea sniffed. 'It is like that, I agree . . .'

At the same moment they heard the first alarm bell, a distant, frantic clanging in the labyrinth of companionways.

'Right.' Andrea stopped. 'Right.' She grabbed Juliet's arm. 'You go straight to the first-class lounge. It may only be a drill, but it's important to do just as we've been told, all right?'

'But surely I can –'

'Just *go*.'

Andrea left Juliet and hurried on down. She was joined by another of the Volunteer Escorts, an elderly music teacher, heading in the same direction.

'What on earth has happened, do you have any idea?' asked the music teacher. She was oddly clothed in a long Viyella nightie, argyll socks, brogues, a gabardine mac and a felt hat.

'I'm afraid I don't,' said Andrea. 'But I feel we should be quick.'

The narrow corridors – the landscape of a nightmare, Andrea

thought — were dark, and as they went down a level, so the smell became stronger. But down here the alarm bells sounded muffled, it was as if they'd entered a lost world, deaf to danger and panic.

Not for long. The two women rounded a corner and came to a howling black abyss where the cabin-class bathrooms had been. A five-hundred-pound torpedo had exploded in Number Five hold on the *Benares'* port side, ripping off the hatches. The Atlantic was pouring into the lower hold and the ship was settling by the stern.

'The Lord is my shepherd!' quavered the music teacher, 'I shall not want, he leadeth me beside the still waters, O Lord! O Lord!'

Usually Andrea would have found this kind of outburst both irrelevant and irritating but now, as she steered her nearly hysterical companion away from the terrible yawning hole and towards their charges, she found herself echoing her sentiments. Just let them be all right, Lord, and I will try and do better.

Sophia was in the doorway of her cabin. Already there was a slight but discernible slope to the floor.

'What's the matter?'

Andrea stopped, trying to bring her breathing under control. When she spoke, she was surprised at the calmness of her voice, a calmness she did not feel. 'The ship's had an accident, and we may need to get off. Are the others asleep?'

'Sander is.'

Andrea stepped inside and shut the door. Maria was kneeling on the top bunk, near the ladder, her round pink face thunderous with suspicion. Andrea ignored her for the moment and continued to address Sophia.

'Do you remember the first-class lounge where we went on our first night — where the captain talked to us?'

'Yes.' Sophia was composed.

'When I've got Maria ready I want you to take her there *at once*. Juliet is already there, so look out for her, and when you've found her stick by her, and do everything you're told whether I'm there or not. Do you understand?'

'Yes.'

'Right, put a coat and shoes on, as many warm things as you can. Maria, come down here.'

Maria snatched up her Wol, a shapeless khaki sausage of cloth with two staring white felt eyes, and came down the ladder.

'Will we perish?' enquired Sophia, doing up her shoelaces.

'Don't be ridiculous!' snapped Andrea, and thought, God forgive me. Clumsy in her haste she helped Maria put on a tweed skirt, socks, a Fair Isle jumper, and her blue tweed coat.

'Shall I put on knickers?'

'Yes – two pairs, I should.'

Maria got some out of her locker. 'These are both over-knickers,' she remarked sensibly, 'they have pockets.'

'Good, good.' Andrea inspected the two girls briefly. 'Right, off you go, there'll be lots of other people going the same way. Sander and I will catch you up in a minute.'

They stood to attention, still a little bemused, staring at her. She clapped her hands sharply in front of their faces.

'Licketty split, off you go!'

They went. The corridor outside was now full of jostling children, some of them laughing, and sharp-voiced, anxious women. Andrea turned back to the bunks and pulled the bedclothes off Alexander's recumbent form.

'Go away!'

'Come on, Sander, we have to go upstairs, quickly.'

She hauled him out and held his staggering, drowsy form between her knees as she pulled on his flannel shorts over his pyjamas. The alarm bells clanged and clanged, like the panicky wing-beats of a trapped bird, desperate and insistent. Andrea was acutely conscious of the bigness of the ocean, miles and miles of heaving, icy black water beneath the fragile man-made hull of the *Benares*.

As she tugged Alexander's jumper over his head there was a sudden lurch and she sat down with a bump on the bedside stool. There was a crunching sound, she had broken his spectacles.

'Whoops, an accident,' she said, picking up the frames and shaking out the loose glass. 'Still, waste not.' She put the frames on his nose and hooked the wire arms around his ears. He blinked owlishly at her.

'Golly, Andrea, I can't see!'

'Don't worry, I'm here. Come on.'

They joined the stampede in the corridor. Up in the first-class lounge there was chaos. It was quite clear that a number of people had been sitting drinking, talking and playing bridge, quite oblivious to the problem. But now a drift had begun in the direction of the lifeboat stations and the atmosphere was one of simmering consternation, erupting here and there into outright panic. Few people were appropriately dressed for a nocturnal adventure on the high seas, and there was scarcely a lifejacket to be seen. Andrea could not see the three girls anywhere. She could only trust to their good sense and hope they had found each other and were doing the right thing. She held Alexander's hand tight.

'Are we sinking?' he asked in his clear, rounded voice, no longer peevish and half asleep.

'Yes,' she said. There seemed little point in half-truths at this stage. Besides, the floor now rose in front of them like a ski-slope.

'Cripes . . .'

'But there's no reason why we shouldn't all be fine if we do as we're told,' she added, for the umpteenth time, wishing fervently that she could see someone – anyone – who looked as if they might issue clear-cut instructions.

Andrea was not a woman who liked to do nothing. When she and Sander had stood in the milling throng for a few minutes and still not spotted the others, she set off in the direction of the deck.

At No. 5 lifeboat station, where the boats should have been slung from the davits for the passengers to climb aboard, certain bright sparks had launched them, and they bobbed far below on the dark, tossing sea. A fine, squally rain blew in the faces of the people on deck. The air flickered and flashed with distress flares. Suddenly, in one of these bursts of sickly pale light Andrea saw the girls, standing in a tight little group a few yards in front. Juliet must have sensed her eyes on them, for she turned, smiled with relief, pointed them out to the others, who did the same.

Her team, as it were, complete, Andrea became entirely single-minded. Ruthlessly she pushed her way to the girls' side, conscious of the kind of highly-coloured insults she had not expected to hear outside Whitechapel coming at her from all sides. She took no notice. The time had come for action. Her job was the safety of the Gordon-Smith children, and she would discharge it. This singleness of purpose made her almost happy.

'Well done, good girls. Now we must get you on to a boat.'

'But how?' Juliet's glasses were dappled with rain. 'Not down that awful ladder?'

'But of course! How else do you propose going down?'

Juliet was a picture of misery. The other three looked at her for a lead. Andrea smiled encouragingly. 'We mustn't dither, we must go.'

She thought — I'm terrified of this sort of thing, so how must they feel? But the nose of the ship was almost out of the water now, giving the sickening impression of a displacement in nature itself. The suction of the dying ship was creating a whirlpool effect which could only get worse.

Andrea grabbed Juliet's arm and thrust her roughly forward to the rail, where a young rating in an oilskin stood to help the hardier souls on their way.

'You first,' she said, 'quick, leg over.'

Juliet obeyed, momentarily more concerned about revealing the tops of her first pair of nylons to the young sailor than about the preservation of life itself.

'Attagirl,' he said. Andrea wondered how long he would remain so sanguine.

'Now you Sophia, quick.'

'I can't, honestly.' Sophia's face was bluey-white.

'No such word, my girl!' Andrea slapped her backside, not altogether comfortingly. 'Get a move on.'

'Come on, sweetheart,' said the sailor, prompting Sophia to burst into tears. But between Andrea's bullying and his soft soap, she was persuaded on to the ladder, sinking out of sight with a tragic expression, but fairly steadily.

'Now Maria, you go, and then I'll bring Sander, he's broken his glasses.'

Gamely, the plump Maria scrambled over. She had stuffed Wol down the front of her coat, and his large white eyes peered out over her top button with an astonished expression.

Andrea peered over the side. The sailor said: 'They'll be okay, lady,' but she wished she felt as certain. The girls' heads bobbed down, Juliet was almost there. The nearest boat looked ominously full, but one of the Lascars stood in the bows, tall and magnificent in his uniform, his arms outstretched encouragingly.

'Now!' Andrea bent down and shouted in Alexander's face. 'I'm going to get my feet on the ladder, and then the sailor will help you over between my arms and we'll go down together, yes?'

'Yes.' He nodded energetically, and she hugged him, felt the cold stub of his nose against her neck for a moment. People were pushing and shouting, she heard a sharp, upper class voice say: 'How typical – there's always someone ready to use children as an excuse to save their own skins, even when there are old people waiting.' She could not be bothered to argue, she hoisted her skirt and climbed over. Amidst all the confusion she had seen to it that everyone was warmly dressed except herself. She had on only her light wool dress and jacket, and brown snakeskin court shoes, all of which were now completely soaked. As her feet felt timidly for the slippery yielding steps of the rope ladder, she knew exactly how she must look – a smart, vain, self-centred woman, bent on looking after number one.

'Come on, Sander!'

She couldn't look down. The weight of the girls further down the ladder made it bounce and swing uneasily, the wind blundered round her, tugging at her wet clothes, whipping her hair into her eyes. From this angle the *Benares* was like a great black cliff face, patterned with slanting rows of lights, looming and listing in the huge unfriendly darkness. Faces were banked at the rails like pale seabirds clustered on a ledge. Alexander found his footing, the reddened hands of the sailor grasping him beneath the armpits as he did so. Andrea braced her arms on either side of him.

'I'll count,' she said, 'and you keep your feet in time with me.'

'Okay.'

She thought how fantastically brave he was, braver than she. 'Ready? Left . . . right . . . left . . . right . . .'

Painfully they progressed down the ladder. A teenage boy and an elderly couple, perhaps his parents, got on above them.

She could not believe such a frail structure would be able to bear their combined weight. She concentrated on the back of Alexander's head, just about level with her nose. The wind combed and parted his neat, newly-cut hair into little points. Suddenly she felt an icy slap of water on her calves. They were almost at the bottom.

'Stay there,' she said unnecessarily. 'Hold on tight.' With trepidation, she looked over her shoulder. The air was full of sounds, a keening of wind and frightened voices, the hiss and suck of the water. The surface, glistening with rainbow-tinted black oil slicks, was already littered with flotsam – a music case, a chair, a plant in a pot, a soft toy (which she refused to identify as Wol).

The boat bearing the girls had already moved away from the dangerous suction of the sinking *Benares*. She could see the white figure of the Lascar steward still standing in the bows, as if in mute, dignified apology for his departure. For a second, Andrea was panic-stricken. The ladder now groaned beneath the weight of ten people, the massive leviathan-hulk of the ship rose above them as if at any moment it might topple and crush them. Beneath her thinly-shod feet the black unfriendly ocean heaved and grabbed.

She put her lips to Alexander's cold, pink ear and shouted: 'Can you swim?'

'Not really.' He turned his head a little. 'Sorry.'

Inwardly Andrea cursed Zinnia Gordon-Smith for having brought up her son in a seaside town without teaching him to swim. She herself had not swum since she had been on family holidays at Sandwich before the last war, and she hadn't been much good then.

'Never mind,' she said. 'Hold tight to me.'

She took another look. There was a large slab of wreckage, part of the hull, apparently, no more than fifteen yards away. It was the only substantial object that she stood any chance of reaching. Putting one arm round Alexander's waist she said, almost brightly: 'Let's go!' and launched herself on to the oily black swell.

They say you don't lose the ability to swim, and this proved true in Andrea's case. It was awkward gripping Alexander and paddling at the same time, but not impossible. She was able to keep them both afloat by treading water. Her expensive shoes came off and drifted down to Davy Jones's locker within seconds. The cold was her worst enemy, she gulped and fought for breath. Her one free arm flailed and beat down the water, but they made no progress. It was the boy who entered the water after them who was the great swimmer, ploughing sturdily past them, smashing and thrashing the swell with strong arms, and reaching the raft of wreckage. Andrea did not dare look back for the old couple.

The boy pulled himself up, and turned, squatting on the edge of the raft and holding out his arms, making beckoning motions with his hands.

'Come on, you can do it!'

He looked odd, dressed in evening clothes, his first dinner suit, probably, complete with satin cummerbund and bow tie, but smeared with oil and dripping wet. Andrea swam for all she was worth, she could feel Alexander paddling too, though his small ineffectual movements were more of a hindrance than a help. The cold of the water was intense and her legs in their thin stockings were becoming numb. She knew if she became frantic she would stiffen up and it would be harder, so she tried simply to keep going, moving by inches, if at all.

When they were perhaps six or seven yards from their objective, the slab of wreckage suddenly lurched towards them, carried by a freak wave. It happened quickly, it was upon them, with all her strength Andrea thrust Alexander forward and upward into the reaching hands of the youth, felt the child's dragging weight transfer from her to him. But as she let go, something struck her a sharp blow on the bridge of the nose. She was so cold that she scarcely felt any pain, just a kind of thud, and a spreading boom like a contained explosion inside her head. This was followed by a falling, drifting sensation as she sank.

'Andrea!' She heard a voice shout, and fancied that it might be Louis, wanting her back. But it was too late, much too late. Finally, Andrea had given up.

During the autumn of 1940, Londoners felt they were being squeezed in an iron fist, compressing the world around them, so that London *became* England, her hard-pressed but still beating heart. It suited them to think that if they succumbed, so would the rest of her. In consequence, since that first terrible afternoon, they had contrived to make their ordeal by fire seem like normality.

As soon as Bill had realized the significance of that lurid glow over the East End he had dashed down into the street and hijacked a seat in a fire officer's control car at the foot of Ludgate Hill. This importunate behaviour was made possible by the fact that his was now a 'name'. He was not welcome in the control car, but he was tolerated. Besides, the fire officer had his mind on other things.

'Christ almighty . . . I've never seen anything like this . . . never.'

'Can your people cope?'

The man shrugged. His square, sensible, moustachioed face was harshly lit by the fires ahead of them. 'God alone knows. I doubt it.'

London's dockland was a snarling inferno. At Surrey Commercial Docks 250 acres of resinous timber, stacked to a depth of over twenty feet and in prime dry condition after the excellent summer, flared and crackled in a jungle of flame. Water pumped by fireboats from a river already choked with burning vessels simply evaporated into hissing clouds of steam as it struck the blaze. The old dockland roadways made up of wooden blocks glowed red like rivers of molten lava. The great black skeletons of burning buildings trembled and leaned before the onslaught of the fire, then tumbled like matchwood, swallowed up in the rushing, voracious flames.

Around this holocaust, little scampering, gesticulating pin-men tried to contain its fury. Out of a fire brigade of 30,000, ninety per cent were wartime auxiliaries, until now scathingly known as the 'Darts Brigade', most of whom had never tackled a fire before in their lives. Never had the expression 'baptism by fire' become more apposite for more people. The streets of the East End teemed with courageous tenderfeet, doing their level best to cope with the stuff of nightmares. The London air-raid wardens and their part-time volunteers set out to tackle a full-scale blitz armed with little more than a scant knowledge of toxic gases, a tin hat marked 'W', and a whistle.

By dusk the London fire brigade had logged a thousand separate calls, and all through the night Goering's airborne armada kept coming, replenishing fires whose intensity made the use of water futile.

By the time Bill returned to his office at eight o'clock on Sunday morning, the view from the windows of the *Herald* was very different. In place of the racing, leaping dance of the hungry flames over Poplar, Whitechapel and Wapping, there was now an acrid pall of smoke and steam, and a wasteland of damp and blackened ruins. But the Darts Brigade had proved themselves.

During the days following that first blitz, 'Invasion' had been the watchword. Home Guardsmen armed with everything from assegais to garden spades had kept watch, and tolled church bells (on their own initiative) to warn of imminent attack. On the south coast roads motorists kept their passes at the ready, bayonets glinted ominously at frequent check points, bugles echoed eerily from hill to hill, false alarms were rife.

But the expected invasion hadn't happened. After three days of intense bombing the Port of London had been closed to ocean-going shipping, and vessels were being re-routed to ports all over Britain. But the mass panic and demoralization of Londoners, so hoped for by the Luftwaffe, was not apparent. On the contrary, as Bill remarked on morning forays into the devastation of the East End, morale rose in direct proportion to the amount of high explosive dropped during the night.

On Sunday 15 September, the Luftwaffe had made one massive final attempt to lure the RAF up into the air for a pitched battle. By midday the best part of a hundred and fifty German bombers had broken through to the sky over central London, the signal for a huge aerial battle. An air corridor thirty miles wide and more than twice as long was packed with thousands of planes, locked together in hundreds of separate dog fights. But by the time the last of the raiders disappeared over the Channel at four o'clock, their losses were considerably greater than those suffered by the RAF. Though the awestruck watchers on the ground could not have known it, the tide had turned. Invasion was no longer likely.

Now, in the second half of October, East Enders had adapted to a new way of life. The first 'Shelter Census' showed that nearly 200,000 Londoners had taken to the underground; whole nocturnal, subterranean communities had been established. Bill, setting out to write a series of features on this phenomenon for the *Herald*, found that shelter life had evolved its own rules and regulations. In some boroughs a shelter admission card was issued, listing particulars of the holder on one side, and on the other a lengthy injunction concerning the pass's removal at any time at the controller's discretion, and adding: 'If not occupied by twelve midnight, bunks will not be reserved for absent ticket holders.'

Inevitably, some public shelters quickly gained a reputation for horrific squalor, while others became almost unofficial social clubs. At Archway Hall in north London Bill joined a queue royally entertained by exuberant buskers.

'It's lovely in 'ere,' he was assured by one elderly lady, accompanied by her husband and an elderly mongrel on a lead. 'We wouldn't miss it for the world.'

'Do you come every night?' enquired Bill of the husband.

'Yes sir, every night. They do you proud here.'

And indeed, there were plentiful refreshments, clean comfortable bunks, and a trio of indefatigable musicians. Though Bill was by no means clear why the Archway Hall should be more immune to the effects of bombing than any other building.

At the other end of the scale was one north-east London tube station, whose night-time patrons were probably safe, but at some considerable cost to health and human dignity. The overcrowding was appalling. Raw sewage ran over the dirty platforms from three buckets which served as lavatories, and couples copulated in full view of hundreds of others, including young children and the very old. The prevailing atmosphere was explosive, continual bickering over places and orders erupted frequently into skirmishes, or fights which spread into bloody brawls, scattering the weak and frightened to fend for themselves as best they could. Latecomers straight from the pubs added to the edginess with their unpredictable tempers, their warbling singing and shouts of fury echoed threateningly round the tiled tunnels and halls, little puddles of vomit and urine lay here and there to trap the unwary. Bill was shaken.

He emerged into the cold dawn streets gasping for air, like a diver surfacing from the bottom of the sea.

But the news from Malta made it clear that whatever Londoners might be suffering, Malta suffered a hundredfold. It seemed to Bill that it was typical of Kate to go out of the frying pan into the fire. He felt a kind of perverse proprietary satisfaction to think of her there, on that small speck of land, in the teeth of danger. And yet he felt her absence as a kind of continuous, violent rage. His need of her was acute and ferocious, and became more so with each day that passed. It was almost as though his feelings, once spoken, had become stronger, like animals released from their cages. His longing for Kate was quite specific: he had only to close his eyes to recall the exact texture of her hair and skin, the taste of her mouth, the feel of her long, coltish figure, the fierce wary expression of her yellowish eyes. He dreamed about her, and awoke sweating and aroused. Sometimes he was in Dulcie's bed when this happened and he would make love to one woman while thinking of another.

The plain fact was that although he continued to spend a lot of time with Dulcie, he had almost ceased to see her. The present woman was actually less real to him than the absent. He was consumed with a desolating sense of waste, as if Kate were a physical part of him that would wither with disuse. He was too old to let that happen. As the blitz on London continued so his determination increased. A fierce, amoral energy swept through him, he wanted to be with Kate, more than anything else he could think of, and he thought of little else. This feeling was quite unlike the loyal and warm affection he had for Dulcie, as different as a domestic hearth from the hungry fires that consumed London. He was helpless before its arrogant, imperative force.

Incidents which might previously have shocked him left him strangely unmoved, as though this one feeling for Kate had drained him of all others. One such was on the morning after a large public shelter in Beaufort Street had received a direct hit. There were no survivors. When Bill got there at eight am, the scene was bleak, grey and sombre, bitterly cold, shrouded in damp autumn fog and clouds of dust as the rescue workers hauled lumps of rubble aside to free the corpses. Among the workers were one or two women ambulance drivers from a nearby depot. Bill went to the assistance of one of them, who was tugging at a huge concrete paving stone.

'Oh, thanks!' She was plump and pink-cheeked and upper class, full of bright, untried enthusiasm.

'Someone under here?' he asked, curling his fingers over the edge of the slab, getting a good grip.

'Almost bound to be I'm afraid. There were so many people inside.' They tugged at the paving stone until the corner began to lift.

'I'll take the strain,' he said. 'You go round and give it a push, then we can lower it this side.'

The girl went round to the far side and began pushing with her hands in Fair Isle knitted gloves. As the slab of concrete rose before their combined efforts, the expression on the girl's face changed from one of effort and concentration to one of sickened horror. When Bill had taken the edge of the now-vertical slab, and was beginning to lower it to the ground, she put her fingers to her mouth in an incongruously genteel gesture and said in a small voice, 'Would you excuse me — I'm awfully sorry —'

Bill nodded, released the stone, and looked at what it revealed. Lying in a kind of trough was the body of a young woman. She lay half on her side, one arm thrown up above her head, her legs spread as if running, in a macabre parody of a swastika. Her half-born baby protruded from her skirt, its small, damp, black head lolling on a fragile stem of neck. The woman's head, arm and thorax were badly crushed, but the baby was unmarked. It had experienced life and death at almost the same moment. Bill found himself staring at it with detached interest. Only the reappearance of the girl shook him out of his reverie.

'We'd better do something with them.'

'Of course.'

She had been sick, he could smell it on her breath, and her face was damp and white, but she had recovered her composure. She went to the demolition truck and collected two of the blue waterproof bags that passed for winding sheets. She was still squeamish, but Bill packaged the mother and baby in the bags, one down over the head, one up from the feet, and tied them in the middle with a length of string.

He spent another hour helping the rescue workers, during which time they uncovered another twenty bodies, some looking as if they had just fallen asleep, suffocated but preserved intact in some freak bubble in the mass of fallen masonry, others crushed and mutilated beyond recognition. And there were the bits and pieces – a leaf-shaped scalp, still greasy with Brylcreem, clinging to the stone which had stove in a man's skull; arms, and hands, with wedding rings; bodyless heads and decapitated bodies still partially clad in warm winter underwear, and corsets, and cardigans. Bill worked and worked until he was exhausted, but not saddened. It was only death, only debris, and at the moment his concern was life.

About a week later he and Dulcie went with Giles and Ernest, at Giles's invitation, to the Strand Theatre, to see some of Sir Donald Wolfit's lunch-time Shakespeare. The bombs had now been dropping on London for fifty-seven consecutive nights and Londoners, perhaps more from defiance than love of the Bard, had swelled the Strand's audience to a thousand a week. Sir Donald's company presented favourite scenes and snippets fortissimo to drown any interruptions whether from the audience, the sirens or the Luftwaffe itself. The back of the theatre had been damaged by bomb blast, so that when the curtain went up a distinct chilly draught could be felt by the audience, but the players had turned even this to their advantage by using the damaged stage-door as a bier during a death scene.

After the show the four of them went to Rules for a late lunch. The restaurant was packed, its clientele enjoying themselves. The good life, rather surprisingly, continued. Newspaper and magazine photographs of the well-to-do eating in smart restaurants and dancing in expensive clubs were not suppressed, perhaps to show that Hitler could no more alter the time-honoured pursuits of the rich than he could cow the ebullience of the poor. Three hundred thousand tons of shipping had now succumbed to Donitz's torpedoes, the classic English breakfast had become a thing of the past, but on this occasion Bill, Dulcie, Ernest and Giles were able to enjoy vegetable soup, braised Scotch beef and charlotte russe.

Bill conversed with Ernest, since Giles and Dulcie were deep in enjoyable villification of some actor of their mutual acquaintance. 'Have you been to see your family lately, Ernest?' he enquired. 'How are they making out?'

'They're spending the night in the tube,' replied Ernest, 'they've got it all worked out. My mum's got a wheelchair, and they've got their own patch down there.'

Giles caught the tail end of this. 'I have suggested that he might like to bring his mother up to us for a while,' he said. 'But he assured me she's happier where she is.'

'I'm sure that's true,' said Dulcie, 'I can understand that.'

Ernest cast her a scathing look. 'Can you?'

'I think so,' said Dulcie stalwartly.

Bill continued: 'Well organized is it, the tube station?'

'Yes it is,' replied Ernest in the same truculent tone. But he liked talking to Bill, the sensation of being interviewed was titillating. 'They've got proper segregated dormitories, a lady doing hairdressing, fruit and veg barrows, you name it. It's like a hotel.'

'I must say,' remarked Bill, 'I've been impressed by some of those I've seen. It's just the sheer weight of numbers that concerns me, and the lack of proper supervision at the entrances, and so on. But otherwise –' he raised his hands, disclaiming – 'a marvellous display of initiative.'

Giles was looking at Dulcie, who was peering over his shoulder at someone on the far side of the room. 'What is it?'

'I can hardly believe –' she craned her neck. 'I think that's Louis Avery over there.'

Giles pulled a face. 'Saints preserve us. Who with?'

Dulcie broke her bread roll, crumbling it delicately, trying not to stare. 'A young couple, she's very pretty.'

Pointedly, Ernest looked over his shoulder. 'Very nice, *très chic*!'

'Mainly just young,' said Bill. 'Steady on, do we want to catch his eye?'

'No,' Giles was emphatic.

'No,' said Dulcie, 'but I'm going to go over in a moment, because I do want to ask about Andrea.'

Bill looked at her in surprise. 'Would that be wise? I mean – he's the villain of the piece, isn't he?'

'I don't think we're necessarily supposed to know that. And I literally never had another peep out of Andrea since Aubrey's wedding in the summer. I'm perfectly entitled to enquire after a friend.'

'It's the wine talking,' Giles said to Bill.

Dulcie ignored this. 'Oh look, they're going, I'd better –'

She slipped out of the banquette, leaving her napkin on the seat, and was already halfway across the room before she realized that the young and pretty girl was not with the young man, but with Louis. It was his arm to which she clung, vivacious and a little arch, while the rather stern-faced younger man stood to one side with his hands in his pockets.

But by the time this awkward fact had borne in upon Dulcie she was committed to making her move, and Louis had seen her. Had she herself not felt acutely embarrassed she might have taken some satisfaction from his brief but genuine expression of dismay.

But it was only brief, he was nothing if not self-possessed. He kept the girl's hand in the crook of his left arm, stretching out his right hand to Dulcie and smiling broadly.

'My dear Dulcie! How altogether delightful.'

'Hallo Louis.' Dulcie stared pointedly at his companion, but Louis rose smoothly to the occasion.

'Let me introduce two young friends – Cynthia Lancaster, Paul Rowlandson. This is Dulcie Tennant.'

Dulcie smiled a little frostily. 'I don't want to keep you, I can see you're just going – I wondered what news of Andrea?'

Louis arranged his small, regular features, which these days were becoming insignificant in his increasingly fleshy face, into the earnest expression more suitable for discussion of his wife.

'You mean you've heard nothing?'

'No. I didn't really expect to. She told me at my brother's wedding that she was thinking of taking a new job, but that was all. Since then – well, I just wondered how she was getting on.'

Louis shook his head. 'Oh, Dulcie.'

The girl Cynthia disengaged herself. 'Shall we wait outside?'

'That's a good idea,' Louis patted her hand, 'I shan't be a

moment.' He watched her go with an indulgent expression. 'A gifted copywriter, that young lady,' he murmured.

'And Andrea?'

He put his hand to his brow and lowered his head, as if seeking the right words. When he at last looked into Dulcie's face his eyes were mournful: 'Dulcie, this is really most unfortunate, neither the time nor the place . . .'

'What on earth do you mean?'

He put his hand on her shoulder and advanced his face to hers so that she could smell the pampered fragrance of his skin. 'She's dead, Dulcie. Andrea is dead.'

Dulcie felt a lurch of shock. 'What?' she said stupidly.

Louis lowered his voice, glancing from side to side with a bizarre air of well-bred discretion.

'I'm so sorry, Dulcie. I was trying to think of a way of letting you know. Terrible.' He shook his head. 'Terrible . . .'

'But how?' asked Dulcie. She was not interested in his self-indulgent maunderings, she knew them to be meaningless. 'What happened?'

'She was on that ship, the *City of Benares*, you probably read it in the papers. It was torpedoed by U-boats – the most appalling loss of life.'

Dulcie vaguely remembered something. 'There were a lot of children, evacuees –'

'Yes, she was a volunteer escort.'

Dulcie could not take all this in. 'Has there been a funeral or anything?'

'There is to be a memorial service.'

'I want to come.'

'Of course. I understand she was rather brave.'

'Yes,' said Dulcie, 'she would be.'

She half-heard Louis make some further pompous, suitably glum remarks, and then some quicker words of self-excuse. She had always got on quite well with Louis, but now she felt that the scales had fallen from her eyes.

She cut across what he was saying. 'Please let me know when the service is to be.' Then she turned quickly and walked back to the others, without saying good-bye.

Bill rose and took her arm as she sat down. 'Dulcie? Christ

Almighty, you look terrible, what on earth was he saying to you?'

'Andrea's dead,' she said, plainly and clearly, trying to give this bleak fact some reality in her own mind as well as theirs. Andrea white and bloated, tossed and swamped in a freezing, mountainous sea, Andrea with her hair draggled, her eyes staring, her mouth gaping. Andrea who had been 'rather brave'.

'Andrea was drowned,' she said again, in the same sort of voice. They reacted sympathetically, in their different ways, hands reached out to her, a little wash of warm, understanding words eddied round her, but could not affect her. The sheer injustice of it took her breath away. Andrea had always *tried*, had fought and coped and endured and not been afraid of unpopularity; Andrea who had even found an unselfish and practical solution to the heartlessness of the dreadful Louis. If this could happen to Andrea, thought Dulcie, then nobody was safe. She turned to Bill. He appeared to be saying something, but she couldn't hear him. She simply said: 'Please take me home.'

'They got no guts!' said Connie to Kate, delivering her usual succinct assessment of the Regia Aeronautica with as much *élan* as if she'd never said it before. 'They know if they come down any closer we biff 'em!'

'I'm sure you're right, Connie.' Kate had her bike propped up in the shade of the cloister by the living room window, and was oiling and cleaning it. Connie, her Maltese cook, stood by her, wiping her huge hands on her apron. The roles of employer and employee were blurred in the case of Connie and Kate, and yet somehow understood by both. Connie had come with good references from a naval officer's wife who had left the island: 'Connie Bazaru is a good worker and quite unflappable,' the reference had said, 'and I have no hesitation in recommending her for any domestic post.'

Connie was a native of Zemola, and her husband Pawli was one of those who, in spite of being too old for the regular army, possessed a shotgun and had enlisted in the Malta Volunteer Defence Force. Pawli was now an important person, and occasionally looked in to see if all was well at the house in Strada Forni, wearing his steel helmet and official armband, his shotgun (free cartridges supplied) under his arm. These visits would throw Connie into a turmoil of emotion. She spent much of her time inveighing against Pawli who, she said, was a shiftless drunk and no use to anyone — 'he make me pregnant so I can't chase him' was a favourite saying of hers — but the sight of him in the service of his country was too much for her. She was wildly sentimental and would break into floods of tears on his departure, even though he was invariably going no further than the town square to check the coffee supplies. On these occasions he ceased to be the cowardly impregnator and became a paragon among family men, prepared to defend hearth, home and country with his life. Connie and Pawli had four children, all married, and Connie was a grandmother several times over, though she herself was only in her middle forties.

Connie was also hugely fat. She wore her fat like a kind of magnificent gown or cloak — it swung and rippled round her in greasy splendour and she was not ashamed of it. And indeed, as supplies on the island grew more scarce, it became a heartening experience to see someone so extravagantly well-larded.

The naval wife's comment that Connie was 'unflappable' was well justified. There was little that troubled or dismayed her. All her considerable emotional vocabulary was squandered on imagined dangers, loves and sadnesses; given a real crisis she reacted with sturdy matter-of-factness. Her cooking was sublime, though to watch a meal in preparation was to kill the appetite at a stroke. Her approach to food was wholly tactile. She kneaded, pressed, slapped, pummelled and fondled her dishes into being with her huge cushiony hands, the same hands with which she adjusted her thick, tangled hair, wiped her brow, scratched her armpits and pulled her sweat-soaked clothing away from her body.

Now Kate spun the pedals of the bike, which seemed to be turning freely again. 'That's better.' She glanced up at Connie. 'Can I do anything for you, Connie?'

'We got nothing to fear,' said Connie, referring more to the war than the domestic arrangements.

'Good.' Kate sat back on her heels, wiping her hands on a rag. Experimentally, she reached up and rang the small blue bell on the handlebars.

'Air-raid warning! Air raid warning!' cried Connie, and laughed her rich, wheezy laugh. She saw her function in the Drakes' household as mainly social, to prevent them from getting dull or depressed.

Since June, a new kind of order had established itself on the island. Though invasion seemed inevitable, the Maltese people had nothing but scorn for the Italians who were so wary of the dockyard barrage that they scarcely came within striking distance. Often, they just dropped their bombs on fields or in the sea and retreated hastily. Not until 16 July had a British aircraft been shot down, bringing the score to 12–1. The arrival of Hurricanes to the airfields of Malta had been the cause of general jubilation, and the civilian population were now so confident that more and more of them gave up the shelters altogether during raids, and would crowd the rooftops and bastions to cheer the defenders on. They were less worried by the inaccurate Italian bombing than by the practical problems which confronted them from day to day. Accommodation had to be found for the refugees from the cities, and the distribution of foodstuffs was a priority, since there had been no replenishment since June. Everyone had a ration card, but so far most had adapted to fluctuating supplies in an *ad hoc* way: farmers milked goats out for a few extra pennies, and when kerosene became scarce people resorted to the *kenur*, an old-fashioned open stone cooker, which could be carried around with one's possessions and lit with sticks.

The authorities' main preoccupation had been the strengthening of the island's defences – swelling the ranks of the Royal Malta Artillery and the King's Own Malta Regiment, forming the Malta Volunteer Defence Force. The beaches now bristled with pill-boxes and barbed wire, the coast roads were pitted with tank traps and minefields. Wherever possible shelters were dug, rather than constructed. Every able-bodied man attacked the rock with pick axe and shovel until by the end of September literally hundreds of official public shelters had been dug, and hundreds more had been tunnelled out by individual families for their own use. New, wartime communities had formed, like the one to which Antonina's family belonged in The Ditch at Floriana, which actually boasted its own boy scout troop.

Kate had speedily found herself an occupation. With Lawrence absent for six days out of seven, and the small, parochial world of Zemola completely dominated by the demands of church and land, it was soon clear that she would be more likely to die of boredom than bombs. She had enlisted in the ranks of Zemola's refugee welfare group, and spent most mornings at the town hall, making huge vats of soup, or typing inventories or lists of names on a bulky, old-fashioned typewriter. She preferred to be more active, and kept her bike in good running order so that she could herself perform the errands, carry the messages and do the menial marketing which Father Fenech would have preferred to give to the local boy scouts. She became a sort of recognized local oddity in her trousers and cycle clips, her hair pushed into an old army beret of Lawrence's, pedalling furiously hither and thither. She put more into her alloted tasks than they merited, because they stopped her thinking of Bill.

It was 22 December, nearly Christmas. Tonight, Lawrence would be back on a twenty-four-hour pass. Her attitude towards his return was ambivalent. It was a comfort to have him there because he was the reality, the here and now, and he loved her, of that there was no doubt. She sank into that love as a child buries its head in a pillow at night, to shut out fears of the unknown and the dark. She wanted to be worthy of it, but she also wanted Bill. She did not understand the position in which she found herself; she felt trapped, baffled and miserable like a wild animal in captivity. The war did not frighten her, it was her ally. The constant raids, the uncertainty and the excitement, created an atmosphere in which her preoccupations went unnoticed. Lawrence came and went in her life, full of exuberant energy, carried on a permanent high tide of purposeful activity in which she could take no part. She was sharply aware that Beth, now magnificently pregnant, was more able to rise to Lawrence's buoyant mood than she was herself. Sometimes she felt that the two of them had formed a special friendship which she could never understand and in which she was not equipped to participate. The possibility of forming a similar, rival alliance with Josh would have been repugnant had it ever entered her head, and anyway, he did not seem to notice anything untoward.

She suspected that Connie intuited a good deal about her. Now she wished her cook would stop standing there, staring.

'Can I help, Connie?' she asked, pointedly.

Connie raised a broad hand, like a plate, and shook her head. 'Is all under control.'

'Have you made up a bed for Mrs Maloney?' She saw that she had her there.

'No, I do it now.'

'Thank you, Connie.'

The house in Strada Forni, and the adjacent convent of which it was part, had a large communal cellar, and it was this built-in shelter which had prompted Josh to suggest that Beth might move in with Kate for the last two weeks of her pregnancy, for reasons of both company and security. The Maloneys' car had been studiously topped-up with precious rationed petrol, ready for the dash to hospital when it came. A little later, Kate was to collect her friend, and Antonina, from Strada Comina.

There was a knock on the courtyard door and Kate crossed the garden to answer it. A man stood there, typically small, brilliant-eyed and hook-nosed like a sparrow hawk. He wore a cloth cap in what Kate was accustomed to think of as Prince of Wales checks, a tartan shirt and a donkey jacket. The cap was pulled down jauntily low, he wanted to sell her something.

'Good afternoon. Yes?'

'*Sahha*. Fish?' He pointed at the small handcart he was pushing. In spite of the strong afternoon sun the fish seemed fresh, the gleaming arched bodies piled on one another in silvery abundance. She thought of Beth — pregnant women needed iron.

'They look nice. Yes, I'll have some, wait a minute.'

She ran indoors and up to her bedroom for her purse. When she came back she found Connie there, engaged in lively discussion with the salesman, gesticulating at the fish, prodding the tartan shirt with fat, splayed fingers.

'What's the matter, Connie?' Kate was irritated.

'I know this man,' said Connie. She rolled her eyes darkly.

'Yes? And?'

'He is not a fisherman.'

'Oh.' Kate looked at the man. He shrugged, take it or leave it. 'Does that matter? The fish look nice and fresh.'

'But where do they come from?' Connie gave her a meaningful look.

'The sea, I imagine. Connie please go and get on.'

'*I* go,' said the little man, and picked up the shafts of the barrow.

'No, I want some!'

While Kate paid him, Connie withdrew, puffing affrontedly. Kate then took the fish to the kitchen and laid them on the table, topped by a small piece of paper on which she had written: 'Connie – supper? Mrs Maloney would like these.'

Later in the afternoon she walked the two hundred yards to the Maloneys' house to collect Beth. Antonina opened the door, smiling her sweet, rather faded, little girl's smile. The plan was that she would join them in Strada Forni to take advantage of the shelter at night, and return to Strada Comina by day to keep the house clean and aired. Kate loaded Antonina into the back of the Maloneys' car, with Beth's considerable luggage, and then assisted Beth, who was by now carrying all before her.

'Do you think I'm even going to be able to get in?' she asked, laughing.

'We could always put you on top.'

'And wreck the bodywork? Josh would never forgive us.'

In spite of her size, Beth had lived up to the maxim that pregnant women are beautiful. She was peachy and rounded, her thick brown hair swung lustrously in spite of a shortage of bathing water, her eyes were bright, her nails unbroken. Kate felt that she must look a dried-up and somewhat androgynous creature alongside her friend.

All the same, she had thrown herself into the care and maintenance of Beth's pregnancy both as a labour of love and as a useful activity to keep her mind off Bill. She came off duty at the town hall at lunch time, and went on duty with Beth, fetching and carrying and foraging and shopping, or just keeping her company. She could not have been more solicitous if the child in Beth's uterus had been her own, though she was glad it was not. Her picture of marriage to Lawrence, even when it had all been plain sailing, had never included children, and still didn't, though she knew he would have liked it. Her slavelike devotion to Beth was a kind of compensation, and Beth had the happy knack of accepting her attentions with a good grace.

Kate leaned across Beth and closed the door. 'How are you?' she asked, releasing the handbrake and letting the car roll gently down the hill to Strada Forni.

'Oh, fine, never better!' Beth put a hand to the back of her neck and lifted her mane of silky hair with one hand, with an air of comfortable, cat-like narcissism. 'I think pregnancy has provided exactly the tranquillizing necessary to put up with all this nonsense. I can honestly recommend it.'

'A lost cause in my case.'

'You always say that.'

'Because I mean it.'

'You sound like my old nanny.'

'I am your old nanny just at the moment.' She stopped the car and put on the handbrake. 'Stay there and I'll come round and help you out.'

As they got out a little dark-eyed nun came out of the convent door like one of the gliding wooden figures on a weather-clock. She smiled at them and raised her hand towards Beth in a graceful, blessing gesture.

Beth smiled sweetly back. 'They make me feel such a swine for not being religious.'

Kate relieved Antonina of Beth's pink vanity case, and a suitcase with a broken lock, tied round with a pair of old stockings. She grinned at her friend.

'You shouldn't worry. It's the time of year, perhaps they think you've conceived immaculately.'

Antonina caught the drift of this, and giggled. In the house, Kate parked Beth in the sitting room, despatched Antonina and the luggage upstairs to unpack, and ascertained that Connie was preparing the fish for supper.

As she returned, Beth said: 'Something smells good.'

'Yes, it does, doesn't it? I bought some fish off a barrow-man this afternoon, but Connie seemed to think he was some kind of gangster, and I wasn't at all sure I'd be able to persuade her to cook it. However, she has capitulated.'

Beth put her feet up on the arm of the small sofa, which sagged beneath her weight. 'Does Lawrence come tonight?'

'Yes, he's got twenty-four hours.'

'How nice.'

'What about Josh?' Kate was more comfortable discussing a different husband.

'Oh, my dear, he's only just gone back. Unless I produce a whole litter or something he won't reappear for ten days.'

'Poor Beth.'

'No, no, to be perfectly honest Kate I'm happier with him out of the way. He fusses dreadfully, worse than my mother – or my old nanny.'

They ate the fish at supper, superbly cooked by Connie, who sulked in her tent, and prettily served by Antonina, her hair caught up at the side in a sparkly plastic clip.

'It's delicious,' said Beth.

Kate put down her knife and fork and smacked her lips thoughtfully. 'Yes, it was nice – but it has an aftertaste.'

'A bit, yes, a little. Nothing to worry about. It's not off.'

'I just wish I could place it.'

'Well this may sound fanciful,' said Beth, picking a scrap of fish off the skin of her plate and chewing it. 'But it's a sort of whiff of charring – although Connie hasn't burnt it or anything –'

'That's it! I know what it is – she said he wasn't a fisherman!'

'I'm sorry?'

Kate picked up her plate and sniffed. 'TNT.'

'For goodness sake!'

'Yes it is, it's TNT, he must have dredged the fish out of the harbour after last night's raid. If that doesn't blast Maloney *fils* out of his corner, nothing will!'

They collapsed, helpless with laughter. Even the arrival of a lowering Connie made no difference, and her staccato enquiry as to whether they'd enjoyed their meal just caused a fresh outburst of hilarity.

At eight o'clock, the siren sounded. On the way down the narrow, precipitous stairs to the cellar, Beth glanced over her shoulder at Kate, and remarked: 'I'm sorry, I can't deceive you any longer.'

'What about?'

'You were right about the TNT.'

Kate turned to Connie who was on the stairs behind her. 'Connie, I think Mrs Maloney is in labour. Could you get some towels and a big jug of water —' she looked beseechingly into the cook's still rather sullen face, 'and anything else we might need?'

Childbirth was an area in which Connie was an expert. In a house full of nuns and young women, she reigned supreme, the matriarch of a large and healthy brood. She cheered up almost at once and trudged back up into the house, taking the whey-faced Antonina with her. Kate could hear her bustling about, chivvying and shouting orders, right back on form. The wail of the siren still threaded through the starry black darkness above the rooftops.

At the bottom of the stairs, Beth caught Kate's arm. 'What on earth are we going to do? This is idiotic.'

Kate felt surprisingly calm. 'We shall be fine. A first labour goes on for ages, doesn't it?'

'Well . . .'

'Of course it does, you'll still be at it this time tomorrow, I'm only taking a few precautions. When the raid's over I'll get you down to the hospital.'

As she finished speaking, Beth's grip tightened on her wrist and her face assumed an almost comical expression of discomfort and anxiety. When it had passed, Kate asked: 'How often are they coming?'

'About every five minutes.'

Kate held her hand, firmly. 'You'll be fine.'

The cellar was large, but low. Though Beth could just about stand fully upright in it, Kate could not. It was, however, quite well equipped with a kerosene lamp, a couple of mattresses, bedding, some tinned food and sweets, a *kenur* (for emergencies only, since the cellar's door was its only ventilation), some first-aid essentials, and a handsome china chamber pot behind a clothes' horse in one corner.

Kate lit the lamp and hung it from its hook in the ceiling, saying, 'Are you going to lie down?'

Beth shook her head. 'No, that's much too final, I'd rather move about a bit.'

They shared the cellar with the nuns. At the far end the

sisters were gathered round a homemade altar — a wooden crate, a lace tablecloth, a crucifix and a nightlight in a saucer — saying prayers. Only one of them turned and gave Beth and Kate a little secret bow and a smile, the rest of them were concentrating on their devotions. Kate found their presence both a comfort of sorts — faith by proxy — and an irritation. Their serene, slightly smug virginity annoyed her, they were so perfectly, irreproachably shielded from the mess of ordinary women's lives. At that moment, Kate could see little merit in the cleanliness and order of spirituality.

Connie and Antonina returned with supplies of towels, and a clean pillow, and two jugs of water, and a kettle which Connie had had the foresight to bring to the boil once in the kitchen so that it could be reheated quickly on the kenur. Seeing the nuns, Antonina went at once to join them, laying on her dark hair a small hankie emblazoned with a picture of Micky Mouse, and kneeling with eyes closed. Connie sucked her teeth noisily.

Beth began to walk slowly up and down, her hands on the area where her hips had once been. Kate fell in beside her.

'They're a long time coming,' Beth said.

'I thought you said every five minutes.'

'The bombers, stupid.'

'Oh, they'll be here. That'll keep your mind off things.' For no particular reason, she added: 'I had a French nanny when I was little. When the Germans were bombing Paris, she used to make me get up in the night and drink cocoa with her in the kitchen, to keep her company. She was much more frightened than I was, funny isn't it?'

'I'd laugh,' said Beth, 'only I've got this bloody great pain!'

Kate stood quietly by her. In a minute or so they continued their walking and now, above the gentle susurration of the nuns, they could hear the approaching bombers. Connie sat on a box by the *kenur*, her huge legs apart, her hands on her knees. At the sound of the planes she rolled her eyes upward and grimaced expressively. If looks could kill, Italian pilots would have rained down on Zemola.

Beth knelt down for the next pain. Kate was conscious of her friend's concentration deepening, she was reminded of animals, who creep away, who increase in dignity and stature as they prepare to give birth. She felt respectful. Beth's eyes were closed, her mouth pursed. Her attractive dimples made two deep clefts in her cheeks, but she didn't make a sound. Kate took her hand and drummed it up and down on her knee, quick and soft like running feet, speeding it up and slowing it down, distracting Beth's body from its turmoil. She had an instinctive knowledge of how to cope with physical pain – you rode it and moved with it so that it didn't catch you unawares. Emotional pain she couldn't handle, she just finished up enclosing it inside her like a snarling, scratching cat, well hidden, but cutting her to ribbons. It was with her even now. She could help Beth, but there was nothing, nothing, that she could do for herself.

As the contraction subsided she asked, 'Do you want to lie down now?'

'No, I'm all right. But I'm leaking horribly.'

Kate looked down. 'What do you want to do? I'll take you upstairs to the lav if you like.'

Beth shook her head. 'It wouldn't help, it's the waters, they'll just keep on coming till we're ankle deep.'

They began walking again, holding hands. The first, distant shuddering of the bombs over Grand Harbour served as a reminder that they were not going to make it to the hospital.

After another three contractions, Beth opted to lie down. She lay on her side and Kate sat on the floor by her, with her arms linked round her knees, looking into her face, just trying to go with her. She felt a great bond of affection with Beth – her unlikely courage, her lisping, self-deprecating humour, even her prettiness that was holding up well under the circumstances.

Beth began to breathe deeply. 'Here we go.'

Suddenly Kate remembered Connie, who had been remarkably self-effacing. She left Beth for a moment and went over to where the cook sat on her box, presiding over the now simmering kettle.

'Connie?'

She looked up, with a stern expression.

'Connie, I wondered – is there something I should be doing? I mean, I don't know the first thing –'

Connie raised a large, imperious hand, her eyes closed for a moment in an attitude of almost sphinx-like detachment. 'You doing fine, Mrs Drake. Is not my business.'

Kate recognized this for what it was, far from being a rebuff, a real sacrifice on Connie's part, and a quite unexpected display of sensitivity.

'I here if you need me,' she added, a little wistfully. 'I boil the kettle.'

Kate returned to Beth's side. One of the nuns had come over, the one who had met them in the street, and waved to them when they first came down into the cellar. Kate saw that she was quite young, with a smooth, dark-browed face full of gentle concern. She had put on a pair of horn-rimmed spectacles which made her seem more of this world.

'Please,' she asked, 'may I help?'

Kate shook her head. 'I don't think so, we'll be all right.'

As if to reprimand her for her presumption there was a terrific boom, like a pile driver being pounded into the floor of the room above, and the nun crossed herself.

'I am a trained midwife,' she added, pursuing her advantage.

'Oh really?' For some reason she couldn't quite explain, Kate felt resentful. She didn't want any assistance. Even had she been disposed to accept the nun's offer, it would have been a mortal insult to Connie.

'Yes,' said the sister eagerly, 'it was my job.'

'But I'm her friend,' replied Kate, in a rather more aggressive tone than she'd intended, and added more gently, 'if you see what I mean.'

The nun ducked her head in a little gesture of understanding, amenable though not submissive, perfectly gracious. 'I understand.'

I wish I did, thought Kate. She sat down again by Beth. 'I haven't asked what you think, as the most interested party.'

Beth laughed. 'I'd much rather it was you than anyone. We can call on the reinforcements if we need them. Oh God in heaven!'

There was a tremendous thunder of bombs up above, and the lamp jiggled on its hook, sending fluttering waves of light and shadow scuttling across the dark ceiling. Kate knew they were probably only random shots, but on an island where the houses were hacked from the same stone as the ground every blow was felt personally. At the far end, near the little altar, one of the nuns was reading aloud, the book held rather primly high, before her face. Antonina sat with the others, listening attentively, her colourful hankie screwed up in one thin, brown hand. The soft, conversational tone of the woman reading aloud trickled evenly through the din, sometimes submerged, sometimes surfacing like a partly buried stream.

'I feel,' said Beth, 'as if I'm being set to music.'

Kate saw that she had lost her prettiness now, she was perspiring and draggled and embattled, but perhaps more beautiful than she'd ever been, or would be again.

'Grand music,' said Kate, 'good sound effects for arriving in the world.'

After another five or six strong contractions – about ten minutes – they heard the steady note of the 'Raiders Passed'.

And as the bells of Malta sounded the 'All Clear', Beth's baby, Douglas St John Maloney, was born, blossoming like a crumpled red rose from his secret place, whole and perfect, crying only briefly, watching the strange world with bright, sightlessly staring dark eyes.

Because his arrival had coincided with the end of the raid, he was like the small seed from which relief and happiness grew. Everyone gathered round Beth as she lay on the mattress, holding him, the nuns' gentle faces were animated by delight and admiration, Connie wept noisily and produced a packet of biscuits, Antonina did little bits of ineffectual clearing-up with a smile like a rainbow.

Kate knelt by the mattress, with her chin cupped in her hands, admiring her handiwork. She felt tired, and peaceful, and satisfied.

'He's lovely,' she said. 'Absolutely smashing.'

'Oh, Kate –' Beth held out her hand and Kate took it.

'No need. I'll go up and make some tea. We'll move you when you've had a cup.'

'I feel so sticky and disgusting.'

'You look wonderful. Don't go away.'

She went up the stairs and into the clear, moonlit dark of the house. The luminous white walls had a watchful air as if they had seen other people, perhaps from the past, while they of the present had been sheltering in the cellar. Through the window of the sitting room, as she pushed open the shutters, she caught sight of the smiling, round-cheeked Madonna. She had that almost-moving air which half-light gives to inanimate objects. The garden was like a sanctuary, small and untouched, the little paving path sprinkled across it like footprints.

She went through to the kitchen. As she made the tea she heard the click of the street door. That would be Lawrence, but she wasn't ready to see him yet. Let him go down and see for himself how clever she had been. The silence was deep, like still water, there was always something hallowed about the quiet after the 'All Clear'. And more than ever, with the approach of Christmas and the slight coolness of the Mediterranean night, her surroundings had a Biblical feel: the square, white buildings of Zemola presided over by the church; the high, serene stars; the baby in the cellar below. Had Kate been a religious person she might almost have fancied that she had assisted at some specially meaningful and appropriate rite.

As she carried the tray across the narrow tiled hall she saw Lawrence's bag and cap by the wall. She felt, as she always did these days, a little start of anxiety, as if he'd caught her out in some treacherous and shameful pursuit.

It was a shock, therefore, when she reached the foot of the cellar stairs, to find that he was not looking for her, or apparently thinking of her at all. The picture that she saw was complete without her. Lawrence, in battledress and unshaven, leaned over Beth. One arm rested on the mattress by her shoulder, as if shielding and protecting her. He was looking down at Beth and her baby with rapt attention, and she in her turn kissed her son's tiny domed head, and returned Lawrence's smile. The nuns whispered discreetly, preparing to go back upstairs; Connie and Antonina looked on benevolently. Lawrence, Beth and the baby created between them a circle in the dim light, a magic circle of which she was not part, and which her arrival could only break.

Hurriedly, quietly, she set down the tray and ran back up to the soothing stillness of the house, and then out into the garden. There was some movement and shouting now, out in the street, people checking up on each other after the raid, but the noise only emphasized the quiet in here. She found that she was shaking uncontrollably, galvanized by something more like rage than misery. There was no one here who knew and understood her. She needed Bill. It was his face she saw as she stood there, his rough, commanding touch she craved. The awful knowledge of the thousands of miles that separated them was real pain to her, she felt each mile like a sharp cut in her flesh. She was alone because he was not with her. He would have understood. She wanted to bay at the moon like a wolf. Instead she lifted her arms and shook them, fists clenched, head tipped back, lips drawn back in a silent scream. Suddenly she became aware that someone was watching her. She turned to see the little dark sister, the midwife, standing with her hands tucked away in her sleeves. She was gone almost at once, conscious of having intruded, slipping into the convent through the door beneath the Madonna.

Kate lowered her arms. As she stared at her hands she suddenly saw, with painful sharpness, what the young nun had seen. A thin, gaunt creature with wild hair, a crazy woman with staring eyes and a snarling mouth, forearms with ridgy muscles and veins like a boy's, nails rimmed with blood, Beth's blood. An outcast.

CHAPTER EIGHTEEN

'But it's a long, long while from May to December,
And the days grow short when you reach September;
And the autumn weather turns the leaves to flame,
And I haven't got time for the waiting game . . .'

'September Song'
Kurt Weill and Maxwell Anderson, 1938

'WHEN will you be back?'

'I honestly don't know. Truthfully, I couldn't say.'

Honestly, truthfully, thought Bill. Why does one always use those words so much when one is dealing in lies?

'You will take care of yourself, won't you?' said Dulcie.

'Haven't I always?'

'Not really. But now you must, for me.'

'Dulcie —' Bill put his hands on her shoulders. The station was dark and cold and noisy, full of the shriek and rattle of mechanized departure that waits for no man. Just behind them the WVS ladies had their trolley and were dispensing tea and wads to a queue of soldiers, so that every few seconds they were bumped and jostled.

'Yes?' She was more than ready for anything he had to say, it was he who could not rise to the occasion.

'Hell, I don't know. It's just that I hate all this.'

'Me too.' In the chill grimy twilight her face was luminously pale. She had on a fur tippet and a little purple velvet hat, and the soft fabrics gentled the outline of her cheek and jaw. She was smiling, her chin lifted, both to return his gaze and to show that she was not giving in. 'And what else?' she asked, almost teasingly.

'I don't know. Nothing.' He took her arm and began to

walk with her to the platform. He was conscious of her beauty, like an armful of summer flowers, those little almost unconscious glances that she drew from other people. In public the theatricality in her was called out, there was the suggestion of a flourish in all she did.

He stopped at the barrier. 'Are you coming on?'

In answer she held out her platform ticket in her black-gloved hand. They walked along the side of the train, threading their way through families, and groups of servicemen, and courting couples, all saying their goodbyes. Her hand was light on his arm, and her step lengthened a little to keep pace with his.

They stopped near the end of the platform, in the no-man's-land where the high roof ended and artificial light gave way to the iron grey dusk of the late December afternoon. The long, silently sweeping arm of a searchlight arced across the darkening sky over London and drowned the tentative early stars.

There had been almost continuous blitz for three months now. The German bombers were becoming less discriminating, Dulcie could no longer be said to be out of the danger area in her flat in St John's Wood. The mansion block had a large basement which the residents used as a shelter, but Bill knew she rarely went down there – she didn't care for that kind of camaraderie under pressure, it wasn't her style. An odd blend of courage and fastidiousness kept her in her own bedroom through most raids. The black-out curtains in her sitting-room were made from a beautiful old velvet evening cloak. She said that rationing was helping her keep her weight down. He didn't know what to make of her.

Now suddenly, *à propos* of nothing, she remarked: 'I'm getting a lot of grey hairs.'

'Yes, a few.'

She laughed. 'The perfect gentleman.'

'You noticed them, why shouldn't I? But there aren't many.'

It was much harder for him to put into words what he wanted to say when she was like this. Her manner and her clothes suggested a spirited young widow, and he wondered if this might have been intentional. He decided not, it would not have been in character for her to put on such a complex front.

She was genuinely trying to make things easier. It seemed gratuitously heartless to call on her to provide even more of what she was so gallantly laying on for his benefit. He felt a louse.

'It might be better,' he said, 'if you didn't think of me while I'm on this trip.'

'Oh? Better for who?'

'For both of us. I'm not used to people waiting for me, worrying about what happens – I'm not sure I can stand the responsibility.'

'Bad luck then.' There was a sharp edge to her voice and she turned her head to one side, pretending to tuck a stray hair beneath her hat. Then she took a hold on herself, turned back, and smiled. 'I understand. Out of sight will be out of mind, I promise.'

'Thank you.'

Somehow he couldn't kiss her, the almost-stifled voice of conscience wouldn't allow that. Instead he took her in his arms, looking over her shoulder at others doing the same thing, longing now to be gone. They drew apart and he picked up his case. Dulcie's cheeks were pink, her eyes shone, she summoned up this incandescent glow to cover her misery.

He climbed on board, and as he turned to close the door behind him she blew him a kiss.

'*Au revoir* Bill!'

'Good-bye Dulcie.'

When he'd put his case up on the rack he went to the window of the compartment to wave to her as the train moved out. But she wasn't there, and when he leaned out she was nowhere in sight; her slim, dark-coated figure had already been swallowed up by the crowds on the platform. He sat down heavily in his seat and closed his eyes. His main feeling was relief. The face he saw was Kate's. But he reflected briefly that though Dulcie constantly protested her own uselessness, her cowardice and triviality, nothing became her half so well as tribulation.

Dulcie went straight to the Charing Cross Hotel, made for the nearest powder room, locked herself in the lavatory furthest from the door and was violently sick. When she had brought up all that was there she sat down on the lavatory seat, took out her mirror and effected what repairs she could, mopping her mouth with a handkerchief, dabbing on fresh scent and re-touching her make up. She was appalled, less by the chilly, trembling nausea than by what the elderly cloakroom attendant might be thinking of her.

When she finally emerged, she was still feeling cold and faint, but at least in no imminent danger of further embarrassment. The thin, grey-haired attendant, Mrs Danvers-like in her high-necked black dress, surveyed her apprehensively.

'Are you all right, madam? Is there anything I can do?'

Dulcie shook her head. 'I'm so sorry. I seem to have picked up some kind of bug, it took me absolutely by surprise.'

'Would you like me to call the nurse? Or a doctor?'

'Oh, goodness no, I can take care of myself,' said Dulcie.

'You go straight home now!' The woman was unexpectedly motherly.

'I expect I shall.' Dulcie adjusted her hat in the mirror. Her face was yellowy white, her make-up seemed to lie on her skin like a sticky mask, covering but not concealing her ugliness. Her stomach bubbled threateningly.

Still apologetic, she put a half crown in the saucer on the wicker table by the door.

'Thank you.'

'Thank *you* madam.'

After the carpeted warmth of the hotel, the bitter cold of the Strand came as a shock, but a therapeutic one, whipping the blood back into her cheeks, restoring sensation to her legs. She walked a little way, but she was terribly tired. The strain of saying good-bye to Bill had taken its toll and now, as usual, he was fully occupied with new adventures while she faced nothing but a dull emptiness. Tomorrow she was due to go down to Lewisham to spend New Year's Eve with Aubrey, Iris and Joe – she dreaded the celebration itself, but quite looked forward to Iris's expert hospitality, her ministrations with food, drink and home comforts. Tonight, she told herself, she would go back to her flat, put cotton wool in her ears and try to have an early night.

*

By the time she arrived home her legs ached, and the nausea had turned into a kind of vertigo. She wanted only to lie down somewhere warm and quiet and go to sleep.

The first thing she noticed was that Fondant did not come running across the hall to greet her with that little 'Prrrp!' he reserved for her alone. The small flat was dark, and utterly quiet.

'Celine? Celine, I'm back!'

There was no reply. Dulcie switched on the hall light, but its solitary brightness just accentuated the empty blackness of the other rooms. Remembering something she went through to the living-room and drew the curtains, and then to the bedroom and did the same there, before turning on any more lights. Her solitary footsteps pattered back and forth.

'Fondant!' She went into the kitchen. The cat's china saucers were on the floor by the door in their usual place, the remnants of some fish skin in one, a circular yellow deposit of milk in the other. Her stomach churned with anxiety and revulsion at the sight of the fish skin. As she stood there, trying to get a grip on herself, there was a timid knock on the front door, which was still standing ajar.

'Yes – come in.'

It was little Miss Comstock from across the landing.

'It's only me, dear.'

'Oh, hallo Miss Comstock . . .'

The old lady dithered in the hallway, fiddling with her knobbly jet necklace. She was always much ornamented, her movements were set to an accompaniment of jingling and clicking. Wearily Dulcie sat down on one of the kitchen chairs.

'Can I do anything for you?'

'No, as a matter of fact I heard you calling your maid –'

'She doesn't seem to be here.'

'No, that's why I popped over.' Miss Comstock advanced a little, her purplish, well-powdered face furrowed with concern. 'Bad news, I'm afraid . . .'

Yes, well, it would be, thought Dulcie. She felt so ill and tired it seemed only appropriate. At least she could not feel much worse. 'What is it?'

'Your lovely cat, he got out.'

Dulcie stared at her. 'But he doesn't go out.'

'No, I know that my dear, but your living-in woman was a little upset, I think she lost her temper over something, and he ran out. I came out to see what the commotion was and he was running down the stairs. I think the front door must have been open – at any rate, your woman went after him, I don't know –'

'Oh God.' Dulcie closed her eyes. 'When was all this?'

Miss Comstock consulted the tiny fob watch pinned to the lapel of her black cardigan. 'I should say, just over an hour ago.'

Dulcie shivered. 'Perhaps she'll find him.'

Miss Comstock brightened. 'I shouldn't be surprised, she was in a terrible state, most awfully upset.'

'Yes, I can imagine.' With an effort, Dulcie stood up, and at once her head span. 'I think I shall go and lie down for a bit, I'm feeling rather off-colour. Thank you so much for coming to tell me.'

She saw the softly-rustling Miss Comstock out of the front door – it was almost as if her false teeth and her fragile, old person's bones were rattling in their loose bag of skin. Dulcie was glad when she'd closed the door behind her. Then, still wearing her coat, she went into the dark bedroom and fell, face down, on the cold, smooth bed-spread. Feverishly, before she fell asleep, she thought of Andrea. Good heavens, she was lucky, at least she wasn't going to die. Andrea had died a terrifying, violent death, she only had the 'flu. But though her brain obediently formed these positive thoughts, she still felt terrible.

When she awoke it was ten o'clock, and she was cold and stiff and her mouth tasted sour. She realized that something had roused her, the sound of voices in the hall. She turned on the bedside lamp, shrugged off her coat, and pulled a jumper out of one of her drawers. She tried to brush her hair, but the feel of the bristles on her scalp made her flinch.

In the hall she found Celine, and a burly red-faced man in a police overcoat. Celine did not somehow present the appearance of guilt and shame which Dulcie had anticipated. On the contrary she looked flushed and excited and her eyes were bright.

Dulcie stood stiffly erect, the accusing employer. 'Where's Fondant?'

'Oh Madame —' Celine's face assumed an expression of almost comical distress which Dulcie found unconvincing. 'He is not used to the roads, he ran out, it was dark —'

'I'm sorry, ma'am,' the constable stepped forward, large and male and whiskery in the small space of the hall. 'He caused a bit of an accident — I was on my bike, I tried to avoid him, but he came right into me.' He had a ponderous delivery, as if reciting evidence in court. Dulcie stared at him coldly.

'This poor man was injured,' said Celine.

'I'm sorry.'

The constable had the decency to look embarrassed. Dulcie noticed that his left hand was bound up in a handkerchief.

'It's not serious,' he said.

'So where is he?' asked Dulcie, looking from one to the other of them. It was the policeman who answered her, he was used to this kind of tricky situation, it was small beer to him.

'I'm afraid there wasn't a thing anyone could do, ma'am. He's dead.'

'Dead.' Dulcie raised her cold hands to her face, rubbing her eyes and forehead. 'I see.'

Celine came fussing over, putting an arm round her shoulders. 'Madame, he was old, perhaps you can buy a new kitten —'

'Don't be ridiculous!' Dulcie shrugged off the arm.

'This lady was doing her best to catch him,' said the policeman in a stolid, self-righteous way.

'I should think so, since she let him out in the first place,' snapped Dulcie. 'Anyway, I don't wish to hear any more about it now. If you would just leave.'

Celine, surprisingly calm, saw the constable out. Some quiet, urgent words were exchanged in the doorway. Dulcie watched them with hatred. As Celine turned back, so Dulcie went into the kitchen. She picked up Fondant's saucers and dropped them in the rubbish pail under the sink, then she went to her bedroom, took the ancient square of pink blanket off the end of her bed, and did the same with that. Only then did she confront Celine again. More than anything she wanted to keep her in her place. There was something disturbing in Celine's unusual composure.

Dulcie's voice was icy. 'I don't feel well, I think I'm getting the 'flu. Would you fetch me a hot water bottle, and get me an aspirin and some lemon barley water?'

'Yes, Madame.'

'We shall talk about this business another time.'

Dulcie went to her room, undressed and got into bed. Her head and all her joints throbbed, and she was more tired than she had ever been in her life. When Celine brought the things she had asked for it was all she could do to raise herself enough to swallow the pills. She wondered idly if Celine and the policeman had put Fondant's body in a dustbin, or if it was still lying out there in the road, a squashed mess of bloody fur.

After she had put the glass down and sunk back on the pillow she became aware that Celine was still standing there, smoothing the palm of one hand with the fingers of the other, fidgeting in a way that Dulcie knew was the prelude to a request.

'What is it?'

'I wonder — since you are feeling so ill, Madame — will you still be going to your brother for the New Year's celebrations?'

Dulcie moaned. 'How can I possibly say, Celine? I need to sleep.'

'Yes, yes, of course.' There was a note of disappointment in Celine's voice, and she began to walk from the room. Her whole manner had been so uncharacteristic that Dulcie's curiosity was pricked.

'Why do you ask?'

At once, Celine was back at her side. 'I wondered, Madame, if you were going to be away, if I might entertain a friend?'

This request was not just unusual, it was unprecedented during the whole time Dulcie and Celine had lived in London. It seemed to Dulcie to be one more clear sign that her world was slipping out of joint.

'Yes. If I go, that is. I see no reason why not.'

'I may cook a little?'

'Yes, so long as you leave things as you would wish to find them.'

'Thank you, Madame, thank you!'

As the bedroom door closed after Celine, Dulcie wondered what had happened to her stern rebuke about Fondant. She turned on her side, and huddled the bedclothes round her shoulders. She was almost glad to be feeling ill because it used so much of her energy, there was none left for unhappiness or rage.

Eventually she fell asleep, sinking into unconsciousness as the long wail of the siren rose above her. Dimly, she heard her door open as Celine looked in, then close. There were footsteps and voices on the landing as the others went down to the basement. Then she was alone in her room in the dark hiatus before the bombers came, confident that if a bomb dropped on her she would know nothing about it. And, anyway, it would be welcome.

She woke in the morning to the news that the Luftwaffe's crack Bomber Group 100 had attacked the City of London. The Thames had been at low ebb, there was a water shortage, firewatchers were off duty, offices, banks and warehouses were empty. Dreadful damage had been inflicted not just on these, but on some of London's finest buildings, and huge fires had burned all night.

Although Dulcie felt queasy and lightheaded, she was not aching all over, so she decided on balance that obligatory cheerfulness in Lewisham would be preferable to remaining here with reminders of Fondant all around, and Celine doubtless sulking over being deprived of her entertaining. On this Monday the 30th she was expected at the shop to help Madame Zoe prepare for the January sale, but New Year's Eve itself she had arranged to take off. She would take her suitcase with her to Zoe Modes and go down to Mapleton Road after work. When Celine saw her case she clasped her hands in delight.

'You are better? You are going?'

'Yes, Celine, I'm going.'

'Have a wonderful time, Madame!'

'I shall certainly try.' Dulcie was aware of how crabbed she sounded, but she couldn't help it. She added: 'I shall be back on Wednesday, Celine. Please remember this is my flat.'

'I will, of course.'

Dulcie had no doubt that she would, she had rarely known Celine in such an amenable frame of mind, and she knew it was not due to guilt about Fondant.

She glanced round warily as she emerged into Abercorn Avenue, half expecting to see the dismal, matted corpse of her pet. But there was no sign of it, and further up near the bus stop a random bomb had scored a direct hit on a row of shops, which put things in perspective rather. On the pavement, amid the broken glass and the rubble and the pathetic bits and pieces, the Incident Officer had set up his makeshift office, and a queue had already formed, asking, enquiring, hoping for the best and suspecting the worst. One of the shops not too badly damaged was a wireless and music store, and the proprietor had put a record on one of the intact gramophones, so that the wheezy strains of 'The Merry Widow' wafted tinnily round the people picking over the ruins of their livelihoods. They seemed not to notice the irony of their musical accompaniment.

After a long and trying day at Zoe Modes, Dulcie pleaded illness and went almost straight to bed on arrival at Mapleton Road. She did in fact feel a good deal better, but so tired she could hardly stand upright. She was shocked to see the extent of the devastation in and around Lewisham, but Iris, when she brought her a tray with homemade vegetable soup and toast, was quite calm.

'There's a public shelter on the corner, but we prefer the basement, we look after ourselves.'

'But the house – your home – don't you worry about it?'

'No point in worrying, what good would that do? We can't move because of the works, so we just have to hope for the best.' There was loud laughter from downstairs, where Aubrey was playing Racing Demon with Joe. Iris smiled. 'He loves to see that boy, it does him the world of good to have the lad's company.'

'I thought the school was being evacuated?'

'No, they're still there. I don't know whether to be glad or sorry, really. It's nice to have him so close, but of course they are right in the danger area – ah well. You have to live for the moment, don't you?'

Dulcie sipped her soup, and smiled. 'I suppose you do.'

'And what may I ask,' said Iris, surveying her sister-in-law with her head rather on one side, 'have you been doing to yourself?'

'Nothing, I told you, I've got a touch of 'flu. In fact I feel better already, better for being here.'

She couldn't bring herself to mention Fondant. She always felt that her spinsterly preoccupation with her pet might seem intolerably trivial to a person of substance like Iris. And they had long since given up raising the spectre of Bill's protracted absences as a reason for depression. So Dulcie deflected further questioning by adding: 'Celine is breaking the habit of a lifetime while I'm down here, and entertaining an admirer!'

Their laughter was interrupted by Aubrey's arrival. Iris rounded on him good-naturedly.

'Au-bree! Don't you knock when you come into a lady's bedroom?'

'Depends,' said Aubrey a little roguishly, kissing his wife's head. He took a piece of toast from Dulcie's tray and munched. 'Besides,' he added, 'that's no lady, that's my sister.'

The following day, New Year's Eve, Dulcie felt once again lethargic, and her stomach rebelled at the prospect of even Iris's wartime breakfast of porridge and syrup. But as the day wore on she felt a little better and by the evening she felt quite able to face some of Aubrey's best Amontillado and a slice or two of the roast chicken for which Iris had eked out meat coupons for weeks past. Thankfully there were no guests, but after dinner they played charades, she and Aubrey against Iris and Joe. Joe had drunk two glasses of claret and was disposed to be flirtatious.

'Did I tell you you look terrific in that dress, Aunt Dulcie?' he said confidentially as they sat side by side on the sofa. 'You honestly don't look your age at all.'

This sally provoked gales of laughter and Joe looked miffed.

'Thank you,' said Dulcie.

'I wish you'd come down to school some time, you'd cause a sensation.'

'I do hope not,' said Aubrey. Dulcie covered Joe's hand with her own.

'I shall some time, of course I shall. It would be a wonderful opportunity to wear an outrageous hat.'

'Do you know,' said Iris, 'you slipped up, Aubrey. We never drank a toast to absent friends.'

'You're absolutely right.' Aubrey rose to fetch the where-withal from the desk in the corner, but by the time he was halfway there the siren went. The four of them took bottle and glasses down to the basement kitchen and saw 1941 come in to the now-familiar strains of the enemy bombers. Iris knitted for the Red Cross, Aubrey and Joe fell asleep on one another, the latter with a foolish beatific smile after kissing his aunt rather too warmly on the dot of midnight. Dulcie sat huddled in her coat, thinking of the absent friends, and allowing herself the luxury of a secret tear over her dead cat.

The merchant ship on which Bill Maguire travelled to Malta contained, most importantly, aviation spirit stored in four-gallon cans; secondly, cloth, soap and medical supplies; and thirdly miscellaneous items such as needles, novels, nappies, baby bottles, pencils and cigarettes. It was a typical Malta run, with each ship carrying a mixed cargo, so that those which got through – and expectations were never high – would take with them a little of everything.

A few of the men on board the *Marguerita* had actually, incredibly, done the Malta run before, had survived and were going back for more. These men did not so much tolerate Bill's presence on board as endure it – no matter what his reputation he was a desk-johnnie. On the other hand there was a grudging respect for his foolhardiness, and an acknowledgement of the need for good press representation which he could provide. No one was rude or unco-operative. Though Bill had a cabin to himself, he ate with the rest of the crew, keeping his mouth shut and listening. In the evenings he played cards below decks when invited, or patrolled the decks and alleyways like a restless ghost. The men of the *Marguerita* could not know it, but it was not his job, on this occasion, which marked him out as different. For the first time, his work was a secondary consideration. The sturdy, phlegmatic courage of the merchant seamen was betrayed by his selfish preoccupation – he cared only for getting to Kate. Their occasional cryptic confidences were wasted on him because he thought of little else but her. For months he'd been like a moth, beating against a window on the other side of which a fierce, unattainable light burns seductively; and with a moth's blind compulsion he had got this job which would either take him to her, or finish him off, which satisfied his sense of natural justice. If he did reach Malta, he had not considered what might happen after that. The expression to burn one's boats had, for Bill, taken on a heady, frightening, new significance.

The convoy of six merchantmen had been labelled 'WS 215', indicating that it was a 'Winston Special' sailing to Egypt round the Cape of Good Hope – a deliberate attempt to mislead the fifth columnists on the docks in England. But it could hardly have been more conspicuous with its accompanying 'nanny' of Royal Navy warships and aircraft carriers. A little grudgingly, the red duster had learned the value of co-operation with the white ensign. Merchantmen were by definition heavy-laden and slow: it was their job to get the cargoes to their destination, and they could do this only by accepting, with a good grace, the chivvying, chasing and cherishing of an escort.

The first part of the voyage was uneventful. The *Marguerita*'s cook, a trim Devonian named Frank Ingles who had done the run before, warned Bill against complacency.

' 'Tez all plain sailing till the Rock, then fuckin' hell breaks out,' was his way of putting it. He and Bill had struck up an unlikely friendship, perhaps due to the peripheral nature of their roles in the scheme of things. Frank had tattoos of palm trees – 'not the tropics, 'tez Torquay' he was quick to point out – on the backs of his hands, and these seemed to waver as he beat batter and chopped onions, as though stirred by a balmy breeze. He told Bill that the ship he'd been on last time had been bombed, but they'd made it to Malta anyway. He had no time for the 'yaller-arsed Eye-ties' as he called them, who rarely came close enough to do serious damage.

'And what if the Germans turn their attention to Malta?' Bill had enquired.

Frank had thrown the last spud into a huge pan with a

splash. 'Then we can all say our prayers, Billy-boy,' was his reply.

They did that anyway, as it turned out. At Gibraltar the convoy had put in for twenty-four hours so that some of the smaller Royal Navy vessels could refuel. While they were there shipboard services were conducted to ask for divine intercession on behalf of the Allies for the rest of the trip.

Bill had little faith in the intervention, tactical or otherwise, of the Almighty, but he was stirred by the sound of hundreds of male voices raised in hymns, and the muted thunder of the same voices in prayer, like the rumble of far-off guns. To begin with he had neither sung nor knelt, but the bigness of the setting, the great ships dwarfed by the Rock, the huge vault of blue sky melting into the distant and dangerous sea, had affected him in the end and he joined in. He closed his eyes and told himself that he was halfway there.

By midday on the following day they were over one hundred miles into the Mediterranean, cutting through the blue waters which the sailors called Bomb Alley, and the Italians the *Mare Nostrum*. From the flagship, the Vice-Admiral commanding the operation sent out a signal to every vessel in the convoy:

'The people of Malta urgently need supplies, and look to us to bring them. From now on, all ships will be in the first and second degrees of readiness. Those on watch must be especially vigilant, and those not on duty must get all the sleep they can. We must not fail those who depend on us. Good luck to all of you.'

Less than two hours after this message had gone out, in the early afternoon, the aircraft carrier *Falcon* was torpedoed. Bill was on deck, he felt the cold metal of the ship's rail tremble under his hands, and saw the glittering sea undulate with shock waves as the blast blossomed and spread beneath the surface. The *Falcon* was no more than half a mile away from the *Marguerita*. As the men yelled and ran to action stations behind him, Bill watched with horrified fascination as the huge, wedge-shaped bulk of the carrier shuddered and rocked, then began to list sickeningly to port. The smooth face of its flight deck tilted steeply, the planes dropping into the sea like flies shaken from a fly paper. In a moment she was on her side, her great red underbelly exposed. Tiny, helpless figures of men slithered into the water, too far away for their panic to have a face, or a sound.

A destroyer had already begun to hunt the sub. There were a series of shattering explosions as she sent down depth charges. But even these were drowned as the sea rushed into the dying *Falcon*, and the air was expelled from her with a cavernous death-groan.

There were to be no more days of swift and steady sailing. The *Marguerita* picked up some survivors from the *Falcon* and carried on, but the whole convoy was now in a state of nerve-stretching alert, and the need to keep in 'station' – a horseshoe formation, with the opening to the rear – was paramount.

All night Bill sat in the crew's mess-room, playing liar dice with Frank Ingles and one or two others. The atmosphere was stuffy and acrid: the *Marguerita* was built to carry goods, her cargo was her *raison d'être*, and men and their comfort came second. The thrumming stillness below decks was punctuated by the periodic boom and shudder of protective depth charges.

Over the next three days one more naval ship, a destroyer, and one of the merchantmen, were picked off at night by submarines. But strangely, by day, the wide blue skies remained ominously empty.

They were only twenty-four hours from the Sicilian narrows, and it was dawn, when the first airborne raiders appeared. And even before the first dive-bomber had begun its howling, plummeting descent, they knew what they were up against: Stukas. Suddenly there was no time to prepare, no space to defend. The smoke and spray formed a swirling fog, and the enemy was so close, so arrogantly effective that it was like trying to beat off a flock of swooping, predatory birds.

The 'fucking hell' of which Frank Ingles had spoken, had arrived. And in the galley, fulminating and bootlace-deep in a mushy green slime of marrowfat peas, Frank told Bill: 'Well, Billy boy, you picked the right time to hitch a lift, didn't you? Looks like we're playing the first eleven now!'

On the afternoon of 11 January, Kate sat in the garden of 58 Bakery Street, minding Douglas St John Maloney in his Moses basket while his mother took a rest.

The Moses basket had seen much service. It had been handed on to Beth by another army wife, who in her turn had had it off someone else after their second child. The raffia was fraying, giving the basket a startled appearance, as if its hair was standing on end after months of blitz.

Inside Douglas (Josh had been quick to point out that St John was a family name, of which his own nickname was a corruption) lay swaddled smoothly in a Viyella sheet trimmed with blue satin ribbon, lightly covered with a cellular blanket. He was totally bald and, as is often the case in the first days and weeks of life, bore a strong resemblance to his father — smooth-headed, regular-featured, neat and clean. He was a good baby, a sunny baby. Often when Kate or Beth went to take a peep after hours of restful quiet they would find him gazing up at them, wide awake, his small wild hands grabbing at thin air, perfectly content.

Kate liked Douglas. Sometimes she thought she liked him even more than Beth did herself but she knew, really, that this was because she was not his mother. Beth had nothing to prove: Douglas was her symbol of success. The birth had been rapid, natural and uncomplicated. Beth had been up and about within thirty-six hours, suckling like a peasant much to Connie's delight, not caring a jot for the fashionable Truby-King regime of rigid four-hourly feeding.

It was a tribute to Douglas's placid charm that he had engaged and held Kate's affections, for she had not been able to rid herself of the idea that she was a pariah. The image of Beth, her baby, and Lawrence so entirely bound up in their mutual and innocent admiration and affection, had haunted her. She had wanted to have her cake and eat it, too: to harbour her secret love like stolen, unusable treasure, but to be comforted by Lawrence's love as well. On the night of Douglas's birth she felt she had jeopardized, if not lost altogether, the latter. The dreadful image of herself as an outcast, an unnatural and unlovable person, which she had seen reflected in the quiet face of the nun, had stayed with her. She had withdrawn guiltily from Lawrence, been cool with Beth. Only Douglas, she thought, who was too young to know better, could accept her.

Now she tweaked back the blue satin and looked at him. He

lay there as quiet as a mouse, not the tiniest movement even to show that he was breathing. Just a little dot of life, and yet all the tomorrows were his, the world created by this war would be his world, and all these doting, anxious adults were only paving his path to adulthood.

It was quiet. Kate could hear the sound of Connie in the kitchen, singing in a breathless, grunting style as she pummelled some dish into submission. Antonina had gone up to Strada Comina, whither the Maloneys were due to return in a few days' time. The shutters of Beth's room on the first floor were closed.

Two nuns came through the narrow door beneath the *Marija*, saw Kate and came towards her. Because of the luxuriance of the plants, and the narrowness of the path, and their long habits covering their feet, the two women seemed to glide slightly above the ground. They smiled at Kate, but what they really wanted was to peep at the baby and this they did, nodding and murmuring in Maltese, full of admiration. Their smooth, indoor-pale faces were ageless. Kate envied them their certainties. She no longer felt the energetic annoyance with the nuns that she had when Beth was about to give birth in the cellar. She saw in them the power of absolute humility – for if you had no pride, where was there to fall?

She heard the street door open, and knew it must be Lawrence, although the dark skirts of the nuns obscured her view. But they moved aside, nodding and beaming, at his approach. Even they were not immune to his charm, thought Kate, I have all that and can give nothing in return.

He came straight to her as the nuns withdrew, melting discreetly through the arched door into the street. He dropped his bag on the ground and bent to kiss her face: she turned slightly aside so that his lips touched not her lips, but her cheek.

'Hallo, you,' he whispered, smiling at her. Then he peered into the Moses basket and touched the baby's cheek with the knuckle of his forefinger. She watched him with that awful, hollow detachment which had come over her like a paralysis in recent months. It appalled her, the ease and suddenness with which real love could turn to shameful indifference. And he would not confront her with it, he was trying to weather it, to ride it, to outface it. She had thought she was not lacking in courage, but she could not tell him about Bill. So their lives crept uneasily forward over a minefield of guilty silence and misunderstanding. When she thought what she had lost, she could have wept. Something in her whined and clawed and howled for attention, but she kept quiet.

He sat down by her on the little raised area round the roots of the fig tree. He wore shorts, and his bare knees looked smooth and youthful. He gave off a pungent smell of sweat and dust and explosives, there was grit in his hair and round his nails.

'How are you?' he asked, still *sotto voce*.

'There's no need to whisper, he won't wake up.'

'How are you?' he asked again, aloud this time, but in a tone that suggested it was a secret matter between them.

'I'm fine. Using the baby as an excuse to do nothing.'

'Convoy's in — some of it.'

'How many?'

'Three, I believe, out of eight merchantmen. And from now on in it's going to be worse.'

'Why?'

'The Germans are in Sicily. They absolutely blasted that convoy. There's an aircraft carrier, the *Illustrious*, in the harbour now I believe. She's absolutely shot to pieces, and they'll be back to try and finish her off.'

'I see.' As usual, Kate felt energized by this kind of news. Any intensifying of danger or discomfort brought about by the war had the effect of diminishing her self-loathing.

'I wish I could be with you more,' said Lawrence. 'You must promise me you'll be sensible and look after yourself.'

'You know me.'

'Perhaps.' She imagined she heard a faintly quizzical note in his reply. But now the baby made a little grunting sound, ticking like a time bomb, the prelude to waking up.

Lawrence glanced at him solicitously. 'Where's Beth? Son and heir's waking up.'

'She's inside, taking a nap.'

'A bad night?'

'No, I don't think so, just feeds . . . you know.'

'Not really, but I can imagine.' He was not wistful, but almost joking. And yet knowing him as she did she overreacted.

'Ghastly,' she said, cuttingly. 'I'm so glad it's not me.'

With obvious relief he looked up and said: 'Here's mum!'

Beth appeared, beaming, wearing a white smock. She still carried some extra weight, but it suited her. She seemed not fat but voluptuous and womanly. She made Kate conscious of her own bones, knobby and prominent as sticks beneath her sun-dried fair skin. She did not tan, but freckled in the sunshine. Beth tanned, and her brownness was like the blush on the skin of a ripe apple.

'Hallo you two!' Her voice was gay. 'Sorry to have deserted you!'

Lawrence stood up to greet her, his narrow shadow falling across the pale blanket in the Moses basket. Douglas gave a little convulsive twitch, as if he could feel the shadow.

'Hail, warrior.' Beth lifted her cheek up to Lawrence's, and he held her shoulders briefly as he kissed her. She came round to Kate and crouched down by the basket.

'What's going on then?'

'Nothing, he's been sound asleep.'

'Long enough,' said Beth. She reached in and lifted her son writhing, bending and grimacing into the sunlight. His wobbly head leaned into the curve of her neck, his tiny crooked legs and out-turned feet kneeling against her shoulder. She spoke over his head to Lawrence. 'Will Josh be coming?'

He nodded. 'If at all possible, tonight. After that I don't know when any of us will be able to get away. I think he feels you should stay here with Kate in view of the new circumstances.'

He went on to explain about the Germans on Sicily, the new and more dangerous phase they were entering. Beth listened, patting the baby's back, made sounds of dismay, laughed shortly, sighed philosophically.

Looking away from them, Kate said, 'I'll cycle into Valletta tomorrow and see if I can find anything in the shops.'

'For God's sake, Kate –' Lawrence was aghast. 'Don't be such an idiot – they're going to be dropping all they've got on the harbour area. Just be sensible.'

'I shall be perfectly sensible,' she said coldly. 'But if there's a convoy in, I might as well go.'

'Kate, you mustn't,' said Beth.

'I want to go.' Kate felt she had been through this scene before, on the night they had discussed Dunkirk. Now, as then, her determination to have her way increased in direct ratio to their opposition. She knew, from half-suppressed movement above her, between them, that Beth had been about to remonstrate further and Lawrence had dissuaded her. Their complicity in protecting her from herself enraged her. She felt like an animal in a net, entangled in its passive folds, so that the more she struggled the more firmly she was enmeshed.

She stood up abruptly. 'I shall go tomorrow,' she said.

She set off the following morning after Lawrence and Josh had returned, with no clear idea when they would next be back. She had endured, miserably, the intervening night, drinking too much at supper to prolong the evening and put off the moment when she would be alone with Lawrence. Away from Beth and Josh they had scarcely spoken, so great was their dread of what each might say. Lawrence had made love to her and she had been unable to respond, but afterwards he was too tired to question her coldness, and had fallen asleep on her shoulder. Before he left he had tried again to dissuade her from going down to the Cities, but she was adamant.

She rode down the bumpy Hamrun road in a kind of self-induced trance of anger and humiliation and loneliness. She thought she might be going mad, that she had some kind of death wish. On the road, most of the traffic was going the other way – the welfare team would be hard-pressed today, and she would not be there.

By mid morning she was standing with the crowd on the bastion of St John Elemosiniere in Cospicua, looking down on French Creek. At the far, outer end of the creek lay the aircraft carrier *Illustrious*. She no longer looked like a ship, but resembled some weird futuristic craft come to rest beside the ancient battlements, her decks and hull a mass of scaffolding, ladders, cranes and pulleys. Beneath this disguise it was just possible to make out the blackened sides of the ship, sparking here and there where welders were at work. The whole edifice swarmed with dockyard workers trying to make good the damage done by the Luftwaffe — firemen, fitters, welders, carpenters — and occasional streams of bubbles on the water near the hull showed where divers were busy below the surface. It was a triumph of determined and courageous teamwork.

Kate glanced round at the people next to her. They were a family group — a man, his wife, and three children, the youngest of whom was perched on her father's shoulders — all come to admire the battered ship which had become a symbol of dogged endurance and hope.

The woman caught Kate's eye and smiled. 'She will be mended,' she said, pointing to the *Illustrious*.

Kate nodded. 'Yes.'

'But the Germans will be back.'

'I expect so.'

Within a few minutes, as if they had made it happen, the siren sounded. There was a large public shelter only two hundred yards away, an ancient tunnel gouged right into the heart of the rock beneath the bastion. The family moved quietly in the direction of the shelter, the small girl still holding on to her father's black, curly hair. Just before they went in the woman looked round at Kate as if inviting her to accompany them, but she shook her head. The people surged past her and round her, and she stood very still. There was a high, grey cloud cover, so the sky was not dazzling. Within a few minutes of the siren's dying away Kate could make out the insect swarm of a large formation, coming in over Grand Harbour from the north. At first Kate thought they were the Macchi 200s flying at an even greater height than usual, but then she realized they were not higher, but smaller. It was her first sight of the Stukas.

She had never been so close to the full fury of the Grand Harbour barrage. As the guns opened up it was like the earth itself exploding, lifting, cracking and bursting with a thunderous roar. The sound was so massive, so violent, that she experienced it as a physical pressure that threatened to crush her, and her eyeballs were seared by heat and blinding flashes of explosive light. She was still holding her bicycle, but now the handlebars were simply pulled from her grasp. Because of the din the bicycle itself seemed to fall weightlessly, soundlessly to the ground, as if it had been made of twigs, not metal.

She was not afraid but exhilarated. It was like running in the dark, or speeding in a car, or yelling in a thunderstorm; the danger became life itself, she felt powerful and strong. She turned her face to the sky and saw the enemy formations like a huge shoal of small fish in a rough sea, somehow holding their course amid the splashing and tearing of the anti-aircraft fire.

A hand touched her shoulder and she glanced round to see a young priest, his black robe powdered in grey dust. His lips moved, and he pointed behind them, towards the conventual parish church, exerting a slight pressure on her shoulder. Again, she shook her head, and he turned and ran back to where his flock were sheltering.

Now the Stukas were directly overhead. They began to peel off one by one and plummet like stooping hawks towards the dockyard, and the *Illustrious*. Their courage was heartstopping. As they descended, on a near-vertical course, they left the umbrella barrage only to fly into a second, even more venomous, from Dockyard Defence and then into a third put up by the Bofors and pom-poms. Every ship in the harbour that could muster a gun began firing, and the Stukas were almost flying down the barrels. Even on the crippled *Illustrious* the covers had been whipped off two of her still-functioning machine guns and a couple of Maltese soldiers were blazing away from among the forest of scaffolding.

The planes swooped to below gun level and now the thunder of the barrage was slashed by the whistling of the bombs, the grating whine as the Stukas came out of their dives, and the thudding impact of explosives.

The yellowy-white buildings of the ancient city of Cospicua seemed to waver and swell tremulously like buds bursting into flower, and fragments of masonry, some of them massive, floated and spun into the air. The rim of the bastion on which Kate stood was torn away, a great avalanche of rock poured down towards the creek not ten yards in front of her.

Kate picked up her bike and ran for the shelter. With her back turned to the harbour she felt that every plane was diving for a point between her shoulder blades. She left the bike just outside and went down shallow steps into the crowded darkness. As she did so, a great slab of rock thrown up by the bombing struck the wall near the entrance. A few seconds later and she would have been crushed to a pulp.

At first she could not see at all. It took her a full minute to adjust to the teeming, twilight density of the shelter, she felt claustrophobic and fought her way to the side where she could press her back against the wall. Here, the noise lost some of its sharpness but could be felt, like body blows, each crash sending a quiver right through the rock and the people who huddled inside it. The air was thick with fear. The ubiquitous fluctuating hum of prayer was punctuated by women's crying, and the shouts of frightened children. Kate's heart hammered — they might be entombed in the bastion, buried alive. Suddenly death seemed inevitable, and she wished she had remained outside, in the light, with her head up. But the raid ended as suddenly as it had begun, like a summer storm. It had lasted only seven minutes. For the first time the people of Malta were loth to emerge, fearful of what they might find. Their worst fears were confirmed when the 'All Clear' rang out; there were scarcely any bells. In place of the usual clangorous chorus there was just the desolate tolling of a few far away, lonely survivors.

In dribs and drabs, chastened and silent, they emerged into the light. The air was full of a fine haze, drifting like smoke — the dust from ruined buildings. The place where Kate had stood was now no more than a rocky outcrop, a tumble of huge stones, some dangerously balanced, coated with dust and splinters of glass and metal. The ground underfoot crunched with debris.

Down below in the creek Kate could just make out the weird spires and trellises of the *Illustrious* — still, miraculously, intact — and the figures of the dockyard workers running back to continue the repair work which had become a matter of national pride.

Suddenly remembering her precious bike, Kate turned back. The black hole of the shelter entrance now looked like the mouth of a boxer after a tough fight, torn and misshapen. But the bicycle was still there, in one piece and functional. The handlebars had been knocked crooked and she grasped the front wheel between her knees and straightened them. Then she pushed it back along the bastion, towards the apex of French Creek, looking for a way down into the town. The haze was beginning to settle. Down on the wharves which had been busy with machine shops and workrooms there was now a blackened honeycomb of wreckage. Great hissing arcs of water played over the devastation, sending up a pungent steam smelling of charring and explosive.

From the wharves a steep, winding path climbed to the ramparts of Cospicua, a path only occasionally broken by a flurry of shallow steps. Little clouds of dust moved over the path so that Kate, looking down, felt that she was standing on a mountain top, above cloud level, or perhaps on the lip of a volcano, gazing into the smoking crater. Several people toiled up the path – two soldiers carrying a stretcher, an air-raid warden, some weary, blackened dock workers in stained overalls.

One solitary figure was going down, walking down the first flight of steps. But he was looking up, surely looking at her.

'Bill!' she screamed. And again, 'Bill!'

She thought he must have heard, but though he still looked in her direction it was plain he could neither see nor hear her. The air was full of voices – shouted orders, and crying, and calls for help – and the rumble and crunch of rubble being shifted as the clearance and rescue operation got under way. He might as well have been on the other side of a canyon. He continued down the path, running now, away from her.

Had it even been him? She stepped sharply back from the edge, suddenly overcome with vertigo, realizing how dangerously far she had been leaning out. Surely, she must have been mistaken? It wasn't possible – and yet for a moment she had seemed to see his face with such clarity, every line and plane of it imprinted on her memory, instantly recognizable. Could she really have been so deluded? She was trembling with shock.

A special constable went by on his bicycle, weaving and wobbling between the piles of wreckage, his whistle swinging round his neck. Blindly she followed him, not trusting herself to ride her own bicycle but using it as a kind of crutch on which she leaned heavily.

The panicky shouting began to subside as she left the bastions and made her way through the ruined streets. Shouting gave way to quiet weeping, the scrabbling of bare hands on rock, the occasional muted moaning of people buried alive.

She found herself at the side door of the magnificent coventual church. There stood the young priest who had earlier exhorted her to take cover. He was talking, with desperate urgency, to two air-raid emergency workers. He glanced at her, recognized her, lifted a hand. His face was bleak, his whole appearance ghostlike under a pall of limestone dust. Beyond him in the dark cave of the beautiful, ornate church, more dust swirled and drifted like ectoplasm. She could see the damage on the outside of the church, the whole side of the building brought to its knees in a meaningless tumble of jagged masonry that spread across the road.

She went up to the priest. 'Is there something I can do? I did a course in England . . .'

He shrugged despairingly. 'No skill is required, just hands to dig.'

She went into the church and turned towards the south-eastern corner, to the right of the high altar. The floor beneath her feet glittered and crackled with a razor-sharp mosaic of coloured glass. The back of the high altar was broken, the great black and gold crucifix spread-eagled, face down on the floor. An elderly man lifted it up and genuflected creakily before it.

More than forty people had sheltered in the sacristy at the priest's instigation, while he had gone to the bell-tower, ready to peal the 'All Clear' when it came, determined to stand with his church in the face of danger. The bell-tower had wavered but remained standing. The sacristy had been destroyed, burying everyone in it. Doggedly Kate began to dig, joining the others – relations, monks from the convent, children, nurses – who had already begun the long process of disinterment. She concentrated absolutely on her task as piece by painful piece they moved the debris, cutting their hands and breaking their nails, not speaking to one another.

After three-quarters of an hour they made the breakthrough. It was actually possible to step through into the artificial chamber in the heart of the fallen masonry where most of the bodies were piled, dead but eerily undamaged. They had died of suffocation. Identification would be agonizingly easy for the husband of this young woman, the father of this toddler in red shorts, the family of this black-clothed grandmother, the sweetheart of this youth with the medallion. Kate was suddenly exhausted. As the rescue workers began to bring out the bodies, and to lay them in a pitiful row in the centre aisle, she left them and went to sit in one of the undamaged pews. She envied the young priest the tears which rushed down his cheeks as he swept aside the broken glass with graceful, domestic movements. She couldn't cry. Too much death.

'Hallo, Kate.'

She looked up. So she had not imagined it. He stood in the aisle at her side, no more than a few feet away. He looked a little thinner than she remembered, though still broad and solid, as if fierce external forces had simply whittled away some of the flesh. There was an angry red map, a burn, down the left side of his face and neck. She stared. The tears she had longed for now blurred his image, it wavered before her like a reflection in water.

'I saw you,' she whispered. She cleared her throat. 'I called.'
'I know.'
'I didn't think you heard me – I thought I'd imagined you.'
'I didn't hear you, Kate, but you called me a long time ago.'

She held out her hand and he took it, tightly, and sat down next to her. 'I made it. I found you.'

'This is terrible,' she said, 'these people are dead. I've been helping to get them out. Please, let's go.'

Clinging together they left the church. In the street he put his arms round her like a vice, so that she could feel the cantering of his heart, strong and insistent. She was completely lost now, willingly lost – she knew neither the time, nor the place, nor what she should be doing. Her world was circumscribed by his embrace. She felt her old self, the one she knew and believed in, leaping up inside her to greet him, like flames fanned from ashes.

'Where shall we go?' he asked.
'I don't know.'

'I've got a room at the Osborne.'

'No, everyone goes there, I should see people I know.'

'Then let's walk, and find somewhere.'

He took her hand and led her down the narrow street at the side of the church – Salvation Street, it was called – and then left, north, towards the suburbs where the bomb damage would be less. Around them the citizens of Cospicua had passed through terror and shock and were beginning to put their lives together again, until the next time. Already a string of washing, small, intimate garments of wool and cotton, hung high over the narrow street like a brave show of bunting. A woman vigorously swept the grit from her narrow hallway, with strong arms like pistons. An old lady and two children set up their stone stove in the street to cook a makeshift late lunch. The high cloud had cleared and the soft winter sunshine helped to restore a sense of normality. The bright golden light gave the devastation an every-dayness, as though it had always been there.

An opportunist tradesman with a donkey and cart manhandled his rickety vehicle over a rampart of fallen masonry and down the other side, calling sonorously that he had hardware for sale. Drawn to a halt the donkey was drowsy and indifferent, standing with one back leg cocked, neck drooping and eyes half closed, his long ears lying sideways like the wings of a dragonfly. Garrulous women emerged from their shattered homes to buy pots and pans and cloths and buckets to help clear up the mess.

Through all this Kate and Bill walked, stumbling and clinging, until Bill pointed, 'There's somewhere.'

The sign said 'Glory Hotel'. The frontage of the hotel was like a shop, with a large window to one side of the door. The window had a rust-coloured curtain running across it at eye-height, in front of which stood an arrangement of plants in troughs and on stands. The only visible damage was to one of the stands, which had fallen over, depositing the plant, with its smooth-sided clod of earth, on the stone floor among shards of bright blue china.

As Kate and Bill approached the door of the hotel, a woman drew aside the curtain in the window and began sweeping up the earth and china with a dustpan and brush. Seeing them, she at once came round and opened the door.

'Good afternoon!'

The woman's generous figure was encased in a red taffeta dress, so that she resembled the pupa of some exotic moth. Her rather pock-marked face was covered with a thick layer of make-up, which could not disguise a robust peasant hand-someness – dark winged brows, intense eyes, an exuberant tangle of rusty black hair like some substance other than human tissue.

'German bombs *and* customers,' she remarked huskily, holding the door for them. 'What a busy day.'

The woman had a strong, intrusive, knowing presence, which Kate wanted to shut out. In the hall was a small, highly polished reception desk, with china ornaments, a brass handbell and a posy of flowers in a tumbler. Around the walls hung a collection of evenly spaced and horribly-framed pictures, some religious, some landscapes, some depicting bottles and loaves of bread. The floor was covered with speckled linoleum. Opposite the reception desk stood a small table flanked by two spindly chairs. One of these was occupied by a young man with a piece of sticking plaster covering his right eyebrow. He was drinking a glass of beer, and scarcely bothered to look up as they entered.

As they went over to the desk another, older man came down the stairs, said something briefly to the woman in Maltese, and left. The place had an air of 'business as usual'.

'You want a room?'

'Yes, a room for two.'

She reached beneath the desk and drew out a dog-eared book for them to sign. She seemed to connive quite readily at their plan, not by a glance or a gesture did she betray any curiosity. As Bill signed the book, Mr and Mrs Maguire, his hand left a smear of reddish-brown half-dried blood, but the woman's face did not alter, and she did not wipe the smear away or comment upon it.

She unhooked a key from the board behind the desk. 'Room five, first floor.'

The room, like the hall, contrived to be both spartan and garish. It was furnished sparsely and cheaply with an iron bedstead, a utility cupboard like a hospital locker and the sort of chair Kate remembered from music rooms at school. But someone had paid a lot of attention to surface decoration, there were more pictures, and bric à brac, and highly coloured cushions, even a stuffed toy with glaring eyes at the head of the bed.

They paid no attention. The first time they did not even undress. Bill simply undid his fly, dragged down her pants and took her with savage speed, his face pressed into her neck, her fingers twined cruelly tight in his hair. But even then he sensed her own ferocious female voraciousness, so different to Dulcie's sophisticated pleasuring. When he had finished, he knew that her energy was only just beginning, like a smouldering fuse. As he came he shouted, but she was silent, quivering and hot. After that, he undressed her carefully, as if unwrapping a present. Kate became languid with excitement, turning and twisting catlike on the narrow bed, alive and dangerous under his hands. She took pleasure in the thinness of her own body against the bulkiness of his, she was rough, then pliant, her eyes burning him up.

For Kate it was release, at last, but there was no peace in it. She knew that when the hot rushing torrent of love finally cooled and stilled, the small voice of conscience would make itself heard. If it could only go on just like this. She couldn't get enough of him. She kept her eyes wide open, staring into his all the time, like a child that boasts it can stare at the sun, the source of energy and light. Long after he was spent she held him, moving against and around him for her own pleasure, pleading, bullying, cajoling, torturing until her energy rebounded on her and she jerked and lay still.

She lay on her back, spread wide, and he on his stomach, his cheek resting on the pillow by her head, his arm flung across her.

The deep, breathing silence in Room Five was accentuated by noises off. Out in the street there was a dry, rhythmic scraping as someone shovelled stones. Somewhere in the hotel a door opened and closed and heavy footsteps ran down the stairs. From the room next door came a bang, a violent creaking, a spluttering burst of laughter.

'You know what this place is, don't you?' he asked.

'I suppose I do.'

'A skin shop. Daughters of joy, sticking to their posts in the face of enemy attack.'

She turned and kissed his forehead. 'How appropriate!'

She began to laugh uncontrollably, rolling away from him and trying to smother her mirth in the counterpane. The hideous stuffed toy lay on the floor and she picked it up and pressed it over her face, her shoulders shaking.

When she eventually calmed down it was to find him watching her with a look of such bleak unhappiness that she could not bear it. She wound her arms and legs tight round him, wriggling and kissing with blind love, like a young animal nosing for its mother's milk, demanding his attention, trying to shut out his difficult, older reflections.

'Oh Kate, my Kate . . . what the bloody hell are we going to do?' There was a catch in his voice. She fell away from him as if he had pushed her, throwing her arms over her face. He thought that her thin, untanned body, thus exposed, was like a child's, the rib-cage sticking out with a sort of fragile toughness, the stomach concave. Deliberately, though he felt her invitation, he did not touch her.

'Well?'

'I can't think about it. I can't.'

'But we have to, if life is to be bearable.'

She brought her arms down and held them across her chest. 'There's something wrong with us.'

'You're damn right there is. I just had to get here, Kate, I'm too far through my life to waste anything, good or bad, right or wrong. I came on that convoy, I knew I'd either be blown to bits or I'd see you, and it was worth it. I didn't care, Kate! Five ships were blown to bits. Men died, we saw them in the water and we couldn't stop, brave men. And all I wanted was you, Kate, and I made it. How can I live with that if we don't make something of it all. Fifteen hundred miles for a lay in a tart's parlour?'

She smiled. 'Fiddling while Rome burns.'

'We *have* to make something of it, there has to be more.'

'I know, I know.'

'We could tell him.'

'I can't – I'm not ready for that.'

'The trouble is,' said Bill, rolling on his back so as not to look at her, 'you love him. The stinking, virtuous bastard – you love him.'

She went to him, laying her cheek over his heart. 'Listen. Perhaps I do, but I don't know that I can live with it. Shall I tell you how he makes me feel? As if he has given me a beautiful but expensive dress that doesn't suit me, that I don't feel comfortable in. I feel I must wear it because he's so generous, and yet every time I tear the dress, or spill something on it, I hurt him and feel guilty. And it isn't my fault, it isn't fair.'

The old, anguished cry of the wrong-doer. He put his arms round her and pulled her face up to his. 'And me? How do I make you feel?'

'Like nothing – like myself. Free.' She kissed his mouth bitingly.

'Greedy.' She settled back on him, watching his eyes close. 'Selfish.' She began to move on him, and he in her, once more lost to everything but each other, the startled round eyes of the ugly toy watching them unblinking from the floor.

CHAPTER NINETEEN

'I get along without you very well,
Of course I do,
Except when soft rains fall and drip from leaves,
Then I recall the thrill of being sheltered in your arms,
Of course I do,
But I get along without you very well . . .'

'I Get Along Without You Very Well'
Hoagy Carmichael, 1939

THEY stayed at the Glory Hotel until late in the afternoon. There was another raid in the harbour and dockyard, but they did not take shelter. The proprietor came up the stairs, rustling in her red taffeta, knocking on doors and calling out in Maltese and English: 'At your own risk, gentlemen!' Between the thunder of the bombing and the harbour barrage there was a rushing sound, like banks of shingle in a high sea, as already-ruined buildings sank still lower. They lay there, buried in one another, loth to disentangle and face the world.

In the end she remembered Beth, who would be worrying, and said in a flat voice, 'You go back to the Osborne if that's where your things are.'

'And what will you do?'

'I'll think. Perhaps you could even come to the house, but I'll let you know. I'll tell them the truth but not the whole truth — that I met you unexpectedly before the raid, that we sheltered together. He doesn't suspect anything, and anyway he's gone back to the airfield.'

'When will he be back?'

She shook her head. 'I don't know, not for days anyway, perhaps longer.'

'You're on your own?'

'No, there's my friend Beth, she's just had a baby. Her husband's in the regiment, at company HQ near Zemola.'

'I see.'

'It's all right, we can work something out, and her being there will help – a sort of chaperone. I must get back.'

She sat up, presenting Bill with the smooth, indented curve of her long back, the spine a swift ripple beneath the pale skin. But when he stretched out his hand to touch her she quickly stood, and began to pull on her clothes.

'Just don't go,' she said. 'I'll call you.'

Heavily, he got out of bed. 'Where would I go? You take two steps and you're in the sea.'

Kate dressed without looking at him. Her clothes were filthy from the earlier raid, and the digging in the church. They seemed to represent the resumption of responsibility, and the squalour of her conscience on display for all to see.

When she turned, he was doing up his shirt buttons. His hands were blistered and cut, and he was making a poor job of it. She went to help him and they clung miserably, desperately together.

'I wish I could be swallowed up in you,' she whispered. From next door came the rasping jangle of an old gramophone record, and someone singing along. 'I wish I could push under your skin and hide there.'

'Well you can't. One thing I can't do is make you safe, Kate. It's not in me.'

They held each other for another precious minute and then left. Down in the hall the young man with the sticking plaster was still sitting at the table, and the woman was with him, perched on the other spindly chair, her legs crossed to reveal a bulging acreage of dark stocking. Rising and crossing to the desk she surveyed them with a sort of benevolent neutrality, and not a hint of coyness.

'You all right?' she enquired, referring to the raid.

'Yes – no problem,' said Bill, fiddling with money. Kate looked away, discomforted. It hardly seemed right that the lubricious patrons of the Glory Hotel should get off scot-free, while less than a quarter of a mile up the hill innocent, hardworking people suffered so.

As they emerged into the dusty brightness of the street, the black shadows of early evening lying unevenly over the heaps of masonry, she suddenly remembered something.

'Oh Lord – my precious bike!'

'Where did you leave it?'

'Outside the church, when I went to help dig those people out.'

'It may still be there.'

They toiled back up the hill, and along Salvation Street to the church. There was no sign of Kate's bicycle, but when she ventured inside to enquire of the priest she discovered it at the back of the church, propped neatly against the wall, unharmed. Remembering what she had been doing when someone had risked their life to rescue her bike, she felt a smart of shame. But when she emerged and saw Bill waiting for her, the shame evaporated.

'I'll go now,' she said. 'And see you again soon.'

She wheeled the bicycle away, and he watched her go, her red hair like a bobbing flame amid the yellowy-white ruins.

Lawrence stood in the deep shadow of the garden at 58 Strada Forni, waiting for his wife. Up the hill the church tolled for evening mass, and from the convent opposite came the gentle rise and fall of the sisters' voices. The air was cool, and dry, faintly smudged with the scent of flowers. In the house behind him he could hear Beth talking to Connie, and the faint, repetitive scratch of the baby's evening crying.

He was afraid. So afraid that he had come back, with no idea of what excuse he would make on his return. The two German raids had come so close together – Kate might possibly have already left the Cities for home, and not have been close to a shelter when the second one began.

And apart from the physical danger which might threaten her, there had been the violence of her mood. Lawrence was all too aware of the inner battle with which his wife had been engaged for months now. He had felt helpless, as if all he could do was keep very, very still, like an animal blending with the background until the stalking danger passed. But it had not been easy, he had just not known what else to do. He wanted to comfort her and reassure her of his love, but her ferocious self-containment had stifled his openness, the very thing which had brought them together. He remembered her saying, long ago, that it was up to him to teach her to love. Now he felt he had failed.

As he stood there, waiting, he did not actually picture her dead, because that seemed impossible. Death would not suit her. If, in an effort to prepare himself for the worst, he tried to imagine her broken, bleeding and lifeless in some bombed-out street, he could not do it. So he stood in the dark, suspended between hope and dread.

After a while he went to the door and opened it, stepping out into Bakery Street. Down the hill, over Grand Harbour the searchlights scanned the night sky. But up here the honey-coloured moon and the stars were big and bright and close, almost like lamps, and in their light he could see her coming. She was on foot as she rounded the corner from Strada Comina, she had had to resort to pushing the bike. But as he watched she mounted again, and pedalled sturdily along, head down.

She did not look up and see him until she was quite close, and then she stopped abruptly, dismounting and leaning the bike against the wall.

'I didn't expect to see you,' she said, in a voice of utter exhaustion. She ran her wrist back and forth over her forehead. He thought it was the closest to being unmanned that he had ever seen her.

'My darling, thank God you're back, I was beginning to think – I can't tell you what I was beginning to think.' Feeling almost reckless – and this for touching his wife – he put his arms round her and felt how stiff and hot she was, like warm metal.

'I was perfectly all right,' she said.

'You should never have gone. I should never have let you go.'

She disengaged herself from his embrace with a fastidious movement, like a cat that does not wish to be petted. 'You couldn't have stopped me. Anyway, it was no good, I didn't get anything for Beth.'

'That doesn't matter. You're back and in one piece.'

He opened the door and they went through, leaving the bicycle in the garden. She walked swiftly into the house.

As he entered the hall, Beth appeared from the direction of the kitchen. 'Is she back?'

'Yes. Tired but okay.'

'I'll leave you to each other then, but supper's ready when you want it.'

'I shall have to go.'

In the living room, Kate was pouring herself a gin and tonic. When she turned to face him her chin was up and she was smiling.

'I'll tell you what happened – I met Bill Maguire.'

'Bill?' He was astonished. 'Good grief, but what on earth's he doing here?'

'He was on that convoy, reporting on the Malta run.'

'He was bloody lucky to get here then. Is he all right?'

'He seems to be.' She took an enormous gulp of her drink and sat down heavily on the sofa. 'He's one of the reasons I was late. We got into the shelter by St John's, and then got talking, it was so extraordinary to see him . . .'

'Of course. Where's he staying?'

'Well, he's *not* really staying, he has to find a way back. But his things are at the Osborne at the moment.'

'That dump. Could he get out here for a night or two?'

'Possibly.' She sounded weary and uninterested. 'I suppose he could have a bed in Strada Comina if Josh is anxious for Beth to stay here. If he's long enough here to make it worthwhile – he'd go out tomorrow if it was possible.'

'Call the Osborne from the town hall and ask.'

'Yes, I probably will.' She drained her drink, and Lawrence stood up.

'Look, Kate, I have to go, I'm AWOL as it is. I'm just so glad to see you back.' He came over and kissed her upturned face. 'You look whacked, get as much sleep as you can.'

'I will. I'm sorry I caused so much worry.'

He kissed her again, he felt encouraged. 'See you soonest. Good-bye darling.'

' 'Bye.'

*

Dulcie encountered Mae Irving in the unlikely setting of a lunchtime fashion show in aid of the Red Cross, held in the home of a Lady Shebbere in Hampstead. Madame Zoe, a professional to her fingertips, had seen to it that the fortunes of her shop continued to flourish even in the harsh climate of wartime austerity. She now employed only one seamstress, and stocked more of the new inexpensive off-the-peg clothes, with a bias towards tough washable fabrics and utilitarian trousers, skirts and jackets, so that even women like Una Roth-Vesey could contrive to look like landgirls if it made them feel any better. Apparently, it did, and the renamed St John's Fashions reaped the rewards of adaptation.

Dulcie had hated all she saw at the show – bulky, badly cut suits, and trousers in cheap materials, skimped so that they didn't hang properly, and dresses that looked limp and tired even on the svelte mannequins.

Afterwards, she talked to one or two friends and customers over mushroom vol-au-vents and sherry, and was about to leave when she was approached by a handsome, busty young woman with suspiciously golden, but well-coiffed hair.

'I hope you don't mind,' said the woman in a confident, pleasantly common voice, 'but are you Miss Dulcie Tennant?'

'Yes,' said Dulcie. 'Have we met?'

'No we *haven't*, though I do know all about you.'

'Heavens.'

'We have a couple of mutual acquaintances. Ernest Marx, and Rex Donati.'

The bizarre juxtaposition of these two names quite took Dulcie aback. The young woman pressed her advantage, and held out her hand. 'How do you do. I'm Mae Irving.'

This rang a bell. 'Oh – are you by any chance a singer?'

'Yes, that's right.'

'I have an idea you were on the wireless from the Savoy one night when I was dining with Giles and Ernest. Congratulations you must have done very well.'

Mae grinned. 'I can't complain. But then I work hard.'

'I'm sure you must do.' Dulcie looked at Mae. She guessed she must be in her late twenties or early thirties and beginning, in her organized, working-class way, to head for the top. At that age, Dulcie reflected, she herself had fled Paris on the verge of a nervous breakdown, having despatched her illegitimate daughter to the ends of the earth, having no savings and no career in which it was possible to take any pride.

'. . . thought I must tell you that I see him from time to time,' Mae was saying. Dulcie brought her attention back to the conversation.

'I'm sorry, I missed that.'

'I've met your friend Rex Donati.'

'Oh yes?' Dulcie was chilly. 'I wouldn't really class him as a friend. And it's absolutely years since I've seen him.'

'He remembers you very well,' went on Mae determinedly. 'Of course I'd seen pictures of him in the *Tatler* before the war, and his mum and dad, but you wouldn't recognize him now. It really brought it home to me, you know, how war changes people.'

This slice of philosophy made Dulcie wonder if she had missed more of Mae's opening remarks than she'd thought.

'Why is that?' she asked.

'He was shot down, the poor love, back in October, but Lord alone knows when they'll let him out, he's like a patchwork quilt.'

'Oh.' Dulcie set down her glass and leaned back against the wall. She still found she tired easily, and the sherry disagreed with her. 'I'm sorry to hear that.'

'Yes. He asked after you, but of course I never expected to meet you, it's such a coincidence.'

'Isn't it? Well, do give him my regards when next you see him.'

'I will, of course, but I think he'd like to see you. He's been in that ruddy face factory such an age, and all the boys, not just him, they get very down.'

It occurred to Dulcie that Mae, tough and worldlywise though she appeared, had fallen prey to the Donati charm.

'I go down to the hospital every fortnight or so,' explained Mae, warming to her theme, 'me and some of the fellas, to play for these dances they have, that's how I met him.' She stared brightly at Dulcie. 'We're going down on Saturday why don't you come?'

'No,' said Dulcie firmly. 'Rex and I have nothing to say to each other and he knows that as well as I do, really. I hate hospitals, I should be utterly useless. It wouldn't serve any purpose.' She returned Mae's stare which now signalled plainly, if good-humouredly: hard-hearted cow.

But Mae said, pleasantly enough: 'Well look, if you change your mind, this is my number of an evening. Just get on the dog and bone and we could go down together in the van.'

'The van?'

'With the fellas, there's plenty of room. I do wish you would.'

'I think it's most unlikely,' said Dulcie, but she took the piece of paper which Mae handed her anyway, and slipped it in her handbag.

In the event, she did ring Mae. Something was happening to her, and she wanted to put off the moment when she would be obliged to admit what it was, to herself and others.

She made two telephone calls in succession, on the Thursday evening after work. Celine was out, as she often was these days, blitz, black-out and all, leaving Dulcie in the complete isolation she so dreaded. This was when she missed Fondant most, following her from room to room, drifting weightlessly on to her lap when she sat down, purring richly from the end of the bed as she removed her make-up. Dulcie first rang Primmy.

'Hallo? Who is it?' Primmy did not have much experience of the phone — one had only recently been installed in the hallway at Globe Road, for the tenants' use — and she tended to shout.

'Primmy, it's me, Dulcie. There's something I want to ask you — could you come over for tea at the weekend, like old times?'

There was a pause. 'I'm on duty. I suppose I could come late Sunday.' Enthusiasm was not in Primmy's verbal repertoire. Dulcie tried to chafe her friend's chilly responses into life with a bribe.

'Perhaps you could stay the night, rather than go all the way home in the black-out. Come for supper instead of tea, and spend the night.'

'I'd rather get back.'

'But you can come?'

'I'll be there about six.'

'Good, I'll look forward to it.'

'Good-bye.'

Dulcie sighed. She hoped that Primmy would be in a more receptive mood on Sunday. She took Mae's piece of paper from her handbag, smoothed it out and dialled the number.

The hospital where Rex was a patient was a special surgical and rehabilitation unit for pilots who had crashed or been shot down, whose apallingly damaged bodies and faces were being remodelled through skingrafts and plastic surgery.

On the drive down Mae and the 'fellas' — Pete on skins, Dudley on the ivories, Geoff on tenor sax — had been at considerable pains to tell Dulcie she mustn't be shocked by what she saw, but their slightly smug manner implied that she probably would be.

'You got a job sometimes to remember they're as normal as you and me underneath it all,' remarked Geoff, who was driving. 'But I just keep thinking it's a helluva lot worse for them than it is for us looking at them.'

'Your friend's not the worst by a long chalk,' said Mae to Dulcie, in what was obviously intended to be an encouraging tone. 'But then he was probably better-looking than most before, if you know what I mean.'

'Yes,' said Dulcie, 'he was good-looking.' She nearly added that he knew it, too, but decided that that might sound vindictive, although it was true.

The weekly social at the Hurst-Waring Clinic outside Haywards Heath took the form of a tea-dance. Since most of the patients were considered to be too repulsive even for their loved ones, a busload of local maidens with suitably placid and resilient natures was imported each Saturday to provide the female element necessary for 'a good time'. These smartly turned-out, fresh-faced young women were getting down from their coach in the front drive when Dulcie, Mae and the musicians arrived in their van. Everybody seemed to know everybody and was tremendously cheerful in the way of people who jointly shoulder tasks too messy or difficult for the herd.

In spite of Mae's flurry of introductions, Dulcie was keenly conscious of her status as new girl. Still, she comforted herself, she did seem to have made the right choice of clothes, a simple but elegant wool dress.

The sturdy local lovelies disappeared in a chattering throng to the cloakroom, and Dulcie accompanied Mae and the band to the patients' lounge. It was a big, light, pleasant room with a view over the grounds to the South Downs, and a terrace outside the windows where she supposed the convalescents sat out in good weather. The rugs were already rolled back, the piano and microphone in place, and teacups and cloth-covered plates laid out on a long table at the side. A good many of the patients were already there, and greeted them with a cheer.

Dulcie was not shocked. What she saw was a room full of anxious, slightly over-eager young men, keen to appear unabashed, imprisoned in wrecked, ugly bodies. Some, in the process of having their noses replaced, had great tubular excrescences of elephant-like flesh in the centre of their faces, awaiting remodelling; others had simply lost most of their features, and looked out from behind masks of crinkly, tissue-fine reddened skin, with little twisted screws of flesh where ears had been, encrusted slits for eyes, mummy-like parodies of mouths and hands blunted into paws or bent into talons.

As the musicians tuned up, Dulcie felt Mae's gaze on her.

'Poor things,' she said. 'Do you know them all?'

'Most of them,' said Mae. 'Your friend isn't here yet.' Dulcie wished Mae would stop referring to Rex as her friend. He had been her keeper, her lover, her enemy, but never at any time her friend. It was odd that such a blameless, noncommittal word should so enrage her.

'Want to come and say hallo?' asked Mae.

'Certainly.'

Mae was good with them, Dulcie granted her that. As they went about the room she dispensed her easy, common, matey charm in a warm and unforced way that dispelled any awkwardness there might have been. She deposited a kiss here and a pat there with the cheerful confidence of absolute professionalism. Dulcie was introduced – 'Rex Donati's friend' – and accepted with a good grace the resultant whoops and bellows.

'All right for some, eh?'

'Donati — the sly bugger! Do the rest of us get a look in?'

'Are you expected, lovely stranger? Hey, someone go and fetch him!'

At this juncture Dulcie felt she should intervene, saying, 'That's all right, don't hurry him on my account.'

This provoked further gales of good-natured laughter, during which the local girls made their entrance, mercifully taking the spotlight away from Dulcie. She went back to the band with Mae and sat down near the piano.

The socializing was in full swing by the time Rex arrived, which was doubtless what he intended. She knew it was him because he was late, and because of the way he leaned in the doorway, hands in pockets, legs crossed with his old accustomed casual arrogance. He was as slim and graceful as ever, but there was a bandage over his head and round his face, with apertures for his eyes, nose and mouth. Dulcie was relieved about this, for the bandage at least left some room for the supposition that Rex might look perfectly normal without it.

She got up and walked round the room towards him. As she approached she could see that his neck, and part of his head where it showed at the back, were an angry, stubbly red. His eyes seemed darker than she remembered, and without lashes.

'Hallo, Rex.'

He stared down at her. Incredibly, he seemed to use his bandage-mask to disadvantage her, to see but not be seen. Same old Rex. 'God in heaven, is that Dulcie?' He spoke not with surprise, but sarcastically, as if she had had an obligation to visit him before this, and had not fulfilled it.

'I met Mae Irving — the singer — the other day, and she suggested I might come down and see you,' explained Dulcie. Don't make me wish I hadn't, she thought, just don't, Rex.

'Splendid girl, Mae, salt of the earth,' said Rex.

'Yes, she seems a good sort.'

'The best.' She knew he didn't mean a word of it. A nurse brought over a cup of tea for Dulcie, and tea in a tall mug for Rex, with a bent straw, such as one might use to drink cocktails.

'Thanks, Paddy,' Rex said, without looking at her. Dulcie

took a deep breath and resolved, now that she had come all this way, to put her best hospital-visiting foot forward.

'How are you, Rex, really? I was so sorry to hear about this.'

'Were you?' He didn't wait for confirmation, but continued, 'Yes, I have at last achieved respectability at the expense of desirability.' Dulcie suspected she was being invited to make an invidious, arbitrary choice, and declined.

'How did it happen?'

'We were shot down near Lancing. I honestly don't remember much about it except that we were doing rather creditably until I ballsed it up.'

'When will you be out of here?'

'Oh Christ, I've got months to go yet, interminable bloody stitchings and patchings and realignments. I shall be a tribute to the surgeon's art, and still my friends won't want to know me.'

'Don't be ridiculous, you underestimate people!'

'I don't. Look, Dulcie, there are three alternatives open to a chap with a face like an open-cast mine. I can become a recluse, and spare everyone the embarrassment of my company; I can opt for the love of a good woman — a plain one who will be only too glad of what she can get; or I can be frightfully sporting, clowning around and cracking endless cringe-making jokes at my own expense to save other people the bother of doing so.'

Dulcie, genuinely disturbed, put her hand on his arm. 'You do exaggerate, Rex.'

'Oh, I exaggerate, do I?' His voice was thin and sharp as a razor blade, and she removed her hand.

'I'm sorry, I shouldn't have come.'

The band struck up a slow number, a foxtrot, and Mae sang in her strong, throaty voice: '. . . They didn't believe me, they didn't believe me . . .' Dulcie stared through a blur at the couples on the dance floor.

'You're spilling your tea,' he said.

'Oh Lord . . .'

'I'll take the cup back to Paddy.'

He did so, and by the time he was back she had been able to dab her eyes with a handkerchief.

'Do you want to dance?' he asked, coldly, in the way that a strict adult might ask a child if it wanted to go to the lavatory.

She tried to make him behave better. 'Are you asking me?'

He shrugged. 'I'll dance with you if that's what you'd like.'

'Thank you.'

He walked ahead of her, between the easy chairs to the dance floor. He walked easily, but because of the bandage he had to move his whole head, like a bird, to see from side to side or look at the floor.

The hospital matron, trim and busty in a navy blue dress, patted his arm and smiled confidingly at Dulcie. 'That's the way, Mr Donati.'

Although she could not see his face, Dulcie could imagine Rex's expression of contempt. Oddly, this awareness generated in her a flash of tenderness, a memory – unbalanced, she knew – of old times. Painful times, but a part of her life, nonetheless, that was over. He turned and she walked into his arms. He had put on a little weight since their days together, probably due to hospital food and enforced inactivity. But he was still a good dancer and they moved together easily and gracefully as they always had done.

A not unpleasant melancholy settled on Dulcie. Bill was gone; Kate was gone; Ralph was dead, her brother and sister married. And here she was back with Rex, a spoiled and ruined Rex, dancing at teatime – perhaps it was all they were good for, people like them. She moved a fraction closer to him, closing her eyes, just letting her mood work on her for a moment or two. But at once he stiffened.

In a minute, when the music stopped, she said: 'I enjoyed that.'

'Did you?'

'Yes, it's quite a while since I went dancing.'

'I expect you feel much refreshed now that you've made your contribution to the war effort.'

'Rex!' His rudeness took her breath away.

'You've done your bit, you might as well be off now.'

'No, I will not. Besides, I came with the band, I couldn't leave if I wanted to.'

'Then I shall. Cheerio, Dulcie. Don't bother to make the trip again.'

He walked briskly away from her, leaving her stranded in the middle of the dance floor. Her face was on fire, she was mortified, insulted. But in a second another partner, his boyish voice at odds with his gargoyle's face, had swept her up.

'At last! I thought the fellow'd never go. May I?'

'Thank you.'

'By the way, take no notice of Donati. Matron assures me he's for the funny farm. Gone to pieces, you see,' he added confidentially, pulling her close. 'I'm made of sterner stuff!'

It was the best thing for her. She danced on, with one grotesquely gay partner after another in a terrible parody of a life she had once known, until it was quite dark outside.

After the ruthless destruction of her benevolent mood on Saturday, Dulcie was in the right frame of mind to be rigorously to the point with Primmy when she called the following evening, though she did take the precaution of arming herself with a Martini and Primmy with a sweet sherry before broaching her subject.

'I'm pregnant,' she announced.

Primmy put her glass down and laced her long, red hands together on her lap. Red, but cool, thought Dulcie, it was funny how fiery-looking hands were often cool, and pale ones warm and clammy.

'Are you sure?'

'Yes.'

'It's quite unlikely you know – in a woman your age.'

'But not impossible. And I am.'

'Have you had a test?'

Dulcie shook her head. 'No, but I don't need to, I'm quite sure about it.'

'I don't see how –'

'Primmy, I've been pregnant before, and I do know what it feels like.'

If Primmy had been in danger of not taking her friend's news seriously, this piece of information brought her round.

'I see, so you're quite satisfied in your own mind?'

'Quite.'

'How far gone are you, do you think?'

'Only a few weeks. I'm terribly sick, and always tired – but the thing is, I want to get rid of it.'

Primmy shook her head and set her lips together in a firm, business-like line. 'You must see a doctor.'

'No, I don't want to do that. It's very early days, I just want not to be pregnant any more.'

'Whose is it?' Primmy's barely-concealed disapproval hung in the air between them.

Though she wanted to, Dulcie did not tell her it was none of her business. 'Bill's. There hasn't been anyone else for years, Primmy, I'm like an old married lady without the privileges.'

'Does he know?' Dulcie shook her head. 'Well perhaps you should tell him – he might marry you if he knew.'

'Yes, he might.' Dulcie gulped down the rest of her Martini. 'But I wouldn't want marriage on these terms, Primmy. I love him, you see.' She soldiered on in the face of Primmy's stern glare. 'I've spent a long time not pressuring him, just being there for him, too long to throw it all out of the window now.'

'I see.' It was plain she didn't. 'And what does he feel for you?'

Dulcie shrugged. 'I don't honestly know. Not as much, I suspect, but I don't mind. We can go on like this for ever, and it's all I want. If I were to tell him about this he would either marry me because it was the decent thing, which I couldn't bear, or I might lose him altogether and that would be even worse. So.'

'You're not giving him the chance though, are you?' said Primmy. She felt a sharp, unaccustomed pang of self-pity. Here was Dulcie turning down these good and worthwhile things when they were offered. Dulcie, confronted with an embarrassment of riches, as she saw it, and interested in none of them while she –'

'I dare not,' said Dulcie. She did not say this fearfully, but emphatically, as though she had weighed the pros and cons with the utmost care and reached an irreversible conclusion. Neither was she going to enlarge on it.

Primmy got up from the sofa, to ease her anger with Dulcie as much as anything else. She went to the window and ran her hand down the join of the curtains, tweaking the two corners neatly together at the bottom. 'You seem to have it all worked out,' she said, a little acidly. 'I don't see why you're telling me.'

'I need your help – to get rid of it.'

Primmy had seen this coming, but even so it was a shock. 'That's silly, dangerous talk! You should go and see a doctor. As likely as not he'd tell you you shouldn't go ahead at your age anyway –'

'Do stop going on about my age!' snapped Dulcie. 'Look, Primmy, I'm sure there must be something I can take so that I can deal with this at home. I don't want to see a doctor, or hear his opinions, or go into hospital, I just want to get on with my life.'

'I see.' Primmy came back and sat down again, perched rather on the edge of the seat, as if poised for flight. 'May I ask what happened last time you were expecting?'

Dulcie made a business of lighting a cigarette. 'I'm stronger than I look – I loathed every moment of it, but there were no complications.'

'And the baby?'

'I had it adopted.'

'You could do that again.'

'No, I couldn't!' Dulcie lost patience, and stood up sharply. In an instant, the delicate layers of friendship and equality laid down over twenty-odd years crumbled like the fragile things they were. Dulcie became again the spoilt, wilful younger daughter of the house and Primmy the secretive, omniscient domestic servant. The two women confronted each other across a void of bitter incomprehension, trapped in an order too established to change.

'For God's sake say yes, you'll help me, or refuse. One or the other! I don't want your advice, Primmy, I want your help, and if you're not prepared to give it to me you can go to hell!'

'I only want to do what's best,' said Primmy, icily.

'Then don't judge me! If you can do something for me, that's fine and dandy. If you can't just say so – and stop looking at me like that!'

Primmy's look revealed Dulcie as a self-indulgent middle-aged woman who had never grown up; who still, after a lifetime of what should have been useful experience, had not changed her ways; and who was still looking to others more responsible than herself to provide an easy way out.

What she said was: 'There's no need to shout.'

Dulcie in her turn saw the slightly puritanical and censorious retainer of bygone years, the shadowy, pale-faced wraith of the corridors and back stairs, seeing all, knowing all, drawing her own severe conclusions.

'Well?'

'I'm sorry, I can't.'

'Right then – fine! Fine!' Dulcie smarted under the humiliation of it. That this woman, a nobody, should have this power and choose to withhold it when she asked her. She threw her hands to her face, not in despair but in a paroxysm of fury, pressing her fingers to her eyes as if to blot out the last few moments. 'You smug cow – get out of my flat!'

There was no reply. When Dulcie looked up, Primmy was not there. She could hear her moving about in the hall in that oh-so-discreet, tidy way that she had never lost. Dulcie stormed out after her, white-hot with fury. She felt better, physically, than she had done for weeks.

'Just go, and hurry!'

Primmy did not hurry, but continued at the same measured pace to button her serviceable dark coat over the scarf crossed over her flat chest, to pull on her wool gloves (handknitted, Dulcie felt sure) and her small felt hat. Then and only then did she turn to Dulcie.

'I'm sorry, Dulcie, but you're asking too much of me. In all my years as a nurse I've not taken advantage of my position, and I won't start now. I'll help you do things properly, through the right channels. But I'm not giving you something that might make you feel ill, and do away with your little baby –' She pecked slightly on the last word, as though it stuck in her craw. 'I'll go now.'

'Yes. Do that.'

'Good-bye Dulcie.'

Dulcie did not answer. She could hardly bear to look at Primmy, so self-righteous and well-darned and respectable, so unimpeachably decent in every regard. She wondered how she had never allowed herself to beg a favour from such a woman. She felt inside herself not only the burgeoning, intrusive life of the baby, but also that subtle change from self-respect to vanity, the one which could stand up to punishment, the other which shrivelled and evaporated when exposed to the fierce blast of truth.

On her way down the stairs, Primmy began to shiver. Like many people who are not normally extravagant with their emotions, extremes of feeling upset had unnerved her. She who had hardly had a day's illness in her life felt quite wishy-washy. Now that she had left Dulcie, her usual commonsense and humanity began to bustle about her brain, setting things in order, opening little windows of perspective and reason to cast light on the turbulent gloom.

By the time she reached the hall, she saw what she had done, and also what the right thing was to do now. Her reasons for refusing help had not been professional, but personal, born of jealousy and spite. What was there in her life that was so wonderful? She had few friends, not many people who needed her, apart from her patients. And yet when someone cried out to her for assistance, what had she done? Retreated primly behind a screen of pious disapproval.

She stood in the dark hall, quite still, her heels together, feeling the currents of pros and cons eddying around her, trying to make up her mind, forcing down the sour, dry pill of pride.

Dulcie opened the door. 'Hallo, you're back. Come in.'

Primmy said: 'I could get you something.'

'Thank you.'

'It won't be pleasant, you won't like it. But if you're only a few weeks gone, it shouldn't take long.'

'So long as it does the trick.'

'It will. I could get it to you during the week.'

'Thank you, thank you, thank you.'

Doris was in the habit of taking her charge down to the tube station these nights, and not only for safety reasons. Quite simply, Doris enjoyed the company. Though her present job had a lot to be said for it, she had to spend so many hours just hanging about the flat with Maria, and she was a gregarious person. She liked to exchange jokes, and sing and roister a bit. Not that Maria wasn't a cheery sort — amazingly so, considering she wasn't a well woman — but Doris needed something a bit more robust in the social line.

The local tube station was ideal as a shelter because it was not yet completed, and was still in a pristine, unused condition. Some nights Doris could almost fancy herself in some big, grand hotel — it was something to do with the wide staircase, and the tiled walls (which, in Doris's imagination, became marble) and the echoing space of the ticket hall, off which the entrances to the platforms led, mysterious and inviting. Also, she liked the feeling of people gathering of an evening, the regulars and the newcomers, the bonhomie and the chit-chat, the pooling of resources. In many ways, the blitz was the happiest time of Doris's life.

At first, there had been the problem of how to transport Maria the few hundred yards to the station. She and Tony had tried walking her, supporting her between them, but the effort had nearly killed her and she'd reached the station white and blue-lipped and gasping for breath. But help had come in the form of an old wood and wicker bath chair belonging to the Dennys downstairs — Mr Denny had bought it for his ailing father — and Doris would load Maria into the bath chair and trundle along at a great rate, often using Maria's lap as a kind of extra pair of hands. Mrs Marx's small, dark head would peer over a mound of magazines, and knitting, and the tartan shopping bag loaded with provisions.

Tony was usually deputed to carry the bedding. Although, officially, people weren't supposed to be sheltering in the station, because it was still under construction, authority had turned a blind eye. There were by now quite a number of servicable wooden bunks down there and Maria, because of her condition, had an informal but permanent claim on one of them. This left the bath chair free for Doris — she spent half the night socializing, anyway — while Tony, like most of the young lads, just dossed down on a bench or on the floor.

The station's nocturnal life became institutionalized. The

locals were resourceful, and their strong family ties and cockney sense of community made them take pride even in this, a hole in the ground. Besides, you never knew whether the home you left in the evening would still be there in the morning, so it was as well to make the best of the available accommodation.

There was as yet only partial lighting in the station, and no crash barriers or railings, but most of the station-dwellers saw this as a positive advantage because it gave plenty of unbroken space. Some of the youngsters brought down an old gramophone and danced, the children and the old did turns, people were happy to provide a little of what they could for the common good, whether it was hairdressing or singing or looking after babies. It became routine for everyone to enjoy some entertainment while they ate – and shared – whatever they'd brought with them. And then there was cards, and gossip and the odd bottle of stout. Doris would make sure Maria was comfortable and then go off on her travels, cruising from group to group, in her element.

Tony didn't much care for the station. He would have stayed with the Dennys in the hallway at Globe Road, but for his mother's pleas, and the fact that he did not trust Doris. Her breath usually smelt of beer even before they left home in the early evening, and by the time they had been underground for an hour or two, the world was her friend. Tony saw it as his bounden duty to remain with his mother, but his sense of grievance against Ernest deepened.

One evening in mid-January they set out as usual, bag and baggage, for the station. It was bitterly cold, with that dank, raw chill that seems particularly to affect cities, where there is only stone and concrete and iron, and no organic matter to give life to the cold. The air was thick with a catarrhal pea-souper, people were trudging spectres, voices and footsteps secret and muffled by the smog. There were a lot of coughs about.

Maria added hers to the atmosphere as they pushed down Globe Road.

'All right dear?' asked Doris automatically. Tony was pushing the bath chair, his mother had the tartan shopping bag on her knee, and a bedroll, and Doris carried another shopping bag and a leaking eiderdown. In the fog, the trickle of feathers from the rolled-up, bulging quilt made Doris look as if she herself were leaking, and might sag and collapse altogether.

'I'm right as rain,' said Maria, stifling more coughs. 'You okay Tone?'

'Yeah, I'm okay.'

They reached the entrance to the station, with its half boarded-up entrance. They were a little later than usual, and there was already a considerable queue including, Tony noticed, the old bugger with the accordion, prancing around like he was the bee's knees.

They took their place in the queue, exchanging greetings with the regulars. The line moved slowly forwards. The man with the squeeze-box came alongside them. He was only fifteen bob to the pound in Tony's opinion, he had a silly fixed smile and a loping, bent-kneed way of walking in time to the music. His hair was parted in the centre and stuck out on either side in two greasy tufts above his purply-red face with its big pocked nose. He played the instrument deftly but abstractedly, as if it were a skill remembered from some previous incarnation, and his goggly eyes rolled moonily. But Maria tapped her hand on the arm of the bath chair and nodded her head in time to the music.

Once behind the wooden partition, at the top of the stairs, they could feel the upward drift of warm air from down below. 'That's better!' said Doris. She put her face down to Maria's. 'Not many brass monkeys out there today, love.'

Tony watched her with dislike. Her noisy, heavy-handed attentiveness reduced Maria to a nonentity, an illusion which was reinforced by her physical smallness beside Doris's huge bulk. Because she could not shout and gesture and trundle about as Doris did she became Doris's thing, a puppet, an appendage, lacking any identity except insofar as she was Doris's charge.

They had a system for getting the bath chair down the stairs. There was no central rail as yet, so they stuck to the side, by the wall, each holding with one hand on to the handle of the chair, lowering it gently down, step by step. The exercise depended on co-operation, for although Maria was light as a feather, the chair was cumbersome. Halfway down there was a wider stair, where they could take a breather. People hurried down, to get a good place, but they circumnavigated the bath chair and there was no crush.

On the halfway stair, Doris looked at Tony. ' 'Ere, do you think this is giving you biceps like Charles Atlas?'

'I bleeding well 'ope not.'

'Go on with you — rather be a ten stone weakling? I like big men,' said Doris. She was puffing heavily. 'Ready for the last lap?'

Tony took the strain to lower the chair over the next step. But as he did so, someone running down the stairs jogged Doris's shoulder. It was only a glancing blow, but her huge, unsteady bulk converted it into a lurch. Her hand slipped off the bar, and the weight of the chair moving forward pulled it out of Tony's grasp, too.

It hurtled forward at a terrifying pace, gathering momentum, bouncing and rocking, but somehow remaining upright.

'Mum! Look out! It's me mum!'

Tony tried to catch it, but people, stupid and slow-moving with surprise, got in his way. The chair knocked over a young woman who began to scream, and her screams, and those of Doris, alerted others in its path, who turned only just in time to move out of its way, watching with startled faces and gaping mouths. Maria's limp, doll-like form jerked back and forth, she had released the tartan bag in order to clutch the arms of the chair, and sandwiches, Thermos, fags and newspaper flew over the steps in her wake.

Only a few yards from the bottom a man had the presence of mind to stick out his hand and grab the arm of the chair. But contrary to his intention the chair, carried by its own momentum, sprang round sideways to face him and Maria was catapulted out, head over heels, bumping and rolling to the foot of the stairs. At the last moment her little stick-like arms, the bones of the hands as delicate and defined as a skeleton, shot out and her head jerked back, resisting the inevitable at the eleventh hour.

For a second everyone just stared at her in horror. The only movement was the slowing spin of the bath chair wheels, turning and ticking on the staircase, and the dripping of the tea from the broken Thermos. From outside on the cold evening pavement they could hear the throb and warble of the squeeze-box man.

'Mum!'

Tony ran down, his face ugly with misery, elbowing people aside. They were respectful, recognizing his prior claim. In his wake, stumbling, wobbling, sobbing noisily, came Doris, still holding the eiderdown, shedding feathers like a great flightless, waddling bird.

Maria was dead. Tony didn't need to feel her heart, or listen for her breathing. Her face, which had been so animated in life, had a rumpled, meaningless, vacated look, the skin of one cheek pushed up in folds by the hard floor of the station.

As other people began to surge round him, exclaiming, commiserating, accusing, Tony sat back on his heels, his stubby hands resting on his knees, the tears trickling slimily from his eyes and the snot from his nose. What he felt was not so much grief as helpless rage. When Doris tried to put her pillowy arm across his shoulders he shook it off violently, and then scrambled to his feet and ran back up the stairs, crouched over as if in pain.

Ernest was in the kitchen when the phone rang. He was making a cheap and cheerful potato and carrot pie, the recipe for which he had found in a women's magazine. For some time now he had been in a rebellious frame of mind, but the simple pleasure of cooking, to the remote accompaniment of some unusually melodious highbrow music of Giles's, had temporarily soothed him. He knew this cosy sense of contentment would not survive the light of day, but he was happy enough to go with it for the moment.

He heard Giles take the needle off the record, and answer the phone. The exchange was perfunctory. Whoever it was on the other end had a good deal to say and was not concerned with conversational niceties. Ernest heard Giles's tone change from welcome and interest to serious attentiveness.

'Yes . . . yes, of course, don't worry . . . I'll tell him at once. Yes, hang on.'

Giles appeared in the kitchen doorway. Ernest did not look

up from his pastry-making: he wished to keep whatever it was at bay.

'Ernest – that's your young brother on the telephone.'

'Tony?' Now he did look up. He had never known Tony use the telephone in his whole life.

Giles came over and took his arm, leading him into the drawing-room, floury hands and all. 'There's been an accident, Ernest, with your mother.'

'Accident?' He could only echo, stupidly, Giles's words. 'How do you mean?'

'You'd better talk to him.'

Ernest dusted off his hands, and a fine, floating mist descended to settle on the Turkish carpet. Gingerly, he picked up the receiver. 'Tone?'

'You bastard!'

'Tony, what happened?'

'She's dead, she's bleeding well dead – she fell down the stairs!'

Ernest couldn't take in the first part of this sentence. 'What stairs?'

'Just get down here quick you selfish, murdering bastard!'

Ernest put down the receiver and sat down on the arm of the chesterfield. 'She's dead,' he repeated dully.

'Oh my poor boy. My poor, poor Ernest.' Giles put his arms round him, rocking him a little from side to side.

'I must get down there,' said Ernest into Giles's cashmere pullover.

'Yes.' Giles released him. 'Take a taxi.' He went to his desk, where his jacket hung on the back of the chair, and took his wallet from the inside pocket. He got out some notes, and tucked them into Ernest's nerveless hand in a fatherly way. 'There. Now hurry and get your coat, it's freezing out there. I'll go on down and get you a cab. By the way – would you like me to come?'

Ernest shook his head. 'No, that's all right.'

When he emerged into the drifting, pressing cold of Piccadilly, Giles was at his side at once, like a guardian angel. A taxi stood ready at the kerb, thrumming patiently in the smog.

'Dear Ernest . . .' Giles touched his face. 'I'm so sorry. Good luck.' Then he opened the door and asked: 'What's the address?'

'Oh – Globe Road, Bethnal Green.'

Giles passed on these instructions to the driver, closed the door after Ernest and tapped on the roof.

Ernest had read one of Giles's books concerning the River Styx and the waters of Lethe, and on his journey down he thought that this must be what they were like – this endless, dangerous dark, and cold, and confusion, this feeling of dread. With the arrival of the smog the streets were crammed with abandoned traffic – buses, vans, cabs and cars – as though their occupants had been spirited away by some terrible, malign stroke of fate. Ernest's cabbie was all for doing the same, but Ernest protested with such violent distress, and was plainly in such a two-and-eight that he pressed on, albeit at a snail's pace, taking circuitous back routes to avoid the worst congestion.

To Ernest in his agony it seemed interminable, but about halfway there the smog began to thin and they made better progress. They did not have to go to Globe Road: as they crawled past the tube station he saw the ambulance, the small crowd – and Tony, standing there waiting for him.

'This'll do.'

He paid the driver abstractedly, forgetting to take the proffered change, and turned to face his brother. In the background he caught sight of the wayward unfocussed mass that was Doris.

'Where is she?' he asked.

'They're getting her,' said Tony. 'You nearly missed her.' In spite of this shaft, his earlier blind fury had given way to a dull misery.

Ernest ran past him, pushed his way through Doris and the others, to whom she was delivering Maria's impromptu obituary, and went into the station. A rope had been slung across at the bottom of the steps, and across the entrances to the platforms, to prevent the curious crowding back. Two St John's ambulance men were rolling the tiny figure of Maria Marx on to a stretcher, covering her neatly with a grey blanket, as though laying a table. To one side stood the bath chair,

It was some minutes before he was able to take a sufficient grip on himself to look out for a cab, and then of course there were none in this part of town. When he did find one he had blundered for almost a mile up the Commercial Road. The cabbie looked at him with undisguised suspicion.

'Albany?'

'That's what I said!' shrieked Ernest.

'All right, squire, keep your hair on.'

Ernest got into the back seat. His chest was tight, his breathing laboured, he let out a little moan of anxiety. The cabbie peered at him in the mirror as they crawled forward.

'Okay cock?'

Ernest nodded, waving a hand to indicate his helplessness.

'So long as you're sure,' said the driver, doubtfully.

By the time they reached Piccadilly Ernest had calmed himself, his breathing had quieted and he had lost the terrible tight, bursting feeling in his chest. However, his recovery did not prevent him from wheezing a little as he told Giles how awful it had all been, and about Tony's unwarranted outburst.

Giles sat on the chesterfield with his arm about Ernest's heaving shoulders. He was thoughtful.

'Poor Ernest. And your mother – I know how close you were to her.'

'Yes, well . . .' said Ernest, fiddling with his cufflinks. He was so glad to be back in the warmth and security and comfort of Giles's flat that relief had almost elbowed out grief. 'I want her to have a decent funeral,' he said.

'Of course, we shall see to it.'

'And there are things to be sorted out – the flat, and the woman I employed to look after her –'

'Yes. And your brother.'

'He can stuff it.'

'I realize he said hurtful things to you, Ernest. But he's only a boy, and he must have been through hell. You'll have to forgive him, he needs you now more than ever.'

It was now Ernest's turn to say: 'Don't make me laugh!'

Giles was patient. 'It's true. And look at things from his point of view – your life has improved out of all recognition, his hardly at all. You were able to pay for a better standard of living for them, but you weren't actually around.'

'I couldn't help that — I was working for you.' Ernest put the very merest emphasis on the word 'working', just enough to remind Giles how things stood.

'Yes, I know. No one's blaming you for anything, Ernest, you've always been a good son to your mother. But perhaps –'

'Yes? Well?' Ernest fixed a reddened glare on Giles. 'Perhaps what?'

'Oh, dear.' Giles got up, and went to the desk to pour himself a brandy and water, lifting the decanter enquiringly in Ernest's direction. When he shook his head, Giles brought his glass back and sat on the chesterfield, but not so close.

'I didn't mean to say any of this now, Ernest. But all this has crystallized something I've been thinking and feeling for a long time. I think you have been too cut off, here with me. I think I should give you your life back.'

'And what,' asked Ernest, 'is that supposed to mean?'

'I think that with the best possible intentions, and . . .' he looked at Ernest, 'for entirely selfish reasons, too, I've made problems for you. I've split your life down the middle, and it's uncomfortable for everyone.'

'No, no it's not –' Ernest moved up to Giles and leaned his head against his shoulder, feeling Giles's hand smooth the hair back from his forehead. 'This *is* my life now, not the other, I don't want any more to do with it.'

'Oh, Ernest . . . you don't mean that. All that — it made you what you are. You'd be wrong, so wrong, just to jettison it. You haven't done, either, up to now, it's one of the reasons you're so — dear to me.'

'So what do you suggest?'

'That you should consider getting a place of your own, perhaps nearer your brother.'

'You want me to move out.' Ernest raised his face to Giles's with a look of tear-stained disbelief.

'I didn't say that. I said it might be better for you.'

'You want to get rid of me.'

'No, no, no!' Giles took Ernest's face between his hands and held it tight in his exasperation. 'Stop twisting everything I say, grow up Ernest. We could still be as close as ever, you could go on working here –'

'And you could go on screwing me during working hours, so that you didn't have to explain me away to your tight-arsed friends in the evening!'

'When have I ever done that? I have never denied you.'

'No, and you've never admitted what we do, either.'

'Why on earth should I? It's none of their business, they don't want to know, and I don't want to tell them. You wouldn't expect anyone else to hang out their private life on the line, so why should we? Besides,' he added, more soberly, 'we're not legal.'

'Ah!' cried Ernest, leaping to his feet, pointing at Giles in what Giles considered his most hammy style but which for some reason he found affecting. 'Ah, that's it, isn't it? Time to tidy things up a bit!'

'Ernest. You have been living here for the best part of four years. Why would I suddenly decide a thing like that?'

'You tell me!'

'You make me happy, there's no one else I want. But I wasn't exactly celibate before I met you, I had to take my pleasures elsewhere. I don't give a damn about the law as long as I don't hurt or offend my friends by breaking it. Nothing could be more moral than two people who care for each other being together. But I think I've been too greedy, I've made it too hard for you to keep in touch with the other people who've needed you. You're very young, Ernest, you need some time and space to find your feet.'

'You pig!' hissed Ernest. 'Hypocrite!'

Giles got up and tried to embrace him, but he fought him off and stumbled wildly for the door, shouting, 'Don't come near me!'

He ran to his room, slamming the door behind him, and fell, sobbing, on the bed.

Kate opened the door of the house in Strada Comina, and they stepped inside. After the harsh, pale light of the street the hall was cool, dark and secret, so that when Bill shut the door they could not see each other but went blindly and instinctively into each other's arms.

He began to unbutton the front of her thin cotton shirt-dress. She felt her breasts, taut and rigid, almost painful with the desire to be enclosed by his hand, and the rest of her melting, throbbing with unbearable fierce impatience.

'Where?' he said.

'Upstairs. Quickly, quickly.'

They stumbled up the narrow, precipitous stairs and into the bedroom. The shutters were drawn, there was a cell-like gloom, just a few thin, horizontal threads of light lay across the rush mat on the floor. They fell on to the bed. Kate made a sound — she scarcely recognized it as her own voice — a throaty, animal keening. Only when they were one, joined, locked together and galvanized by the same current of awesome passion — only then was there any relief. With Bill rooted in her she felt the duplicity, the shame and guilt burned out of her. Then she was truly herself, and no part of her hidden. But their climax, as ever, was quick, and explosive and followed by a terrible hurtling descent into desolation so that she needed more, and yet more of him, unable to assuage her need except by feeding off the energy they created together. And as before she was blinded and deafened by lust — she could not hear Bill, or see him properly, but only feel him around her and in her. She sought concealment in him, domination over him, fusion with him, and finally those things were impossible. Only utter exhaustion halted them, when the sun had moved round and there were no more streaks of light on the floor. They were trembling, drained, soaked with sweat, and saliva and the fluids that had burst and poured from them, scarred and bruised like the two battered survivors of a stormy shipwreck. After a while some energy crept back, and with it a consciousness of time and place, an awareness of each other, little scattered handfuls of quiet words to restore some kind of normality.

'It feels as though it's been waiting for us,' said Bill.

'It's all ours until you have to go.'

'It won't be long.'

'I know.'

'Your friend Beth — does she know?'

'She may guess, but even if she does she wouldn't say anything. We can live in each other's pockets — everyone does here — and no one will think anything of it. Least of all Lawrence.'

'Lawrence.'

The name fell between them like a stone into still water. But he took her in his arms and kissed her ferociously, as if damning his conscience to hell. There could be no 'for ever' in all this. Just, if they were lucky, times when they could be together. Always might be too long for them, they'd burn each other out, there'd be nothing left.

'Hopeless,' he said. 'Hopeless.'

'Nothing's hopeless.'

'We are. We're a lost cause. We can't make each other happy, but we can't do without each other either.'

She didn't answer. He looked down at her, and her face was impassive, averted from him. But when he bent and brushed his lips on her cheek he could taste salt and realized that she was crying – crying for him.

Kate got back to Strada Forni to find Beth eating supper and Connie fulminating in the kitchen.

'Hallo,' said Beth. 'Back at last. I hope you're prepared to make your excuses to Connie.'

'I'm sorry, we got talking.'

'That's all right.' Beth eyed her. 'All settled in?'

'Yes. Beth, it's so good of you and Josh to let Bill stay there.'

Beth shrugged. 'It's a good arrangement, we're only too happy.'

Connie stumped in with a plate of cooked chicken and tomato salad. 'Is dry!' she announced, slamming the plate down in front of Kate.

'It looks delicious, Connie, thank you.'

'It's too damn dry!' snapped Connie.

When she'd gone, Kate addressed herself hungrily to her supper while Beth, who had finished, watched her.

'What's he going to do?' she asked. 'I mean, how long will he be here, and how will he fill his time?'

'He's got his story about the convoy to write,' said Kate. 'And he wants to get up to the airfield with Lawrence and see what's going on there. Apparently a plane's going out with some war office brass early next week, and he's hoping to get out on that.'

'I see. Kate—'

Something in Beth's voice made Kate look sharply at her.

'Yes?'

'Forgive me asking, but what exactly . . .?'

Beth's question was mercifully cut short by the sharp, crackling voice on the radio: *'Twissija Ta Habit Mill Arja!* Air Raid Warning!'

CHAPTER TWENTY

'Sahha . . .'

Maltese greeting and farewell

A WEEK after their previous conversation, Dulcie met Primmy
for lunch. Or at least they furnished themselves with
sandwiches and went to one of Dame Myra Hess's concerts at
the National Gallery. The venue had been Dulcie's idea,
although she was no devotee of classical music, because she
hoped the exchange might be less awkward for both of them if
it took place on neutral territory and in front of several hundred
captive witnesses.

In fact, it was an even better idea than she could have hoped.
The stirring strains of the Polonaise and other, more melancholy
and romantic Chopin pieces, soothed their spirits, so that when
the concert ended they were disposed to be calm and practical.

Primmy handed Dulcie a worn manilla envelope containing
a brown glass bottle. Half a dozen villainous-looking ovoid
capsules rattled in the bottom.

'When you're ready,' she said, 'take two. Half an hour later,
take another one.'

'I see. Thank you.' Dulcie tucked the package into her
handbag.

They walked together, in the departing crowd, as far as the
Gallery's entrance hall, and then Primmy turned to her, saying,
'Well then, I'll be going. Would you like me to be there?'

'Oh no!' Dulcie at once felt she had sounded too emphatic,
and added. 'No thank you, it's a kind thought, but I shall
manage.'

'It won't be pleasant.'

'I never thought it would be.' Dulcie's face was white, but composed.

'You know, it isn't too late to –'

Dulcie beamed at her. 'I mustn't keep you, Primmy. I'll call you soon. 'Bye!'

Primmy was back on the ward at two. She was irritable and out of sorts, and saw her mood reflected back at her from the faces of her nurses, who scurried away like frightened rabbits at her approach. She even looked on her patients with a jaundiced eye this afternoon. Silly women. Most women were silly, she reflected as she made her rounds, inspecting lockers and charts, tweaking curtains and plumping pillows and peering disparagingly at stagnant flower water. They wanted it all ways. The ones with families made out they were martyrs to their children, always confiding in her how lovely it was to be having a nice rest, even if they had had half their stomachs removed. The ones without children told her it had always been their dearest wish to have little ones, but it Was Not To Be. If their kids had been evacuated, for their own safety, they wanted them home. The single ones wanted husbands, the married ones complained of loveless drudgery. They were either hypochondriacs or they left their conditions so long unattended that there was nothing medical science could do. On the ward, they were sluts. Give me men any day, Primmy thought grimly, peering into a toilet bowl full of soggy cigarette ends and stained cotton wool.

By the time Mr Baucher, the consultant, arrived for his afternoon rounds, Primmy's patients were sitting up in their smooth, neat beds as po-faced as graven images, hair brushed, faces washed, bedpans emptied and flower water changed – a tribute to the ward sister's art. Their usual garrulity had deserted them in the east wind of Primmy's mood, she had coerced their loose tongues, their untidy minds and messy habits into a state of pristine order for the benefit of Mr Baucher.

'You seem to be running a tight ship here, Sister,' he remarked jovially, but Primmy did not smile.

'Thank you, sir.'

'Now let's see what goes on *under* the covers, shall we?'

Primmy, watching the consultant's plump backside as he walked in front of her to the first bed, decided she hadn't much time for him, either. And tomorrow she had to attend a funeral.

Maria Marx was laid to rest by the Reverend Robert Hollis in the sooty graveyard of St Cuthbert's, at the end of Globe Road. Bobby Hollis had been approached to conduct the service (on Tony's insistence and to Ernest's chagrin) because he had been kind to Maria in the distant past, and was the only priest with whom she had had even a nodding acquaintance, and the incumbent of St Cuthbert's had gracefully given way.

There were a large number of mourners at the funeral. This was partly because Maria had been a popular member of the community, and partly because so many of the locals had lost loved ones, and homes, with not a scrap left to show, let alone to bury, and this funeral served as a kind of communal paying of respects to the dear departed.

The crowd was a blessing as far as Ernest was concerned. A good many of the local people, especially those from the region of the Institute and Pear Tree Court, had not seen him since the old days, and his stock was still high with them. Their sympathetic affability came between him and Tony's sceptical stare, and the starchy glances of the nurse.

Ernest had not been able to prevent Giles from accompanying him. Since the awful night of Maria's death the question of Ernest's future had not been mentioned again. The anger and mistrust were still there, on Ernest's part, but had been by tacit mutual agreement driven underground for the time being. Giles had rather regretted having made his move at a time when Ernest had been distressed to begin with, and had been gentle but firm in the matter of the funeral.

'I feel a kind of responsibility,' he had said. 'You must allow me to perform my small penance.'

'So long as you don't hang round me too much,' had been Ernest's ungracious response.

Giles had smiled. 'I shall be discretion personified, just your aged employer.'

When the time came, however, in spite of his churlishness Ernest was bound to admit that Giles's presence was a comfort. He managed what might have been an awkward occasion with natural grace and dignity, and it was plain that people took to him in spite of his affluent appearance and posh accent. That, of course, was class, reflected Ernest, something money couldn't buy — and he did not find the notion comforting.

As they moved away from the graveside in the late afternoon, Giles and Ernest found themselves walking by Primmy. Reluctantly, because Giles obviously expected it, Ernest introduced him. To his astonishment, Primmy said: 'Aren't you a friend of Dulcie Tennant's? I'm sure I've heard her mention your name.'

'That's right!' said Giles, delighted. 'How clever of you to have remembered it. Dulcie and I are old friends, though I haven't seen much of her lately. Tell me, how is she?'

Primmy thought of what Dulcie might be doing at that very moment and replied: 'Quite well, so far as I know.'

'She should get married,' confided Giles, in the nearest he came to a *faux pas* all afternoon. 'Have you met her Bill?'

'I can't say I have,' replied Primmy. 'And what will you do now?' she asked Ernest. She had not really intended to speak to him at all after their last encounter, and she only did so now to avoid further discussion of Dulcie. Her nervousness made her sound more censorious than she intended.

'Do?' Ernest stared coldly at her.

'I mean, shall we see more of you? Young Tony's on his own now.'

Ernest could feel Giles's attention on this exchange, even though he wasn't looking at them.

'I'm keeping the flat on in Globe Road for the time being,' he replied in a somewhat lordly manner. 'And Doris can stay on and housekeep for him. It's up to him what he does, he's not a child any more.'

'So you're not coming back?'

'Not going back, no.' He slightly altered her words to suit his purposes.

Primmy turned back to Giles. 'I have to be going. It was nice to have met you.'

'Yes — and who knows, perhaps our paths will cross again.'

This struck Primmy as a possibility too remote to warrant comment so she simply said, 'Good-bye.'

'Good-bye.'

Giles and Ernest walked with the others back to the Ross where tea, beer and refreshments had been laid on. In the refectory the gathering began to exude the steamy, rich sentimentality of a true cockney wake, and even Ernest was not immune to its effects, redolent though it was of a past which he so determinedly disowned. He became quite lit up, so that the small core of grief over the death of his mother became simply the nucleus of a great aura of mellow golden light. When Merle sat down at the piano he stood on the fringes of the group that gathered round and listened as they sang old, haunting songs about husbands and wives and love and loss, and he was one of several who had recourse (though only discreetly, in his case) to a handkerchief.

After a while he sought out Giles. He spotted him sitting at the side of the hall, deep in conversation with Bobby Hollis. Both men were perched on spindly-legged hard chairs which gave them the air of two genteel elderly wallflowers at a dance.

They looked up as he approached, and Bobby Hollis reached behind him and pulled forward a third chair. 'Ernest – come and sit down.'

'Thanks, but shouldn't we be going?' Ernest glanced at Giles.

'That's all right for a minute or two.'

Reluctantly Ernest sat down on the edge of his seat.

'We've just been talking about you,' said Bobby amiably, unaware of the minefield he trod. 'I've hardly had time to say how sorry I am about your mother. She used to come here occasionally years ago, you know, drop in for a bite, or just a cup of tea and a fag. Then for some reason she suddenly stopped turning up, I don't know why . . . but I shall always remember her because she was so pretty and lively.'

'It was good of you to do the honours,' said Ernest.

'Not at all, not at all, as I say . . . and you? You're not coming back to this part of town, I suppose?'

'Everyone keeps asking me that,' said Ernest, brushing at the knees of his dark trousers with an elegant hand.

'And what's the answer?'

'I've got a good job elsewhere.'

'Ah, of course!' Bobby lifted a hand to indicate that Ernest should say no more. 'Mr Huxley has been saying how valuable he finds the work you do for him, but I gather you've become so proficient he feels he can't keep you fully occupied!' Bobby was laughing but Ernest shot a suspicious glance at Giles.

'In the end,' Giles said, 'a young man has to make up his own mind what he wants to do. I've told Ernest his life is his own, he owes nothing to me, and any feelings of loyalty would be entirely misplaced.'

'I'm perfectly happy with things as they are,' said Ernest threateningly. He bitterly resented the fact that the two of them had been discussing him in his absence as if he were a capricious child. 'Now let's go.'

'You can't just go,' Giles reminded him. 'These are your guests.'

By the time the party broke up, the guests flowing away from the Ross on a tide of everlasting friendship, Ernest had lost his earlier feeling of mellow good will and was out of sorts. Tony, on the other hand, who had kept away from him all afternoon, was pie-eyed. As Ernest approached him to say good-bye he crossed the Rubicon that divides euphoria from nausea. His affable grin widened and emitted, apparently without muscular contortion, like the face of a gargoyle after a rainstorm, a pungent flood of semi-digested corned-beef sandwiches, strong tea and light ale. Ernest was disgusted. Doris, who was nearby, let out a shriek of mirth.

'Attaboy, Tone – that's christened 'im!'

In spite of his revulsion at the spectacle of his brother staggering drunk and throwing up, this incident did serve to re-establish some of Ernest's authority.

'Look at you!' he snapped scornfully. 'If you could see yourself.'

'I feel bloody 'orrible . . .' mumbled Tony.

'Serves you right. This was supposed to be your Mum's funeral, not a great big piss-up,' reprimanded Ernest, choosing to forget his own earlier excesses. 'I'm ashamed of you.'

Doris bundled over with a tea towel and began to dab at Tony's shirtfront and trousers. 'Now, Ernie, don't be too hard on him, he's only a lad, he's got to start some time.'

'Start what? Being a lush?' Earnest poured scorn on Doris's homely philosophizing, but it was water off a duck's back. 'Anyway, I'm off now.'

'Rightie-ho, duck,' responded Doris.

'And you, Sunny Jim,' Ernest stabbed a finger at the damp and unfortunate Tony, 'no more beer till you're man enough to hold it!'

On the way out, Giles remarked, pleasantly enough: 'Is that Doris the right woman for the job?'

'She's okay. She's cheap and cheerful.' With this summary of Doris's qualifications Earnest closed the subject.

At the tube station a queue was already forming. Ernest said nothing but walked quickly past, keeping his eyes to the front.

At about the same time that Maria Marx's funeral tea was breaking up, Dulcie was getting things organized at her flat. She was businesslike – it was important to her to have things ready and neat.

Saturday night was ideal, Celine was out and she did not have to get up for work in the morning. She drew all the curtains and tuned the wireless into the Light Programme, turning up the volume so she could hear it in the bathroom.

In her bedroom she undressed, laying her clothes neatly over the chair, and put on her dressing-gown. Then she tied back her hair in a blue chiffon scarf and sat down at the dressing-table to remove her make-up. The only lights were the one over her mirror, and the one in the bathroom: her stage was spotlit. Music wafting from the darkened sitting room reminded her of the sort of person she was, unsuited for motherhood. 'Dance little lady, so obsessed with second best, no peace you'll ever find . . .'

She applied the Ponds cold cream and began to remove it with short, outward-sweeping strokes of a cotton wool pad. Wiping away the brave face, she thought, doing away with the mask, exposing the base metal. It was an oddly satisfying ritual, she was calmed by it. She thought quietly and lovingly of Kate. She drew no comparison between that long-ago rejection of her child and this calculated snuffing-out of the tiny agglomeration of cells in her womb. That had been a different life, another woman. Kate — *her* Kate — was alive, and no one could take that away from her. Then, she had dismissed Kate for reasons of weakness and selfishness, but had miraculously been granted a second chance, quite undeserved. What she was about to do, she would do for love, in the full and certain knowledge that she was right to do it, and that if Kate were ever to hear of it, she would understand.

When her face was quite clean, bare and slightly greasy in the lamplight, she removed her rings and earrings, laying them neatly beside her hairbrush. Then she picked up the brown glass jar, unscrewed the top and took out two capsules, replacing the top afterwards. They lay in the palm of her hand smooth and secretive as birds' eggs.

She picked up the Martini she had prepared for herself, placed the first capsule on her tongue and, watching herself in the mirror, swallowed it; then she did the same with the second and gulped down the rest of the Martini rather too fast, so that her ears sang. Finally she turned off the lamp next to her and sat quietly, the bottle in her lap, the bright square of the bathroom door shining across the hall.

The pain came as a surprise. She had prepared herself for a shock, a cudgel-blow, something sudden and violent. But instead of that it crept up on her stealthily, almost slyly, like a snake, wriggling beneath the fragile barrier of preparedness that she'd built round herself. It squeezed and crushed her so that she bent double, her face contorted. The glass bottle fell to the ground and rolled in an arc on the floor under the stool.

When the first pain receded a little, withdrawing with reluctant, sucking slowness like water down a plughole, Dulcie went across to the bathroom and turned on the taps. Mercifully, the water supply which had been temporarily cut off by bomb damage in Hamilton Avenue was now back on. She pushed the door to, but not shut, and as the next pain started she removed her dressing-gown and climbed into the water: some primitive, animal instinct had told her which element would be most comforting. But the sight of her small, pale body stretched out in the white bath unnerved her. It looked so impossibly unworkmanlike, it was a body designed for pleasure, not pain.

Now she could actually see the subcutaneous rippling and tightening as the pain began to do its work on her. Tears of fear rushed down her cheeks. It had begun, and she was powerless, now, to stop it.

A loud burst of laughter came from the wireless as some variety show got underway – Richard Murdoch, Arthur Askey, Tommy Trinder, the people's favourites. And in the bath the first feathery tendrils of blood appeared in the water.

It took two hours. The comedy programme finished, there was more music, and the news, and a woman explaining how to get the best from your rations, and a short play about a couple who did not appreciate each other. Dulcie did not listen, but neither did she make a noise. Half-way through the siren went and she heard someone, probably Miss Comstock, knock on her door. Surely she must be able to hear the wireless, and so realize that someone is in. But then again, Dulcie rarely went to the basement. She gritted her teeth and hoped whoever it was would go away which eventually, after a second timid knock, they did. Dulcie pulled herself out of the water and sat hunched and shaking on the lavatory, pulling her towel round her shoulders.

Afterwards was worse. When she had rubbed her upper body, and the moisture had mostly dripped and evaporated off the rest of her – she could not bend down – she put on her dressing-gown and set about clearing up, creeping and stooping like an old woman. It was a far more humiliating penance than the suffering inflicted by the capsules, but she had to get it done before Celine returned. She heard the high drone of the bombers coming in from the south-east and the sound reminded her of Bill. Well, she had done it for him. She had made the decision and gone through with it, and now it was over.

Lightheaded, with trembling legs, she mopped and scrubbed until her arms ached. She had had the foresight to buy a tin of Chemico and a cleaning cloth so that Celine would not notice any sudden reduction in supplies. Her stained bath towel and the bath mat she rolled up and stuffed in the bottom of her wardrobe, and she replaced the bath mat with a clean one.

Then she put on a clean nightie, slippers and her dressing-gown and hobbled through to the sitting room. She felt battered and bruised as if she had been knocked down by a bus. She pictured her insides as a mass of fresh, red, raw surfaces which every time she moved scraped agonizingly against each other. Exhaustedly she sank down on the sofa and picked up a magazine. She would have liked a hot drink, but did not have the energy to get it.

The print danced in front of her eyes like a swarm of tiny black insects. Her mind's eye was full of the blood-swirled water, the awful debris, the violence she had inflicted on herself and the small comma of life that had been inside her. She could hear the bombing, but it seemed much further south tonight — poor Aubrey and Iris. The thought of their decent, upright, public-spirited lives acted on her like a stiff drink. It was over now, she must be positive. She determined to wait up for Celine and they could have a cup of Ovaltine together. Such a cosy female get-together would be comforting for her and allay any suspicions Celine might have about the clean bath mat.

The 'All Clear' sounded at eleven, and Celine returned shortly afterwards, not, apparently, much put out by having spent most of her evening in the public shelter near Swiss Cottage.

Dulcie had been dozing when she heard the door open and close. From the waist down she was now stiff and numb, and her head ached. When she called out her voice sounded shrill after so much silence.

'Celine? I'm in here!'

'Coming, Madame!'

Dulcie arranged her features in an expression of amiable welcome, laying the open magazine on her knee as if she had been absorbed in it and only just put it down. But Celine, when she appeared, was far too excited to notice anything. She entered the room with that larger-than-life brightness that the goer-out has in the eyes of the jaundiced stay-at-home. Dulcie's carefully prepared smile felt stiff and stale in the face of such obviously genuine high spirits.

'Madame — I have something to tell you!'

Dulcie stretched out her hand and patted the arm of the

chair next to her. 'Come and sit down then, and tell me. Shall we have a hot drink or something?'

But unfortunately Celine did not seem to hear this suggestion. She bustled over and sat down on the edge of the chair, her usually stodgy features transformed by an expression of almost girlish delight. '*Voilà*, Madame!'

Because Dulcie was looking at Celine's face she did not at first notice that she was holding out her hand. Even when she did see the wagging fingers they indicated nothing to her until Celine exclaimed, giggling: '*C'est une belle bague, n'est ce pas?*'

She lifted her hand now, to admire it herself, fingers spread, palm towards Dulcie. But the use of French — which they reserved for moments of special intimacy, when they were women together, not mistress and maid — caught Dulcie's attention. In a second she had put the pieces of the jigsaw together: the tiny glitter on Celine's plump finger, the giggle, the girlish radiance.

'Why, Celine! You're not . . .?'

'*Oui*, Madame — yes, it is true! I am going to be married!'

With an ecstatic sound — laughter bubbling on the edge of tears — Celine fell into Dulcie's arms, kissing her on both cheeks, burbling incoherently about her happiness after so long, beyond her wildest dreams, the sort of man she had given up hope of ever meeting.

Then she sat up again, abandoning Dulcie, thin and pale and shocked on the sofa, and proceeded with happy selfishness to recount the whole story, how it had begun on the fateful night of Fondant's accident — it was the burly policeman, of course — how his own wife had died some years ago, leaving him alone (for they'd had no children), how wonderful it had been for both of them to find each other.

'Oh, Madame!' she cried, her hands clasped beneath her chin. 'I still cannot believe it! My only sorrow is that I must leave you, after so many years!'

She sounded anything but sorry. It was well after midnight when she finally ran out of steam and went to bed. But her abrupt exit did at least enable Dulcie to make her way to her own bedroom at a snail's pace, without provoking comment or enquiry. The bedroom was cold, the sheets chill and smooth. She heard Celine use the bathroom, but apparently her cleaning-up had been thorough, for she came out again after a moment or two, humming happily, and went straight to her room.

With a shock Dulcie realized that she was still bleeding freely, the short journey from the sitting-room had caused a minor flood. Furtively, miserably, she went to the bathroom and effected repairs with toilet paper and sanitary towels, then returned to her room and changed the bottom sheet, faint and trembling with tiredness. At last, she put the sheet with the towel and bath mat in the wardrobe and sank into bed.

But she did not sleep until four o'clock, and then only fitfully. When at eight o'clock she heard someone at the door, the sound made her skin jump and flinch as though she'd been threatened with violence. But Celine, in the best of humours, sounded welcoming. There were voices in the hall and a light tap on the bedroom door.

'Madame – you are awake?'

'Not really. What is it?'

Celine entered with exaggerated delicacy and tiptoed to her bedside. 'It is your friend, Miss Dilkes – she is here from the hospital to see you.'

'Oh, Primmy . . .' Dulcie tried to pull herself up, failed, and flopped back on the pillow. 'Celine, I've got an awful headache. Perhaps you could draw back the curtains and show her in here?'

'Certainly.'

Celine pulled back the curtains, admitting a rush of sparkling pale winter sunlight. Dulcie noticed she was wearing a coat.

'Have you been out already, Celine?'

'Yes – to mass.'

'Of course, it's Sunday.' The absence of church bells these days – their tongues stilled until they could peal either for invasion, or for peace – made Sunday a day of the deepest silence. Dulcie never went to church, but she missed the bells.

Primmy walked briskly in and stood self-consciously to attention while Celine closed the door after her. As well as her handbag, she carried a large wicker basket.

She glanced around appraisingly and came over to Dulcie.

'You've done it, have you?'

Dulcie nodded, closing her eyes against the bright, hard sunshine.

'Would you like me to have a look at you?'

Dulcie sighed. 'You might as well.'

'I'll go and wash my hands.'

When she'd finished examining her, Primmy took another jar of tablets from her handbag and put them on Dulcie's bedside table.

'They're painkillers, use them very sparingly, or not at all unless you're very sore. How do you feel?'

'As if I've been run over. But relieved — oh Primmy, *so* relieved.'

'Good,' said Primmy shortly. 'It's a great shock to the system. You should stay horizontal for a day or two, to let everything settle down.'

'I can't, I must get to work. I need my job and I've been late a few times recently what with feeling so awful.'

'Very well, but be sure to get to bed early at night.'

'I'll do my best.' Dulcie searched around to find a change of subject. 'Celine's leaving.'

'Is she?' Primmy sat down on the edge of the bed, with her heavily-shod feet neatly together. 'Not a bad thing, I suppose, it'll be much cheaper for you not to have a living-in maid. Get yourself a nice comfortable charlady instead.'

'Perhaps . . .' Dulcie realized it was pointless to try and explain to Primmy the feeling she had of the layers of her life being peeled away. She dared not complain any more to Primmy, she felt so impossibly, ignominiously beholden. 'She's getting married, to an English police constable,' she added.

'Well you never know,' said Primmy, 'maybe she won't want to stop working altogether — she could pop in while you're at work and do a couple of hours about the place, she might be glad of it.'

'Primmy, you don't understand!' Dulcie spoke with such emphasis that she felt a little gush of blood between her legs, reminding her to take care. 'You don't understand, this is her dream, the one she thought would never come true. She'll have her own home, she'll be a queen in it, cooking and cleaning and making curtains and looking after her policeman. She's just a *petite bourgeoise*, the very last thing she'll want is to come back here, even for a few hours. I shan't see her again.'

'No great loss, to my mind,' was Primmy's stony rejoinder. 'Anyway, I brought something with me.'

She fetched the basket and Dulcie watched dully as she opened it. 'I found it on a bombsite on my way out last night. It's been in my office on the ward for twelve hours, may God forgive me.' So saying, Primmy put a kitten on the bedspread, next to Dulcie's legs.

'Oh, Primmy . . .' Dulcie lifted her head from the pillow. 'Oh, it's the utterest heaven.'

The kitten was tiny and ugly, with a minute triangular spike of tail and large ears. It was mainly black with a large splodge of greyish-white over one side of its face, which gave it a snub-nosed, piratical air. Its eyes were glass-green and brilliant in its undistinguished face. The moment it was placed on the counterpane it began to knead the bed with its small front paws, purring powerfully. Its purr had a rattling, syncopated quality, unlike Fondant's rich drone.

'Bless its heart!' Dulcie could not take her eyes off it.

'I don't know what I'm going to do with it,' said Primmy, watching the kitten dispassionately. 'I don't know what came over me to pick him up in the first place.'

'You couldn't resist him,' said Dulcie, picking up the kitten and holding him before her face where he wriggled like a furry spider.

'I think I'll put him back where I found him on the way back,' said Primmy, eyeing the two of them.

'You can't do that!' Dulcie was aghast.

'I can't have a cat with my job — I don't like animals about the place anyway.'

'Then he must come to me — you must leave him here.'

'You've already got a cat. One's enough.'

'No, no I haven't!' Dulcie told Primmy about the dreadful evening of Fondant's disappearance and how, ironically, it had led to Celine's departure too. 'So you see I'm bereft, absolutely. He'll be the answer to my prayers, just like Celine's policeman.'

Primmy looked doubtful, but not impossibly so. 'And there's your job.'

'I can train him to be an indoor cat, just like Fondant was, I should enjoy doing it.'

'He's a stray.'

'But only a tiny one, a baby. He and I will soon shake down.'

'Well . . .'

'You know how I loved Fondant – oh Primmy you can't put him back on a horrid bomb site!'

'If you're sure.'

And so, with both parties knowing exactly how things stood, the transaction was made in such a way that Dulcie appeared to be doing Primmy a favour.

The kitten, still purring jerkily, spread its back legs and wet the counterpane.

'Rather you than me,' said Primmy. 'I hope you'll both be very happy.'

A week after Bill's arrival at the house in Strada Comina he was told that he would be able to fly out in a couple of days' time from Hal Far. It was also arranged for him to take a lift on the supply lorry with Josh (who had been on a twenty-four hour pass) and to spend some time with Lawrence at the airfield. It seemed all over almost before it had begun.

A kind of pattern had emerged in the intervening days. Kate would call on Bill on her way to the welfare centre in the morning, leaving just before Antonina arrived to do the housework. At midday she would come back and they would have another two hours together. Sometimes, if Beth had a rest in the afternoon, she would creep out and join him, often just lying on the bed, watching him as he wrote. In the evening he would come down and join them for Connie's cooking at supper, after which Kate – getting bolder before Beth's knowing look – would walk back with him up the hill and snatch a few more hasty, precious minutes in the house.

All their meetings were characterized by the violence of their physical passion, and also by a dreadful wordless desperation. They rarely spoke at any length, they seemed only to be able to reach each other on a deeper, darker level, a level where wit and warmth and affection and loyalty counted for nothing.

Their couplings — it could not have been called love-making — were heedless of gentleness, care and finesse, and yet they were insatiable. Greed and gratification simply increased the appetite. Sometimes he would be waiting for her in the hallway and would take her there and then, standing up, against the wall, the pair of them grunting and straining like rutting animals.

But if there was no tenderness, there was no guilt or shame, either. They seemed to inhabit a separate world for that week, where ordinary rules of behaviour and conscience did not pertain. She observed, with absolute detachment, that he was two different people — one of them reserved for her, the other for the rest of the world. In the evenings, when they ate supper with Beth, she was reminded of her first meeting with him — he was voluble, amusing, a first-rate raconteur, a man of experience, someone to whom others naturally listened. Beth was fascinated by him.

But with Kate he was silent, and wild, a man in the grip of an obsession. And she was the same, a madwoman who wanted only to feel him always there, between her legs, a part of her. On a night of continuous heavy raids they copulated in the yard, the walls shuddering around them and the sky split by exploding shells and the red trails of tracer bullets, and hoped that they could die in that way, blown to pieces and so freed from each other.

On the morning he left for Luca she was with him as usual. They stood clasped, tightly, in the middle of the room, listening to the lorry pull up in the street, and Josh's brisk knock at the door.

She said: 'You must go.'

'*Au revoir.*' He kissed her. He never told her to take care of herself. Then he was gone, and she heard him talking and laughing to Josh, easy and confident and professional, back in that other world.

The lorry revved and roared, and drew ponderously away. She stood there in the middle of the room, bereft, lifeless, desolate, a statue, unable to believe that it was ending.

Only the sound of Antonina opening the door caused her,

instinctively and automatically, to move. She went down the stairs, and heard her voice speaking greetings, making excuses, saying good-bye.

She left the house and walked up the hill in the already fierce heat to the square. The little town was quiet, and the exhaust-trail of the lorry still hung in the almost traffic-less streets of Zemola. It was Saturday, 16 January – Kate reminded herself of days and dates like a prisoner in a windowless cell, because it was hard to keep track when every day was the same.

In the square she paused. From inside the church came the inevitable sea-swell of morning mass. A small café was open for breakfast, and a tradesman sat at a table with some cronies, playing dice, his hand-cart with vegetables and hardware and bric-à-brac standing next to him. A group of children kicked a ball about. Arms reached from an upstairs window to drape bits of washing over the wrought-iron balustrade, other arms pushed shutters back, like flowers opening in the morning sun. There had been some bomb damage in Zemola, but in the main the villages had got off lightly. The number of people left homeless had been few, and all of them had family within walking distance, so they had been quickly re-absorbed.

For a moment, relishing the sunlit quiet of the square, and not wishing to exchange this solitariness, in which she could still feel Bill, for the bustle of the town hall, she sat down on the church steps. She had received a letter from Dulcie during the week with the news of Andrea's death. She could scarcely believe that the person who had made such an impression on her all those years ago, who had befriended her in London and given her such understanding and practical help, was no more. No more chances to express thanks, or appreciation, or affection, no more Andrea.

News generally was scarce, and when the odd letter did get through it was always at least as out of date as Dulcie's had been. *The Times* of Malta kept up with the war news, and quirky items from England such as the football scores and the state of food rationing – perhaps this was to make them feel better about their own shortages — but the sense of being cut off and increasingly isolated was acute.

It was literally months since she'd heard from Thea, but she gathered things were not going well, with staff shortages, and the demands of the war taking Jack away from home often. Even with the farm reduced in size the workload would be heavy, with the pressure to grow 'food for the boys' and Kate could well imagine Thea's lonely, exhausting days, the endlessness of the jobs that had to be done, the wearing diplomacy needed to keep the few remaining workers. She herself would quite have relished that kind of challenge, but for Thea it would be one long battle, disguised by a slightly distracted smile, a manic, amiable energy. It would get her in the end.

Kate rose and walked slowly across the square. Her absolute aloneness at this moment gave her a feeling of strength — without the clutter of other people's unwanted sympathy, or criticism, or concern, or dependence she could make her life work for her. If Lawrence had appeared before her at that moment she would have told him everything, without demur, she would have been fearless, honest, direct.

As it was, she had to confront the clutter and confusion of the Food Distribution and Welfare Organization in Zemola town hall. The town hall itself was a handsome building put up, like the church, entirely by private subscription and endeavour, about twenty years before. But because it was built of the same materials as everything else, and in an elaborate baroque style, it seemed older. The committee room where the welfare team had set up their operation was down a corridor to the right of the main entrance. Adjoining the committee room was a large walk-in store cupboard. Until recently the cupboard had been used to house the paraphernalia of Zemola's band club, which had been bombed out of its premises in Zachary Street. But since 10 January, with a fresh influx of refugees from the cities, it had been commandeered for the welfare group — medical supplies, bedding, donated clothing, a few tinned and dried foodstuffs, precious cakes of soap.

The scene was a familiar one. A group of women stood near the open door of the store cupboard, arguing vociferously while a harassed clerk, Mr Fredu Gonzi, his spectacles held together on the bridge of his nose with Elastoplast, tried to impose order by consulting neat lists in an exercise book. It would certainly be a waste of time — Mr Gonzi had shown before that an education and neat hand-writing were no weapons with which to combat the matriarchs of the Three Cities in full cry.

In the committee room itself were two other relief workers — another army wife, Louise Carpenter, and a Maltese secretary, Marianne. They would be joined later by the parish priest, making the team fairly representative of the governing body in Malta, wherever it was to be found — the church, the educated Maltese, the British and the militia (or in this case, the wives of the militia). There were about a dozen mattresses on the floor, and one or two dilapidated bunks and cots. At the far end of the room was a door giving on to a small kitchenette, on the right, a lace-curtained window, shutters half-open on to the street. In the far corner a woman sat breast-feeding a baby and a sad-eyed old man with a walrus moustache turned some green beads over and over in bent fingers. In the middle of the floor three sallow, doe-eyed little girls played five-stones. The two volunteers were engaged in rolling up the mattresses and bedding and stowing them against the walls for the day. Louise Carpenter saw Kate and came over.

'Kate, thank God you're here.'

'Why? What's up?'

'Nothing especially, but it was cold here last night and we're out of paraffin so there's been nothing hot to eat or drink this morning. Everyone is in a vile mood.'

Kate smiled at Louise. She was the perfect army wife — tolerant, sporting, hard-working, wholesomely attractive, a little older than Kate. Women like Louise believed wholeheartedly in the mystic communion of The Regiment, and the sacred duty of the women who married into it. She wouldn't be half so pleased to see me if she knew what I'd been doing, reflected Kate. Louise worshipped Lawrence.

'Never mind,' said Kate. 'The paraffin man comes this morning, doesn't he? I'll go out and get some.' She desperately needed something to do.

'But we need you here!' wailed Louise. She was horribly over-tired, her kindly face was positively gaunt with strain.

'It's all right, he's not here yet,' said Kate tartly. 'Why don't you take a breather while we see to this, and I'll go and help Mr Gonzi sort out the Amazon hordes as well.'

'Well . . . maybe I will . . . in a minute or two.'

'Now!' Kate was commanding. Louise withdrew gratefully.

After about an hour, during which time she and Marianne restored cleanliness and order to the committee room, rescued Mr Gonzi from the matriarchs and set him to the allocation of billets, a task more suited to his talents, Kate saw the paraffin man pull up in the square. On his way up the hill he had already accumulated a queue of about thirty people. Although she was quick in fetching the two large cans from the kitchen and getting outside, Kate found herself thirty-fifth out of fifty.

At the head of the queue the paraffin man plied his trade with a keen sense of his own importance, filling each can, bucket and jug with agonizing slowness from the large drum on his cart. His thin donkey munched hay lethargically from a nosebag. Many of those queueing were children, who simply left their cans in place and played around, weaving in and out of the adults, bumping and screeching. Some of the older girls were secretive, huddled together in a whispering group, cardigans pulled round thin shoulders, bony brown legs emerging from frayed hems, black hair hitched and bunched in coloured slides and lengths of ribbon.

She had almost reached the head of the queue when the flag above the town hall went up, and from the Rediffusion loudspeakers came the familiar, crackling warning, first in Maltese, then in English. With practised speed, but no panic, the queue dispersed. Kate went back across the square to the town hall, to help get the families down into Zemola's one public shelter. She stood in the crowded darkness, alone, fists clenched and eyes closed. Left behind, on the corner of Strada Zachary, seventy or so containers stood in for their owners in an orderly line, while at their head the paraffin man's donkey stood sentinel, still munching from his nosebag.

The airfield was not what Bill had expected, even from Josh's description on the way up — 'like a scrap metal dump in a desert' was how he put it — and this was because it emphasized for him the island's smallness. When the *Marguerita* had hobbled in with her comrades to a hero's welcome in Grand Harbour the filthy, battered men on board had been awestruck by the splendour of their surroundings. Here, indeed, was safe harbour, a fortress of fabulous beauty and strength, a place created by nature and enhanced by man for his protection. Tiny though she was, Malta was magnificently equipped to withstand attack from the seas. As the merchant ships had crept in under the sheltering wing of the bastions of Valletta, even Frank had left his galley and come on deck, stirred by the cheering column of people that wound along the walls high above them. The Torquay palms on the backs of his hands had been damp with wiping away tears, his mouth set grimly to counteract its shaking. Bill would never forget it.

But here, inland, things were very different. Luca was simply the central part of a sprawling complex of runways, including Taqali to the north and Hal Far to the south, linked to the latter by the recently constructed Safi strip. All around the airfields and runways were the splinter-proof aircraft pens which it had been Lawrence's regiment's job to build and now to maintain. The pens were made of limestone blocks salvaged from ruined buildings, bolstered up with sand-filled oil drums. From a distance they looked something like sheep-pens in the fell district of England, the kind of rough, stony structure that Bill was more accustomed to associate with snow than with continuous sunshine. As the supply lorry rattled round the outside of the airfield towards base, Bill could see slit trenches between the pens, and the long snouts of anti-aircraft guns at regular intervals along their route, the gun crews waving cheerfully as they went by.

They had dropped Josh off at HQ, and three or four more at points along the way, so that by the time they reached Luca Bill was the only passenger. As the lorry stopped it was at once surrounded by men and he was almost trampled underfoot in the unloading process.

Bill had determined to treat his meeting with Lawrence as nothing more than a business exchange. This was what he had come to do, and Lawrence was his means of doing it. But he had forgotten just how much he liked Lawrence, and how very different the idea was from the man himself.

'Bill – you bugger, it's good to see you!'

'Lawrence. Thank you for arranging this.'

'I've arranged nothing. I'll introduce you a bit, and then you're on your own.' He beamed, engagingly. 'I could hardly believe it when Kate said she'd met you – you were lucky to get here at all.'

'Very lucky.'

'Still in the Maloneys' house?'

'Yes, I've been most grateful for that. It's enabled me to get my writing done in peace –'

'Peace!'

'Well – even bombs can be preferable, or less intrusive than people, sometimes.'

Walking alongside Lawrence, Bill wondered, dispassionately, why Kate should prefer him to her husband. Lawrence was the sort of lucky, well-spoken, good-looking young man who should by rights have been spoiled, but who instead managed to turn his good fortune into something that elicited in others not envy or resentment, but liking and admiration. He had a quality of good-humoured innocence which defended him like the toughest shield. Here was a fellow who could have married any doting, pretty, amenable girl he wanted, but who had instead chosen to throw in his lot with Kate. That in itself showed that bright, shiny niceness concealed deeper waters – and Bill remembered how once before he had feared for Lawrence, without realizing that one day he himself would pose the threat.

The officers' mess to which Lawrence now conducted him was no more than a large, funnel-shaped dug-out – smoky, smelly, and overcrowded. Further north at Taqali the airmen and officers had the use of the Marsa Club. Here there was the dug-out, which could not possibly have accommodated everyone, surrounded by a sort of shanty town comprising tents and makeshift huts built of sandbags, rubble, tarpaulins and old oil drums. The field kitchen, where the quartermaster was now checking the recently-arrived stores, was a lean-to of corrugated iron and planks. A hand-painted notice on the back wall stated that 'Cold days' were Wednesday and Friday.

'To save fuel,' explained Lawrence. 'The food's not bad on the whole, what there is of it. I'm billeted here,' he indicated the remains of a small building which had been patched up with rock and tarpaulin, 'with a couple of others – and you for tonight. Quite palatial by the standards of the day. Dump your bag and I'll show you around.'

Bill did so. The inside of the building had a pungent, farmyard smell – goat – and every sign of having been dilapidated long before it received the attention of the Luftwaffe.

When he emerged again into the sunlight he asked Lawrence: 'What exactly is your role here – I mean, the role of the army?'

Lawrence grinned. 'You may well ask. Officially, we're on airfield defence, but we've had to learn road-mending and aircraft maintenance. Really, apart from the gun crews round the harbour and on the edges of the airfield, there's not much we can do. The enemy is only ever up there –' he pointed at the sky. 'It's incredibly demoralizing for the men. We had to find a job that was practical and active so that the soldiery didn't waste away with boredom. When the Stukas first dive-bombed the main runway it looked as though it would be unusable for weeks. The infantry filled in the holes and had it operational by the next morning. Now, we can keep it constantly repaired, no breaks at all. In addition to which we can get a plane refuelled, rearmed, and back in the sky in a matter of minutes, working with the airmen.'

'And in between – like now?'

'In between we build, and dig, and make good, and fill shells and generally act as nannies to the whole operation.'

They walked to the nearest dispersal point together, Lawrence showing Bill the different operations in progress. All the men were scruffy – it was almost impossible to tell the officers from the men – most were bare chested and all were unshaven, since Gillette blades had become precious as gold dust. Here and there the pilots – distinguishable because they wore slightly more clothes – sat about reading, or playing cards, or just waiting. Someone had salvaged some ricketty chairs from somewhere, the kind to be found in church halls and waiting rooms, but their presence simply heightened the air of unreality that the whole place had for Bill.

Here, on the bare, gravelly shoulder of the island he was conscious as he had not been before of tiny Malta's isolation.

The unkempt runways, the makeshift pens, the dug-out, the occasional shocks of prickly pear or wiry daisies — none of it seemed to have solidity or permanence, those characteristics which made Grand Harbour so reassuring. There was a sense of painful exposure. The yellowy-white ground held and reflected the brightness of the sky, the lumps of limestone gave off a glare. The men in their polyglot uniforms were like creatures who had been dropped from the passing spaceship on to the bleak and dusty surface of an alien planet. The likelihood of anything purposeful and hostile homing in on this naked plate of rock seemed remote. But if once it did — Bill could not imagine how any trace of order still remained, with such frail defences and so little cover, and he said as much to Lawrence.

In reply, Lawrence thumped the ground with his heel. 'There's your answer — she's solid rock. They can make a few pockmarks in the ground, which we can fill in, but there's nothing to burn, and good underground shelter. Also, an extraordinary spirit, which you may have noticed.'

Bill remembered the arrival of the *Marguerita*. 'Yes, I have.'

'The Maltese themselves are incredible, they seem to be able to take anything and still dust themselves off and start all over again as the song has it. The rock and the people, they're both made of stern stuff.'

They were passing an enclosure where half a dozen soldiers were standing at a table loading and making up belts of cartridges for aircraft. The scene had the peaceful, practical air of a domestic task, like children shelling peas. The men laughed, and one of them whistled a gay, warbling tune.

When the high, continuous, tuneless whistle of the air-raid warning sounded, Bill witnessed an incredible change of gear. The place which had seemed so exposed, so vulnerable and unprepared, and the men he had thought so oddly out of place, were suddenly transformed. As the pilots scrambled for the aircraft, so the soldiers began to push the planes from the pens. Within a minute of the whistle sounding the first planes were airborne, as the scattering of glittering dots appeared in the blue sky to the north.

The aerial battle Bill witnessed at Luca was not like anything he had seen before. For sheer closeness it took the breath away, the sky was splashed with bursting shells and criss-crossed with vapour trails that seemed near enough to touch, the planes swooped and engaged so near the ground that the pilots were clearly visible. The runway seemed to burst open along its whole length like a perforated water pipe, great fountains of dust, rock and smoke rising into the air, the Stukas emerging from their dives in that sickening dead spot, after the howl of their descent, when the pilot actually blacked out. The hand-to-hand drama of it was mesmerizing. Someone yelled at Bill to take cover, but he was transfixed. When a Junkers bought it and reeled across the sky, spinning and spewing smoke and fire, he could not refrain from letting out a whoop of delight.

He had almost forgotten Lawrence when he saw the two trucks bumping and trundling out on to the runway. The battle was still raging, the noise ferocious, the smell of cordite and burning strong. The lorries with their bumbling, unhurried progress looked quite defenceless. This was the nannying and road-mending of which Lawrence had spoken. Bill climbed up on to the side of one of the pens, squinting through the smoke as the soldiers scrambled down and began there and then to haul rocks from the back of the lorry, and from the runway itself where they had been scattered by blast, and to fill in the first of the half dozen or so craters.

Bill shook his head. 'Bloody wonderful lunatics – wonderful.' He thought it took a special kind of dogged, trusting courage to commit yourself to a task like that, absolutely without protection or the means of retaliation, just so that others could put up a good fight next time. Incredibly, they filled in two craters, under constant fire and with the ear-splitting stutter and whine of dog-fights going on overhead, before the lorries trundled back to the sidelines to load more blocks.

A Hurricane taxied down, and was instantly ushered into its pen by the waiting soldiers, reminding Bill again of a sheep chivvied by eager collies. Reversed in, it was overhauled in a matter of seconds, the armourers swarming over it festooned with cartridge and shell belts, screwdrivers between their teeth like daggers; the radio fitter, earphones on, changed the crystals; petrol was passed hand over hand along a human chain and poured into the tanks through a lined funnel. When the plane eventually roared back into action, the pilot giving it so much throttle that the tail lifted long before he gave it its head, a lone armourer still clung to one wing, frantically screwing down the last machine-gun plate. As the plane started to move he flung himself clear, and rolled away from his snarling, stinking charge just in time.

The raid lasted twenty minutes. Three planes – two Junkers and one Beaufighter – had come down, to join the spiky, blackened remains that dotted the airfield zone. Bill was stunned. For sheer spectacle he had seen nothing like it. The bombs that fell on London each night, drifting down from the dark skies like the weird fruit of unseen trees, were nothing like this. Londoners took their punishment bravely, but when your enemy was as close as this, he became more real – no wonder the Maltese fought back.

Lawrence ran up to him. 'Bill – you're okay?'

'It was extraordinary, I've not seen anything like it –'

Bill saw the danger reflected on Lawrence's face before he heard its approach. A Messerschmitt, one of several which had encircled the island and crept in 'beneath' the AA guns along Malta's south-western corner, suddenly swooped in on the row of aircraft pens, so low it blocked out the light, its machine-gun spattering bullets over the men who had been servicing the aircraft and now, too late, dived for the slit trenches. It had seemed to come from nowhere.

Lawrence leapt up and Bill felt himself caught by the jacket and pulled bodily down to the ground. His cheek and jaw ground into the rock, which he could feel vibrating as the Messerschmitt's bullets, and those of another close on its tail, sprayed all around them. Only when they had passed did he realize that he and Lawrence were locked in a kind of embrace, Lawrence's shoulders shielded his head, one hand still firmly held his lapels.

Dazedly they sat up. Lawrence looked beyond Bill, exclaiming, 'Christ. What a mess.'

The scrambled to their feet. In the pens immediately next to them there appeared to be no serious casualties, mostly cuts and abrasions where the men had flung themselves down at the last moment. Gingerly Bill felt his own face, the bottom left-hand corner of which was already beginning to stiffen painfully.

His hand came away covered in blood. Lawrence had moved away, checking for casualties. Curiously, Bill looked at the side of the pen where less than a minute before he had been sitting. The rock, and the sandbags that flanked it, were pitted with bullet holes.

The next day, Sunday, after a night of extreme discomfort in the goat shed, Bill left Luca. To his astonishment, there was an outdoor church service in progress. Whether or not attendance was obligatory, almost every man seemed to be present, respectably turned out. Hymn books were distributed and the chaplain stood on a trailer with his organist – a subaltern at the harmonium – next to him. Bill's admiration was tinged with scepticism – what if the Luftwaffe returned now? But the sky was overcast this morning, so perhaps there was no threat. Lawrence stood at the back of the 'congregation' round the trailer, singing lustily: 'Soon, soon, to faithful warriors comes their rest . . .'

Bill had the use of a shared bike for his return journey. He was to leave it at the Osborne for collection by another officer next day. The bike was rusty and unbelievably ancient, though for some obscure reason it had recently been given a new bell. He strapped his bag on to the back mudguard and waited while the final 'Allelujahs' crashed out confidently. Heads bowed virtuously as the chaplain gave the blessing, a rumbled 'Amen' and then Lawrence was coming over to him, smiling.

'So you're off.'

Bill shook the proffered hand. 'We have to be opportunists of necessity in my profession.'

'I'm glad you were here.'

'You're doing an incredible job – I'll try and do it justice for the folks back home.'

'I'm sure you will – and safe journey.'

'Thank you.' He turned to go, the ancient bike squeaking complainingly at his side. Neither of them had mentioned the incident of the Messerschmitt. After all, this was war, these things could happen at any time, one could not give them any particular significance.

'Give my love to Kate, won't you?' Lawrence called after him. 'If you see her on the way through.'

As he entered the house, and closed the door after him, she appeared at the head of the stairs. She was rather in the dark, he could not make out her expression.

He said: 'I'll just get my things together.'

As he ascended the stairs she turned, and walked ahead of him into the bedroom. The sheets were rumpled and flattened.

'I came to lie on your bed,' she said stiffly, doing so now.

He turned his back on her – it was actually painful for him to do it – and began to collect and pack his few possessions. Her terrible, dead inertia was more agonizing than any protestations of desire or grief. As he moved about he could feel that lifeless presence at his back. He was killing her, and himself, wasn't he? But to carry on as they were would surely mean to destroy each other too. Heavily, he turned to face her.

'I saw Lawrence.'

'Of course.'

'He loves you.'

'Yes.' They could acknowledge that fact, but it meant nothing to them, it was simply a form of words.

'He said I should give you his love if I was passing through.'

'I don't want it!' she hissed. It was the first time she had betrayed any feeling, and now she stood.

'I think –' he paused, and passed his hand over his face, trying to collect himself. 'I think you must accept it. He saved my life. And I have to go. There's nothing else we can do at the moment.'

'There is!' She grabbed the front of his shirt. 'I could come with you!'

'No, you couldn't.' He was deathly matter of fact. 'You wouldn't be allowed on the plane.'

'You don't care. I *hate* you.'

He struck her, hard, with his closed fist, catching her on the point of the jaw. Her head snapped back, she staggered, but held her ground. The only colour in her face now was the yellow fire of her eyes and the tiny ooze of dark blood where her teeth had driven into her lower lip.

'Go ahead and hate me,' he snarled at her, 'you'd do better to hate me. Hate me! Hate me!'

He grabbed her hair as he shouted at her, and wrenched her head from side to side, he felt her fingers gouging his shoulders as if she wanted to tear his flesh, just to keep some for herself. He felt literally torn apart, he had never known such rage or such pain.

'Leave me!' With a last superhuman effort he threw her away from him and she fell on her back on the bed. She lay motionless, awkward as a discarded puppet, her legs splayed, her head and neck eerily angled. She might have been dead, and for one terrible second he thought he might have killed her, but then he saw her narrowed eyes, just yellow slits, stalking him, challenging him as he left the room.

The journey from the centre of the room to the door was the longest he had ever made. His legs were leaden, as if he were wading, literally, through the slough of despond, a black, sucking mire of misery dragging at his feet and draining his energy. He did not look back, for he felt that like Eurydice, if he once did so he would be lost.

Kate lay, watching the dark rectangle of the door through which he had disappeared, and it felt like the black emptiness inside her which spread and widened, threatening to engulf her utterly. His receding footsteps on the stairs were like drops of water falling into that void. The final, dead sound of the front door closing after him was the last shutter closing on consciousness. She blacked out.

CHAPTER TWENTY-ONE

'The way your smile just beams,
The way you sing off key,
The way you haunt my dreams,
No, no! They can't take that away from me . . . '

'They Can't Take That Away From Me'
George and Ira Gershwin, 1937

DULCIE was pleased to find a bench by the trees on Parliament Hill free. She sat down, huddling her coat round her. It was 1 March, cold, bright and bracing, still winter really but with a hint of spring in the light, and bursting along the branches of the trees. Her favourite bench was free probably because no one else would be fool enough to sit around in the chilly wind that boomed across the face of the heath.

But Dulcie, warmly wrapped up, liked it here. She came quite often at weekends, for a walk along the hilltop with its lovely, lofty view over London. Until now she had never much cared for fresh air and exercise, considering the benefits of both to be greatly exaggerated, but these days it did her so much good just to be away from the buildings, high up on this vantage point with the wind on her face. Other people, out doing the same thing, with running, barking dogs, and kites, and children shouting, provided a sense of companionship without responsibility: she could be alone but not lonely, as she sometimes felt in town. Even the war seemed to be something that took place 'down there'. She left its danger and inconvenience behind as she climbed South Hill Park and emerged, breathing deeply, with pink cheeks, on the open grassy shoulder of the hill.

She felt serene. Her fears about Bill were allayed because she had bought the *Herald* once or twice (something she did not normally do, on principle) and had seen his story on the Malta Convoy. It had been on the front page, accompanied by a photograph of Bill, and datelined Gibraltar. She assumed this meant he was on his way back. She had not bought the paper again — that would have been tempting fate — but had settled back to wait, as peacefully as she could, for his return. The successful termination of her pregnancy, now that the memory was fading, had made her serene. She was confident she had done the right thing, there had been no regrets. One day during their shared future she would tell Bill, not using the information as a weapon in an argument, but as a way of showing how much she loved him, and how well she understood him. For now it was her secret, giving her confidence and strength. If she felt down, she would picture how his face would look when she told him, and hear his voice, full of emotion, saying: 'You did that for me?'

'Dulcie?'

She heard the real voice at almost the same moment as she conjured up the imaginary one, and for a second she was confused, as if she'd been caught red-handed in some humiliatingly self-indulgent activity. She was glad of the strong wind which might account for the redness of her cheeks.

'Bill! I was just thinking about you. I don't believe it . . .'

He sat down by her and kissed her cheek, and his scarf — the same old hand-knitted muffler that he often wore — whipped round their necks, binding them together.

He looked concerned. 'What are you doing sitting here in the freezing cold?'

'I often come here these days, I like the view.'

'Well, shall we walk? You forget, I've got used to higher temperatures.'

They rose together and he put his arm round her shoulders, rubbing her arm with his hand as if to restore circulation. She was completely happy. Her patience had been rewarded by his sudden, almost magical appearance at her side.

'When did you get back?' she asked.

'Oh — about a week ago.'

'A week ago?' she was aghast. 'You mean you've been in London a whole week and you haven't even telephoned me.'

'I'm sorry. I've been tearing about like a gnat in a paper bag. I'm glad I found you, though.' He squeezed her shoulders.

They were walking down the far side of the hill, towards Highgate Ponds, the water shone a bright, steel grey in the wintry light.

'How did you find me, then?' She was teasing him, trying to make him feel uncomfortable. 'I mean, how long would you have wandered around town hoping to bump into me by chance?'

'Now that's not fair. I went to your flat, as a matter of fact, and disturbed Celine with an admirer —'

Dulcie burst out laughing. 'He's more than her admirer, he's her fiancé! They're getting married next weekend!'

Bill looked suitably stunned by this information. 'So you'll be shot of Madame Defarge at last.'

'Sadly, yes.'

'At any rate, she told me you'd probably come up here, so I followed on the off chance.'

They walked a little way in silence, and then he added, 'You've got another cat, I see.'

'Yes, Fondant was run over. My friend Primmy found that one, he was a stray. I don't know where I'd be without him.'

'My poor Dulcie . . .' she thought he sounded unnecessarily sad. 'What a lot of changes in your life.'

'Not at all!' She became gay. 'And the best one is that you're back. I read your article — that's how I knew you were all right.'

'If you read it then you'll also know it was a pretty close thing. Our convoy exactly coincided with the Germans setting up shop on Sicily, so the whole of the last day or so of the journey was hellish. Those merchant sailors are heroes — I never want to go through that again.'

They were now at the water's edge. Dulcie stooped and picked up a twig, throwing it into the pond where it bobbed and spun on the choppy water. 'And Kate?' she asked lightly. 'I don't suppose you've any news?'

'Yes, I saw Kate.'

She turned to him with an expression of delighted disbelief. 'You actually saw her? I don't believe it!'

'Malta's a very tiny place, very parochial, the odds are well in favour of any two people bumping into one another.'

'And how was she? And Lawrence? How were they, were they happy?'

Bill noticed that happiness came first with Dulcie, rather than safety or health. He scooped up a handful of small stones and began to shy them at the stick.

'Everyone there is in an extraordinary mood,' he said carefully. 'They're exalted almost – the tougher things get the higher their spirits.'

'Oh yes,' that seemed to satisfy her, he was always struck by the pride she took in her niece. 'That would be right for Kate, she positively thrives on adversity.'

He hit the stick fair and square, sinking it, and she cried, 'Good shot!' and clapped her hands, but it bobbed back up again, frail and resilient. He linked his arm through hers and began to walk along the path that runs beside the ponds. If he had ever supposed that he could simply carry on as before, he knew now that it was impossible. The love he bore Dulcie depended for its very existence on honesty, and a friendly ease they had with each other.

'Why don't you and I get out of London for a day soon?' he suggested. 'I'm sure we could both do with a good break – and there are things we should talk about.'

'That would be lovely.'

'Any suggestions? Somewhere the petrol quota and the banger will get us without letting us down.'

She considered. 'I know – I have to go to Celine's wedding next Saturday morning. Why don't we go down and see Joe at school – I promised I would – and then we could have a night at some nice country pub, or something – what about that?'

The completeness of this plan took him aback rather. 'I hadn't honestly seen it as a chance to fulfil family obligations . . .'

'Only one – I did say I would, and I shall never get round to it on my own. Then we could have all Sunday to ourselves.'

It seemed better to give in gracefully. 'All right, why not.'

'I'll tell the school we'll be down in the afternoon. It's something we can do for Kate, you see.'

'Yes,' he said, 'I see.'

*

As if to ensure that things were made as difficult as possible for him, Dulcie looked marvellous when he picked her up at the register office on Haverstock Hill the following Saturday. She wore a coat and dress that he'd seen many times before, but topped by an especially dashing snap-brimmed hat. It was not her usual style of hat, being altogether more crisp and mannish, and it made her seem independent and debonair.

'That's a nice hat,' he commented, as they drove away.

She tweaked the brim rakishly and glanced at him. 'I'm glad you like it. I told Joe if I visited him I should wear a smart hat.'

'In that case he'll approve. And the wedding?'

She waved a hand. 'Those kind of weddings are depressing — but Celine and her beau were like a couple of lovebirds, so what does it matter?'

'Would you have gone on with them if you hadn't been coming out with me?'

'I might have done — but I am coming out with you, so that's that! Celine's pursuing happiness like a madwoman, so why shouldn't I?'

'No reason.'

At Hartfield House there was a rugger match in progress, which Joe advised them it would only be common courtesy to watch, though Bill suspected that this had more to do with showing off his personable aunt to the members of Upper School who had been turned out to cheer on their side. Various red-nosed, bright-eyed friends were brought over and introduced, and Dulcie responded with just the right mix of charm and humour.

'What very nice boys,' she said to Joe, as they walked round the pitch for the fourth time, praying for the final whistle which would signify Hartfield's resounding victory over Elsmere College.

'They're not a bad bunch,' conceded Joe. 'They've been dying to meet you.'

'Oh?' Dulcie smiled at him. 'Why was that?'

'I told them you were a corker.'

'Is that a compliment?' Dulcie looked to Bill for confirmation.

'The highest.'

'Then I hope I didn't disappoint.'

'No I shouldn't think so,' replied Joe, ever-cautious.

Bill felt more than somewhat *de trop*. He had scarcely met the boy before, and his ill-defined position as Dulcie's henchman was not calculated to smooth the road to friendship. It was this slight awkwardness which prompted him to suggest the cinema when the match eventually finished. The idea was greeted with warm enthusiasm, and Rupert Govan elected as the friend who would accompany them. The local fleapit was showing one of the Road films with Hope, Crosby and Lamour, alluring as ever in a sarong, and though Bill suspected the boys might have preferred something more stirring, they seemed to enjoy it well enough.

After a substantial fish and chip tea they took them back to school. In the car on the way Dulcie said, 'You know Bill has seen Kate and Lawrence? He went on a merchant navy ship to Malta.'

There was no mistaking the pride in her voice, but Joe was unimpressed. Bill knew he lost points for not being in uniform.

'I never hear from her,' said Joe.

'There's hardly any traffic in and out of Malta, except for essential supplies,' Bill explained. 'But she's very well.'

'I remember your sister,' said Rupert, 'she was a sporting kind of girl.'

'Heavens!' Dulcie lifted her eyebrows and looked over her shoulder at the two boys in the back seat. 'What does that mean?'

Rupert blushed slightly, he was an extremely polite boy. 'Just that she looked the outdoor type.'

'Oh yes, she is,' said Joe gloomily.

'The first time I ever saw the two of you,' said Bill, 'Kate was doing cartwheels in the middle of the Unter den Linden in Berlin, she was absolutely splendid.'

'I didn't think so,' said Joe. 'I could willingly have died.' Then he added, as though fearing he had been disloyal: 'She's a lot braver than me.'

'What about your mother and father?' enquired Dulcie, changing the subject. 'What news of them?'

'Oh, they're okay,' replied Joe, in the elliptical style of the fifteen year old. 'They generally complain about the farm, so that's nothing new.'

Bill glanced at the boy in the mirror. 'Do you miss them?'

'No — well, yes, I do sometimes. But of course Uncle Aubrey's been very good to me, and Mrs Drake, too.' Anxious not to be unfair, he added: 'And of course your family, Govan. I'm very lucky really.'

This dutiful appreciation touched Dulcie, it rather reminded her of Aubrey as he used to be, so painfully polite and proper, though she had not at the time found it a touching characteristic in her brother.

'What would you like to do when you leave school?' she asked, with genuine interest. Because the interest *was* genuine, and also because she was beautiful, this did not come across as the 'auntly' question it undoubtedly was.

Joe was surprisingly emphatic. 'I'd like to go back, and work the farm.'

'Really? I would never have thought that of you, Joe. You seem such a European, far more than Kate, for instance.'

'I didn't use to want to,' he said. 'But I do now, as I get older.'

Dulcie looked ahead again to hide her twitching mouth. 'Then I hope that's what you do, Joe, when this horrible war ends and we can all get on with our lives again.'

Back at Hartfield House they shook hands all round — except that Dulcie did plant a kiss on Joe's cheek — and the boys said 'good-bye and thank you, sir' and departed to their study.

'Aren't they funny?' said Dulcie as they drove away. 'They don't have a frivolous bone in their bodies. It seems sad to me, somehow, Joe is bowed down with cares and he's only a child.'

They found a pub on the way back where they could have dinner, Bill having explained that he had to spend time in the office the next day. She had accepted this quite happily, he noticed, there was some change in her, a sort of peacefulness. The fact that they had only just been with Joe, and spoken of Kate, turned out to be a blessing in disguise, for Kate's name came quite naturally into the conversation as they sat at their table by the fire, drinking coffee.

What she said was: 'I wonder if they'll start a family, Lawrence and Kate?'

'I couldn't say.'

'No, of course not, but wouldn't it be nice – think what an august relation I should be then!'

'I suppose you would.'

Not until they were back in the car for the last stage of their journey did he say to her: 'Dulcie, there's something I should tell you.'

He felt, but could not see, that she turned towards him, smiling. 'That sounds ominous.'

'It wasn't meant to, though I can't pretend I relish any of this.'

He heard her fumble in her bag for cigarettes and lighter. 'Do I really have to know, then?'

He cleared his throat. 'I think so, just because I value our friendship.'

'I see.' Her voice tightened a little. 'You'd better carry on then if it will make you feel better.'

He knew it would not, that it would cause only distress to both of them, but that it had to be said. If he left the matter unspoken it would undoubtedly poison their relationship in the end, he was sure of that. His feelings for Kate were so strong, but so confused, that if he allowed them to go underground he would go mad. Maybe, just maybe, Dulcie would hold out her arms and say she understood. For so long she had been there for him, he seemed suddenly to see her clearly for the first time. He remembered how she had looked the day he left for Malta, on his madman's mission. Heroic, she had appeared, there had been a quality of real grandeur and gallantry in her demeanour that day. Yes, he must tell her, and hope they could ride it out together.

'Well?' Her voice was thin and sharp.

'Dulcie –' He pulled in to the side of the road, in the entrance to a field gateway, and switched off the engine.

'Yes. I'm listening.'

'When I was in Malta I told you I saw Kate.'

'Yes.'

'It was more than that.' He fumbled frantically for the right words, and found nothing that would serve. He fought shy of 'love'. His own word, compulsion, was the closest he could come to expressing what had happened, but he suspected Dulcie would find that evasive.

So, 'We were lovers,' he said tamely.

'I see.' She was much too quick. 'And before? Before you went.'

'Just once.'

'You went to Malta to see her, then?'

He hesitated. 'Yes, I did.'

He was still grasping the steering wheel, peering out into the darkness, not looking at her. He heard the click of her lighter and her sharp intake of breath on the cigarette.

'You risked your life to see Kate . . .' She sounded almost reflective, her reaction so far had been one of almost eerie composure. He wanted to crack that composure, to make this exchange more real. He put out his hand to touch her in the dark, but she snatched it away as if electrocuted.

'No! Don't you dare!'

'I'd like to try and explain to you —'

'I'm sure you would!'

'I think we both were — are — a little mad. I needed to be with her so badly, I could think of nothing else. I actually hate myself for it, in a way, for being so dominated by that need, and for jeopardizing her happiness because of it.'

'And Kate? How does she feel?'

He covered his face with his hands, shook his head slowly from side to side. 'The same. I don't think it's going to change, or go away.'

'But she's married.' The tone of almost prim chastisement sounded odd, coming from her. 'She's married to Lawrence.'

'I know. They're both young, they've got years to make it work, and they might succeed. But Kate and I must keep our distance if they're to have a chance.'

'Vain, aren't you?' Her voice was whip-thin and stinging with jealousy and scorn, he shrank before it. She didn't, couldn't understand. 'Tell me,' she said, 'what was it like when you left? What did she say?'

The question hung in the darkness between them. He saw

again Kate's dead-white face, the blood on her mouth, felt her fingers clawing at him, heard his voice screaming 'Hate me!' How could he tell her that? 'She wanted to leave Lawrence and come with me,' he said flatly. 'But it wasn't possible. Malta's a fortress under siege and she's trapped on it.'

'So having had your fling you left her there to pick up the pieces. And then you have the shameless gall to come cringing back here to me and expect to be welcome, damn you!' She was panting, breathless with pain and rage. He knew now that he had made a fatal, wrong-headed mistake, that she could never forgive or understand, because he had not the words to express what had passed between him and Kate.

'I want you – I want you to think the best of me –' he said, brokenly.

She gave a sharp, barking laugh. 'I'm sure you do! I'm supposed to pity you for all your terrible sufferings in the name of seduction.'

'There was no seduction.' It was the bare truth, but it didn't stand a chance.

'Take me home,' she said. 'I'm not used to hearing confessions.'

'Dulcie, I'm so terribly sorry.'

'Are you? Are you *really*? Just take me home.'

'I will. But I just want to say this – I didn't have to tell you, Dulcie. I chose to tell you because I care about you, because we trusted each other. Kate and I –' he felt, rather than saw her flinch – 'we're like a pair of scorpions, stinging each to death while –'

'While you bed her.'

He ignored this. 'But we were *happy*, weren't we? We're good for each other Dulcie, we're nicer people because of each other, and that counts for something, I think. I promise – I swear – that I shall try not to see Kate again, because it causes such pain, not least to ourselves. I can't say it will never, ever, happen again, because if I saw her, or met her somewhere – I don't know. I pray to God it won't happen. I'll do everything to prevent it. I *promise* that, Dulcie, to you, and I never made a promise like that to anyone before, man or woman. That's how much I want your understanding. Please.'

Through all this she sat staring straight in front of her,

expressionless, and when he finished she said nothing but: 'Take me home.'

As they drew up outside Harrow Court, the siren went and she said, without looking at him: 'You'd better come in.'

'No, that's all right . . .'

'Don't be ridiculous, there's an air-raid on,' she snapped.

As usual, she did not go to the basement, though they met several others on the way down. The flat was cold and dark, the kitten, Blitz, was yowling with hunger. Bill stood in the kitchen watching Dulcie as she fed it. He had spent so much time here, with her, he had become part of her life, too, but now that was over. He had to force himself to face the fact that this was the last time he'd watch her do these small, everyday things. He said nothing, he had already said too much. The painful, accusing silence, which had accumulated over the long journey, filled his head like dark water.

'Would you like some tea?' she asked, almost spinsterish, pulling off her hat and laying it on the kitchen table.

'Thank you.'

Without the hat, which she had worn all day, he could see how pale and tired she was, her face drawn and lined, the mouth set.

Apparently the siren had been a false alarm, or at worst caused by a single plane, for they heard no bombing and in another fifteen minutes the 'All Clear' sounded.

They drank their tea at the table, both with their coats on, and in silence, like two strangers in a station buffet. When they'd finished she took his cup and said, 'You'd better go now.'

'Yes.' He rose and stood leaning on the back of his chair. 'Shall we see each other again?'

She stared at him with an expression of scorn. 'I suppose it's just possible.'

She went into the hall and stood holding the door for him. As he paused by her, she said, more quietly and calmly. 'Don't forget you're not the only one who cares about Kate. She's very dear to me. I can't hate her. If she needs you as much as you say, perhaps you owe her something. In spite of Lawrence.'

'Dulcie, please –'

'That's all. I'm awfully tired.'

*

The next morning early, the phone rang and rang, but she did not answer it. She sat in bed with Blitz on her lap, stroking him firmly until the intrusive summons at last stopped, in mid-ring, as if stifled. She continued to stroke the kitten, but she was bathed in sweat.

It rang again, later in the morning, and she ignored it once more. But when it rang for a third time, at about six o'clock she thought it might be someone else, and cautiously lifted the receiver.

He was calling from a telephone box. Because he was anxious, he began to speak even before the coins had dropped, and she only heard the last few words of the sentence.

'. . . leave you like that. I wanted to know how you were.'

She knew she should put the receiver down then and there, and have no more of it. Instead, she said stiffly, 'You know very well how I am.'

'Can I please come over and see you?'

'No! No.'

'Tomorrow, in the evening?'

'No, not then either. Never.'

There was a pause. 'Is that what you really want?'

She took a deep breath. 'Yes.'

'But we were such friends — always such friends. We had such good times together. It's not as if either of us have that many people clamouring for our attentions.'

She couldn't answer.

'Dulcie? Dulcie, I'm sorry.'

'It's all right . . . please don't say that . . .' She was in tears now, but she kept her voice under control.

'Perhaps we'll run into each other.' The sugary words on the bitter pill of desertion.

'Oh, I daresay . . .'

'*Auf wiedersehen*, then.'

They both held on for a second, perhaps he was waiting for her to say something else. But she didn't, and he put the receiver down at his end. She looked at the black earpiece emitting its long, empty, rattling tone.

'Good-bye, Bill.'

She just hoped, fiercely, passionately, that Kate if she had any choice at all, would choose happiness, and reach for its high, bright fruits with both hands, even if she took a fall in doing so. Because in the long run anything else was shabby, dismal compromise.

On the Friday evening she attended a small drinks party at Giles's flat. When he had asked if Bill might come too she had been able to say, with apparent calm, 'I wouldn't know, we don't see much of each other these days.' And he, being the good friend he was, had not enquired further.

She was glad to be going out. During the week she had taken the major step of replacing Celine. The hall porter, an elderly, but still stately ex-RSM named Manners, had taken the liberty of enquiring after Celine, and how the wedding had gone. The fact of her departure firmly established, he went on to say that his wife was 'in the market for a bit of domestic work' should Dulcie be interested, which she most definitely was. They had agreed on an hour and a half per day, starting that Wednesday. Mrs Manners was hardworking, spotless, discreet and motherly — she had two grown-up sons in the Royal Navy. Also, to Dulcie's considerable relief, she liked cats and was happy enough to see that Blitz was fed and his tray clean before she left.

This small practical advance cheered her somewhat. She thought perhaps she should look at herself in a different light, as a kind of highly-organized single lady out at business. But getting ready to go to Giles's party she quickly abandoned that idea, and put on a pretty, though unfashionable, dress of lilac taffeta, which Bill had liked.

Ernest greeted her, apparently in excellent spirits. 'Dulcie — you look wonderful!' He peered round the landing. 'No Bill?'

'No Bill.' The sword twisted in her vitals, but she smiled almost flirtatiously.

'All the better for the rest of us, is what I say. Come in, come in.'

He was at his most engaging, acting the *enfant terrible* but with such assured charm that everyone smiled at him, and Dulcie was no exception. She knew that things had been turbulent between Giles and Ernest, and that the recent death of Ernest's mother had been the cause of further friction, but tonight it seemed that all was sunshine and light.

In the hall, when he had taken her coat, Ernest whispered to her, 'Come to my room a moment.'

'Why?'

'I've got something, something on offer to selected guests only.'

'What is it?' Still laughing she allowed herself to be led to Ernest's bedroom. He shut the door after them, put his fingers to his lips and tiptoed with exaggerated care to the wardrobe, taking a box from the top and setting it down on the bed.

'Here.' The box was full of nylon stockings. 'How many – one pair, two?'

'*Ernest!* Where did you get them?'

'From the nylon fairy – and I do use the term advisedly.'

'You're the end.'

'Go on –' He took out three pairs and held them out to her. 'I mean, I shan't be using them, shall I? Not tonight, anyway . . .'

'Well, thank you.' She took the stockings. Ernest's black market contacts were known to be legion, but Dulcie was uncertain by what means he cemented those contacts, or paid them. You never knew where you were with him, he was like two different people in one skin – the defensive, touchy, ambitious East End youth, and the fey, flirtatious joker, always on the *qui vive*. She liked him like this, but she didn't trust him.

He came over to her, and sniffed her hair, closing his eyes and inhaling deeply, like a Bisto kid. 'Mmm . . . you smell gorgeous.'

'And we should join the party.'

To her astonishment he put his hands on her breasts, and brought his face close to hers. 'You're so pretty, Dulcie. Give us a kiss.'

Calmly she took his wrists and put his hands back at his sides. 'That'll do, Ernest.' In spite of her calm she felt hideously vulnerable and alone.

'What's the matter?' He seemed genuinely taken aback, as though he could see nothing whatever wrong in his behaviour. She tossed the stockings back into the box.

'Just behave yourself.'

'I can – do both, you know.' He gave her an arch look. She was suddenly rather afraid, and moved towards the door.

'I don't doubt it, Ernest, but you don't have to prove it to me.'

'And you don't want the stockings?'

'No. I want to see Giles.'

'Of course, of course!' He sprang past her and opened the door with a flourish. As she passed him she looked into his face, with its bright dark eyes and luscious mouth, the hair a little disarrayed and falling in a black comma over one eyebrow. His expression was elated – amused even – and, she thought, more than a little mad.

There were about a dozen people assembled in Giles's drawing-room, among whom Dulcie saw the Southgates, and Mae Irving, the latter accompanied by a well-known, elderly impresario. There were a couple of army officers with their wives and a small group who were instantly recognizable as actors.

Giles greeted her with her favourite dry Martini, kissing her warmly as he did so.

'It's wonderful to see you – I thought I saw you come in a few minutes ago, what's Ernest been doing with you?'

She opted for the truth but not the whole truth. 'Dangling black market nylons under my nose.'

Giles frowned. 'I wish he wouldn't.'

Dulcie lifted her drink. 'Come on – everybody does.'

'Yes, but he's so – well, it doesn't matter. Come and meet people.'

Dulcie got into conversation with Mae, and the impresario, Wally Buxton. She was used to being out and about without Bill – he had been away so much over the past two years – so that in itself did not worry her, and she tried not to dwell on the permanence of their separation. If she found herself thinking 'I must tell Bill that' she simply changed the subject quickly. Like a bereavement, she had not yet come to terms with the completeness of the break.

At one such awkward juncture she asked Mae: 'How's Rex Donati, have you seen him?'

'Yes,' said Mae, 'I've been down there two or three times since.' She turned to Wally. 'Dulcie and I have a mutual acquaintance at that hospital I was telling you about. He had another operation just before the last time I was there. They took skin from his backside, apparently, to put on his cheeks –'

'Will you ladies excuse me?' asked Wally, withdrawing.

'No bottle,' was Mae's comment. 'Anyway, he's been giving them all a bit of trouble down there from what I gather.'

'A bit of trouble?'

'He's a bit, you know –' Mae put her index finger to her temple and made a screwing motion. 'Not responding as they hoped.'

'He was very vain,' said Dulcie, plainly.

'Yes, well, it can't be very cheery to see your pride and joy all messed up and put back together again, can it?'

'No. No, it can't.'

'Anyway,' said Mae sanguinely, 'I'm not going down there any more. I'm off on tour, round the RAF camps and that, entertaining the lads!' She embellished this last with a suggestive roll of the eyes and wiggle of the hips. 'I shall enjoy myself!'

'I'm sure you'll cheer them up,' said Dulcie truthfully. 'It must be nice to do what you enjoy, and to be doing a bit of good at the same time.' She thought of her own 'war work' more than twenty years ago, which had definitely come into that category.

At this point their conversation was interrupted by the sound of raised voices on the far side of the room. At least, Ernest's voice was raised, and as the assembled company fell silent and looked to see what the commotion was about, he raised it still further.

'Thrill?' he was saying. 'What do you mean, thrill? I'm his secretary.' He was addressing Patrick, one of the actors, a pleasant, quiet-mannered young man, now looking severely discomforted.

'I just thought,' said Patrick, smiling round at the others, enlisting their support, 'that to see a writer's work when it's straight out of his head, so to speak, that must be quite a privilege.'

People had turned away, seeing nothing of consequence, but Ernest brought them snapping round again.

'Privilege?' His repetitions, Dulcie felt, were like the strands of a frayed rope, breaking one by one. She glanced at Giles, but he was quietly offering drinks, and ignoring Ernest.

'Perhaps you don't feel that,' said the actor, disarmingly. 'I think I should find it enormously exciting.'

Dulcie felt for him, the poor man was trying to pay Ernest a graceful compliment and it was rebounding on him quite hideously.

Mae, always unselfconscious, called out: 'Give over, Ernest!' but he was well into his stride now.

'Oh you would, would you?' he snapped, cutting across the faint, determined murmur of rival conversations. 'You could always have a go, since he can't wait to get shot of me.'

'Now, Ernest, you know that's not true,' said Giles quite lightly, handing a gin and tonic to Donald Southgate. 'Another one, Clara?'

But Ernest continued to harangue the unfortunate Patrick. 'You'd find it exciting, would you, to be the skeleton in some old pansy's cupboard?'

'Ernest!' Mae stormed across the room. 'Shut up!'

He pushed at her with one hand, without looking at her, and she staggered back, slopping her drink down the front of her dress. Giles rushed to her side, mopping her with a silk hankie, people's expressions changed from polite unconcern to dismay.

'That's what it is though, isn't it?' snarled Ernest rhetorically, addressing the whole company now, sure of his captive audience. 'And everything's fine and dandy so long as no one mentions it. I must remember how lucky I am to be working for the great man of letters, a lad like me from the East End. What a load of crap!'

The two army types took a step or two forward, clearly feeling the time had come for the men of action present to show their mettle, but Ernest picked up a large potted African violet from the top of a bookcase and cast it on to the floor. The resulting explosion of soil and china stopped the officers in their tracks.

'He's an old queen!' screamed Ernest in their astonished faces. 'An old poof! He picked me up on the Embankment, and you could tell it wasn't the first time he'd done it, either. But it's all okay, isn't it, because he's a cultured fucking gentleman. Job? What job?' He kicked at the violet, sending earth spattering on to Mae's dress and the officers' trousers. 'Fucking's the job! He doesn't want me sat at the desk, he wants me in bed, he wants to screw me till his eyes pop out!'

Finally running out of breath Ernest stood there panting, his face glaring white, his hands clenching and unclenching at his sides. If it had not been for the pure venom of his accusations he would have appeared almost comical, a parody of inarticulate fury.

One of the officers said, 'Now come along, old man . . .'

Otherwise, there was complete silence. Dulcie held her breath. She was aware of a grouping of forces. The separate reactions of the people in the room to Ernest's outburst were linked by one common factor – their liking for Giles. She could feel it binding them together as they stared at Ernest, feel its warmth and strength combining to defend and protect this man who really, now, had no defences left of his own. Silence was their greatest weapon, and they maintained it. You could have heard a pin drop.

Ernest kicked again at the debris on the floor.

'You lot – you don't know you're born!' he said, but Dulcie could sense the anger draining from him, he was a little less certain. He took a couple of steps back, pushing his hands into his pockets, his thumbs sticking out like a pair of six guns. He was, Dulcie observed, actually affecting the mannerisms of the western hard guy, backing threateningly out of the saloon he has just wrecked, watched by the frightened bartender, the poker players, the saloon girls and cowboys . . . He was in a world of his own.

'You make me sick!' That was the parting shot at the bottles behind the bar. Still moving backwards, his legs slightly straddled, Ernest reached the door. Then, abruptly, he turned and flounced out, slamming the door after him. His footsteps crossed the hall, and they heard the front door, too, crash shut.

In the awful, shamed silence that followed Ernest's departure Giles knelt down to salvage the African violet. Only Mae had the courage to say, loudly, 'Silly little devil. I need another drink.'

Amid the discreet murmur of people saying they really ought to go, Dulcie bent down to help her friend scrape up the loam on to a folded newspaper.

'It's all right,' he said, half apologetically. 'It's all right, he's got to come back, his things are here.'

After they had all gone — even Dulcie — Giles went about his flat, clearing away the glasses and the dirty ashtrays, straightening the furniture and plumping the cushions. When everything was ship-shape he went to the bedroom, and lay down fully clothed on the bed, and waited.

It was very quiet, there was no blitz, and eventually he fell asleep. At about two in the morning he was awakened by the key in the lock. In a few seconds he saw the outline of Ernest's rumpled form appear in the doorway.

'Giles . . . ?'

He did not reply.

'Giles, I'm sorry . . . I didn't mean those awful things I said. You know me, I get carried away. I had too much to drink . . . Giles?'

Ernest came a little further into the room, at first swallowed up in the darkness, then looming into view, pale-faced and anxious. 'Are you asleep?'

'No.'

Ernest knelt down by the bed and rested his cheek alongside Giles's on the pillow. 'Do you forgive me?'

'No.'

Ernest laughed nervously, he thought Giles was having him on, trying to make him crawl. He was prepared to crawl.

'What do you want, blood? What do you want me to do, Giles . . . ?' his hand wandered down the bed and came to rest lightly on Giles's upper thigh.

'I want you to go.'

Ernest laughed again, this time with more confidence. 'No you don't, you said so yourself. That's *my* line.'

Giles took the straying hand in his own, and sat up now, reaching to switch on the bedside lamp behind Ernest's head. Still holding his hand, he stroked Ernest's black hair. He had seldom wanted him more, nor found him more alluring. But he surprised even himself with his unforgiving determination.

'I do, Ernest. I do this time. I've even packed everything for you.'

Ernest shook his head. His fine dark eyes shone with tears. Giles was affected, not so much by the tears, which he knew to be turned on, but by Ernest's transparency. It was that scheming, theatrical precocity which had first drawn him to Ernest. Now, however, he'd had enough of it.

'Your case is at the end of the bed,' he said. 'There's more, of course, but if you contact me in a few days' time we can arrange to hand that on. There's a month's salary in there, of course.'

'But, Giles —' Ernest was wheedling, not yet completely panicked, 'it's two in the morning, where can I go?'

'I told you, there's cash in the case. Go back to wherever you've been since seven o'clock. Go home. Go anywhere.'

'But —'

'Get out!'

Suddenly, Giles stood up. Ernest, thrown off balance, fell on the floor on his backside, his face comically startled.

'Hurry up now, I want you out in five minutes!'

Ernest, scrambling to his feet, tried a new tack. 'Or what? Out in five minutes or what?'

Giles thought swiftly and opted for the most straightforward threat at his disposal.

'Get out, Ernest, or I'll give you a hiding.'

Giles left the room, and went into the drawing-room, sitting down on the chesterfield. Pain writhed and chewed in his stomach like a tightening rope. He'd pay for all this *Sturm und Drang* tomorrow and there would be no Ernest to cook bland, appetising little meals to tempt his dyspeptic appetite.

After a moment Ernest appeared, wearing his overcoat over his suit, and carrying the suitcase. In his other hand he held what appeared to be a letter.

'Have you thought all this out properly?' he asked, somewhat loftily. He now seemed to be in the persona of the cool customer, the man who holds the cards and calls the tune. Giles was infinitely weary of his posturings.

'Yes,' he said, 'I've thought it out properly. I don't need to think it out. Please go, I'm tired, and don't forget to give me your key.'

Ernest felt in his trouser pocket and held out the key, and Giles rose and came over to take it.

'Perhaps you'd like this, too,' said Ernest, handing him the letter, 'I got it this morning.'

'What is it?'

'A letter from that Holy Joe at the Institute. Another of your little plans to put me back where I belong.'

'I'm sorry . . . ?' Giles was quite baffled.

'You'll find out.'

Giles crossed the hall and held the door open for him saying, 'Good-bye, Ernest, and good luck.'

As Ernest passed Giles he stopped, his face only inches away. 'You bastard,' he hissed, clearly feeling that even now it was not too late to send home one final shaft. 'You heartless, hypocritical old bastard.'

'Take care of yourself, Ernest.'

Finally, Ernest crossed the threshold, and Giles closed the door after him. He unfolded the letter and scanned it quickly. Bobby Hollis, typically uncircumspect, had written to suggest Ernest take on some of the secretarial work at the Institute, since it was in 'his part of town' and had piled up horribly since the departure of Mrs Drake for Malta.

By halfway down the stairs Ernest found himself wondering if he might not take up Bobby Hollis on his offer, and perhaps approach one or two theatrical contacts on the side . . .

Giles, heartbroken, stood leaning against the closed door, the letter on the ground at his feet, the spacious comfortable rooms of his flat in front of him, terrifyingly empty.

A fortnight elapsed between Bill's departure and the return of Lawrence to Strada Forni. During this time the Luftwaffe and the Regia Aeronautica pounded the airfields of Malta almost continually. But, incredibly, it was a time of optimism on the island, for not only was Malta withstanding the attacks, she was actually increasing her offensive activity. People said to one another that things could get no worse, if they could survive this they could survive anything – they were invincible. Even on the battered airfields the holes were filled in and the planes kept operational, and dangerous, against overwhelming odds. Among the blackened skeletons of aircraft which littered the interior of the island were at least as many German and Italian as British. Parachute mines were the latest enemy device for creating havoc and destruction, but even these had been put in perspective by a group of enterprising Maltese youths from the village of Raxxa in the north, who had succeeded in separating the silk from its deadly passenger and hawking it in Valletta and the Three Cities as dress fabric.

With Douglas now nearly two months old, Beth, presumably subject to the same wave of optimism as everyone else, moved back to Strada Comina and the exigencies of the slit trench. Antonina left with her, only too delighted to have the baby to herself again, and to be free of Connie's ascerbic surveillance. Kate was on her own.

The feeling that she had during this odd, solitary period was that she had been in some other place, unknown to anyone but her, and from which only she knew the way out. No one could help her, because they did not recognize the existence of this other world. The sense of isolation was devastating. She saw Beth's departure as a kind of throwing down of the gauntlet – Beth suspected something, and was tacitly challenging her to fight her way out of whatever trap she had got herself into.

She could, and would, do it. Kate was someone whose battles had to be fought physically. With Beth no longer there she spent nearly all day working at the town hall, and assisting at the newly formed 'Victory Kitchen' which provided hot meals for people subsisting on meagre, ever-decreasing rations. She helped out at Zemola's tiny school and so became like a female pied piper, always with a clutch of children in attendance. She would work until she was so tired that even the siren didn't wake her, and Connie would come into her room in high agitation, to shake her and bellow in her ear: 'Mrs Drake! Get up and come down!'

Like someone emerging from an addiction to a strong drug, she had to wean herself off Bill, and also to admit to herself that the addiction would always be there. The tough, practical side of her threw up its hands in horror at the willing slavery into which she had sold herself, but recognized that she would submit to it again if she had the chance. So, there would be no more chances, she would see to it. While Bill had been there, there had been no time or energy for anything but him, he had stood between her and the rest of her life. He filled her horizon. With Lawrence, she could stand at his side, looking at the rest of the world, ready to take it on. But when Bill was there, *he* had been her world, and no other had existed.

Nevertheless with Bill gone, and nowhere else to go, nor anyone else to turn to, she was thrown back on herself. Some vestiges of conscience returned and, oddly, she reserved its pangs more for Dulcie than for Lawrence. Loving was so easy for Lawrence, he gave it freely and drew it to him, it would always be a part of his life. This may have been unfair of Kate, but that was how she saw it. Whereas for Dulcie love had come late, a stranger. The experience of love had changed Dulcie, and caused her to change her life. She had laid her love on the line and expected little in return. No one knew this better than Kate, and yet she had thrown out that knowledge along with understanding and even common human decency in taking Dulcie's man. If she *had* taken him — she could only hope that somehow this interlude in all its terrifying intensity would turn out to be a chimera, that order would reassert itself, and the chain remain unbroken.

So Kate made her decision to excise Bill from her consciousness. But it was not easy, and she suffered. Her resolve hardened like a wound that healed gradually and with pain. With the almost perverse courage that had characterized her many times in the past she rubbed salt in that wound — she allowed of no hope, no vague changes or future possibilities. There would be no more Bill.

On the Saturday that Lawrence came back on a forty-eight hour pass, a dance had been organized for such members of the regiment who could attend, at the Union Club in Valletta. The Club had been hired for three hours in the afternoon, the regimental band would play, refreshments would be laid on.

Josh had arranged for the four of them, with Louise Carpenter and her husband, to attend the dance – all of them contributing to the cost of the petrol to get there.

Kate made a special effort, putting on her dress and make-up carefully, adding a brooch he had given her, like a disguise. But he saw through it at once.

'Hallo, tiger.' He kissed her and then turned her face to the light. 'Kate – what have you been doing to yourself? You look terrible.'

'Do I?' She glanced in the mirror. 'I thought I was quite presentable.'

He came and stood alongside her so that they both confronted their reflections, his arm round her narrow waist.

'I love you, you're beautiful – but you look ill. Are you ill?'

'No. I'm rather tired.'

'You do too much.'

'Not nearly enough.'

He laid his cheek against hers and closed his eyes. His smiling, open face looked sadder and older when he did that, she wondered what had possessed him to choose her, of all people. She felt stiff and nervous. When he turned her towards him and embraced her she stepped back, saying, 'I've only just got this on! And the others will be here soon.'

'You're right, there's time enough.'

Time enough, and how she dreaded it, the final seal of treachery, the last word in deception.

But the dance acted as a kind of lens, through which she saw Lawrence in a different light. Or at least the old light. It was fun, everyone was there in a holiday mood, to enjoy themselves while they could, and to hell with tomorrow. It was the first time since coming to Malta that Kate had seen so many of the people she'd met at their wedding in Palestine; she was surrounded by support and affection, giving her back a more pleasing picture of herself than the one she'd been confronting for the last two lonely weeks. She was almost disposed to share Louise Carpenter's view of the regiment as a kind of extended family, affording friendship and protection when all else failed.

And watching Lawrence she observed afresh his remarkable capacity for happiness, and for engendering happiness in others. Now, when he danced with Beth (who had left Douglas in the doting care of Antonina) she saw that his smile was one of appreciation of the good things in life, of which a pretty friend was just one, and nothing more. She did not have the energy to be miserable when everyone loved and laughed so. And tomorrow they could be dead.

When she herself danced with Lawrence she found it hard to be stiff and withdrawn in his arms. He was warm, and alive, and loving. He was *there*. She closed her eyes and tried to cut out everything, past, present, other times and places, in order to concentrate on this real closeness, this love she did nothing to deserve and did not have to earn.

Somebody nudged them on the dance floor. 'Necking again — you two don't change!' And she opened her eyes to find that his eyes were on her face.

'Don't we?' he asked.

'Don't we what?' A cold wash of anxiety flooded through her.

'Change.'

'Not in the way he means.'

'I hope not!' He swung her round. 'It struck me how long it's been since I saw you laugh. You've been in another country, Kate.'

She didn't answer. It was so close to the truth that he might have read her heart.

The interlude ended. The siren sounded soon after the dance finished, as they were piling back into the Maloneys' car, but they took no notice of it. A daytime raid would mean either the harbour or the airfields, they were blasé. Only Beth was anxious, impatient to be back.

'Come on, darling!' she urged Josh as he struggled to start up the motor.

'For God's sake, woman!' Josh was in excellent humour. The car started with a roar. 'There you are. It's the first time you've been out of that chap's sight for two months and you're pining for him.'

'I'd just rather be with him if there's going to be a raid,' Beth insisted.

'No one is going to pound Zemola at five-thirty on a Saturday afternoon,' agreed Ben Carpenter. 'I'm sure you need have no fears.'

'I know how the poor girl feels,' said Louise. 'One simply likes to be *there* . . .'

She went on to enquire after Antonina and her family, and the conversation became general, about the shortages and how much worse they would get. Louise had queued the whole of the previous afternoon for some stewing beef, and had been by no means certain which animal it came from when she'd cooked it. Kate added the story of the explosive fish, and they came back to babies, and the night of Douglas's birth.

It was as if, without knowing why, they were paying their final respects. As they climbed the Hamrun Road they could see and hear the raid up ahead, in the direction of the airfields. By the time they were on the steep hill into Zemola the raiders had passed, but not before a random bomb had been dropped somewhere further up, to the north of the church.

'Hell . . .' exclaimed Ben Carpenter, and hell was what it felt like as they crawled closer, approaching the fog of smoke and dust that hung over the street. Rescue workers in tin hats passed them, running faster than the car, there was shouting up ahead.

Because Josh couldn't see to drive they climbed out, and Beth and Josh went on ahead. The church bells began to toll the 'All Clear', but to them, waiting in dread, it sounded like a funeral knell.

One of the rescue workers ran down, and Lawrence caught his arm. 'Which house? What number?'

The man shook his head. 'It fell behind Strada Comina — there is some damage, a lot of rubbish, but no one dead, we think.'

'Thank God.'

In fact, the man was almost right. The bomb – one solitary, random bomb – had dropped in the narrow alley between the backyards of Strada Comina and those of the street that ran parallel and behind it. The blast had folded the outer walls of the gardens backwards, away from the alley. In two of the three houses affected, the people were sheltering with family nearby. In the third house, Antonina had been in the slit trench with Douglas in his basket. Hearing the 'Raiders Passed' and not concerned about waiting for the bells, she had run into the house to fetch the yelling baby his bottle. During the two minutes she spent indoors, the baby had fallen silent, buried beneath several tons of limestone rubble.

On the open hillside to the north of Zemola, where the lattice of dry stone walls gave way before an area of uncompromisingly rocky and barren heath, there was a shrine. Kate and Lawrence had seen it, often from the 'battlements' of Strada Comina – no more than a mound of stones with a narrow door, and a crucifix standing by it. Sometimes the crucifix was adorned with flowers in a jam jar, though you never saw anyone there.

The next morning – the day after Douglas's death – they left the Maloneys, because they felt there was no more they could do, and walked up the hill to the shrine. They didn't talk, or touch, but kept in step, side by side. Strangely, it was the closest they'd ever been, as if the blast that had buried Beth's baby had literally thrown them together.

The night had been terrible. It was Josh, not Beth, who had wept like a child. 'I never got to know him!' he kept saying over and over again, and there was nothing they could say to comfort him. Beth had been stiff, and white, and terribly composed, but she had let Kate take the hysterical Antonina down to Connie in Strada Forni. They'd made tea for the rescue workers who laboured in the yard, and tried to be practical. There had been no body, to speak of, but perhaps that was a mercy. In the morning Louise Carpenter had come back to stay with Beth and Josh for a while, and Kate and Lawrence had come out here.

When they reached the top of the hill, the shrine appeared even smaller than it had seemed from a distance, a dusty little makeshift affair, the crucifix leaning drunkenly, its base dislodged by bomb blast, though there were a few orange marigolds in the jar on the ground.

Lawrence tried the door. It wasn't bolted. 'What do you think? Shall we go in?'

She nodded. Immediately inside the door a steep, narrow flight of steps led down into the ground. On a shelf were candles and matches. Lawrence lit one and they went down the steps, leaving the door open behind them. There was a smell of damp, and stale incense, that became more claustrophobic as they neared the bottom.

The room itself was tiny, and hideous. The bust of Madonna and Child which took pride of place had all the aesthetic grace of an advertisement for baby food — Mary was represented as a busty, red-lipped, smug young housewife and the infant Christ was podgy and pouting with a mass of unlikely ringlets. There was no mysticism, or magic, in the images, or in the crudely painted religious pictures on the walls — they reminded Kate more of the Glory Hotel than of any holy place.

Lawrence held up the candle, and moved it from right to left, and up and down. 'What a place,' he said.

Kate shivered. 'I hate it.'

'Yes, but look . . .'

He crouched down, holding out the candle in front of him. On the floor below the ugly statue was a mass of small offerings. There were posies of dried flowers bound with ribbon, candles, books, pieces of cheap jewellery, carved models of people and animals made from wood and stone, even sweets carefully wrapped in colourful paper. There must have been fifty or more of these little presents, laid out there in the dark, probably never seen except by those who placed them there, not intended for show, but given with love.

Kate knelt down by Lawrence. 'You're right. It doesn't matter that it's not pretty.'

He passed her the candle. 'Hold this a minute.'

'What are you doing?'

'We should leave something.' He took out his cufflinks, and held them in his palm. 'Now you.'

At first she couldn't think of anything, but then she remembered the brooch she had put on the previous afternoon — she was still wearing the clothes she had worn for the dance. She unpinned it, and together with the cufflinks he put it with the other presents, and set the stub of candle, still alight, on a blob of its own wax beside them.

Then they went back up the dark, narrow stairs together, into the sunlight.

PART THREE
1945—46

CHAPTER TWENTY-TWO

'There'll be bluebirds over
The white cliffs of Dover, tomorrow,
 just you wait and see . . .
There'll be love and laughter
And peace ever after, tomorrow,
 when the world is free . . .'

'The White Cliffs of Dover'
Nat Burton and Walter Kent, 1941

STELLA Drake, rising two and a half and stark naked, was implacable as only a child of two can be. Her brows beetled. Her jaw jutted. She held her arms stiffly at her sides, fingers pointing down rigidly. Kate fancied that if she'd patted her daughter hard enough on the top of her head she would simply have driven her down through the floorboards like a nail.

'I. Want. Er. BATH!' she shouted.

'Well. You. Can't!' responded Kate, trying to make a joke of it. And then added, more briskly. 'Not tonight, there isn't the water for it. And if you don't have a bath,' (here she became shamefully wheedling) 'there'll be more time for a story —'

'No!' This was the foremost word in Stella's vocabulary, and one she used with all the considerable force at her command.

'Come and put this on anyway,' said Kate, holding up her daughter's nightie, 'or you'll get cold.' She stretched the neck of the nightie and peered through it, eyes rolling. 'Boo!'

'Stop it.' Stella turned her head away with magnificent disdain. Rejection of this order always made one's efforts at appeasement look particularly foolish, and Kate lowered the nightie. Impatience and admiration filled her equally as she returned Stella's frosty glare.

'Come along Stella, hurry up please or I shall be cross and I don't want to be cross.'

'No!'

A figure appeared in the bedroom doorway. 'Look!' cried Kate with relief, 'here's Aunt I. What will she think?'

Iris made an unlikely *deus ex machina*, but Stella ran to her with arms outstretched, her face crumpling into an expression of the utmost pathos. 'Aunt I! Mummy's cross!'

'I expect she is.' Iris scooped up the complainant. 'And why would that be, I wonder?' Briskly, affectionately, she sat down on the edge of the bed, took the nightdress from Kate, slipped it over Stella's head, added dressing gown and slippers with dazzling *legerdemain*, and said again, 'Hm? What do you think?'

Stella had already forgotten the point at issue, and slipped down off Iris's knee. Kate ran her fingers through her hair.

'Actually,' Kate said, 'Mummy has been displaying the patience of a saint, in the face of considerable provocation, trying to explain to madam why there's no hot water.'

'Well, bless her soul, she doesn't understand about the horrid fuel shortages,' said Iris fondly, in a tone that parodied itself just enough to avoid being cloying. 'How lovely to be that age, so beautifully selfish.'

'Hmm.' Kate glanced across at her daughter, who was inspecting an old Hornby engine on the floor near the chest of drawers. 'She's that alright.'

'She wouldn't be normal if she wasn't,' said Iris with a calm, indulgent air. Though she'd never had children of her own, she was a naturally motherly woman. As an afterthought, and in very much the same tone, she added: 'Aubrey sent me up to tell you the Russians have taken Warsaw.'

'Hooray! Marvellous, marvellous!' Kate leapt to her feet and flung her arms in the air with a whoop.

Stella copied her. 'Hooray, hooray, hooray!' Kate picked her up and enfolded her in a bearhug but she at once wriggled and kicked to be free.

Kate sat down on the bed and kissed Iris. 'Oh, the end really *is* in sight, isn't it? We're not just fooling ourselves.'

'No indeed.' Iris smiled at her. 'They played the Polish national anthem on the wireless just now – it was stirring stuff, I must say.' She picked up Stella, who had come over, clutching a book. 'Who knows, my poppet, you may be able to have that hot bath come the spring. And now are we going downstairs to read a story to your Uncle Aubrey?'

'Yes, read Tom Kitten – and all his buttons burst!' Stella's conversation was peppered with free-ranging literary questions.

Kate looked on gratefully as Iris carried her now beaming daughter from the room. 'Iris, are you sure?'

Iris flapped a hand at her. 'You come down when you're good and ready, my dear. What time do you expect Lawrence?'

'I don't know – when I see him.'

'You take your time.'

Kate listened to Iris going down the stairs singing, a little breathlessly 'When the red, red robin comes bob, bob, bobbin' along . . .'

She began to clear up the debris of the last half hour. Though she was never made to feel less than warmly welcome at Mapleton Road, she usually brought Stella upstairs at this time, to get ready for bed and allow Aubrey some peace and quiet while the six o'clock news was on. It was the time of day when Aubrey most resembled his premarital self, sitting stolidly with his pipe, flanked by the fire (lit at ten to six and not a second sooner) and the wireless, and occasionally a glass of something, concered with affairs of state. All developments in the various theatres of war would be faithfully reported to her when she came downstairs and tonight, in view of the news about Warsaw, there would probably be sherry all round. Nor would Aubrey mind in the least being climbed on by his great-niece, who liked the whiskers in his nose, and his signet ring, and the shiny toecaps of his shoes in which she could see her face.

Kate picked up the engine which had been Aubrey's, then Joe's, and was now Stella's; the bricks and the wooden miniature village; the doll and the knitted outfit Iris had made for her; the pencil stubs, and the brown paper bags on which Stella had been scribbling; the long-defunct chicken alarm clock and Stella's clothes – a blue kilt and red jumper with white ducks (another confection of Iris's), blue socks, Chilprufe vest and pants. She put the toys in the box at the bottom of the wardrobe, and closed the door. As she did so she was presented with a picture of herself in the long mirror: Kate Drake, wife and mother, twenty-nine years old, standing here in this room where once she had despaired of ever being happy again when she first entered it in the summer of 1936.

She put her daughter's clothes on the chair and went to the window, adjusting the curtains and the black-out closely over the long panes criss-crossed with anti-blast tape. Then she had stared out of this same window at the high, close-together houses, and the tall gloomy trees, and the long narrow garden with its overgrown borders and primly enclosing walls, and her heart had sunk within her. Now, for the moment, this place was home, and she was happy to be here. Here was warmth, affection, stability (if not actually safety in this, the year of the buzz-bomb), a place where she and her daughter were undeniably part of the family. She shared this once-hated room with Stella, the child's narrow divan stood against the wall in the corner. A tapestry screen, which had once stood in the drawing-room, but which Iris had banished – 'too gloomy, dear, like a funeral parlour' – stood folded near the bed, ready to be pulled round it when Stella had gone to sleep.

It was 17 January, 1945. They all dared to hope, now, that the end had begun. The great pincers, the Russians to the east, the British and Americans to the west, were tightening gradually, inexorably, across Europe, closing on Berlin. But as if to banish complacency shortages grew worse and the enemy attacked with more than usual venom. Rocket raids were frequent and fearful, fuel was scarce, rationing tight, and the black-out, with all its attendant hazards, could not be lifted.

The shortages did not bother Kate overmuch, after Malta. She and Lawrence had remained on the island until early '44. They had been there through the worst of the siege, long after the date initially set for surrender, when the resistance of a starving population and garrison had been artificially prolonged by the arbitrary halving of rations in June 1942. Beth and Josh too had stayed on, but there was not to be a younger brother or sister for the much-mourned Douglas. In early '42 it was Kate, not Beth, who became pregnant. The wives and families of army personnel were moved out of their homes and into St

George's Barracks for safety, only to be bombed out of there, too. Kate, never large in her pregnancy, due to her natural thinness and starvation rations, had helped organize and care for those families now obliged to live in underground shelter accommodation. For days there had been virtually no bedding, no milk for the infants, and scarcely any food. But they had regrouped, and organized, and survived. And not only survived, but contrived to be cheerful too.

In April, the Luftwaffe had bombed the villages in a short, murderous raid at midday which had shaken Maltese society to its foundations, and spawned dozens of stories that were to be the stuff of legends. It was the day after this raid that Bill Maguire saw the Maltese flag hoisted in salute over the offices of the *Daily Express* in Fleet Street, and he and others had stopped where they were for a moment, hatless and at attention, in recognition of a tiny island's fortitude.

Five days later the King awarded Malta the George Cross. When the island's new governor, Lord Gort, arrived in May he had brought it with him, and it had been put on display in Palace Square in Valletta. Everyone who could had gone to the presentation ceremony, and joined the queue to see the cross. They had all felt very close then, not just those who were already friends, husbands, lovers, but all of them, servicemen and civilians, British and Maltese, men and women. Love and bravery were in the air like music, making individual problems, and even personal losses, seem small and unimportant.

But in spite of honour, things got worse. In June, out of a convoy of seventeen ships, only two reached Malta, and just a few days later the Germans took Tobruk. Tiny Malta seemed to stare starvation and defeat in the face. In August the biggest single convoy ever assembled sailed from Britain: five merchantmen made it to Grand Harbour, to a heroes' welcome, and the dreaded 'target date' was put off indefinitely.

Lawrence broke his left wrist and leg in a fall on the airstrip during a raid – he'd been lucky not to be killed – and spent a few days in the military hospital in early September. No sooner had he come out than Kate was admitted, to deliver herself of a daughter in the noisy corridor which passed for a labour ward, under the sergeant-majorish surveillance of a strapping Maltese midwife. The midwife's obstetric skill had consisted in barking at her charges to pull themselves together and get on with it, which either reduced them to hysterical tears or galvanized them with fury. Kate was of the latter persuasion. The baby made her appearance in three hours flat, and Kate discharged herself the following day. She and Lawrence had laughed like drains to think of the picture they made, he with a crutch, his arm still in a sling, she walking gingerly clutching her wailing newborn — what a snapshot for the folks back home!

They had called their daughter Stella — Kate's choice, because during her labour she had been able to see a little oblong of night sky through a window high in the wall of the corridor, and a sprinkling of soft Maltese stars, low and bright like candles in a dark church. Always, after the fierce crash and flash of a heavy raid, you half-expected the sky to be empty, the stars blasted to kingdom come. But when the 'All Clear' rang out, and you looked up, there they were, above it all in every sense, shining calmly away and putting it all in perspective. Kate knew the name was a fanciful notion, but then she herself had such a plain name, devoid of any romance or imagination, and she was disposed, suddenly, to do better for her own child. Kate pictured her natural mother as a stern, unbending kind of woman, kindly but downright, to have given her that name. Lawrence was not so sure — look at Shakespeare's Kates, he used to say — but she was not persuaded. Her own name was dull — but her daughter would be called after a star.

All through October the Luftwaffe stepped up its anti-Malta activity to curtail harassment of convoys taking supplies to Rommel's Afrika Korps. Life for Kate and Lawrence and their new baby, and for everyone else, became a scuttling, dodging affair, not so much concerned with the preservation and maintenance of life as with the cheating of death. Little Stella, hungry, cried and cried, but seemed like her mother to be fuelled by a kind of built-in rage, and somehow grew. The island's goats, once so precious for their milk, were slaughtered and put in soups and stews for the hard-pressed Victory Kitchens. A civilian population for whom bread, made from imported flour and grain, had been quite literally the staff of life, had to accustom themselves to eating only a few ounces per head per day, and to drinking hated powdered milk. There was scrupulous fairness and universal fortitude. Belts were tightened, and life went on.

At last the tide had turned. At the end of that month Monty was victorious at Alamein. By the third week in November, with only twelve days' worth of food, and five days' worth of high octane fuel left on Malta, four more merchant ships got through. The garrison had gone a full five weeks past the target date for surrender, and showed no signs of giving up.

Shortly before Christmas there had been an announcement over Rediffusion by the Food Distribution and Enforcement Officer, concerning a special seasonal issue of supplies. They had waited with bated breath, their ravenous imaginations running away with them – chicken, pudding, mince pies, crackers? The bonus would consist, Mr Nalder informed them solemnly, of candles and baked beans. The whole island had collapsed in hysterical laughter. What explosions there would be! Fit to rival the enemy bombs and the harbour barrage all rolled into one!

On 23 January 1943 they received the news of the fall of Tripoli. They'd been back in Zemola then, and there had been a great celebration in the village square, with the town band assembled and playing for the first time in years, and streamers and bunting hanging from the balconies, and dancing. Everyone had gone, and the Drakes were rewarded by the spectacle of mighty Connie Bazaru dancing in a passionate embrace with the diminutive Pawli, his grizzled head pressed to her vast bolster of a bosom, the patriotic tears streaming down her face. It had been a night to remember.

And, sweetest of all, one day in September the proud Italian fleet had sailed into Grand Harbour to surrender beneath the ramparts and bastions of Valletta.

They'd been back in England a year now. Before returning they had managed to meet up with Thea and Jack in Cairo for a few days. Old Robert Kingsley had died, and Jack had been over to settle his affairs and attend the funeral. Since both he and the Drakes were in transit, it seemed an opportunity to introduce the Kingsleys to their son-in-law, and granddaughter. Travelling had been a nightmare; there had actually only been two nights when they'd all been together, but Thea had been enchanted with Stella. Jack, who was weary, and more preoccupied than ever, appeared to withhold judgement, causing Kate yet again to wonder what it was in her that repelled him, but which she could not alter. The meeting had been edgy and only partly successful, they would have needed months, years, not hours and days, to reacquaint themselves with each other after so long a time when so much had happened.

When they did get back to England they first had a short leave in the west country, before Lawrence was posted to a training job in Aldershot. The idea was that Kate and Stella should stay on in the relative safety of the rented cottage, but after a few weeks of separation, isolation, and boredom, Kate decided that the dangerous south-east, near Lawrence, was infinitely preferable to the cosy south-west without him, and moved up to Mapleton Road as a self-invited guest. Aubrey and Iris had been bricks, doubtful about the wisdom of such a move with a small child, but unable to disguise their delight at having them both around. They were full of plans – Aubrey was going to sell up, when the war ended, they were going to go to the seaside, Hastings or Sandwich, and start a high-class boarding house. Their excitement over these plans was almost childlike, though privately Kate had the greatest difficulty in picturing Aubrey as a *maître-d*.

She had taken Stella down to see Loelia Drake, now very thin and frail, but as game as ever, and quite determined not to move. 'An old biddy like me is much better staying put,' she would say. 'Pour me another of those, my darling.'

Joe had left school, and joined the RAF. He was training as a radio operator at an air base in Sussex, and it was on a visit to Loelia's that he'd come to meet his new niece. Kate had been at first tickled, then impressed, by this serious, dashing, uniformed young man. He reminded her so much of Jack, it was almost eerie. And after years of starchiness, he had grown-up enough to kiss her goodbye.

Of Bill she had seen nothing. She did not even pick up the *Herald* in case she saw his name. Her first meeting with Dulcie filled her with dread – what had happened? Might he even be there, still at Dulcie's side? Without him, commonsense and concern for Dulcie's happiness prevailed — she wanted the picture to be complete, and harmonious, with Dulcie happy and herself free from guilt. But she knew that if she saw him, looked into his eyes, touched his hand, heard his voice, she would be lost, hurtling once more headlong into that dark and mindless place of passion which only they inhabited, and where no ordinary love could reach.

But when Dulcie came down to Mapleton Road, there was no Bill. She seemed rather tired and brittle, and she drank a lot, but she dispelled Kate's gnawing anxiety almost at once, by saying airily: 'If you're wondering about Bill, we parted company.'

'Oh, *Dulcie* — I'm sorry.' Kate had prepared herself for this a thousand times, but now that it had come there seemed to be no words that would adequately express her sorrow and self-loathing. Down in the kitchen she could hear Stella and Iris prattling to each other over preparations for lunch. Cosiness and normality, soon to end, she thought.

But: 'I sent him packing,' said Dulcie.

Kate looked up at her. 'But I thought — but why?'

Dulcie shrugged, and ran her fingers round the rim of her glass. 'It was that work of his I think, in the end. It was like being a sailor's wife, all that waiting and worrying. I'm really not suited to it you know. I was losing all my other friends, I was so dependent on him and he was hardly ever there. After he came back from Malta we only met up by accident, you know — he never rang me. Imagine!' She gave a little tripping laugh that made Kate's skin start out in goose pimples. 'I think that was when I realized I was being a fool, and told him as much.' She swallowed her drink. 'He didn't put up much of a fight, I'm bound to say.'

Kate whispered: 'But you loved him.'

'Yes, but who knows what *that* means, it's the world's most overused word, isn't it? And I always knew he didn't care in the same way for me — it was a one-sided affair whichever way you look at it. So there you are, and here I am, still going strong, as you see!'

She smiled brightly at Kate, who said: 'Just the same, I'm terribly sorry.'

'Enough! *Fini!* I want to see more of my little great niece, she's much more interesting . . .'

Bill had never been mentioned between them since. Their relationship was more guarded, more careful, more tactful than it had been. Something had been lost, but it was safer this way.

As for Kate and Lawrence they had struggled and fought their way back to each other's side through the dark waters of secrecy and ignorance. Carefully, they had begun to rebuild a partnership based on love on his side, good intentions and respect on hers. The respect had become affection and now she could once more say she truly loved him. The grim privation of the siege on Malta and the shocking tragedy of Douglas's death had finally stifled selfishness. And Stella's determined, inexorable growth, in spite of everything, reminded them daily of how much they had to be grateful for. If Lawrence had any suspicions, he did not voice them. It seemed they had weathered the storm.

A little later she went down to the drawing-room to collect Stella and put her to bed. She found Iris, busy with her inevitable knitting, and Stella sitting on Aubrey's knee. The small fire was still burning, though Kate knew it would be allowed to go out the minute Stella had been taken upstairs.

The room was very quiet. Aubrey was reading William Shirer's *Berlin Diary*, a book that had kept him engrossed for some days. Stella sat on his knee, absolutely still and silent, staring at *Tom Kitten*, copying. From time to time she gave her great-uncle a covert glance from beneath her thick black lashes, but he did not notice. Kate was intrigued by this ability of his to be massively detached. If Stella had been on *her* knee, there would have been no question which book would have occupied her attention.

Hearing her come in, Aubrey did not look up, but said: 'This fellow claims the Germans never wanted a war in '39, can you credit it?'

'He must know dear,' said Iris equably.

'Why must he?' Aubrey lowered the book. Stella stared raptly into his face at point-black range. 'Just because the man's in print? It makes fascinating reading, I don't deny that, but it's plain as the nose on your face that Hitler was spoiling for a war from the moment he came to power.'

Kate remembered the Olympics. 'I agree.'

'He was there, though, after all,' put in Iris. 'At the time.' She finished a row and measured her work with a tape measure.

'That doesn't mean anything,' said Aubrey firmly, closing the book and reaching for his pipe and tobacco pouch – the cue for Stella to get down. 'The perspective of history is more often right than the eye-witness when it comes to the grand pattern.'

'I dare say you're right,' said Iris blandly, starting another row. The grand pattern was of less interest to her than the one created by her clicking needles.

'Stella,' said Kate to her daughter, who had sat down on the hearthrug and was untying Aubrey's shoelaces. 'Bed-time.'

'No, I don't want to.'

'Come on now, no nonsense.'

'No!'

Iris stuck her needles into the ball of wool and stood up. 'Your Daddy's coming home tonight, Stella,' she said, scooping her up, 'and the quicker you get to sleep the quicker you'll see him in the morning.'

She passed Stella to Kate, who felt her daughter warm and smooth and wholesome in her arms, like a fresh loaf or a sun-ripened apple. To her, there was nothing like the natural beauty of a small child, even a cross and complaining one, wriggling like a worm.

'Can I give Aubrey a kiss?' She craned away from Kate towards her great-uncle.

'Uncle Aubrey,' corrected Kate. She took her over and lowered her so that she could deposit a kiss on his cheek, which he lifted and tilted away from his lighted pipe.

'Good-night soldier,' he said absently, his mind still on William Shirer. 'Sleep well.'

Iris came into the hall with them. 'Good-night my precious!' She embraced Stella lavishly. 'Oh but she's gorgeous. Let's hope we have a nice quiet night so that Daddy's not too late.'

It was a forlorn hope. As Kate tucked the sheet under Stella's chin, the siren wailed, and Stella bounced back up with obvious delight. 'Downstairs! Hurry up!' she crowed. She was across the landing and halfway down the stairs before Kate had even grabbed her dressing-gown and slippers. As she ran down to the basement kitchen in her daughter's wake, Kate realized that hers was a child who had never known anything but war, and that there must be millions of others like her — children to whom peace would be a strange, dull time when it came. Since the introduction of the V1s and V2s, raids were frequent and more random than ever before. Robot planes, buzz-bombs, doodle-bugs — the things had many nicknames, but only one function: to kill. And since they exploded even when shot down, there was virtually no defence against them.

Although the kitchen at Mapleton Road was not completely below ground level — the windows looked out into the area at the front, and beneath the wooden garden stairs at the rear — it was the next best thing to an underground shelter. Aubrey had a supply of old mattresses, pillows and sofa cushions which he used to insulate the windows and doors, and everything they might need was down there — food, drink, warmth, a wireless, some books and toys for Stella (who loved it) and chairs and rugs so that they could spend all night there if necessary in reasonable comfort.

When Kate arrived, Stella was sitting in her 'house' under the kitchen table, with her teddy, Iris was knitting near the stove, Aubrey still reading his book. It was as if the three of them had been simply lifted, like toys, by some giant hand, from the drawing room, and placed down here.

As she closed the door she heard the distinctive *thrum-thrum* of a rocket as it made its wayward descent. Iris looked up briefly, needles poised. Often a rocket that seemed close was as much as a mile away, the noise was deceptive. But the blast effect was so violent that buildings and people over a wide radius were literally shaken to the core.

Kate sat on a chair by the table. She could feel Stella's small fingers creeping up her leg, doing Incy Wincy Spider. The noise became louder as more rockets came over — the tail-light of one seemed to pass within feet of the window, it seemed it must explode in the back garden, but when the thunderous crash came it was a few hundred yards away. They felt the house waver and tremble, bricks and mortar made as insubstantial as cardboard.

'Oh dear,' said Iris, referring to the nearby explosion, and then 'Damn!' as she dropped a stitch, and dexterously retrieved it.

Stella poked her head from under the table, near Kate's knees. 'Mummy! Hallo!'

'Hallo, darling. What are you doing?'

'Giving Pooh his malt.'

'Good.'

'Do you want some?'

'No thank you, darling.'

'It's good for you!'

'Oh . . . all right . . . thank you.' Kate pantomimed swallowing radio malt off an invisible spoon, as the walls of the house threatened to implode under the force of the raid. 'Mm, jolly good,' she said.

Because the noise was now something they were used to, she heard at once when somebody knocked on the back door.

'There's someone there!' She pushed her chair back, and it fell over as another explosion shook the ground like an old carpet. She went out to the scullery and opened the door, which was in the alleyway at the side of the house. It was pitch dark, but the sweeping beams of the searchlights, and the yellow glow from a nearby fire, revealed the white and anxious face of Beatrice Fisher, warden of the local shelter.

'Beattie – what's up? Come in, quick.'

Kate closed the door after her. Beattie was coated with grey dust, and her eyes were reddened and streaming.

'Kate, we've been hit – there's only one usable room left, and I'm not sure it's stable. I've got twenty there, women and children, can I bring some of them over?'

'Of course!'

Stella appeared at Kate's side. 'Hallo Beattie.'

'Hallo darling . . .' Beattie stared distractedly at the small figure in her blue dressing-gown. Aubrey and Iris came through from the kitchen, and Kate turned to them.

'That was the shelter that got hit – Beattie needs somewhere for some mothers and children. They can come here, can't they?'

'Aubree!' Iris took her husband's arm. 'You get along there right now and lend a hand, I'll get the kettle on.'

Kate said: 'I'll come too. Stella, you stay here with Aunt I. and help her get ready, we've got some people coming.'

'Who's coming?'

'Some boys and girls with nowhere to sleep.'

She shrugged on one of the assortment of old jackets that hung on the inside of the door. Then she, Aubrey and Beattie ran up the alleyway and into the road. Already they could see the heavy rescue lorries and fire engines in grim attendance, and the great hissing arcs of water playing on the heap of masonry which had been the entrance to the Cholmondeleigh Road shelter.

Lawrence had left the barracks at four-thirty. After a long wait in the rain, he had got a bus to the station. At about six an already overcrowded train had pulled in and he had somehow found himself a place in the corridor, uncomfortably close to the door of the toilet, where he was continually jostled and trodden on by the lavatory's patrons. Every jolt and rattle of the train as it went over points or even, very occasionally, built up speed, sent a shudder through the people packed inside. Lawrence, as almost last in line at the end of a carriage, received the accumulated force of some fifty bodies banging against each other. Half an hour into the journey there was a derailment further up the line, and they all had to get out at a halt in the middle of nowhere and wait in the freezing cold for a relief train which would carry them in approximately the right direction on a branch line. When the relief train came it could only take about half of those waiting, and Lawrence had no alternative but to stand down in favour of family groups, exhausted and embattled mothers with grizzling, fed-up children. In the end he left the halt, walked down to the road and hitched a lift on a lorry as far as the next station, where it would be possible to get a train to London, though no one knew when. He had at last squeezed on to another train at about eight, and after three more unexplained delays they reached Lewisham.

*

In the wake of the buzz-bomb raid Lewisham was full of feverish, badly-lit, panicky activity. It was bitterly cold, and the air-raid wardens and rescue workers, with their pale helmets and their breath smoking, were like creatures from another planet in the fitful dark. There had been two big explosions in the area, one near a cinema in the local shopping parade, which had caused a lot of damage, but few casualties; the other, they told him, on the public shelter on the corner of Cholmondeleigh Street and Mapleton Road.

He began to run, barging past people, half-apologizing but soon forgetting to do even that. He ran down the shopping parade where window-dummies from a dress shop lay in stiff, affected attitudes among the water and rubble and splinters of glass on the pavement. Propped against the shattered doors of the cinema was a sign, rather pathetic now, informing the public that in the case of a raid they might return and see the rest of the performance using the same ticket, but that the ticket could not be used for any other performance, and that on no account whatever was there to be any queueing during a raid. The inside of the local Woolworths resembled hell's mouth, a black, smoking cave where people blundered about like lost souls, shouting to each other through the drifting smoke.

At the end of the parade Lawrence turned right, and now he could see the shattered shelter on the corner. There was a huge crater in the road, which the police had already cordoned off. There was an air of aimlessness about the rescue workers as though they had done all they could. Lawrence's heart pounded and his mouth was dry. He ran to the corner and looked up Mapleton Road. It was so close to the disaster, and yet looked the same as always, stolid, suburban, unruffled. It was not without its battle scars – three houses in the road had been hit in the past few years – but already the sites had settled down. In the summer, weeds sprouted through the chinks in the broken brick walls, the wasteground foamed with pink willow-herb. Where the dentist's surgery had been a neat board had been erected, directing patients to his new premises. Most of the ugly trees had survived, their trunks now emblazoned with a girdle of white paint to help pedestrians and motorists in the black-out.

Lawrence tore up the road, his case banging against his legs. Since the 'All Clear' had not yet sounded he guessed they would still be down in the kitchen. Where water had streamed along the pavements from the firehoses it was already freezing over and as he turned into the side alley of Number 43 he slipped and barked his hand and face on the wall, and fell over, knocking for six two of Iris's three dustbins. One of these was her 'scrap iron for Spitfires' bin, contributed to by the local children, the other her 'pig for victory' bin, containing a glutinous swill of household scraps to feed the pig in which she and Aubrey had a third share. What with the deafening crash of assorted saucepan lids and kettles hitting the concrete and Lawrence's stream of curses as he landed on all fours in the potato peelings, his arrival advertised itself.

As he struggled to his feet, brushing pulpy vegetable matter from his trousers, the door was opened by Aubrey, in a thick cardigan and slippers, pipe in hand.

'Lawrence, my dear chap . . .' Aubrey let him in, looking him up and down. 'Good God, what have you been doing to yourself?'

Lawrence put up his hand and felt blood on his cheek. 'Nothing, I fell over.' He laughed, with relief, because they were obviously all right, Kate was all right. 'There's a war on out there, you know.'

Aubrey put his hand on his shoulder. 'Don't we know it. Come in.'

Lawrence put his case and cap on the floor and followed Aubrey into the kitchen. There must have been eighteen people in there, all women and children of assorted ages, and a small rodent in a cage on the kitchen table. Lawrence was so taken aback that he could not at first make out his own wife and daughter until a piercing scream of 'Daddy!' cut through the hubbub, and his knees were gripped by small, vice-like arms.

He bent down to pick up Stella, and tried to kiss her, but she was twisting and turning, pink with excitement.

'We're having a party! Kevin's brought a rat!'

'Has he indeed, well there's a thing.'

'It's called Micky.'

'Good. Where's Mummy?'

'There!'

Kate was on the far side of the room, carrying a large baby with a drooping nappy. She was grimy and dishevelled but her eyes sparkled.

'Hallo, you,' he said to her. 'Taking things quietly I see.'

'That's right.' She raised her eyebrows. 'If you could see yourself!' Still carrying the baby, she came over to him and he put his free arm round her.

'Pooh,' said Stella, 'that baby smells.'

Lawrence put his daughter down. 'Yes it does.'

Aubrey passed them, saying something about tea in the pot. Lawrence leaned over the head of the reeking baby and kissed his wife.

'You shouldn't be here, I've said so before,' he whispered.

She shrugged. 'They all are.'

'I don't love them.'

'Well you'll have to put up with it,' she said. 'It would take more than an old buzz-bomb raid to separate us.'

He knew that was true. There was something, he suspected, which might one day separate them, but bombs were not part of it. Bombs he could cope with.

It was the small hours before Mapleton Road returned to normal, and Kate and Lawrence got to bed, but they were not too tired to make love. Indeed, in this new phase of their marriage the phrase 'to make love' had a special aptness and meaning, it was as if they literally reaffirmed and regenerated love when their bodies were joined, sealed the trust they had in one another, reiterated the promises of the past. And Lawrence could still bring Kate ecstasy, his promise of the gift of happiness, made so long ago and which she had thought so rash, had been honoured. The greatest sweetness and bliss she had ever known had been in his arms, and was still to be found there.

And they talked, lying close in the dark, keeping their voices down because of Stella, asleep behind the screen.

'Do you love me?' he asked.

'Yes, I do.'

'Do you get fed up here without me?'

'Yes. And I worried tonight, with the raid — I didn't know where you were.'

'Think how I felt when I saw the shelter had been hit . . .'

She kissed him. 'It's going to end soon though, isn't it?'

'It looks like it. It's just a case of hanging on. You know I'd feel happier if you and Stella weren't in the thick of it.'

'But then I'd never see you. I need to see you.'

She often said this, or something like it. To Lawrence it sounded almost as if she couldn't believe in him unless he were physically present, it was one of the several different nuances in her attitude to him which warned against complacency.

Now he held her tight in his arms, her face pressed into her shoulder. 'You'll never know how much I love you,' he said. 'Never.'

It had been a bad night, one of the worst. But it was a habit of Primmy's, if she had the time, to get out of the flat as soon as possible on these occasions, to exorcize the horrors of the raid. She considered herself a hardy soul, but the cold was almost worse than the doodle-bugs at the moment. Individual raids came to an end, but the winter seemed to be going on for ever, and without much means of combating it.

At least today they had opened the emergency coal-dump up the road. A little late, really, in February, but better late than never. There were lots of people heading for the dump with barrows, boxes, bags, even prams, to collect whatever they could cart away. The privations endured by some people were beyond belief. The East End was desolate, laid waste, and each day there were new gaps and holes and rubbish heaps where homes had been. And this area especially had a haunted feeling since the terrible disaster at the tube station in January of last year. Two hundred or more dead, one of the worst single disasters of the war, and young Tony Marker among them. Hardly a family was left untouched. Primmy detected the hand of fate in all this somewhere. Even if that no-good Doris had not been too pie-eyed to hang on to Maria's wheelchair that night three years ago, Maria would still have died. The poor got it in the neck, and that was it. God knows where Doris was now — she'd been in the pub when it happened.

Primmy's own family was much diminished. Her brother Eddie had died a year ago, a peaceful natural death, unaffected by the war. But her other brother, a merchant seaman, had been torpedoed in '41. And Lisbeth and Jim had lost their eldest boy and been bombed out of their home a few weeks ago. It could have been worse, the shop wasn't badly damaged, just the first floor flat, and they were being accommodated by neighbours down in Southwark. It was on Lisbeth's account, or at least her daughter's, that Primmy set out this morning. She had heard that a greengrocer in the Commercial Road had some oranges, and that Dixies' Department Store was selling off a stock of sheets. Both these commodities were in demand and Primmy had no intention of missing out on them. She was a determined shopper, not averse to the occasional dabble on the black market, provided she did not feel she was being 'done'.

Primmy went first to the greengrocer. She noticed that there were no oranges on display, but there was an interesting-looking wooden box at the back, under the till.

'I heard you had some oranges,' she remarked, with a keen look at the box.

'No lady, no oranges.' This was a game the greengrocer was pleased to play, even with regular customers, and Primmy was not deterred.

'Come on Mr Hodges, what's back there in the box?'

'I'm keeping 'em back. Making 'em last.'

'What for? Hitler's birthday?'

This wrangling went on until Primmy finally affected pique and turned to walk away, whereupon Mr Hodges prised off the lid of the box and supplied her cheerfully enough with a couple of nice Jaffas.

The linen sale was another matter. There must have been over a hundred women gathered round the main entrance of Dixies', and every one of them just as determined as Primmy. Sheets were going at between three and four pounds for a pair of singles, and woolly blankets for about the same each. It was as well there wasn't much traffic, for the steely-eyed queue spilled right across the road. Primmy waited until eleven o'clock, queue-barging expertly from time to time, and was rewarded with the purchase of three sheets, a pair of unbleached singles of mediocre quality and one good linen sheet which might cut down into a small pair for a child's bed. She considered she had done well for five pound ten.

As she left the shop, she spotted a young man on the fringes of the queue. He wore a hat, and a smart overcoat, and carried a kind of large attaché case or Gladstone bag, the contents of which were attracting considerable interest. Once he put his hand in and pulled something out, the corner of a white sheet, and smiled warmly at the tired women. They smiled back, they were a soft touch. And Primmy recognized that smile. It was Ernest Marx.

She was incensed, not by Ernest's being a spiv, but by his bare-faced cheek in plying his trade down here, in his own manor, not a mile from where his mother and brother had died. He was a callous piece of work, and no mistake. But in the moment that it took Primmy to plan what she would say – and there was plenty – he had moved down the line, and round the corner of the shop, where the tail end of the queue still waited stoically. She began to push her way through the throng at the front of Dixies', but by the time she reached the corner and looked down the side road he was not in sight. A small green van puttered away, as if cocking a snook at her.

Primmy shook with frustrated fury, her morning was tarnished. She rounded on the woman nearest her, who was holding a couple of sheets, obviously pleased with her purchase, demanding, 'Did you buy those from that young chap who just drove off?'

'Yes –' the woman displayed them. 'Good stuff, that is. Saved me poor old feet any more of this.'

'Let's have a look.' Primmy was peremptory, but she was not in Women's Surgical now, and the woman was irate.

'Get off, whotcher doing?'

Primmy peered disparagingly at the sheets, but they appeared to be of unimpeachable quality.

'Get off!' the woman repeated, snatching her precious sheets to her bosom. Her cronies, gathering round, some of whom had also bought from Ernest's Gladstone bag, looked equally hostile. Primmy felt suddenly foolish. After all, they had a perfect right to pay more for sheets if they wanted to, and she might well have done the same – if only it hadn't been *Ernest*.

With dignity, she withdrew. On the way home she passed two American military policemen, bulky and sinister in their greatcoats and gauntlets and white helmets. One of them was black as the ace of spades. Primmy averted her eyes. The world was changing, and not for the better. There were too many foreigners about, when Primmy had always thought they were fighting to keep them out.

The foreigners had the opposite effect on Giles Huxley and Dulcie as they emerged from the cinema into Leicester Square one Saturday in mid-April. Slightly dazed by the glories of Olivier's *Henry V*, they saw the West End as a vibrant and wonderful place, a rich stew of cosmopolitan humanity. The place was packed with overseas servicemen – Americans, Poles, Canadians, Australians, Free French – as if London were the hub of the world. Because there was so little traffic, the swell of pedestrians flowed freely right round Piccadilly Circus itself, so that the boarded-up monolith of Eros was like the handle of an enormous spinning top.

Giles took her to Fortnum's for tea. They ate wafer-thin bread and scrape in the solid, unchanging comfort of the restaurant where she had first met Kate for lunch.

'Did you enjoy it?' asked Giles, pouring tea.

'It was wonderful – I needed my hankie.'

'And to think that thousands of children grow up thinking the Swan of Avon is a boring fellow who writes in old-fashioned English.'

'I did. I grew up thinking that.'

'But now you know better!'

It had indeed been stirring. The great exhortation on the eve of Agincourt was more potent than any recently-devised propaganda, Dulcie had had a huge lump in her throat. They had been through so much, all of them, and now the end was in sight. And it was the warmest spring in years. In the space of a few days they had gone from winter coats to summer dresses, and where just a week ago daffodils were being sold at a shilling for a single bloom, you could now buy a whole sunshiny, glorious bunch for one and three. It was nearly summer, nearly peace. But as the war ended, they were only just beginning to understand its price.

'Those terrible, terrible pictures . . .' said Dulcie. She could not get them out of her mind, they were like bitter black smoke obscuring her vision. She stared at the frilly trumpets of the flowers in the middle of the table, but kept seeing skull-like faces, shrunken bodies like marionettes, and eyes sunken and dark with suffering.

'Man's inhumanity to man,' said Giles. 'With a vengeance. We must all bear some guilt, never feel complacent.'

She looked away. 'But so many thousands . . . and how many more, that we don't know about yet? I can't even imagine so much killing.'

He put out his hand and covered hers. 'Don't. Don't try, Dulcie. Our concern, surely, must be life. We're coming out of the tunnel and into the light. The best thing we can do is to deserve our light and life.'

She looked back, and into his eyes, smiling. He was her dearest friend. 'What a nice thing to say.'

She wondered if Giles felt as she did, since he had been alone. He was always so gracious, so dignified, she had never once heard him complain, so she tried to be the same. They had seen a lot of each other recently. But she hurt, oh how she hurt, not a day went by but that she thought of Bill, and missed him. Giles spoke of light and life but she felt she was without either.

'It's true,' Giles was saying, encouraging her. 'After the war will be grim, and grim without excitement, what's more. Things aren't going to change overnight. It's important to be cheerful.'

'I suppose so.' She touched the daffodils gently with her fingers, because it was a way of taking her hand from his without giving offence. 'Aren't these beautiful?'

He leaned forward. 'Beautiful like you, Dulcie. And like you, wasted in a stuffy tearoom.'

She laughed gaily. 'Tearoom? This is Fortnum's! And I'm not wasted — I've had a lovely afternoon.'

He surveyed her with great tenderness and perspicacity, his head a little on one side. 'Are you lonely, ever?'

She shook her head, the world's most practiced liar. 'No.

Especially not since Kate and Lawrence have been here, and my beautiful Stella. I enjoy them. I concentrate on being peaceful.'

'Oh, how you concentrate on it,' he said, but not unkindly. 'You see now, I was right about Kate.'

'Dear Giles, you're always right. But you'll never know just how terrified, how *guilty*, I felt when she first arrived. You'd never let yourself get into a position like that, so you simply can't understand.'

'I could imagine, though.'

'And you've been marvellous — all these years, keeping my secret, not interfering . . . the perfect friend.'

'Hm.' He bowed his head in a little graceful nod of acceptance, but when he looked at her again his expression was serious and searching.

'Tell me, Dulcie,' he said. 'Do you ever feel the need to share your life with someone?'

'Not really.' She smiled brilliantly at him, a smile was always her defence against hurt or intrusion. But added: 'Not for a long time.'

'I'm asking to share it,' said Giles. 'Would you marry me?'

Because of his directness, and the precious friendship that had been theirs for so many years, she was not taken aback. She even sustained the smile as she said, 'No, Giles.'

He became warmer, more insistent. 'We're such dear friends, so fond of one another. Think what a pleasant and lovely life we could have together.'

She knew it was true. Pleasant and lovely . . . it was like a phrase from the Bible. And that was the trouble. It *was* almost holy, the ultimately bloodless and civilized arrangement for two good-looking, worldly, slightly jaded friends to comfort each other, to enjoy a pleasant and lovely decline into old age. She remembered Bill and felt her heart would break.

'I can't settle for it,' she said, and her voice shook. 'Don't stop being my friend Giles. I couldn't bear to lose you. But I can't settle for companionship, no matter how . . . pleasant and . . .'

She picked up her napkin and covered her mouth. Giles brushed her cheek with his fingers.

'Don't cry, my lovely,' he said. 'Nothing will change. We shall be friends always.'

The following day, Sunday, Kate took Stella to visit Dulcie in the afternoon.

'Dulcie!' cried Stella. 'Where's Blitz?'

'Asleep on the sofa, darling, now don't disturb him too much.'

Kate laughed at her. 'Are there degrees of disturbance?'

'There are with cats,' Dulcie insisted. 'They are splendidly impassive for just so long and then — pfouff!' She made a little sound and a gesture that were entirely French. 'Would you like a glass of wine? Or something stronger?'

'No thanks.'

'I think perhaps . . .' Dulcie retrieved a half-full glass from the kitchen, and linked her arm through Kate's as they went through to the sitting-room.

The sun poured in. Stella had sat herself down on the sofa and dragged the wretched Blitz on to her knee where he now lay draped, with a martyred air. Dulcie placed herself next to them, and put her arm round Stella's shoulders, hugging and kissing her head. Predictably, Stella shook free.

'Don't!'

'Have you got a kiss for me? Stella?'

Stella offered a cheek, and Dulcie kissed it. Kate saw that her love for Stella was painfully intense, but she was hopelessly bad at expressing it. Stella was forever shrugging her off, pushing her away, dodging her embraces. It hurt Kate to see it, but Stella was too young to be prompted, and Dulcie would have been cut to the quick if advised to hold back. Her advances rebuffed, she tended to fall back on endless small presents as a means of courting Stella's affection — Kate remembered the *petits cadeaux* of her own childhood — and Stella, acquisitive in the way small children are, milked this tendency for all it was worth.

'How are you?' asked Kate, as Dulcie set down her glass and lit a cigarette. 'The end's in sight now — are you looking forward to a life of normality again?'

'Normality?' Dulcie blew smoke in an affected way. 'I shan't know what to do with it.'

'The black-out ends on Monday,' said Kate. 'I really think that means more to me than anything.'

'Yes, that's true . . . dear old London all lit up again. Yes, I shall like that.' She took a sip of her wine as Kate watched her. Before, she would have said bluntly: What's the matter? Why are you always drinking? But now she could not do it, not only because she was more tactful, but because she didn't want to know the answer. She allowed her aunt to suffer privately, she did not have the moral courage to cut out the bullet that caused the hidden bleeding. And she didn't like herself much for it.

Stella put both hands round the cat's neck and attempted to lift him. He was a dead weight, his eyes closed, his spiky ruff of black fur sprouting round her squeezing fingers. Kate leapt up and rescued him.

'Stella, for heaven's *sake*, you must not do that to poor Blitz.'

'I love Blitz,' said Stella.

'Yes, but he won't love you if you strangle him. Be gentle, stroke him nicely.'

Astonishingly, the cat settled down once more on Stella's knee and she stroked him with somewhat over-firm movements, flattening his shoulder blades with every vigorous caress.

'Shall I tell you something?' said Dulcie.

'Go on.'

'I had a proposal, yesterday, a proposal of marriage.'

Kate was thunderstruck. 'Dulcie! Who?'

'Giles Huxley. I've told you about him.'

'Yes.' Kate could deduce nothing from Dulcie's expression which was almost studiedly impassive. 'So? What did you say?'

'Oh I said no, of course.'

'Is it of course?'

'Yes.' Dulcie sighed. 'He's my oldest and dearest friend, but marriage isn't for friends, is it?' She looked at Kate with sudden, penetrating sharpness. 'It's for lovers.'

Kate felt uncomfortable before her aunt's look. These days Dulcie always seemed to be both artificial and slightly out of control, the artifice like a fragile layer of ice on a dark lake of unhappiness. One had to walk carefully.

'I'm sure you're right,' said Kate. 'But weren't you tempted at all?'

'No my darling,' said Dulcie, but her eyes were a little too bright. 'Not one bit.'

There was an awkward silence which Stella broke, asking, 'Dulcie – have you got a surprise for me?'

'Goodness, now let me think . . .!' Dulcie put her arm round Stella again and this time, with a present in the offing, she was not shaken off.

'Dulcie, you give her too much,' said Kate. 'She's a mercenary little beast.'

Dulcie ignored her, and continued to address Stella, whose head was pressed against her shoulder and whose face which Kate, but not Dulcie, could see, bore an expression of unfettered greed.

'Go and look on my dressing-table, in my bedroom, you know where it is. By my hair-brush you'll see a little box. Now you bring that box to me and we'll see what's inside.'

Kate watched dubiously as her daughter tipped the long-suffering Blitz unceremoniously on to the floor and ran out of the room.

'What on earth is it?' she asked.

'Wait and see – just a little something.'

Stella returned with the box and handed it to Dulcie who made a great business of undoing the tiny clasp, and lifting the lid. At once Stella pulled out the small, shiny object, deserted Dulcie and rushed over to Kate.

'Look what I've got!'

Kate was aghast. 'Dulcie, for goodness sake – it's a ring!'

'I know what it is, sweetie, and I don't in the least want it.' Stella put the ring on her thumb and held up her hand. 'Look!' A single diamond, surrounded by petal-like diamond chips, flashed in the spring sunshine.

'It's lovely,' murmured Kate. Stella skipped about, enormously gratified. Kate leaned forward and said, urgently: 'Dulcie I really can't let you give her that, she's only two and a half years old, and it must be so valuable, I mean where did you get it?'

Dulcie flicked a graceful hand. 'It's worth money, but it has no value for me, it's one of my spoils from Rex. I've had it for ages and not worn it. It's the only thing of his that I took when I left. I'd like Stella to have it. You wear it for her until she's grown up.'

'I don't think so!' Kate grimaced. 'It's just not me.'

'Then put it away for her. But I should much rather she had it. It will be something for her to remember me by.'

'Now you're being morbid, what's that supposed to mean?'

'I don't know . . .' Dulcie appeared to muse, then laughed. 'I'm just a foolish, indulgent great aunt.'

At the end of April 1945 Ilse Bauer had left her apartment in the Metzallee, and her job, and gone to live with an ex-waitress friend, Walda, in her house in the northern suburbs of Berlin. The job had gone first – she had not actually left it, but been relieved of it – and without the incentive of the work at the Kafe Wien the stairs had become such a trial that she scarcely ever went out. Around her, the centre of Berlin was systematically flattened. Since Christmas, the prowling hunter-bombers of the western allies had ranged the skies over Berlin, destroying at will every target that came into their sights, unhampered by the Luftwaffe. The notion of *Berliner Luft* – that sweet and special air peculiar to their city – was now a bad joke to Berliners. *Berliner Luft* meant smoke, and dust, and the smell of death.

But a surprising number hung on. Before she was finally persuaded by Walda to move out, Ilse was in the habit of making the painful trek down the stairs and out into the street, to join the queue for whatever food was available. When the *Jägerbomber* whined overhead the more agile housewives leapt for cover into the nearest tenement block. But Ilse couldn't move quickly, and on many occasions had simply stood in the street, eyes closed and legs throbbing, her shopping bag clasped to her chest, wishing it would end. She had been rewarded for these acts of literally blind faith by the inevitable redistribution of the queue when the raid was over – she generally managed to gain at least four or five places, at the relatively small cost of a few scratches, and scorched eyebrows. She was immobile, fat and old and helpless, but there seemed to be an invisible shield around her.

Still, she was glad to accept Walda's invitation, even though it did mean abandoning most of her things. She did not delude herself that the tenement in the Metzallee could survive much longer under the continuous bombing and strafing, and she was pleased of the company. Walda and her fourteen-year-old daughter Marianna had a small house on the north-western edge of the city. Theirs was the very last house in Kurt Ebermann Strasse, and beyond the road was a scrubby field where the children used to play, with a wood on the far side. Walda could remember taking Marianna to pick bilberries in the wood when she was younger – they used to cover the ground in a hazy purple and green carpet – but now the wood was blitzed and broken, just a collection of skeletal black trunks through which the enemy might, at any moment, appear.

Walda was younger than Ilse. Her husband and her older son were in the army, though neither had achieved the elevation of Ilse's Tomas who was in the SS and looked *wunderschön* in his black uniform. Not that either woman had seen her menfolk in more than a year, and Ilse would certainly never have boasted about Tomas. He was still her good boy, she received money from him as regularly as circumstances would allow, but she would dearly have loved to see more of him, and to have the opportunity to show him off.

Ilse was very sensible of the kindness done her by Walda. She took care to earn her keep, to help around the place in whatever way she could. Walda had one other lodger, an elderly teacher called Herr Edrich, who had worked at a local school until it had been closed down in '41. Herr Edrich had TB, so that although he was only in his early fifties he appeared much older, and it made Ilse think she was quite lucky, for though her legs were bad she was still basically healthy. She would go into his room to clean and tidy up, and amuse him with her well-embellished stories of life at the Kafe on the Ku'damm, revolving her large sagging hips in parody of the tarts, singing vampishly with slitted eyes and pouting mouth, making Herr Edrich laugh till he coughed and had to calm down. The raids still crashed and whined around them, but the devastation was not quite so bad out there, they felt they only had to hang on.

For they knew the war was over, really, and no one in the

house on Kurt Ebermann Strasse cared much that they had lost. Marianna said that at school they were being given lessons in something called National Politics, a kind of last-ditch stand to grab the minds of the young, but Marianna dismissed the lesson with a wonderfully scornful laugh. Ilse, though a little shocked, also admired Marianna, who was both pretty and spirited. Even if they had lost the war, there was hope yet for the Fatherland if Marianna was typical of her generation.

By 23 April the front was so close that many Berliners were bicycling to battle in the morning. The main defence of the city was in the hands of the Berlin home guard, the *Volkssturm*, comprising boys under sixteen and men over fifty. Berliners were tough and patriotic, they had taken everything the enemy could throw at them in recent months, but still most of them knew that fighting was useless. When on the 23rd the last issue of the *Volkische Beobachter* featured a final message from the Führer on its front page, they half hoped for some dignified acceptance of the inevitable. But it was not to be. *'Be warned!'* they read. *'Anyone who undertakes actions that weaken our capacity to resist, or who propagates or even approves such actions, is a traitor! He is to be shot or hanged on the spot!'*

They were most of them too tired to care. How could their capacity to resist be weakened any more than it was already? The Berliners were a punch-drunk, frozen, starving people, staring at a mighty, advancing army from behind a single line of old men and little boys. They were not defeatists, but they were realists.

That night self-appointed executioners roamed the city. On the corner of Kurt Ebermann Strasse the body of a fifteen-year-old youth dangled from a lamppost, with a cardboard sign tied round his neck: 'Look at me. I am a traitor'. Herr Edrich and the three women had cowered in terror as they listened to the bully-boys going about their business. It was almost as if they took pleasure in it, as if they were punishing helpless people for their own failure to win the war. In Ilse's mind it raised the ghost of *Kristallnacht*, when the stormtroopers had run riot in Berlin, till the pavements had glittered with glass, and they'd had a foretaste of the enormous engine of power which Hitler had at his command. Now it appeared there was to be no respite, no graceful giving in; they were to be attacked on both sides.

That night they lay low. And afterwards, they continued to wait for the inevitable end. And what they hoped against hope, what they prayed for with all the fervour at their command, was that the Americans would get there first. The other possibility — the Russians — was almost too terrible to contemplate, so they scarcely mentioned it, even to each other.

On the last day of April Marianna was confirmed, in the front room of Walda's little house. She wore a cut-down and altered white dress of her mother's and looked lovely, and they managed to collect quite a number of flowers so the room was appropriately festive. Walda gave Marianna a nice prayer-book, and Herr Edrich had made a special bookmark with elaborate Gothic lettering. They all tried hard to concentrate, and take comfort from the ceremony, and the holy words, and the sacrament. But enemy artillery was whacking away from just beyond the wood now. And when the first tanks came into view the following morning, they were Russian.

There were a few dozen German soldiers dug into bunkers in the field – a handful of real regulars, so they thought. These men had a bazooka, and fetched the first tank a tremendous broadside. Ilse, watching from Herr Edrich's window, could not contain a whoop of delight. The Russians must have rifled a store, for as the men fell from the tank they released a shower of sweets and bars of chocolate. Astonishingly, the Germans left their gun and ran out of their bunker to pick up the scattered sweets. Ilse watched in horror as the next tank, and the next, emerged from the wood and simply picked them off. The moment of hysterical euphoria was over as soon as it had begun.

They shut themselves in the cellar. Herr Edrich kept on coughing and every time he did, after a long and agonizing effort at restraint, the harsh barking sound made their nerves leap, and their bodies break into sweat. They were so weak, so physically weak, they none of them felt they had any more resources to draw on. If they could just sit there quietly, in the dark, maybe no one would come.

Five minutes later they heard a door burst ooen – it sounded like the side door, from Walda's kitchen. They held their breath as noisy uneven footsteps clattered across the hall. A thump. Silence. Herr Edrich wheezed, spluttered, coughed, and the footsteps clattered down the stairs.

It was a German soldier. Walda, hysterical with relief, then panic again, utterly lost her presence of mind and screamed at him.

'Get out!' She waved her fist. 'Get out, do you want us all shot? If they come and you are here, they'll shoot us all, get out at once!'

'My friend is badly wounded, can I bring him down – oh please!'

Ilse saw that this was no regular, but a boy of no more than sixteen. The men in the field, by whom they had set such store, were just Hitler *Jugend*, given a two-week training and a fancy new title. This youth was just a child in his distress, he was almost in tears, there was dark, viscous blood on his grey tunic and a packet of milk chocolate sticking out of his pocket. Ilse thought of her Tomas. She could not bear it. Heavily she got up and staggered over to him, putting her hand on his shoulder as much to support herself as to comfort him. Her feet and ankles were dropsical, bulging over her shoes.

'Run along and get your friend, but be quick . . .'

He clambered up the stairs, two at a time. The others stared at Ilse as she turned back to face them, but no one accused her, or complained. Fear sapped their energy.

The thump they had heard earlier must have been the boy's friend being lowered on to the hall floor, for in less than a minute there was a dragging shuffling progress down the stairs, and the two of them reappeared.

Ilse had never seen anything so dreadful. The second boy – it was quite impossible to tell his age – had no face left. Where once his face had been there was now just a featureless red and black mess. From some deep, still-functioning source came a stifled, gargling sound. His hands waved in vague, spasmodic movements like the limbs of a newborn infant. His hair – it was blond – was caked with blood and blood ran in strange, swirling tributaries in his remaining ear. The first boy sat with the awful travesty of a head on his knee, leaning over as though if he were close enough his friend might, by some miracle, be able to see him. He whimpered, and pleaded, and besought him to come back. They all sat watching, shocked, unable to help. Ilse took off her black cardigan and gave it to the boy to mop up some of the blood, but it was only a gesture. Childlike, he blew his nose on it.

Upstairs, all around, there was heavy shelling, and shooting, a hellish din. Yet every one of them in the cellar could pinpoint the second when the wounded boy died, when the awful soft creaking sound of his flooded throat finally ceased. The silence, though it was only a tiny pocket of silence in a world of noise, was almost palpable.

Confronted with the worst, the first boy behaved with dignity. He covered his friend's shattered face with the black cardigan, and laid him neatly on the floor. Suddenly commanding, he said: 'I'm going to take a look. Please stay here.'

But Marianna was peculiarly excited. When he had disappeared she skipped up the stairs after him, and the others were too slow to stop her.

The boy was at the front door, crouched down, so Marianna went over the hall and into the front room. She went to the window, drew aside the thick net curtain and peeked out.

She was confronted by the horrific spectacle of the open fly of a Russian soldier as he relieved himself over the small flowerbed beneath the window. For just a moment, there was a strange imbalance of power. The young girl peeping open-mouthed from behind the net curtain was actually less taken aback than the barrel-chested Russian sergeant hastily buttoning his equipment back into place.

But the natural order soon re-established itself. In a flash Marianna's saucer-eyes had taken in a squad of perhaps fifty Russians just beyond the garden, some riding on lorries, others just milling about in the quiet cul-de-sac. On the far side of the road were tanks and artillery, contrasting oddly with the suburban walls and hedges.

She dropped the curtain, raced across the room and into the hall. As she did so the front door flew open with a crash, the German boy was thrown backwards, there was a second bang and his body leapt and convulsed, black blood seeped on to the threadbare carpet. A picture, dislodged by the report, fell from the wall, glass tinkled. Marianna screamed and ran for the cellar stairs, aware of those big, dark forms following her, loud voices, the splintering and crashing as the small items of furniture in the hall were wantonly kicked and thrown aside.

Sobbing with terror she reached the foot of the stairs, the Russians close behind her. They took in the scene at a glance – the dead boy, the frail elderly man, the fat old woman and the young girl hysterical in her mother's arms. The sergeant, the one whom Marianna had seen first, was munching the chocolate which had been in the boy's tunic pocket. There were two others with him. Ilse thought they were like bears, great Russian bears, dark and heavy and unshaven and brutish. She felt that the very passivity of herself and the others, their helplessness, was an incitement to violence. These men were natural aggressors, and they were natural victims. They stood no chance.

When he'd finished the chocolate, the sergeant pushed up his sleeve, revealing a thick forearm, covered in black hair, around which were at least half a dozen watches. He tapped the watches, then pointed at them.

'Watches!' he growled, in case they hadn't understood him. As the three adults fumbled to undo their straps he said something in Russian to one of the others, who ran back up the stairs.

Silently they held out their watches and he took them, stuffing them in his pocket. In a minute the man who had gone upstairs returned, carrying Herr Edrich's alarm clock which generally stood on his bedside table. The sergeant took it from him, and as it did so the alarm mechanism was suddenly sprung and a piercing trill rang out. To their astonishment the sergeant, clearly startled, hurled the clock to the ground and shot it to pieces. Replacing his revolver, he nudged the battered clock gingerly with the toe of his boot, and the others looked down at it equally warily. The Russians' naivety was not comforting. Like drunks, they were unpredictable and might do anything.

Abruptly, as if ashamed of the incident, he came forward and hauled Herr Edrich to his feet, indicating that he should go upstairs, and that the others should follow. As Marianna went by he tweaked her cheek with huge, black-nailed fingers and smiled, and she managed a small smile back.

In the hall, pale spring sunlight streamed in through the shattered door, but the carpet had a great dark patch of blood on it, like a shadow. In the garden several more Russian soldiers loafed about, smoked and talked, and on seeing them, cheered. From the direction of the kitchen came a soldier carrying one of the taps from the sink. He held it up, talking excitedly, and turned the top. When nothing came out he exclaimed in irritation, tried again, then finally threw it with great force at the wall where it made a considerable hole in the plaster, and lodged for a moment before clunking to the ground.

The sergeant shook his head and then brought his attention back to the terrified party from the cellar. His eyes rested on Marianna. He pointed at Walda, who stood with her arm round her daughter.

'Frau, komm!' he said.

White-faced, Walda stepped forward, but he shook his head testily, and placed her arm back across Marianna's shoulders, pulling them both forward.

'Komm!'

Those two short, simple words, spoken by a Russian peasant turned conqueror, were to become the most feared command in the city. On that fine spring morning alone Walda and Ilse were raped many times, and Marianna many times more. Herr Edrich, a sick man, and an intellectual, who had never slept with a woman, was forced to watch.

At about midday the Russians had had enough, and indicated to them that they wanted the house for a billet. Other people were being turned out of their houses all along Kurt Ebermann Strasse. They were allowed to take nothing except what they stood up in, and as they left they could hear the soldiers in the kitchen, clearing the cupboard of the small supplies that were left there.

They headed west for a few miles, but as a group they were in no fit state to walk. They went west, because they thought that by doing so they were heading away from the Russians, but the

Russians had already surrounded Berlin, there was no escape. Even the quiet suburbs of the city were unrecognizable, a lunar landscape of blackened craters, and dust and random piles of rocks, with fires burning untended and unquenchable, feeding on the ruins.

Ilse could only shuffle and plod, with frequent rests. She was shocked, but she had the sensation of having sunk about as low as she could get. She had always been philosophical – surely things could get no worse? The Americans or British would be here soon, tomorrow or the day after, then the war would be over, the rule of law would be reasserted. Yes, things would get better.

Herr Edrich was dying. He could scarcely stop coughing now and his face was white and greasy with sweat, like dead fish. But he was game, Ilse noticed, he tried to be their leader, as befitted the only man in the group, the only one not already subjected to violence. Yet he was desperately ill. They none of them had strength or courage beyond what was required simply to drag their own battered bodies along, and keep themselves from giving up.

Walda, like Ilse, was keeping a brave face on things, probably because she was used to doing so for Marianna's sake. Marianna herself had sunk into an almost catatonic state of shock, stiff-limbed and wide eyed, far more terrible to witness than weeping or hysteria. The fine independence of spirit which Ilse had so admired was completely broken, she was like a staring doll. She no longer seemed to be inhabiting the same world as the others. Ilse could not bear to see it. She remembered the faltering, trusting smile that Marianna had given the Russian sergeant when he pinched her cheek. Oh, it was not just virginity that had been snatched away, but innocence and honesty and joy.

After a time they found themselves in one of the *Villaviertel*, one of the better class suburbs where the rich and the professional classes lived in imposing stone houses set in large gardens. The bomb damage was much less severe here, many of the houses were untouched, and there was a park, and an artificial lake, from which the tail fins of a fighter-plane – they could not tell whose – stuck up incongruously. The big villas had a hollow, deserted air, probably everyone had fled, or was watching in terror from behind curtains, or from attic windows.

Herr Edrich called a halt. He leaned against a wall, holding his handkerchief to his mouth and raising his free hand as if it was necessary to excuse himself and hold their attention. But where would they go? They stood and stared at him, lifeless as waxworks, hoping that when he finished coughing he would have some masterplan to offer, something to work a miracle.

'I think we might stop here,' he offered at last, dabbing his lips. He was so polite, genteel, almost like a down at heel bank clerk in his shiny suit and homburg. 'We could find somewhere to sleep in one of these large houses, I feel sure. Does everyone agree?'

They nodded. They couldn't have walked another step anyway. The garden of the great house into which Herr Edrich led them had once been stately and formal but now, with the spring, was beginning to be overgrown. Here and there clumps of daffodils and tulips sprouted through the fresh green grass and weeds. Big, gaunt evergreens overhung the ragged lawns – cypress and pine, forbidding and funereal. On either side of the front door two stone mastiffs sat with their lips curled in a permanently arrested snarl, their bodies patched with lichen and moss like green mange.

No one answered Herr Edrich's polite knock, and the door was not locked. They went in, aware they were trespassing, too exhausted to care, not really knowing what they would do if some irate householder tried to turn them out. But the hall was empty, the handsome furniture dusty, the tall plants drooping and desiccated. The four of them stood in the middle of it feeling that they had stumbled into a place sanctified by tragedy, but they didn't speak – they were stifled by misery and fear. Herr Edrich bravely advanced on the nearest closed door, opened it and looked in. At once he closed it again.

'Study,' he told them, almost as if he were an estate agent, pointing out the property's many assets. He opened the next door and stepped inside, rather more boldly. They watched, and from his face they could read more than they wanted to know. Ilse shuffled over to him and peered over his shoulder.

The occupants of the house had committed suicide. It must have been poison, for there were no marks on them, they were greeny-white, stiff and still, side by side on the brocade-covered sofa, she in her fur coat, he in a good suit, with a watch chain. A fluffy black and tan dog, a pekinese, lay dead on the cushions next to the woman. The bodies were just beginning to rot, the merest sweet stain of putrefaction seeped through the stale, enclosed air. At the far end of the room, the curtains were drawn, but the lamps were lit.

'God in heaven . . .' whispered Herr Edrich. 'God bless and save us . . .'

Ilse was more practical. Indeed she was less shocked by the sight of these two well-heeled cadavers than by that of the horribly altered Marianna.

'Come,' she said, taking his arm. 'Let's cover them and shut the door. It's good for us, we can stay here.'

They went in and covered the bodies with the fur hearthrug. Then they shut them in.

They found a little food in the larder, and there were plenty of beds; it was clear they could camp in the villa quite effectively for a while. Due to the bomb damage there were no services, so that evening they lit a fire in the corner of the garden and cooked a piece of bacon – only slightly rancid – that they had discovered, and a few ounces of hard bread. They felt almost safer out of doors, where they couldn't be trapped, as if they had at least some chance of running away. All around them the sack of the city by the Russian army continued, there was the continual crump of guns, the chatter of machine-gun fire, the flare and flicker of burning buildings. But, for the moment, they were safe.

Later that night they went back into the house and collected bedding together in one room and tried to sleep. Herr Edrich coughed and coughed, and began to talk to himself. Walda dozed. Marianna lay stiff and still, wide awake, Ilse could see the child's eyes shining in the dark. She hitched over to her side. 'Marianna . . . why don't you talk to me a little bit? Why don't you cry?'

Marianna shook her head.

Ilse felt for her hand, but the girl shrank away as if her touch were poison. 'If you keep it all inside, you will be ill. You should cry, it's nothing to be ashamed of.'

But she just rolled away and lay with her back to Ilse. Before dawn they heard the noise of heavy vehicles in the road outside, and then there were the soldiers, kicking the ashes of the fire, looking up at the windows, passing round a bottle. During the night Herr Edrich had died, so he did not have to watch a second time as the three women were made the spoils of war.

Ilse had thought that the western allies would arrive within two days. In fact, it was nearly two months before the first American jeeps and tanks bowled into Berlin, and during that time she and Walda and Marianna learned a lot. They learnt that ugliness was not a complete protection, but it helped a little, so they systematically disfigured themselves, especially Marianna, hacking off their hair, cutting their faces and allowing their bodies to become soiled and repulsive. They wore hats, and makeshift trousers, neither of which the Russians liked. Too late they realized that they would have been safer at the top of a tenement block in the centre of the ruined city than in the elegant stone villa, because the Russians were mainly peasants, used to one-storey buildings, and did not like heights. They rarely went beyond the first floor. There was an attic at the villa, but it was musty and pitch dark, they could not stay there all the time, and Ilse could not manage the stairs. They tried to keep Marianna in the attic as much as possible, taking her out for fresh air when the coast was clear, like a prisoner.

The greatest prize was a baby or a toddler, that was the only safeguard. Pregnant women, old women, sick or injured women, were all fair game. The only woman the Russians would not touch was the woman with a baby in her arms or a toddler by the hand. So when Walda discovered that there was such a woman in a house up the road, a woman with a one-year-old baby, they struck a bargain with her – she could come to the villa, share their resources, use the attic, provided they could take the baby with them when they went out. Never was a baby given so much fresh air. The miserable Fritz was wheeled and carried out by whoever was foraging for food, or whoever just wanted a walk, and the Russians would pet him and sometimes give the woman with him, whoever she was, a lump of bread or a cigarette. Fritz's mother, Ilone, was young and strong, and helped them bury the bodies of the villa's two owners and their dog.

Their sweetest moment was when a horse came into the garden. The Russian army had brought many horses, pulling supply wagons and even gun carriages – stocky, shaggy creatures with long manes and broad backs. One evening Ilone saw one of them cropping the grass, and called Walda and Ilse.

'Look!'

They stared, hardly believing their eyes. Food on the hoof, kilos and kilos of it.

Ilone's brother-in-law had been a butcher before the war, and she had one or two vague ideas about how to approach the task. They made a very rough job of it – by the time they had finished they were covered in blood and viscera, but they were as elated as savages at a tribal rite. Death to the Russian horse! Walda nipped out to tell other people in the road, and everyone came along and went away with something, till there was nothing left but the head, hooves and tail, and that evening they ate like kings, chewing and tearing and smacking their lips with very special relish.

The next morning, however, when Ilse confidently set out with Fritz and her ration card, to queue for whatever was on offer, there were a couple of Russians in the garden of the house next door. One of them jumped over the wall at her, holding the horse's tail above his head, like a helmet plume.

She smiled amiably, and he returned her smile. Even Ilse could smell herself, and she knew what she looked like. She did not expect trouble. The soldier bent over the low wooden pram and made an amusing guttural sound at Fritz, while his friend looked on. Then, abruptly, he pulled her hands away from the pram handle and jerked his thumb in the direction of the wall.

'Frau, komm!'

CHAPTER TWENTY-THREE

'Every time we say good-bye I die a little,
Every time we say good-bye I wonder why a little;
Why the gods above me,
Who must be in the know,
Think so little of me, they allow you to go . . .'

'Every Time We Say Good-bye'
Cole Porter, 1944

VE DAY, 8 May, dawned bright and sunny, though there had been a heavy thunderstorm in London overnight, so that the effect was of a hopeful smile after tears. And the relief was so great at this, the official order to be happy and celebrate, that normally reserved people wandered the streets with silly smiles on their faces, unable to believe it.

Kate and Stella were alone at Mapleton Road for a while, because Aubrey and Iris had gone up to town very early to attend the thanksgiving service at St Paul's. There were plans for later in the day; Dulcie was due to come down, and Joe and Lawrence were hoping to be there for a party in the evening. There was to be a children's tea-party in the afternoon in Cholmondeleigh Road, one of many in the area, to which Kate was going to take Stella, who was keen to renew her acquaintance with Kevin and his rat. She was positive the rat would attend, though Kate had tried to explain that it was unlikely.

Just for now Kate was relishing the peace and quiet. She sat on the garden steps watching Stella potter about with her black tin doll's pram, and was perfectly content. All around, beyond the garden, the air was full of the sounds of celebration — church bells, and bands, and people calling and shouting and laughing, older children running about in the streets infected by the rare spectacle of adults in a state of carefree euphoria. Out in Mapleton Road staid Mr Treece was up a ladder helping to hang red, white and blue bunting – last used at the coronation – on the ugly trees, which seemed to submit with a bad grace to this indignity, like plain bridesmaids forced to wear frilly dresses. Kate felt privileged just to sit there in the sunshine, with her daughter playing happily on the grass below, and soak up the happiness. When the telephone rang she was slow to answer it because she felt almost drowsy, drugged with well-being. Then she had to move quickly, running down the steps to pick up Stella and take her indoors with her, out of habit, in spite of loud protests.

'Hallo?' She was breathless.

'Darling – hallo.'

'Lawrence!' She smiled to hear his voice and to picture him smiling on the other end of the line.

'I don't know why I rang –' He broke off, as if he were laughing, she could hear a great racket in the background. 'At least I do, it was just to say I love you, and I'll be with you later on this afternoon.'

'What time?'

'I don't know exactly, I have to pick up Mother first. But I won't be late.' There was a silence. 'What are you doing?'

'Sitting in the sun, watching Stella – nothing.'

'Are you lonely?'

'Hardly!' she laughed. 'I was enjoying the peace, literally.'

'I'll see you later then. Good-bye darling.'

'See you later.'

She returned to her seat on the garden steps. Stella was crouched with her back to her, her head sunk between her knees, laboriously picking the pink-eyed daisies where they sprouted in the long summer grass at the edge of Aubrey's vegetable plot. Against the sunny wall at the back of the border that flanked the cinder path, the passion flower which Lawrence had given to Kate nine years ago was now a mature climbing plant, romping all over the stern red brickwork in a riot of growth, in spite of stringent cutting back each autumn. With the sound of her husband's voice still in her ears, Kate had no difficulty in seeing in the flourishing plant a metaphor for her marriage. Between them, in spite of adversity, and temptation, and the fearful separations of war, they had created something that would last. Its roots went deep and its hold on life was strong. And perhaps now, with the coming of peace, they could turn their faces to the light at last and enjoy what they had made.

'Mummy – wake up!'

Kate had not been asleep, but daydreaming. Stella stood on the step below her, holding a posy of wilting daisies with extremely short stems.

'I picked you a bunch.'

'Aren't they lovely?' Kate took them.

'Go on then –' Stella pushed at her mother's knees. 'Put them in water. You've got to look after them or they'll die.'

The thanksgiving service was magnificent. Aubrey and Iris, although their seats were well back in the cathedral, considered it to have been worth every moment of the long awkward journey and the queueing. They especially enjoyed singing all the verses of the national anthem at the end of the service. Aubrey damned all their knavish tricks and confounded their politics in fine style – Iris had never before noticed what a pleasant bass-baritone he had. It was as if the famous dome, which had survived so much, a symbol of London's pride and endurance, would simply lift off and float away like a great balloon inflated with the nation's jubilance. Iris also dabbed her eyes a good deal, because all the little boys were back in the choir after several years' exile, and the shrill, silvery resonance of their voices rang round the cathedral like angels' trumpets. She thought of how lucky she was, her future with her husband spread before her like a pleasant meadow, full of shared delights, and she tucked her hand into the crook of his arm, quite overcome with emotion.

Dulcie arrived at Mapleton Road before Aubrey and Iris got back, and Kate took deck chairs down into the garden. There wasn't a lot of space for sitting these days, what with Aubrey's patriotic rows of well-ordered vegetables, so they set the chairs up on the cinder path.

'Do you have plans?' Kate asked almost idly. 'Now that there's room for plans.'

'As a matter of fact I do!'

Kate glanced at her. 'What are they?'

'I'm going to get in touch with your parents and see if they would put up with me for a bit.'

Good heavens!' For some reason this was the very last thing Kate had expected.

'There's no need to sound so astonished. Thea is my sister, after all.'

'But what made you suddenly decide to go — I somehow can't picture you there.'

Dulcie laughed. 'Neither can I, I'm not exactly pioneering material, am I? But I do need to take stock, and get away, and the more different the setting the better it will be . . .' Stella handed her her doll and Dulcie held it on her knee, adjusting its woolly hair. 'Isn't she lovely, what's her name . . .? No, I need a change, Kate. I can hardly go on being a shop assistant for ever, Good Lord I shall just turn into a thinner version of Madame Zoe! Perhaps if I get right away from everything some wonderful plan will present itself to me.'

Kate watched her as she spoke. She was still beautiful, still well dressed, but there was a kind of desperation about her. It was no good denying it, her life was an empty one, Kate herself could not have stood it for one moment. There had been a time, when Dulcie was with Bill, when a new Dulcie had emerged. She could not bear to think that she herself might be the cause of this reversal. They had, she and Bill, both been subject to a kind of madness. What if he had told Dulcie, had felt compelled to speak, had thought it kindest to be cruel? Now his presence hung between them like an evocative scent. They did not look at each other but at Stella, who had reclaimed her doll and was pushing daisies into her hair.

'Besides,' Dulcie said, almost as if she had followed some of Kate's thoughts and was trying to change the subject, 'as you get older, your family become more important to you again, you need them more, I expect you will find the same.'

'Perhaps.'

'They heard the front door open, cheerful voices in the hall.

'Thank God,' said Dulcie. 'Now we can decently have a drink.'

That evening they assembled to celebrate. But inevitably, because it was an ending as well as a beginning, and because the future was uncertain, they found themselves looking back as well as forwards, and their joy was tinged with melancholy. As always it was the young members of the party who forced the others to recognize the passing of time. Stella, who could not remember her grandparents, who thought of this house as Aunt I's, and could not hear the echoes of other voices, the tremulous summons of the past that eddied in every corner; and Joe, now a young man, who had brought a girl with him! None of them could get over the girl, it was as if none of them had ever fallen in love themselves, so wondrous was the spectacle of Joe with his girl. She was tiny and dark and devastatingly pretty and her name was Joan. She was also a nice girl, who adored Joe, and who confided with mock shame to Iris that she could not so much as boil an egg. Iris promised to teach her, but Joe had the look of a man content to live on kisses.

Loelia Drake was there, representing the old guard, but she was now very lame and stiff, and had to sit in a big chair in the drawing-room while other people came to her, like a queen giving audiences. Only Dulcie, Kate saw, could not mesh, nor be part of it, though she tried so terribly hard. She drank rather too much, and smoked a lot, and talked and laughed loudly, but everyone seemed to have someone of their own who was just a little more important to them, so that in the end they turned away from Dulcie, fond of her but not fond enough, keeping their love for another person. And who could blame them on this special day?

When they sat round listening to the huge crowd singing *Land of Hope and Glory* outside Buckingham Palace, while the King and Queen, and Winnie himself came out on the balcony, Kate looked round to see that Dulcie wasn't there.

She crept out and found her in the hall, standing very straight and still by the door, almost as if she had been about to leave and something had stopped her. Kate went to her and saw that there were tears on her cheeks, but that her face was drawn tight, resisting them. Kate put her arm round her.

'Don't cry, Dulcie,' she said. 'We're all here. You have all of us.'

But she knew it was not enough, and Dulcie could not trust herself to answer, so they stood together, Kate's arm about Dulcie, until she was composed enough to rejoin the others.

Primmy, dressed for work, picked up the cat, Blitz, and carried him downstairs, along Globe Road a little way, and on to the bomb site. It was the end of August, and going to be a beautiful day, the desolation of Bethnal Green was bathed in a wonderful hazy, promising dawn.

Primmy watched as Blitz prowled about selecting a suitable spot for his ablutions. Though she took her duties as cat-minder while Dulcie was abroad extremely seriously, she drew the line at a cinder-tray in her nice clean flat. She had never been keen on pets, she did not consider that human habitation should be made smelly and insanitary by their presence, but since she had rescued this particular cat in the first place she could hardly say no when asked if she would give him a home for a few months. She had even grown quite fond of him, she liked his tough, piratical air, and the rattling syncopated purr with which he greeted her when she got back from the hospital.

But a cat-tray she would not resort to so, twice a day, she took the trouble to bring him out here and supervise while he did his business. Sometimes, when she came off duty it nearly killed her, the standing about. She was getting bad veins in her legs – an inheritance from her mother whose own legs had resembled a map of the Nile and its tributaries – and by the end of the day on the ward they throbbed murderously. Primmy bitterly resented this sign of weakness, she had always considered herself as strong as a horse, able to work forever. She literally could not imagine a future without work. Her work was her marriage partner, no matter how hard it drove her, she still depended on it.

Now, this morning, she looked forward to arriving at the hospital and slipping into her routine that was so satisfyingly smooth and well-oiled, a machine that she kept in peak condition by her own efforts. It was where she was at her best. She gazed around. There were still a few election posters stuck up here and there, reminding her of her political treachery. Primmy, who believed in a ruling class, was a lifelong Tory, and Winston Churchill had no more fervent admirer. But with the war over, housing was a key issue. Her own sister Lisbeth's family had been rehoused in a dreadful prefab – they were pathetically glad to have it, but it made Primmy hopping mad to think what they had lost. So she had voted Labour and hoped they would stick by their promises, or she would never forgive herself or them.

A van drew up in the road and disgorged the four German POWs who came every day to work on this patch. They were clearing it and assembling the still-good bricks into neat piles, and levelling the ground for rebuilding. They were always accompanied by a young British guard but they were obviously trusties, for the relationship between guard and prisoners seemed entirely amiable and relaxed. At first their presence had aroused a certain amount of good-natured local curiosity, posses of staring children and watchful, whispering women. But now they had become just another feature of the post-war landscape.

They nodded and smiled at Primmy, and one of them called 'Good-morning to you!' and gave her a little wave. She inclined her head with careful politeness. It was always the same one who said good-morning when he saw her, and though she scarcely liked to admit it even to herself, her reaction was not the one of lordly indifference which befitted the women of a conquering nation. On the contrary, she suspected that on more than one occasion she had blushed. Blushed!

The prisoner in question was tall and dark with a thin, rather sad face and gentle eyes. He was without question younger than Primmy but she sensed in him a maturity and sensitivity beyond his years, which set him apart from the other men in his group. There was something courtly about him, she found herself wondering what he had done before the war, and what he thought of it all . . . and then she would twitch her shoulders and purse her lips in annoyance at herself.

While the prisoners removed their tools from the van she turned her attention back to Blitz. To her horror, he had gone.

For a moment she gaped in disbelief at the place where only a moment ago he had been tidily scratching soil into a neat heap. She gazed around: he was nowhere in sight. She ran forward, calling his name, without the smallest hope of getting any response. She could not imagine how she had been so negligent and stupid. Glancing at her watch she saw that she would be late if she did not go. Hot with frustration and anxiety she turned and began to stumble back towards the road. She was so agitated that she almost bumped into the tall, dark German, who at once leapt back with something astonishingly like a bow, one hand resting on his spade as if it were the poshest gold-topped cane.

'I'm sorry,' he said.

'I've lost my cat!' blurted out Primmy. She was devastated. She knew she should not be talking about it to him, but it just came out. Already she could see the guard coming over, keeping an eye. So as not to get the prisoner into trouble, she addressed her next remark over his shoulder to the guard.

'I lost my cat — someone else's cat that I was looking after!'

'Is that so?' replied the guard. 'I expect he'll come back.'

'But I have to get to work.'

'Don't worry, we'll keep an eye out for him,' said the guard. Primmy realized she was making a complete fool of herself and made to go, but the German said quietly: 'I too have a cat at home, and often he roams and I don't find. But when he is sufficiently hungry, he returns. A hungry cat will return.'

She looked at him and he smiled — gently, warmly, encouragingly.

'I do hope so,' she said. 'He belongs to someone else.'

'We shall be here all the day,' he said. 'We keep a look-out.'

'Thank you. Thank you very much, I would be grateful.'

Her cheeks burning, she went back to lock up her flat, and then hurried to the bus, not daring to look at the prisoners again.

When she returned in the evening Mrs Denny popped out as she crossed the hall. 'Miss Dilkes — I've got your cat!'

'Oh Mrs Denny, bless you, thanks ever so much.' Primmy felt quite faint with relief. She went into the Dennys' overcrowded living-room and there was Blitz sitting on the settee, with a length of string tied loosely round his neck.

'What happened?' she asked, picking him up and cuddling him. 'Did he just turn up on the doorstep?'

'No he did not!' said Mrs Denny. 'One of them Germans brought him round, one of them that's been working on the site.'

'Oh really?' said Primmy.

'And 'e left a note for you.'

'Oh.' Primmy took the scrumpled piece of paper that Mrs Denny handed her and put it in her pocket. She was absolutely tingling all over with embarrassment. Carrying Blitz she went to the door, and added, 'Thank you very much for minding him for me.'

'Don't mention it.'

'Good-night then.'

'Good-night.'

She positively scurried upstairs and dumped Blitz on the floor. Then she smoothed out the scrap of paper and read what was written on it. He had beautiful handwriting, symmetrical and flowing.

'Dear Fraulein – a hungry cat returns, as I told you. Perhaps you should keep him on a string in future to avoid more escapes. Possibly I see you tomorrow.'

Primmy's heart, with the elephantine stiffness of long disuse, creaked into life and managed to skip a beat or two. He had without doubt the most elegant handwriting she had ever seen, it was like getting a bunch of flowers. Primmy was not a fanciful or sentimental person, but she could not ignore the peculiar aptness of this coincidence. Once again a pet of Dulcie's had been the indirect cause of – well, of a meeting. In Celine's case it had led to marriage. Primmy did not anticipate anything even remotely like that, but she did find herself looking forward to tomorrow with more than usual eagerness. The immediate future took on a gay and unpredictable aspect. It was as though Dulcie had left, along with her buccaneering cat, a little legacy of her own seductive glamour.

Primmy glanced at Blitz. He sat on the table – a favoured vantage point, strictly not allowed – his tail wrapped round his legs, eyes half closed, basking in a patch of evening sunshine.

On this occasion she did not sweep him off the table, but coaxed him down with a saucer of milk and watched quite benignly as he lapped it up. Evening sun streamed in through the window.

One evening in mid-September Thea Kinglsey stood in the drawing-room of her house in Gilgil, simply trying to summon sufficient good-humour and resolve to go out and join her sister on the verandah. She hated herself for being so grudging over what was, after all, just a simple act of friendliness.

Of course she had expected changes after eight years. Typically, Jack had been uninformative after his visit in '43 — 'She seems fine' was the best he could do, and she'd had to be content with that. But the woman who sat out there now had more in common with the brittle and self-obsessed girl of their childhood days than the woman Thea remembered from 1937. She had grown very thin, and in middle years it didn't suit her, her face was becoming gaunt. She had the look which in other women Ralph had been wont unkindly to describe as that of 'an organ grinder's monkey'. Certainly her style had not deserted her, but there was a pathos in such elegance now, as if Dulcie knew she had no audience. She tried too hard.

Thea could not bear it, she suffered agonies on Dulcie's behalf but was at a loss to know how to help her. The visit so far had not been a success. Thea at least had been delighted to receive her letter, and only too eager to have her to stay, to try and build on what had seemed such a promising rapprochement eight years ago. She had had visions of them becoming real friends at last, as sisters should be, of moving into calm and sunlit waters.

But from the moment Dulcie arrived it was as if she were there against her will. She seemed unable to relax, didn't sleep well and was forever moving about at night in her room so that Thea couldn't sleep either. She drank like a fish and smoked like a chimney, which was not in itself any crime except that she seemed to glean no pleasure from either. She constantly expressed admiration over the surrounding countryside but appeared also to be afraid of it, and could not be coaxed away from the house and verandah except for occasional drinks and dinner parties with friends. On these occasions she had been more herself, and charmed everyone, but the minute they were over she had seemed edgy and nervous again, and had wanted to stay up and drink all night when they got home, and Thea and Jack were exhausted. Of course the considerable burden of keeping Dulcie company had fallen on Thea. Jack, irritated beyond measure, simply withdrew behind a protective smoke-screen of work and male preoccupation. The tension in the house was excruciating. No limit had been put on Dulcie's stay, naturally, Thea wouldn't have heard of it, but now the coming days, weeks, months, so warmly and willingly offered, stretched ahead like a life sentence.

Jobi, the new house boy, appeared on the verandah with a tray on which were the whisky, sherry decanter, soda syphon and glasses.

Thea heard Dulcie's voice: 'Oh, that is kind, how lovely, I'm just not used to all this service. Yes, do pour me one, only a little soda, just a splash, that's it!' Her bright, jangly laugh rang out jarringly. Thea could just make out Jobi's amiable, baffled expression. But he was no simpleton, he was crafty, and he had the measure of Dulcie, whose approach to the African servants swung wildly between saccharine friendliness and capricious rages. The first bought her no favours, and the second was water off a duck's back.

Thea went out on to the verandah and Dulcie at once turned to her. 'Thea, how nice. The little boy just brought the drinks, can I pour you one?'

Thea smiled and sat down on the other side of the small table. 'Yes, thank you.' She took the glass of sherry Dulcie handed her. 'What have you been doing this afternoon?'

Dulcie lit a cigarette and turned and tapped her small gold lighter on the table top. 'Oh, this and that . . . amusing myself . . . I could ask the same of you.'

'I had to do some work in the garden,' said Thea. 'I'm sorry if I deserted you. You must find life here very dull.'

'Nonsense.'

'I expect Jack will join us in a minute. He's always so busy – he works too hard, really.'

'I know, I know. Poor Jack.'

There was a silence, embarrassed on Thea's part, contemplative on Dulcie's. She finished her drink.

'I wonder, do you mind if I . . .?'

'Help yourself, please.' Thea watched her pour a large whisky and barely alter its colour with a spit of soda. She took a deep breath. 'Dulcie, I wonder if we shouldn't have a proper talk –'

'Oh look!' Dulcie waved her cigarette airily, dropping hot ash on her skirt and not bothering to brush it off. 'Talk of the devil!'

Jack came along the verandah from the direction of his office. Seeing him through her sister's eyes over recent weeks had brought home to Thea how he had aged. The elegant ascetic young man had gone for ever now. His hair was receding slightly at the temples, accentuating his widow's peak, and there were deep vertical clefts between his brows and at the corners of his mouth. He had recently begun to suffer from blinding headaches and been obliged to wear glasses for driving and all close work. It pained Thea to realize that people meeting him for the first time would see a thin, tired, frowning man in glasses, obviously careworn, and would never guess at the slim, red-haired, dashing officer she had married at the end of the last war.

'We were just saying you work too hard,' Dulcie said, pulling his sleeve to make him sit down. It was a new manifestation, this constant touching and tweaking of hers, and Jack loathed it. Thea could not look. Cornet waddled along from his basket outside the drawing-room door and slumped down with a grunting sigh: she busied herself stroking his broad, slit-eyed head.

Jack spoke, severely polite. 'There's a lot of work to be done. I'm sorry if I appear anti-social.'

'*Pas du tout*. All work and no play, though,' said Dulcie.

'Anyway, I'm here now.' He helped himself to whisky, subjecting the bottle to a quick, but noticeable appraisal as he did so.

Thea wished he wouldn't do that. To draw the fire, she said brightly: 'I was wondering whether we might go into Nairobi for a weekend while Dulcie's here, she hardly had time to see anything on the way from the coast. We could stay at the

Norfolk for a night, and perhaps have dinner at the Muthaiga . . . what do you think?'

She could not gauge her husband's expression in the sudden near-darkness. But Dulcie at least was enthusiastic.

'That sounds a wonderful idea, I should enjoy that!' She finished her drink, and her hand moved towards the tray, but Jack had put the bottle on the ground by his chair.

'We could think about it,' he said cautiously. Thea knew the problem was cash, but she did not want him to say that in front of Dulcie. She wanted him to be, for that moment, what he certainly wasn't, the genial host.

'You could combine it with business,' she urged cheerfully. 'And we could all do with a change.'

He stood up to light the hurricane lamp, and smiled down at his wife. 'We'll see.'

As he sat down Dulcie leaned across to touch his knee. 'You'll take us, won't you Jack,' she said. 'For old times' sake?'

Jack crossed his legs, thus moving his knee well beyond Dulcie's reach. 'Possibly.'

'Lovely!' Dulcie clapped her hands, then leaned conspiratorially towards Thea. 'How can he resist the two of us?'

'Quite easily, I should think.'

Dulcie referred herself once more to Jack. 'How gratifying it must be to know that the pair of us were wild about you – and still are!'

Thea stroked and stroked Cornet's head, he was in an almost trance-like state from all the attention. But Dulcie had no intention of leaving it at that.

'It only seems like yesterday doesn't it?' she went on, with a gay, musing inflection in her voice. 'Though one can hardly imagine that the same sort of fuss would be made in today's progressive world.'

'I really do think it's best forgotten,' said Thea, very gently. She heard the sharp scrape of a match as Jack lit a cigarette. She simply couldn't look at him, she longed for the earth to open and swallow up the three of them. How could Dulcie behave like this?

'Rubbish,' she said now. 'We've all been forgetting about it for years, in the true-blue British tradition. We ought to be able to laugh about it now! I *was* a little bitch, wasn't I? I mean not just for doing it, but for telling. That was what really *infuriated* everyone, that I wasn't ashamed!'

'Very probably,' said Jack. 'But I was. And as for laughing about it, I don't feel inclined to. It caused a lot of people a great deal of unhappiness, it was no small thing.'

'Well Jack, if you say so . . . might I have another drink?'

'No.'

'Jack!' Thea was mortified. Jack pushed his chair back and stood up.

'Isn't dinner ready?'

'I expect so.'

Dulcie was ready now to be deflected from her collision course. 'Dinner it is . . .' She got up unsteadily and followed Jack into the house. Thea turned out the light.

In the dining-room Jobi was waiting, watchful and immaculate in the white *kanzu* he put on at dinner time. Dulcie had taken Jack's arm. Being rather drunk made her prettier, her face was flushed and softer, her eyes bright. With the utmost courtly dignity Jack showed her to her place. His impeccable manners were almost more painful for Thea to watch than if he had openly berated Dulcie for her behaviour, they seemed to underline the gulf that had widened between them. She did not know who to comfort first.

Dulcie ate almost nothing. Halfway through the meal she abruptly left the table. When Thea followed her she met her leaving the bathroom, as white as a sheet and distinctly shaky on her feet.

'Dulcie . . . are you all right?' She put her arm round her, but the gay, forced affection had now gone, literally down the drain.

'No, I'm as sick as a dog – for heaven's sake, what does it look like?'

'Can I get you anything?'

'No.' Dulcie mopped her face with a small white hankie. 'I'm sorry if I spoiled dinner.'

'You didn't.'

Dulcie looked at her sceptically. 'Dear Thea, so tactful. I'll go to bed now anyway and give you both some peace.'

'There's no need –'

'Good-night.'

Thea returned to the dining-room. Jobi was setting out the cheeseboard and biscuit barrel. Jack, looking tense and white, was holding his knife poised between his finger and thumb, tapping out a rhythm on the tabletop. His eyes flicked up to her as she entered and Jobi glided discreetly from the room.

'I can't take much more of that,' he said quietly.

'I know . . .' she sank down in her chair and looked at him helplessly. 'I do know.'

He leaned forward. 'It's not your fault my darling.'

'I asked her here.'

'She asked herself.'

'I know, but – if she needs me, if she's unhappy and wants to come I can hardly refuse. I didn't want to refuse.'

'I realize that.' He looked away for a moment in exasperation. 'But what's the matter with her? You said that when you last saw her she was in good form, and she seemed perfectly all right when I was over last. I mean, what ails the woman?'

'I don't know. But perhaps when she's been here a while longer she'll begin to tell us things.'

'Tell us things – Jesus wept! I just wish to God she'd keep quiet for five minutes.'

'That isn't fair, you hardly see her all day.'

'I take care not to.'

'Then don't complain.'

'Why the hell shouldn't I complain?' Jack pushed his chair back violently, threw his napkin on the ground and went to the sideboard. But instead of pouring himself coffee he rounded on Thea. 'This is my house – our house – and she is behaving atrociously. She's drunk every night, she seems to think she can say what she likes irrespective of our feelings. She's making life a misery, Thea!'

'I'm sorry.'

'And we don't have the faintest idea when she might oblige us by leaving.'

'I couldn't ask her to leave, Jack. She's my sister, she's family – and there's Kate.'

'Yes, damn it, there's Kate!' He slammed his fist down on the sideboard so that the lid of the coffee pot jumped. 'Of course it's only a matter of time before that comes up, God knows what she's storing up for us on that subject.'

'That isn't fair,' Thea was almost in tears. 'She hasn't mentioned it.'

'Give her time, give her time.' He laughed sourly. 'What idiots we were ever to suppose that she could accept a thing like that without throwing it back in our faces at some time or another.'

'But Jack, I think she's very unhappy, ill even, I'm quite sure she'll tell us the reason if we hang on.'

He sighed. 'Oh my darling . . .' He reached out, now, and took her hand. She felt in his touch and saw in his expression the changes that more than twenty years had wrought in all of them. 'All your geese are swans, aren't they? And God knows, always have been.'

Much later that night, after they'd gone to bed, they were rudely awakened by a loud crash from outside, at the back of the house near the kitchen. Cornet began barking hysterically in the corridor and even the dogs in the pen at the end of the drive started up in sympathy. Jack leapt up, dragged on a dressing-gown and went out of the screen door on to the back verandah. Thea pulled herself up in bed, glancing at her watch: one-thirty. She rubbed her eyes, her head ached.

In a moment Jack came back in. 'You'd better go,' he said curtly. 'It's your sister.'

'Oh Lor',' Thea scrambled out and felt for her sandals. 'What on earth is she up to?'

'I haven't the remotest idea, nor do I wish to find out. I don't trust myself.' He got back into bed and reached, with an air of finality, for his book and glasses off the bedside table.

Thea went out, closing the door after her. Cornet, hearing her familiar footsteps, deduced that the matter was in hand and fell silent. Ahead of her, in the direction of the staff quarters, she could make out a pale figure like a wraith, flapping about in the darkness, and hear Dulcie's voice raised in protest.

'Dulcie!' She went down the steps at the end of the verandah. It was cool and she shivered. 'Dulcie, what's the matter?'

Now she could hear her sister's shrill, imperious voice: 'Come out whoever did this, it's an absolute disgrace! Boy! Would you please come here and explain to me —'

'Dulcie!' Thea ran over to her and tried to put her arms round her, but she was all wayward limbs like an insect, impossible to hold. From the black bush a solitary bird gave its mocking, hooting cry like the laugh of a ghost.

'Dulcie, what on earth are you doing out here at this time of night?'

Dulcie was in a diaphanous nightdress, and carrying a white linen frock over her arm. She smelt strongly of whisky — it was plain she had sought out the confiscated bottle once more since dinner. When she turned to face Thea it was without surprise, she was completely bound up in her own drama.

'Look at this!' she shrieked, holding out the dress. 'Will you look at what that idiot black boy has done to my dress.'

Thea gazed at it distractedly, it was just a dress. 'What?'

Dulcie shook it under her nose. 'He's ironed it with creases down the sides! I shall look like a cardboard cut out! I'm simply livid, he must do it again!'

Thea laughed with relief. 'Oh, don't worry. He's new, he's still learning. You can show him tomorrow and he can do it again under your supervision. Don't for goodness sake disturb him at this hour.'

But she was already too late. A bleary-eyed and aggrieved-looking Jobi appeared at the door of his house.

Thea smiled brightly. 'Not to worry Jobi, no trouble, you go back to bed.' She tried to take Dulcie by the arm, but found herself resisted and cast off with surprising strength. Jobi's wife and his two young children appeared next to him, a cluster of dark, accusing faces. Dulcie stormed over to confront them. Her pale hair stood on end and what with that and the floating nightie she resembled some avenging spirit come back to seek retribution.

'Look at this!' She held up the dress for Jobi's inspection, a gesture which he treated with monumental impassivity. 'You have made a complete mess of one of my best dresses. Do you see what you have done? Do you see?' She pushed her face towards his with that air of aggressive petulance that Thea remembered so well.

'Dulcie —'

'Leave me alone!'

Thea had a feeling of *déjà vu* about the whole thing. The situation would have been almost laughable if it had not contained so many echoes of past confrontations. The expressions of Jobi and his wife became increasingly baleful in the face of Dulcie's tirade.

'. . . I might have known not to expect normal standards of work in a dead and alive hole like this. Has no one ever shown you how to do this job properly?'

'Yes, they have.' Jack came forward and took her firmly by the arm. Thea did not know whether to be pleased or appalled by his arrival. 'Come back into the house now Dulcie.'

Jim the gardener, and the cook, and several more *totos* had appeared to add weight to the opposition. Thea was acutely aware of their heavy, watchful silence, their solid, blacker bulks in the darkness as she and Dulcie and Jack stood white and conspicuous, spotlit by the yellow light that spilled along the verandah from the bedroom door.

What happened next was what Thea least expected. Dulcie turned and looked at Jack for a moment, and then collapsed, sobbing pitifully, into his arms. The dress, the cause of the uproar, was dropped, forgotten, on the red murram pathway, so it would need washing again anyway.

Jack spoke a few restrained words in Swahili to Jobi and then turned, with Dulcie still weeping against him, and walked back to the house. Thea picked up the dress, smiled apologetically, hesitated for a moment, then followed. She knew they were being watched as they retreated in disarray. She felt, as she did increasingly often these days, threatened by the Africans. There seemed to be a more considered resentment in their attitude, a real dislike which didn't take much to fuel it. She was sure that the three of them – Dulcie with her wild and insulting accusations, Jack with his somewhat haughty propriety, and she hovering ingratiatingly in between – must represent the three aspects of white society least calculated to improve the situation.

She closed the bedroom door after them, and shot the bolt. Then she released the frantic Cornet, who grunted and panted protectively round them as they made their forlorn way to the drawing-room. Jack turned on a lamp and helped Dulcie into a chair. His manner, as at dinner, was fastidiously polite. Thea stood holding the dress.

'It's all right darling,' she said. 'I'll look after Dulcie.'

He looked dubiously from one to the other. Cornet whined. 'Are you sure?'

'Quite sure.'

As he passed her he nodded his head minutely in the direction of the drinks table, and lifted a hand. 'No,' he mouthed.

Thea went and sat down by Dulcie, who was hunched over, her elbows on her knees, her head in her hands. Her shoulders seemed pitifully thin and pointed, her blue-veined wrists thin and brittle as twigs. Thea put her arms round her and this time was not pushed away. Dulcie felt insubstantial in her embrace, like a bird, just bones wrapped in skin.

'Dulcie, we can't go on like this. Please tell me what's troubling you, you're not well.'

Into her shoulder, Dulcie said: 'Could I have a drink?'

'Don't you think—'

'Thea, please. *Please*.'

The desperation in her voice was too much for Thea. She went to the table. The contents of the bottle had dropped by about an inch since before dinner. Thea poured her a small one and topped it up with a generous measure of soda. When she took it back, Dulcie was sitting up, and when she handed her the glass she drank half the whisky down at once.

'You're not having one?' She looked almost accusingly at Thea.

'I don't want one.'

'Lucky you.'

'What's the matter?'

Dulcie pulled a bitter face. 'I love the way you ask that, as if I could answer you in one sentence, and you could sort me out in another, and that would be that.'

'We have to start somewhere, we have to make a beginning.'

'But miserable people are such a dreadful *bore*.'

'You won't bore me,' said Thea. 'That is one thing you've never, ever done.'

*

At a quarter to four Thea crept back into bed and put her arm round Jack. 'Jack? Are you awake?'

He grunted. 'I am now.'

'Can you listen for a moment?'

With a mighty sigh he turned on to his back. 'All right. What did she say?'

'First of all – do let's go for that weekend. Please say yes, please, for me.'

'My God, she's so spoilt!' Although he was whispering, the vehemence in his voice was explosive. 'It's incomprehensible to me how a woman can reach that age and still expect to be pandered to and indulged as if she were a child. Not content with drinking the place dry and causing mutiny among the *watu*, she keeps you up all night and expects to be carted about on a bloody progress!'

'You're too harsh, and you haven't heard yet, you don't know her story.'

'Tell me then. And it had better be good.'

'She was in love with this man Bill. Do you remember I told you about him, but he wasn't there when I was over in '37. It was why she was so happy and contented then, she truly loved him, she was transformed—'

'Pity she couldn't keep it up,' said Jack, but he felt for his cigarettes and lit one, prepared at least to listen.

'But she made a mistake. She got pregnant.'

'Good God. At her age?'

'It was two or three years ago. At any rate, I suppose she felt like you that it couldn't happen, and that's exactly why it did.'

'If you say so.'

'But she got rid of it. Think of it, Jack, she got some of those awful pills and got rid of it by herself at home because she didn't want to lose him – she didn't want to seem to be forcing his hand. I think it was so brave of her.'

'Well –' Jack looked at her, and his face was gentler now, his voice more tender. 'Brave or foolish. But I admit they're often the same thing.'

'You see,' Thea was encouraged, she took his hand, parting the fingers and stroking it. She knew how straight he was, how honourable, that he would do the right thing if she could just persuade him what the right thing was. 'You see, she resolved not to tell this man, this Bill, she just wanted everything to carry on as before when he got back. She didn't mind if she wasn't the great love of his life as he was of hers, provided they could be together. But when he did come home he told her he had fallen in love – really in love – with someone else. She was a married woman, there was nothing he could do, but he said they needed each other and if the time ever came when they could be together he would have to be with her.'

Jack watched her face. 'And so?'

'She realized that she couldn't settle for second best. She couldn't tell him about the baby she had got rid of. And she knew that this other woman deserved happiness too, proper happiness and real love. So she told him to go and she hasn't seen him since.'

There was silence. Jack ground out his cigarette and turned back to her. He lifted his hand from hers and brushed her throat and chin with his fingers. His voice was sad when he spoke.

'My darling . . . she should have got over it by now. She's a woman of the world, God knows. She should be able to cope, don't you agree?'

Thea avoided his eyes and withdrew from his touch. 'You haven't heard yet who the other woman was.'

He smiled at her. He loved her. 'Surprise me,' he said.

At the end of the week, they went into Nairobi. The drive in was a much improved and abbreviated affair these days, due to the new tarmac road over the escarpment between Naivasha and Nairobi, built by Italian prisoners of war. As the car hummed along Dulcie seemed to blossom, to take real heart from the prospect of a couple of nights in a good hotel, and dinner at the Muthaiga country club. But neither Thea nor Jack set much store by her apparent high spirits. The days and nights since she had unburdened herself to Thea had been almost more harrowing than those which preceded it. She had been at pains to behave, like a child trying to earn a treat, and somehow though they all three now knew her story, they could not discuss it together, the cross-currents which had been set up over thirty years ago formed a kind of mesh which held them fast. So they had been polite, more tolerant of one another, more thoughtful, but not one jot closer.

On the way up the winding road that led south from the rift valley Dulcie turned and gazed out of the window.

'Look at that, it's so beautiful. Jack, could you stop just for a moment while I take a photograph?'

'Certainly.' He braked and pulled in. 'But be warned, these African views look like nothing in a snapshot — just a great expanse of nothing.'

She gathered up her camera and opened the car door. 'Never mind! *I* shall know what it looked like in the flesh, and a photo will serve to remind me.'

Thea got out and joined her, while Jack sat sideways in the driving seat, his legs stretched out in the sun, smoking a cigarette. Dulcie bobbed and sidestepped, trying to get the view to her liking. Two Kikuyu women were toiling up the hill, each carrying a mountainous burden of firewood, held in place on their backs by means of a head strap. Beneath the straps their faces were dour and creased, faces of quite young women who had long forgotten vanity. A little behind the two women walked a man wearing a brown and orange cotton tunic and threadbare English blazer. He carried a small switch. All three kept their course, and Dulcie and Thea had to step aside to let them pass. The women did not acknowledge them by so much as a blink, though the man lifted a pale, seamed palm, and grinned. Beside those women Thea thought that Dulcie, who was probably older than both, looked like a sunflower in her yellow and white sundress.

She took three pictures, and then lowered the camera, pointing. 'That's what I've tried to get in — what is that?'

There was a small building at the foot of the road at the bottom of the escarpment, its stubby tower outlined against the hazy coppery plain beyond.

'It's the Italian Chapel of Thanksgiving,' said Thea. 'The prisoners built it when they'd finished the road. They had the first service there at Christmas about two years ago. I always think it has the loveliest position, just where a chapel should be, with that spectacular view.'

'Yes — although it looks out of place.'

Like you, thought Thea. Just like you, small and romantic

and somehow irredeemably European. Whatever are you doing here?

It seemed that Jack, too, was thinking that, for he got out of the car and came over to them. He thrust his hands in his pockets.

'I can remember bringing young Kate over here, in the wagon,' he observed gruffly. 'No road then.'

Thea held her breath, but Dulcie said: 'I wonder what she thought of it all.'

'She went a touch silent on us. She's not easily overwhelmed, but I think she was then. As a great many people have been before her, and will be yet.'

They all three gazed out over the lovely hot, shimmering plain, but they were piercingly aware of each other.

Jack cleared his throat. 'You should be proud of that daughter of yours, Dulcie. She has character.'

It wasn't much of a compliment, as compliments went, but it was enough to provide them, those cautious middle-aged people, with their moment of truth. Dulcie made a considerable business of returning her camera to its case, before saying quietly: 'Yes, I know.'

It had been said. The unutterable had been mentioned, and there had been no pain, they had contrived to emerge with dignity. As they went back to the car Thea took Jack's arm and kissed his cheek. There were two patches of colour on his cheekbones. Only she knew what it had cost him, and she loved him for it.

They drove on in a silence that was not strained, but tranquil and understanding.

If the Rift Valley had changed little since the day Kate first saw it in 1922, the Norfolk Hotel had. Post-war Nairobi was booming, there was a whole new influx of would-be settlers on the run from Attlee's austere socialist Britain, and for the wealthy, cosmopolitan whites who had always been there the wind of change was as yet no more than a tickling breeze. Work flourished and play abounded. The Norfolk was no longer simply a saloon-style watering hole and transit camp for farmers and hunters but a thriving international hotel, the hub of an expanding East African tourist trade.

At the Norfolk, Dulcie looked more at home than she had for weeks, Thea and Jack rather less so. The three of them had rooms in the hotel's row of cottage apartments, overlooking the garden at the back. In the centre of the garden was a big cage filled with an assortment of jewel-coloured native birds, and an immaculately restored and polished ox-cart to remind people of the old, pioneering days. Days which Dulcie was not interested in considering. In these surroundings she blossomed like the rose, she drew admiring glances, she was sparkling, she was in her natural element.

Over lunch on the Saturday they were suddenly approached by old acquaintances of the Kingsleys, Piers and Vera Dalhousey. Dulcie was in especially buoyant form, after a morning's shopping with Thea, and away from Jack, and was extolling the virtues of the Norfolk's sumptuous lunchtime buffet when the Dalhouseys hove in view.

'The Kingsleys, God rot them!' was Piers' characteristic greeting. He pulled a chair from a neighbouring table and joined them. 'Mind if we muscle in?'

A waiter, seeing the general drift of things, brought a second chair for Vera.

Jack smiled, a shade frostily. 'Piers, Vera, what a surprise. Er — may I introduce my sister-in-law, Dulcie Tennant? She's over with us for a while from home.'

'Is she now?' Piers squeezed Dulcie's hand in both his large, brown paws. Vera shook hands more coolly.

'How do you find us,' she asked. 'To your liking?'

'Oh, the country is superb,' said Dulcie with a smile. 'But I'm not at all sure it would suit me to live here. I don't think I should fit in, somehow.'

'Too damn right you wouldn't,' bellowed Piers. 'And that's a compliment, eh Jack?' He bellowed with laughter. Jack smiled thinly.

'Who's for another bottle of wine? Boy!'

'Piers, you're at our table, I'll buy the wine.'

Piers snorted again and grinned at Thea. 'Still a stickler for protocol, the old man, I see.'

Thea turned to Vera, and asked something about a race-meeting. Their conversation, though spoken in English, might as well have been in mandarin Chinese for all Dulcie understood of it. She felt their world encircling them as hers encircled her; they were all too old now to break out of their separate worlds. She also saw, and noted automatically, that Vera Dalhousey must once have been a woman of leonine good looks, but that now, though she was still handsome, she was coarsened and hardened by the exigencies of her life in Kenya. Rich she undoubtedly was, her large, rough, capable hands sported two impressive diamonds and her clothes, shoes and handbag were old but quality. But her hair was dry, frizzy and colourless from years of exposure to harsh sunlight and her skin, Dulcie thought, ruined. She recalled how she had envied Una Roth-Vesey her golden tan, but looking at Vera she was quite glad she had stayed out of the sun in her youth.

'. . . we could make a party of it!' Piers was suggesting. His eyes bulged towards Dulcie in a look she knew and recognized all too well. 'Hear that, my dear –' he addressed his wife, 'the four of us will have dinner together at the Muthaiga tonight and make whoopee like the old days.'

'I don't know Piers,' said Thea, 'we thought just a quiet family evening.'

'Quiet, who wants to be quiet? You don't want to be quiet, do you Dulcie?' He beamed at her and Dulcie cringed and shrank inwardly from him. But outwardly she was gracefully enthusiastic, the model relative and guest.

'It sounds delightful, what a nice idea. I've been far too quiet for too long.'

'See?' Piers was triumphant. 'Woman after my own heart, always game for a party.'

Thea could do no more, she was powerless before Piers' elephantine boisterousness and Dulcie's misplaced politeness. Thea disliked Piers. He was half the man Jack was, but he had done twice as well, if success was to be judged in pounds, shillings and pence. Since the days when Vera had wrestled with the ill-starred pet cheetah on their lawn near Gilgil, Piers had given up farming himself, though he still owned some land. He now made most of his fat living from running safari tours, and stage-managing unfortunate animals so that people might eventually be able to use their heads for trophies, their legs for umbrella stands and their feet for paperweights. There was about Piers an intrinsic vulgarity. What Vera made of him was not clear. His amorous adventures were numerous and much bruited about, and Vera was reckoned to be a brick to put up with it all. Especially as she was the genuine article, blue-blooded, with acres in the shires back home.

Looking at the group seated round the table, Thea could see all too clearly what role Dulcie filled in Piers Dalhousey's plans for the evening.

Neither Jack nor Piers could any longer have been said to be typical of the membership of the Muthaiga Club. Indeed, if they had applied at the present time they would probably have been turned down, Jack for not being part of the right social group, Piers because the Dalhousey escutcheon was now well and truly besmirched by commerce. But both men had joined more than two decades ago, when their credentials had been impeccable.

The Muthaiga in those days had an international reputation founded on its willingness to turn a blind eye to the whole spectrum of libidinous behaviour. In its heyday, any amount of damage could be incurred, without rebuke, in the club's bar, provided those concerned had the money to pay for it. As a centre for extra-marital fornication it was unrivalled. 'Are you married or do you live in Kenya?' was a conversational gambit, not entirely facetious, which had had its origins in the bar and on the tennis courts of the Muthaiga.

As a building it was no more imposing than any other pleasant colonial country club. It was an attractive, pink-washed single-storey building a few miles from the centre of Nairobi, set in pleasant grounds. Inside, the decor and ambience were certainly not indicative of excess – gracious, flowery rooms with Grecian columns, polished floors, chintzy furniture, sporting prints.

Piers, however, when out for the evening, was disposed to call to mind the good old days. 'Now let me tell you Dulcie,' he confided, taking her arm as they walked into the dining room, 'we raised hell in these hallowed halls in our time, isn't that so Jack?'

'You certainly did Piers.'

'Hah!' Piers brayed with laughter. 'Good old Jack!'

'For goodness sake Piers,' remonstrated Vera. 'Stop boring poor Dulcie with your dreary reminiscences.'

Thea stuck up for Jack. 'He wasn't as good as all that,' she said. 'I can remember some mornings after that he's probably forgotten, and a good thing too!'

They all laughed, even Jack, because he knew his wife was only trying to show that he, too, had once been a gay dog.

They sat down to dinner. Thea caught Dulcie's eye and smiled encouragingly. Even now, there was something about her sister which signalled not just that she was single, but available, always available; that interest shown in her might repay quick and delightful dividends. Thea remembered how she had used to envy that quality in Dulcie, that silent siren call with which she so effortlessly summoned the opposite sex. But now it seemed like a curse rather than a blessing, there was no escape from it, Dulcie must be constantly wary and on her guard, constantly finding ways of deflecting and rejecting without giving offence. She had no peace.

Over dinner they talked about the war, and interest centred once more on Dulcie as she came from London, and the Dalhousey wanted to know what it had been like there through the blitz. Dulcie was expansive, even amusing, about it.

'I'm afraid I found the worst thing was the general discomfort,' she said, 'the endless shortages, and making do, and the dark. I'm sure that's what got most people down in the end. Danger's exciting, after all, but discomfort – well, it's just uncomfortable!'

They all laughed, and Thea put in: 'But surely the people in the worst hit areas must have lived in fear of their lives?'

Dulcie demurred. 'Yes, of course, I suppose mine is a selfish point of view. But quite ordinary people seem to rise to the occasion when it's asked of them, whereas an endless round of dreariness wears down even heroic types.'

Piers guffawed heartily. 'I like that,' he announced. 'That's the spirit of British womanhood for you!' He was seated between Vera and Dulcie, but it was Dulcie he leaned towards, like a plant towards the light, dwarfing her with his bulk, swamping her with his exuberant lechery. He was a big, broad-shouldered man who had always been handsome but was now becoming merely florid. His tanned face was reddened by good living, but his yellowy-white hair was thick and glossy, he exuded a venturesome masculinity. It was just, thought Thea, that he made Dulcie look so terribly fragile. The sight of Piers with Dulcie seemed to encapsulate the very conditions which had brought Dulcie low, which had somehow ensured that while she had seemed capable of everything she had finished up with nothing.

She's *not* spoilt, thought Thea. She may ask a lot of us, but what else can she do, we are all she has now.

'So tell me how long you'll be staying over here,' said Piers.

'I don't know –' Dulcie glanced at Jack. 'A little while longer if they'll have me.'

'We haven't even considered her going,' said Jack stoutly.

'It's years since we've had any real time together,' added Thea. 'There's a lot of ground to make up.'

'You know,' said Piers, turning to Vera, 'we should have these good people over to dinner as soon as may be.'

'Certainly, any time they like,' replied Vera, not extending the invitation herself, or even endorsing it, but simply passing it back to her husband to do with as he liked.

Piers waxed expansive. 'Next week then? Saturday? How about it?' He looked into Dulcie's face. 'I can show you just how comfortable we can make ourselves out here when we really put our minds to it.'

Dulcie smiled, but she felt suddenly quite sick with claustrophobia. She had never felt her isolation more keenly. She gazed about her at the low-ceilinged, elegant dining-room, white cloths and silver, and shining glass and impassive, watchful black faces. Beyond the windows the deep, palpable African night sighed and waited like a black sea where the patch of yellow light ended. Piers' great heavy shoulder pressed against her bare arm, beneath the table his trousers rasped her leg uncomfortably. He was an intrusion, a threat, an insult. She could scarcely breathe for the loneliness and revulsion she felt at that moment.

'I wonder – would you excuse me for a moment?' She got up, steady and careful, conscious of Thea's concerned look, Jack's more wary.

The men rose, and Jack said: 'Are you all right Dulcie? Can I come with you?'

She put her hand out to stop him, practiced grace and poise covering her panic. 'Please, there's nothing the matter. I just need a breath of air, I shall be back in a couple of minutes, I promise.'

She sensed, or saw with her peripheral vision, that Thea would have come anyway, but that Jack detained her. She was conscious also of the little susurration of speculation and polite concern as she left, threading through the tables. She was a little light-headed but not this time, she realized, from drink.

Because she didn't know her way around, or where else to go, she left the building by the way they had come in, crossing the entrance hall and going out by the main door into the car park.

She didn't know what she intended, only that whatever she had said, she could not go back in. She realized that she was quaking all over with a sort of ague, her teeth chattered, she was in shock. She had told Thea everything, everything. And so now presumably Jack knew as well. There were no secrets left, and the terrible thing was, they couldn't help. They did their best, but they were powerless. She was beyond help. She was nothing, insubstantial. She felt that like the Little Mermaid of the fairy tale she might simply be dissolved into foam or spray. The only two people for whom she might have had substance, who had given her a sense of worth and value, for whom she had borne real, unselfish love — those two had gone, she had no more claim on them, she had forfeited her right to their love.

She wanted Bill so much that she was in physical pain, cramping with longing and the sense of loss. Her heart thrummed and she was dizzy, she was stumbling, bumping off the sides of the parked cars.

In the dark on the far side of the car park a man appeared, pocketing his keys, walking towards her. A stocky man, grey-haired, smiling at her, welcoming her. It was Bill, he had come. She had wanted him so much that he had heard her and come for her. She smiled back, began to run, and to stretch out her arms, she was delirious with joy.

She neither saw nor heard the car that swung through the

gates. All she saw as she drew closer was the startled white face of the man — not Bill — caught in the flooding glare of the headlights. And then something like a great wave of water buffeted her, lifted and threw her to the ground. Her last sensation was neither fear nor pain, but bitter, bitter disappointment.

Thea ran out of the dining room, across the hall and into the car park. Other people surged and eddied just behind her, curious but respectful. The man looked up from where he knelt beside Dulcie, horror-struck. The pale-faced young couple stood by their MG, the girl crying, wiping her eyes and nose on her gossamer stole.

'I'm so terribly sorry,' said the kneeling man. 'I don't know what to say. Who is she? She just ran towards me as if she knew me, she was screaming something — she didn't stand a chance.'

'We honestly couldn't do a thing,' said the youth who had been driving. 'She ran straight out as if she hadn't seen us.'

'Who is she, who knows her?' said the first man again.

Thea crouched down by her sister. There was a black smudge up the side of her pale silk dress, and a trickle of purplish blood coming from the corner of her mouth, it looked almost black against her white skin. But nothing could dim her beauty. Her still pallor was almost luminous, like the reflection of the moon on dark water. The whispering and chattering ceased as everyone looked at her. Thea adjusted the skirt of Dulcie's dress, which had been wrinkled up by her fall, and stroked the soft, fair hair that was still fine as a child's.

'It's all right,' she said. 'I know it was no one's fault. No one could help it. But she was someone a lot of people loved.'

CHAPTER TWENTY-FOUR

*'Bei der Kaserne, vor dem grossen Tor,
Steht 'ne Laterne, und steht sie noch davor,
Une alle Leute soll'n es sehn,
Wenn wir bei der Laterne stehn
Wie einst Lilli Marleen,
Wie einst Lilli Marleen . . .'*

'Lilli Marleen'
Hans Leip and Norbert Schultze, 1944

KATE walked back from the NAAFI stores in Charlottenburg with Stella. It was December '46, nearly Christmas, and she carried a huge bag of shopping. Stella, keen to help but also self-interested, clasped two of the wrapped manufactured cakes, gooey with ersatz cream, which were off ration at the NAAFI. The cakes were her abiding passion: peace for Stella and millions of other children was literally sweet. It was late afternoon and bitterly cold. So cold that it hurt to breathe, every intake of the freezing air seemed to solidify in the nose and throat, turning every tiny hair and delicate membrane to brittle ice. Kate's hands, in two pairs of gloves, were already numb, she felt as though she would have to prise her fingers from the plastic handle of the shopping bag when she got home. Her feet, encased in stockings, two pairs of socks, and unbecoming fleecy boots were in agony as the sub-zero air ate through the protective layers.

Kate bent over Stella. 'All right darling? Shall we try and run a bit?'

'No, I'll fall, it's slippy.'

'Stamp when you walk then. March like Daddy, it'll keep your feet warm.'

'They *are* warm!'

Surprisingly, Kate knew this was probably true. Stella's cheeks and nose were apple-red, and her eyes bright. Her straight-cut fringe, where it emerged from her blue woollen pixie-hood, was spiky with frost. But she rarely did feel the cold until it was too late, until it suddenly made her whine with misery, and then they would run home, watched by thin, blue-lipped German children in threadbare coats and shoes lined with cardboard, who hadn't the energy to run anywhere.

The road along which Kate and Stella walked was flanked by ruins. Ruins were the order of the day in Berlin, they were virtually institutionalized, you almost ceased to see them. Every building was a wreck, to a greater or lesser extent. Many of the houses and apartment blocks in this road had been reduced to rubble, and where buildings still stood they were mostly windowless, and pitted with holes from small-arms fire like faces disfigured by smallpox. Some were just shells, burnt out, with the roofs blown away so that metal girders and wooden joists stuck up into the sky as though the buildings' hair stood on end, which well it might.

But people lived here, life went on with a kind of bizarre normality. There were families carrying on with their day to day lives, not just in the remaining buildings but in the ruins themselves, in the interstices between one broken wall and the next, in buried cellars and boltholes. There were Christmas trees standing in many of the gaping windows, not bought ones of course, but young fir trees hacked down in the woods around the lake at Gatow. The British had a club at Gatow. When Kate and Lawrence had dined there recently with friends they had driven past a trudging line of Berliners, some on their way into the Russian zone to search for potatoes, others carrying their Christmas trees over their shoulders. You couldn't but wonder at the human spirit when you saw those trees, decorated with bits of ribbon and tiny candles.

Ritually, in spite of the cold, they stopped by the municipal tennis courts which had been frozen over for skating. There were all sorts of people on the ice, some swooping and swirling expertly, others stumbling and falling over and laughing at themselves. Kate could see why so many took pleasure in the ice – skating was itself a kind of freedom, like flying, it must be easy to forget for a while as you sped and rushed and shouted to your friends.

But she and Stella soon got too cold just standing and watching, and set off again. On the corner of their road a couple of *steppke*, street urchins, were playing about. Their companion was a haggard little girl with a pinched face, her thin hair scraped to one side in a trailing ribbon. They played a kind of tag. The boys would shout '*Frau, komm!*' and run after her, pulling at her ribbon and her coat while she struggled and laughed, trying to keep her clothes on.

Stella watched in admiration. 'They're playing Russian soldiers,' she said, 'can I play?'

'Certainly not!' said Kate sharply, and then added, 'it's cold, we must get home for tea.'

She tried to hurry past the children, but already she could see from the corner of her eye that one of the boys was coming towards her. She steeled herself, dragged on Stella's hand, resisted her attempts to slow down, to turn and welcome the boy. But it was too late.

'*Zigarette, gnädige Frau? Zigarette bitte? Schokolade?*'

'I'm sorry,' said Kate, 'I don't have any. *Kein Zigarette.*'

'*Schokolade bitte?*'

Stella tugged her hand. 'We've got some chocolate, Mummy, give the boy some chocolate, go on!'

'We're not supposed to.'

The boy addressed himself to Stella. 'It is Christmas,' he pronounced carefully, he was a seasoned campaigner.

'Yes, it's Christmas!' shouted Stella. She handed him one of the wrapped cakes, his eyes flicked up to Kate. She was beaten.

'Very well, I have a little chocolate.' She set down the shopping bag and began to rummage, clumsily, with her cold gloved hands, among her NAAFI purchases. She found a slab of chocolate and would have broken it into pieces but her fingers were too stiff, so she gave him the whole thing. The boy took it with a skinny, purplish hand.

'*Vielen dank!*' He ran back to the other two and they fell on their loot like wolves.

Kate felt almost sick with anxiety and degradation. She felt like this almost every time she went out. As she and Stella walked away she heard one of the boys — he couldn't have been more than nine – remark sneeringly, *'Ist ja zum kotzen . . .'* It's enough to make you puke.

They had expected to walk the streets of Berlin like conquerors, but it had not turned out like that. Even when the Drakes had arrived, eighteen months after the end of the war, the devastation was such that the city the Allies had dreamed of bringing low was scarcely recognizable as a city. The job begun by the bombers in the last year of the war had been triumphantly finished by the Russian tanks and artillery. Berlin was a nightmare place, inhabited by a people who could suffer no more than they had done already. For a great many of the Allied families posted to Berlin that year, the sweets of victory turned to dust and ashes in their mouths.

When Lawrence had first come out with the battalion he had lived at his place of work, the old German army barracks at Spandau. But when Kate and Stella arrived the three of them had been allotted the requisitioned house in Charlottenburg. They were only to be in Berlin a few months, because the authorities had a low opinion of the Allied soldiery's ability to withstand the temptations of fratting and the black market in this notoriously wicked city.

There were specific orders to treat the Germans as a vanquished, not a liberated, nation, in spite of the fact that they had been hailed as liberators after the horrors of the Russian occupation. The no-fraternization rule was rigorously enforced by the British army. It was not permitted to give lifts to Germans, to supplement their rations, or to assist them in any way that was not strictly in accordance with their role as victorious army of occupation.

The colossal programme of denazification ground on its way, and in the meantime it was strictly forbidden for the Allies to employ ex-Nazis in any capacity whatever. Lawrence and Kate had initially taken on a cook, Waltraut. She had been conscientious and efficient, painfully quiet and self-effacing. The awful pallor typical of most Berliners was in Waltraut emphasized by a skin complaint, probably due to malnutrition, which manifested itself in a spotty rash down the centre of her face. There were great sweeping dark shadows under her eyes, and her greasy black hair was caught back in two slides. She was also, apparently, a long-standing member of the Nazi party and had been taken away, weeping and protesting innocence, in spite of Lawrence's attempts to speak up for her. Both Kate and Lawrence had been shocked by that, and torn in two directions. It was hard to equate the unspeakable horrors of the death camps with a frightened, sick woman who had cooked your supper for you.

Waltraut had a son, Heinz, a lad of seventeen or so who was severely tubercular. He came to sit in the Drakes' kitchen, to watch his mother and keep warm, and he was pathetically bereft without her. So Heinz now became one of the several ex-officio members of the household in Charlottenburg for whom Kate, regardless of memos and directives, stretched her rations to breaking point. They took on a nanny, Hildegarde, for Stella, because they felt duty-bound to provide as much employment as possible. Hildegarde travelled in from Spandau on the tram each day, and though unlike Waltraut she was 'clean' it would have been hard to imagine a more natural collaborator. Hildegarde was plump, scruffy, genial and flexible in her attitudes, one of the few Berlin women to have successfully ridden the storm, though whether due to fortitude or turpitude it was hard to say.

In the miserable Waltraut's place came Gisela, as living-in cook. Gisela was beautiful, lustrously Titian-haired and with a figure that had retained its voluptuousness in the teeth of near-starvation. Not only was Gisela beautiful, she was clever, she had been the medal-winning student at her school at the outbreak of war. But now at twenty-two she was the breadwinner for the remnants of her family who lived in a semi-derelict tenement in the hard-hit suburb of Kreuzburg. In spite of a brain and qualifications which would have brought her a prestigious job under normal circumstances, she happily cooked and cleaned for Kate because it was a regular wage with plenty of perks. In addition to which, when she had washed up Kate's and Lawrence's dinner each night she discarded her apron, put on her good shoes and went out to ply her trade as a 'cigarette girl' in the clubs and bars on the Ku'damm and Kaiserdamm. Here she bartered her sought-after favours for the universal currency of the day, tobacco. The cartons of Lucky Strike and

Players thus acquired bought some decent food, and occasionally fuel and soap, to supplement her family's rations. Gisela was the provider. So when on her occasional weekends off she could not be present at family meals, nor attend church, her proud elderly parents no longer had the will to reprimand her. Whatever took Gisela out, brought the food in. Because of her they had managed to keep a few pieces of good china and silver, whereas so many of their friends had been obliged to trade theirs for less durable essentials.

There were five grades of ration card distributed to the civilian German population, increasing in value in direct ratio to the usefulness of a person's job. It therefore followed that women and the old commonly held the Number Five card dubbed, with typical graveyard humour, the death card. One could hardly blame the young, strong and presentable women for doing what they could to make life more bearable.

And Kate did not blame them. If ever she had needed an object lesson in the futility of war, Berlin provided it. It made her former feelings of pride, or patriotism, of a united struggle against the forces of evil – feelings which had literally replaced food in Malta, and kept them alive – seem hollow and ridiculous. All around were sickness and starvation and despair; little girls who had never been children, and little boys who acted out the rape they had seen inflicted on their mothers, sisters and grandmothers by the Russians.

The unspeakable discoveries of the concentration camps were more terrible than the human brain could encompass. But here, and now, Kate could find no one to blame.

When they got back to the house it was getting dark. They could hear the wretched, tinny tinkling of a small bell – an old man was begging near the back door. Gisela, tough as only those who have suffered themselves can be, was giving him short shrift. Stella was all for giving him the other cake, but Kate was firm this time, hurrying her in through the front door and up the stairs to Hildegarde's extravagant embrace, while she went through to the kitchen with the shopping.

Heinz sat at the kitchen table and Kate smiled briefly at him and then continued as if he wasn't there. She and Gisela unpacked the shopping, and she made him a sandwich. He was like a dog, helpless and grateful, watching her with soulful eyes.

From outside the door came a clattering and scrabbling. Gisela made an impatient gesture.

'Already I have told him to go!'

'Yes, I know.'

'Perhaps if Madame tells him . . .?'

Kate hesitated. The scrabbling became louder as the old man rummaged deeper in the dustbin. 'No,' she said. 'That's all right, he'll be gone in a minute.'

The evening proceeded, with tea for Stella, and then the decorating of their own small Christmas tree after Hildegarde had helped at Stella's bathtime and gone to catch her tram home. Gisela's father was a skilled craftsman in wood; he had made some especially beautiful tiny tree decorations, filigree angels and snowflakes and reindeer, for which Kate had paid in cigarettes, without a conscience, but also without telling Lawrence for it might have placed him in an invidious position.

Gisela, who was laying the dinner table, had to be fetched, of course, to admire the tree when it was finished.

'You must tell your father how lovely his decorations looked,' said Kate. 'We shall treasure them always.'

'Oh yes,' said Gisela. 'He can make things, but he is slow.' And that was as much as she was prepared to say on the subject. She picked Stella up and kissed her on either cheek, and rubbed her nose with her own, she was a very affectionate young woman. 'Good night little Stella.'

'Good night Gisela, sleep well.'

'I guess so,' said Gisela, whose most profitable customers were American, and who existed on less than four hours' sleep a night.

Kate had got Stella into bed and had begun reading to her when she heard Lawrence's car arrive. There were the usual good-nights between him and his driver, Corporal Baker, and then the sound of the front door, and his footsteps, quick and eager in the hall.

'Hallo up there!'

'Hallo!'

He ran up the stairs and appeared in the doorway of Stella's tiny bedroom. The greeting he received from his daughter was less than warm.

'No Daddy! Mummy's reading, wait a minute!'

Lawrence, who had been about to hug her, withdrew respectfully. Kate was sitting curled up on the floor by the bed, and he leaned across the book she was holding and kissed her.

'What sort of day?'

'Daddy be *quiet*!'

'Tell you what, why don't I take over?' suggested Lawrence.

'Go on then, you read.' Stella was testy with impatience, she watched with ill-disguised annoyance as Kate handed over the book to Lawrence. He made himself comfortable on the bed, leaning back against the wall. He seemed large and protective in battledress in the tiny lamplit room. Stella, frowning in concentration, huddled against him. She wore a blue and yellow Viyella nightdress bought, and subsequently smocked by hand, by Iris.

Though Kate knew she was being freed to have a moment or two on her own, she could not tear herself away, but remained there, watching the pair of them.

' ". . . as for the Rat," ' read Lawrence, ' "he was walking a little way ahead, as his habit was, his shoulders humped, his eyes fixed on the straight grey road in front of him; so he did not notice poor Mole when suddenly the summons reached him, and took him like an electric shock . . ." '

Kate loved them, Lawrence and Stella, her family. Not a big family, but a tight ship, a trim and formidable fighting unit. She felt herself, so often and for so long her own worst enemy, soften in contemplation of her husband and daughter. She had not thought it possible to love Stella more than she had done for the first three years of her life, but since receiving the letter from Thea, she had done so. The shock of that letter still reverberated in her heart more than a year later. It had literally changed her life. Or at least it was as though her life had had one pattern, which she had understood and suddenly a giant hand had shaken the components, like a child's kaleidoscope, to form a new design. The same people were there, the same pieces, but the whole was utterly different.

Thea had told only her, and she had kept that trust. No one else knew about Dulcie, she had not permitted herself the luxury of unburdening herself. It was as if by struggling with it alone she in some way repaid a little of the debt she owed her mother: she, too, could keep a secret, no matter how painful, and she would do so for Dulcie. And, for Dulcie, she would love Stella as no daughter had been loved before. Stella would not be spoiled, or cosseted, but she would have at her disposal every ounce of strength and resourcefulness and determination that Kate could muster, she could stand on Kate's shoulders to reach the stars. Watching her daughter now, Kate was struck by her looks. She was not a beautiful child so much as an arresting one. Her face, with its typically English high colour, was lit by an uncompromising and enquiring intelligence. Even at four and a bit she did not suffer fobbing-off, or evasion. She was courageous, she took life on the chin. Kate felt her own heart swell and glow, so much so that she half-expected to see a yellow radiance emanating from her sweater. In Stella she had found peace, the torch was handed on.

' ". . . the call was clear, the summons was plain. He must obey it instantly, and go. 'Ratty!' he called, full of joyful excitement, 'hold on! Come back! I want you, quick!' ". . .'

Lawrence read this passage energetically, with a great deal of expression, and then glanced at Stella for her reaction. Her response was to nudge his arm to continue, her eyes still fixed on the page.

Lawrence had changed. In his middle thirties he had acquired gravitas. Their time in Berlin had shown Kate her husband in a new light. The necessarily delicate role of army of occupation had not brought out the best in everyone, but it had done so in Lawrence. The quality in him which had been just charm, the ability to make others happy, had now fleshed itself out into a real talent for diplomacy, and more than that, a humane wisdom. Some people were clever, thought Kate, others brilliantly talented, or natural leaders, but it was given to few to be wise.

Lawrence had wisdom. She still, even now, did not know how much he knew or suspected about the past, about Bill. She hoped that if he harboured questions he would continue to keep them hidden, for she doubted her ability to deny her feelings. To disturb the feelings might also be to breathe life into them, for she knew that they had not gone for ever, but simply lay there secretly, hidden beneath layers of intervening experience, and other and different kinds of love, piled up like leaf-mould in a deep wood, soft but easily removed. If they were laid bare they might spring up, like the dragon's teeth of mythology, and become armed men, and injure them both, fatally.

He turned the page, and looked over the top of the book at her, conscious of her gaze resting on him. He was heavier these days, his face was broader, there were creases round his eyes, his jaw was more set. The moustache was no longer the stylish affectation of a pleasantly vain young man, but entirely fitting. He still smiled, though, in such a way that his scalp moved back, and all the lines smoothed out of his face, and Stella had inherited the smile from him.

'What a look that is,' he said now. 'Explain that look.'

She shook her head. 'Sorry, daydreaming.'

'Go *on*, Daddy!' Stella pulled his nose. 'Stop talking to Mummy.'

Kate got up. 'You must let Daddy go soon, darling, Gisela will have his supper ready.'

'Oh, please, a little bit more . . .'

Lawrence returned to the book. 'Hang River Bank and supper too!' he declared triumphantly.

Kate saw that she had, for the moment, lost, and left the room.

Downstairs, the dining-table was ready laid. Gisela met Kate in the hall. She wore her white evening apron over a blue dress.

'Madame, are you ready for dinner?'

Kate smiled at her; she knew she was itching to be gone.

'Yes, Gisela, you can dish up, the Major will be here in a minute, he's just reading to Stella.'

'Ah, she likes her books,' said Gisela. She was artfully made up, and her dress had a sweetheart neckline which revealed the lush rise of her upper bosom. Dressed to slay the patrons of Micky's Bar, dressed for cigarettes.

Kate put her out of her misery. 'It's all right Gisela,' she said, 'you can go when you've dished up, we'll look after ourselves.'

'Thank you, Madame.'

'That's quite all right, we'll see you in the morning.'

'*Gute nacht*, Madame.'

Kate went into the sitting room and sat looking at the Christmas tree, and listening as Gisela put supper on the table. Then her quick, eager footsteps pattered across the hall; she would already be removing her apron, smoothing her brows, pulling down the neck of her blue dress. But Kate knew that no matter how long Gisela's night of nefarious dealings and alliances, no matter how blistered her feet in one more pair of American nylons, sweat-stained and danced into holes, she would still be in the kitchen first in the morning, to make them all breakfast.

Over supper, Lawrence said: 'I'm sorry to have to say I've got to attend a reception tomorrow night. It's not wives.'

She shrugged. 'I'm not bothered. I've got all the presents to wrap, lots to do. Will they give you something to eat, do you think?'

'There will be the usual bakemeats, I suppose.'

'Only I could boil myself an egg and let Gisela have the evening off.'

Lawrence lifted his eyebrows. 'If the girl needs a rest she should stay here, not go shimmying off down the Kurfursten-damm.'

'I know, but still, it's Christmas, and she's so pretty, I don't like to think of her just hanging about in our kitchen.'

'No, no . . .' He laughed at her. 'I shall have had plenty to eat, give her the evening off by all means. I'm sorry about this damn do, but it's the Control Commission and I must go, the season of good will and so on.'

'Of course.'

The following evening Lawrence had spread, and consumed, about as much good will as he could take, when he suddenly caught sight of a familiar face on the far side of the room. The shock of seeing that face was so great that for a moment he didn't believe the evidence of his own eyes. For that moment he craned and peered trying to ascertain whether it was, whether it could be – but it was a moment too long, and the man had said his good-byes and gone. Then, of course, Lawrence was absolutely sure he had been right, that it had been him. He set down his glass, and said to his companion, a worthy but dull official of the Commission, 'Look, I'm so sorry but would you excuse me? I think I've just spotted someone I know and haven't seen for years.'

He was aware that, though true, this sounded like the limpest and most threadbare of excuses, but he couldn't help that. The official, to his credit, took it in good part.

'Happens all the time at the moment, doesn't it?' he said, and lifted his glass, 'Carry on.'

Lawrence began to elbow his way none too carefully across the room, but the crush was terrific, and expanding by the minute under the influence of good and plentiful liquor. When he reached the other side, by the door, there was no sign of the man who had just left.

The room where the reception was being held was on the first floor of a once-grand old house, now requisitioned by the Commission. From the landing a broad staircase swept in a graceful curve down into the well-lit hall, laid out in black and white tiles, like a chessboard. Lawrence crossed the landing and ran down the stairs, past a wall on which the ghosts of family pictures, long since sacrificed to the *Zigaretten Wirtschaft*, marched in shadowy squares and oblongs.

He crossed the great hall and pushed open the heavy door. A light, stinging snow was falling, the air seemed to reverberate with the cold like struck steel. A row of handsome cars, Mercedes, Bentleys and Rolls, stood parked by the kerb, massive and shining like unused warheads under the silent onslaught of the snow. In one or two of them army drivers sat, huddled in their greatcoats. A pretty girl climbed hurriedly out of one of the cars and walked briskly away, her collar bunched up round her neck, her feet tap-tapping in impossibly high heels.

Lawrence went down the steps on to the pavement. From behind him shafts of yellow light poured from the windows of the house, illuminating the faces of a woman with two small children, who stood looking in. The woman pointed, picked up the smaller of the children, a boy, and held him aloft so that he could see better. Lawrence glanced over his shoulder and saw what they saw, people laughing and enjoying themselves innocently enough, smoking and drinking, some of them eating, all secure in warmth and comfort and light. He looked back at the woman. Her face was utterly impassive, it held no trace of envy or resentment, she was simply allowing her children this glimpse of another world. At that moment, forbidden or no, he would have given her something if he'd had anything on him to give. Instead, when he caught her eye he smiled, and spread his hands: 'I'm sorry . . .' And she shook her head, forgiving him.

Lawrence returned to the reception, and encountered the official, Anstey, near the door, about to leave.

'Any luck with your erstwhile acquaintance?' asked Anstey.

Lawrence shook his head. 'No, I was too late.'

'Anyone I might know?'

'Well . . . I suppose you just might. It was — at least I thought it was — a chap called Bill Maguire.'

'Yes, that's right,' Anstey was matter of fact. 'Bill Maguire of the *Herald*, he was here tonight. Where do you know him from?'

'Oh, way back.' Lawrence waved a hand to indicate how unimportant it was. 'He passed in and out of our lives.'

'Yes,' Anstey pulled a rueful face. 'My wife does that.'

Lawrence failed to laugh, so Anstey added: 'If you want to contact Maguire I believe he's staying with some other chaps from the press corps at the Hotel Ziegler in the Kaiserdamm.'

'Thanks. But I don't know if I shall bother. It was such a long time ago.'

'He's a funny sort of cove,' mused Anstey, helping himself to a vol-au-vent from the salver handed by a white-faced waiter. 'I've encountered him a couple of times recently and he's absolutely obsessed with the idea of finding some woman.'

'Oh?'

'Yes, an old flame I imagine, that he thinks might be in Berlin. It's quite an *idée fixe* with him. Actually, I think he's a bit potty.'

*

It was as well that wives were not included in the Commission's reception, for that evening Stella developed a cold. She streamed and spluttered and coughed with the sort of near-relish that only the very young can bring to bear on discomfort. She was still not asleep when Lawrence got back. Kate came down the stairs and met him in the hall.

'Hallo – how was the party?'

'You didn't miss anything.' He put his arms round her and kissed her mouth, and then her neck, through her hair. She smelt slightly of Vick, and Friars Balsam. 'You smell just like a nurse.'

'Starchy?'

'No, sexy.'

'Well I am a nurse at the moment, Stella's streaming, I was with her when you came in.'

'I'll go up. You've been the ministering angel all day, and I've hardly seen her.' She watched him go up the stairs, heartstoppingly handsome in mess kit. The sheer pleasure of his coming home to her at night was something she experienced afresh every time. She was lucky, so lucky.

Stella was sitting up in bed. On her chest of drawers a nightlight in a blue china saucer guttered and wavered as Lawrence opened the door. Her teddies were clustered round her on the pillow like a guard of honour, straight-backed and beady-eyed.

'You should be asleep,' he said. 'What's up? Coughing?' He came and sat down on the edge of the bed and put his hand on her forehead, underneath her fringe. She was not hot, but her eyes were reddened and her breathing stertorous.

'Do you want a drink?' he asked.

She shook her head. 'I'm all full of drinks and I can't taste them.'

He smiled. 'Me too.'

'You look nice.'

'Thank you.'

'Why are you wearing those tight trousers?'

'I've been to a party.'

'What sort of party?'

'A dull one.'

She surveyed him suspiciously, not believing any party could be dull. 'Will you read me about Mole and Ratty?'

'All right.' He picked up the book and gave her legs under the blanket a shove. 'Budge up. Just a few minutes, and then you must try and go to sleep. Okay?'

'Okay.' She threw her teddies on to the floor and pulled her pillow round against the wall so that she could sit next to him in comfort.

Kate heard Lawrence, doing his stuff. ' "Mole's face beamed at the sight of all those objects so dear to him, and he hurried Rat through the door, lit a lamp in the hall and took one glance round his old home" . . .'

About ten minutes later she heard the door close, and the creak of the stairs as he came cautiously down.

He crossed to where she sat on the floor surrounded by wrapping paper, and kissed her again. She was very conscious of his strength and love, his ability to soothe and ease her, to make this rather grim place into a home just by his presence. She was peaceful.

'I think she'll settle,' he said. He went into the dining-room and came back carrying a glass of whisky. 'I'm sorry, did you want one?'

She shook her head. 'No thanks, I'm past it.'

'No you're not.' He sat down on the sofa, and held out his arm, he looked tired. 'Come and sit by me.'

She did so, and they sat quietly together for a minute or two. Gisela was long gone, and there was no sound from Stella's room.

After a while he broke the silence by saying: 'I saw a face from the past tonight.' As he said it, he looked at her face, which was in repose, like calm water. He dreaded breaking that repose, but knew he could have no peace unless he did so.

'Oh? Who was that?'

'Bill Maguire.'

There was no change in her expression, she continued to gaze at the tree as she had been doing, but he thought he felt her stiffen. 'What did he say?' she asked lightly.

'That's the silly thing, I never got close enough to speak to him, he was just leaving when I caught sight of him.'

There was the merest current of relief transmitted from her. He went on: 'I spoke to a chap who's bumped into him a couple of times recently. It's possible to contact him apparently, at the Hotel Ziegler.'

'Maybe we should.' It was impossible to tell from her tone whether this suggestion was made genuinely or with reluctance.

'I don't know, it's been such a long time, is it worth it? And it might be embarrassing even, with regard to Dulcie. I think we should leave it.'

'Perhaps.'

'This fellow told me that Bill's obsessed with finding some woman or other, an old flame was how he described it, who might apparently be in Berlin.'

'Oh.' Now, suddenly, she looked at him and he saw with a shock that there was real desperation in her face, it was like walking into a familiar room and finding it ransacked. He put his arms round her and she clung to him with wild, frightened strength, and he knew he had been right.

'I love you,' she whispered. 'Don't forget that I love you.'

The next morning, when Lawrence had gone, Kate organized the still-snuffling Stella into tidying her room, a task she quite enjoyed since it involved first emptying every drawer, cupboard and shelf. Under Hildegarde's genial and none-too strict supervision the job became a game.

With the two of them occupied upstairs, and the severely hung-over Gisela snapping at Heinz in the kitchen, Kate busied herself sorting out and wrapping the toys donated as presents for the children's parties to be given by the Allies on Christmas Eve. There were a great many, people had been very kind. Some had given nearly-new things that had belonged to their own children, others had made dolls and dolls' clothes, some had managed to buy new toys. It was hoped that every child in the city would attend one of the parties, and receive a special present.

All morning Kate sorted and wrapped, concentrating. When Hildegarde brought Stella downstairs for an early lunch she went to the NAAFI to do her shopping. When she got back Stella had relapsed somewhat, so she gave her half an aspirin and instructed Hildegarde to get her into bed, for a sleep if possible. As she went to the kitchen to find something to eat for herself the army ration lorry arrived. Along with the usual packets of Pomm dried potato, tinned fruit, vegetables and meat there were some extras for Christmas, so she and Gisela spent half an hour emptying the boxes, putting stuff away, making a cup of tea for the half-frozen lorry driver. She tried hard to keep busy. Never had she been so conscious of how little there was for her to do here, her unused energy prowled and snarled inside her like a caged cat, and she feared it. With Stella asleep and all the available jobs done, she tried to ring Beth Maloney, whose flat was only a mile or so away, to ask her over that afternoon, or to see if they could visit her when Stella woke. Anything, anything. But there was no reply.

She was sitting by the phone, and the house was absolutely quiet. The phone seemed actually seductive, lying there so smooth and silent, the receiver moulded to receive her hand, the mouthpiece curved secretively to receive her words, and carry them to someone else.

In the end, she gave in, as she had known she would. She lifted the receiver and dialled the number of the Hotel Ziegler.

For more than a month Bill Maguire had been trying to track down Ilse Bauer. Now, at last, he was almost there. It had been a wearisome and a harrowing search. The block in the Metzallee had been razed to the ground by bombs, so his next step had been to go to the Kafe Wien and see what they knew. They had been guarded and surly, there was a new proprietor and he wanted nothing to do with the past, or the old regime. But one of the waitresses had seen Walda, and told Bill that Ilse had left the Metzallee before it was bombed and gone to join Walda in the suburbs. Astonishingly, Walda and her daughter were in their own house. They had been able to move back there soon after the Americans arrived, apparently, though there hadn't been much left in the way of fixtures and fittings. Walda told him about their camping out in the big house in the *Villaviertel*, about the depradations of the Russians, about the horse they'd slaughtered – she'd become very excited, almost elated, because it had been so terrible and they had come through it. But on the subject of Ilse she was more cautious. No, she was no longer here, they had been unable to persuade her to stay, although she had not been herself, she had taken it hard. She had wanted to get back into the centre of the city where she belonged and where she felt safer . . . Walda had shaken her head in disbelief and sadness. Ilse had been a tower of strength, but in the end it had been too much for even her broad shoulders to bear. But where was she? Bill had asked. He wanted to find her, to help her, he had known her for years, where was she?

Walda said she had been hoping to go back to the Metzallee, but when Bill told her it was bombed out she had no other ideas. He could try asking at any local shops, she suggested. So Bill had returned to the Metzallee and asked around, and in the end it was an unknown *Hausfrau* in a queue, who, overhearing him making enquiries, had told him where Ilse was. But there's nothing you or anyone can do, she warned him, there are plenty like her and there's nothing you can do for them.

The building wasn't far from the Metzallee, a tall, narrow apartment block, bleak and institutional, with none of the Metzallee's vestigial grandeur. It was not badly damaged, apart from the roof, but the high hallway was dark, and smelt unpleasant.

As Bill arrived, a little old *Hausmeister* came out of the door on the right of the hallway and looked him up and down suspiciously.

'*Ja, was ist los?*'

'Do you speak English?'

'Of course.' The sarcasm was unmistakable.

'I'm looking for Fraulein Ilse Bauer – I believe she's at this address.'

The man stared at him oddly. Then he said: 'She's up there.' He stabbed a finger directly upwards, towards the sky. 'At the top.'

'Thank you. Is she in?'

'She is in, always,' said the man.

Bill crossed the hall. There had once been a lift, but now the shaft was a gaping, empty hole, made only marginally less dangerous by the positioning of an old metal bedstead across the aperture. A single hawser dangled in the darkness like a hangman's rope. Against the wall near the *Hausmeister's* apartment door was a pile of wood — pieces of fences, and notice-boards, and chopped-up wooden crates — and a very small bag of coal.

Bill went up four flights of stone stairs, until the light shining through the damaged roof of the building told him he was as near the top as it was safe to go. The stairway was chill as a tomb and had a tomb's atmosphere of neglected stillness, an unnatural, untouched tranquillity.

On the top landing there were two doors. One stood wide open to reveal a small empty room with part of the ceiling missing. As Bill looked the wind caught the door and slammed it shut, as if the very fabric of the building was disposed to be secretive.

The other door was closed. He knocked on it. There was a long, heavy silence, shaken only by the boom and howl of the wind through the shattered roof. Bill crossed the landing and glanced down the stairwell. He saw, briefly, the skull-like, upturned face of the *Hausmeister* in the darkness far below, peering at him through the spiral of iron bannister. When Bill turned back, the door was ajar. Either the wind had blown it, or someone had opened it while he had been looking elsewhere. Tentatively he pushed it wide, stepped in, and closed it softly behind him.

He was in a large, low room, a kind of spacious garret. There was one window, set in the eaves, but it must have been broken, for it was covered with sheets of cardboard, roughly tacked in place. On the far side of the room, in the steep angle where the roof sloped down, stood a sagging bed. Somebody was sitting on the bed. Apart from the bed there was only a small table with an upturned box by it, and a chair, perhaps rescued from a dump or bomb site, which had once been upholstered but was now a bony, listing wreck. It was appallingly cold, a cruel, knife-edged wind sawed at the cardboard sheets at the broken window, and between the ill-fitting floorboards. There was an air of almost palpable dismal neglect, the place smelt of damp, and dirt, and unclean bedding and mouse droppings. In a corner near the window was a two-ring gas stove, but there was little evidence of cooking — one blackened saucepan, some dirty plates, a chipped cup, and an open tin with a spoon sticking out of it. In a box on the floor were some cabbage greens, turning slimy and rotten, adding their smell to the rest. Bill addressed himself to the shapeless, motionless figure on the bed. In the gathering midwinter dusk he could not make out who it was.

'Ilse? Is that you?'

There was a sudden, awkward flurry of movement. The figure on the bed lay down, knees bent up. He could make out the white splodge of face turned in his direction. One bulky arm made a beckoning movement. He stepped forward but he was afraid, there was a bitter taste in his mouth. It was like answering the summons of a corpse. When he reached the side of the bed, Bill lit a match and held it up.

'Ilse?'

It was Ilse, but she was scarcely recognizable. The face he knew so well was disfigured by dirt, and scabs, and strange thin white scars. But most of all Ilse was altered by the most terrible fear he had ever seen. She wore a strange old knitted bonnet pulled down low over her brow, and the eyes that looked out from beneath the rim of the bonnet were the terrified, snapping eyes of a trapped animal. Her nose and chin were drawn together by the seamed and sunken purse of her toothless mouth.

He was shaken to the core. He knew he should touch her, reassure her, but he couldn't bring himself to do it. The match burnt his fingers and he dropped it, and crouched down by the side of the bed.

'Ilse, it's me, it's Bill. I've found you.'

Her haunted eyes flicked over his face, but he saw that she didn't understand. She let her knees drop apart and pointed to her crotch. Bill realized with horror the implication of the gesture. And yet in contrast to her ghastly attempt at seduction, she seemed to have armoured herself in layers of filthy clothing, it would have been impossible for any but the most brutal and determined ravisher to have his way with Ilse. She wore several frayed, stained sweaters and a man's heavy jacket; a long scarf was wound round her neck, and there were black mittens on her bent hands. Her legs were encased in trousers — the old Ilse had never worn trousers, considering them unfeminine — which seemed to have been stitched together from the remnants of other garments, for the two legs did not match. Apart from her face, and the ends of her fingers, the only area of skin to be seen was the inch or so between the bottom of the trouser legs and her heavy boots. The boots looked like old army issue, they were not a good fit, and were curled and split. She had no socks on. The smell rising both from her body, and the clothes and mattress, was indescribable.

Suddenly he felt her hand reaching and grabbing at him, trying to force a way between the buttons of his coat, and he leapt up in disgust. Partly to disguise his shameful rejection, he went back to the door and felt along the wall for a light switch. He found one, and pressed it, and a single bulb over the sink in the corner flickered and came on.

Resolutely he went back to the bedside and crouched down again, bringing his face close to Ilse's, to excise from his vision the terrible room, the filthy clothes, the stained and stinking bed, so that he could see just her eyes. They were still clouded, and uncomprehending, but when she reached out her hand this time he grasped it and held it tightly.

'Ilse. Look at me. It's Willi, remember? Remember the motorbike, and the picnics, and the fun we used to have? Remember me!' This time it was an order. In his frustration and despair he became rough, he took her shoulders and shook her so that the flaccid skin of her cheeks trembled, the vacant eyes were lit by panic. He shouted at her: 'Ilse! Ilse, come back! It's over, come back!' He was rewarded. From the corner of one eye a tear swelled, oozed, and trickled down the side of Ilse's face into the grubby wool of her bonnet, dividing into greyish tributaries as it went.

Now he put his arm round her, and did not notice the dirt, or the smell, nor did he feel any revulsion but only triumph. 'Ilse, it's all right, it's over. I'm here now, I'll look after you, you mustn't cry . . .' He felt her shaking and shuddering, thought he heard his name, borne on a tide of tears, but when he lowered her onto the pillow he saw that he had lost her again. She gazed at him in confusion and fear, her lips moved in a soundless babble.

He stood up, and leaned over her, holding her shoulders. 'I'll come back,' he said loudly, trying to print his words on her mind, to cut through her terrified imaginings and make himself understood. 'I'll come back very soon. I'm going to look after you now.'

He felt in his pocket for a packet of cigarettes and handed them to her. He had absolutely nothing else to give her. She took them and stuffed them under the pillow.

'I shall come back,' he said again, but she seemed truly terrified now, huddling back against the wall, peering and muttering.

He closed the door after him and went down the damp, echoing staircase. It was snowing again, and flakes floated down the stairwell and settled on the steps. At the bottom he paused. He honestly did not know what he could do, he did not know where to begin, he was daunted by the task of reclamation that lay before him. But who else did she have? And who else did he? As he stood there the *Hausmeister* reappeared with an expression that said 'Don't say I didn't warn you'.

Bill looked at him, acknowledging the fact. 'She's ill, she shouldn't be there.'

The man shrugged. 'She will not go. It is kinder to leave her where she is.'

'What is the matter with her?'

'She was raped many times, she is syphilitic. Up there, she still hides from the Russians.'

'She should be in hospital.'

The *Hausmeister* closed his eyes and shrugged. There was in his manner something gracefully accusing, he found Bill's sympathy for Ilse ironic.

'We do what we can,' he said. 'We would not let her starve. But we too have troubles.'

'Of course. And thank you. I didn't mean to accuse you of neglecting her, she's not your responsibility. I will help her now, she is an old friend.'

'Very good, *Meinherr*.'

'Can I ask you –' Bill hesitated – 'what are the cuts on her face, do you know?'

The *Hausmeister* nodded. 'My wife also has scars like that.

Many women must cut their faces — to be unattractive, you see, it's safer.'

'I see.' Bill was acutely discomforted in the face of the man's cold, appraising look. 'I shall come back tomorrow. In the meantime, if you can —'

'We shall make sure.'

'Thank you. I'm afraid I have nothing at the moment, but when I come back I shall bring something for your family, to repay your kindness.'

'Very well.'

Bill went out into the street. The snow was beginning to lie, softening the black, jagged city in a drift of dense white. In the yellow lamplight the flakes twirled and span, dervish-like. It was getting colder.

Bill sat on the small, straight-backed chair by Ilse's bed, watching her as she slept. She was in a ward with eleven others, and some of them had visitors, but it was still quiet, voices were lowered, only a few bedside lamps had been lit.

He was bone-weary. He hadn't even had the energy to remove his coat, and melted snow trickled from it and on to the floor, like unstemmed tears. The old scarf Ilse had knitted for him years ago was still round his neck. He had the beginnings of a sore throat. Outside the window the snow was now falling densely, swiftly, silently, real Christmas Eve snow.

This morning — it felt like centuries ago — he had moved heaven and earth to get Ilse the hospital bed. The interesting thing about suffering was that it bred less, not more, sympathy and understanding. People became pain-hardened. In the end it had been his press card which had done the trick, but even then their attitude to the new patient when she had been brought in had been one of almost cynical fatalism, they had seen it all before.

Nevertheless her face in repose was childlike in its sedated calm. She had been efficiently cared for and cleaned up, her face scrubbed and her hair washed, cut and combed back neatly off her brow. That alone seemed to have brought her back within reach, she looked more her old self. Probably the old nightmares would attend her waking but for now at least she was peaceful.

Back at the Hotel Ziegler the press crowd were well-entrenched in another evening's impromptu celebrations. The usual group were ranged along the hotel's bar, in the company of one or two attractive German girls, watched impassively by the barman. He was a boy of eighteen or so with a skeletal, blueywhite face, the embodiment of bitter, silent reproach.

They'd been waiting for Bill, but there was a general cheering and hailing as he appeared in the foyer. As he crossed to the lift, the girl at the desk called to him.

'Mr Maguire – there is a telephone message for you.'

'Oh?' He went to the desk and took the piece of paper she handed him. He must have stared at it quite stupidly for a while, because the receptionist touched his arm lightly, and had obviously spoken once already.

'Mr Maguire? She asks you to call her back.'

'Yes, I will. Thank you.'

He still stood there, staring at the piece of paper. All his energy was used up by the need to absorb this second, and even greater shock. His hands trembled. The girl, fiddling with keys and letters in the cubby-holes behind the desk, looked over her shoulder at him.

'The telephone is free, sir.'

'Thank you.'

He went to the kiosk on the other side of the foyer, by the entrance to the bar. Someone called, and held up a glass, there was laughter, but he looked right through them.

He dialled the number, and she answered almost at once.

'Kate.'

'Hallo.'

'Is he there?'

'No – he's at the school this evening – there's going to be a children's party there tomorrow.'

Bill closed his eyes. Words said nothing, they were just sounds. He could almost feel her, though, her tension and longing over the humming wire.

'Shall we meet?' he asked.

A Flower That's Free

'When?'

'Tomorrow.'

'All right. In the afternoon, Lawrence and Stella have to be at the party, but I can make some excuse . . .'

'Say where — somewhere we both know, not in the centre.'

She said the name of a place. 'All right,' he said. 'I'll be there.'

Christmas Eve, *Heiligeabend*, was destined to be one of those days when the light never properly broke through. The early morning was more than usually dark and cold. The snow had settled and frozen overnight, so that it was now covered by a crust of ice. A few flakes, whipped up by the wind, darted in the air. The sky was heavy and opaque, promising more of the same later.

Before Lawrence left, Kate said to him, 'I might be a bit late at the party, I'm going to meet Beth and do some last-minute shopping. I'll tell Hildegarde to bring Stella.'

He looked at her, trying to print her face, her look, everything about her, on his mind. Just in case.

'Fine, have fun. I'll see you later then.'

She did not reply, but kissed him.

Lawrence felt her kiss on his cheek as he walked out to the car. It seemed to burn there, he put up his hand and touched the place where her lips had been. Corporal Baker stood holding the car door, shuffling his feet in the snow. 'Morning sir! Bit parky, sir, for the nippers coming to the party.'

'We'll have to make it worth their while then, Corporal.'

'That's right, sir!'

Baker slammed the door after him, and ran round to climb into the driver's seat. The car moved north-west, in the direction of the barracks. Outside the windows the suburbs were unbelievably bleak, caught in the grip of winter, no possibility of change. There were the usual people out and about, trudging, dogged. Some — the lucky ones — going to their last day's work before the Christmas holiday, others simply engaged on the ceaseless daily quest for the necessities of life. Lawrence wondered idly if it was sheer hypocrisy to hold a Christmas party for the children of such hard-pressed

752

people, when what they really wanted was bread and potatoes and coffee and meat for the pot. But a treat could brighten life, and shed an afterglow to soften suffering, perhaps.

But it was Kate who dominated his thoughts, with the terrible vividness of something already lost. He was no fool, he knew the score. He had deliberately, even wilfully, given her this opportunity to make a choice. But he was not being entirely unselfish. He remembered, in the early days of their marriage, how captivated he had been by the air of freedom she had seemed to carry with her. He could almost pinpoint the moment when it had gone, and why. Though they had, he knew, reached calm and happy waters, he could not bear to think that Kate's presence in his life was no longer the result of a free and willing choice. If he was courting disaster by precipitating that choice, he could not help that. At least, by tonight, he would know.

In the early afternoon Kate kissed Stella good-bye as Hildegarde was dressing her in her party clothes.

'Aren't you coming? I thought you were coming.'

'I shall try – but I might be late. Daddy will be there.'

'I want you to come too.'

'I shall try, I promise.'

Kate set out to walk to the *Olympiastadion*. It was a long walk, but she had done it before, with Stella and the old pushchair, on fine afternoons in the autumn. It had been fun for Stella to run along the great curving covered walkways, and shout in the echoing tunnels, and to stare up at the massive, expressionless statues.

Though it was only three o'clock when she got there, the afternoon was already darkening. The stadium was deserted. The wind, aching with snow, blustered and howled among the tiers of seats, and snow had drifted on the flights of steps. The swimming pool was bleak and empty, a death trap. Icicles hung in a fantastic parody of white fire around the lip of the bowl which had held the Olympic flame. She came into the stadium by the main entrance, and looked around at the great, empty concrete bowl. On the far side of the field, where the massive stone horse stared out over the *Maifeld*, two solitary labourers were engaged on repair work, she could hear the clank of a pick and shovel.

And she could see Bill. He sat halfway along, on the left-hand side of the stadium, where the Tribune of Honour had sat ten years ago, when this desolate place had reverberated with noisy expectation. From this distance she could make out no detail, nothing about him, but she knew it was him. He sat very still, in spite of the cold, his hands in his pockets. But as she began to walk along the upper terrace towards him he turned as if he had sensed her presence, his face pale against his dark coat and scarf. In her pocket she felt the letter, like a talisman. 'Help me,' she thought, 'to do the right thing.' But she knew that in the end she could only help herself. She had freely and voluntarily walked into the situation which for years she had most dreaded and longed for, willingly exposed herself to the temptation she had most feared.

Yet her sense of the inevitability of this meeting was strong. She was possessed by an almost ritual sense of calm.

He stood up to meet her as she walked down the steps towards him. Her first reaction was one of shock – he had aged so – but it was all shot through with desire and remembrance so that the poignancy of it was almost unbearable. He was nearly fifty, she remembered, only a few years younger than Aubrey, but he looked older. His face was drawn and drained, and his hair, which had always been grey, was wild and unkempt. He held his shoulders hunched slightly against the bitter cold, and his eyes watered, perhaps also from the cold. There was about him such an air of desolation, of time having slipped away, and chances missed, that she wanted to put her arms round him then and there, and say: 'I want you. I've always wanted you. Now we must be together.'

But she did not, and he made no move to touch her. He tried to say something, but his voice was husky, so he cleared his throat.

'Kate . . . I'm glad you came.'

'Did you think I wouldn't?'

'I thought you might not. How did you find me?'

She stared at him, puzzled. 'I heard that you were looking for me.'

It wasn't true. The irony was exquisite. He had not been looking for her, nor had he even known she was in Berlin. But she must have misconstrued something she'd heard, and taken, as ever, the initiative. Her directness moved him unbearably so that at last he put out his hand to her, and after a tiny hesitation she took it. He drew her against him and kissed her cold face, and her lips that were warm from being shielded by her scarf. Around them, the desolate emptiness of the stadium was like the closest, most intimate privacy, the clang of the workmen's shovels away down in the snow seemed to emphasize their isolation.

Still holding her hand, he led her down into the mouth of the entrance tunnel, where they were more sheltered. It was down here that he had followed her, and found her, when she had left the stadium with her grandfather that day ten years ago. He had been struck then by her air of fierce independence. Now he saw that she had altered. Her hair was no longer like fire, but like autumn leaves, a soft brown lit only here and there by red. Her face had filled out slightly, her mouth had softened, she had grown up in some way that puzzled and saddened him. She had lost the painful rawness, the angry vulnerability, or she had it under control. He could only imagine the courage it had taken for her to come here, but to imagine it made his heart race with wild, furious hope.

'I must tell you something,' said Kate.

Carefully, she took Thea's letter from her pocket. It was folded in just the same way as when she had first taken it from its envelope, the creases were worn almost through. Bill watched her thin hands, without gloves, as she unfolded the sheet of paper. It flickered and fluttered as a blast of wind suddenly moved through the tunnel.

'What is that?'

'It's a letter from my – from Thea. I don't know if you heard. But Dulcie is dead.'

'Dulcie?' He shook his head, turned away. 'How was this – when did it happen?'

'I got this letter about a year ago. She died last year when she was staying with Thea and Jack in Kenya. She was knocked down by a car.'

'Knocked down –' He was unmanned, he put his arms over his face.

'I know,' she went on. 'I know – it seems so cruel, so terribly arbitrary.'

'Yes. Yes, it does. Dulcie of all people . . .'

'But there's something else you should know – something else Thea told me in her letter.'

He looked into her face and saw there a flash of the old Kate in her eyes, the Kate who would have torn the flesh from his bones rather than be parted from him.

'Yes?'

'Bill – Dulcie was my mother. My real mother. I am Dulcie's daughter.'

For Bill, like a blind person suddenly restored to sight, the shock of seeing things as they really were was almost too much. What had only been confused half-impressions were suddenly so sharp, so clear, that they dazzled painfully on the inner eye. No wonder, no wonder . . . So much that had seemed perverse was now sublimely logical, so much of his behaviour that he had considered straight and honest now looked like the basest and most twisted cruelty.

And now it was he who could have ripped his own flesh from his bones. He was filled with a repugnance so powerful that bile rushed into his throat and he gagged and covered his mouth. He walked away from her, struggling to gain mastery of himself, while she stood very still, watching him. When he returned he was shaking, he couldn't control his voice, the words burst out of him on a terrible roar of distress.

'Why didn't she tell me? Sweet Jesus, why didn't she tell me?'

She fixed him with her eyes – so steady, and fierce and challenging. 'Would it have made any difference?'

'Oh God – I don't know! How can I know?'

'It would have made no difference. *I* know.'

'A lost cause – you're right, Kate, we were. What have we done to her?'

She didn't answer him directly, but spoke evenly, not reading from the letter but gazing down at it as if it were her source of strength. 'She got rid of the baby she was expecting because she thought it would keep things the same between you and her. That was while you were in Malta —'

'Dulcie was expecting a baby? My baby?' He could hardly encompass the thought.

'Yes. But she was frightened she'd lose you if you thought she was pressuring you. She was prepared to do anything to keep you, you see.'

'Oh Christ. Christ forgive me . . .' His voice sank to nothing beneath the weight of his guilt and misery. But Kate's continued, evenly.

'But when you got back that time, you told her about us — no, don't say anything, it doesn't matter now, whatever your intentions. Don't. But when you told her, she realized that she'd left herself with nothing. Except that —' her voice caught, but she brought it under control and went on: 'Except that she wanted me to be happy and if you — if you could make me happy she had no alternative but to send you away. She wanted more than anything for me not to compromise, or be trapped in some second-best thing. Not to make the mistakes she thought she'd made. So she told you to go.'

Now she folded the letter and replaced it in her pocket, as if she had no more use for it. Her air of finality was frightening, as if they had reached some point from which there was no turning back.

'I remember,' he said. 'I remember her saying that I wasn't the only one who cared for you, that it was your happiness at stake too . . . The stupid bitch!' He turned and slammed his fists into the wall. 'If she'd only just for once let that pretty mask of hers slip, she didn't even give us a chance to do the decent thing.'

'We wouldn't have done it,' Kate said simply. 'We weren't responsible. And afterwards, when you left Malta . . . Well, we haven't seen each other since, until now.'

'Until now. No.'

'She never told anyone,' she went on. 'The only people who knew about me were Giles and Thea and Jack. I was never to know. She felt she'd forfeited the right to honesty the day she let me go. What she must have suffered when I came back to London, I don't know — and even worse after Malta — she always made out she was a coward, but it wasn't true. She was incredibly brave.'

Bill felt despair ebbing from him and there, where it drew back, the first grains of hope. 'But if what you say is true,' he said, with new urgency, 'and your happiness is what she cared about most, don't we owe her something, the two of us?'

She shook her head. 'I don't know.'

'You do!' He took her in his arms and was stunned by the thunderbolt shock of her closeness after so long. His strength and certainty grew. He could feel her thin and alive and quaking with life under her thick coat like a butterfly waiting to emerge from its chrysalis.

'She gave up love so that you could have it, she bargained for you, it was a straight exchange, wasn't it? And yet she had to watch you settle for something less —'

'No! Something different!'

'Kate for God's sake — we know what we are, what we have. Are you telling me it's not so? Are you going to stand there and deny it?' He clasped her neck as if he would strangle her, forcing her to look at him. She shook her head, there were tears in her eyes.

'No. But it wasn't love. And we weren't happy.'

'Happy!' He spat out the word contemptuously, releasing her roughly so that she staggered. 'Happiness — who cares about it? When we're together we *live* Kate, we feel and we live and we burn, we're above happiness, whatever that is. I'm right, aren't I?'

She nodded dumbly.

'And why did you come here today?' he shouted. 'Why did you ring me after so long?'

'I heard you were looking for me,' she said.

'But I wasn't!' He was triumphant. 'I wasn't looking for you, I was looking for someone else, and I found her, a woman I knew from many years ago. I didn't even know you were in Berlin. And yet here you are.'

'They said it was an old flame,' she whispered, overwhelmed by her mistake and its implications.

'They were wrong. She was dear to me, but there was no

flame.' He touched her hair. 'You're the flame, and you always will be.'

She pulled away from him and began to walk slowly down the tunnel, away from the stadium. He pursued her and caught her wrist, he could sense the dividing line between victory and loss as delicate and fine as a single hair. His need of her roared in his ears like a rising flood, he was filled with violent energy, he would *make* it impossible for her to go.

'It was *you* who found *me*, Kate, because you've been waiting for me all this time – we've both been waiting – and surely that letter tells you what you have to do!'

'I love Lawrence. And Stella, my daughter Stella.'

'You may love them, but you *need me*!' He shouted at her and she sank against him, weakened, her forehead against his shoulder, shaken to the core by a rampaging cross-current of feeling. Beyond the tunnel the tumbling, freezing air was darkening all the time, as if shutting off their escape.

Kate, feeling his arms around her, and the power of his formidable desperate longing, was nearly helpless. She was drowning, drowning, she could not see the light.

'I offer you nothing Kate,' he said against her hair. 'Nothing but what we together can make. I'm just a door standing open for you. All you have to do is walk through, and you're free!'

'Free . . .?'

'Yes! Think of Dulcie, and then decide.'

She pulled back from him. 'I do think of her, Bill.'

'Then will you, *will* you, come with me?'

Outside, from some distant, undamaged suburban church, the first bells of *Heiligeabend* began to ring. Firmly, he took her hand, and together they walked from the tunnel.

At the children's party, held in the gymnasium of the infants' school in Charlottenburg, Lawrence held his daughter by the hand and watched as the German children received their presents. Just behind Lawrence and Stella stood Hildegarde, beaming and benevolent, she had enjoyed herself.

A very English Santa Claus sat on a spindly-legged school chair and handed wrapped parcels from two sacks – the officers' wives had sorted the presents according to age. Behind him were a group of about a dozen helpers — wives, teachers, Red Cross officials — happy because the party had gone well. Kate was not among them.

The party had been a success. It had not seemed, as Lawrence had feared, either inappropriate or vulgar. The children had had a wonderful time. Now, all the lights except those on the Christmas tree had been turned off, and the faces of the children, tense with excitement, shone like pale flames. The tea tables, strewn with the debris of the feast — cracker wrappings, and crumbs, and greasy plates and smeary glasses — were pushed against the walls in the dark. One by one children came forward and were patted or kissed by the bespectacled Santa — Drum Major Watts — and whispered their thanks, and disappeared in a flurry of rustling to unwrap their treasures.

Lawrence glanced at Stella. She was watching the proceedings with stern — even scowling — detachment. She wore her red velvet party dress, with white socks and bronze leather pumps. Hildegarde had brushed her hair till it shone. Lawrence was filled with love for her, and fear. He put his hand on her shoulder, and bent down and whispered, 'Your turn soon.'

She didn't look at him, but whispered back fiercely, 'I don't want to — I don't want a present.'

'Why not?'

'I'm not like them,' she said.

And indeed, no amount of coaxing and cajoling on the drum major's part would get her an inch closer to him. She remained adamant. As Santa left, to rousing cheers from the rest, Lawrence asked her again: 'Why didn't you want a present?'

'Where's Mummy?'

'She'll come soon I expect.'

Hildegarde caught his eye and pulled a face. 'She is not at all pleased about Mrs Drake being late, sir.'

'So I see.'

He was filled with sickening cold dread. As Hildegarde took Stella's hand he felt himself usurped, perhaps for a second time. The party was almost over, and she had not come.

The infants' school head teacher, Frau Inkermann, stepped forward, pressing her hands together for silence, preparatory to making an announcement.

'And now, everybody! It has been such a lovely party, and all the children have enjoyed it so very much. They would like to say thank you with two German carols they have prepared. And if you know them, then you may join in perhaps *Kinder – bitte.*'

She lifted both hands, beckoning the children forward. There were about forty of them, from two years old to eleven, the little ones had to be pushed forward by their mothers. When they were assembled in a semi-circle Frau Inkermann seated herself at the piano and played a chord.

They sang '*O Tannenbaum*', and then '*Stille Nacht, Heilige Nacht*'. At first, the listeners maintained their cheerful, indulgent smiles, but it wasn't a moment for pretence. As the children reached the final verse their voices became thin and breathy, and there was a good deal of coughing and sneezing. Frau Inkermann waved a hand, indicating that the adults should join in, but somehow no one could manage it. And when the singing ended it was not just the children who blew their noses.

Afterwards they drove home, with Corporal Baker for once quiet at the wheel. Stella sat staring out of the window, her fingers laced on the lap of her best blue coat.

'Daddy.'

'Yes?'

'She didn't come.'

'No.'

'Why not?'

She turned to look at him, and he couldn't meet his four-year-old daughter's eye. The world outside the car seemed vast – black and cold and empty. The absolute weariness of defeat engulfed him. But Stella had asked a question, and the very hairs on the back of Corporal Baker's neck seemed to be listening for his answer.

'I don't know,' he said. 'I honestly don't.'

Hildegarde was not due back until Boxing Day, and Gisela was supposed to be off-duty once she had served supper.

Lawrence sent her home, having first located the present Kate
had wrapped for her — nylons — and suffered her tearful thanks,
and watched her smother Stella in kisses.

When he at last had the house to himself he first changed,
and then ran Stella's bath and sat and talked to her while she
was in it. He must be reliable, and ordinary, he must get
through the bedtime rituals, then he would let go. Away from
the highly charged atmosphere of the party Stella was
better, and of course it was Christmas next day, there was a
stocking to be hung up and all the attendant speculations and
prognostications. Christmas! Beth and Josh were supposed to
be coming to lunch, and others for drinks in the evening, and
what if Kate simply did not come back? What would he say to
people, how would he live through the day, and the next? He
realized now just how great the risk was that he had been
taking. He had taken it, he supposed, because he had been
sure she would come back. He had been absurdly over-
confident. And he had told himself that if Kate left it would
be better than if she stayed as some kind of prisoner of
conscience. He had been grand and magnanimous, and a
bloody fool. Now he realized that he wanted and needed her,
on any terms. Probably he had been wrong to keep quiet so
long, never to confront her with his fears — what had he hoped
to gain by that, what had he been playing at? He hadn't
wanted to trap her or possess her, but in being careful had he
simply failed to show her how deeply he cared?

He pulled Stella's nightie over her head. He felt as if each of
these small domestic, unaccustomed actions was a kind of
drug, keeping him going, keeping him from collapse. He
dreaded their completion.

Stella picked up the book, found the place, and handed it
to him. Then she clasped her stocking — an old red and black
rugger sock of Joe's — and took up her usual position, pressed
up against him. She seemed surprisingly calm and content.

'I expect she'll be back soon,' she said.

He did not answer, but began to read: ' ". . . forthwith their
shrill little voices uprose on the air, singing one of the old-time
carols that their forefathers composed in fields that were fallow
and held by frost, or when snow-bound in chimney corners,

and handed down to be sung in the miry street to lamp-lit windows at Yule-time—"'

He paused, thinking he had heard something, then went on, reading the words of the Christmas song, a little self-conscious with the verse.

'You ought to sing it,' said Stella.

'I don't know the tune.'

'Mummy knows the tune.'

'I'm sorry.'

He skipped the rest of the carol, and continued: ' "The voices ceased, the singers, bashful but smiling, exchanged sidelong glances and silence succeeded — but for a moment only. Then, from up above and far away, down the tunnel they had so lately travelled, was borne to their ears in a faint musical hum the sound of distant bells ringing a joyful and clangorous peal . . ." '

'Here's Mummy,' said Stella. 'Make room for her.'

Lawrence looked up at her over the book. She seemed to shine, there was snow on her hair, and on her coat and scarf which she had not yet taken off. Her eyes were as bright as candles and her cheeks glowed. She was entirely beautiful, she lit up the room.

'Go on, Daddy,' said Stella.

He held out his arm and Kate came and sat on his other side. Though her outer clothes were cold he could feel the warmth of her body inside them, she radiated that light, that warmth, as she had always done. She had come back.

Stella stretched out an imperious hand and pointed to the Latin words that headed the page.

'It says Dulcie,' she announced, proud of her new reading.

'No,' said Lawrence. ' "*Dulce. Dulce Domum.*" '

'What does that mean.'

'Home,' said Lawrence. 'It means sweet home.'

ACKNOWLEDGEMENTS

The author and publisher are grateful to the following for allowing them to quote song lyrics:

MEMORIES OF YOU
by Andy Razaf and Eubie Blake, 1930
© 1930 Shapiro, Bernstein Inc
All rights controlled by Lawrence Wright Music Co Ltd for British Territories excluding Canada and Australasia.

SOMEONE TO WATCH OVER ME
Composer: George Gershwin
Author: Ira Gershwin
© 1926 Harms Inc
British Publisher: Chappell Music Ltd
Reproduced by kind permission.
© 1926 (Renewed) W B Music Corp
All rights reserved. Used by permission.

WORLD WEARY
Composer and author: Noël Coward
© 1928 Chappell Music Ltd
British Publisher: Chappell Music Ltd
American Publisher: Chappell Music Company
Reproduced by kind permission.

IT'S ONLY A PAPER MOON
Composer: Harold Arlen
Author: Billy Rose and E. Y. Harburg
© 1933 Harms Inc
British Publisher: Chappell Music Ltd
© 1930 (Renewed) Warner Bros Inc
All rights reserved. Used by permission.

AUF WIEDERSEHN SWEETHEART
words by John Sexton & John Turner
© 1952 Peter Maurice Music Co Ltd
Reproduced by permission of EMI Music Publishing Ltd.

OUT OF NOWHERE (YOU CAME ALONG FROM)
Composer: John Green
Author: Edward Heyman
© 1931 by Famous Music Corporation
Copyright renewed 1958 & Assigned to Famous Music Corporation
British Publisher: Famous Chappell
American Publisher: Famous Music Publishing Companies
Reproduced by kind permission.

FOR ALL WE KNOW
by Sam Lewis and Fred Coots, 1934
Reproduced by permission of CBS Songs.

THE CLOUDS SOON ROLL BY
Words and music: H. Woods/G. Brown
© 1932 renewed Shapiro, Bernstein and Co Inc
Lawrence Wright Music Co Ltd for British Territories (excluding Canada and Australasia) incl. Continent of Europe, and Shapiro, Bernstein & Co for remaining territories. Used by permission.

BLUE MOON
by Lorenz Hart and Richard Rogers, 1934
Reproduced by permission of CBS Songs.

THE FOLKS WHO LIVE ON THE HILL
Composer: Jerome Kern
Author: Oscar Hammerstein III
© 1937 T. B. Harms Company
Copyright renewed c/o The Welk Music Group,
Santa Monica, CA 90401. International Copyright secured.
All rights reserved. Used by permission.
British Publisher: Chappell Music Ltd
American Publisher: T. B. Harms & Co
Reproduced by kind permission.

SMOKE GETS IN YOUR EYES
Composer: Jerome Kern
Author: Otto Harbach
© 1933 T. B. Harms Company
Copyright reserved c/o The Welk Music Group,

YOU ARE MY SUNSHINE
Words by Jimmie Davis & Charles Mitchell

STORMY WEATHER
Words and music: T. Koehler/A. Arlen

LONDON PRIDE
by Noël Coward

SEPTEMBER SONG
Composer: Kurt Weill
Author: Maxwell Anderson

I GET ALONG WITHOUT YOU VERY WELL (EXCEPT SOMETIMES)
Composer and author: Hoagy Carmichael

All Futura Books are available at your bookshop or
newsagent, or can be ordered from the following address:
Futura Books, Cash Sales Department,
P.O. Box 11, Falmouth, Cornwall TR10 9EN.

Please send cheque or postal order (no currency), and
allow 60p for postage and packing for the first book
plus 25p for the second book and 15p for each additional
book ordered up to a maximum charge of £1.90 in U.K.

B.F.P.O. customers please allow 60p for
the first book, 25p for the second book plus 15p per
copy for the next 7 books, thereafter 9p per book.

Overseas customers, including Eire, please allow £1.25
for postage and packing for the first book, 75p for the
second book and 28p for each subsequent title ordered.